Choices Made

A Tale of the Gwerin

By
Scott William Simmons

This book is a work of fiction. Any references to historical events, real people, or real locales are used fictitiously. Other names, characters, places, and incidents are the product of the author's imagination, and any resemblance to actual events or locales or persons, living or dead, is entirely coincidental.

ISBN 978-0-615-88382-3

To see more work by Scott William Simmons visit
www.facebook.com/ScottWilliamSimmons
or
www.galleryscott.com

Cover art by Joe Phillips www.joephillips.com

Tony
Thank you for encouraging my creativity and
for putting up with the chaos it brought to our home.
I love you.

Contents

Chapter 1
The Ganeamha Flats

Salt and sand. For as far as one's eye could see - an immeasurable expanse of salt and sand.

Because, well over a thousand years ago, the goddess Cavanna commanded that the oceans and seas of this world be drained, leaving behind vast basins full of shifting sands, interspersed with extensive plains of salt, baked hard in the sun. While, by the good graces of the pantheon that watched over the Gwer, life still flourished on the continents of this world where the Gwerin deities used their power to keep the land alive while they strove to bring peace to its people.

The Ganeamha Flats, once called the Ganeamha Ocean, had become part of one continuous desert now covering the world of Gwer. A desert that now stood between its major continents and kingdoms, keeping a once warring people, a war originally started by the gods, separated from each other as they struggled to find the peace that the gods had forced upon them.

Early on the flats were treacherous at best and there was a time when crossing them would have been all but impossible. But the gods, pleased upon seeing peace finally take hold among their children, gave the Gwer a rare gift of flight. That gift, along with the ingenuity of its people, brought travel back to the kingdoms of Gwer.

***

Although the Ganeamha Flats were a barren wasteland, one could not say it was void of life, because life could be found traversing its expansive landscape.

A barge, its shadow flickering over the light brown colored sand, had been flying over the Ganeamha Flats for the past two days. The ship and its crew had left the kingdom of Ardane and were making for their own homeland, the kingdom of Birr. Not only had their trading been successful, the barge's holds laden with goods for market, the ship was carrying the younger prince of Birr and his entourage back to Kinsale, the capitol of Birr.

"Prince Dar. The captain says we should be reaching Kinsale within three days. He also said that once we pass through Murra's Maze we should at least see the mainland by midmorning tomorrow."

The twenty-two year old turned at the sound of his lieutenant's voice, the man having found Dar Banning leaning over a railing on a balcony on the stern of the barge. Lieutenant Cahl Goban remained at the entrance to the barge where he joined two of his soldiers from the Royal Guard who had been watching over Banning during his sojourn out onto the balcony.

The prince nodded to his lieutenant and without saying a word, returned to watching the starkness of the Ganeamha Flats roll underneath them. Aside from a dust devil that had formed yesterday, the past two days of flying over the desert had proven to be uneventful. Passing through the canyon known as Murra's Maze would be the only break to the monotony of a bleak landscape until they reached home.

Not that Dar Banning minded. For this was the first time he had ever left Birr and he had been allowed to go unescorted by his parents. A big milestone in the young man's life since Banning had gone to meet the ruling family of Ardane and to be introduced to their oldest son, all hoping that the two were compatible for marriage. Banning couldn't help but sigh in frustration knowing that this was only the first of many more encounters to marry him off to the right prince that had been lined up for him. A marriage into another ruling family which would bring prestige and status for whatever kingdom that his family found suitable for him. A marriage to another man that would be suitable to the needs of his family and their ever growing empire called Birr.

And soon enough, Banning would be home, dealing with his family and the politics that made up his life in Kinsale. A life that was truly not his own, a life that belonged to his parents for the moment, until his eventual betrothal when he would then become the property of another.

Banning closed his eyes and sighed once more as the warm winds blowing through the flats whipped at his blondish, brown hair, which at this moment had much more freedom than he did.

"What a shame." He said, opening his eyes and staring off into the distance. "I'm enjoying the solitude of being out here too much. How about you Goban? Are you enjoying the flats?"

Lieutenant Cahl Goban walked over to the balcony to stand at Banning's side, grasping the railing as he leaned over to watch as they flew over the desert which was some thirty feet to forty feet below them.

Escorting the prince to and from Ardane had been Goban's first assignment as a lieutenant and the thought of being in such an open space as the flats, with only a handful of men to protect the prince, had left Goban feeling on edge for most of the trip. He scratched at the side of his jaw, wiping away sand that had stuck to his face before answering him, wishing they had more coverage and more men around them.

"I must admit Milord. It will be nice to have solid land under my feet again."

Banning leaned forward and rested his elbows on the balcony's railing. "That will be soon enough." He said wishing that this trip would have lasted longer than it was going to as the barge began to slow its momentum and started to bob slightly in the desert's air currents.

"We must be near the Maze." Goban said as he leaned over the balcony on his left side and tried to catch a glimpse of the massive canyons that would soon be dwarfing over them.

The landmarks now before them, Murra's Maze, was a series of canyons standing between the kingdoms of Birr and Ardane and were once covered by what was the Ganeamha Ocean which was drained away by the goddess Murra. The mountain range had only been discovered when the kingdoms of Gwer were given the gift of air travel and movement between the continents once again resumed. The range, named for the goddess herself, stretched for several hundred miles across the land. With flights through these canyons, riddled with channels, switchbacks and dead ends only made possible by the single passage that was eventually discovered that meandered through this mountain range.

Even though the barge had already passed through Murra's Maze on the trip out to Ardane, Banning and Goban couldn't help but be impressed by the vastness and grandeur of it as the Maze stretched off into the horizon in either direction from the ship. The sheer walls of the Maze, casting shadows across the barge, with the air becoming much cooler as they neared the range's main passage. And as they moved into the main tunnel, numerous openings and minor arteries began to appear on either side of the channel that wove their way from the main passage. Goban couldn't help but pray silently to the gods, grateful that the Gwerin that first learned to fly had taken the risks, with some of them sacrificing their lives as they became lost in these tunnels, so that a course could eventually be mapped for future generations, his, to be able to safely fly through here.

"I wonder why a colony was never established out this far." Banning mused out loud as they flew by an overhang of rock, on their left hand side, that seemed to have once been the crumbled remains of a natural bridge that had spanned the two sides of the canyon.

"No water. At least, it's never been found out here that I know of. There's no reason to live out here when Murra will not grace your land with water. The captain says," Goban's voice trailed off as a flash of light caught his attention when sunlight seemed to be reflecting off something in the shadows, near the overhang. Goban shaded his eyes with his right hand, trying to get a better look at what might be out there in the canyon causing the effect.

"What's that?" Banning asked as he too noticed the odd irregular lights.

"Don't know." replied Goban. He squinted a little harder because he could just make out the movement of what he thought were large birds when he saw two more objects making their way towards them from their right. "Gliders!" he shouted, grabbing Banning's arm as soon as he recognized the men in their winged, flying suits. "Quickly! Get inside!"

"Why? What's going on?"

"We're under attack!" Goban yanked Banning away from the handrail and was pushing him towards the doorway when a small dart zipped through the guardrails on the balcony and embedded itself into the planks where Banning had just been standing. The two guards who were still standing at attention near the doorway to the balcony rushed forward, drawing their weapons.

"Don't let them through!" Goban ordered to his men as he pushed Banning into the hallway.

Goban cursed under his breath as he steered Banning towards the bridge, dismayed over the small group of soldiers he had to protect the prince from this attack. For now he ignored Banning's worried gaze as they rushed towards the prow of the ship, ordering the barge's crewman and their own soldiers they passed along the way to grab a weapon and prepare to defend the ship and the prince, against the impending attack.

What was he going to do?

This singular thought began to overwhelm the lieutenant as he and Banning stormed onto the bridge, startling the barge's captain, Thear Ibor, and his crew.

"Captain!" Goban, who had yet to let go of the prince, huffed heavily, while leaving Banning to stare wide eyed out of the floor to ceiling curved window that made up the front and sides of the bridge. "Gwerin in glider suits are attempting to board us! You need to get us out of here!"

Captain Thear Ibor, who had noticed some type of movement in front of the barge before the men's interruption, now had Goban's statement to confirm his own fears.

"On it." Ibor turned to the man standing in front of him, the man who was steering the barge. "Croft, pick up speed and get us through the Maze as fast as you can."

"Aye." Croft replied, his voice sounding distant with an odd fluidic echo, as if he was trying to talk with his mouth half full of water. Croft's hands were also resting on grey metallic orbs that were about the size of a child's ball, which were perched on wooden columns to either side of him. The orbs, or lodestones, were the gift from Barra, the god of the earth. The union of stone, wood and flesh allowed the Gwerin to steer their vessels by their wills alone, moving it in any direction the ship's steersman desired.

Croft, whose eyeballs were a solid metallic grey, mimicking the mystical orbs he was holding onto, involuntarily squeezed said orbs a little tighter as he forced the barge to move faster. Unused to the barge's increase in speed, both Banning and Goban grabbed onto handrails attached to the bridges wall as the vessel pitched slightly while it picked up momentum.

From their vantage point the men on the bridge watched as several more pirates tried to land on the main deck of the moving barge, with one of the raiders stumbling and rolling over the edge of the deck while his companions were able to maintain their footing when Croft shifted the barge again. And though the crewmen and guards were trying to defend themselves, and their ship, with swords and daggers, they were easily falling prey to the more agile pirates and their rain of poisoned darts as they flew onto the barge's main deck to land and join their comrades who had started this attack.

"Damn!" Goban cursed. From the assault he was watching unfold in front of him, the lieutenant knew they would not last long against their attackers. He walked over to Banning and none too gently, in his own fear to protect him, grabbed him by the forearm. "We need to get you out of here my prince." He then said to his charge. "My advice to you, in case we get separated, is that we try to make it down to the storage hold and make a break for it through the loading bay."

Turning to the captain, Goban asked if the man could find someplace to land so that they could properly defend themselves.

Ibor ran a hand through his graying hair, furrows creasing his forehead as he tried to think of a way to not only save the prince, but his ship as well. "We'd have to slow down or the ship could break apart at this speed."

"I don't care," Goban shouted, "we need to. . ."

"Captain!" The crewman acting as lookout at the main window shouted and started pointing out the window. "To our port!"

All heads turned to watch as a ship on their left hand side moved out of the shadows. The ship looked to only be three to four decks high, painted a dull gray and shaped like a large flat wing. With a design to cut through the winds, this ship was made for stealth and speed and as it flew into the main channel it tried to fly on top of the barge, trying to force it down and land.

Cahl Goban cursed again, not caring who heard him this time, as the barge dipped sharply to avoid this new attack.

***

The ship attacking the barge was called the Shaefra and its crew had spotted the Birrnian barge almost a day and a half ago as the ship was making its way across the flats. The Shaefra easily kept pace with the barge as it stayed out of view from any of their lookouts and from the heightened senses of their steersmen. And once Emmis Daigh, captain of the Shaefra, knew that they could only be heading towards Murra's Maze, he had his ship circle around the barge and made their way to the only channel that cut safely through the Maze.

The Maze's channel was very familiar to Daigh because he had travelled through it on more than one occasion, and he left a group of his men at the entrance, while he had the Shaefra fly into the nearest artery that shot off from the main channel. Two of those men that he had left behind were perched on the overhang that the barge was about to fly under.

"They're almost underneath us." One of the two pirates said when he noticed the barge in the channel heading in their direction.

The two men began preparing their suits for flight; tightening straps on arms and legs and making sure that their small pieces of lodestones were wrapped tightly against the palms of their hands.

"Signal the others and Captain Emmis. Get ready." The second man replied while he cocked a poisonous dart into his hand crossbow.

The first pirate took out a small mirror and aimed it further into the channel, reflecting sunlight off of it, warning their companions of the barge's arrival. He was responding to a second group of men on another ledge when his comrade informed him that the barge was passing under them.

"I'm all set." The pirate said as he pocketed the mirror and quickly twisted his head from shoulder to shoulder, snapping his neck as he tried to relieve the tension that was knotting his back. "Jump!"

Both men leapt off the rocky ledge and spread their arms and legs, their eyes glazing over when they gripped the small pieces of lodestones in their hands. As they took to the air the black fabric between their limbs and torso tightened, turning into sails, capturing the wind and keeping them aloft as they flew towards their goal.

While in the air they slowed their descent and began gliding towards the barge when another group of pirates jumped from a different ledge and began flying towards the barge, quickly gaining on the slow moving vessel. Several figures could be seen standing on a balcony on the bow of the barge and a few more men were seen walking across its main deck.

Unfortunately, the Shaefra's run of good luck must have come to an end because it seemed like two of the Gwerin standing on a balcony at the rear of the ship were looking in their direction with one of the men pointing up at them before they backed away from the balcony's railing, moving towards the door that led back into the main cabins.

The pirates loosened their concentration on the lodestones, their bodies cutting through the air with no force to keep them aloft, so they could aim and fire their weapons. The first pirate missed one of the two men as they turned to run inside while the second was able to hit one of the guards in the thigh. The fast acting poison rendered the guard unconscious so that he slumped to the ground in a state of oblivion. And not having time to reload his weapon for a second time, the pirate who had missed his target joined with his lodestones to slow his flight slightly so that he could bodily slam into the other guard, sending him back into the wall and knocking the wind out of him so he too collapsed to the ground. Once the pirates had landed, they moved the prone bodies of the members of the Royal Guard into the main cabin section and closed the door to the balcony and prepared themselves for the fights that they would encounter on their way to the barge's bridge.

***

"There's the signal Captain. The barge has moved into the gorge."

Captain Emmis Daigh looked over at his crewman who was acting as lookout at his bridge's main window. The crewman's keen eyes had spotted a signal from the two men who were hiding in the main channel to Murra's Maze.

"Excellent." Daigh stood up from his chair and walked a couple of feet to the woman who had been sitting in front of him. "Okay Vinnia." He said to his steersman. "You know the drill. Take the Shaefra out slowly. We don't want to spook them."

"Aye, Captain." Unlike her counterpart that was steering the barge, El Vinnia was seated in a fairly comfortable chair on the Shaefra's bridge. It was well padded, with the back of the chair about shoulder height for her to lean against. And the arms of the chair were at a slight downward angle from the back with the Shaefra's lodestones resting in wooden indentations at the end of the them. Vinnia had had her hands resting casually on the stones, a fingernail on her right hand tapping one of them lightly, but grasping them as soon as her captain gave the order to fly. Once connected with the stones her eyes started to glaze over, a dark grey fluid rolling over the whites and the pupils of her eyes, turning them into tiny metallic orbs. Perfect reflections of the arcane objects she was holding onto.

The crew adjusted their weight as their centers of gravity shifted when Vinnia lifted the Shaefra off the ground. She easily moved the ship, into the tight confines of this smaller offshoot of a channel that was slightly wider than the Shaefra itself, to a location where the bridge's crew would have a better view so that they could watch for the barge as it moved through the channel.

Daigh wanted a better view as well. So he walked over to the main window that stretched from floor to ceiling, a feature commonly found in these flying vessels, to watch the barge's progression with his crew.

A crewman who was acting as lookout for the bridge, and standing on the left hand side of the large, round window, turned at his captain's approach.

"You can just make out two of our men flying in from behind the barge." The man said while pointing with his left hand at two dark shapes flying out from the deep shadows of the rocks.

"I see them Lhoyt." Daigh said to his second in command. "Must be Brady and Dow. We left them at the entrance to the channel."

Several new specks caught Lhoyt's attention. "There's another group towards the front of the ship."

Daigh had been watching Brady and Dow disappear behind the barge, but turned at Lhoyt's remark and looked to where he was now pointing and scowled. "Too early, too early. What were they thinking?" Anger flashed across his face, turning it a deep red, a red as fiery as his hair, as he stalked back to his chair and sat down. "Fools! Get ready to move us Vinnia."

"Aye, Captain." She responded, hollowly.

Daigh looked back over to his second in command, "Lhoyt, go make sure the men are ready with the grappling hooks. I don't feel like chasing this thing all the way back to its gods' forsaken berth."

"Aye, aye, Captain." Lhoyt said, beckoning for another crewman to come and take his place at the window as he left the bridge.

The new lookout wasn't long at the window before he turned to Daigh. "Captain! Looks like they're picking up speed!"

Daigh's fists slammed down onto the arms of his chair. "Damn!" They came down a second time. "Damn!" He frowned, a knot painfully forming in his lower back as he leaned forward in his chair, hoping for a better look out the window from the safety of his seat. "Get us moving Vinnia."

Vinnia responded to Daigh, her voice soft and fluid as one word escaped her barely moving lips. "Aye."

The barge came into view as Vinnia moved the Shaefra out into the main channel and Daigh could just make out some of his men trying to land on the barge's main deck. He cursed under his breath as the prow of the vessel lifted up and then tilted to the left as it began to move faster. And as the barge passed them, Vinnia forced the Shaefra to gain momentum and altitude, as she tried to move the Shaefra over their target in the hopes of forcing them to land.

The barge tried to stay ahead of the Shaefra as the gorge angled sharply to the left, sending many of the barge's crew and the pirates attacking it staggering across its main deck. But Vinnia was a masterful steersman and took the turn by pivoting the back of the Shaefra to the right and pushing it forward, the ship's timbers groaning under the stress, forcing Daigh to press his thighs against his chair to keep himself in place while his crewman at the window grabbed onto a vertical brass rail that was on the side of the window so he wouldn't stumble to the ground. Vinnia soon began to perspire as her concentration became focused on increasing the Shaefra's momentum, making it buck and vibrate uncomfortably as if it was hitting small bumps in the air. Under Vinnia's deft control the pirate ship did begin to gain on the barge and as soon as they were close enough Vinnia used its wedge shaped hull to slowly move in on the barges portside.

The barge rolled to the right, exposing its lower hull to the Shaefra for a moment before it righted itself again and dropped several dozen feet as it tried to avoid the Shaefra on its left and from hitting the rocky wall on its starboard side. Vinnia took the opportunity to move the ship forward, keeping it apace with the barge, but stayed a little back so that their mark could still be seen out of the bridge's window. And with the ship tilted at this angle towards the barge Lhoyt and his men should have a better vantage point to attack the other ship.

Lhoyt had just made it down to the weapons room when the Shaefra banked towards the barge, sending him sliding the rest of the way into the room. Fortunately he was able to grab onto the door jamb to stop from falling and not one to lose an opportunity, bellowed orders for his men to fire their weapons. As if on cue, grappling hooks with cables attached to them and as thick as a man's arm, were loosed from their ballistae, cutting through the air as they flew towards the barge. The first two hit their marks. One hook skipped across the barge's main deck, sliding backwards until it caught on the ships railing with the other hook slamming through a shuttered window on the upper part of the hull, sending broken wood into the barge and latching onto something solid within the vessel.

As Ormin Lhoyt's men shot a third cable at the barge their target dropped violently out of the air and began to move under the Shaefra. The unexpected move dragged the attached pirate ship down with them. The third hook missed its mark completely, its line snapping taut as it swung backwards to trail behind the pirate ship.

On the bridge Vinnia tilted the Shaefra into the pull of the barge so its hull wouldn't get ripped open from the strain as the barge tried to escape.

The move caused one of Lhoyt's ballistae to snap its moorings and slammed against the hull, just missing its operator who had been holding onto the weapon to keep steady as the Shaefra banked violently.

Lhoyt, who had stepped away from the door to join his men at their weapons, was thrown into the hull, his right shoulder and left hand taking the full force of his weight as he tried to protect himself from getting hurt. As pain shot from his right shoulder down his arm Lhoyt couldn't help but drop to one knee as a wave of nausea came over him.

"Release the cables." He groaned, slipping as he tried to regain his footing. "They'll take us down with them if we don't."

His men scrambled across the shifting floor to the ballistae and began disconnecting the cables from the weapons. The first loose cable zipped free and disappeared behind the Shaefra. The second cable was released from the intact ballistae but the ship swung and pivoted on the last cable still connected to the barge as it still tried to evade the Shaefra. The ship creaked and the hull seemed to bow under the strain put on it by the connection between the two ships.

Continuing to fight back nausea from the pain in his arm, Lhoyt staggered to the damaged weapon to help his man there where the crewman was trying to squeeze his right hand into the space between the ballistae and the wall to get at the release mechanism for the cable.

Lhoyt stumbled into the ballistae as the ship shook. It seemed Vinnia could barely keep the ship aloft and stable in the air as she too struggled to separate the Shaefra from the barge. Lhoyt knelt at the weapon and held onto it with his left hand. His right arm was numb; he couldn't feel anything below his shoulder and he couldn't lift it or get his fingers to close completely. His arm was useless.

"Come on Mac! We're shaking apart here!"

"I'm trying sir!" The crewman's eyes were closed and his teeth were clenched in pain as he tried to force his right hand and fingers into the tight space between the ballista and the wall. "But it feels like the pin and gears are embedded in the wall." Mac grunted as he kept digging at the hull around the mechanism with splintered wood biting into his fingertips and the palm of his hand. The gears and wall quickly became slick from the blood seeping from his wounds and the sweat from his hand.

"Shit! Davis! Anyone!" Lhoyt shouted over his shoulder to the men left in the room. "Cut the cord! Use a knife, something, just cut us loose from that fucking thing!"

Davis and another man stumbled into the ballista as the Shaefra groaned and slid sideways. Davis grasped the stock of the ballista, a long knife in his right hand ready to use on the chord that was keeping them attached to the barge. Suddenly their feet left the floor as the pirate ship was dragged out of the air by the barge when it dropped towards the bottom of the gorge. Davis and Lhoyt were able to maintain their grasps on the ballista as the Shaefra tried to stop its plummet but the man who had run over with Davis, lost his grip on the weapon and rolled away, landing on his back and sliding across the floor as the solid surface broke his fall. Mac, whose hand was pinned between the ballista and the wall, keeping him steady and in place, was thankful the weapon hadn't moved and for not crushing his hand or him for that matter.

Lhoyt gasped in pain from being rocked against the ballista and moved his left hand across the weapon as he felt for a better handhold. "Davis, come on man! We can't take much more of this."

Davis grunted, his concentration focused solely on saving himself and the ship. With some force, he was able to slide the knife between the cable and the stock of the ballista and started moving the knife in a sawing motion. The cable slowly began to tear, the strands of the tightly woven, hemp chord separating as the knife sliced through it. Davis clenched his teeth as he struggled to push the knife even more quickly through the remaining strands of chording. Unfortunately, the Shaefra bucked violently and the knife twisted in Davis' sweaty hand, the blade slipping flat under the chord. Davis cursed loudly and, letting go of the ballista, used both hands to twist the blade back into place.

Davis had almost cut through the rest of the rope when it snapped from the tension placed upon it by the two ships as they tried to get away from each other. Everyone in the weapon's room was thrown into a free-fall for the briefest of moments as Vinnia lost control over the Shaefra. Davis tumbled backwards, the knife falling from his hands and bouncing across the floor while Lhoyt maintained his grasp on the ballista as it shifted away from the wall and scraped across the floor. Mac, who had the good sense, and luck, to pull his hand from between the weapon and the wall, scrambled across the floor as the ballista rolled towards him. The stern of the ship suddenly began to rise, with everything and everyone changing direction as they now slid forward. The Shaefra began to move into the dip it was thrown into, leveled off and finally came to a halt in midair.

Even though it seemed like Vinnia had gained control of the ship, Lhoyt wasn't ready to let go of his grasp of the weapon as he tried to catch his breath. He sat there and watched as Mac grabbed a dirty rag from the floor and wrapped it around his bleeding hand while Davis crawled over to the crewman who was still lying prone on the floor. Davis knelt by the man's side and gave him a quick once over, checking for a pulse and broken bones.

"Sir, I think Ross is just unconscious. Has a nasty bump on the back of his head though. No blood that I can see." Davis said, looking over to his commander.

"Good." Lhoyt stood shakily and grabbed his right elbow with his left hand to keep his useless arm from flopping around and steadied himself by leaning against the ballista and surveyed the damage. Aside from the mangled weapon he was near, the part of the hull it had scraped against, and the missiles and tools scattered across the floor, the room seemed to be intact. Looking at the mess and thinking back over his long career of serving with the captain, Lhoyt could not remember when such a simple raid had gone so wrong.

"Mac, go find Cook and get her here to have a look at Ross." Cook not only prepared the meals on the Shaefra, she doubled as the ship's doctor and she also brewed the sleeping potion used to attack the crews of the ships they raided. "And have her take a look at that hand of yours. I don't need you crying about getting your job done because of some splinters."

"Aye sir." Mac gave his commander a half-hearted smile, rubbing sweat from his forehead as he left the room on his errand.

Lhoyt was heading out of the door too when the Shaefra started to move again and turned back the way they had flown as it started a slow descent. Lhoyt grabbed the door jamb and looked back to Davis who was trying to get Ross into a more comfortable position on the floor.

"At least we know Vinnia is alright. I'm going to go check the rest of the ship before heading to the bridge." Lhoyt's arm throbbed uncomfortably and he winced in pain a he forced his fingers to move slightly, a gasp of pain escaping his lips. "If I know the captain, we're still going after that barge so we need to get ready. Davis, as soon as Cook gets here, get your mask and be ready to board the other ship."

Davis nodded and mumbled an aye sir as Lhoyt left the ballista room. "That ship better have something worth all this aggravation." Lhoyt thought as he headed for the stairs, making his way to the lower deck and to find as many men that were still able, to prepare for the raid.

***

Vinnia was worn out. It had taken all of her strength and skill as a steersman to keep the Shaefra aloft and not have the ship plummet to the ground as the barge fought to escape their towlines. She had almost passed out when the Shaefra broke free of its entanglement. But using what little strength she had left, found the will to control the ship and kept it from skipping through the air and slamming into the rock walls of the gorge. Vinnia's head throbbed with a pain shooting from around her eyes to the back of her head and something wet was dripping from her nose and running down her upper lip. El Vinnia soon had the metallic taste of blood in her mouth as she tried to lick the moisture away. Unfortunately she could not raise a hand to clean her face because to remove even one hand from a lodestone would mean to lose control of the ship, allowing it to fall out of the sky. So the blood poured freely and dribbled down her chin as she turned the Shaefra back towards the barge which had landed a ways back. Vinnia coughed several times, trying to clear her throat so she could breathe, not caring that she was spraying blood across her blouse and lap.

During the attempt of subduing the barge, the crewman who had been acting as lookout lost his grip on the railing and had tumbled across the floor of the bridge. Daigh risked a run to him from his chair and dragged his crewman back to the main window where he kept firm grips on the railing and his dazed man. His crewman, Orin, was just a little shaken up, not seriously hurt, and he was able to grasp the rail himself and ride out the rest of the wild ride.

From where he now stood bracing himself against the rail, Daigh, not caring what was happening outside, watched as Vinnia struggled to gain control of the Shaefra, and grew fearful for all of their safety when the pallor of her skin turned a clammy grey and blood began to drip from her nose. When the Shaefra began to slow and leveled off in the air, Daigh patted his crewman's back, asking if he was okay and when he got a nod in the affirmative from the man, rushed over to help Vinnia, who coughed again as she tried to keep the blood out of her mouth and clogging her throat.

Upon reaching her Daigh pulled a handkerchief out of his vest pocket and gently wiped her face. "Get us down Vin. Nothing fancy." Vinnia only nodded as Daigh looked over to his crewman still standing at the main window. "Orin, get some water and a couple of towels so I can clean Vinnia up. And find Nolan so he can replace Vinnia after she lands the ship."

"Aye, Captain." Orin replied and quickly left the bridge on the errands he was given.

Daigh hadn't flown the ship but he felt just as exhausted as Vinnia looked. He rubbed his face in his hands, huffing into them and then dragged them across his long tapered ears and through his reddish brown hair and pulled his wavy locks tight against the base of his neck. He then tried to reach the middle of his back, between his shoulder blades, and rubbed at the knot that had formed there as he walked back to the main window.

Vinnia was bringing the ship down to land and Daigh could clearly see the barge and cursed at the sight of it. For the barge had landed but was listing to starboard with a large wedge of sand pushed between its hull and the canyon wall. A furrow trailed behind the vessel from where it had plowed into the ground when it had escaped from the Shaefra. It looked like there was wreckage not far behind the barge, near a large outcropping of rock jutting from the sandy floor. Daigh pounded the wall near the window with the clenched fist of his left hand and then propped his fist and forearm against the wall so he could rest his forehead on the window as his ship moved closer to the barge.

"Looks like they've lost some of their hull." He said out loud, more to himself than to Vinnia. "I don't think Brady or the others made it to the bridge to land the ship." He turned to look at Vinnia and saw that there was a little bit of color returning to her face and it looked like her nosebleed had stopped. "There's plenty of space in front of the barge for us to land." He said as he turned back to look out the window. "Can you sense it?"

"Not, yet." She gurgled as she coughed up more saliva and blood. The taste of it was making her nauseous and she was trying not to swallow it for fear of vomiting and losing her control over the lodestones. She smirked around the mess on her face. "Try." She said woodenly. "One piece, land. No walk. Home."

Daigh chuckled as he pushed himself away from the window. "That's kind of you, Vin. The walk home from here would be a killer."

"Aye."

It wasn't long before Orin returned with towels and the bowl of water Daigh had asked for. "Captain, Nolan should be here in a moment or so. He was getting himself ready to board the other ship and fly it but I told him he was needed here to replace Vinnia. And I passed Commander Ormin in the hallway on his way to organize the crew for the raid. He seems to be having trouble moving his right arm and he said Ross is out cold. Said he'd get Cook up here once she's done tending to Ross so she could take a look at Vinnia."

"Good." Between the men who attacked the barge and his uninjured crew still on the Shaefra, Daigh hoped to have eighteen, maybe twenty men ready to raid the barge. And with Nolan sitting in for Vinnia, Daigh didn't know how he was going to get the barge back home. A terrible loss in revenue since the barge could have been used by his employer for shipping or sold for profit. "Not far now Vin." He said as he watched the ground quickly coming up to meet them.

"Yes." She hissed, sensing the land below them. She also sensed Orin near her who was dipping one of the towels into the bowl of water, ringing it out so that he could clean her face. "Wait." She whispered as he reached over to touch her. "Landing." She coughed.

Orin stopped and held onto her chair, his and Daigh's stomach rolling as Vinnia slowed their descent rather quickly, sending a rumble through the ship with loose items rattling or falling as the Shaefra landed, none too gently, onto the sandy floor of the gorge. And as Vinnia let her hands slip off the lodestones and slumped forward in her chair, Orin carefully pushed her back into a sitting position and began to wipe her face of its mess. Vinnia reached out and grabbed Orin's wrist with a shaky hand and pulled the cloth to her mouth, sucking water out of it to only spit phlegm and blood back into the towel as she tried to rid the tinny taste from her mouth. Her crewmate rolled up the mess and dropped the towel onto the floor.

"Thanks." She whispered hoarsely.

Orin only nodded as he bent to grab the other clean towel he had left on the floor. "Let me clean you up a little more and then we'll get you out of here."

Daigh continued to look out the window, trying to assess the damage to the barge while Orin tended to Vinnia. Even though the ship they had attacked was listing to one side, he could see two of his men who had glided onto it during the attack run easily across the barge's deck to the railing and began signaling them that they were okay. Daigh turned and walked over to Vinnia, giving her right shoulder a squeeze noticing that more color had returned to her face and telling her that she had done a good job.

Vinnia looked up at Daigh and gave him a week smile. The influence of the lodestones had cleared from her hazel eyes and had left them puffy and red. She rolled her head to the left and pursed her lips and took a couple of deep breaths as she tried to not pass out from exhaustion.

Knowing that Vinnia would be in good care with Orin, Daigh walked over to the back of his chair and grabbed the mask that was hanging by a hook; by decree from his employer, he and his crew were to keep their faces hidden during their raids. But, unlike the bandanas with eyeholes that most of his crew wore, Daigh's mask was a little more ornate.

Made of shaped leather, the mask had the usual eyeholes with it peaking in the middle where it sat across his nose and curved downward from the nostrils and outside of the cheeks to end in points, leaving his mouth and beard exposed. The leather had been stained a dark bluish black and the strips to tie it around his head were made of shiny black silk. Daigh's mask was very stylish and extravagant, not so much utilitarian, and would have been more appropriate at a masquerade instead of being used as a disguise for a raiding party. But then again, Daigh did his best to make sure all of his attire had a little flare.

"Orin, I'm going down to the bays, so you need to stay with Vin until Cook and Nolan arrive. Once they get here I want you to stay as lookout for Nolan because we might need to leave sooner than we think." Daigh said to his crewman while putting on the mask, knotting the silk at the back of his head and letting the remainder of the long strands of fabric fall between his shoulder blades.

Orin stood to look at his captain, twisting the dirty towel in his hands. "We'll be ready to fly at your command."

"Good." Daigh tugged at the green velvet of his vest and turned to leave the bridge only to find Lhoyt, his second in command, standing in the doorway with his right arm in a sling resting up against his chest. Daigh could also see that Lhoyt's fingers, which were dangling out of the sling, were swollen and red. And whoever had helped him with the sling had also helped him with putting on his mask; a dark purplish fabric with eye slots, covering the entire top of his head and knotted in the back.

"What happened to your arm Commander?" Daigh asked Lhoyt as he joined him at the doorway.

"Got slammed against a wall. Cook says I should be fine though." Lhoyt stepped back out into the hallway so that Daigh could leave the bridge and followed his captain as he started walking down the hallway, making his way towards the main stairwell that lead down to the storage bays. As they were walking, Lhoyt raised his right arm slightly and tried to move his fingers, grimacing in pain from the failed attempt. "Just need to not use it for a couple of days."

"And how did the rest of my ship fair?" Daigh asked Lhoyt as the two men reached the stairs.

"Ross was knocked out cold and Mac did some damage to his right hand too. But Cook says they'll be fine although Mac won't have use of his hand for several weeks." Lhoyt replied. As they headed down the stairs, Lhoyt trailed his left hand across the railing to maintain his balance during their descent. "The rest of the crew came through with only a scratch or two. We did lose a ballista. It was ripped from its moorings when the barge tried to pull us out of the sky. That's how Mac injured his hand; trying to release the pin holding the grappling hook and its cable attaching us to that barge. It'll have to be replaced and we'll have to check the hull where the ballista slammed into it and make sure that section doesn't need to be replaced. Other than some broken jars of wine and water, the ship came through fine."

"Well, once we're airborne, get a crew together and have them brace the damaged part of the hull and to make sure that the rest of our weapons are secure. I don't want anything else falling apart before we get back to port for repairs."

When Daigh and Lhoyt reached the bottom of the stairs, they continued walking towards the stern of the ship where the main storage bay was located. The bay had doors that could be opened to the outside, allowing supplies and crew on and off the Shaefra while it was grounded or not docked near a pier. Upon entering the bay, Daigh found that his men had already opened the hatch and had left doors wide open. A warm breeze was blowing in from the canyon and the wind dried the sweat on Emmis Daigh's exposed cheeks and neck. Unfortunately his shirt stuck to the perspiration on his chest and he tugged at his clothing as he tried to get them into a more comfortable position.

The bridge of Lhoyt's nose began to itch and he stuck a finger underneath his mask to scratch it as he looked around the bay, noticing only a couple of men in the large room organizing boxes and barrels that had been knocked out of place. "Looks like most of the crew has already headed outside."

"Then let's not keep them waiting." Daigh said sourly. "The sooner we're done with this salvage, the better off we'll be."

Daigh stepped off the ramp and walked over towards the large group of men who were waiting for him while Lhoyt turned to look back into the bay, whistling and gesturing for the men still working in it to stop what they were doing and to join the rest of them outside.

"Alright. This raid didn't go according to plan but you know the drill." Daigh said to his men as soon as they had all assembled around him. Let's go relinquish that ship of its crew and get it back up in the air as soon as possible so we can be on our way. Thankfully Vinnia brought us down close to the barge so we won't have far to run.

While Daigh gave his pep talk to his men, some movement out of the corner of Lhoyt's eye caught his attention. Turning, he saw that one of their men must have found a way off the barge and was now running in their direction. The crewman hadn't undone the wings to his glider suit so the clothe billowed between his arms and torso, making him stumble a little as he crossed the forty foot stretch of sandy floor spread between the downed barge and the Shaefra. Lhoyt caught Daigh's eye and nodded towards the incoming man.

"Looks like Brady, Captain." One of the other men, who happened to be standing next them, said to Daigh and Lhoyt.

Not wanting to wait for Brady to cross all the way over to them, Daigh started to make his own way towards the man and motioned with a hand for the rest of his crew to get to work. Men in masks ran by Brady, some patting him on the shoulder, as they headed for the barge where another man stood to show them how to get into it. Lhoyt fell in behind his captain as they approached Brady.

"What happened?" Daigh asked Brady when he stopped in front of them.

Brady, who was winded, bent over for a moment, putting his hands on his knees and inhaled deeply while he tried to catch his breath.

"Sorry, Captain." The man huffed. "They were prepared for us. They must have seen us flying in and they had an armed escort on board. Took us a little longer to dispatch them so we could get to the bridge."

As Brady stood, Daigh put an arm around his shoulders, steering his man towards the barge. "An armed escort?"

"Yes." Brady said, unbuckling the straps for the wings from his arms so that the fabric from them hung only from his back, allowing him to move a little more easily. "There must have been about ten of them sir. Royal Guards of Birr, I think, if I read their insignias right. So far we've only found sacks of grain and bolts of fabric in their holds, so we're not sure why they are on this barge and what they were protecting."

"Have the men search the captain's quarters. If there's anything of value worth hiding it should be there or in a room close to it." Lhoyt suggested.

Daigh and his two men were almost three quarters of the way to the barge when the captain was surprised to already see several of his men coming around the far side of the barge with what looked like the large sacks of grain Brady had described thrown over their shoulders, struggling with their burdens down a small hill of piled sand that had been created by the barge's landing as they began to make their way back to their own ship.

"Why are they taking the cargo off of that ship when we can just use it to fly everything back?" Lhoyt asked as several of the men passed them by, some nodding to their captain and second in command as they made their way back to the Shaefra with the stolen supplies.

"The barge isn't going anywhere Captain." Brady began to explain to Daigh as more men appeared from around the barge, some with more sacks of grain while others were balancing long bolts of fabric across their shoulders. "We were heading to the bridge when we heard the grappling hooks striking the barge and that's when they dropped the ship out of the air. Sent us all flying for a moment. The barge was descending when we got to the bridge and that's where their crew tried to put up a good fight. Then there was no time to switch steersman so we had no choice but to keep their man awake and continue to fly the ship so it could land." Brady continued with his commentary as they walked around the back of the ship to its starboard side. "Thought the landing would be smooth but the steersman saw that outcropping back there and purposely side swiped it. And he swiped it good." Brady ended his story by pointing up at the side of the barge.

Daigh stopped and looked up to where Brady was now pointing and cursed loudly because a large section of the starboard hull had been torn away, leaving a jagged gash almost forty feet long and wide enough so that two decks were now exposed to the elements. Daigh sighed in frustration, knowing full well he wouldn't be needing Nolan nor anyone else to fly this broken ship.

Lhoyt shook his head. "Whoever tries to fly this will be fighting with the winds while they're up in the air and we couldn't keep anything in those exposed rooms because it would just get sucked out of that hole. Why, it even looks like another section might give way once it gets aloft. What a shame. Looks like it could have held a lot." Lhoyt picked up a piece of planking sticking out of the sand and poked at its splintered side before tossing it away in disgust. "Looks like our bonuses will amount to next to nothing from this venture."

Brady's shoulders slumped. He had been the man in charge of the first assault on the barge and knew he might be the one taking the blame for the raid turning into such a fiasco. He continued with his explanations. "For their size, Commander, they weren't carrying that much cargo. That's why we're hauling all of their stores over to the Shaefra. It shouldn't take us long to complete the task. And with their crew out for another hour or so we should be long gone before they wake."

"This day couldn't end soon enough." Daigh thought as he scratched the back of his head. Looking around the field of debris, he noticed that the barge's crew had already been laid out under an overhang of rock that made up part of the gorge wall where they would be protected from the sun. It was routine for them to leave the crew of a commandeered ship behind; no kills, no prisoners, just take the property. Because, with no killings and no hostages taken, there would be less likely of a reason for someone to come after you in search of retribution.

"Any casualties among them?" Daigh asked Brady as he walked over to the unconscious crew.

"No one dead. Some of them have bumps and bruises and might need to be looked at, but it's nothing Cook can't fix if she has the time.

I'm sure their crew will all walk away from this." Brady said matter of factly as they reached the thirty bodies lying prone on the ground. "We did lose Siv. He fell off the deck of the barge when they first tried to evade us. We saw his signal from the top of their main deck so he's not that far from us. Says he's hurt though. Told him to hold tight and we'd get him as soon as we're done here." Brady looked down the row of bodies and pointed towards the last of them. "The military ones are at the end."

Glancing down, Daigh slowed his pace as he walked past the row of sedated men with Brady at his side while Lhoyt had stopped to watch the progress the other men were making as they exited the barge through a set of hanger doors in its side.

"Did you manage to grab the stones off of their bridge?" Lhoyt called over to Brady.

"Yes Commander." Brady had turned slightly to look at Lhoyt while Daigh continued on of his inspection of their captives. "First things we took off the bridge when we realized it was probably not going to fly again. Had the stones stowed with some other non-essentials that we found and they should have been sent over to the Shaefra by now." Brady turned and walked back over to Daigh who was now inspecting some of the unconscious men lying in front of him.

"You were right." Daigh said to the man while he continued to inspect the soldiers in front of him, using his booted foot to drag a cloak off of one man to get a better look and his armor. But he didn't have to keep searching for clues because the insignias woven into their cloaks and the markings hammered into their breastplates definitely marked them as members of the Royal Guard of Birr.

Thinking that he was finished with the inspection, and not seeing anything of real value on the bodies, Daigh started to walk back to Lhoyt. They needed to get things wrapped up here to be on their way and out in the openness of the flats where they could quickly get swallowed up by the desert.

Casually, as if he was comparing exploits with a drinking companion, Brady pointed to a young man lying next to one of the soldiers. "Oh, and these were hiding behind some sacks of grain in the same hold with several other guards that might have been protecting them. We took them down quite easily but I think they were all hoping to make a break for it through an outer entrance when they landed."

Daigh really didn't care where they were found or what they had been doing during the attack when something about the sleeping crewman caught his eye. He looked at the man and frowned as something about this Gwerin gnawed at the back of his memory. Why should this the man, boy, be so familiar to him? His frown deepening, Daigh squatted to get a closer look at the man.

This Gwerin certainly looked much younger than the rest of the men laid out before them; a man who seemed to be in his early twenties. Certainly not unheard of when such merchant ships as this one commonly had entire families as its crew.

Daigh continued to scrutinize the boy, whose head was tilted to the left with his mouth slightly open, giving him the appearance of sleeping peacefully, even though he had just been knocked unconscious by one of Daigh's crew. The boy's left arm was still red and a little swollen from where the needle like dart had struck him. Daigh couldn't resist the urge to move the young man's tussled blondish brown hair from his eyes while he also inspected the boys clothing which seemed to be of a better cut than the rest of his crewmates. And as he was fingering the fine linen of the boy's shirt, a glint of gold caught Daigh's eyes. Lifting the boy's right hand, he found that he was wearing a ring on his index finger. And it was not some common band on his finger, but a signet ring with the crest of the royal family of Birr.

That's when memories from his past began blurring his vision and why he knew this face. A face quite similar to that of another man he had been intimate with for many years oh so long ago.

"The hair is a little darker and his ears are a little longer," Daigh thought as he laid a hand on the boy's chest, a strong steady heartbeat vibrating against his fingertips. Quite unlike the one now racing within his chest. But so much like him, oh so much like him.

"Captain?" Brady asked, curious as to why Daigh had become so entranced with this sleeping figure.

Daigh looked at Brady and gave him a reassuring smile. "Well, I think we have found what the guards were protecting."

"What did you find sir?" Brady assumed something precious had been hidden on the sleeping crewman's body.

But Brady was taken aback by his captain's announcement, as he patted the unconscious Gwer's shoulder. "This happens to be one of the princes of Birr. The Companion's son if I'm not mistaken."

"Really, Captain?"

Daigh looked down at the prince's face, resisting the urge to run a hand over his cheek as more memories of a past he had never truly forgotten threatened to overtake him. "Yes, I'm quite certain."

"What's going on?" Lhoyt asked as he walked over to them, wondering what had caught their attention and what they were quietly talking about.

"The captain says we found royalty, one of the princes of Birr." Brady explained to his commander.

Lhoyt found himself beginning to frown. "Is that so?"

Daigh gently cupped the prince's right hand again and raised it so Lhoyt would see the boy's knuckles and the gold ring resting on one of them. "See." Daigh said as he looked up at Lhoyt. "He wears the family crest of Birr."

Lhoyt scratched the back of his head with his left hand, annoyed and quite fearful by this new discovery. "All the more reason for us to leave as soon as possible, Captain. You know once this group is missed, the flats and the Maze will be swarming with their royal fleet."

Daigh looked down at the prince once again, whose hand he had yet to let go of, and watched the soft fluttering of his eyelids, relishing the memories that Banning's presence was conjuring up and looking at a future that, could have been, should have been his.

"You're right." Daigh said as he scooped up the prince into his arms. The boy moaned softly and instinctually nestled against his chest, as the stood and shifted Prince Banning into a more comfortable position. "Get everyone back to the Shaefra with whatever they are carrying and we'll abandon the rest. And as soon as everyone is aboard we'll leave.

Impulsively Lhoyt caught Daigh by his forearm as he started to walk by with the unconscious prince in his arms. "Captain? What are you doing with him?"

Daigh stopped to look at his commander, a boyish grin spreading across his face. "He'll be coming with us. Make sure,"

"What!" Lhoyt stammered, forgetting his place and interrupting the captain, while Brady sucked in air in surprise at this turn in events. "You know the rules Captain! No prisoners."

Daigh shrugged off the hand of his commander and continued to walk towards the Shaefra with his burden. "There will be an exception today." Daigh called over his shoulder for Brady. "If we don't bump into Cook on the way back, find her and send her to my quarters. We're going to need to keep the prince out until we get back to port."

"Aye Captain." Brady replied, a look of confusion clouding his face as he looked to Lhoyt for help.

"Captain!" Lhoyt called out again in the hopes that his raised voice might wake the sleeping prince. It it did not. "This is wrong! You're putting all of our lives in jeopardy!" Lhoyt ran the few feet between them and grasped Daigh's arm again, forcing the man to stop. "Daigh, you're being foolish! Like you say, if he is one of the princes of Birr then we don't need clans Aerin and Dar out here looking for us! And what will Lord Argus think of all of this?"

Daigh stopped and yanked his arm out of Lhoyt's grasp. The joyful smile on his face turning quickly into a scowl, for the man knew full well that if his hands weren't full he would have struck his commander. But Daigh turned away and continued walking to the Shaefra. "We won't be telling our employer."

"But?"

Daigh stopped and looked at Lhoyt as his patience slowly evaporated in the arid air of the canyon.

"You heard me Commander." Daigh growled. "No one will tell Lord Argus Berach about this. That is an order. Are we clear on this?"

"Aye, Captain."

"Brady?"

"Yes, aye, Captain." Daigh's crewman stammered.

Daigh continued on to the Shaefra, passing several of his crew who had stopped hauling the stolen goods from the barge to watch the commotion between captain and commander. But Lhoyt didn't leave the curious men idle for long as he rushed over to them and ordered them to get what they were carrying back to the Shaefra so they could leave this gods' forsaken place.

***

Thear Ibor, captain of the downed barge, moaned and threw an arm over his face to block out the sun that seemed to be beating down on him. And when he went to drag himself up off the floor of the bridge he thought he was lying on, Ibor's hand sunk into warm sand, disorienting him even more.

And as foggy remembrances of the attack and his men struggling against masked assailants came back to him, Ibor suddenly felt cold and clammy as bile rose in the back of his throat. Ibor struggled to roll onto his hands and knees and, as quickly as he could, began crawling away from where he had just been laying, not getting very far before he started to vomit. Once his stomach was empty and the dry heaves stopped, Ibor pushed himself into a sitting position and wiped his mouth with one sleeve of his shirt before rubbing his face with hands. But he quickly grabbed his knees with his hands, doubling over and sucked in air as another bout of nausea threatened to overtake him. Ibor thanked the gods he was able to keep the second wave down and closed his eyes, jamming his hands into the sand to steady himself. And once the pounding in his head subsided a little, Thear Ibor forced himself to stand and took a look at his surroundings.

What he saw wasn't good, as a dull humming filled his ears and his head grew numb with his vision blurring as he staggered while he fought his own body from the effects of blacking out. Once his vision cleared again he saw that all of his men were only a few feet away and scattered around him. Most of them were still unconscious. Though several of them had already come to and seemed to be just as disoriented as he was.

One of the men he was grateful to see awake was Moro Croft, his steersman who had been on duty during the attack. Croft was seated with his arms hugging his legs and his head tucked between his knees.

"Steersman, how are you feeling?" Ibor said as he stumbled over to Croft while he tried to avoid stepping on one of his comatose crew.

Croft looked up. "Been better Captain." That's when Ibor noticed that the front of Croft's shirt was wet and flaky while the sand in front of him was slowly absorbing the remains of his vomit. The smell alone threatened to make Ibor throw up all over again. Of course Croft reddened in embarrassment at his crudeness and forced a weak smile onto his lips, as he pulled from his eyes the wavy, dark brown hair that was plastered to his face. "I could use a bath."

"I think we'll all need a bath after this trip." Ibor said as he squeezed Croft's shoulder to steady himself once more as he continued the survey the situation. That's when he saw the barge. His heart sank at the damage for most of the hull was missing on its starboard side with another section looked as if it was ready to fall off in a light breeze. He let go of Croft's shoulder as he sighed in frustration. Thankfully there was a port within a day's reach once they left Murra's Maze. Although, with the condition that the ship was in, they would be flying slowly so that they would not fall apart before they reached the town.

Ibor heard Croft grunt in pain and looked to see his crewman trying to get onto his feet. Ibor helped him by grabbing the man underneath one of his armpits and held his steersman, as he went into a coughing fit, and prevented him from falling. Once Croft finished coughing and caught his breath and looked to be keeping his balance, Ibor gave him some orders. "Take whoever's capable of walking and get into the ship and try to assess what other damage it has. I'll see to the crew and get them back onto the barge."

But Croft stopped Ibor from leaving.

"Captain," Croft said as he took off his soiled shirt, crumpled it into a ball and wiped down his face and chest with what seemed to be the cleanest part of the shirt. "I saw Lieutenant Cahl up and about and he seemed to be mumbling something about Prince Dar. I don't think the prince was out here with us and the lieutenant eventually ran around the back of the barge to go looking for him."

"Damn! Croft, try to wake more of the men and start a search for the prince in the barge. I'll be back to help you as soon as I can!" Ibor called over his shoulder as he started to head in the direction the lieutenant had gone.

"Aye, Captain." Croft mumbled at Ibor's back as he dropped his ruined shirt to the ground and knelt beside the man who had been lying next to him, gently shaking the man, as he tried to rouse him.

And while Croft was following his captain's orders, Ibor had made his way to the stern of the barge, slipping down a slope of sand the ship had created during its landing. Ibor was standing and wiping sand off of his hands when he caught sight of the lieutenant, who was standing in the middle of the empty channel, staring off in the direction they had flown in to get here.

"Lieutenant!" Ibor shouted as he ran towards the man. But Goban didn't turn at the captain's call. Either he hadn't heard Ibor's shout or Goban was choosing to ignore the captain. "Lieutenant?" Ibor repeated as he reached Goban's side.

Cahl Goban looked awful. His olive skin was a pasty white as were his lips which had lost most of their color. Goban's short, dark hair was plastered to his head from sweating and there seemed to be sand in it from where Goban might have run his hand through it. And his cloak had a large, wet, messy stain on one side of it.

"They took the prince." Goban finally replied after Ibor spoke his name one more time.

"Are you sure?" Ibor asked, hoping that Goban was wrong.

"He was in the main hold, standing by my side, when we were attacked." The lieutenant turned to look at the captain and that's when Ibor noticed the dark circles under the man's eyes and the pained look on his face. "The prince wasn't with us when I awoke and I couldn't find him in the barge's hold. The only tracks I could find led here, away from the barge. Probably to where the other ship had landed after it attacked us." Goban said, pointing down to the many tracks and large indentation left from the pirate ship that could still be seen in the sand as the soft winds moving through the channel tried to obliterate them.

"Well, they couldn't have gotten too far." The captain replied, hoping to sound encouraging. Ibor turned to look in the opposite direction, avoiding Goban's gaze for a moment. "Once we get onto the flats we should be able to find them."

"We've been out for almost two hours." Goban interjected.

"What?" Ibor turned to look back at the lieutenant. "That's impossible!"

The commander walked away from Ibor and pointed upwards at the sun which was well on its way to setting behind the cliffs of Murra's Maze.

"Well take a look Captain! Tell me I'm wrong!" He spat before folding his arms across his chest and looking back towards the way they had flown into the channel, wishing that his gaze could drag the escaping pirate ship back to them.

Ibor walked over to Goban and put a hand on his shoulder before gently turning the young lieutenant to look at him. "Let's get back to the barge. We're only a day's flight from Portroe and once we're there we can alert the guard and start a search for the prince."

Anger flashed across the lieutenant's face.

"Are you mad? What we need to do is get back to the barge and start looking for him now! Now! I'm not going to fly a day out of the way, probably in the wrong direction, so we can come back hoping to find some signs of the prince!"

"I understand that Lieutenant Cahl. We just won't get very far with that gaping hole in the side of my barge. What we really need is another ship and more help to find him."

Looking Ibor in the eyes, his voice deepening, becoming hard like the stone surrounding them, the commander said, "Hole or no hole, we will start looking for the prince. Even if we have to strap your steersman down to a single plank of wood so he can fly us around, we will continue to look for Dar Banning!"

"But Lieutenant!"

"Captain Thear," Goban growled. "I'm not asking you. I'm ordering you to look for the prince. Like I said, that barge of yours can fall apart for all I care. We will be going after the prince now! Is that understood?"

Cahl Goban was one of the youngest lieutenants in the Royal Guard, just twenty-nine, and this had been his first mission; a mission that should have been routine, where the Companion's son had been placed into his care. Knowing these things, Ibor understood this would be the outcome even though he had held onto a small shred of hope that reason would win out.

"Very well Lieutenant." Ibor sighed. "We will start searching for the prince as soon as we can."

But their disagreement was interrupted by a shout from behind them and as both men turned at the sound, they found the barge's steersmen running towards them.

"What is it?" The captain shouted as he and Goban ran to meet the steersman on his way over to them.

"The lodestones! They're gone!" Croft huffed.

"What! You're mistaken!" Goban shouted as he grabbed the steersman by both shoulders and shook him.

"No, no Lieutenant." Croft said, wincing in pain as Goban's fingers dug into the bare skin of his shoulders. "While we were looking for the prince I sent someone up to the bridge to make sure everything was intact. The man returned saying that they weren't on their bases and couldn't be found on the bridge at all." Croft hissed as Goban squeezed harder as he took out his own frustration and anger on the innocent steersman.

But Ibor quickly pulled one of Goban's hands off of his man and forced the lieutenant to face him. "Pull yourself together man! Getting angry with my crew isn't going to make this situation any better."

"I'm sorry Steersman." Goban let go of Croft's other shoulder and stepped away from the two men in frustration as he tried to get his emotions under control. "I didn't mean to lash out at you."

"No worries Lieutenant." Croft said as he rubbed at the red handprints now on his shoulders.

Goban looked at Ibor. "Well Captain, I guess we have no choice but to go to Portroe now. How long will it take us to get there on foot?"

The captain chewed on his lower lip as he thought through the distance and not really wanting to answer Goban because flying to Portroe was one thing; to walk through Murra's Maze and the open desert was another. "If we are lucky, it should take us about four to five days to get to Portroe on foot."

"That long?" Goban lost his composure, his shoulders slumping, a defeated look filling his face at the thought of how he would be explaining this to Banning's father and his partner, the Lord Aerin Riocard of Birr.

"Yes. Depending on the weather, it could be more or it could be less."

"Well." Goban said as he stared beyond Ibor and Croft, and blinked away tears of frustration that had formed in the corners of his eyes. He ran a hand through his hair, dislodging some of the sand that had been in it, the grains bouncing off his red cloak, disappearing and to be lost among the multitude of sand on the channel's floor. "We should see how the rest of your crew and my men are doing and see what supplies we've been left with."

"I agree." The captain said as the three men turned and headed back to the barge. The sun was starting to sink beyond the tops of the cliffs and a cool strong breeze began to blow through the gorge, stirring up the sand.

"We'll move quicker if we leave most of your crew and the injured here. I can leave most of my men behind to protect them." Then Goban snorted and looked at the captain. "They can also protect what's left of your barge too."

Goban's quick thinking gave the captain a glimmer as to why this young Gwerin had been made a lieutenant so quickly. Hopefully that promotion would not be the demise of this man. Nor his. Ibor patted one of Goban's armored shoulders. "Don't worry lieutenant, we'll find the prince."

Goban looked at the older man for a moment then turned back to look at the barge where they could see the barge's crew and his own men sorting through the debris that was strewn about it. Goban's right cheek twitched involuntarily as he thought about his failure in his duty to Prince Dar and to the royal family.

"I hope you're right Captain, I hope you're right."

Chapter 2
Kinsale
Capitol of Birr
Lord Riocard's Library

It took Captain Thear and Lieutenant Cahl, along with five other members of the captain's crew, almost two days to make their way through Murra's Maze. Taking very few breaks as they stuck to the shadows of the cliffs and forcing them to walk on through the night. But once they were out in the open desert, their struggle began as they crossed over ever shifting dunes of sand with a sun that relentlessly beat down on them from a cloudless sky.

On board a ship you could stay inside and avoid the persistent wind. But here the wind was all around them, pounding them with sand so that they had no choice but to wrap cloth around their heads and mouth while keeping hands in front of their eyes to protect them from the sands bitter sting. Their ordeal out on the Flats continued for about a day and a half when, by the luck or whim of the gods, they were spotted by a small vessel flying across the desert from the west. Exhausted and dirty, they explained who they were to the vessel's captain, who immediately flew them to Portroe to get help.

The city of Portroe was a way station of sorts for ships flying to countries surrounding northern Birr, with a large garrison and several ships maintained by the Royal Guard as its protection. Upon their arrival to the city Ibor sent four of his crew back to his downed ship on vessels manned by members of the Royal Guard. And as word spread throughout the city of the attack, several locally owned vessels followed on the heels of the military ships out into the desert to lend aid and protection to the damaged vessel with its injured crew.

Ibor, Goban and Croft, who had also made the trek with his captain and the lieutenant, were immediately taken to Kinsale by another of the Guard's ships. The flight from Portroe to Kinsale took two days. Two more days of frustration for Cahl Goban, two more days lost looking for his charge.

Now, after being escorted to Aerin Riocard's library, the captain and lieutenant stood before the Royal Family. Lord Aerin Riocard, the ruler of Birr, sat at his desk while his companion Dar Fionn, the father of Banning stood behind him, a hand tightly clenching the leather of Riocard's chair. Riocard's own son and the half-brother of Banning, Prince Aerin Manus, and Mair Betrys, the mother to both princes, who also happened to be the High Sagartta to the goddess Cavanna, were also in the room. Another young man in the livery of the Royal Guard stood quietly at the doorway to the library, his arms crossed over his chest as he and everyone else in the room listened to Ibor and Goban recount their ordeal.

"And when we awoke we found ourselves lying outside of the barge." The captain explained to his liege lord who had one hand stroking his bearded chin, while his partner Fionn began to fidget behind him. Riocard's son, Manus, was standing at the left side of his father's desk with his right hand resting on top of its surface, while watching the two men standing in front of his father. Manus' mother stood at the only window in the room which took up the entire wall behind Riocard's desk. Her back was to everyone while her gaze was lost over the city. Thear Ibor found the quiet demeanor of the family disconcerting. The only one with any sign of emotion being Banning's father who was struggling to keep himself composed, and sighed as he readied himself to continue with his story.

But before Ibor could continue, the lieutenant put a hand on his shoulder, interrupting him so that Cahl could take over in the telling of their tale. Cahl Goban felt he had been the primary person charged to protect the prince and right now he did not want someone else talking for him and taking responsibility for his failure.

Fearing that he would lose his composure in front of Banning's family, Goban stared ahead with his back straight, hands clasped behind his back, as he avoided contact with everyone in the room as he spoke. "As soon as I awoke, I noticed Prince Dar missing from my side, where he had been while we tried to escape from the attack, and began searching for him. The only tracks we found led back to where the other ship had landed." Goban blinked and looked at Riocard who met his gaze with his own. "They must have taken him my Lord or we would have found him wandering somewhere near us."

"Whoever attacked you knew what they were doing." Riocard said, interrupting Goban with his deep voice, laying no blame on either man's head. "Fortunately no one was killed."

"That we know of." Mumbled Manus, who, unlike his father, was all too willing to blame the lieutenant for his brother's disappearance, freely giving the man an accusatory eye. But Manus had always been quick to anger and rage now filled him as he thought of his missing younger half-brother and of how he should have gone on this trip with him so that it was he who should have seen to his protection.

"Your brother is still alive." Betrys said as she turned away from the window to face her oldest son. "Blessed Cavanna assures me Banning is still alive and I feel no emptiness in my heart when I think of him."

"Then have Blessed Cavanna tell you where he is so we can go rescue him." Manus quipped as looked at his mother from over his shoulder.

Betrys smiled sympathetically at her son. "You know that she cannot. You of all people know it is not for the gods to interfere in our lives as they once did, but to give us their guidance. If you have so easily forgotten your history of the wars that were fought across the lands in the name of the gods, then go down to the wharves and wonder why the oceans are dry. Be thankful Cavanna even let us know that your brother is still alive."

Fionn looked at his foster-son sympathetically as Manus crossed his arms and turned to glower at some rows of books. Everyone who was close to the Aerin clan knew of Manus' devotion and what might be considered over protectiveness of his brother. They also knew about his more than slight disdain for the gods.

"Do you think the Mendens could possibly be moving their attacks further north?" Fionn finally asked, hoping to find an answer as to why his son was missing.

"Not likely." The captain, who had flown the Flats most of his life, said as he commented on their age old enemies from the south. "If it were the Mendens, they would have killed or taken all of us as slaves and burned the barge." Ibor looked at Riocard. "More likely these raiders are the same ones that sporadically attack vessels from Amarra and the smaller kingdoms to the east of us."

"I thought these raids had lessened since Iniscarn started selling its military out as escorts across the Flats." Manus queried as he looked to his father for an answer.

"True, the attacks have become fewer over the years." Riocard replied in response to his son. "All the more reason they might be spreading out to find new areas and ships to raid. We'll have to consider persuading our merchants to move in convoys with escorts from the Guard for a while." He thought out loud, as he started to consider strategies to protect his people.

Manus' face darkened at his father's supposed callousness. "That doesn't help Banning now." He growled as he slapped the top of his father's desk. "What is wrong with you?"

Aerin Riocard ignored his son's brashness as he stood and looked at the young man. The Lord of Birr was half a head taller than his son. Broad shouldered, who had always been an impressive man and whose presence could fill a room. Just like it did now. "Unfortunately, your brother isn't my only subject or my only problem. I, we, have a whole kingdom we need to consider protecting."

"Manus," Riocard continued, his tone softening as he watched the pained look filling his son's eyes. "We'll need to get a ship and crew together and ready to fly back to the barge. I am sure that the Guard that were already sent there should have everything under control and have helped Captain Thear's men through their ordeal. But I think you should go to see how they are doing and I think the crash site will be the best place for you to start looking for your brother."

"Me?"

"Yes. As much as I want to be the one to go and search for Banning, my place is here. So I want you to be one who leads the search for your brother. Rest assured I will not be sending you alone."

Riocard looked at his captain and lieutenant. "Ibor, get the Camalain ready for flight. It's an older ship but you have flown it before and it is large enough to hold a large crew. Lieutenant Cahl, the ship should have enough space to hold its crew and about thirty guards. Pick the best soldiers from my own men. You'll be leaving by dusk."

"Yes M'lord." Goban replied, stunned that he was being told he would be going back out on this search. Goban had certainly thought he was going to be demoted and sent to some far off garrison after losing one son. Not to be sent out to help protect the other.

Riocard easily read the look on Goban's face. "Lieutenant, whoever attacked you knew what they were doing. It also takes courage to be willing to brave the Flats, the way you did. You are a good soldier and now both of my sons need you. Is that understood?"

"Yes M'lord."

Riocard turned back to his son. "Manus, go to the temple of Barra, search out the Sagart Seb Cullen and request that he join you on this venture."

"You want me to fetch a sagart? The last thing we need on this trip is a priest." Manus snorted.

"Your impetuousness borders on heresy!" Betrys snapped as she looked at her son, anger clouding her eyes and her voice. "At times you go too far in your lack of respect for the gods and now is not the time to lose favor with them."

Lack of faith in the gods was an ongoing argument Riocard had had with his son for the past several years now and their discussions usually ended in a stalemate. This lack of faith in his son was a disappointment and a source frustration to the ruler of Birr.

"Your mother is correct." Riocard agreed. "Sagart Cullen has always been a friend to Clan Aerin and priest to our deity, Barra. The god and his brethren have blessed Birr with peace and unity for almost a thousand years. Show some respect and do not be so glib about the gods and those who serve them!"

Embarrassed at his own outburst and being called upon it by his two parents, Manus acquiesced to the two of them. "Forgive me father, mother. I didn't mean to offend and was only concerned that we would lose time if we have to go to the Inner City in search of one sagart."

"Nonsense." The High Sagartta said as she walked over to her oldest son, an expression that might be considered tenderness replacing the anger that had been there, and ran a hand through his dark, shoulder length hair. Manus looked at her as she continued to talk to him. "There is plenty of time to get the good sagart while others prepare the Camalain for your journey, and retrieving Sagart Cullen should not take you long if you head over to the Inner City now."

"But I still have to pack my own gear." Manus stammered, still looking for a reason not to fetch the man and to hopefully leave without him.

"I'll see to it personally and have your gear and clothing stowed into your cabin." Fionn chimed in. "All will be ready before you return from the temple."

Knowing that he had lost this battle, Manus sighed. "Very well."

"And take Kael with you." His father added as he nodded to the other young man still standing by the doorway. "Kael, we'll make sure your gear is taken care of too."

"Aye, Milord." Karam Kael said as he moved away from the door jamb as his friend left the side of his father's desk and approached him.

Riocard waved a hand, dismissing Manus, his friend, as well as Ibor and Goban from the room. Betrys walked back to the window, ignoring Fionn as he collapsed into Riocard's chair, covering his face with his hands.

Riocard walked over to stand behind his companion and rubbed his shoulders, pressing down on the knots in the middle of his shoulder blades. "Don't worry, we'll find him" He said reassuringly.

"But he could be anywhere." Fionn murmured.

"Still, we will find him and have our family whole."

Betrys turned to look at the fathers of her two sons, hiding the contempt she felt for the two of them. For, even though they believed in the gods, she was becoming more and more unsympathetic in their lack of control over Manus and his outspokenness against the gods. Especially when it came to his lack of devotion to Cavanna. In her heart the goddess Cavanna, the mother of them all, came first. Even before her family.

"You must trust in the gods for they have a plan for him." Betrys said sagely, her hands clasped in front of her. "They have a plan for us all."

Fionn looked at Betrys and frowned at the woman who bore him his only son. Even though he loved his son dearly, and if the choice had been his own to make, he never would have chosen Betrys as the mother of his child. Never. He turned away, not caring if he offended the High Sagartta and openly voiced what was in his heart. "I would have been just fine if their plans had not included my son."

***

After leaving the library, the captain and lieutenant went to organize the Camalain and to gather the men needed for the journey while

Manus and Kael left the castle and headed through the part of city now referred to as "Old Kinsale" so they could catch a tram into the Inner City.

"Sorry." Kael said as they walked down the main street to what was once the main thoroughfare to Kinsale.

Manus looked at his friend. A frown etched his face and his blue eyes were darkened with concern for his younger brother and only grunted a reply to Kael.

The two had met after Kael's father, a member of the Royal Guard, had been transferred to Kinsale from their home in Cliefden and had quickly become fast friends. And over the years Kael had learned to interpret Manus' dark moods, knowing that avoidance was the best tactic for them. Unfortunately there was no way of skirting around this one and tried to look for something positive within this situation.

"Your mother is the High Sagartta to Cavanna. You must know the goddess would have told her if Banning was in any real danger."

That was certainly the wrong thing to say because Manus' face darkened even more, the corners of his lips trembling slightly and his forehead furrowing in rage.

"Do I?" He snorted. Men who recognized the prince bowed and moved out of their way as they crossed an intersection, a small tavern on one of its corners, and continued towards the outer wall that was still several streets away. "Some mother! Being high sagartta didn't help to stop the attack nor protect Banning. And did the most holy Cavanna tell us where he is? No! And by the grace of Cavanna we now need to go and find him ourselves!"

They turned a corner, walking down a side street containing a mixture of homes and shops, in silence. But only for a moment as Manus' tirade started up once again. "The gods love to interfere in our lives when it suits their needs! But when we need their help, they willingly ignore us, making sure we have no choice but to take care of ourselves." Manus clenched his fists, his fingernails biting into the flesh of his palms. "As far as I'm concerned, the world would be a much better place without them and their whims muddling our lives."

The two men came to the end of the street they were on and stopped as several carts drawn by pack animals crossed their path on the street that was running perpendicular to the one they were on. Once the team of animals and their burden cleared they could cross over and be at the defensive wall that surrounded Old Kinsale. Almost diagonally across from them a sloping buttress extended from the street up to the top of the wall, with a flight of stairs leading up its spine to the tram station above.

As Manus started to cross the street and headed towards the station, Kael grabbed his elbow and stopped him. "You don't mean that? Those things you said about the gods? We wouldn't be here if it wasn't for them and you know they created us. And they did save us from killing ourselves!"

Manus shrugged off Kael's hand and continued across the street to where other citizens of Kinsale were making their way to and from the tram.

"For all we know we were here and the gods stumbled across us!" He said sarcastically. "The only thing the gods did was to save themselves from themselves in their endless bickering and warring. We just happened to be the tool they enjoyed using the most and if we had died off from their fighting they would now have had no one to worship them."

It wasn't until Manus stepped onto the curb on the opposite side of the street that he realized Kael wasn't with him. He turned and saw that his friend was still standing at the corner, the cobbled lane now a rift between the two of them. Manus knew Kael kept a shrine to several of the gods in his room and that in his anger he had crossed a line with his friend. Sighing in frustration, Manus hunched his shoulders and shrugged his hands into his pockets and walked back over to Kael.

"Now I'm sorry." He said when Kael finally looked at him. "You know I do believe in the gods. I just don't have any faith in them. You should have known that by now."

"I know." Kael said grudgingly, giving in to his friend.

Manus smiled at Kael's acquiescence and, placing a hand on his friend's shoulder, steered him across the street. They continued on in silence as they started up the stairs, passing several men who were making their way down the stairs, and came to a large landing at the top of the buttress.

This section of the buttress and the surrounding wall had been reconstructed into a station for the tram system that connected what was now called Old Kinsale to the rest of the city that had been built across the strait that once separated the island where Capitol had originally been built from the mainland. There were two tram tracks that went directly into the city while a third rail stood a little away from the others; all of which were powered by lodestones. A bridge that had been built over five hundred years ago, could also be seen below them, extending across the channel to the newer part of the city that most of the population used to commute between the new and older part of the city.

The two friends passed by several groups of men waiting for the next tram and headed towards the shuttle sitting quietly on the third rail. This rail and its car were reserved for the royal family, although it was Manus' mother who used it the most for traveling primarily between her home at the temple and the royal castle where Riocard, Fionn and her two sons lived. The car was protected by several guards, two men and one woman, who came to attention at Manus' approach. Manus saluted them as he walked by and went through the open door of the car with the female guard following them into the tram and seating herself in the pilots chair at the front of the cabin while one of the other guards closed the door behind them.

"To the temple please." Manus said as he and Kael sat down.

"Aye, Prince Aerin." The guard replied as she placed her hands on the lodestones, her eyes glazing over, as she lifted the car to take them to the Temple to Cavanna.

The track they were moving on briefly paralleled the bridge over the channel and they could see many Birrnians moving back and forth along its path, making their way home or to do business in some of the more exclusive shops housed in the older section of Kinsale. But once they were across the channel, the rail veered east while the other two tracks continued on to different destinations within the city. The royal tram moved through a small fortification built in the outer wall, a regular stop for Manus' father, then traveled back into the city to pass a stop in the merchants' district, followed by the stop at the Temple to Cavanna.

As the tram moved silently along, past its first stop and on to the temple, Manus leaned forward, resting his elbows on his knees and stared off into the distance as he rung his hands, lost in thoughts of finding his brother and getting him home safely. Kael on the other hand was slumped in his seat, his legs stretched out in front of him while he fingered a chain around his neck, watching Manus out of the corner of his eye. Kael had several charms on that gold chain, each representing the gods Barra, Aodhagen and Cillach and as was his habit, he rubbed each charm as he said a silent prayer to the deities, wishing he had something positive to say to Manus that he would find helpful.

Karam Kael knew his friend was strong willed and it showed in almost everything he did. Manus was always quick to anger, slow to smile and almost always brooding about something. And as he found his way into becoming a leader, Manus' commands were direct and usually quite stern, although he was always there when his men needed him and he supported them no matter what, receiving their devotion. So it was no surprise that his father, Lord Aerin Riocard, seemed to always comment on how much Manus was like his grandfather, the old lord of Birr.

But unlike the old lord of Birr, his belief in the gods was a belief without faith.

Manus believed that the gods had done more harm than good for the Gwerin race. Their senseless destruction of the oceans and seas to create peace had been self-serving, resolving only the conflict they had created amongst themselves.

Gods who felt no guilt in using their worshipers as swords and shields in their great wars that had once spanned the centuries, had once preyed upon each other as they tried to dominate the people of Gwer. The gods knowing that the Gwerin were about to wipe themselves out and in doing so, would have most likely ended their own existence. Cavanna, the chief among them, couldn't even convince her brethren to come to a truce to save themselves', so with the help of the few that would support her, she banished seven of the pantheon, one of them being her own mate, to another world.

But Ciaran, the god of mischief, the creator of chaos, and one of Cavanna's brothers, had remained behind with his followers to sporadically harass, enslave and sometimes kill the other peoples of Gwer. "A reminder of whom we used to be and that we should always work on keeping the peace with our neighbors." Manus once drawled as he mimicked one of his mother's countless sermons doled out to him as to why the Mendens were allowed to remain. But Manus felt no qualms about cursing Ciaran and his followers, only wishing that they would have left with the others.

Why, there was once a time while sitting in a pub drinking beers, Manus had mused, quite loudly and to the discomfit of Kael, that they hadn't been created by the gods but had been found by them and been "enslaved" by the gods to serve their purposes. Kael quickly shushed

Manus whose words were slurred and whose mug was raised into the air with ale splashing out, hoping no one who noticed the prince's tirade would take him seriously.

"Worrying about me again?"

Kael blinked, startled in the middle of his daydreaming, only now realizing that Manus had turned and had been looking at him for a while. "What do you mean?"

Manus smirked, his eyes glittering with just a hint of joy, as if he had caught Kael in some mischievous act, before turning back to look out the window and the vista of Kinsale as it passed by them. "You always rub your charms and begin to mouth prayers when you start to worry about me."

"I was not praying." Kael said, laughing in embarrassment. But Manus began to recite a devotion that Kael usually said to Cillach, the god of war, that had just come out of Kael's mouth.

"I guess I did then." Kael looked down and realized he was holding his charm to Cillach between his fingers. He looked at it and the other charms dangling from his necklace before raising them for Manus to look at. "You see? I've worried about you so much that I've almost rubbed Cillach away." Kael's eyes clouded over as he looked at his friend who was squinting and pretending to be concerned about the charm he was holding between his fingers. "Of course I worry about you. Manus, not only are you my friend but you're the closest thing I have to a brother."

Manus looked awkward in the face of Kael's honesty. "Thanks." He whispered, his voice lost for the moment, not truly happy with his friend's honesty, and not knowing what else to say, offered to buy Kael a new charm of Cillach so that his friend could envision him when he prayed.

"Thanks, but these are fine." Kael placed the necklace back under his shirt and patted the charms against his chest before reaching over to scratch the middle of Manus' back. "And don't worry. If you can't trust in the gods at least trust in us and that we'll find Banning."

Manus, unable to say anything through his jumble of emotions only nodded as he looked down at his feet.

But their conversation was interrupted by the guards garbled, dull, hollow announcement from the front of the tram that they had arrived as the tram slowed and bobbed slightly, coming to a stop at the only landing platform built on the side of the large complex that was the Temple to Cavanna.

The two young men stood as the tram's door was once again opened from the outside and walked out onto the platform where several guards could be seen. Here at the temple the Royal Guard was comprised all of women. And it was women who guarded most of the inner wall of Kinsale that was the women's district.

"Wait for us. We shouldn't be long." Manus commanded to the guard who followed them out of the tram.

"As you wish Prince Aerin." She replied to the backs of both men as they headed into the Temple to Cavanna.

The Temple to Cavanna, as well as every temple in Kinsale, was connected by the wall that surrounded the inner city that made up the women's district with a parapet running the length of the top of the wall. A route that would be the easiest way for Manus and Kael to reach the Temple of Barra while skirting the city traffic below them.

Once they left the confines of Cavanna's temple they walked above several blocks, the women's district on one side of the wall, the men's on the other, before reaching the temple of Maat, goddess of the air and winds. Here the walkway wrapped around the outer wall of the goddess' temple with flags of cerulean, Maat's color, flapping from the upper levels of the temple.

As they followed the path that the parapet took around the temple, the bazaar and merchants' quarters came into view below them. Shops, taverns and inns made up most of this section of the bustling city on either side of the wall. The smell of cooked foods, along with the voices of Birrnians haggling in the marketplace wafted through the air. And with everything that had been going on that morning, Kael hadn't found time to eat and now just thinking about the food being cooked below made his stomach rumble loudly from hunger. He just shrugged his shoulders unapologetically when Manus looked at him in annoyance as his stomach rumbled again.

Thankfully the Temple to Barra was next in line along the wall and could now be clearly seen only several blocks away. The temple was large, almost a town unto itself, and built of granite. Its center was a vast space that was open to the sky and had a network of buildings attached it that branched off on either side of the temple's walls. And since Barra was the god of the earth, many of those outbuildings housed guilds and workshops for the cities masons, potters and sculptors. As a matter of tradition, visit any city, town or village anywhere in Birr and one would find a temple devoted to Barra and his craftspeople sited near a bazaar or market square so that their products could be readily available to sell to the public. And as the two neared the temple the incessant sound of hammers striking against stone and on metal began to fill the air.

The rampart they were on eventually came to end at a landing which was dwarfed by a tower with its entrance protected by two men and two women of the Royal Guard. The guards immediately recognized the prince and came to attention and saluted him before stepping aside so he and Kael could pass into the tower. The walkway continued on across the front of the temple, hidden from the streets below by a façade on the temple wall while to their left a flight of stairs led down into the temple complex. Manus and Kael took the stairs and exited into a guardroom on the ground floor and after passing by several more guards, walked into a hallway outside of the room. The hallway joined a main corridor where acolytes and sagarts were going about their daily business. Many of the priests recognized the prince and bowed their heads respectfully as the two passed by them.

"Excuse me Sagart." Manus said to one of those priests. "Could you tell me where I could find the Sagart Seb Cullen?"

"You might be able to find him in the gardens Prince Aerin. He usually goes to one of the smaller glades to pray at this time of day."

"Thank you." Manus replied to the sagart who bowed to the prince before walking away.

"Well, it sounds like it should be easy enough to find him." Kael remarked as they also continued on their way.

"We'll see." Manus said a little doubtfully as the two followed a corridor with an archway eventually appearing on their left. Sunlight poured through the opening as Manus and Kael passed underneath the arch and walked onto a granite colonnade that encircled the gardens. The gardens were the Temple to Barra and they created a park with paths leading through trees to open areas where anyone, man or woman, could come to meditate and pray to the god of the earth. But then again, most of the temples built to the gods were open aired structures with the exception to this being the temples to Cavanna; her temples were libraries that housed the breeding records of almost every child born since the "Great Rift" had united the world.

"So, where to?" Kael asked as he and Manus stepped onto the lawn surrounding the gardens and found several paths leading away from them and disappearing into the vast stand of trees directly in front of them.

"I think I know where we can find him." Manus said as he headed for a path on their right. "Seb Cullen use to be the sagart that would join my father on his adventures onto the flats. And always before a trip, he would come to the temple to meditate and there was one particular spot that he and the sagart liked. Father made sure I came and prayed for Barra's protection when I went on those trips with them." Manus slapped then scratched the back of his neck, chasing away a bug, as he and Kael passed an open space of lawn where several men were seated quietly on the ground as they meditated.

"It's been a while since I've been here." Manus said quietly. A slight twinge of shame filling his gut at the negligence he had shown to their clan's deity.

"Me, I prefer to pray at the Temple of Aodhagan." Kael replied, stating the obvious about who his family was devoted to as he tried to change the subject. Kael knew that his friend used to visit here with his father and on more than one occasion Manus had invited him to come along and pray with them. But now, Kael sensed Manus was becoming maudlin and hoped to staunch the bitterness and anger that would usually follow by prattling about his own ambling musings.

"I thought you said you preferred worship at a tavern not far from Aodhagan's temple"

"What?" Kael asked, caught off guard by the comment.

But Manus continued with his jibe as they continued to follow the wooded path. "Oh, not the tavern itself but someone you met there. What was his name? Bru? Brick?"

Kael sighed, fondly remembering the attractive man Manus was talking about. "His name was Breck. And you know it was nothing. Why, he left the next day to go back to his father's estate in Glenmur."

Manus chuckled. "Well, with that look on your face I'm sure you have a place to stay if you ever decide to head inland."

"I'm sure." Kael screwed up his face in annoyance before sighing wistfully as he once more remembered the short lived yet frenetic encounter with the boy from Glenmur.

"We're here." Manus said, interrupting his friend's reverie as a small path appeared to their left among some tall grasses with two tall, weathered stones flanking the path before it entered into a small grove of trees. Without saying a word Manus took the path that would hopefully lead him and Kael to the sagart.

Even though it looked like the glade had just entered could comfortably hold about twenty or so worshipers seated on the ground, Manus and Kael could see that it wasn't that big. The lawn was a rich green and manicured, surrounded by a vast grove of old river birch. The trees, slightly thicker than a man's torso, grew straight and the bark of their trunks were a slivery grey as the trees stretched almost fifty feet into the air. The trees' leaves rustled softly and branches creaked in the faint breeze moving through the glade, obscuring any noise and setting this shrine apart from the outside world.

There were two statues in the glade. The first in all his manly perfection was Barra and at the other end of the small glade was a statue of his sister, Ennaya, the goddess of all living things. A man wearing the robes of a sagart, shades of brown, tan and off white, colors that represented the earth, stood in front of Barra's statue. The sagart was bald with a neatly trimmed, grey goatee covering his chin and looked to be in his sixties. A cane was held in his left hand that was keeping him steady on his feet while his right hand was outstretched in prayer. The men could see that his eyes were closed and there was a look of serenity on his face while he communed with his god Barra. Manus immediately recognized the gentle, insightful man and knew they had found his father's friend, their family's sagart, Seb Cullen.

"Ah, hmm, excuse me Sagart." Manus stuttered. For now that he was here in the glade Manus could almost feel a faint hint of Barra whispering around him and he was now loathe to interrupt Seb Cullen while he prayed.

Cullen opened his eyes and turned to look at the two men and smiled. "Prince Manus!" he said with familiarity, using the prince's personal name instead of his clans. "Your visit is a surprise! You know it has been a while since you have been out to temple." The sagart said as he headed over to them while walking with a limp he now lived with after his left leg had been injured in an accident. "Kael. It is good to see you too." Cullen said to Manus' friend who nodded politely to the sagart's greeting.

But when he noticed the distressed look appear on Manus' face, and fearing that something might have happened to Manus' father, Cullen couldn't stop himself from asking, "What is it my prince?"

"Banning is missing." Manus' voice shook as he made the statement, his guard slipping and pain showing on his face as talked to the grandfatherly man.

"What do you mean?"

Manus cleared his throat and looked away, watching little motes of pollen flickering in the sunlight, tossed about on the faint breeze moving through the glade, while he pulled himself together. Manus then proceeded to recount the story Captain Thear and Lieutenant Cahl had told them in his father's library; of how pirates had raided the ship, and of how his half-brother was the only one taken as a hostage during the attack. Cullen listened and watched the prince intently while Kael, who had already listened to this story once before, moved about the glade as he pretended to inspect some plants and statues, but all the while listening to the subtle hint of pain and anger in his friend's voice.

"Now father is gathering a force to find Banning and he would like you to be a part of it."

"Certainly." Cullen replied. He had been the sagart to Manus' family and a friend of his fathers for decades. To not help the Aerins in their time of need was out of the question. He began walking, limping, towards the path that would lead out of the glade. "When do we leave?"

"Father expects us to leave by dusk. Sooner if possible." Manus replied as he and Kael followed the sagart and joined him on the path. "We'll have several steersmen on board flying the ship day and night so we can reach the site where they were attacked at as soon as possible."

"Of course. I do not need much so leaving by the end of the day will not be a problem. I just need to leave word with the high sagart and will head over to the port to meet you." Cullen explained as he hobbled along.

Even though Manus was sensitive to the man's infirmary, he was beginning to see it as a liability. What had his father been thinking of when he ordered that he fetch the lame sagart for this trip? Manus found himself thanking the gods that they did not have to walk all the way there.

"My Prince?"

"What!" Manus snapped, realizing he had allowed himself to be distracted by thoughts of the sagart being a burden instead of listening to the man. He turned to look at Kael for help who was looking back at him, who also had a look of shock on his face at Manus' rudeness.

"The ship. I was asking you what the name of the ship is and where it will be berthed so I can find you."

"The ship?" Manus mumbled, looking down at his feet, embarrassed at his outburst, as he tried to recollect his thoughts and remember its name.

"It's called the Camalain, Sagart." Kael interjected, coming to his friend's aid. He patted the priest's shoulder to get his attention, momentarily distracting him from Manus. "The ship is berthed at the docks near Old Town. And not to worry, we won't leave without you."

"Ah, the Camalain. A fine ship that I have flown on during past adventures with your father." Cullen looked back to Manus, who, after the stress of the day, had somewhat composed himself. "Manus," Cullen said quietly, sympathetically. "Do not let me keep you. Like I said, I do not need much so why don't you two go take care of what you need to and I will be at the docks as soon as I can?"

"Very well Sagart." Manus said as he picked up his pace and passed by Cullen with Kael in tow. "We'll see you soon." Manus turned, giving Cullen a weak smile and a half-hearted wave. Kael also nodded back to the priest as they headed back to the main path that led into the gardens.

"Oh, Prince Manus! One more thing!" Cullen shouted, getting the young men's attention before they were out of earshot. Manus turned to look back at him, a frown covering his face at being stalled once again. "Do you mind if I bring someone along?"

"Yes, yes! I'm sure we can always make room for another sagart or a temple guard." Manus turned away and started back down the path, waving his hand in the air, not bothering to stop or turn to look back at the priest this time. "Do what you think is right!"

"Thank you, my Prince." Cullen said softly as he stopped walking and watched as the two friends picked up their stride and started to run through the gardens. Cullen sighed, watching them disappear around a stand of trees and once again limped down the path.

***

As soon as the men had left the glade a heavy silence crept back in and a bird landed on the lawn and began poking about the ground looking for worms. The bird hopped about, as birds have always done, thrusting its beak into the soft dirt, like a sword into flesh, looking for prey. It stopped, rustled its wings and sent out a trill to fill the void of the previous voices as a gentle breeze rustled through the trees.

But a voice, soft and feminine with a faint lilt of youthfulness, bodiless, danced on the air. "Their prince could be anywhere by now. They could search for an eternity and never find where he has been taken."

The wind changed direction, not a common occurrence, as it swirled about the glade, sending the pollen into a glittering dance. Another voice, as masculine as the other was feminine, filled the glade with its bravado. "Not to worry Ennaya. They will find him."

The bird continued on its quest for food, ignoring the voices as it hopped around the statue of Ennaya, the wind swirling a little more forcefully, tossing some loose brush into the air. "You know she is watching you Barra. And you know the law. Stop meddling in their little problems."

"Tsk, tsk, Ennaya. You know that my meddling has protected many lives from the clutches of Ciaran and his followers."

While the conversation continued between the two gods the bird, about halfway between the statues of the brother and sister, found a worm. The worm put up a fight as it was pulled from the ground. But it was short lived as the bird pulled the long, wriggling creature out into the open and swallowed it whole. Chirping a song of victory, the bird hopped twice before spreading its wings and flying away, carrying itself upwards on the gods' voices.

"Barra! Do nothing!"

Chuckling, solid in its confidence, bounced through the air again.

"Ennaya," Barra whispered. "If you had been paying attention you would have realized that saying such a thing would mean nothing."

***

After making arrangements with Barra's high sagart so that someone could perform his services while he would be away, Cullen made his way to his own home, that was part of the temple grounds, packed belongings he thought he would need on the journey, then headed to the Stone Masons' Guild to enlist the help of that someone he was hoping to take with him.

The Masons' Guild was only a street away from the temple but it spread across several blocks of the city. Creating a small neighborhood of its own where most of the buildings consisted of large workrooms on the ground levels with residences and dorms for apprentices on the upper floors and creating a sort of small village nestled within Kinsale. And, even though many men were out on the street for a midafternoon break, a persistent sound of hammering could be heard echoing out of open doors from many of the workrooms, as Cullen walked down the Guild's main street in search of his help.

Cullen hadn't gone too far into the neighborhood when he saw a guildmaster that he was friendly with standing outside of a large warehouse with several young men, most likely apprentices, who were gathered around him as he rolled a large chunk of marble in his hands, explaining how to polish the stone so its veining and color could be enhanced. As he approached the group, Cullen raised his cane to get the guildmaster's attention and to make some inquiries after the person he was seeking. Cullen thanked his friend before walking another block and turned right onto a much quieter street that was all walls and shuttered windows and headed for the warehouse that blocked the far end of the street and turning it into a dead end.

The warehouse's large double doors were open, allowing sunlight and a warm breeze to flow in and the sound of sweeping and someone whistling to float back out. Cullen smiled at the pitchy, erratic tune and stopped at the entrance to look in. Moving around some work benches was a man in his early twenties whose back was to the entrance as he swept the floor. There was one block of marble, a deep grey flecked with quartz standing next to one of the benches. It's top section had been carved into a squatting gargoyle while a worker's rag dangled from one of its clawed feet. Although the gargoyle seemed to be just about finished, it appeared to be flawed; a piece where one of its shoulders met a wing had been chipped away, most likely one of the many bits of marble lying on the ground.

"So they have you cleaning the workroom today, Liam?" Cullen said as he walked into the room, startling the young man whose whistling ended abruptly as he stopped sweeping and turned at the sound of Cullen's voice.

"Hello father." Liam said to Cullen, giving his father a weak smile as he held the broom in front of him. "I guess cleaning the shop is my punishment for today."

"Oh?"

Liam walked over to the gargoyle, his father trailing behind him, and ran a hand over the broken shoulder of the sculpture. "Master Rahl had asked me to smooth off some burrs on the left shoulder and, well, you can see how I took a little more off than I should have."

"Sorry Liam."

Liam looked at Cullen, shrugging in resignation, the head of the broom smacking against the base of the damaged statue.

"Don't be father. It was a test. A test that I failed. Master Rahl knew the rock was flawed and wanted to see if I would catch the imperfections. Master Rahl wasn't bothered by the mistake and said that the shoulders can be lowered and should still look fine after the sculpture is reworked. Still, I should have caught the flaw." Liam shrugged again, careful not to knock the statue with his broom again. "So I get to sweep today."

Cullen poked at a small piece of marble on the ground with the tip of his cane, wondering why Liam had given up wood carving, which he had always been much better at. Far better than he was at stone carving.

"Well, if Rahl Kanter says it can be fixed then I am sure he will be able to fix it. Do not be too hard on yourself Liam. You are an apprentice and it takes years of practice to know what rock will do when you take a hammer and chisel to it. You know that skill is not something you learn overnight."

Liam sighed as he rubbed the back of his neck. "I know. Still, I should have seen the flaw."

Cullen closed his eyes and shook his head. Not knowing what else to say to his son, Cullen came out with what brought him here. "Well, it sounds like you could use a break."

"Sorry father." Liam said as he ran a hand through his curly black hair, sending stone dust falling to the ground. "I don't have time for a break right now. Once I'm done here I still need to go help the others finish packing a shipment of stonework that is going to Ealga, and the gods only know what Master Rahl will have in store for me after that's done." Liam continued sweeping, moving his new pile over to the one he had started before his father arrived. "I'm sorry father, but I think a break is out of the question for today."

Cullen ran a hand over his bald head. "Well, the break I'm thinking of would be much longer than an hour or two."

"What do you mean?"

Cullen then proceeded to explain the kidnapping of Prince Dar Banning, the expedition being undertaken to look for him and how Lord Aerin Riocard had asked for Cullen's aid in helping them to find his foster-son.

"And Prince Aerin Manus, who will be in charge of this mission, has allowed me to bring help, so I thought of you."

"Me?"

"Yes you. I thought you could help." Cullen smiled as he held up his cane, using it as an example as to why he needed help. "I'm not as young or as spry as I used to be."

Liam stopped working and propped the broom against the damaged sculpture and walked away from his father.

"Me?" He repeated. "I'm sure there must be another sagart from the temple that could be of more help to you than me." Liam said, hoping to find a way out of helping his foster-father, as he turned back to look at him. "Or a temple guard. You know a guard would protect you better than I ever could. I know I'll be useless on this expedition so why don't you pick someone else?"

Cullen walked over to his son and put a reassuring hand on his shoulder, giving him a tight squeeze. "Liam, you are twenty-four and you have yet to leave Kinsale. Don't you think it's time to leave the city to see what is outside of these walls?"

"I have so left the city!" Liam said defensively. "I've been on errands to some of the fortresses that surround Kinsale."

"I stand corrected. You've never left the island. I know going on a search is never a good reason, but now there is an excuse for you to see some of the world. Instead of holding up in these workrooms every day?"

"But it's safe here." Liam said as a pained look crossed his face, thinking about the disruption to his life that this journey would be.

Cullen sighed as he patted Liam's shoulder again, understanding what was going on. "The raid on your village when you were a child was unfortunate, as was the death of your real father. But Barra saved you and kept you safe until you were found, and I willingly took on that duty and since then you've become a son to me so please listen to what I have to say; do not hide behind these walls and protect yourself from the outside world. You will miss out on so much. Please, my son. Come with me so we can together find the prince."

Keir Liam looked at the man who had taken care of him for most of his life. But now, even if he would be with his father, the thought of leaving Kinsale and its safety frightened him. He sighed in resignation. "Is that an order?"

"Of course it is not."

"How long will we be gone?"

Cullen looked down at the ground as he tapped the floor lightly with his cane before looking back at his son. "I honestly do not know. It might be days or it could be months. I can only assure you we will be gone until we find Prince Dar."

The thought of being gone for what could be a long time wasn't very reassuring. Especially when Liam liked the routine his life had taken, a quiet home life with some free time for himself here and there. Though he was struggling with the skill, he liked working for Guild master Kanter, whom he didn't want to disappoint by falling behind with his training. It was all very daunting he thought as he picked up the broom and took some more swipes at the floor with it, sending dust swirls across its surface. But then again, he didn't want to let his father down or think of him as a disappointment.

"Very well. If it means so much to you, I think I can pull myself away from all of this."

Noticing the fear still lingering in Liam's eyes, Cullen smiled as he did his best to be reassuring. "Thank you. I am sure the Royal Family will appreciate what you are doing for them. I know I do." Cullen turned to leave, Liam following right behind him, and at the door he stopped and picked up his pack and looked at his son for one more time. "I have already packed what I need for the trip. Go home and get what you think you will need for a week or two and I am sure the ship will be well provisioned in case there was something we overlooked. I am heading over to the tram just outside of the merchants' square and that is where I will be waiting for you. But hurry! Prince Aerin wants to leave as soon as possible."

Liam watched his father limp back up the street, his pack rocking back and forth across his back due to his irregular gate. Liam called out to him, not to offer assistance, for his father would probably turn it down, but to let him know there was something he needed to take care of before going home.

"Father! I just need to lock up here and find master Rahl to let him know I will be away for a while."

Cullen stopped and turned, Liam just catching the wink his father gave him. "I have already spoken to the guildmaster. Everything is all set for you to leave so lock up, go home and get your belongings. And do not worry Liam, seeing the world is not so frightening as it seems and it will change you."

Liam put a hand on the doorframe as he watched his father walk down the rest of the street and turned the corner as he headed for the tram station. He looked down and tapped the doorframe with his booted foot before looking up again.

"Who says I want to change?" He whispered into the air as he closed the doors to the workroom.

Once he was home Liam made quick work of packing, throwing a couple of pants, several shirts and a cloak into his backpack. He also grabbed his canteen that he would fill with water from the communal well in the courtyard. He packed his small carving kit along with several small pieces of wood, as he figured he would have plenty of free time to do some woodcarving and thought that this would be a good way to make his time on the Camalain go by faster.

Now that he was all packed, Liam walked back into the main room of the home he had shared with Cullen and took a look around with its tan colored walls and dark wooden furniture. It had been almost nineteen years since Cullen had brought him here and eventually adopted him. Here, in this home, he felt safe, secure, and he didn't want or feel the need to worry about the outside world. But now, his father asked for his help and it was time for him to leave for a while.

Liam slung the pack over his shoulder as he made ready to leave and stopped at an alcove to the right of the door. The alcove was the home's shrine, its interior painted in a deep blue, with a statue of Barra housed within. And it had become a ritual for Liam to say a prayer to the god as he left the house for the day. No matter what the hurry, today would not change things as Liam placed a hand on the statue and closed his eyes, standing silently for a few moments as a warm wind blew into the house through the open front door.

He lingered longer than he normally would, his hand tightening on the bronze icon as he whispered the words, "Barra, take away my fear."

As he let go of the statue Liam looked around the room one more time, hoping to draw some strength and security from the place he had learned to call home. Adjusting the backpack over his shoulder, Liam stepped over the door's threshold and closed it behind him.

And as the door clicked shut a shadow of no distinct shape and cast by nothing in the room, formed and then flickered slightly in the afternoon sunlight streaming in through the windows. A man's voice, just as elusive as the shadow, softly floated through the empty room.

"Strength and a safe journey Liam. Strength and safe journey."

***

Once Liam met Cullen at the station, the two took the tram and sat in silence for the entire ride as the car made its circuitous route to the station, where they had to then make their way to the docks that were outside of Old Town. A larger wharf had been built adjacent to the newer section of the city, but it was here that the Royal Guard had most of its ships stationed so they could be in a better defensive position to protect the castle and it was here that Kael had directed Cullen to find clan Aerin's private vessel.

Stopping only briefly to get directions to the Camalain from the guards at the wharf's entrance the two men were directed to the last pier on their right.

Liam stared in awe at his surroundings as they walked to their destination. For off in the distance several stone towers with large ballistae on their roofs and slits in their walls for archers flanked the piers, with very thick walls of granite extending about a third of the way across the now sand filled bay. Each wall ended with another large tower. Their roofs were flat and held a brazier filled with wood and oil so they could be lit at night for travelers to find their way into the protected bay.

"Watch yourself!" Someone shouted as a hand shot out and forcefully stopped Liam in his tracks. For Liam had been so busy looking around that he almost tripped over some sacks in front of him. Fortunately a dock worker had stopped him just in time to prevent him from tumbling over them.

"Sorry." Liam stammered. The dockworker nodded politely, slapping his gloved hands together before proceeding to pick up one of the sacks and slung it over one of his broad shoulders before turning and carrying it across a plank to a ship berthed nearby.

Cullen had continued up a ways before realizing Liam wasn't behind him and was now waiting for his son to catch up to him. "We're not far now." He said to Liam.

"Where's the ship?"

Cullen raised his cane and pointed further down the dock. "There. The Camalain is the last ship on the left."

Unfortunately Liam was disappointed at what he saw for he assumed they would be flying in a war vessel, bristling with weapons and covered in metal plating from stem to stern. Instead, they seemed to be approaching what looked like an antiquated yacht. From what Liam could see of it, its deck looked to be elliptical with a rounded hull and the ships main deck was small and tapered towards the stern of the ship where it seemed that most of the living quarters were housed in a raised cabin section. The yacht did look like it might have been brightly painted in shades of reds and gilded at one time, but age and the elements had blasted its colors to a dull finish, exposing the ships carved wood in many places. A brass rail also surrounded most of the main deck but time had taken its toll on it as well, tarnishing it to a dull, pitted black.

"Not what I was expecting." Liam said out loud.

"Oh?" His father replied. "Well, do not let its looks deceive you. Lord Riocard's father, Aerin Broll, built this ship in his younger days so that he could explore the flats. The Camalain can hold almost fifty men; soldiers and a crew to man it. There are ballistae on the stem and stern of the ship for defense and with the ship not plated there is less weight for a steersman to hold up in the air so it flies faster and it is much easier to maneuver." A faint smile crossed Cullen's lips. "I have been on many adventures in this vessel. As a matter of fact, I was on the Camalain when we rescued you at Fomor."

Liam looked down, disturbed at being reminded of his former home. "I don't, I don't remember being on it."

Cullen looked at his foster-son who had always been a sensitive child and had remained so as he had gotten older. "Of course you would not remember; you were only five. And everything happened quickly after that as we tried to save as many villagers as possible. And with all that was going on why should you remember a boat?" They were now closer to the Camalain and Cullen pointed out two Gwerin standing nearby while workers moved about them, loading supplies onto the vessel. "Let's go. There are Prince Aerin and Captain Thear.

As they walked over to the captain and the prince, Liam was relieved to see that he would at least know another person on board the Camalain. Captain Thear was a friend of his fathers and the two of them had been on many missions with Aerin Riocard when the current ruler of Birr was just a prince and his father still ruled over Birr. Thear Ibor was a friendly man who loved to talk about his three sons, all sailors of the skies like himself; two captains and a steersman. Captain Thear would regale Liam of the adventures that he or his sons had been on and occasionally would give Liam a souvenir or a coin from some foreign land that Liam kept in a small clay bowl in his room at home.

And, even though Liam had met Lord Aerin when he had visited their home, he had yet to meet his son and was surprised that he didn't seem to be much older than himself. The prince looked to be almost as tall as his father, a little over six feet and he had a head of dark, wavy, shoulder length hair. And as they got closer to them, Liam noticed he also had the same blue eyes as his father. The prince could not help but look regal garbed in the armor of the Royal Guard with his hands crossed over his chest as he watched Captain Thear give orders to the men that were still loading supplies onto the ship.

The men were so busy with getting the crew and ship organized that they did not notice Cullen and Liam approaching until the sagart cleared his throat to get their attention.

"Ah, Sagart. Glad to see you have arrived." Manus said, acknowledging them.

"Yes, Cullen." Ibor said as he stepped over to clasp his friend's hand. "It is good to see you. Especially under such unfortunate circumstances. And Liam, it is good to see you too. How have you been?"

Liam, who had been carrying both his and his father's pack had fallen a step behind his father, hoping to avoid being part of the conversation. "I'm fine Captain. Thank you." He replied, fumbling with the packs as he dropped them to the wooden planks of the wharf so he could give his arms a rest.

Liam also noticed the prince looking at him with a squint in his eye and a frown forming on his face.

"I'm sorry, I don't know you." Manus said hesitantly.

Cullen stepped aside and motioned for Liam to join the group. "Prince Manus, this is my son Liam. Keir Liam, this is Prince Aerin Manus."

"Your Highness." Liam said as he bowed quickly to the man. But being in the presence of the prince made him nervous so Liam stuck his hands in his pockets and turned his gaze to the ground.

But the prince continued to look at him. "I don't remember you having a son."

"Well, Liam would really be my foster-son, Milord." Cullen said as he patted Liam's shoulder to get his attention, looking at him proudly. "But it has been so long that Liam has been in my life that I consider him my own flesh and blood." Cullen turned back to the prince. "Your father has met Liam. I am sure he must have mentioned him to you."

Not one to be overly polite and more concerned about preparing the Camalain for travel, Manus shrugged his shoulders. "Sorry. Maybe he did but I don't recall." He looked at Liam, giving him a half-hearted smile as he watched several crewman carrying crates onto the ship. "So, are you here to see your father off?"

"Uhmmm."

"Liam is going with us, Milord. He is the help I had requested of you." Cullen interjected quickly.

"Help?" Manus stood a little taller, crossing his arms over his chest again, a stern look directed a Liam. "You're not in the Guard?" He asked, thinking he knew the answer already as he gave Liam's pedestrian appearance a once over; his shirt slightly frayed at the sleeves with several tears sewn tight by an unskilled hand with dust embedded in the creases of his clothing, as if he had just come from laboring.

"No." Liam replied, confirming the obvious.

"A sailor? Maybe a steersman we could use to help fly the Camalain?" He asked hopefully.

"No."

Manus' eyes narrowed and the scowl that had formed on his lips deepened. "Of course, you're an acolyte to Barra. Or maybe to one of the other gods, who will give you guidance so we can find my brother?"

Manus' disdain was all too apparent so Liam dropped his gaze to the ground at once feeling embarrassed and ashamed of his chosen profession. "No M'lord." Liam replied, his voice shaking out of fear and humiliation. "I'm an apprentice, in the Stone Masons' Guild."

"What! Really, Seb Cullen?" Manus said, feeling quite annoyed with the sagart over this situation. "You've brought a family member with no useful skills as aid? You know we are searching for Banning. Not going on a holiday!"

Cullen stood tall, a pillar of unmovable granite, against the onslaught on Manus' wrath. "I know the nature of this trip and Liam is here to help me."

"And what about me, Cullen?" Manus turned to look back at Liam who had yet to raise his head again. "And what value do you have to me? How will you help in finding my brother?"

Liam looked up at the prince and even though they were about the same age, Manus had the air of authority of someone much older and his anger only added to making him seem monstrous. But from the depths of somewhere, a snide remark escaped his lips. "That's exactly what I asked my father."

Cullen frowned at Liam's rudeness and hit his son's ankle with the butt of his cane to quiet him. "Milord, it was Barra who whispered Liam's name in my ear when I prayed for help on this venture. For some reason, the god thinks that Liam needs to be with us."

"Really?" Manus said doubtfully as Liam gave his father a quizzical look of his own. Manus turned to get the captain's opinion but Ibor was smart enough to have stepped away during the conversation, paying attention to what was going on board his ship, and waiting for the event to come to an end.

"Yes." Cullen said, not backing down from Manus' scrutiny. "Would you deny Barra a tool that might help us to find your brother?"

"No, I would not deny any help Barra has to offer us." Manus said sullenly. "But let me be perfectly clear. This is not an excursion where your son gets to enjoy the sights. He will work like everyone else. Is that understood?"

"I would not have it any other way my Prince." Cullen agreed.

Liam remained quiet, shuffling his feet, not looking at the two men while they discussed him, for he was feeling more dejected about being here and he certainly regretted not having said no to his father as he began to see weeks or maybe months of misery before him.

Finally looking up he saw that Captain Thear had walked back over to the group and was watching him. A sympathetic look was on the captain's face. And knowing that the prince couldn't see him, Ibor gave Liam one of his fatherly smiles, mouthing silently that things would be okay.

Ibor straightened up just in time as Manus turned to look at him. "Captain, have someone escort the sagart and his son to the quarters that they will be sharing."

"But, Prince Manus, the cabin is. . ."

"That's an order Captain."

Ibor sighed as he scratched the back of his head. "Aye, M'lord."

Thankful to have a reason to momentarily step away from the group and hide his annoyance over the prince's decision to have Cullen and his son share a room, Thear Ibor scanned the main deck for a crewman and spotted Croft helping load the cargo onto the ship. Whistling to get the man's attention, he gestured for Croft to join them on the wharf.

"Tomorrow you will start working for the captain." Manus said, addressing Liam and Ibor when the captain returned to the group. "If there happens to be any spare time, we'll see about scheduling some weapons training for you. So, unless your father or I happen to need you, you will report to the captain and his crew. Is that understood?"

Feeling distraught over how things were turning out, Liam only nodded his ascent to the prince.

"Very good. You're dismissed." Manus said, ordering Croft who had reached the group to take the two men to their quarters and returned to making arrangements with the captain.

Croft nodded to the prince politely and as the two men joined him he took Cullen's hand in greeting. "Sagart, it is good to see you again. It has been a while."

"It is good to see you too Croft. Yes, I think it has been almost four years since you have been around."

"That long? Well the captain has been keeping me busy. Flying here, flying there. You know how it is. And is this Liam?" Croft whistled and pulled Liam into a friendly embrace. "My you've grown! How old are you now? Eighteen? Nineteen?"

Although he stumbled a little in Croft's clutches, for he was once again carrying his and his father's packs, Liam smiled, blushing at Croft's attention. For Liam had met Croft when the steersman joined Captain Thear's crew almost fifteen years ago, when Croft was in his early twenties. Croft, who had no family of his own in Kinsale, would occasionally show up at their home with the captain when he came to visit or when Liam saw his father off on some journey that Captain Thear was commanding. Now, in his mid-thirties, Croft seemed to be still acting like that young man he had met long ago. A man that was still very friendly and quick with a smile.

"I'm twenty-four now." Liam answered his friend.

"You're that old now?" Croft said, acting surprised at the answer. He removed his arm from Liam's shoulders so the young man could maintain his balance as they walked over one of the two planks connecting the pier to the Camalain. He looked back and gave Liam a wink. "Well, I'm sure you must have a lot of suitors knocking at your door."

"No." Liam replied, a little embarrassed by the remark. "My apprenticeship has been keeping me busy so I've been pretty much keeping to myself."

"Oh, well." Croft said nonchalantly as he slowed his pace and put an arm around Liam's shoulder again as they crossed the ship's deck. "Maybe we will have to make sure it stays that way."

As Croft was escorting the sagart and Liam across the deck they passed Kael, who watched the trio make their way towards the cabin section. He quickly crossed over to the wharf and headed right to Manus.

"Who was that?" Kael asked, interrupting Manus and Ibor with whatever they were doing. For while he had been crossing the Camalain's main deck Kael had spotted Cullen and Liam, especially Liam, approaching the prince, and watched as the conversation, at least on Manus' side of it, become heated. Kael did wander closer to the railing of the boat in the hopes of hearing their conversation better but whatever was being said was drowned out by the sounds of the crew shouting to each other and supplies being dropped onto the ship's deck.

"Mmmm, what?" Manus replied, looking up at his friend. Manus had been lost in thought, going over what he knew needed to get done so they could leave and had already forgotten his conversation with the sagart and his son, moving on to items he deemed important. "Who was who?"

"Who was the one with the sagart?"

"The boy?" Manus asked becoming slightly annoyed when he realized who Kael was asking about. "That was Liam, his son. He's the "help" Cullen wanted us to take along."

"Liam." Kael said, liking how the name rolled on his tongue. He said the name again eliciting a sour expression from Manus. "I didn't know the sagart had a son."

Manus, trying to ignore Kael's new infatuation, had pulled some pieces of paper from his pocket that he had scribbled notes on and he began double checking them to make sure he had what he needed for the trip. "Foster-son. I think father had mentioned the sagart had a son, but I have never met him before until today. Unfortunately he's just an apprentice in the Stone Masons' Guild. Nobody useful."

Kael looked back over to the Camalain, hoping to catch another glimpse of Liam with his tanned skin that covered what looked like an athletic body, already memorizing the mess of curly black hair that fell to the nape of his neck. But the three had already disappeared into the cabins. "Well," He said wistfully, already anticipating his next run in with Liam. "He seems older than a boy."

Manus looked at his friend out of the corner of his eye and shook his head in disgust, already knowing what was on Kael's mind. Because it was the only thing that was always on Kael's mind. "Something tells me he's not your type." Manus replied as he crumpled the papers and tossed them to the ground.

"And what type is that?"

"Easy, for one." Manus said, snorting at his own joke. "Also, he seems as timid as a hare and his father, who will be on board, is a sagart."

Kael shrugged, taking the observation as a non-issue. "Sagarts have needs too, you know. You don't think the esteemed Sagart Cullen hasn't had his own share of lovers?"

Manus' expression soured at the turn of the conversation as he crossed his arms over his chest. "That's a vision I don't need to have. Besides, that boy is pretty much useless to me, especially the way he is now. So I'll be having him help the captain and his crew." Manus nodded to Captain Thear, who had once again taken several steps back from Manus and Kael as he tried to ignore how they were talking about his friends.

"Captain, keep him out of my way as much as possible. Hopefully somewhere where he can do as little damage as possible. At some point I want you or another of the guard to train him using a dagger and a bow. Hopefully he at least knows what they look like."

Kael smiled and began to describe what he wanted to train Liam in but was short by Manus' shout.

"Kael! Keep your hands off of him! Is that understood or do I have to make it an order?"

Kael raised his hands up in the air, a look of feigned innocence covering his face. "What? I was going to say bow. You know I'm one of your best archers. And if no one can touch him how's he going to get trained in anything?"

Manus kicked at the ball of papers he had dropped earlier, sending them tumbling across the wharf, annoyed with his friend and now wanting to be done with this conversation. He was about to give his friend some choice words before boarding the Camalain but was interrupted by the captain.

"Prince Manus, your family is heading down the pier." The captain said as he nodded to the group heading their way.

Manus turned to look and sure enough, his father, mother and Fionn, with a small armed escort of about a dozen men were walking towards them. Members of the Royal Guard who were on the pier stood at attention while dockworkers bowed and moved out of their way so the royal family could pass.

"I was hoping we could have left without them showing up here." Manus sighed, frustrated at the entourage heading his way. "Captain, I need you to have the men pick up the pace and finish loading the ship so we can leave once this formality is over." The captain nodded his ascent and walked away to follow through with the prince's commands just as Manus grabbed his friend by the arm. "Kael, you're with me."

As they walked to meet his parents, Manus forced a smile onto his face. He knew his parents meant well by coming here and that this voyage would be long, as well as dangerous. It was just that, searching for his brother would be the most important thing he had ever done in his life, and every minute here was time wasted, the sooner they could leave, the better chance they had at finding Banning.

***

"And these are the living quarters of the ship. At least, most of them." Croft said as he led Cullen and Liam through a door into the three storied building that was the main cabin section of the ship. They entered into a hallway that was a little over three feet wide. A tight squeeze if two men, especially armored, had to pass each other.

"This floor houses most of the quarters for the crew and guard." Croft continued to explain during his tour as doors immediately appeared to their right and left. They were about halfway down the hallway when they came to a stairwell to their right, with a flight of stairs running up and down into the ship. Croft grabbed the railing and proceeded to climb them. "The stairs going down lead to the "facilities" and most of the storage bays. And in case of inclement weather, or if you don't like being on the main deck while the ship is moving, there's a hallway that runs underneath the main deck and will lead you from here to the bridge. The captain's and my quarters are over in that section near the bridge."

As they came to the landing on the second level Croft stopped and pointed up the stairs. "The galley takes up most of the third floor and because there are so many of us, I don't know if the cook will be keeping a schedule for meals, so it might just be first come, first served." Croft stepped into the hallway of the second floor and pointed down towards the rear of the ship. "The prince and Master Karam have their quarters on this level and there's a smaller cabin over there with members of the Royal Guard. And this is your room." Croft had only taken a few short steps to a door on his right and, since all the cabins had pockets doors, he slid it open. Croft looked in and stepped away so they could have a look inside. "What do you think?"

The father and son stood on either side of the door jamb and poked their heads into the room. The cabin looked to be almost six feet wide by ten feet long. A bed, which was built against the hull, took up most of the space, being three feet wide and maybe a little over six feet long. A desk with a stool took up the rest of the length of the wall. Daylight was pouring in from two portholes; one in front of the desk and the other one over the bed. And the only storage seemed to be a row of three drawers built underneath the bed.

"Ah, my usual room." Cullen remarked as a matter of fact as if he couldn't see the actual size of the room.

"But there's only one bed!" Liam said, deciding to state the obvious while giving Croft a look of dismay.

Like his captain, Croft was also embarrassed by this cramped situation. "Sorry. Orders were you two were to share this room."

"The room is not too bad." Cullen said as he went into the cabin and sat down on the bed. Cullen couldn't help but admit to himself that was he enjoying his son's discomfit.

But Cullen's good humor only frustrated Liam even more. "Do I at least get some blankets and pillows or do I have to sleep on this bare floor in my clothes?"

Croft couldn't help but let a small chuckle escape from his lips as he listened to Liam's voice crack and become pitchy as the young man tried to deal with this situation. "No, no. I'll take you to a storage locker later and we'll get you as many blankets and pillows as you want."

"Great!"

Croft's chuckle became a little louder, bouncing through the empty hallway as a thought came to him. "You know Liam, there's enough space in my bed for two if you don't mind sharing the space with me."

Cullen tapped the cabin floor with the butt of his cane and frowned at the steersman.

"Oh! Why only in a brotherly way of course." Croft said to the sagart. Although he had made the comment in jest, Croft knew Liam's story and, even though he was older, still thought of him as a younger brother that needed protecting.

Cullen understood Croft's jibe and his feelings toward Liam. The sagart just didn't want another excuse for more unnecessary disdain to be heaped onto Liam's shoulders by the prince. "Thank you for the offer Croft, but I am sure Liam will be just fine sleeping on the floor of this room."

Croft tapped the floor of the cabin with the heel of his boot, eliciting a dull thud from the scuffed, wooden floor. "The floor does sound comfortable Sagart." Croft couldn't help but look at Liam and give him a wink. "But, if you ever change your mind."

"I think that will be all for now Croft. Let Liam and I stow our gear and get settled in and we will catch up with you later."

"Very good Sagart. Besides, we should be leaving soon and I'm sure the captain will want me back on the bridge." Croft patted Liam on the shoulder and whispered the words good luck into his ear before turning away and heading back to the stairwell, the sound of his footfalls slowly fading as he went down the stairs.

Glumly, Liam walked into the room, pulled out the stool from under the desk and sat down. "I don't know father. This room is no bigger than a closet." Liam rung his hands as he looked out the porthole, just catching a glimpse of a frigate as the late afternoon sun reflected off its metal plated surface, all oranges and reds, as it left the fortified port. "Does the prince really expect us to share this space?"

"Liam, my boy, we are only expected to sleep here. We have the rest of the Camalain to move around on for the rest of the time. We just have to rough it for a while."

But the prince's earlier rudeness, the claustrophobic room and not wanting to be on this voyage were already beginning to take their toll on Liam. He ran a hand through his hair, scratching his skull, something he did when he was tired, and began begging his father to let him go home before they left port.

Cullen looked at Liam from where he sat on the bed before sliding his cane through the straps of his pack and hauling it onto the bed and started to pull his belongings out. "Liam, if you really do not want to be here then you really should go home. I am sure you can make it off the ship before we leave and I will see you when we get back."

"But, I thought you said you needed me." Liam said as he stood, hesitating for a moment as he picked up his pack and threw it over his shoulder.

Cullen snorted loudly, finally beginning to lose his patience with his son. "Go home Liam. We have not left port and you are already miserable and I have no interest in going down that road with you. There is too much work that needs to get done and if you're not going to be useful then just go home."

Liam lowered his head and closed his eyes, embarrassed with his own childish behavior, and gripped his pack a little tighter, unsure of what he really wanted to do. "I'm sorry father, I," But Liam stopped in mid-sentence as he stumbled slightly and grabbed onto the desktop to steady himself when the Camalain began to ascend, turned and pulled away from its berth.

"Well," Cullen said as he stood, putting his weight on his cane so that he could keep himself steady. "It looks like things have been decided for you. For some reason I do not think the prince will be turning this ship around for you." Cullen headed for the doorway. "Come, Liam. Let us go on deck and watch as we leave port."

"I think I'll stay here for a bit. I'll put our belongings away and I wouldn't mind relaxing for a bit before the prince puts me to work."

"Suit yourself." His father replied as he slid the door shut, leaving Liam to his solitude.

Liam went to Cullen's pack and knelt by the bed as he took the rest of his father's gear out of it and started to stow them away into the drawers underneath the bed. From out of the porthole over the bed, Liam could see that they were moving steadily away from the piers, with Old Kinsale falling behind the Camalain as the ship approached the opening in the defensive wall to the port.

Liam stopped and left the unpacking for a moment and sat on the floor pulling his knees up with his arms wrapped around them and lowered his head onto his knees and closed his eyes.

"Wish I could stay here the entire trip." He thought as the Camalain made for the open desert of the flats as his once simple life being left behind. "Wish I could be home. Barra, I wish I could be anywhere but here."

Chapter 3
The Temple to Cavanna

After seeing her eldest son off on his journey, Mair Betrys returned to her home at the Temple to Cavanna. She was deep in thought, praying for Manus' safe return as she walked through the temple corridors, making her way to her personal apartments with two attendants, females in the livery of the Royal Guard trailing closely behind her.

The High Sagartta maintained an even pace through the temple, pretending to be oblivious to the bows she was receiving from the other priestesses or the salutes from the guards who were roaming the corridors as she mulled over Manus' departure.

Manus.

Her eldest son. Manus.

Aside from his looks, which he had inherited from his father, Betrys didn't think he was much like the man at all. If anything he seemed to be more like his grandfather, the great and deceased, Aerin Broll. Broll had been a passionate man who has demanded much from others as much as he had from himself. And never once had the man yielded to the will of others. All of which were strong reasons why Manus' grandfather had turned Birr into such a strong and powerful nation.

But Manus' aloofness and his pragmatism came from her. How Betrys wished that Manus' father, who was thoughtful and introspective, could have been more like the elder Aerin. Someone she would have willingly mated with over and over again.

Banning on the other hand was exactly like Fionn, his own father. In looks and in personality. Her youngest son, though he had been trained to handle weapons, was more of an intellectual, and who had been groomed to be married off for the benefit of Birr and his clan. Sadly, when Betrys looked at her youngest, she saw very little of herself in him.

Still, she was proud of her sons, she even adored them. For Manus would one day rule Birr while Banning, hopefully, would become a companion to a prince of either Ardane or Tuame. Two male lives that had the mark of her hand on them. Guiding, nudging them as much as a Gwerin women could with a male.

And helping them, especially Banning, would certainly help stretch her reach as High Sagartta into their neighboring kingdoms. Granted, countries such as Ardane or Tuame had their own high priestesses but a pairing with her youngest would only allow her to strengthen her own personal empire and strengthen Cavanna's doctrine in either land.

Yes. Betrys was very proud of her sons, proud of her creations. Proud because love would be too strong of a word for her to use.

Betrys was lost in thought, planning out her ever growing empire, as she turned a corner and ran into an obstruction. Betrys was surprised, the wind knocked out of her as she instinctively grabbed at the object that had hit her. One of her guards grabbed the priestess by her shoulders as she stumbled backwards, preventing her from falling. Looking down at what was squirming in her arms, Betrys found a pair of bright green eyes staring up at her.

"I'm sorry, High Sagartta." One of her priestesses said, huffing as she came running up to the group, immediately retrieving the child from Betrys' grasp. Turning the boy to face her, the woman said to the boy, "Now Wyllym, what have we said about running in the Temple?"

The boy lowered his head and hunched his shoulder, his voice escaping his lips in hushed tones. "Not to, Sagartta Althea."

"Correct. Now please apologize to the High Sagartta for bumping into her." Althea instructed sternly as she turned Wyllym back to face Betrys.

Shocked, afraid at whom he had run into, Wyllym began to shake and tears welled up in the corners of his eyes at the thought of being punished for not paying attention to where he was going. "I'm sorry High Sagartta."

Betrys couldn't help but smile warmly at the child, a crack forming in her aloof exterior, as she was reminded of her own children and how rambunctious they acted when they were Wyllym's age.

"Thank you." She said to the boy as she looked to Althea, who was retrieving what looked like a sack of belongings from where she had dropped it in the adjacent hallway. "And where are we off to today Althea?"

Althea slung the sack over her shoulder as she answered her superior. "Wyllym has come of age and his father is here to take him home."

Betrys knelt so she could be at eye level with Wyllym, whose eyes widened in surprise and fear at the High Sagartta being so close to him. She cupped his face in her hands and wiped away a stray tear with her thumb as it made its slow path down his cheek. "So you are five? Congratulations!"

Wyllym beamed, his voice rising in pitch, his fear evaporating, forgotten by the new question, as he raised his right hand, fingers spread wide to help emphasize what he had to say. "No High Sagartta, I'll be five on Sabadain!"

"Will you not be attending the Ceremony of Departure?" Betrys asked the boy, straightening his shirt and running a hand through his mop of brown hair as she looked up at Althea because the question was really directed at her.

"No." Althea responded. "Unfortunately the next ceremony is scheduled for the end of this month and Wyllym's father, who is a vintner from Esra, is here now to deliver wine to market and the gentleman said he would be hard pressed to make the trip back in several weeks because of other deliveries that will take him out of the area. So, we saw no reason to hinder Wyllym from leaving now with his father and joining his family."

Wyllym, becoming bored with the conversation between the adults, fished a string bracelet woven with some stones out of his pocket and started to try to single handedly tie it around his wrist.

Betrys, noticing the child's failed attempts took the bracelet from Wyllym and tied it for him.

"Esra? Esra is less than a day's flight away. It is a shame you and your father will miss the festivities." Betrys said to Wyllym as she knotted the bracelet and adjusted it on his wrist. She also noticed how the simple trinket had been woven with several different colored strings. And how the stones were all of a rusty color and how someone had also taken the time to paint little symbols for Cavanna and several of the other gods onto their surfaces. A charm like this was quite a common thing that a birth mother usually gave their sons on their day of departure.

"Is Wyllym one of yours?" Betrys asked Althea as she stood.

The aged sagartta chuckled at such a thought. "No. I have had my three. Thank the gods. No, Wyllym belongs to Colene. He is her first and Colene has become somewhat overly attached to the child and is having a difficult time with his leaving. Fortunately she is with child again and it will help to change her focus from this one. Especially if this second child happens to be a girl."

"Wyllym has been in many of my classes so I offered to take him to his father who should be in the courtyard by now."

"Then I should not keep you any longer."

"Well, Wyllym, it is time for you to go." Betrys said as she placed her hands on Wyllym's shoulders and quite impulsively, which was not like her at all, Betrys pulled him into a hug and squeezed him tightly. "Remember, say your devotions and always keep Cavanna close to your heart."

"I will." He mumbled into her blouse.

Betrys turned Wyllym and handed him back to Althea. "And do let me know how Colene is fairing."

"Yes, High Sagartta." Althea bowed slightly before continuing on with Wyllym in tow.

The child remained well-mannered as they continued down several corridors, passing other sagarttas with children in their care and several more women dressed in the garb of the Royal Guard. Of course Althea had not let go of Wyllym this time, curtailing his rambunctiousness, as they made their way through the rest of the temple. But she could not contain the child, nor tried to, as they entered the courtyard and Wyllym spotted his father.

"Papa!" He shouted as he tugged his hand out of Althea's and started running across the courtyard.

Several Birrnians standing in the Temple courtyard turned at the boy's shouts of joy, but only one of them smiled, recognizing the little boy.

"Wyllym!" His father replied, laughing with joy at the sight of his son, as he knelt to capture Wyllym in an embrace. "Are you ready to go?"

"Yes!"

"You will not get far without your clothing young man!" Althea shouted across the courtyard. A broad smile blossomed on her face at the sight of the two as she approached them. "Master Luaid I presume?"

The man stood, scooping up Wyllym in his arms while balancing him on his right hip. Wyllym's father also had a smile on his face that was just as wide, if not wider than Althea's. "Yes Sagartta. But you can call me Sloan. Once again, thank you for allowing me to take Wyllym home early."

"Yes, well, the high sagartta was disappointed the two of you would miss the Ceremony of Departure. But she does understand the circumstances." Althea replied as the three began to walk towards the main entrance into the city.

"That is good. My father has scheduled several more deliveries for me to make over the next several weeks and it was either get Wyllym now or in a couple of months. So either way I would have missed the ceremony."

My, he likes to chatter, Althea thought, finally understanding where Wyllym got his gregarious personality.

"Oh so you do not run the vineyard?" Althea inquired, already knowing the answer to the question.

Sloan chuckled, before answering the sagartta's question. "No. My father enjoys being in control and is not yet ready to give up running the vineyards or our wineries. He still loves being in the field so why stop him? And grandfather is here too." Sloan said to his son as he adjusted him on his hip.

"Mor is here?" Wyllym asked, his eyes widening as he sucked in air in surprise.

"Yes, Mor is here and is waiting for us on our barge. Imagine that, Mor took a whole day off just for you."

Wyllym could only giggle in delight, his little feet involuntarily kicking his father's buttock and thigh.

"My father felt guilty about having us miss his ceremony so he wanted to do something nice for us." Sloan explained to Althea as he readjusted Wyllym again, forcing him to stop his erratic movements. "He knows of a nice place to eat in the bazaar and offered to take us there before we leave for home."

"Hopefully they have a good wine selection." Althea quipped, eliciting another laugh from Luaid Sloan for it just so happened that

Sloan's family supplied the inn they would be visiting and several others within Kinsale with its wine.

The three had reached the main gate to the temple courtyard and stopped at its entrance where Althea could see an open aired coach waiting just outside of the gate and assumed it was for Luaid Sloan and his son. "Well, good luck to you and may Cavanna bless your family."

"Thank you Sagartta. Oh, I almost forgot. Even with all the traveling my father has in store for me I have scheduled a pairing. I think it is within seven or eight weeks. Do you think Sagartta Colene will be available again?"

"Unfortunately, no. She is already with child again. It was the reason why she couldn't make it today." Althea smiled warmly, hoping her aged charm might cover up the semi-lie she had just told the man.

"Oh. I was hoping to have the same mother for Wyllym's brother. Or a sister, of course, if that was Cavanna's will. Again, thank you Sagartta." Sloan replied before turning and walking to the waiting carriage.

Wyllym shifted in his father's arms again, wrapping his hands around Sloan's neck so that he could look back at Althea, his eyes round with excitement at the thought that his new life was about to begin. Wyllym raised a hand to wave goodbye to the priestess. One of many women who had a hand in raising the child. A woman he would probably never see again.

Althea smiled, returning the gesture. But she was already forgotten by Wyllym who was being helped by his father into the carriage and already grilling the man incessantly, not allowing his father to answer one question while his voice filled the air like a flock of chattering birds. Althea watched the two for one more moment before turning and heading back into the courtyard, beginning to forget the two just as easily as she had been forgotten.

***

It wasn't until Betrys entered her apartments, with one of the guards stationed outside of her quarters closing the door behind her that Betrys began to relax.

As she passed through the foyer into the living room, Anice, one of her personal servants, entered the room with a cold glass of smari in her hands and handed the drink to the High Sagartta. Betrys took a sip and smiled because Anice had added some alcohol to the berry juice, giving the sweet drink a slight bite as it slipped down her throat. "Thank you, Anice."

The woman bowed, her hands clasped in front of her as Betrys moved past her. "Your sister is here High Sagartta. She is waiting for you on the patio outside of the dining room."

Anice fell in behind Betrys, following her down a short corridor that passed a door leading into the kitchen and opened into the small informal dining room.

"Is Cait here too?" Betrys asked of her servant.

"No High Sagartta. Word was sent to the merchant of a problem with a shipment that had just arrived at her warehouse. Mistress Solvo left less than an hour ago and suggested that you should eat without her."

"Very well. My sister and I will eat out on the patio tonight. If you have not prepared dinner, I think something simple would be nice."

Of course Anice had cooked a meal, and Betrys knew this as well for the smells of fresh baked bread and cooked meat had escaped from the kitchen as they walked by. But Anice simply bowed again in acknowledgement to the change in menu and turned back towards the kitchen as Betrys stepped onto the patio.

Betrys was just in time to watch the sun begin its slow decent behind the mountain range to the west, painting the sky with a coppery glow while the clouds overhead were fired in shades of red and yellow as the mountains facing Kinsale fell into a deep shadow of dark blue, almost purplish as night came to claim its territory. Admiring the gods' hands in this, Betrys rubbed the side of her neck as she tried to remember the last time she had watched such a spectacular sunset.

"How was the sendoff?"

"Predictable." Betrys replied to the voice that came out of the shadows that were being cast by the temple walls over the patio. Anice had yet to light any of the lanterns so the only illumination for the patio came from the dining room doorway, several windows and another entrance at the far end of the long balcony.

"Very curt and polite. Diplomatic. The way it should be." Betrys called out as she slipped back into the dining room to retrieve a candle so she could light some of the lanterns. "Mihra, did Anice forget you were out here?" Betrys asked her sister upon her return.

"No, I told her not to bother." Betrys' sister replied as she finally became illuminated by the glow of the lanterns. In the soft light Betrys could see her sister sitting on one of the couches made of dark woven wicker surrounded by ornate tapestried cushions and brightly colored pillows. A table of the same woven wood was in front of her with another couch on the opposite side of it with several chairs scattered around the patio.

After completing her task Betrys looked upon her younger sister once more, the candle light reflecting off her dark hair, pulled back from her face, and giving her pale face a warm glow and the cataracts covering her eyes a yellowish tint.

"I wanted to sit here in some peace and quiet while I waited for you. Sometimes the lamplight at the corner of my eyes can be such a distraction." Mihra explained.

Betrys understood Mihra's misgivings about the lighting because her sister had been born partially blind. The cataracts covering most of the front of her irises only allowed Mihra able to see greyish shapes or harsh bright light from the corners of her eyes.

Betrys had been seven when Mihra had been born, and her mother, who was also a sagartta to Cavanna, knew immediately of her daughter's blindness, calling Mihra special. Then again, her mother would tell the two of them they were both special and that the gods had plans for them both.

But Mihra did seem special because as an infant her blindness never seemed to be a hindrance as she navigated the furniture around their home. And when she was old enough to walk, Mihra took to opening doors and running down hallways, climbing stairs like any other sighted child as she explored the large mazelike structure of the Temple to Cavanna. Of course theses escapades brought much distress to her mother and the other priestesses. But for some reason Mihra had been born with this need to escape her caretakers and explore a world she would never be able to truly see.

In the end, their mother was right for Mihra was special. But it wasn't until Mihra could talk, and a chance conversation overheard, that Betrys realized how special her sister was.

For Betrys was woken one night by the sound of several voices coming from her sister's room. And thinking that something might be wrong, Betrys got out of bed to see what the commotion was. Upon entering the room Betrys was shocked to find Mihra sitting upright, alone, in the dark room in middle of a conversation. When she was questioned, Mihra only giggled, yawned and curled up in a ball and went back to sleep as if her sister had never been there.

And when Betrys brought up the odd incident to her mother the next day, her mother only smiled and explained how not only Cavanna, but all the gods, talked to her little sister. That the gods had been there Mihra's birth, always visiting and singing to her while she had lain in her crib in her dark little world. They had been the ones guiding Mihra around the apartments and the temple halls. So, in the hopes of there being some sense of normalcy for the time being, the only people who had known of Mihra's gift, was their mother and the current High Sagartta to Cavanna.

The gods never left Mihra's side and were always helpful and friendly. Their voices acting as beacons of light in a world flooded with darkness.

But once Mihra reached the age of maturity she found out that the god's friendship came with a price. Because what they wanted from Mihra was for her to become their oracle, their voice to the Birrnian people. And not really having a choice, Mihra's routine soon became one of sitting on a stone pedestal in the center of Garradh dhe Dia, the Garden of the Gods, dispensing the gods' judgments to the many petitioners that came seeking guidance, with every word spoken by Mihra written down by temple scribes. Her weighty words documented for future posterity so that all knew that the gods walked among them.

At times the gods were orderly, with only one or two of them wanting to talk through her to their disciples. And then there were days when a group of them would want to talk. Each clamoring over the other, a painful cacophony in her head, so that their voices could not be clearly heard.

Then there were those stretches of days that would go by where Mihra found herself sitting in the garden in total silence, while men and women milled about as they too waited for the gods. Waiting to be needed and heard by their deities.

The people who came before her and the sagarttas from the temple praised Mihra for her gift and continuously told her how lucky she was that the gods wanted to commune with her. On those occasions Mihra would smile politely in return, for her eyes revealed nothing, keeping secret how much of a curse her gift really was.

And Betrys, who was also within earshot of many of those compliments, would smile as well. The high sagartta hiding the resentment she felt for her sister and her gift, wishing it was her who spoke to the gods; not just Cavanna, but all of them. And it was this slow, simmering resentment that pushed Betrys to compensate for this slight by the gods and by striving to become Cavanna's High Sagartta.

"Have you asked Cavanna or the others about Banning?" Betrys asked her sister as she sat down on the couch across from Mihra.

"I have tried, but the gods have not answered my questions." The blind woman sighed frustrated that she did not have the answer Betrys wanted to hear. "Actually, they have been quiet for some time now and even the scribes are getting bored of sitting and waiting. What about you? Surely Cavanna has said something about Banning to you."

"No. Just the same reassurances that he is well. Thank you Anice." Betrys said to her servant when she arrived with a tray of meats, cheeses, sliced fruit and some of the fresh baked bread. A pitcher of smari was on the tray along with a glass for Mihra. Anice bowed and left the patio, allowing Betrys to serve herself and her sister.

"Here." Betrys had the filled glass out in front of her and as Mihra stretched to retrieve it, Betrys grasped the unadorned hand, wrapping it around the glass. "There is a tray of food in front of you too."

"Yes. I can smell the bread." Mihra said as a smirk formed on her face. "And Maat is here describing to me what is on the tray." To emphasize this, Mihra reached out for one of the small plates that was also on the tray, picked up a fork and placed some salted beef and several cheeses on it. "They will not tell me where my nephew is but they will certainly help me to find my way around a tray of food."

Betrys hissed in surprise, always shocked at how flippant her sister could be. "Careful sister! Your rudeness borders on blasphemy!"

Mihra chuckled at her sister, her high sagartta. "Do not worry Betrys. The gods seem to find my bouts of sarcasm amusing." And the goddess Maat seemed to be in agreement with Mihra because a slight breeze swept across the patio, setting some small copper bells that were dangling in the corner to softly ringing. "Trust me. The gods will let me know when I have gone too far."

"But do be careful." Betrys reiterated, silently asking for forgiveness from Maat as she placed food on her own plate. "It is not our place to question the whims of the gods. If not for the sacrifices

Cavanna made for us we would not have been graced with this eternal peace."

Mihra remained silent, ignoring her sister's comment as she bit into a piece of cheese.

The two continued to sit in silence while they ate, enjoying the warm clear night while the sound of muffled voices and soft laughter floated up from the gardens that surrounded the temple.

Forgetting herself for a moment, as the alcohol in the smari loosened her tongue, Betrys mumbled, "Someone else should have gone."

"Who should have gone where?"

Betrys looked over to her sister. "What?"

"Who should have gone where?" Mihra asked again.

Betrys took a sip of her drink as she composed her thoughts, staring at her sister who, for someone that was blind, seemed to be staring very intently at her, with Mihra's glazed eyes eerily reflecting the surrounding lamplight and making the moment awkward.

"Someone other than Manus should be leading this search for Banning." Betrys replied as she tilted her head back and looked up at the stars that were making their appearance in the sky.

"Oh? I thought you felt he should go."

Betrys stood and walked over to the railing to look down on the temple gardens. The lawns were lit by lanterns and by their faint illumination Betrys could see the dark shapes of women sitting on benches and the ethereal movement of couples, only noticeable by the lantern light reflecting off of jewelry on wrists and ankles. Like mythical woodland willow-the-wisps, Betrys thought, that were floating along her garden paths.

"There were several generals in the Guard qualified to conduct the search but Riocard was adamant that Manus be the one in charge of this search." Betrys explained to her sister while watching the sparkling movement below her.

"Even Fionn could have led the search for his son." Betrys smirked as she pushed herself away from the railing

Mihra couldn't see her sister's offensive facial expression, but she could definitely hear the subtle edge to her voice. "Fionn is not a warrior."

Betrys walked back to the couch and sat down. "No. But with enough of the Royal Guard at his back he would have been just fine. Of course, Riocard did not want him to go either."

"Really? Why not?"

Betrys picked up a piece of cheese and ate it, savoring its sharp salty flavor before replying.

"Riocard felt that more guards would have been needed just to protect Fionn. Too many guards. And he did not want the search to be slowed down by Fionn's inexperience in military affairs which is a shame because Fionn is the most disposable out of all of us."

Mihra grimaced at her sister's comment. Although Betrys had mated with the man to conceive a child, the coupling had only been a matter of convenience and a way to maintain her influence over the ever expanding kingdom, no empire, of Birr. Mihra, on the other hand had always found Fionn to be pleasant and likeable man. And in this case Mihra couldn't help but agree with Riocard.

"Well, that does make sense Betrys. If Manus is to rule Birr one day he should be out there on his own making important decisions and where he can have Gwerin follow him without Riocard over his shoulder correcting those decisions. Banning's kidnapping is an unfortunate circumstance, but this gives Manus the chance to prove himself as a leader."

Betrys sighed as she leaned back onto the couch, stretching her arms over her head and her legs out in front of her. Though she would have liked to have Fionn's influence over Banning removed, in her gut, she knew that her sister was right.

"Besides," Mihra continued, interrupting Betrys' thoughts. "Manus adores Banning. He would do anything for his brother, including searching all of Gwer for him."

"Yes I know." Betrys closed her eyes as she thought that there might now be a chance for her plans to unravel. If she needed to lose a son it should be Banning. He was the least valuable of her children. And he always would be.

Unfortunately Mihra was right about Manus and would spend years looking for his brother. Manus would Waste time, energy and his own life in the pursuit of finding Banning.

"And that is what worries me."

***

Banning stumbled, falling to his knees as the barge lurched forward and tilted sideways while in midair as it tried to escape from the attacking ship. Shouts of panic and men calling for help filled the corridors, and the sounds of several large objects pounding against the hull and the snapping of wood and groaning metal reverberated throughout the vessel.

"Steady my Prince." Goban said as he helped Banning to get back up on his feet. "We must get you to safety."

Sweat covered Goban's face and his forehead was creased with worry. With a sword in his right hand to protect his charge, Lieutenant Cahl maintained his grasp of Banning with his left hand as he guided the two of them down the corridor.

"We must get you to the storage bays as soon as possible! Hopefully we can get off the barge from there." The lieutenant informed the somewhat disoriented Banning as he led the prince down a stairwell that would take them to the lower decks.

They had reached the lowest level of the ship when the barge began to rock violently, the timbers overhead creaking in distress as the ship tilted to the left and right. The corridor also felt like it was getting warmer, with tendrils of thick black smoke swirling around their ankles while the very air around them became oppressive, making it difficult to breath.

Suddenly screams filled the air as the barge began to roll on its side with Goban losing his grip on Banning, who was tossed backwards down the corridor as the lieutenant had tried to steady himself. As Banning landed on his back and continued to slide backwards, the remaining hanging lanterns that were lit went out, leaving him in darkness. Banning could only moan as he tried to sit up, as pain shot through his shoulders and the back of his head. The barge eventually leveled off but still continued to rock violently. Banning wrapped an arm around his head to protect it from smacking against the wooden floor as he reached out with his other hand, hoping to at least touch one of the corridor walls so that he could steady himself.

While he tried to roll to the right, the barge tilted to the left and dropped out from under him. He hit the floor on his back with the wind being knocked out of him again. Banning found himself beginning to slide once more as the barge rose at an odd angle. The only control

Banning seemed to have was in holding back tears of frustration as he tried to wipe the sweat from his face.

"Goban!" Banning tried to shout the lieutenant's name, but it came out as a weak whisper. He wasn't even sure anything came out of his mouth at all. "Goban?"

"Prince Banning!" The lieutenant's shout cut through the stifling darkness. But his second shout seemed more distant. As if Goban was moving in the wrong direction.

Banning tried calling out to him. But a faint croak was the only thing he could force from his lips.

"Banning! Where are you my Prince?" A new voice called out from the darkness. A voice that sounded like it could be Captain Thear's. Thankfully he seemed to be close to Banning. Or at least, it seemed so as Banning tried to again raise himself. But he was having a difficult time of it for his head was spinning, or the barge was spinning, he couldn't tell anymore as more sweat trickled down his forehead as he called out the captain's name again.

Banning rocked in frustration because he could still hear the captain and lieutenant calling out for him. But the two seemed to be moving in the wrong direction, their voices becoming muffled even as Banning coughed, forcing the words, "Here, here . . . help!" out of a throat that was dry from the heat and the ever increasing smoke. Words that were swallowed up by the darkness.

Suddenly, Banning gasped in surprise as he felt hands grasping at him. At first he thought it must have been either the lieutenant or the captain who had finally found him. But, instead of being helped up, he found himself being pushed roughly back to the ground. Banning tried to reach out for a forearm of his attacker to push them away and free himself, but he couldn't find one, his hands only grasping at air.

"No." Banning gasped, his head rocking from side to side. "No. No!" Banning shouted as he finally found his voice, his hands balled into fists as he fought his unseen attackers before trying to raise himself onto his elbows.

Finally winning his freedom from his unseen attackers Banning struggled to stand and found himself sitting in a bed. Feeling completely disoriented Banning let himself fall back into the soft, oversized bed as he tried to catch his breath. Laying there he found his legs were tangled in several blankets and he was soaked in sweat.

Banning brought a hand to his face to wipe it clean before running his hand through his damp hair as he tried to place where he was.

Raising himself up against several pillows that were on the bed and kicking the heavy blankets away from his legs, Banning took a look around at his surroundings. On the left hand side of the bed was a table and on it sat a lantern, which was lit, but slightly shuttered, allowing a faint light into the room. A mirror was hanging on the left wall and it reflected some of the lantern light around the room and he could see a red flickering light emanating from the opposite wall. Turning, Banning saw, just beyond a little sitting area, a fireplace which had probably kept the room warm which was now only a glowing pile of embers.

Deciding to get out of bed and explore the room Banning swung his legs off of the bed and realized for the first time that he was not wearing his own clothing. Instead of being in his traveling clothes, he found that he was wearing thin dark blue cotton pants that reached below his calves and he had on a white sleeveless shirt. Thankfully, he thought, either the lieutenant or one of the other crew must have been around and had helped him change into something more comfortable to sleep in once the attack had ended.

And as he stood, Banning felt a little wobbly with a sharp pain shooting through his lower back. He must have been curled up in the bed for a while for his back to hurt so much so he kept one hand on its surface until he adjusted to standing again. Taking a deep breath, he walked over to one of the chairs in front of the fireplace, his calves tight from lethargy, with those few steps uncomfortable as he made his way across the floor. It was then that he noticed a wardrobe against the opposite wall from the bed and decided to walk towards it, hoping to get the blood flowing through his legs again.

Moving across the room Banning noticed that the floor was one solid piece of stone, which was cool to the touch as his feet padded over it. The floor also seemed to have that same coloration as the stone walls which were covered with thick embroidered tapestries. And when he reached the wardrobe he saw that it was made of a dark stained wood and had been heavily carved with images of trees and woodland scenes and upon opening the wardrobe Banning found more clothes hanging in it. None of which were his own.

"Well, not the barge and this is definitely not home." He thought as he closed the wardrobe doors.

"I don't even think I'm back in Ardane." Banning bent over, trying to touch the floor with his hands as he tried to get some more of the stiffness out of his back. "Now to see where I am." He thought as he stood and headed for the door to the bedroom.

The door, which was on the same wall as the mirror, was made of wood with a dark red stain with intricate detailing carved into the bronze doorknob. Hesitantly, Banning reached out for the knob and found that it refused to budge as he turned it to the left and the right, his hand slipping over the knob's intricate detailing. Trying the knob of the door once more Banning began to panic as he questioned why someone would want to lock him in a bedroom.

"Hello! Is anyone out there?" Banning shouted as he began to slap the solid door with the palm of an opened hand. "Hello!"

Banning immediately heard the clicking of a key as it turned in the lock and he backed towards the bed as the door swung in and a man, about six feet tall with tanned olive skin and clipped black hair, walked into the room while a second man, with fair skin and a bandaged right hand, could be seen standing out in the hallway.

"Can I help you, Prince?" The man asked as he stopped just beyond the threshold, blocking the only exit out of the room.

"Yes." Banning said slowly, not recognizing the man nor the one still out in the hallway. Angered that he had been kept in a locked room Banning said with as much confidence as he could muster to be taken to meet with either Lieutenant Cahl Goban or Captain Thear.

The man in the room turned to his companion in the hallway. "Mac, go get the captain and let him know the prince is awake and is asking for him."

"You sure, Davis?" The one named Mac frowned at the request.

Davis chuckled at the questions. "Go ahead now. We'll be fine."

As Mac turned to leave, Banning couldn't help but notice the dagger on the man's belt. A common sight on a barge because a sharp instrument always came in handy, but quite unsettling on the waist of a stranger. Looking down he saw that the man named Davis was wearing one too, making Banning unsure of what he should do. Common sense told him to move further into the room, putting some distance between himself and the man with the weapon, but that would also put him further away from the door and escape if that were an option. So Banning took a chance and remained standing where he was near the side of the bed.

"You said you were getting the captain. Where is Lieutenant Goban? Is he okay?"

Davis crossed his arms and leaned against the door jam, shifting his hip so the dagger he had at his side slipped behind him, out of view, and smiled warmly, almost mischievously at Banning, a twinkle to his eyes as he sideswiped Banning's question. "Not to worry, the captain will explain everything."

But Banning was savvy enough in court politics to notice this simple foil and decided to take another stab at the man. "I don't remember you from the barge, err, what was your name again?"

"Davis, Prince Dar."

"Davis. Right. Like I said I don't remember you from the barge, and I apologize for not recognizing you or your friend. So I was wondering, what were your duties while aboard Captain Thear's ship?"

Davis' smile didn't leave his face as he rubbed the cleft in his chin. He looked to be a man who would be considered attractive; with his athletic build, rugged looks and cavalier attitude. All attributes a man or woman would find disarming. But Davis' penetrating gaze, the flecks of green sparkling in his hazel eyes, was starting to make Banning feel like some small defenseless prey being stalked by a wild animal.

"I wasn't on the barge. But the captain will explain it all to you."

Banning walked over to the wardrobe so he could pretend to examine some of its carvings and to avoid the uncomfortable feeling of Davis' gaze.

"How long have I been asleep?"

"The captain will explain it all."

"And where are we anyway?"

"The captain will explain it all." They both said in unison, Davis chuckling, his white teeth exposed as he moved away from the door jam, crossing his arms over his chest while Banning rolled his eyes and fidgeted with one of the bronze handles on the piece of furniture.

"The captain will explain it all." Banning mumbled one more time, not caring that Davis could hear his snide remark.

"What will the captain explain?" A new voice asked from the doorway.

Turning, Banning found another man standing in the doorway next to Davis.

A third man that Banning didn't recognize from being on the barge. This one had reddish hair, beard and mustache with wisps of gray at the sides of his mouth. He was somewhat older than most of Captain Thear's crew, but not as old as the captain himself. He was also dressed more formally than Davis or his companion; dark trousers, grey linen shirt and a black velvet vest embroidered with silver thread. Obviously he was a man of some importance and not a deckhand from the barge.

The red headed man put his hands into his vest pockets as Banning approached him.

"Yes, I was waiting for Captain Thear. The other man," Banning pointed to Mac who was now standing in the doorway, "was going to get him for me. I was hoping the captain could tell me what happened to us and where the lieutenant of my guard is."

"Why don't you leave us for a moment?" The man said to Davis as he placed a hand on his shoulder. Davis nodded and stepped away and closed the bedroom door behind him, leaving Banning and the newcomer alone in the room. "Please, Prince Dar, have a seat." The man pointed towards the sitting area in front of the fireplace. "Hopefully I can answer your questions."

Banning obliged his host, captor, and sat down while the man went over to the fireplace and threw some logs on the smoldering embers before kneeling so he could blow on them, waiting until the fire took.

Turning he smiled at the prince as he took the chair opposite to him, and noticing some soot on his vest, he began wiping the dirt off of his meticulous outfit. "How can I be of service to you, Prince Dar Banning?"

That the man knew him by his name bothered Banning, but he forced himself to ask his questions just the same. "Well, you can start by telling me why you're here talking to me and not Thear Ibor, or Lieutenant Cahl Goban for that matter. They were the men in charge of my entourage and I would most like to speak to them."

"Yes, about that." The red headed man said as he continued to primp himself a little more and, ignoring Banning's initial question, he asked his own. "What is the last thing you remember?"

That question caught Banning off guard and he stopped for a moment to think. "The last thing I remember was that the barge was under attack." He paused again because the nightmare he had just woken from was still fresh in his mind, muddling his memories of the incident. "I think, no, I know Lieutenant Cahl was escorting me to the lower levels of the barge so we could escape." Sweat formed on his brow as he tried to remember all that occurred. "I think the barge started to fall out of the air. Then. Nothing." Banning shook his head. "I don't remember."

Daigh, who had been staring intently at Banning while he recounted the attack, quietly thanked the gods while Banning struggled to remember what had happened. It did seem that the prince was telling the truth about not remembering the rest of the attack nor did he seem to recognize him or his men. Leaning forward, he rested his elbows on his knees and clasped his hands and looked down at the floor for a moment before staring back up at the prince who had remained silent after trying to recount his tale.

"Well, Prince Banning, may I call you Banning?" Daigh asked, and not waiting for a response continued with his deceit. "You were lucky, Banning. On our way back from Birr, we found you wandering through Murra's Maze."

"We were attacked in Murra's Maze."

The man smiled sympathetically, almost fatherly, at Banning. "Yes, well, the Maze can be a dangerous place to travel through and it's not uncommon to be attacked by pirates while in the Maze."

Relieved that they had been rescued, Banning asked to the whereabouts of the barge's crew and his personal guard.

"Alas, we only found you." Daigh frowned. "It is safe to assume your captain must have been quick enough to drop you off and then fly away as a diversion. And if you were truly attacked, there is no way of telling where your captain flew his ship or what happened to it because the Maze is riddled with channels that travel endlessly before turning into dead ends. A wrecked vessel could be lost in there for days. If the ship can be found at all."

"And what of my Lieutenant? Surely they would not have left me alone in the Maze."

The man scratched at his beard as his gaze moved over to watch the fire spread across the dry logs in the fireplace. "Like I said, we only found you."

Banning looked at his savior, who seemed to now be avoiding him. Banning remembered that Croft, the barge's steersman, had mentioned on several occasions how the flight through Murra's Maze would be routine. That the captain had traveled through the channel on a regular basis. Banning was finding it hard to believe that the men his fathers' had sent to protect him could get lost so easily. The story just didn't seem right and the feeling of being trapped and helpless started to overpower him again.

"Well then, I owe you my thanks for saving me sir."

"I am Captain Emmis Daigh. But you can call me Daigh."

"Captain? Well Captain." Banning said, using the man's title as he stood, because he did not want to use the man's given name. "We were about a day or two from the mainland when we entered the Maze so we shouldn't be too far from where you found me. If you could, please send word to my family that I am fine and that we have gone back to search for the others."

Daigh also stood, raising his hands and halting Banning in mid-sentence. "Steady Banning. Unfortunately any type of search would be most difficult right now."

"Really? And why is that?"

"Well, for one thing, we are not in Birr and the second is that you have been unconscious for the past five days.

Banning sank back down into his chair, stunned as he tried to comprehend what Daigh had just told him. "Five days? I've been asleep for five days?"

Daigh also sat back down. "Yes, well, we only just reached my home last night and I wanted to keep you sedated until we could figure out how badly injured you might be."

"You what? How could you?" Banning said as he realized that he was probably very far from home. "If it's a ransom you are trying to get from my family."

Daigh shook his head and sighed, feigning mock injury at the accusation. "Prince Dar, it's not like that."

"Oh? Then how is it?"

Daigh hesitated as he continued to look at Banning, who was grasping the arms of his chair tightly, his brown eyes wide with fear and their corners glistening with moisture, while he tried to control his breathing.

So much like his father, Daigh thought, unable to pull himself together, his tongue feeling swollen in his dry throat while it felt like a large rock had made its home in his stomach.

And after all this time, a single thought of Banning's father could still cause him so much pain. "My Prince," Daigh began, stuttering over what he wanted to say and as he tried to gather his thoughts, he was interrupted by loud banging on the bedroom door.

"I said I did not want to be disturbed!" He yelled at the intrusion. But the banging started again. Daigh stood and, growling under his breath, stormed to the door and threw it open

"Davis, I told you not to disturb us!" He shouted, but his rage faltered as he found a third man standing in the hallway; a man who was not one of his own crew. A man dressed in the garb of the local militia.

"Sorry Captain." Davis whispered as he took a step closer to Daigh, quickly nodding in the man's direction. "He insisted that I interrupt you so that you could go with him. Says you been summoned."

"Summoned?" Daigh turned pale as he grasped the door in his right hand. This was not a good sign that a request such as this was coming so quickly after their arrival. Daigh looked questioningly at Davis who was just as pale as his captain.

"Wasn't me, Captain." Davis replied, understanding what Daigh was trying to find out. Mac only shrugged his shoulders in confusion and shook his head in the negative when Daigh's gaze fell upon him.

Daigh motioned for the guard to step forward and, as quietly as he possibly could, informed the guard he had some unfinished business to attend to before he could answer the summons.

But that was not good enough because the guard frowned and glowered at the captain while his knuckles whitened as his grasp tightened on the spear he was carrying.

"Now." The man mouthed silently and pointed down the corridor with the weapon, forcing Mac to take a few steps back so he would not get hit with the butt end of the spear.

Banning couldn't see what was happening from where he was sitting so he stood and walked over to the opposite side of the bed where he could get a good glimpse into the corridor. A vantage point where he could just make out that there was now a third person in the hallway.

"What is going on Captain Emmis?"

Daigh turned quickly to face Banning and closed the door slightly, blocking Banning's view into it the hallway. "Nothing of importance Banning. Unfortunately I have been summoned to a meeting which I cannot refuse. I will return as soon as possible. "

"But you haven't answered any of my questions! I demand that you tell me what is going on!" Banning stammered as Daigh opened the door to leave.

Daigh turned to look at Banning, smiling reassuringly at him as if nothing was amiss.

"I am sorry but all of your questions must wait for the time being." Daigh, whose gaze never left Banning's, shot a hand out into the corridor and dragged Davis into the room. "You are definitely disheveled and a little ripe from your ordeal so Davis here will show you to the washroom. There you will find a tub to refresh yourself and feel free to use any clothes you find in this room. Unfortunately, neither Davis nor Mac has answers to your questions." Daigh finished as he dug his fingers into the man's bicep. Davis only grimaced in pain and nodded in agreement with his captain's orders.

"But Captain?" Banning responded as he hurried around the bed so he could reach the door.

"Sorry." Was all that Daigh said as he pushed Davis into the room and slammed the door shut behind him. Daigh's underling immediately stood in front of the door with his arms crossed over his chest as he guarded his captain's escape from the bedroom.

And not caring what happened, Banning grabbed the doorknob and yanked the door open, the bulk of the wooden door smacking into Davis and sending the man forward into the room. Mac, who had remained out in the hallway, ran in front of Banning and blocked him from leaving the room while Davis grabbed him by his shoulders. Banning twisted in the man's grasp and looking to his left he was just able to catch a glimpse of two men turning the corner.

"Captain! Daigh!" Banning shouted, to no avail for the man with all the answers had left.

Banning looked at Mac who seemed to be avoiding his gaze by looking down at his bandaged hand while fiddling with one of the knots that kept his fingers bound together.

Davis patted Banning's shoulder, the prince turning to look at him, a forlorn look in his eyes. "It's not all that bad." Davis said to him reassuringly.

"Really?" Banning said as he glowered at Davis.

Daigh's crewman only shrugged because he really didn't know what to say and decided that silence would be most prudent. He sniffed, looked at Banning and sniffed again. "You do smell a little ripe Milord. None too pleasant if you know what I mean." He said as he winked at the prince and pointed him in the direction of the washroom.

Stunned, frustrated at his own impotence, Banning dropped his head into his hands while Mac looked at Davis wanting to know what to do. Davis only shrugged at his companion and turned Banning out into the corridor, sniffing again at Banning's foul odor, as he steered the prince towards the washroom.

***

After leaving his villa Daigh was quickly escorted to the home of his employer, the leader of the small nation of Iniscarn, the Lord Argus Berach. It was Berach's great grandfather who had founded the kingdom several hundred years ago and it was his son, Berach's grandfather who came up with the idea of raiding vessels from other kingdoms, then hiring out his own soldiers as escorts to protect the ships they had just attacked as a means for his very small empire to survive. The venture had proved worthwhile and profitable and the attacks continued to this day.

Upon entering Argus' home, they continued on to Berach's library, passing the ruler's daughter in the hallway.

"Hello, Captain." The young woman said to Daigh as she approached the two men.

"Good afternoon, Gwyn. I'm here to see your father."

"I know." Gwyn smirked as she passed the men.

"How is he?"

Gwyn stopped and looked back at Emmis Daigh, a man she had known for almost her entire life. A man she liked. And who wouldn't? For it was a rare day when the captain was not full of bravado and swagger, going out of his way to charm any person that he met. Unfortunately, today was not one of them.

"Do you really want to know?"

Daigh snorted and gave Gwyn a halfhearted smile. "Not really." He replied.

Not wanting to be forgotten nor, to be reprimanded for neglecting his duties, the guard, none too gently, poked a finger into Daigh's side and nodded for him to move forward. "Sorry Mistress, but I have my orders." The guard politely said to Argus' daughter.

"Must be new." Daigh said and winked at Gwyn as he put a hand on the guard's shoulder and directed him to once again lead the way.

There was the brashness that Daigh was known for, Gwyn thought, as she continued on to do her own errands.

The library wasn't that far from where they were and after walking up a flight of stairs they arrived at its closed door.

"After you." Daigh said to the guard, who was new to Berach's household. But the man only nodded and pointed at the door for Daigh to go first. "Well, if you insist." Daigh whispered as he knocked on the door.

A voice shouted from the opposite side of the door, demanding for him to enter.

Daigh took a deep breath, opened the door and stepped into the room. "You wanted to see me, M'lord?" Daigh asked hesitantly as he shuffled to one side as the guard reached in and closed the door behind the captain. Daigh saw that Argus Berach was seated behind his desk while there was another man seated in one of the two high backed chairs in front of it.

Berach looked up from the papers he was rifling through and glowered at Daigh. "Sit!" He snapped and pointed to the empty chair.

As he went to do as he was told, Daigh looked over to see who was in the other chair and hissed in surprise as he noticed that it was his second in command, Ormin Lhoyt. Daigh felt like he had been kicked in the stomach at this obvious betrayal. He stared at Lhoyt, hoping to catch his eye but the man kept his head lowered as he tried to avoid his captain's gaze by looking down at his hands.

"Are you going to sit Captain?"

Daigh was so stunned at seeing Lhoyt here that he forgot what he was doing. "Yes, M'lord." He said as he sat down and faced the Lord of Iniscarn.

Berach looked at the captain as he gathered his own thoughts. He was so angry from what he had learned of Daigh's duplicity, his stupidity, that all he wanted to do right now was reach over his desk and to strangle the man. His lips tightened as he tried to control his rage before taking a deep breath to talk.

"So, your second in command says you picked up more than just goods on this last raid of yours. What else did you find that was so precious that you did not want to share with me?"

Daigh could not help but look back over to Lhoyt whose skin had become white with fear. Lhoyt was so pale that Daigh could make out the faint scar he had on his lower lip and chin from an injury he had received some time in the past. Lhoyt looked up at him for a moment, his lips moving as if he wanted to say something, but returned to lowering his head and picking at his fingers.

"Captain! What did you find?"

Daigh coughed slightly and shifted in his chair uncomfortably before he responded. Looking at the man who was not only his liege lord but his employer, began to explain how they had found one of the princes of Birr.

"Really now? And which one did you find?"

"The Consort's son. Prince Dar Banning."

Berach ground his teeth, already aware of this information. "And what is the law when it comes to the raids?"

"We are to take no prisoners M'lord."

"No prisoners." Berach stood and placed the palms of his hands onto the desk and leaned forward, forcing Daigh to look at him. "No prisoners at all!" He bellowed as spit flew from his mouth. "I do not care if the goddess Cavanna was lying naked in front of you, begging for you to take her! We take no prisoners!"

Berach sat back down and looked at both men. Daigh's commander looked like he was about to crumble into a pile of dust, waiting to be blown away by the winds of Berach's wrath, while the captain himself just stared unblinkingly at the wall behind his desk.

"Really Daigh?" Berach said, turning back to look at the captain, once again ignoring Daigh's second in command, who he now wished he had dismissed before reprimanding Daigh. "What were you thinking?"

"My Lord, I. I." Daigh faltered, realizing there was no way he would be able to lie his way out of this situation. "I am sorry M'lord, I acted impulsively."

Berach pushed the papers away from him in annoyance. "To say the least you fucking fool! And by the way, I know all about you and Dar Fionn.

Now it was Daigh's turn to go pale, shocked by Berach's knowledge of his secret. For though it was true, very few Gwerin knew about the romance he had with Banning's father over twenty-five years ago. A romance that happened before the man became the consort to Aerin Riocard. But Lhoyt had known. He was one of the few people he had told. And it was now obvious that Lhoyt had been the one to tell Lord Berach.

"Now this fool," Berach waved a hand in disgust in Lhoyt's direction. "He had the common sense to tell me what happened during the raid."

"My Lord, I can explain."

"Oh, shut up Daigh!"

Berach sighed, flummoxed over the entire situation. "We had a good thing here." Had, Berach thought angrily as the scowl deepened on his face.

While this small kingdom struggled to survive in the middle of nowhere, it was his grandfather's idea to raid unsuspecting ships traveling across the flats. But it was his idea to also then sell the goods his men had looted in his own markets to make a profit.

Berach's grandfather also had the good sense to then approach those same kingdoms and merchants to offer the services of his military as escorts against those "unknown" pirates, and selling those services for a price.

"But there have been two rules!" Berach said, ignoring the confused look on the men's faces as he continued on with the conversation that he had started in his head. "We kill no one and we take no prisoners. When everyone is left unharmed, there is less of a chance someone will come looking for us. Daigh, you disobeyed our most important rules!"

"I know M'lord." Daigh mumbled.

"I know? I know! By the gods Daigh, your stupidity may well ruin us all! We do not need Birr or the clans Aerin and Dar finding out that it was us. You kidnapped one of their sons! If, when, they find out who did this, how long do you think it would be before they attack us to retrieve him? Iniscarn is a small kingdom and you of all people should know that we would not survive for long against the might of Birr!"

Daigh just sat there and took Berach's verbal attack for he was at a loss for words and knew that everything Berach said was right.

"Fool!" Berach snapped before he stood and paced in the tight space behind his desk. "Stupid fool! We were on the verge of ending the raids and becoming legitimate."

Lhoyt finally looked up, not really comprehending what Berach had just said. "My Lord?" He asked, forgetting himself.

"We have finally become profitable." Berach stopped and raised his hands into the air as he preached this good news to the men. "And Inchinver is now one of the largest port cities, with one of the most famous bazaars in the northern hemisphere."

Berach stabbed a finger into the desk to drive his point home. "There's no reason for us to steal anymore. We have done well as escorts for the smaller kingdoms around us. Our new commodity is our military and selling ourselves as protection to our neighbors. After almost two hundred years of living on this spit of land we are finally seen as a legitimate country. A kingdom to finally show its colors among its equals. A couple of more months and the raids would have been completely over. And now, with one stupid, impulsive act, you've ruined everything!"

A loud knock on the door interrupted the ruler's diatribe.

"Come in!" Berach ordered as he sat back down.

Gwyn, Berach's daughter, entered the room carrying a silver tray with a silver service set on it, the bitter aroma of caff filling the library as she placed the tray on a side table in the room. Berach turned back to Daigh as his daughter ignored the three for the moment and poured the hot drink into two of the cups that were on the tray.

Berach raised his right hand, pointing his index finger at the Daigh, stabbing it in the air with emphasis, wishing that he could draw blood from the man, while he spoke. "You need to fix this Daigh. I do not know how you're going to, and I don't want to know, but if you still want to stay in my employ, you need to fix this mess."

"Now I want the two of you out of my sight! Get out of here!" He waved the men away as Gwyn placed one of the cups in the front of him.

"Aye M'lord!" Lhoyt mumbled hurriedly as he got out of his chair, relieved to be escaping Berach's wrath.

Daigh gave no response of his own, about to follow Lhoyt out of the room just as Berach called out to him.

"Daigh." Berach said as he picked up his cup. "Over the years you have been an asset and a friend to my family. But make no mistake, if you fail to fix this, and if is a means to putting things to right, I will kill you myself."

Daigh only bowed his head, accepting Berach's words as truth, before turning to leave so he could catch up with Lhoyt.

"Guard!" Berach shouted to the man who had remained outside of his library. "Go fetch Urnin Saul for me. He should be waiting down in the kitchens."

The guard, who had heard most of the one-sided conversation through the closed door, and was now quite fearful for his own hide, gave a quick salute before scurrying away to retrieve the man his leader wanted.

Gwyn walked over to one of the vacated chairs, the second cup of caff in her hand, and sat down. She brought the cup to her lips and took a sip while looking at her father, who was pulling together the papers he had scattered across his desk and tried to stack them neatly.

Gwyn took another sip as she waited patiently for her father to finish what he was doing.

"I would get rid of the man now if he wasn't so good at what he does." Berach finally said, once again picking up his cup and holding it in his hands. His eyes took on a distant look as he thought of what he would now need to do to protect his kingdom. Berach took a sip from his cup.

"Fool. He has gone too far this time."

"Don't worry father, Sioda will watch over us."

"Now you are teasing me." He said to his daughter. "Sioda may be our patron deity, but the god is fickle at the best of times. It would be better to beg Murra to release the seas and wash us away to hide this idiotic crime."

"But father, that would not be good for business."

Berach chuckled. Thankfully Gwyn had her mother's sense of humor. Maude, Gwyn's mother and his mate, had passed away several years ago and it was on days like today, when his country seemed to be spinning out of control, that he missed her wit and sensibilities.

"No it would not." Berach replied to his daughter.

The two of them sat in silence for several minutes, each drinking their caff, both lost in their own thoughts; Berach trying to run strategies on protecting Iniscarn and his, investments and Gwyn, wondering what her father had up his sleeve to protect them. Because, what she had learned from her father and from her grandfather, when he was alive, was that there should always be a back-up plan.

Gwyn was still waiting for some type of response from her father, an idea to save them, when she noticed that he had finished his caff and the silver cup was sitting empty on some forgotten papers, so she stood and retrieved the pitcher from the side table so she could refill his cup. And as she was pouring, a gruff voice sounded from behind her. "You called for me Lord Argus?"

"Yes, Saul. Come in and have a seat."

A chill ran down Gwyn's spine as she watched the dark shape of Urnin Saul walk into the room, only turning her head to politely nod at the man as he sat down. Saul, who spent most of his time outside, had a ruddy complexion from the sun and his eyes were so dark that it was difficult to distinguish his irises from his pupils. Saul was tall and broad shouldered, incredibly muscled so that Gwyn always thought of him to be built like a wild tarbh from the plains of Amarra. Saul only lacked the horns of one of those wild herd beasts. And even though Saul worked for her father, Gwyn knew she would not want to meet the man in a dark alley, nor a lit one for that matter.

"Gwyn, Saul and I have some business we need to take care of so why don't you go and give us a couple of minutes to chat."

"Certainly." Gwyn replied. Saul gave her his regards as she brushed past him as she all too willingly made her escape from the man's menacing presence.

Berach called after her to close the door and when he was sure she had left the area he explained to the man that they had a problem.

Saul only nodded for Berach to continue.

But Berach wasn't ready to continue and instead asked Saul how things were progressing with Na Lomahn.

Saul shifted in his seat.

"Well, one wharf is just about finished and we are continuing with the fortifications of the ravine and the cavern." Saul said in a voice that sounded like rocks tumbling in a wooden barrel as he explained the happenings in Berach's newest venture. "Also, a new tunnel was found leading into another cavern. The new cavern is not as big as the main one but there is enough space to make it livable or we can turn it into warehouses."

"And it's off the main tunnel?"

"No. The second entrance was found further east from the main cavern and well hidden behind some outcroppings of rock. Fortifying the entrance while making sure it remains hidden won't be a problem and I have men looking for ways to connect the two caverns so there will be as little outside movement as possible.

"The cistern that needs to get built, on the other hand, is going to be a problem. We keep finding cracks in the basin, so we might need to consider bricking in the entire thing or we could do what your grandfather did when he founded Iniscarn: build some underground water towers while trying to get the cistern to work. Or we could keep a ship loaded with barrels of water docked at the wharf. We keep hoping to find some underground pools of water, but Murra is not being generous with her gift of life."

Berach swore, doing his best not to curse the water goddess, wishing that water could have been found on the island that his men had discovered in the northeastern wastelands of the flats.

"And has any construction started in the main cavern?"

"No. I assumed we had some time to start planning out the borough where your people would be living." Berach's look told him otherwise. "What's going on? Is there a new deadline?"

"Tomorrow." Berach said sarcastically.

Saul watched Berach as he rolled the word around in his head. The Lord of Iniscarn was running a finger around the lip of his cup while looking at the top page of a stack of papers, making Saul wonder if this was some sick sense of humor and that he was just waiting for some punch line to follow. None seemed to be forthcoming so he asked. "Tomorrow?"

"Yes, tomorrow." Berach replied, the second cup of caff was not sitting well and was starting to turn to acid in his stomach. Tomorrow. Even the word tasted bitter in his mouth. "We need to start moving everything and everyone to Na Lomahn, tomorrow."

Berach leaned back into his chair and steepled his fingers of his hands in front of him as he quickly explained the kidnapping of Banning and of Daigh's involvement in it.

"Saul, we should have had two, maybe three years to finish construction but now, thanks to Emmis Daigh, we need to move much more quickly."

This revelation was certainly not what Saul was expecting and only nodded as Berach ran off a checklist for him. "The raiding vessels we have berthed in Maum need to be gone by tomorrow night. And make sure you have the holds on those ships filled with as many supplies as you can carry because it will be a while before any of you can return."

Saul sat quietly and listened as Berach continued. "There are several ships out on the flats looking for marks and are not expecting to return back to port for several weeks. So, as soon as they return I'll have them redirected to you. Also, most of the dock workers who have been maintaining those ships will be going with you.

"That is a lot of people M'lord. How am I supposed to house them?"

"You will have to use the ships for now. Most of the crew will have to double up for the next three days on your flight to Na Lomahn and, once there, try to empty the cargo bays as much as possible and turn them into sleeping quarters. It will be wise not to send out as many raiders, better yet, none at all for a while, and to use the extra manpower to push these projects along."

"I understand M'lord."

Berach stopped for a moment, his jaw tightening in anger as he thought of Daigh's indiscretion.

"Another thing. The Shaefra will be going with you and I want it dismantled. Strip it down to its hull and turn it into spare parts and scatter its timbers across the flats. Just make that fucking ship disappear."

Berach grabbed a clean sheet of paper, dipped a pen into the inkwell sitting on his desk and started writing. "Emmis Daigh has his own personal ship and I am giving you orders to have it conscripted into service as his new vessel. Maybe this will teach him a lesson." Berach signed the letter and passed it to Saul. "Leave this with the dock master in Maum. Tell him to give it to Daigh when he goes looking for the Shaefra. You and I are done here for now. I will see you in a month or so when I come out to Na Lomahn to see how things are coming along."

Saul nodded, stood and left the room, folding the letter and pocketing it as he walked out into the corridor.

Berach watched as Saul headed down the hallway, rubbing his temples wishing that the throbbing that had been there for hours would go away.

Once she was sure that Saul had left their home, Gwyn headed back to the library, only to find its door still open and her father sitting quietly, his head cradled in his hands, the paperwork he had glimpsed briefly, all but forgotten again. Gwyn hesitated for a moment before she rapped lightly on the door and called out softly, "Father? Are you alright?"

Berach looked up at her as he struggled to put a smile on his face for his daughter. "Yes, I'm fine. Come in and have a seat."

Gwyn did as she was told. As she sat down she could not help but notice his haggard appearance; Berach's eyes were pinched and lines of exhaustion creasing their corners and a vein on his temple was throbbing and his complexion was pallid. All this from one of Daigh's juvenile indiscretions?

For there had been many so called indiscretions, and when Gwyn was a child and while sitting on her father's knee, Gwyn delighted to hear her father's stories about Daigh and how brash and foolhardy the captain had been when he was younger. This kidnapping was nothing compared to some of the adventures Daigh had been on while in father's service so there had to be something else that was bothering him.

"How bad is it?" She asked quietly.

"Mmmm?" Her father replied distractedly. "Oh, it's not as bad as it seems dear. It's that, sometimes I just want to kill the man. And this is one of those times. His little escapade could not have come at a worse time for us."

"Why? What is happening?" Gwyn asked as she leaned forward in her seat.

Berach stood and walked over to the empty chair in front of his desk and sat down, pulling the chair closer to his daughter's. He reached over and grasped her hand, her palm cool and dry under his fingers.

"Gwyn," Berach sighed as he looked away from his daughter. "the world has been changing and we need to start changing with it. You see, we are doing so well hiring ourselves out as escorts that there is no need to keep the pirating operations going. So I have decided that it is time to have the raiders disbanded."

Gwyn found the statement hard to believe because pirating had become a family tradition. "Disbanded? Are you sure?"

Berach looked back at his daughter as he explained the new world that was growing about them. "The kingdom of Birr has become stronger. Their continent has been united under Riocard for the past twenty or so years and they are now stretching their influence over other nations. And more of their vessels are roaming the flats and it is becoming harder to find marks that are flying solo."

"And those fanatics who worship Ciaran, the Mendens, seem to be increasing their attacks again. There are reports from many of our southern neighbors that the Mendens are moving north and that they are raiding the villages that are in their path. We do not need the rest of the world thinking we are the ones doing the killing or that we are working with the Mendens. We need to be united and on friendly terms with our neighbors. So, I am having Saul dismantle our raiders and having many of the ships overhauled as escort vessels. I thought we would have time to do this one ship at a time but Daigh, damn him, has pushed my hand. The entire operation needs to be broken down as soon as possible. If Riocard ever finds out his Consort's son is here then I am sure we will have Birrnians poking through everything. So, the sooner everything is dismantled, the better off we will be."

Gwyn reached over and encircled her father's hand with both of hers. "Is there anything I can do?"

"No. Urnin Saul is more than capable of handling things for us." Berach smiled reassuringly, hating the lie he was telling his daughter. "One day all of this will all be yours and with the raiders gone there will be no reason for you to be always looking over your shoulder the way I and your grandfather had to. Trade and escorting will be the focus for Iniscarn now. We need to make it work!"

"You know you can count on me father. We'll build Iniscarn into a kingdom to be reckoned with!"

"I know," Berach said as he ran a hand over the back of her head, remembering the little girl, who had turned into this young woman at his side. "I knew I could count on you."

***

Lhoyt and Daigh had only walked several blocks from Berach's villa, in an uncomfortable silence, when Lhoyt sheepishly, and stupidly, made an attempt at making conversation.

"Well, that didn't go half as bad as it could have."

Daigh wished Lhoyt could have kept his mouth shut because Lhoyt's voice brought the sound of his own blood pumping heavily to his ears. Growling and losing all composure, Daigh punched Lhoyt in the stomach, the man doubling over in surprise and pain as Daigh swung again, hitting Lhoyt in the face, sending the man sprawling across the street. Daigh quickly strode over to Lhoyt and grabbed him by the front of his shirt and hauled the man to his feet and swung him up against a nearby wall, knocking the breath out of Lhoyt as he connected with the building.

Daigh, his face only inches from Lhoyt's, shouted at the man, spittle flying everywhere. "Half bad! How bad did you think it could have been?"

Lhoyt cringed in Daigh's grasp, fearful of getting hit again.

"Daigh, Captain." Lhoyt stuttered as he tried to catch his breath, overwhelmed by the pain in his gut, the throbbing in his left eye where Daigh's fist had hit him and the burning feeling in his scraped and bloody palms when he tried to stop himself as he fell to the ground. "I. . ."

But Daigh growled, not wanting to hear Lhoyt's voice, and pushed him up against the wall again to stop him from talking. A dull thud was heard and Lhoyt hissed through his teeth as pain shot through the back of his head when it connected with the wall once again.

Daigh was getting ready to push Lhoyt again when he caught movement out of the corner of his eye. Turning he found that a group of men and women had stopped in their routines and were now watching their altercation. There were mutterings among them, discussing the appalling scenario, and several among them even looked like they were considering intervening and separating the two. But Daigh let go of Lhoyt, who slumped to the ground, and took several aggressive steps towards the crowd.

"What! You look like you've never seen two men having a disagreement before!" Daigh crazily swung his hands in a shooing fashion at the onlookers. "Go on! Get out of here! The show's over!"

The crowd began to disperse, more apprehensive of the maniacal man now directing his anger at them. Save for one older man who went to go help Lhoyt up, who was stopped in his actions by Daigh. "Screw! Mind your own business!" The man suddenly alone and fearing for his safety, quickly turned and followed the retreating crowd.

Daigh went back to Lhoyt who had pulled himself up from the ground and had propped himself up against the wall, a bloody hand covering his left eye. Daigh, who fought the urge to throw another kick at his second in command, started shouting more expletives about how he could so easily betray him.

Lhoyt looked at him with his good eye then dropped his gaze and shook his head, knowing that anything he had to say, or telling the captain how he felt for him, would not be helpful.

Daigh tucked in his shirt and then tugged his vest back into place before he started to pace in front his second in command as he began to rant. "I told you! I told the whole crew not to say anything! I had this all under control!"

Daigh stopped to look at Lhoyt who was wiping dirt off of his bloodied hands.

"We've known each other for a long time, Lhoyt. I thought you were more than my second. I thought we were friends."

"We are." Lhoyt mumbled miserably.

Daigh laughed sharply. "You have a fine way of showing it. You've ruined everything!"

Lhoyt looked at Daigh, his left eye had swollen shut and the skin around it was beginning to darken and streaks of blood marked his cheek from where his palm had rested against his face.

"What have I ruined?" Lhoyt spat out hoarsely. "There's been nothing to ruin?"

Daigh pushed Lhoyt back up against the wall again. "Watch your tongue!"

"Why? Are you going to hit me again?"

Daigh pushed one more time at Lhoyt before letting go of him and moved away from the man.

But Lhoyt felt like he had nothing to lose at this point and decided to plow ahead. "I know that man was the love of your life but it has been over twenty five years. When are you going to realize you should just move on?"

"Phaw!" Daigh shouted to stop Lhoyt but he knew the man was right and that his ongoing infatuation over Fionn was ridiculous, childish at best. He just didn't want Lhoyt to be right.

But Lhoyt ignored Daigh's exclamation and continued. "Captain, we were lucky this time. You disobeyed the law and you could have not only gotten yourself killed, you could have had us all killed!"

Lhoyt winced as he rubbed the left side of his head, his left eyeball moving underneath his lids, which wouldn't open anymore and his cheek was shaking involuntarily. "You never should have taken his son, Daigh. He doesn't love you anymore and maybe he never loved you at all."

Pain shot through Lhoyt's arm as Daigh grabbed him and squeezed tightly, twisting it at an odd angle.

"Don't push your luck." Daigh hissed and shoved him away and started to walk away from Lhoyt. "You know what? From now on I want you to stay out of my life! Just stay out of it!"

As he stormed away, Daigh couldn't believe how angry, how incensed and hurt he was by Lhoyt's betrayal. Not to mention how his loss of control and assaulting his second in command infuriated him.

But, damn Lhoyt! He should have turned a blind eye and stayed indifferent to the situation. Just like the rest of his crew had.

Unfortunately he couldn't get rid of the man because he needed Lhoyt's pragmatism and ingenuity on the Shaefra. Daigh just wanted the man to stop acting as conscious to his personal life.

Daigh fumed as he started to make his way home so that he could finish his talk with Banning, hoping to come up with an idea on how to salvage something from this fiasco he had created. But nothing inventive was materializing, and out of frustration Daigh ducked into the first tavern he came across.

It was only mid-afternoon and the tavern was somewhat crowded as Daigh strode up to the bar and slapped some coppers onto it and sullenly ordered ale from the barkeep. The man nodded, poured a mug from a keg behind the counter for Daigh, and took the appropriate amount of money from him, leaving several coppers behind.

Daigh grunted his thanks to the man and wrapped his hands around the mug and stared into the amber liquid, hoping for an answer to his problems to bubble up to the surface. But none seemed to be forthcoming so he took a long pull from the mug.

Daigh still had no answers to his predicament and was unsure of what he was going to do as he finished his drink. So fishing in his pocket he pulled out two more coppers and annoyingly banged the mug on the counter. When he did get the barkeep's attention, he just swirled his finger in the empty mug and pushed his money forward. Displeased by Daigh's rudeness, the bartender poured another mug and none too gently pushed the mug towards Daigh, splashing his hands with some of the drink. This counter attack brought Daigh out of his dark reverie.

As he watched the man raise his wet hands in surrender, the barkeeper only shook his head and tossed Daigh the rag he had at his waist. Daigh wiped his hands and mumbled his thanks and held out the rag for the man to take back.

"One of those days?" The barkeeper asked as he lifted Daigh's mug to clean the counter in front of him.

Daigh snorted and gave the man a slight smile. "You can say that. Just the beginning of many of those days.

"Well, good luck through them my friend." The barkeeper said as he wiped the coins into his hand and pocketed them before heading towards the other end of the bar where a group of men and women had come in and were hailing him over to be serviced.

Daigh took a sip from his new drink then went back to staring absently into the ale. What were the answers? Damn! He knew the answer. He should have left Dar Banning on the barge, instead of taking the boy and picking at the scab to a very old wound. Daigh felt numb and with his eyes fixed ahead, focusing on nothing, took another drink from his ale.

"Fionn, after all this time." Daigh mumbled as he took a longer pull from his drink, remembering their last day together, as it swirled to the surface of his memory, like the bubbles in his ale, like it had just happened yesterday.

"Why?" He mumbled again.

"No. We have to stop." Fionn's voice echoed in his head from out of the past.

"What, why?" Daigh said, looking for a response, not realizing he was talking to no one, not really caring that his misery and the alcohol he was drinking began to numb his senses.

But the word pounded in Daigh's head; why? For he and Fionn had been lovers twenty-five years ago. And now it was a memory that once again becoming all too painfully clear for Daigh.

"You know this isn't right." Fionn said, his blond hair reflecting the faint light from the moon overhead, a pained look in his eyes as he wedged an arm between himself and Daigh as he tried to separate their embrace.

An embrace that Emmis Daigh had longed no yearned for since he had followed Fionn out of the province of Talamh Shar, the last and the largest of the western kingdoms to hold out against the advances, albeit peaceful, of Birr.

Those long standing rulers of Birr, the Aerin clan, had learned long ago that in a time of peace, that unification could be brought about by money and the prestige that usually came with it.

And the monarch of Talamh Shar, the Lord Dar Selden, was no exception to this rule. If anything, prestige was at the forefront of his thoughts because Dar Selden had been fortunate in that he had been gifted by the birth of three sons.

The two oldest of Selden's sons were already married off and it was agreed upon by him and Lord Aerin Broll that they would succeed as dukes ruling over Talamh after his passing, his kingdom being split into two provinces for the sons; Talamh East and Talamh West. In return for this grand gesture, Selden's youngest son, Dar Fionn, would become the companion, the consort, to the only heir of Aerin Broll, his son, Riocard; a marriage of two clans that would finally unite the continent of Birr, turning it into a vast kingdom, only to be ruled by Aerin Broll.

Unfortunately there was one problem and his name was Emmis Daigh.

For Dar Selden had known of his youngest son's relationship with Daigh because the boys had been courting for several years. And, even though the Emmis' were a wealthy and well respected clan, the Aerin's were far a richer and a much more powerful clan in which case Selden's entire family would benefit from this venture.

So, as treaties were signed and ceremonies prepared, Fionn was told to break off his relationship with Daigh.

Of course the Emmis clan understood the situation. But Daigh was devastated by the break-up. But after three years of courting and no proposal forthcoming from Daigh, something was bound to happen. Sadly, such is the case when one eventually waits too long for the right moment to propose to their lover.

So a month after accepting the Dar's proposal, Aerin Broll, along with his son, Riocard, traveled to Seruth, the capital of Talamh, for the introduction of the two young men. Their meeting was amicable and polite, very politic, to the extreme pleasure of both fathers and so it was agreed upon for Fionn to return to Kinsale, the capital of Birr, where the two men would be given some time to get to know each other before their union.

Daigh, incensed by his dismissal, and against his own father's wishes and his own better judgment, made the decision to follow Fionn to Kinsale. Once there Daigh easily learned that Fionn was living at the Temple to Cavanna. So finding him would be easy. It would just be another thing to figure out how he would be able to see his lover.

Daigh stalked the public grounds of the temple for a little over two weeks, hoping to catch a glimpse of Fionn. With his vigils being fruitless Daigh was starting to lose hope and was considering making the painful trip back home, when one day, by the grace of the gods, he stumbled across Fionn in the Garradh dhe Dia, the temple's Garden of the Gods. Fionn's face lit up like the new day sun and took several quick steps towards his jilted lover before remembering where he was and stopped, a mask of indifference replacing and hiding the joy he felt at seeing Daigh.

But Daigh, who had found his prize, would not be deterred so easily by the wall Fionn had put up. Daigh, born with the gift to charm, promised to be on his best behavior, and was able to coerce Fionn into agreeing to spend the day with him.

But what to do about the Royal Guard who were now watching over Fionn's movements? The two soldiers that the young men were obliged to take out into the city so that Fionn could visit with an "old friend"? Thankfully they did not have to worry too much because the guards were generous and gave them some liberty, staying out of earshot of their conversations as they wandered the streets outside the temple.

Daigh's soul was filled with joy and he silently thanked the gods for having Fionn standing by his side once again. As was Fionn, who shared in a joy that couldn't be expressed as the two men toured the city.

Daigh eventually began to reminisce about their time spent in Seruth, finally getting Fionn to crack a smile and laugh over casual days gone by in their homeland, with Daigh's face lighting up from joy in Fionn's laughter. Daigh also remembered how Fionn had looked so forlorn in the temple gardens and it took all of Daigh's self-control not to reach out and hold Fionn's hand as they walked along the bustling streets of Kinsale.

But as the sun set over Kinsale and street lamps were lit, the somewhat forgotten guards once again made their presence known, informing the two that their time was up and that Daigh should be moving on. Daigh knew that once he walked away from the love of his life, whatever he and Fionn had shared for the past several years would be over. So Daigh, who pleaded and flirted a little with the guards, explaining how this might be the last time he would see Fionn for a long time, got the guards to grudgingly allow them ten more minutes of solitude to say their goodbyes before Fionn had to be escorted back to the temple.

So as the guards walked away towards the street corner Daigh made his move and shoved Fionn into a little walled unlit alley and pulled him into an embrace. Fionn, who was caught off guard, knew he should have resisted, but yielded as Daigh pushed him against the wall, grabbed the back of his head and kissed him. Fionn quickly gave into his yearnings, his upcoming union all but forgotten because he too had missed Daigh, and wrapped his arms around Daigh's waist, the heat from each other quickly chasing away the coolness of the night.

Fionn, knowing in his heart that this was the man he wanted to be with, kissed Daigh even harder and pushed a hand under his lover's shirt, eliciting a moan as his fingers ran over naked flesh, rubbing the small of Daigh's back and forcing his hand past his belted trousers, grabbing his buttocks, urging Daigh to ground harder into him, his hot breath billowing against Fionn's tapered ear.

Alas, need and want are two totally different things and reality began to reassert itself as images of his father and Riocard flashed in Fionn's head. Fionn closed his eyes, trying to wish the images away as he removed his hands from Daigh's pants and moved them up his back. He did not want to let go of Daigh, but he knew his family must come first. A family that would benefit immensely from his marriage into the Aerin clan and family that he did not want to shame.

And like a soft breeze brushing against Daigh's skin, he whispered, "No."

"Mmmm?" Daigh mumbled, not really hearing the word as he moved down to kiss Fionn's neck.

"No. We have to stop." Fionn repeated breathlessly as he wedged an arm between himself and Daigh.

Daigh straightened while still holding onto Fionn and looked at him. "What? Why?"

The look of pain in Daigh's eyes, the frown forming on his lips that were bruised from their kissing and his arms still holding onto him tightly were too much for Fionn.

"You know this isn't right." Fionn reiterated as he tried to separate their embrace.

But Daigh would not let go and held on tightly to Fionn's waist. "This isn't right? You know it is!" He let go of Fionn only to grasp the sides of Fionn's head with his hands. "Please!" He whispered as he tenderly rubbed Fionn's cheeks with his thumbs. "Please, stay with me! Let's try to get away now while the guards aren't looking!"

Fionn grasped one of Daigh's hands with his own and turned it to kiss its palm before looking at Daigh, holding tightly onto his hand.

"And where would we go? Back home? Not only would I be an embarrassment to my family, you would shame your family too."

"Who cares?" Daigh replied as he grasped Fionn's hand with both of his and brought Fionn's to his mouth, taking time to kiss each knuckle. "We don't have to go back to Seruth or Talamh Shar. We don't have to stay anywhere in Birr for that matter. As long as we are together, living in a cave would be fine with me."

A faint smile crossed Fionn's lips at the thought of running away with Daigh. An enticing thought; to give it all up for the man he loved. "I can't." He said as he dropped his gaze to the ground. "My father, my family has everything at stake because of this union to Prince Aerin. No, I will not be the one to disgrace them."

"But?"

Strengthening his resolve, Fionn pulled his hand out of Daigh's grasp. "No. I will not betray my family! We missed our opportunity and now my father has chosen someone else for me."

"Are you saying this is my fault?" Daigh asked in frustration. "Your father has always been amicable towards me. Like a fourth son he used to say. And we agreed there was no rush for us. How was I supposed to know the almighty rulers of Birr would come to Talamh looking for a mate for their prince?"

"Please." Fionn whispered. "You are not making this any easier and you know we are both at fault for this."

"Is everything alright Prince Dar?" Startled, both men turned to see Fionn's escort staring at them from the entrance to the alley. Daigh stuck his hands in his pockets and tried to shift himself into a more comfortable position as he did his best to hide his arousal for Fionn from the two men.

"No, we are fine." Fionn said to the men as one of the guards walked towards them. "I am ready to go."

"Fionn." Daigh said painfully as he grasped Fionn's shoulder, stopping his lover from walking away, still hoping beyond hope that Fionn would not leave his side.

The move was a mistake because the ringing of steel filled the air as the guards drew their swords and stepped into the walkway to defend their charge from Daigh's advances.

But Fionn shouted in panic as he put a hand up to halt the guards from attacking Daigh.

He turned back to his now ex-lover and said with as much force as he could muster, the words like daggers digging into his gut as he said them, "We are through! Go back to Seruth or wherever you feel you need to move on to. Maybe you can go find that cave of yours. Whatever you do, it would be wise for you not to come back here anymore."

Daigh stared dumbly at Fionn, not comprehending what was being said nor the sarcasm thrown at him as Fionn turned to leave. This wasn't happening. Daigh didn't want it to happen, so he took a step forward, hoping Fionn would change his mind but one of the guards blocked his movement, the flat of his palm landing solidly on Daigh's chest.

"You heard the prince." The guard growled at Daigh as the young man tried to push the immobile hand blocking his path off of his chest.

His back to Daigh, his trembling voice echoing in the corridor, Fionn asked the man detaining Daigh to escort him back to where ever he was staying. Inhaling deeply, and rubbing at his face to wipe away the tears clouding his eyes, Fionn continued to walk down the main street with the second guard right on his heels as they disappeared into the night.

The guard who had remained with him grabbed Daigh by the shoulder and forcibly led him out onto the street and in the opposite direction the other two had taken.

"Alright lover boy, your fun is over." The Birrnian guard said with a smirk on his face. "Just to let you know, Prince Dar's father warned us about you. You don't know how lucky you are that you got that last kiss goodbye."

"I do."

The guard only coughed loudly before asking Daigh where he was staying.

"Docks." Daigh replied in a rough whisper. "I'm staying at an inn near the docks." He said a little louder.

"Then the docks it is." The guard, whose hand had not left Daigh's arm stopped the forlorn man and roughly turned Daigh around to face him. "And if I were you, I would disappear at first light." He shook Daigh, making sure he had his attention. "Is that understood?"

Daigh felt like he was floundering, his world crumbling around him and the only thing he knew was that, at this moment, he couldn't get out of Kinsale soon enough.

"Yes." He finally said, clenching his teeth as he uselessly fought to hold back the tears that were rolling down his cheeks. "I'll go."

"Mmm." The guard acknowledged throatily as he continued down the street, his hand still gripping Daigh's arm, though not as roughly as it had been. Daigh simply allowed himself to be led away, not caring where the guard eventually dumped him.

"You okay mate?"

Daigh blinked, a stray tear running down his face only to drop silently into his ale before remembering where he was and looked up at the man tending bar who had walked back over to him and was now watching him while he cleaned a mug. How long had the bartender been watching him while he picked at a very old wound?

"No. I'm fine." Daigh replied to the man, trying to force a smile on his face; and failed.

That's when Daigh realized the tavern had become much more crowded with men and women standing around him, talking boisterously as people tried to be overheard over the laughter that was filling the air. Daigh hunched his shoulders and grasped the mug tighter as he tried to escape the merriment flowing around him. But to no avail because the sounds and the groups of people only emphasized how lonely he felt. Camaraderie that reminded Daigh of how he had continued to long for a man he could never have. Daigh took another pull from his ale, before looking around one more time, his frown deepening as he realized he couldn't avoid Fionn's son any longer. Reaching into his pocket, he placed a silver crown on the counter, way too much money for a tip, and squeezed his way through the other patrons as he left the tavern.

The trek across the streets of Carnuaimh had become tortuous for Daigh as he stumbled home. For with each step that he took, each a burden as he made his way closer to home, Daigh found himself stopping several times as an idea came to him on how he might clarify why he had brought Banning here instead of taking him home to Kinsale. Unfortunately, because of the alcohol or because of the truth, Daigh's schemes didn't even sound believable to himself.

He even began to draw stares from passersby's as he stopped one street only a block away from his villa and began to mumble to himself while pacing back and forth. Throughout his alcohol induced one sided debate the only thing that made sense to Daigh was to tell Banning the truth. At least, he thought as he rounded the corner to approach his home, as much of the truth as possible without it sounding like the kidnapping that it was or to implicate Lord Argus Berach in the pirating ventures.

Upon entering his home Daigh felt another drink, on top of the ales he already had, might help to fortify his nerves, and wanting something stronger this time, Daigh headed for the dining room and the liquor cabinet within. As he was poured himself a glass of squilla, Daigh could hear several voices in conversation echoing down the hallway from the kitchen. Quickly gulping down some of the bitter liquid and refilling the glass, Daigh walked into the kitchen and found Mac, Davis and Banning standing around a counter, eating.

Their conversation ended abruptly and an awkward silence filled the room as Daigh approached them and took another sip from his drink while he looked at the men. Daigh also thought he saw a conspiratorial look in the stares they gave each other (and he would be right because they couldn't help but notice Daigh's glassy eyed expression and flushed face) as they silently picked at cold meats and boiled eggs from a plate on the counter. The three men also seemed to be trying to avoid his gaze, looking down whenever he tried to catch their eye.

Polishing off his drink in consternation, Daigh walked out of the room, leaving them in the lingering silence as he retrieved the decanter of squilla from the dining room, pouring himself another drink while making his return to the kitchen.

"So, are we having a party?" He asked with a smirk on his face.

"Sorry, Captain. Just having some dinner." Davis said around a mouthful of food. "Once the prince had cleaned up, he told us he was hungry and, since he had only been fed broth for the past several days, I saw no reason not to get something more solid into him."

"No. No. You did right." Daigh said with a slight hint of a slur beginning to enter his voice. He looked at Banning who was staring back at him while Banning took a drink from a mug that was in front of him. From where Daigh stood he noticed the prince was barefoot, wearing black pants and a dark purple shirt that brought out the color in his golden brown eyes and there was a shine to his light brown hair from the lit candelabra overhead. Banning was a little shorter but more solidly built than his father. But the resemblance between father and son was still there. A disturbing look that brought up more of the past, chasing away the warm hearted smile he had put on his face.

"Give us a moment." Daigh said to his men as he swayed a little, his hand reaching out for the counter to help steady his balance. Mac and Davis who were relieved at being dismissed, yet concerned at leaving Banning alone with their captain in his current condition, nodded and left the room.

"Feeling better?" Daigh asked as he picked up a boiled egg and bit into it.

Banning returned his mug to the counter, a little uncomfortable at being left alone with Daigh because he had read Daigh's smile as lascivious and was unsure of what would be expected of him, especially in the man's current state.

"Yes, thank you." Banning finally replied as cautiously as he could. "The bath was quite refreshing."

"Good, good." The faint smile had returned to Daigh's face and as he looked down he noticed that his glass was once again empty. Daigh was far beyond feeling lightheaded and there was a hum rolling through the back of his head. Staring down into the bottom of his empty glass Daigh resisted the urge to try and pour himself another drink.

"Sho, where to start?" Daigh said, the slur in his voice getting thicker.

Banning rolled his eyes, realizing that Daigh was on his way to being, if not already, drunk and that there was nothing sexual going on or going to happen at this point. So Banning answered Daigh's question with one of his own. "How about at the beginning?" The prince said with a smirk. A smirk that remained on his face as he watched Daigh's head droop a little and bob from side to side, words forming silently on his lips as he seemed to struggle with what to say.

"You could start with why we're in Carnuaimh and not Kinsale." Banning offered Daigh as a beginning to his story.

When Daigh looked at Banning questioningly, trying to piece together in his muddled mind how the he had figured out where they were the prince jerked his head to the side and said, "There was a window in the bathroom your men let me use to wash. Carnuaimh is the only city I know of that is built on the walls of a gorge."

"Yesh, well you being here is pretty much the middle of the story." Daigh said as he picked up one of the boiled eggs, bit off half of it, before popping the rest of it into his mouth and slowly ate it before as a soft chuckle escaped his lips.

"Please!" Banning interrupted, angry that the man he rightly believed was his captor was now becoming a drunkard. And not knowing what would happen to him, Banning couldn't keep the tone of fear from creeping back into his voice. "If I am to be ransomed for some reward then let me know what you want so I can go home!"

"No. No ransom." Daigh sighed, rubbing his face with his hands. "First of all, I am sorry and I beg forgiveness for what I have done."

Now that remark caught Banning off guard. He didn't know what he was expecting but he knew it wasn't supposed to be an apology. After a moment he asked Daigh to go with his explanation.

Daigh tapped his glass against the counter, the blurred image of it coming into focus, and decided to pour himself another drink. Anything so he did not have to answer Banning.

"So, what do you know of your father's life before he became consort to the great Aerin Riocard?"

Banning thought for a moment, even more confused by this next question, and just shrugged. "I don't understand what my father's past has to do with this."

Daigh took another sip of his drink and rolled the glass in his hands, watching the red liquid swirl inside. "Well, my family is from Seruth and we were quite friendly with yours." Daigh raised the glass and finished off the squilla in it. "As a matter of fact, your father and I were lovers."

"What? You? My father?"

"Yesss." Daigh slurred as he held up his right hand, scrunching his fingers into a number. "Three years. We were together for almost three years before he was sent to Kinsale by your grandfather." Out of annoyance, he pushed at the glass in front of him. "Good ol' Dar Seldon married off your father to clan Aerin so he could keep his greedy grasp on Talamh Shar after its unification with Birr."

"Then why didn't you just take me home?" Banning whispered, already knowing his father's marriage to his foster-father was mostly one of convenience. As his marriage would one day be.

"That bastard didn't care one bit about our feelings for each other." Daigh said, ignoring Banning's question. "I followed your father to Kinsale and begged him to run away with me. I begged him. I would have taken him anywhere." Daigh's voice shook as he held back tears. "But your father, always an honest and honorable man, refused to bring shame to his family." Daigh snorted as he poured himself another glass of squilla, most of it spilling onto the counter. "I truly loved your father. I still love him. So when I saw you. . ."

"What do you mean? When you saw me?" Banning asked suspiciously.

"By the time we landed so that we could reach you." Daigh explained. "I do not know how long you had been out there by the time we found you or even how long you would have survived on your own.

I do know the gods were with you on that day Banning." He looked down as he began toying with his glass again. "And when I saw you, I just couldn't believe the resemblance. I knew exactly who you were."

Daigh brought the glass to his lips before he realized he had already finished off the squilla in it. Closing his eyes, he sighed. "We should have looked for your ship or taken you back to Birr. But, I thought. I don't know what I thought. I really am sorry." Finally some bit of truth escaped his lips because he was sorry. Sorry for the trouble he had caused for himself and for the ire and disdain he received from Lord Argus Berach. "I should have taken you home to your father. Where you belong."

Banning was very dubious about the story he had been told, especially when it was coming from a man who was obviously very drunk. Except for stories about his uncles and life with his grandfather, Banning had never really heard his father talk about anyone from his past. Banning had met members of clan Emmis, on several trips back to Seruth, but none had ever mentioned Daigh's name, but Banning couldn't deny that Daigh's emotions did seem genuine.

"Sho now to fix thiss mess." Daigh slurred, interrupting Banning's thoughts.

"Well, Captain Emmis, it's obvious the best way to fix this is to take me home." Banning replied in annoyance.

Daigh smiled, missing the tenor in Banning's voice, not really able to make out the expression on Banning's face anymore. "Yes. Obviously." He agreed as he turned to walk away from the counter, but the squilla and the ale he had earlier drunk, had taken their toll on him and Daigh stumbled slightly, his legs wobbly, all feeling in his feet lost to him.

Thankfully Banning reached out and caught Daigh by the arm and held onto him until Daigh placed his other hand on the counter to steady himself.

"So much like your father." Daigh said, looking at Banning through glassy eyes.

Banning turned red, embarrassed by the comment, and looked around the room for a moment. It was obvious that in his drunken stupor Daigh probably thought he was thinking those words instead of having said them out loud.

"So when do we leave?" He asked the captain, interrupting the man's thoughts once again.

"My Prince, I'm thinking it would make sense if I went to Kinsale on my own to talk to your father.

"How does that make any sense?" Banning said as he scowled, thinking that there must be some ulterior motive for him to be left behind.

"I'm sure your Royal Guard is out searching for you and how will it look if we get boarded and they find you on my ship? Put to death on the spot. No. I think the best way of keeping my head attached to my shoulders would be to go alone and have one of your ships return with me to Iniscarn. A formal escort for your return home to Kinsale."

"I don't know."

Daigh chuckled at something only he had found humorous and might have fallen over again if he hadn't been holding onto the counter.

"My Prince! Banning!" Daigh shouted a little too loudly. "How have I wronged you? You are in my home as a guest and you have been well taken care of. Why, my own personal physician has cared for you." Of course, on the Shaefra, Cook was everyone's physician.

Daigh frowned. "Have Mac or Davis made any untoward advances at you?"

"No."

"Have we harmed you in any way?"

Banning snorted. "You did keep me asleep for almost a week."

Daigh shook his head. "We kept you sleeping so we could make sure you had no injuries and were well rested. Banning. Please. Trust me on this."

Banning straightened up and crossed his arms over his chest as a thought came to him. "Very well. But I have one condition; I wish to speak to Lord Argus."

That sobered Daigh a little. "Lord Argus Berach?"

"Yes. Since I am not your prisoner and you won't be taking me home just yet, I see no reason not to let Lord Argus know that a prince of Birr is in his kingdom."

Daigh fretted with his vest, picking at a piece of lint that wasn't there before he before informing Banning that Berach knew that he was here.

"He does?"

"Yes. As a matter of fact, I am in his employ and he knows all about this situation. Lord Argus was the one who called me earlier today and it was his idea that you stay in my villa. He thought you would be more comfortable in the home of an ex-countryman than in the halls of his mansion."

"Just the same, I would still like an audience with him."

"Very well, I will let him know of you request." Daigh said as he tried to look at Banning through puffy eyes. "But he is a busy man and I'm not sure when he would be able to see you."

"Be that as it may, when will you be able to talk to him?"

"Tomorrow. I will talk to Lord Argus tomorrow before I leave to see your father."

Somewhat mollified, Banning grudgingly thanked Daigh. And as he was toying with the plate of food, Banning asked the man if any servants would be around to help him around the villa.

"No. I have no servants, but several of my crew help me here when I have a need. And since you have already met Mac and Davis I see no reason why they shouldn't stay to help you around here. Unless there is some reason you disapprove of them."

Banning knew that no matter what he said it would be Mac and Davis who stayed behind and the two men had treated him well, so he smiled politely as he tried to be sociable. "They will do. As a matter of fact, I've read much about your city; with its bridges that span the canyon's wall and the spectacular sunsets. A tour of Carnuaimh by your men would be most appreciated."

"Unfortunately a tour of the city is out of the question." Daigh said as he picked at his vest again, wondering how he would keep the prince hidden from view. But it was hard to think with his head pounding and he was feeling dizzy and the only thing Daigh wanted to do right now was to lie down. "Carnuaimh and Maum have many military training grounds and storage facilities that are off limits so I would not want you stumbling into someplace you don't belong. I think it would be wise if you stayed in my home and waited for my return."

"Do your men not know their way around the city so they can avoid those restricted areas? Your denial seems highly unreasonable, especially if I am a guest and not your prisoner. I see no reason to keep me hidden away."

Daigh put a hand to his forehead, barely able to hear Banning over the pounding in his head and he was starting to feel nauseous. "Please, Banning."

Banning couldn't help but notice that Daigh wasn't looking well and in his drunken stupor Banning felt that this might be the only time he had the upper hand in dealing with this man, so he decided to play the only card he had up his sleeve. "Please! Or what?" He demanded loudly. "Will you beat me the way you did your crewman earlier this afternoon?"

Daigh swayed and through his eyes that wouldn't keep anything in focus, watched as Banning defensively backed away from the counter.

"Mac! Davis!" Daigh bellowed, not realizing how loudly he shouted or that he had no reason to because the two men had only removed themselves to the dining room. There they could eavesdrop on most of the captain's conversation because they wanted to know what truths and lies he was weaving for the prince and they wanted to be able to back him up if Banning ever questioned them.

"You called Captain?" Davis asked ignorantly as he and Mac entered the room.

Daigh forced himself to stand a little straighter as he talked to his men. "Was Lhoyt here?"

"Yes Captain."

"What did he say?" Daigh asked as he tried to gauge his men's reactions to the question. Unfortunately, Mac who had always been the quieter of the two men was looking down at the tiled floor while tapping the base of the counter with his foot while Davis stared back at him, his face devoid of any expression.

"Nothing, Captain. Only that you two got into a row over something. He came back, grabbed his kit from his quarters and said you could find him staying with some friends off Market Row. If and when you need him, that is. If you don't mind me saying Captain, he was pretty banged up."

Daigh scowled, angry that he now had one more mess to clean up. "We had a disagreement and I let it get out of hand. Nothing to concern yourself about." Daigh said without looking at Banning. "Forgive me, Prince Dar. Unfortunately, you are seeing me at my very worst."

Banning shrugged nonchalantly as he tried to be the one in control over this situation. "How you treat your men is of no concern to me. Only how I will be treated and what I will be telling my father upon my return to Kinsale. So, do I have liberty to see the city or will I be kept as a prisoner in your home?"

"Captain," Davis interrupted, putting a hand on the captain's shoulder to stall him from saying anything and to steady the swaying man. "Giving Prince Dar a tour of the city will not be a problem. There is much to see and keep us busy in Market Row and we will certainly stay out of the areas Lord Argus deems off limits. You can count on Mac and me not to get Prince Dar into trouble."

With his head spinning and the feeling that he was going to pass out, Daigh was finding it easy to acquiesce to the prince's demands, especially if his men watched where they took him.

"Very well." He finally said, waving a hand in the air. "Now if you'll excuse me."

Daigh took a step to leave the room, but stumbled as he let go of the counter and he would have fallen if Davis hadn't caught him.

Davis held onto Daigh tightly, who was slumped against his chest and beckoned for Mac to help him with their captain. Davis handed Daigh to Mac, draping the captain's right arm across Mac's shoulders so the man could grasp Daigh around his torso.

"Get him to quarters. I'll be right there to help you with him." Davis said.

And as Mac stumbled into the dining room, the captain mumbling incoherently, Davis turned back to face Banning. "If you go through the door behind you and follow the hallway to its end, you will find a game room. The outside walls of the room are all glass so you will be able to see Carnuaimh and the part of the city that's on the opposite wall of the canyon. And at this time of the night most of the city should be lit up by now. Once Mac and I are done with the captain we'll come down and join you. If you are up to it, we can play a couple hands of cards. They do play forte five in your land?"

"Yes. My father taught my brother and myself how to play. Though it's been a while since I've played. Don't worry, I'll find my way to the room and wait for you there."

"Oh, and one more thing if you don't mind that I speak my peace." Davis said before Banning could leave the room.

Banning nodded his ascent so Davis continued. "I'm not one for flowery words of formality so I will just say it. After all these years apart, the captain still has serious feelings for your father. I don't know why, but he still does."

Davis sighed and started again, not sure if Banning understood what he was trying to say. "The captain is usually much more reserved and always looking out for his crew and it's very rare when he gets like this. But when he lets go, like he did tonight, it's not uncommon for him to reminisce about your father."

Davis shrugged as he put his hands into his pants pockets. "Aside from his scuffle with Lhoyt, and you didn't hear it from me, but I think that scuffle has been a long time coming, the captain does mean well. If you don't want to trust the captain you can trust me that you will be kept safe while you are with us."

"You know," Davis said over his shoulder as he left the kitchen to go see how Mac had faired with their captain. "Any one of us would be lucky to find someone who would love us the way Captain Emmis loved, still loves, your father.

***

Daigh was not the only one who had found his way into a tavern on his way home that afternoon. For as Daigh was on his stool, pining away over his lost love, Urnin Saul was walking into another tavern on the other side of Carnuaimh, stopping at the entrance, scanning the room until he found who he was looking for.

A man, almost as heavily muscled as Saul, with just as dark skin and jet black hair sat at a table on the far end of the room with his hands wrapped around a mug of ale. When Durdst Cabot noticed his lover crossing the room, he smiled and raised his mug in greetings.

"So, how are things going?" Cabot asked in a voice that was just as accented as Saul's.

"Well, things have gotten somewhat interesting." Saul dragged the other chair out from under the table and sat down, rubbing his chin while he mulled over what had learned at Argus Berach's villa.

"How so?" Cabot gestured towards the barman, held up two fingers and pointed down at their table. The bartender nodded and grabbed two mugs and began pouring new drinks for the men.

"Argus Berach wants me to move his operations to Na Lomahn. And he wants it done now." Saul leaned back in his chair and kicked at one of the table's legs in annoyance. "His pet, Emmis Daigh, has fouled things and now all the ships, their crews and anyone else involved in the raiding operations needs to be shipped to the base as soon as possible."

Cabot whistled, surprised at what he heard. "But it's not finished? What happened?"

Saul began to recount his meeting with his employer and the gossip that was floating around the villa. He stopped momentarily when the bartender arrived with their drinks and grabbed one of the mugs, taking a long pull from it while Cabot thanked the bartender and handed him a silver piece, telling him to come back shortly with two more ales. When the man had walked out of hearing distance, Saul continued with his story, both men laughing viciously as Saul described Daigh's fall from grace with the Lord Argus Berach.

"Kidnapping Prince Dar?" Cabot chuckled as he finished his drink. "It is a shame we could not use this information to our advantage. But what of our men hiding in the hills of Na Lomahn? And what do I tell Captain Villis? He and Lord Lyro thought we had two more years using Lomahn as a camp into the north."

"Do not worry." Saul assured him, knowing full well they could not afford to lose the only foothold their people, the Mendens, had into the northern desolations of the flats. "I can give you one, maybe a two day head start before I start sending anyone to the camp."

Saul was tapping the table, trying to hammer out the evacuation of both the raiders and his own people when a thought came to him. "Wait!" He said, pointing a finger at Cabot. "Leave several of the men behind with supplies. The caves we are using are well hidden and as long as there are no ships about they should be able to remain so."

And as another idea came to him, Saul couldn't help but chuckle, "Berach wants me to dismantle the Shaefra, the vessel Daigh was flying when he kidnapped the prince. Leave a steersman behind and a handful more men. I'll get them into camp somehow and when it is time to dispose of the Shaefra, I'll have the ship dumped out on the flats for Captain Villis to retrieve." Saul chuckled again. "Why let the ship go to waste? Oh, and make sure you leave a pair of lodestones with the steersman because I'll need to return with the ship's original ones so it looks like the Shaefra has truly been dismantled."

"Saul, you are a genius." Cabot's laughter mingled with Saul's. "I am supposed to rendezvous with the captain soon so I will let him know of these changes."

Saul frowned as he let go of his mug and stretched his hands out to grasp those of Cabot. "Hopefully you won't be leaving too soon?

Cabot smiled wickedly at the question. For although he and Saul were mates, their time together was always sparse and sometimes short lived. "I'm not the only one who needs to leave on errands." And watching Saul's frown deepen he squeezed his lover's hands to get his attention. "I've already paid for a room for us."

Saul smiled, anxious to leave the tavern, he bowed his head and closed his eyes and whispered, "May Ciaran watch over and hide us from our enemies."

"Preserve our endeavors and smite our foes." Cabot whispered.

Saul let go of Cabot's hands and raised his mug, finishing off his drink before calling out to the bartender for their next round that they would be taking upstairs with them.

***

"I just bumped into Daigh as he was leaving. He looked awful."

"I know." Berach said to his daughter around a mouthful of food.

Even though Berach had been able to sleep through the night, he still had a haggard look that was hard to ignore. But he was doing just that, ignoring how he felt, as he went over some paperwork and not bothering to look at his daughter as she sat down at the kitchen table, trying to use those reports as a distraction from yesterday's events.

"And he didn't seem happy." Gwyn added as she reached over and pulled some of the papers towards her; the reports being on the production of some new escort vessels and an inventory of lodestones to fly them. The numbers were good for the two but Gwyn knew they would eventually need to find a new vein of ore to mine to keep their ships aloft, or face the eventuality of trading with another country for the means to fly their ships as their fleet expanded. "He said the Shaefra was being scrapped for parts and that if he wanted to stay in your employ he would need to use his own vessel from now on."

"Yes." Berach snorted as a smile formed on his lips while he signed his name on several pages. "I figured I would tell him now instead of him being surprised when he reached Maum and found the Shaefra's berth empty." Berach couldn't help but snicker again at the punishment he had exacted upon Daigh. "Serves him right."

Berach slid more paperwork towards his daughter. "Squilla production is down at one of our farms not far from here. Do you mind going there today or tomorrow to see why things are tapering off?"

Gwyn looked at the paperwork. Her father was right about the farm not being far from Carnuaimh, it being only about an hour outside of the city. Gwyn had plans on leaving Iniscarn tomorrow and a stop at their property could be easily made on the way to her ship at Inchinver, the main port of Iniscarn. "That won't be a problem. And how did things go between Daigh and the prince?"

"Better than I thought they would have gone." Berach smiled, finding some humor in this fiasco, as he stabbed his fork into some meat from a plate he was using as a paperweight for yet some more of his paperwork. "I guess the good captain told the prince of how he has been mooning over his father for all these years. He made up some story of finding him in the desert and bringing him here for his protection, and apologized." Berach laughed. "A drunken apology by the looks of it."

"And the prince bought it?" Gwyn asked doubtfully as she folded the farming report and pocketed it.

Berach raised his eyebrows in a shrug, agreeing with his daughter, and wondering about the naiveté of the prince from Birr.

"Seems so." He said, not bothering to look up from the report he was now reading. Manpower was down at the docks in Maum, more so now that he was moving men to Talamh Shar. So he would need to relocate work crews from the docks at Inchinver until workers could be found to replace the missing dock workers and carpenters. "Daigh told the prince he would be leaving him behind while he went to talk to his father. Told the boy it would be safer this way."

"Really?" Gwyn was still skeptical about the entire situation.

"Really. I know if I found you on a strange ship from another kingdom, I would probably run the captain through with my sword first, before asking him what had happened. It will be safer this way for Daigh. Regrettably, the prince would like an audience with me."

Gwyn looked at her father incredulously. "He didn't implicate you in his escapade?"

Berach shook his head as he wrote notes for the transfers he would need to make so Maum stayed properly staffed for not only were his raiders berthed there, it was also the main port for his military fleet. All the more reason he needed to not let the production of his ships fall behind during this forced exodus.

"No. Just that he was in my employ and that he did something stupid while working for me. So, of course, Dar Banning would like to talk to me now." Berach couldn't help but frown, wondering where he would find the time for such an audience.

"What?"

Berach huffed. "I don't have the time, nor do I want to entertain this prince. He is not even the legitimate heir to the throne of Birr. He's just the son of the consort. He has no value whatsoever."

"To you." His daughter replied, for she knew her father's moods and when business was not looking good, he would get cranky and not give his full attention to the matter at hand. "He is still a prince and his good word about us to his parents might have value to us."

"I know, I know." Berach said as he waved his fork at his daughter. "That is why I told Daigh to use this incident as a way of getting some of our vessels stationed in one of their ports on the other side of Murra's Maze and to see if they would use us as escorts through it. We'll see how the good captain handles that."

"All the more reason for you to meet with this Prince Dar."

"Yes, I know, I know." Berach said in annoyance at his daughter's persistence before a smile formed on his lips as an idea came to him. "I know." He said as he looked at his daughter. "You can talk to him for us."

"What? Me?" Gwyn asked in surprise. She moved her chair back as if to get up, the chair legs squealing as they scraped across the stone floor. "I've only dealt with our trade partners on deliveries or with an emissary while they have been visiting you. You've never had me deal with any of the royalty before." And she hadn't because most of the trading agreements with their neighbors had been established by her grandfather long ago and, being isolated in the middle of the flats, her father usually traveled to visit most of these kingdoms; usually without her.

"Father, I don't know if I'm ready for this."

Berach smiled reassuringly at his daughter, ignoring her discomfort. "All the more reason for you to start by entertaining this one. Besides he's not really royalty, more like a prized piece of livestock to be traded for something better."

"That's not nice." Gwyn frowned at her father's rudeness.

"But true. His only value is in who he will be married to and how the Aerins and the Dars will benefit from his union. He is the consort's son. No more, no less."

Not happy with the outcome and seeing a loophole in her father's plan, she asked, "And what do I tell him about you not wanting to see him?"

"Well, give him my apologies and let him know I needed to go to Maum to take care of some issues there."

"And you'll just hide out in the villa until he is gone?" She asked disgustingly.

"No." Berach said as he began collecting his papers and stacking them together. "I will be going to Maum."

"What? You can't be serious?"

"Saul is in the middle of dismantling the raiders, our crews will be short staffed while they help him, and production of our military vessels seems to be falling behind. I most certainly should be there to put everything back in order and it gives me a reason not to deal with Prince Dar Banning." Berach explained as he moved his plate of half-finished food retrieved the paperwork from under it.

"But, my trip to Lahunne is scheduled for tomorrow!"

Berach stood and tapped the papers against the table as he tried to neaten the pile, smiling in mock sympathy at his daughter. "I'm sure you can squeeze him in before you leave."

"And the squilla farm?"

"Sorry, can't be helped." Berach gave Gwyn a peck on the cheek. "Welcome to running a kingdom." He added as he walked away.

"Thanks." Gwyn said glumly as she crossed her arms and sunk her chin into her chest, sulking at her predicament as her father left the room.

***

For the first time in over a week, Banning had a night of sleep that hadn't been drug induced and when he awoke he found that his bedroom door had remained unlocked and upon opening it found the smell of fried food filling the hallway. Retracing his steps from the night before Banning found Davis at a stove frying eggs and bread in a skillet with Mac pouring steaming caff into some cups.

Banning was greeted warmly by the two men, who informed him that Daigh had left over an hour ago, both men chuckling over the fact that their captain had still been a little drunk when he left, and how their second in command, Ormin Lhoyt would be staying with them.

As he was moving food onto plates Davis suggested they should hang out at the villa for the afternoon and they would give him a tour of

Market Row around sunset when things would get more colorful. Having nowhere else to go, Banning shrugged and said that was fine.

Fortunately, Mac and Davis were turning out to be quite friendly and after Banning got himself cleaned up they escorted him to the main terrace of the villa, where Banning found himself on the upper level of the house with the city spread out below them and across the gorge. Obviously Daigh had done well for himself Banning thought as Mac guided him to the terrace's railing where he received a finger tour of the city, with Mac pointing out Market Row three levels down on the ledges, and several other areas of interest he thought Banning might like to see during his stay. Mac also mentioned that the cities temples were on the outskirts of Carnuaimh and both men were willing to take Banning to any of them if he wanted to see them or if he had a need to give devotions.

And while Banning was listening to Mac, Lhoyt joined them on the terrace, with Davis going to greet their commander, only stopping when he got a dark look from the man. But a dark look was all the man could give because the skin on Lhoyt's left cheek and around his eye was a livid purple and it looked like he had a cut across his nose. Lhoyt grunted sourly at Mac and Banning who silently turned back to the railing to watch what was happening on the streets below them, leaving the commander to the solitude he seemed to want at the moment.

Davis had also gone back to join the men at the balcony but he hadn't been there long when they heard a new voice from behind them. "Oh. Here you are."

The three men turned to see who had joined them just as Lhoyt quickly rose from the chair he had just sat in.

"M'lady." Lhoyt stammered and bowed his head to the young woman who now stood before them.

"Hello Lhoyt." Argus Gwyn said as she approached him. "My guard knocked several times and since there was no response, and the door was unlocked, I let myself in. I hope I am not interrupting anything."

Lhoyt bowed his head again out of embarrassment. "I'm sorry Mistress Argus. One us of should have stayed downstairs. We just weren't expecting company."

"No worries. But what happened to you?" She said as she examined his face. "Piss off a lover?"

Davis snorted as he watched his commander turn bright red, accentuating the bruises on his face. Davis' chuckle caught Gwyn's attention so she headed across the terrace towards the three men at the railing with Lhoyt in tow.

"I'm sorry, I don't know you two." She said to the men who were flanking Banning.

"Mistress, may I introduce Clune Davis and Ilwin Mac" Lhoyt said from behind her, each man bowing when their names were given. "They are crewman in Captain Emmis' employ." Being in Emmis' employ also meant that they worked for Gwyn and her father. "The young man between them is Prince Dar Banning. Prince Dar is from the kingdom of Birr."

"It is a pleasure to meet you, Prince Dar." Gwyn said as she held out a hand for Banning to take.

"Prince Dar," Lhoyt said, continuing with the introductions. "This is Argus Gwyn, daughter to our Lord Argus Berach."

"The pleasure is mine." Banning replied as her took hand. A hand that felt warm and dry in his. Banning could not help but smile at her attractiveness; her hair long and black and wore lose down her back, with strands of her locks moving slightly in the breeze that was crossing the terrace. Her eyes were a dark green that seemed to sparkle and she was slight of build, almost an inch or two shorter than he. She wore a buttoned vest, no shirt underneath, and leather pants made from some soft skinned animal. Banning's smile broadened, matching Gwyn's, as he realized he had yet to let go of her hand.

Considering that he was the son of a consort, Gwyn was expecting to meet someone on the soft side. Instead she found someone who looked like he took care of himself. His borrowed clothing draping pleasingly over his body, her hand quite comfortable as it was enfolded by his. Quite comfortable. And for a moment she forgot she was here as a diversion and that several other people were standing around them. Reluctantly, she withdrew her hand and asked Daigh's men to leave so that she and Banning could have a moment to talk privately.

"Certainly, Mistress." Lhoyt said and motioned for Mac and Davis to follow him, the three men walking to the other end of the terrace, leaving the prince and their princess alone.

"I want to apologize for the circumstances which have brought you here." Gwyn said as she turned to look over the city. "But I do hope that we can make your stay here amenable."

"Thank you." Banning replied, taking Gwyn's apology at face value, as he too turned to look over Carnuaimh. "Will your father be arriving too or will you be taking me to see him?"

Gwyn tilted her head to look at Banning. "Unfortunately, no. We are having production problems at our dockyards in Maum. Since my family takes a hands on approach to ruling our kingdom, my father felt he needed to be there to oversee what could be done to rectify some of the issues. He does send his apologies for not being here to meet with you."

Banning turned, resting his butt against the low wall the made up the railing for the terrace and crossed his arms over his chest, frowning. "And I am supposed to find it amenable that the ruler of Iniscarn cannot make time for me?" He asked.

"Forgive us Prince Dar." Gwyn said as she turned her back to the city too. "I begged my father to see you. Sadly, he can be quite stubborn when it comes to running our kingdom. If it's any consolation, he did send me as representation for our family. But I am sorry that I am not what you were expecting." Gwyn smiled demurely, thankful that she had not had to lie, at least that much, and shrugged her shoulders, sympathetic to Banning's plight.

Banning looked down at his feet as he tried to gather his befuddled thoughts. Befuddled because Argus Gwyn was standing close enough to him that their shoulders were almost touching and close enough that he could smell the fragrance she was wearing. A fragrance that was subtle, with just a hint of something spicy to catch your attention. Nothing flowery like the scents his mother or his aunt wore, but it enticingly clung to him as he turned to look at her.

"No, you were not what I was expecting." He said as he smiled. "But I think I can forget my disappointment."

Banning thought his gaze might be lingering a little too long on the princess so he looked from her for a moment, only to find Lhoyt glowering at him from the wall he was standing against. His eyelids were half closed, his left eye almost closed completely from yesterday's assault, and his lips were pursed into a tight little line. Not sure why, Banning felt that if Lhoyt could, he would probably throw him off the terrace.

Becoming uncomfortable under the commander's scrutiny, Banning turned his own gaze onto Mac and Davis, the two men having found a table to sit at the other end of the terrace. Davis had removed the bandages off of Mac's injured right hand, taking time to inspect the sutures in his palm while rubbing his fingers. "I don't know if I should feel threatened by you or if your people do not find me threatening at all." Banning said watching Mac close his eyes as Davis picked up his other hand to massage it as well.

"You truly are safe here Prince Dar." Gwyn whispered as she too watched Mac and Davis. "They seem quite friendly."

"I think they are lovers." He whispered back conspiratorially.

"All the more reason to not feel threatened, especially if Captain Emmis' men are this comfortable around you. Prince Dar, we Scarnians are just a hardworking, simple people.

"Banning, call me Banning, Milady."

Gwyn smiled. "And please, call me Gwyn."

"So what do they have planned for you?" Gwyn asked Banning, who seemed to have started to relax a little, while nodding at his guards.

"For now, only dinner in Market Row this evening."

"You will enjoy that because many of the inns and taverns in the Row are terraced. Dinner under the starlight is quite enjoyable here."

"Well then, maybe you can join us?"

Gwyn frowned. "I would like that very much. Unfortunately my father is not only a hard taskmaster on himself but on me too. Once I leave here, I need to finish preparing for a trip to Carnuaimh and to run some errands for my father."

Banning's smile soured. "Well, thank you for the obligatory hello. Let your father know I am sorry I have inconvenienced the both of you. Just remember, you weren't the one hauled to some unknown location, then left behind when I could have simply been taken home."

Gwyn put a hand on his forearm and squeezed slightly. "I really am sorry for this imposition. But if there was anything I could do, I. . ."

Banning couldn't help but notice as her hand tightened on his arm that her green eyes seemed to sparkle mischievously.

Gwyn smiled up at him. "How would you feel about going on a trip?"

"What do you mean?"

Gwyn explained how her father had her flying out to one of their farms on the outskirts of Carnuaimh. "Nothing exciting. Just a cactus farm for the making of squilla. The trip to the farm will be far from exciting. But, after that, I am going to Inchinver and then flying on to

Lahunne to deliver merchandise to my uncle who lives in one of the city states. Would you like to go?"

"You make deliveries?" Banning asked, eyeing her skeptically.

Gwyn couldn't help but laugh. "Of course! We all work here, including me." Gwyn dramatically puffed out her chest. "Why, I have been captain of my own vessel for over a year now and will probably do so until my father relinquishes control of Iniscarn. So what do you say? Do you want to stay cooped up in Captain Emmis' villa or do you want to go for a ride?"

Banning frowned, tempted by the thought of leaving. "I'm not sure. Your Captain Emmis has left and he will be expecting me here upon his return. And what will your father think of me off with you?"

Gwyn giggled like a little girl, drawing the attention of Emmis's men from across the terrace. "We won't tell them." And when Banning looked askance at her she said. "Don't worry. I will leave a note for my father. I'll leave it on his desk so he sees it when he gets back from Maum."

"I don't know."

Throughout the entire conversation Gwyn's hand hadn't left Banning's arm and she used it as an excuse to move closer to Banning, their bodies almost touching. "Haven't you ever jumped?"

"Jumped?" He asked.

Gwyn was about to explain how, for sport, her people flew in special suits with chips of lodestones in their hands when she realized her error in that she might remind Banning of the recent attack upon him by her people. Gwyn kept the smile on her face, her hand remaining on his arm, while silently cursing herself for her stupidity as she tried to think of something to get out of this situation,

"It's a saying we have here." She finally replied, going with the simplest answer she had. "Haven't you ever taken a chance on something, knowing full well you could fail, that you might have made the wrong decision and that you will be worse off when you had first started? Have you ever jumped?"

Banning chewed at his lip because he knew the answer to that question and he was sure he didn't like the answer. His father, his mother and his foster-father had his life planned out for him and he was just a puppet following their lead. Why even his brother Manus had expectations of him that would help Manus rule Birr when it was his time. Was his life ever going to be his own?

"No."

"Then, Banning, take a chance and jump. What's the worst that could happen? Your family will have to wait a little longer for you to get home? That Captain Emmis will be more embarrassed than he is already? Jump, Banning." Taking one more jab, she whispered, "Jump."

Banning unfolded his arms, forcing Gwyn to let go of him as he placed his hands on the small wall behind him. He looked upwards, at the blue strip of sky that ran over the city that was nestled in the shadows of the canyon walls. What did he have to go home to? Nothing, except returning to his quiet life at court, waiting until a suitable partner could be found for him. A pairing that would benefit his family and one that would most likely keep his kingdom secure as a power in the world.

"How long would the journey take?" Banning continued to look up at the sky, watching as a cluster of clouds sailed by.

"The flight to Lahunne takes almost two weeks to make. Give or take two or three days depending on where and how long we stop." Gwyn began to explain. "We can cut through Murra's Maze or fly around them. It's up to you, but I usually fly north then west around your kingdom. Thanks to the Mendens, flying south is becoming a much more dangerous route to take."

"By the time we reach the Lahunne City States, Daigh should have spoken to your family and if you want, I can return you home instead of flying back here."

Banning had made his decision and just shrugged as Gwyn listed his options. "Home or back here. Either way, I don't think it will matter where or when you return me. Oh, but there is one thing." He said as a thought occurred to him. "I need clothing. Master Ilwin and I are almost the same size and he has allowed me to borrow some of his belongings to wear over the next couple of days. I just can't see him giving up his wardrobe for me to take on this trip."

Gwyn fished into a small pocket on the side of her vest, pulled out a coin and handed it to Banning who turned it over in his hand as he inspected it. The coin seemed to be made of brass, tarnished from being constantly handled and the stamps on it were a little worn. But Banning was able to still make out a balance scale with two crossed swords below it; a symbol that was on both sides of the coin.

"That's my families trading marker." Gwyn explained as Banning ran a thumb over the coin. "Have the men take you to a clothier in Market Row so you can square away some clothing for yourself. Just show the merchants this coin and tell them to have the bill sent to me."

"You're too kind. When I get home I will make sure my family reimburses your expenses."

Gwyn clicked her tongue. "Think nothing of it. Consider it the beginning of making amends for the imposition you have been put through."

"Thank you. And what of them?" Banning said as he gestured towards Daigh's crew.

Gwyn pushed herself away from the railing and headed towards the men in question. "Let's find out." She said to Banning over her shoulder. "Excuse me, Commander Ormin. I'll be leaving for Lahunne tomorrow and I have invited Prince Dar to join me."

"I'm sorry Mistress?" Lhoyt said as he stepped away from the wall hoping he had heard Gwyn wrong. But he knew he hadn't when Davis stopped in the middle of re-wrapping Macs hand as both men paid attention to the conversation. "Do you think that is wise? What will your father or Captain Emmis think?"

The princess shrugged. "I'm sure my father will be fine with Prince Dar as a guest on my ship and he will be well protected there. I just wanted to leave word with you and your men for when the captain returns."

"But M'lady, we were instructed to take care of the prince and to keep him safe here. I do not think Captain Emmis will be happy to return and not find the young prince at home."

Gwyn looked at Banning, giving him a conspiratorial wink. "And what would you like to do Prince Dar?"

"Considering I have never been to the city states I would most certainly enjoy a trip to Lahunne." When he saw that not only Lhoyt, but Mac and Davis were frowning, he added, "If you like Commander, why don't you and your men come with us. I am sure Mistress Argus can find room for you three and, since I am bereft of my own personal guard, you can take their places."

"I don't know about that." Lhoyt said, silently cursing the appearance of Dar Banning and the trouble he had brought upon their heads, as he mulled the idea of going with them over in his head.

"Besides," Banning continued. "I would hate to think what Captain Emmis will do to you if I am not here. Don't you think you will be much safer with me and the princess for a while?"

The not so subtle reminder of the assault he received yesterday at the hands of the captain made Lhoyt scowl, making his cheek throb in a dull pain as the bruised skin stretched while a dull emptiness filled his gut.

But Davis stood up, leaving the bandages dangling from Mac's hand, interrupting Lhoyt. "Begging your pardon, your Highnesses." Davis said to Gwyn and Banning. "Protecting the Prince Dar was Mac's and my first priority. I think it is sound judgment for us to go with you for your protection. Besides," He said as he looked as Lhoyt. "I would like to keep my face in one piece too. So what do you say Commander, you going to stay and wait for the captain or come with us?"

Lhoyt didn't answer. Davis had no idea what he was asking of him. None of them did. Because the last thing Lhoyt wanted was for Daigh to think less of him than he already did. Unsure of what to do, and not wanting to explain himself, Lhoyt scraped the heel of his shoe against the granite floor of the terrace.

"Ormin Lhoyt." Gwyn said as the tone of her voice deepened, a stern look appearing on her face as she spoke. "There is plenty of room for three more men on my vessel so I command that you and your men will act as personal guard for Prince Dar. And I command that you will act as his escort on our trip to the Lahunne City States. Is that understood?"

Lhoyt sighed and nodded with a mixture of relief and resignation as the decision was taken out of his hand, while Davis slapped Mac on the shoulder in excitement jarring his right hand that was still raised in the air with its semi wrapped bandages dangling.

"Good." Gwyn said curtly. "I've given Prince Dar one of my markers, so when you take him to Market Row, make sure you find him clothing and whatever else he may need for the trip. I suggest you head over there soon."

After receiving quick nods in the affirmative from Daigh's men, Gwyn continued to detail out her plans to them. "I have to stop at Shandon Farm on our way to Inchinver so we'll be leaving first thing in the morning. Have all of your gear ready and we'll meet at the port. We'll be flying by skiff instead of taking a tram so we can make the detour."

"Aye M'lady." Lhoyt replied.

"Good." Gwyn turned to look at Banning. "Now, if you'll excuse me."

"M'lady." Banning said, halting Gwyn in mid step. "What are the possibilities of having dinner together tonight?"

"I would like that very much." Gwyn said as she smiled warmly at the thought. "But, I do need to get ready and to send word to my men that we will now have four guests on board. Do not worry; tomorrow morning and the beginning of our trip will come soon enough, in which case we will be seeing plenty of each other for a while."

Banning gave Gwyn a slight bow. "Very well then."

Gwyn looked over at Lhoyt again as a thought came to her. "Why don't you use my marker and take the prince and your men to The Mantle tonight for dinner." She turned back to Banning, who had not left her side during the conversation. "The Mantle is one of the best inns in Carnuaimh. Their meals are superb and the view from their terraces is spectacular."

"You are too kind." Banning replied as he bowed again, flattered by the gift for all four men. "Until tomorrow."

Gwyn nodded, turned and walked towards the stairwell leading down into the villa. Banning couldn't help but notice she seemed to now have a bounce in her step as she walked away. He stood there, watching her back until Gwyn all too quickly disappeared down the stairs.

Chapter 4
Kinsale
Aerin Castle

"Any word from Manus?"

"Mmmm?" The ruler of Birr murmured distractedly.

Fionn had found his partner in the castle's map room, whose back was to the door when he had entered the room. Riocard had sheets of crumpled papers in his hands that he was holding behind his back while looking at a painted map of Gwer that covered most of the floor of this large room.

"Manus. Has he sent any word to you yet?" Fionn replied, slightly annoyed that Riocard had not heard him the first time.

Riocard met Fionn's annoyance with his own. "No, of course not! It has only been two days since they left. Even if Manus pushed himself and his crew, I don't even think they could reach the barge by now." Riocard returned his gaze back to the map on the floor, shuffling his feet as he moved around a small continent that was southeast of Birr. "You know Manus will send word as soon as he can."

Fionn couldn't help but huff in frustration as he crossed his arms over his chest, giving himself a hug of reassurance as he walked into the room. "I know, you are right. What are you looking at on the map?"

"Belmar. We just received word that a village on the kingdom's northern side was attacked a little over a week ago." Riocard walked over to a stack of shelves built into one of the walls and retrieved a wooden Gwerin. The figure was about two feet tall, painted black, holding a sword and shield and it was posed as if it was attacking an unseen foe. Riocard placed it down where the village of Colp, on Belmar, was marked on the map and walked back to the shelves and retrieved two black vessels from the wall. He walked to a continent that was south of Belmar and placed the ships on it.

Fionn walked over to where Birr was on the map, staying out of Riocard's way as he watched his partner work. "What happened to them?"

"Several vessels filled with armed men raided the village at night. Most of the villagers were lucky and escaped into the hills during the attack. But almost all of Colp's port was raised to the ground."

Fionn was shocked by the decimation Riocard was describing even as he continued.

"A half dozen of their ships were taken and they lost the lodestones from many more before they were destroyed." Riocard un-crumpled the papers and looked at them again. "They found some murdered villagers but it seems that many, many more Belmarns are missing. From the looks of it, the raiders were a Menden slaving party."

"Are you sure?" Fionn shuddered at the thought as he stepped closer to Riocard.

Riocard looked at his partner. "The report from Lord Tavin Lorne says they found a couple of dead raiders, all of whom had tattoos that ran from their left shoulder to the middle of their backs. Tavin Lorne writes that the rune of the god Ciaran was one of the tattoos inked on their shoulder blades and that the rest of the tattoos were most likely markings for the clans they belong to."

Fionn turned pale as he listened before speaking his worst fear. "Do you think it was the Mendens who attacked Captain Thear's ship?"

"I doubt it." Riocard said, hoping to stop Fionn's speculation. "For one thing, the attack was too far to the north and had it been Mendens, the rest of our men would have been also taken or killed. No," Riocard said as he walked to stand on the north eastern part of the map. "Somebody else has taken Banning."

The Lord of Birr continued to walk around the map as he ran strategies against more attacks and devised defenses for his people in his head.

"It has been over fifteen years since the Mendens were daring enough to attack one of our own villages. Not since they raided Fomor on the southern part of Birr. And until now, they have been content to attack only vessels flying through the flats. What has changed?"

"What do you mean?"

Riocard ignored the question as he turned away from Fionn and walked back to the shelf and picked up a red soldier that was holding a spear while standing at attention. Riocard found himself irked by Fionn's question. He seemed to be finding himself irked by Fionn more and more as the days wore on and only wanted to hide his displeasure of his partner from his partner.

Of course Riocard sometimes needed to remind himself that Fionn had been third born into the Dar family and as the youngest son he had not been trained in military strategies because he was not expected to rule. Nor had Fionn bothered showing any interest in any of the arts of war during their union.

The Lord of Birr took the figure he was holding and placed it down onto the continent of Kinsale and stood there for a moment. "When they attacked Fomor we were fortunate enough to unite the southern kingdoms in defense against the Mendens, hunting down their slaving parties until they retreated back across the Bitter Wastes. The decimation should have left the fear of us in them, but they seem to be growing bolder again."

"I remember." Fionn replied, for they had already been married by then. "Mendes is an isolated kingdom and who knows what goes on in their world behind the sandstorms that make up the Bitter Wastes. Or maybe, this is just the will of Ciaran."

Now it was Riocard's turn to ask, "Ciaran?"

Fionn may not have known much about the craft of war but he was definitely schooled in the history of the gods. Not that he brought up any of his interests nowadays because he had learned a long time ago that if what he knew had no value in benefiting Kinsale then Riocard had very little interest in what Fionn might have to say.

"Well, the Mendens still follow the old ways of Ciaran. Maybe they are out attacking for sport or they are following the whims of the god of chaos that they still worship."

Riocard walked around the map as he mulled that thought over. "But why destroy a peace that has lasted for so long?"

Fionn Shrugged. "Why not? Ciaran and his followers were left behind for a reason. Why not beat against the peace the rest of us have worked so hard to build?"

Riocard chewed on the knuckle of his right thumb as he listened to Fionn's conjectures. Riocard knew he didn't want Fionn to be right. If the gods chose to fight amongst themselves again it would mean the collapse of Birr and many other kingdoms as the religious sects fought against each other and for dominance for their deities. What would happen to Birr and how could Aerin Riocard keep such a large kingdom together?

Riocard squatted onto the balls of his toes, resting his arms on his knees. He looked at the wooden soldier with the sword, wishing it was a real Menden so that he could wrest its secrets from it and know if and when a new attack would come. "We will need to send word to our southern villages and outposts to prepare for an eventual attack. It might even be wise to stop flights across the flats to the south and have our people stick to the mainland routes for a while."

"Don't you think halting travel is a little severe?"

Riocard stood. Tired, he twisted from side to side as he tried to release the tension that had knotted the muscles in his lower back. "It will not be severe if it saves the lives of our people."

"Well, I think to tell the merchants that they cannot trade with our southern neighbors would be more detrimental to us. More so than trying to save their lives. See here?" Fionn said as he walked to the southernmost tip of Birr and pointed down. "Tuame is only what, a two days flight from us? And Belmar. It is about the same distance away from Tuame. There is no reason why the flights cannot still be made, especially if our merchants hug our neighbors' coastlines. I am sure, if we ask Tuame, we could negotiate for a route over their mainland."

Riocard knew Fionn was right. Sighing, he walked to the opposite end of the room and tossed the papers he was holding onto a table stacked with rolled maps and more scattered papers. He started searching through the morass of scribbled notes and ledgers, moving them with a finger as he looked for information on the status of Birr's military.

"Maybe there is a way of creating a caravan, guarded by our fleet that could fly from Birr to Tuame. Maybe we could even strike a deal with the Tuameens to travel together to Belmar. We just cannot afford to empty our garrisons for the sake of some merchants trying to traffic their goods."

Riocard turned back to the floor as he looked at two other kingdoms sitting on the eastern edge of the Ganeamha Flats. "I can concede to travelling to our closest neighbors. So, unless a merchant wants to be daring, I think traveling to Gurund and Kerma are out of the question. At least for now." Out of frustration, he slapped his hands against the table. "How I wish Manus was here." He said out loud, now sorry that he sent his son out into danger.

Fionn on the other hand stiffened at the reminder of the absence of his own son. Knowing he was impotent in finding Banning and that an argument with Riocard about the search would be futile, he changed the subject and asked his partner if he needed help with anything else.

Oblivious to the change in Fionn's voice, for he had learned to ignore the emotions of the people around him, as the burden of ruling a large kingdom lay heavy on his shoulders, Riocard walked across the map as he plotted out movements of man power from inland to some of the coastal towns. "If you do not mind, assemble my generals and have them meet me here so we can discuss tactics and the defense of our people. Also, send word to the magistrate of the southern province and let him know what has happened in Belmar. Let him know we'll be sending help his way as soon as we can."

Fionn nodded and headed towards the door. He stopped and looked back at Riocard. "Do you want me to inform Betrys too?"

"Of course. Her guard makes up almost half of the defense for Kinsale and she has her own caravans she will need to protect. I am afraid difficult times might be coming our way and we all will need to be prepared."

Fionn, forgotten by his partner, who continued to walk across the floor map of the world while murmuring about Birr's defenses, left the room. Once again his own world of solitude closed in around him while Fionn silently prayed as he walked down the corridor, making his way to the courtyard and the barracks that made up the defensive wall of the castle. The prayer was routine and to no one god in particular for it seemed the deities had stopped listening to Fionn's prayers, ignoring his own personal dreams, a long time ago.

***

Fortunately for the Camalain and its crew, the flight across the flats proved to be uneventful. The prince also had been wise enough to have three steersmen on board, one of them being Moro Croft, and Manus pushed them to move the ship as fast as they could go, only stopping long enough for his pilots to switch shifts. Thus they arrived at the sheer walls of the canyon in the middle of the night on their second day out on the flats. The ship continued to fly north, keeping the maze on their starboard side as they slowly made their way to the main entrance of Murra's Maze.

Nobody slept that evening, not even Liam, who was woken by the commotion of the Camalain's crew and the prince's guard as they shouted to one another, running through the corridors as the dark shape of the maze appeared on the horizon under the pale light of the moon.

Liam, following many of the crew, made his way onto the main deck and found his foster-father standing at the starboard railing. The sky was blotted out on their right and the wind keened softly as it pushed itself between the ship and canyon.

He went to stand next to his father and ran a hand through his hair, trying to flatten the mass that was standing in all directions from sleeping on it. Liam also rubbed his face as he tried to stifle a yawn, his father looking at him and smiled before turning back to watch the wall of rock as the steersman guided the Camalain close enough to the cliffs. So close that Liam could almost reach out and touch stone.

"Aren't we flying too close?" Liam whispered, not wanting to draw the attention of the members of the Royal Guard now standing to the left and right of him and his father.

"A competent steersman will keep us from hitting those walls." Cullen replied. And, as if in response to the sagart's remark, the

Camalain banked to port as an outcropping of rock appeared in front of them. Father and son grabbed onto the railing so they would not lose their balance while Cullen continued with his explanation. "Flying this close will make it easier for us to find the entrance for someone who is unsure of its location and it will help us blend in with the shadows cast by the Maze, especially this late in the evening. From a distance we should not be seen at all."

"If we're lucky."

Cullen and Liam turned at the sound of the new voice, while the soldiers around them quickly came to attention.

"Prince Manus." The Sagart Cullen said as both he and Liam bowed their heads in respect to the young man.

The prince, followed by Lieutenant Cahl Goban, came to join them. "At ease." Manus said to his men who were milling about with the father and son. "Your father is right, being this close to the Maze should hide us from prying eyes. We don't want to be attacked the way my brother was, so we should be on our guard." Manus nodded to the lieutenant, the statement not only a reminder of his failure at protecting Banning but also silent command.

"You heard the prince!" Goban said to his comrades, ordering them to retrieve their weapons and gear, leaving Cullen, Liam and Aerin Manus alone at the railing. The prince took a moment to brush away locks of his dark hair from his face which was being whipped about the wind before going to stand on Cullen's left side, grasping the railing with his right hand, allowing the silence to continue as they watched Murra's Maze slip by the Camalain.

This was the first time since they had left port that Liam was in the presence of the prince. Granted, he had seen Aerin Manus here and there as he went about the duties he had been given but, to have him standing several feet away, made him feel very uncomfortable.

Quite quickly the silence became unbearable for Liam. "Is there anything you need me to do M'lord?" He asked.

Manus turned to look at him. The prince's blue eyes were cloudy. At least they always seemed to have a dark look, a reflection of the mood he always seemed to be in when they were turned towards Liam, and replied, "I do not need anything of you. But I do know the crew on the bridge will not be leaving anytime soon. Why don't you go to the galley and get them something to eat and drink."

"Aye M'lord." Liam said in relief, and bowing quickly, he left his foster-father and the prince standing alone on deck as he headed inside.

The prince and the sagart continued to watch the canyon move by them as the steersman piloted the Camalain around outcroppings and some rubble that appeared in front of the ship's path. The wind was all too happy to be the only voice heard as the two men continued to be lost in their own thoughts for the time being.

After a while, the sagart spoke. "He is a good man."

His own thoughts now interrupted, Manus looked at the older gentleman. "Who?"

"Liam. My son."

Manus frowned at the reminder of Liam, whom he thought of as an unnecessary burden, and waved his hand in annoyance. "I am sure he is Sagart, but I do have more pressing matters on my mind than the goodness of your son."

Cullen only nodded in response to the remark.

"As a matter of fact," Manus said as his grasp on the rail tightened as the ship tilted slightly to port. "I'm more curious if Barra has passed on any more information to you."

Cullen frowned. Manus was one who seemed to have a need for quick answers. Something cut and dry to solve the problem at hand for Manus really was like his grandfather, a man whom Cullen had known well; everything black and white, no in between, an answer always needed at hand.

"Only that we are moving in the right direction." The priest replied. "That we should go to the crash site. Your brother is alive. Of that I am sure."

Manus found the information somewhat positive but scowled just the same. "Then why not just take us to my brother? Why this game of going back to the wreckage and starting from scratch?"

"I do not know Milord." Cullen tapped his cane against the deck's planking. "For one, maybe Barra wants to teach us patience."

Manus' scowl deepened as he questioned the sagart's implication.

Cullen raised his right hand to calm the prince and quickly put it back down onto the railing as the Camalain dipped to port. He didn't trust himself to keep his balance while holding onto his cane before continuing on with his sermon. "Only to believe and trust in your faith in the gods. Not to rely on them for your needs and to solve problems for yourself. The gods are not tools only to be taken out of a box and used when needed and then put away until they might be useful again."

Feeling somewhat embarrassed, Manus swallowed hard and looked sideways at Cullen who was still watching the canyon move by them. The sagart's words hit close to home when it came to how he truly felt about the gods. Tools to be used.

And not good tools at that, Manus thought as he turned back to watch more of Murra's Maze slip by them. The movement of the rock and the soft hissing of the wind had an almost hypnotic quality. "Is my lack of faith that obvious?"

Cullen replied without turning to look at the prince. "Only to someone who has known you most of your life Milord. You forget. I remember the days when you would come to devotions with your father. And it has been a long time since I have seen you at temple. Have you switched deities?"

"No."

Cullen continued. "I know this is a search for your brother, but also try to see this as a search for your faith."

Impatience welled up in Manus again over the lecture he was receiving. "Sagart Cullen. Do you really think I even have time for this?"

"Now take Liam for instance." Cullen said, not too concerned that he was interrupting the prince.

"What? Why are you changing the subject? And what does your son have to do with my faith?"

"Because my son is the exact opposite of you. His belief in Barra is so absolute, that it takes up almost his entire life. He tries very hard not to see what is going on around him. He uses Barra as a reason not to leave Kinsale, let alone the temple. That is one of the reasons why I wanted him to come on this voyage."

"I don't understand."

Cullen sighed. "Liam has had a rough childhood at the hands of others and he has tried to isolate himself from the rest of the world. He needs to realize there is more to life than just work and prayer. Just as you need to realize that you need to find some of your faith. This could be the reason why we need patience when it comes to finding your brother."

"Patience is not one of my virtues." Manus pushed himself away from the railing. He had stayed longer than he had wanted and knew that he should make a round of the Camalain before heading to the bridge. "I will give what you have said some consideration. Now if you'll excuse me." The prince gave Cullen a slight bow and walked away.

Cullen returned the bow and since he was not needed for anything at the moment, he turned back to watch the Maze and to listen to the wind, its voice sounding melancholy, as the Camalain flew by.

***

For the past two days the only job that had been given to Liam was to head down to the galley and to take care of the roots for the daily meals. The cook, a man about his foster-father's age, and prone to few words, would hand him a knife, point at the vegetables and simply commanded him to "Peel those". And sitting next to said pile of vegetables was a large metal bowl with tepid water in it and it was Liam's correct assumption to just to place them in the bowl after they had been peeled so they could soak before being cooked.

This morning, Liam was fortunate to find the cook in the galley at such an early hour. The man had risen with the rest of the crew and, not one to waste time, coupled with the fact he had flown through Murra's Maze far too many times for him to count, had immediately gone to work. Liam found the cook kneading a large ball of dough on a counter covered in flour and when Liam mentioned the prince wanted caff for the bridge crew, he nodded at two pots of boiling water that were sitting on the stove and directed him into a pantry where the bitter grounds were kept.

The cook, who had assumed Liam should have found his way around the galley by now, became slightly annoyed when Liam asked him what to do next. How could someone not know how to make caff? So the cook grunted out instructions as to where to find a press and how to make the drink and where to find a tray and cups for it.

When Liam inquired about some food to go with the drinks, the cook pointed, with a hand caked in dough, to a stack of large drawers and just gave a sharp "In there." Inside the middle drawers he found small honey cakes stacked between sheets of waxed paper. Liam also thought he remembered seeing plates in the pantry and found what he was looking for and went back to stack the cakes on one of them. Once he readied the tray Liam gave his thanks to the cook who only grunted as he began to divide the dough into small loaves as Liam headed towards the stairs in the hallway.

Carrying the loaded tray, Liam decided to take the corridor that ran under the main deck instead of trying to cross the open deck with his arms full. Still, he was nervous as he descended the two flights of stairs, the clay cups clinking loudly as he tried to keep his balance, almost losing the tray when the Camalain sharply tilted to port as it moved past some unseen obstructions.

Except for the several members of the Royal Guard who smiled warmly at Liam, moving aside so he could carry his burden unhindered, Liam was thankful that the rest of the crew were at their posts, embarrassed to be seen as a new member of the kitchen staff.

When he arrived on the bridge, Liam found the crew quietly staring out the window. Liam couldn't help but gawk as well for the sky had lightened slightly to a deep indigo on the horizon while remaining an inky black above. The black silhouette of Murra's Maze continued to pass them on the right. And the only way Liam could even tell they were moving by the canyon was that its outline changed shape against the sky.

Liam was so enthralled by the vista that he was not prepared when the steersman almost missed an outcropping of rock and the Camalain suddenly slid to the left, sending Liam off balance and setting the items on the tray to rattle obnoxiously.

Most of the crew turned at the noise but returned to looking out the window when they found that the sounds and their creator were harmless. The captain, along with Moro Croft and Karam Kael, who were also on the bridge, continued to look at Liam as he took a couple more tentative steps into the bridge.

"Sorry Captain Thear." Liam said, apologizing for creating a disruption. "The prince thought you and your crew might like something to eat and drink."

"Thank you Master Keir." The captain said politely, using Liam's family name. "There's a table to your left that the tray can go on."

"Yes sir." Liam said as he walked over to the table, which, not having any legs, was more of a thick shelf bolted to the wall. The table's surface was about three feet deep with a small shallow basin on its right side. A pair of metal arms and a set of stationary forceps were mounted above the table's surface. Liam had seen several of these in the galley and, with watching how the cook used them, Liam knew enough to place the tray onto the table and pushed the pitcher of caffe between the prongs of the forceps, keeping it stationary and with no chance of being knocked over. Liam carefully lifted the cups and plate of honey cakes and rotated the thin metal rods over the tray and locked them into place so the tray wouldn't move around on the table. Once that was done he put the food and cups back down onto the tray.

"The cups and plate can go into the basin." Croft said as he walked over to Liam and grabbed two of the honey cakes and immediately bit into one. He tousled Liam's hair with his free hand. "Just get out of bed?" He mumbled around a mouthful of food.

Liam swatted Croft's hand away in annoyance and put the cups and food where he was told. Croft chuckled and gestured for Liam to follow him along the wall of the bridge, his hand trailing across a brass rail, tarnished and pitted that ran the circumference of the bridge. They walked back to where Croft had been standing on the left side of the bridge where Liam grasped the railing lightly as they watched the landscape move by.

Out of the corner of his eye, Liam saw the prince's friend, and member of the Royal Guard, Karam Kael, staring at him. Unlike the prince, who always seemed to be in a sour mood, Kael had been amiable over the past two days; saying hello or asking him how he was doing if they passed each other in a hallway or bumped into each other in the dining hall. Liam found these chance exchanges disconcerting and had done his best to avoid the man. Now though, looking at Kael through the corner of his eye, Liam wasn't sure he could read the look on the man's face that he was receiving.

"Should I leave?" Liam whispered to Croft as he once again tried to flatten the clumps of hair that his friend had got to standing again.

"No, you're fine." He replied as he wiped crumbs off his face. "If the captain didn't want you here he'd tell you to leave or find something for you to do." Croft bit into the second cake he still had in his hand.

"Why aren't you steering?" Liam asked, changing the subject.

"Well, not my shift." Croft replied as he popped the rest of the second cake into his mouth. "And it's a good thing too because Jensen's family is from the northern coast." He explained as he nodded to the steersman who was seated in the middle of the bridge. "So he is more familiar with the Maze than I am."

Liam only nodded as Jensen steered the Camalain to starboard around the cliff face of the Maze. The cliff turned out to be a long arm of mountain with the main body of the maze now taking up the whole of the horizon. A thin strip of sky with a sprinkling of stars could be seen above the black ridge line.

"Take us across the flat." Captain Thear commanded.

"Aye." Jensen replied, his voice sounding distant and smooth from his joining with the lodestones.

"Are we far from the Maze's entrance?" Liam asked Croft.

"If we were flying to it from Portroe I could give you a good guess as to where it might be." Croft replied as he got rid of the crumbs from his hands by wiping them on his trousers. "Unfortunately, I'm not familiar with this part of the mountains." Croft leaned against the rail and began tapping the brass with his fingernails.

Liam found the tinny, plinking sound annoying, as did the captain, who looked in their direction and made a coughing sound to get their attention.

"Sorry." Croft replied to Ibor. However, after several minutes, Croft's nervous habit started again.

"Hsss! Croft!" Liam whispered a little too loudly. Croft stopped, looked at him and shrugged. The steersman crossed his arms over his chest and leaned his butt against the handrail while, from across the bridge, Liam could see Kael looking at them with a smirk on his face. Liam immediately returned to watching the view outside of the Camalain, hoping to once again be ignored.

The silence finally ended as several of the bridge crew took a moment to pour some caff or to grab a bite to eat as Murra's Maze loomed larger on the horizon. Soft spoken conversations broke out among the men standing around the table as the captain felt confident enough to have Jensen increase the speed of the ship. Instinctually, Liam tightened his grip on the railing while Croft, unfazed by the movement of the Camalain, kept his casual stance against the bar.

And, as the ship once again neared the Maze, Aerin Manus walked onto the bridge. Several of the crew nearest him murmured greetings as the prince took a look around, both Liam and Croft nodding to the man when he looked their way, before walking over to Captain Thear to make some inquiries on what was going on, and then made his way to stand near his friend.

For some reason, seeing the prince made Liam feel uncomfortable, small and out of place in front of this man of royalty. Liam certainly felt as if he should be doing something other than hanging out with his friend, whose job it was to be on the bridge, anything to get himself out of the presence of Prince Aerin Manus.

"I should go." Liam said nervously as he let go of the brass rail and began to walk away from Croft.

"Why?" Croft asked curiously. "Got more vegetables to peel?"

"No, but I'm sure there's something I could be doing."

But Manus interrupted his escape from the bridge. "There's no need to leave Seb Liam. Be at ease and watch the view for now. I am sure there will be plenty of work for you in the upcoming hours."

"Thank you, M'lord." Liam replied as he went to stand near Croft. The steersman immediately put his right arm around him and squeezed his shoulder, setting Liam off balance. Liam didn't know what was more uncomfortable; the prince acknowledging him in front of everyone else, the fact that he had been called by the wrong clan name or that a friend of his family now had an arm casually draped over him in front of the eventual ruler of Birr, making a spectacle out of the two of them. Liam sighed quietly, distressed by the situation and if there had been a hole nearby he would certainly crawl into it and hide from everyone.

But no one seemed to care, with the exception of Kael and the prince, who were whispering to each other, while everyone else's attention returned outside as Jensen neared the Maze and again began to steer the ship in a northerly direction.

Liam couldn't help but notice that the horizon had lightened to a pale cerulean and the stars were beginning to wink out as the morning light overwhelmed them. Thankfully in an hour or so Jensen would not be the only one who could see where they were going.

"What do you think they are talking about?" Croft asked in a whisper as he drummed his fingers against the young man's right shoulder.

"Who?" Liam whispered back, not taking his eyes off of the emerging landscape outside of the Camalain, though he did know who Croft was talking about.

"The prince and his sidekick." Croft whispered back conspiratorially.

Liam was amazed at Croft's audacity, acting like someone in his teens, not his thirties. "It's not polite to stare." He replied.

"Well, they keep looking over here."

Liam reluctantly turned and saw that Kael, who was still conversing with the prince, was once again looking over at them. Karam Kael smiled at Liam, who reddened in embarrassment, when they caught each other's eye, before quickly returning to look back outside. And when Liam shifted his gaze away from the window he could just make out that Kael was continuing to look at them. Liam once again gave his full attention to the sunrise and Murra's Maze moving quickly by them and shrugged in Croft's arm. "Who cares?"

"I do." Croft chuckled. "You know, I'm thinking that Master Karam might have a thing for me."

"You?" Liam screwed up his face in disbelief. "I find that hard to imagine."

Croft made a mock frown. "And why do you think that?"

Liam shrugged again, missing the humor in Croft's voice. "I don't know. Seems to me they are most likely thinking of new chores for me to do. Maybe something to make this trip even more miserable."

"I don't know." Croft replied, a slight twinkle in his eye. If only Liam could get over being afraid and intimidated by the majority of people he was meeting on this journey and just tried to enjoy himself, Croft thought. "I just don't know." He repeated. "What could possibly be worse than kitchen duty?"

And what could possibly have been said across the room that would keep Kael's attention focused on Liam and Croft?

"I think you got his name wrong." Kael whispered to his friend.

Here we go again, Manus thought, rolling his eyes in annoyance. "Whose name did I get wrong?" He whispered back as he watched the Camalain begin to fly parallel to Murra's Maze.

"Liam's clan name." Kael replied. "The captain called him Keir Liam, not Seb. I don't think he's the sagart's natural son."

Manus thought about that tidbit for a moment and shrugged. "Maybe. I don't ever recall the sagart having a companion nor my father ever mentioning one. The Temple to Barra does have an orphanage and it is known for always taking in strays. Maybe the Sagart Cullen decided to take on a project all those years ago."

"Do you think they are a couple?" Kael asked his friend, as he watched the two men on the opposite side of the bridge. Croft had an arm draped over Liam's shoulder and was tapping it lightly and noticed that the two seemed to be whispering about something.

Manus huffed, perturbed by the question. "I'm surprised you haven't found out by now."

"I have tried to talk to him." Of course he meant Liam. "But every time I see him in a hallway or the galley he just mumbles and scurries away." Kael suddenly stood up straight and a wide grin swept across his face. "Hey!" He said, jabbing Manus. "He's looking over here!"

Manus looked back over at the steersman and Cullen's foster-son, but Liam had already turned away from them and was back to looking out of the Camalain's main window. The steersman, Croft, on the other hand, was looking back at them, nodding at the prince, who returned the gesture.

"You're wasting your time." Manus said to Kael. "If you're that hard up, I'm sure you can find someone else on board to play around with. Unless you're looking for some type of project."

"No, I'm not!" Kael frowned. "Don't you find him attractive in the slightest?"

Manus shrugged off the question, already tired of the direction the conversation had been taking. He returned to watching the sunrise outside of the Camalain. "Sorry. My priority is finding my brother. Besides, he's not what you usually go for. And you have said it yourself; he doesn't seem outgoing and looks like he gets spooked by his own shadow."

Kael, sobered by the reminder of Banning's disappearance, still allowed a hint of a smile to escape at the description of Liam he had once given.

"I know." Kael replied as he leaned closer to Manus. "Along with his looks, I think it's those things that are making him attractive. I don't know, there's just something about him that I find appealing."

"I don't know either." Manus replied sarcastically.

Annoyed by the quip, Kael shot back, "Well, not all of us have the good fortune of having the opportunity to pick our mate from all the royalty of Gwer."

"Trust me. If you think having your parents pick who," Manus began but was interrupted by Jensen.

"There." The steersman said, in his stilted voice, meaning that something was outside. One of the drawbacks to joining with the lodestones was that one's speech became stilted, condensed into barely understandable one word phrases. "There. Ship."

Even though they were still a distance away from whatever he could see, conversations on the bridge ceased as everyone became intent on whatever Jensen was able to see outside. By now the sky had lightened considerably and Murra's Maze had become a mixture of deep blues and rusty browns in the morning light with openings intermittently appearing in the mountain's side as Jensen flew by. Other than that, nothing else could be seen with the naked eye.

Ibor walked over to his steersman and put a hand on the man's shoulder. "Are we close to the main entrance?"

"Yes."

"Continue towards it but slow down and move us out onto the plain."

"Aye."

As the Camalain flew back onto the flats, Captain Thear walked over to the main window and unhooked a spyglass that he had attached to his belt, and with a twist of the canisters, extended it so he could place the instrument against his right eye to scan the horizon.

Manus had followed the captain over to the main window and stood by him, asking if he was able to see anything.

"I think so. Yes." The captain replied. "I can see the entrance and there's one, no two ships outside of the pass."

"Let me see!" Manus held out his hand for the spyglass, with Ibor handing it over to him and pointing in the direction Manus should look. At first Manus didn't see much of anything while he focused the lenses. Then, "Yes, I see them. There are definitely two ships out there. Looks like one them is hovering while the other looks to be grounded." Manus continued to adjust the spyglass as they flew closer. "They look like a couple of sloops. Much smaller vessels than ours."

Liam did his best to see what was going outside as the tension began to fill the room. Croft had pushed himself away from the railing, waiting for a command from his captain, while Kael, who had all but forgotten them, had put a hand on the pommel of his sword. The prince's friend now seemed tense and nervous, ready for a fight. Lieutenant Cahl, who had remained stolidly at the entrance to the bridge, absently took a couple of steps forward into the room, while Liam grasped the railing tighter as he became fearful of moving.

Liam was beginning to wonder why he was here and why he didn't resist his father's insistence on being on this journey, when Manus shouted, "Wait!" He seemed to be having trouble focusing the spyglass so he turned to Jensen. "Jensen! Stop! Stop the ship!"

"Aye." The steersman replied, his voice sounding like a rock being dropped into a pool of water, no recognition to the prince's urgency.

Manus returned to scanning the horizon through the spyglass while everyone swayed slightly as the Camalain came to a halt. "The second ship is rising." Manus reported back to everyone. "The sloops are turning in our direction." He removed the spyglass from his eye to look at the captain, a nervous edge to his voice. "I think we've been spotted."

The captain nodded and was about to send the Camalain into an evasive stance, so the ship could escape an attack if necessary, when Croft stepped forward and pointed out the main window. "What's that?" He asked.

From the direction of the sloops, a small slip of light could be seen glittering on the horizon. And even though it was visible to all, Manus returned the spyglass to his eye.

"It's a signal. Yes. Yes! They are asking who we are." The prince explained to the bridge crew, his grasp on the spyglass tightening as he recognized the flickering pattern of lights. "And they're giving the code for the Royal Guard. Those ships are ours!"

Manus removed the spyglass from his face as he began to give orders. "Captain, get the ship back into the shadows of the Maze. I want to make sure those men are able to see any response we give."

"Lieutenant, find Gwion and get him on deck. He knows the code the best out of all our men. Instruct him to let them know we are here to help, but don't let them know that I am here until we're sure of their intent. I'll stay here for now and decipher for Captain Thear. Kael, go get our men ready for an attack."

Goban nodded to the prince in acknowledgement while Kael gave his friend a curt "Aye" as the ship moved closer to the cliffs. As he was leaving the bridge, the lieutenant passed two of the Royal Guard, commanding one to follow Kael and to help him organize the rest of their men. Goban had the other man remain so he could protect the prince.

Liam, who had returned to watching the signaling lights, was surprised to hear his name called out.

"You! Master. . . Liam. Can you handle a weapon?" Prince Manus asked him.

Liam turned pale. What could he say other than the truth? "No."

The prince scowled, unable to hide his disappointment at the answer, and looked like he might have had something sarcastic to say. Instead he commanded Liam to stay on the bridge where he would not only be safest but out of the way of his men if any trouble did arise.

"Aye M'lord." Liam replied. But Manus had already returned to watching the signaling, and had begun tapping the spyglass against his thigh, irritated by not being on the main deck to command his men.

Thankfully, Croft turned to give Liam a wink and a smile in reassurance as he brought a finger to his lips, suggesting he should stay quiet for now, and Liam was all too willing to listen to his friend and stay out of the way in silence.

The signaling had continued from the sloop, while Manus gave out his commands, and then stopped. Several long minutes went by before the lights started again. And to Liam's untrained eye, the lights looked much the same as before, but to the prince, the pattern had changed.

"Looks like Gwion replied to their call and must have asked where they hail from. They are telling us that they are from Portroe." The flashing from the sloop stopped once again; a sign that Gwion had started up his signaling again. Then their flashing started once more, as did Manus' narration. "I think Gwion must have told them we're from Birr. Maybe even from Kinsale." He looked over to Captain Thear as the pattern repeated itself. "They're telling us to remain here and they will come out to meet us."

"Do you want us to land?" Ibor asked the prince.

"No." Manus said as he walked over to the captain and handed him the spyglass. "They say they are ours but I want us to be ready to fly in case it's a trap. I'm going to head up so I can be on deck with my men while we wait for those ships." The wait wouldn't be long because the sloops had already become large specks advancing across the horizon. "Don't let them box us against the Maze and head out onto the open desert if we're attacked."

Ibor only nodded to the prince as the man left the bridge before turning to Jensen to give some commands.

Now that the prince had left, Liam, feeling a little daring, and walked over to Croft. "What should I do?" He whispered to his friend.

Not turning as he too was intent on watching the ships outside the main window, Croft replied, "Stay here. The prince was right about you staying on the bridge. This will be the safest place for you for the time being. If anything does happen, try to stay by my side."

"Okay." Liam said as Jensen moved the ship to port while keeping the sloops in view. The steersman kept making slight adjustments to the Camalain's position as the ships quickly converged upon them, moving the ship so they wouldn't be flanked by either sloop.

Fortunately, the ships did stop several hundred feet away with the lead one starting to signal them again. The lights started, stopped, and then started again.

"What are they saying?" Liam asked Croft.

"Not sure." Croft said as he too watched the flashing lights. "They're using a military code, not a mariner's. But I'm sure we'll know their intent soon enough."

Liam let the silence linger as the sloop doing the signaling moved a little closer and, for a ship that was smaller than they were, seemed quite threatening. It looked like the sloop had at least one level below its main deck and no cabin above because several large ballistae were mounted across its main deck. Morning light reflected off metal covering the prow of the ship and the metallic shafts that were aimed at them. Amongst the weaponry a soldier with a large lantern was working its shutter as he conversed with Gwion on the Camalain.

The man on the sloop suddenly stopped working the lantern and waved across at them. Liam noticed that the captain and Croft seemed to relax a little and after several moments someone could be heard running through the corridor outside of the bridge as a soldier, a little out of breath, arrived to talk to them.

"The prince says to let them come alongside." The man huffed, before quickly turning so he could return to the main deck.

After several moments, the bridge's crewmen watched as the sloop's weapons were lowered, and the ship flew alongside to dock with them, disappearing from view, with the second ship flying in to take up a defensive position about them.

Soon, shouting could be heard coming from above deck as members of the Royal Guard from the sloop began talking to their comrades on the Camalain. The prince must have also revealed himself to the soldiers as well because the yelling not only got louder, but a little more exuberant and more frantic, with the vessel still hovering in front of them, suddenly turning away as it moved over to take a position on their portside. Just as quickly, the first ship was in front of them again and took up a position of defense on the Camalain's starboard side.

"Well, that's a positive sign." Croft said to no one in particular as the smaller ships and the Camalain resumed their signaling. "Looks like we've found some friends."

"Indeed it does." Seb Cullen said as he walked onto the bridge to join the group.

Captain Thear turned at the sound of the sagart's voice. "You have word?"

"Yes." Cullen said as he limped over to the captain. "The prince says you are to move the Camalain forward until we can see the men on the other ships. They will be watching for a signal from the bridge to proceed forward. Prince Aerin said a wave should suffice to get their attention. And, as soon as the sloops start to move, we should follow them into the Maze. The prince will be remaining above deck for the time being and will keep the men at the ready in case there is trouble."

"Understood." Ibor turned his attention back to his steersman, placing a hand on the man's shoulder. "Jensen, move us forward, slowly, until we can get a good view of the men on the other ships."

Jensen's only response was to begin flying the Camalain into the space left for them between the sloops.

"You." Ibor said as he pointed to one of his men who happened to be standing near the main window. "When we get close enough so that we can see men on those ships, I want you to do what the prince suggested and wave. Hopefully that will be enough to get them moving."

"Aye, Captain." The crewman said before turning back to watch as the Camalain slipped into its new position. Sure enough, a man on the starboard vessel could be seen holding a spyglass with it pointed at the bridge's window and when Ibor's man thought they were close enough to be seen he began waving an arm over his head as he tried to get the man's attention.

The guard on the sloop saw him and waved back to them then turned to someone on his own ship. His vessel then began to move forward, followed by the other one that was hovering to their left.

"Okay, Jensen. Follow them." Ibor commanded his steersman.

"Aye." Jensen replied hollowly, sending the ship forward.

"Not too close. Pull back just a little." The captain instructed as the Camalain kept pace with the two sloops because Thear Ibor wanted to make sure they could slip away if necessary. "Good. This is fine Jensen."

As all three ships made their way to the entrance that would cut across the Maze, Cullen walked over to Croft and his son. The sagart acknowledged the two as he joined them to watch their flight across the flats.

"So what's the good word from above?" Croft asked of Cullen.

"Sadly, none were spoken that were good." The sagart replied. Liam, who was standing between them, kept his silence as he listened. "Instead of hovering here and getting a report, the prince was more concerned with getting to the crash site and looking for signs of his brother."

"Makes sense." Croft replied as the flashing signals once more appeared from the sloop that was on their right. It was obvious that Prince Manus was going to stay in touch with his men on the new ships. "Better to not be out in the open and we should be safer once we're inside the Maze."

"The cover of the Maze didn't help you the last time." Liam said, stating a fact as his fears began to overtake his common sense. To his right, his father hissed at him reproachfully. Turning, Liam looked at Croft who was staring off into space with a pained, lost look on his face. Liam was mortified. "I'm sorry Croft. I wasn't thinking."

Croft looked at Liam and gave him a wan smile. "But your words were true. At least, this time, there will be more than one ship to help when it comes to defending ourselves."

At this point, Liam didn't know what to say to his friend. Liam had always had this habit of speaking the obvious, especially when it wasn't needed, and usually at the wrong times. He also knew that Croft would have done his best to not only save the prince, but to save the crew of the barge as well. Liam wasn't sure how to say that or if it would sound sincere after his blunder so he just dropped his head, staring down at the planks of the floor.

"Hey." Croft whispered as he put a hand on Liam's back, who looked back at his friend. "Seriously, no harm done. Okay?" Croft stared at him until Liam gave him a half-hearted smile and nodded. "Besides," Croft continued as he gestured out the window. "We're here."

Liam looked up to see that Murra's Maze had now taken up the entire landscape ahead of the Camalain, and with most of the sky lost from view, morning light still revealed all the cracks, crevices and sheerness of the Maze. And in the center of it all, a dark opening that sunlight had yet to reach split this mountainous region.

"That's it?" Liam whispered.

"Yes." Croft replied as all three ships began to slow their approach to the entrance. "Quite impressive."

Liam couldn't help but agree with his friend. Not only was the vastness of the Maze impressive, but so too was the entrance cutting into it. The opening they continued to approach now took up all of the view out the window and from where the sloops were positioned Liam guessed that all three vessels could fly into this part of the Maze side by side. Now, some sunlight could be seen spilling into the canyon so that ledges and small openings were exposed, pock marking the sheer walls of the Maze.

"How long does it take to fly through here?" Liam asked.

"About a day and a half. Less, if a steersman knows the twists and turns of the Maze."

"And what do you think they're doing?" Cullen interjected as the two sloops in front of them slowly came to a halt just outside of the entrance. The Camalain, following their lead, also stopped.

Captain Thear had that same question on his mind. "Jensen. Anything?" He asked the steersman, the only man in the room that might a have any chance of seeing something they couldn't.

Jensen's only response was, "Third."

"What's a third? What does he mean?" Liam asked, forgetting that he just should have been quietly observing the situation.

"Probably means that there is a third ship out there somewhere." The captain answered over his shoulder, not too concerned that it was Liam who was posing the question. "Croft, what do you think?"

As a steersman, Croft was all too familiar with the gibberish that bubbled out of his own mouth when he was flying a ship, and agreed with the captain and his assessment.

But the bridge crew didn't have to wait to see if Jensen was correct or not because a third ship, slightly larger than the two sloops, emerged from the canyon, blocking its entrance. Fortunately, the signaling continued between themselves and their guide, with the new vessel peppering the conversation with some signals of its own, so the assumption was that the new ship was not a threat.

Except for the slight pacing of the captain behind Jensen's chair, everyone remained quiet, with Liam wondering what would happen next as he watched the vessels pass information to each other. Fortunately Liam and the rest of the crew didn't have to wait long before the prince, along with a member of his guard, returned to the bridge.

"Not to worry, Captain." Manus said as he approached Thear Ibor. "That third vessel is one of ours and it will guide us into the Maze. When the skiff starts moving, we'll follow it in and the two sloops will take up rearward positions behind us."

"Aye."

From their view of the outside, the crew could see the flashing lights stop on both the sloop and the larger vessel. And after a moment, the skiff sent several quick flashes, pivoted and flew back into the channel that would snake its way through the Maze. Manus nodded to Captain Thear who then ordered his steersman to follow the new ship.

Everyone on the bridge watched as the two sloops vanished from sight as the Camalain passed them and took up a position behind the skiff. As the sheer walls of the cliff blocked out most of the morning light, Liam couldn't help but tense as he thought of the two vessels now blocking their only means of escape. Liam did see several lights flare to life on the lead ship, giving him and the other non-steersmen something to focus on as the shadows of the maze deepened. Not only was the faint glow reassuring, Liam also assumed that the Camalain and the vessels behind them had done the same and had lit lanterns of their own.

Finally, after several minutes had passed, Liam's foster-father broke the silence. "Prince Aerin. How long do you think it will be until we reach the wreckage?"

"We should reach the site by mid-afternoon." Manus replied to the sagart without looking at the man, for he was intent on paying attention to the progress they were making and his thoughts were of finding something that might help in locating his brother. "From what my men have said, it looks like Steersman Moro flew the barge quite a ways into Murra's Maze before crashing it."

Liam looked at Croft, who only returned his gaze with a blank look and a shrug. Like Manus, Croft was lost in his own thoughts, remembering the attack and trying to figure out if there was something he could have done differently that would have saved the ship and Prince Manus' brother.

"Is there anything you need us to do?" The sagart asked because he had been on several searches, among other missions, with the prince's father, and knew that now was not a time to be idle.

"As a matter of fact, my men have the ship well-guarded, so it should be safe for everyone else to get back to their duties. And, unless absolutely necessary, I would suggest staying off the main deck for now."

"Understood." Cullen replied, for everyone on the bridge.

"Well," Croft said, as he raised his hands over his head and let out a long yawn. "My shift is next so I think I'll try to grab a few winks of sleep before I have to relieve Jensen. And you might want to think of taking care of that hair." Croft reminded Liam while pointing to the unruly mass on his head.

Liam self-consciously ran a hand through his hair once again, not realizing he was making it worse. "I should get cleaned up and probably make my way back to the galley."

His father agreed with him. "You will be just as safe in the galley as you would be here. I have flown with old Crogan before and he knows how to use a sword much better than he uses a butcher's knife."

"Then why is he in the galley?" Liam asked.

"Because, whether we like it or not, we all have a job to do and that's his. Now run along." Cullen urged.

"Yes father." Liam replied as he left the bridge, followed by Croft who bid him a good night, even though it was early morning. Liam once again followed the main hallway that ran below the main deck and made his way back to the cabin he and his father were using as their sleeping quarters, grabbing a towel, some clean undergarments, another pair of pants and a brush, before heading down to the washroom at the back of the ship.

But Liam wasn't the only one with thoughts of getting cleaned during their momentary lull, for several other men had already formed a short line in the hallway as they waited their turn to use one of the two shower stalls that made up the washroom. Liam couldn't help but notice that the man in front of him was bare-chested, with a towel thrown over one shoulder and who acknowledged the young man with a smile as he got into line.

Liam returned the gesture to the man, whose name he didn't know, leaned up against the bulkhead and, not knowing what to do, turned his attention to the far wall and started counting the cracks that had formed in the old varnish on the paneling.

"So, you the sagart's boy?" The man next to him asked as he tried to make some small talk with Liam.

"Yes." Liam said nervously as he quickly glanced at the man before returning to his vigil of the wall.

Of course the crewman who had spoken to him had known who Liam was and that he had been mostly keeping to himself over the past several days, and being of the friendly sort, he tried again. "Name's Gorman." Jerking a thumb at the other two men in front of him, he named them as Manton and Yarrow. Each man greeted Liam as his name was given.

Liam politely gave his name in return.

"So, what's the good word?" Manton asked as he joined in on the conversation. He was standing only in his undershorts while Yarrow was similarly dressed like Gorman; trousers and no shirt. Since his arrival on the ship, Liam couldn't help but notice that the crewmen and the soldiers on the Camalain seemed to be quite comfortable being half naked around each other when not on duty. Something Liam was finding very uncomfortable.

"Word?" Liam asked because he was not sure what the man was asking.

"Yeah. Any word on the prince's brother, Dar Banning?" Manton asked again.

The door to the washroom slid open, and a man drying his hair with a towel, stepped out and Yarrow quickly went in, closing the door shut behind him.

"Has your father said anything about the search?" Manton continued.

"No, nothing. I probably know just as much as you do. Maybe less, I think. Has the captain said anything to you?"

"Just sent word to get to our stations as soon as possible. Got to be ready for anything." Gorman replied as he scratched his hairy chest.

"Guess it's a good thing we have the Royal Guard on board to protect us." Liam said as he continued his conversation with the two men.

Gorman and Manton laughed good-naturedly at his remark. "I guess it is considering we are all members of the Guard." The door to the washroom opened again as another man left the room. Manton gave a quick goodbye before he headed into the washroom and the vacated stall.

"I didn't know you all were part of the military. I meant no offense, I just thought most of you were sailors." Liam explained to Gorman while he fumbled with his towel as it began to fall out of his hands. The towel now dangling from a hand, Liam hugged his pile of belongings a little tighter.

"None taken." Gorman chuckled, amused by Liam's naiveté. "All of us may not be wearing the uniform, but we have been in the service of the Royal Guard for many years. As a matter of fact, I have been in the service of clan Aerin since I was about your age. So, if anyone tries to board us they will have a tough fight on their hands."

"Gods willing, that won't happen." Liam said nervously as Yarrow opened the door to the washroom. Yarrow hadn't wasted any time in the shower and was still drying off his chest and shoulders as he left the room.

"All yours, Gor." Yarrow said to his friend as he passed him and Liam on the way back to his room.

"And not to worry Master Liam," Gorman said as he moved away from his place in the hallway so he could go wash. "You're safe on the Camalain. This ship is a den full of wolves and we won't back down from anything that' thrown at us."

Liam only smiled, not thrilled at the thought of the ship being invaded, as Gorman slid the door closed behind him, leaving Liam alone in the hallway waiting his turn. Closing his eyes, he tried to listen to the muffled sounds of Gorman's and Manton's voices coming from the washroom although the closed door and the sound of running water drowned out most of what they were saying. But Liam wasn't trying too hard and the resonance of their muffled conversation and the bobbing of the ship slowly began putting him to sleep.

Unfortunately, he didn't get long to doze in the hallway because, just as quickly as Yarrow left, Manton slid the door open and exited the room. Obviously Manton was not one to be shy because he was now standing in front of Liam with the towel wrapped around his waist, using his right hand to keep it in place while his underwear was balled up in his left.

"Next." He said to Liam with a smile as he padded down the hallway, a trail of wet footprints left in his wake.

"So, we meet again!" Gorman chuckled as Liam entered the room and slid the door closed.

"Looks that way." Liam grinned nervously as he went over to the bench bolted near the left hand stall that was empty and placed his belongings on it. Glancing out of the corner of his eye, Liam could see that Gorman was standing underneath the showerhead scrubbing his face so he quickly took off his own clothing and hastily got into the stall, his fingers slipping on the latch as he closed the door. Turning on the water Liam hissed in surprise as cold water poured over his body. He was quite shocked, his teeth chattering uncontrollably, because it hadn't been like this the other day when he had taken a shower, and stepped out from under the water as best he could as he waited for the water to become more bearable.

"With so many men showering at once, it's usually like this in the morning. The water might get warmer," Gorman said over the shoulder high partition, watching Liam's discomfort and laughed in good humor as he closed his eyes and stood under the cold water again. "Then again, it might not."

Liam's gaze became affixed to Gorman as the man turned underneath the pouring water. Because, like most Gwerin men, and as a member of the Royal Guard, Gorman had an athletic build. He was chiseled and brawny and Liam was finding the man's closeness and nakedness overwhelming. As he found himself uncontrollably aroused by the man, he hurriedly grabbed the soap from its dish on the stone wall, and took a step underneath the bitingly cold water. Lathering himself wasn't helping his condition. If anything, touching his own goose pimpled flesh was making his arousal worse. So Liam pivoted underneath the running water so that he was facing away from Gorman in the hopes of hiding his interest.

"Guess I've been spoiled." Liam chattered nervously, aware that the only sound now filling the room was the sound of the splashing water from the two showers. "I've only had to share with my father and when he traveled I would have the washroom all to myself. Need to get used to using a common one."

The only response Liam got from Gorman was an "uh-huh" as Liam continued to keep his back to the man. Liam knew he was being rude, but he didn't know what else to do as his heart pounded heavily in his chest, while feeling flustered, wishing that the water would get warmer.

"Well, better get used to it." Gorman finally replied. Liam realized the man must have thought he was being rude too because the tone of Gorman's voice had become flat, less jovial and friendly. "You're not going to find much privacy on this ship."

Liam twisted slightly, doing his best not to expose himself, but Gorman had turned away from him as he also continued to wash. Liam knew he should apologize and explain that he wasn't trying to be rude, but at that moment the door to the washroom opened as another man entered the room.

"Oh, sorry Gor." The newcomer said as he recognized his comrade. "I didn't know both stalls were taken."

"No problem Burton. Just finishing up. I'll be out in a minute."

Burton ducked out of the room, closing the door behind him as Gorman shut the water off and stepped out of his stall. And as he grabbed his towel to dry himself, Gorman looked over at Liam who was hugging himself, his hair hanging over his eyes, while he shook slightly under the falling water. "Finally getting used to the water?" He asked, giving Liam a curious stare as he ran a towel over his chest and abdomen.

Liam brushed the hair out of his eyes to look at the man, not knowing what to do or say. He was so embarrassed by this situation that he unwittingly looked down at himself. He had thought he would have had the opportunity to escape the washroom once Gorman had left the room, but now he didn't know what he was going to do now that there was someone else waiting to shower.

"Ahh, so that's the problem."

Liam looked up and found that Gorman had stepped over to his stall and was looking in at him. Liam was now thoroughly mortified and shook even more under the showerhead, wishing there was some place for him to hide.

Gorman gave Liam a sympathetic, albeit a mischievous eye, as he stepped away and continued to dry himself.

"You know, at your age, if you aren't getting those on a regular basis then there should be a problem." Gorman chuckled. "As a matter of fact, when I was your age, I walked around with my hands in my pockets most of the time hoping no one would notice what was going on in them. See?" He said teasingly, as he took a step back and quickly exposed himself to Liam. "Now you've got me doing it too."

"I, uh," Liam mumbled because Gorman's nonchalant attitude with his own sexuality had thrown him off kilter. But then again, Liam knew this was the norm for his people, even though he had done his best to avoid the world around him and had also done his best to not be intimate with anyone. He had done well up until now, Liam corrected himself, as the thought of leaving the stall and exposing his nudity to someone else was scaring him immensely.

But Gorman, a man in his early forties, was not unsympathetic to Liam's plight. "Here." He said as he draped Liam's towel over the stall door. "You should dry off before you shrivel up into nothing in there."

Liam forced himself to move and turned off the water and then grabbed his towel so he could dry himself, while staying in the stall, of course. Gorman didn't even bother covering himself as he also placed Liam's clothes on the door. "When you're all set we'll both leave. Okay?"

Liam mumbled his ascent as Gorman started to put on his own pants, not bothering with his underwear and walked over to the polished piece of metal on the wall that was the mirror, and ran a hand over his dark, close cropped hair, sending droplets of water across the counter.

Poor Liam, not wanting to hold the man up any longer than he needed to, quickly got dressed, adjusting himself as best he could as he put on his underwear and pants. Liam didn't bother throwing his shirt back on; he added it to the pile of his belongings so he could hold it in front of himself. Hopefully the bundle would hide his embarrassment from everybody else. Once dressed Liam informed Gorman he was ready to go.

"What about your hair?" Gorman asked, noticing that the young man's hair was still dripping wet, while pointing to the brush Liam had in his hand.

Liam shrugged, sending water trailing down his back. "I can take care of it later."

"Relax." Gorman said reassuringly. "Dry your hair off and brush it if you need to. It shouldn't take too long."

Drying his hair and trying to have a semblance of control over it was just a formality for Liam because his black hair was naturally curly and did whatever it wanted to do, usually falling in a mess in front of his eyes. Still, running the brush and his hands through his hair was at least a halfhearted attempt at keeping it from looking unruly.

And as Liam shifted to find a decent reflection of himself in the beaten metal, the door slid open.

"Hey, either you guys done yet?" Burton said as he poked his head in again. "There's a line forming out here again."

"They're both free." Gorman replied as he wiped the back of his neck with his towel.

"Come on." Burton said over his shoulder to the man behind him as they both entered the room. Gorman took a step back and Liam watched out of the corner of his eye as Burton moved by them and went towards the shower stalls. The two crewmen wasted no time getting naked and jumping into the vacated stalls with gasps of shock escaping their lips as the cold water poured over them.

"You know Gor, you and your friend could have left us some warm water!" Burton said as he dunked his head underneath the shower and began to wash himself.

"Sorry mate. Was like that when we got here." Gorman picked up Liam's belongings and held them out to him. "You all set? Good."

"Let's go." Gorman put a hand on Liam's shoulder, herded him out of the room and closed the door behind them. Five more men were waiting to use the showers and Gorman swapped pleasantries with them as he and Liam walked by.

As they turned the corner and headed for the stairs leading up to the living quarters, Liam stammered, "I, uh, I'm sorry about that. You know. In the shower?"

Gorman chuckled as he rolled his underwear in his towel and held the wadded bundle in his right hand. "I meant what I said. Don't worry about it." Gorman chuckled again. "Anyway, as a rule, the longer we stay on the flats, the more of those you'll be seeing around the stalls."

Deciding to change the subject, Gorman asked Liam his age.

"Twenty-four. I just had my birthday this past Juliach."

Gorman laughed, something that seemed to come easily to this man, and smiled warmly at Liam. "Twenty-four! Me, I'm forty-three. You got anyone back home?"

"Anyone?" Liam asked as they started to climb the stairs to the upper levels. Then it dawned on him what Gorman was asking. Liam decided to lie, or at least tell a half truth, because who he had and what he wanted were two different things. "No, no one."

"Well, you're young yet." Gorman said over his shoulder. "I have a partner. His name is Verrim Heath and he is onboard too. Been together almost fifteen years. I'll introduce you to him later if you haven't met him by then."

"Okay." Liam said as they reached the landing to the floor that housed most of the Royal Guard.

"Well, here I am." Gorman said as they moved to one side of the corridor so several men could head downstairs. "Need to finish dressing and get to my station."

"I should probably get to the galley." Liam replied as he started up to the next level where his cabin was located. "I'm sure the cook has something waiting for me to do by now."

"Well, don't let Crogan work you too hard." Gorman said as he headed down the hallway. "It was nice to meet you, Liam." Winking slyly at Liam and telling him to take care of himself.

A thought came to Liam, so he took a couple of steps back down the stairwell and called out to Gorman, halting the man before he entered his own cabin.

"Gor! Do you think we will be on the flats for long?"

For the first time since he met the man, Gorman frowned. "I hope not Liam. We'll know for sure once we reach the crash site. But I hope not." And not having anything else positive to say, Gorman told Liam he would see him later, walking into his own cabin and sliding the door shut behind him.

With the thought of remaining out on the flats on his mind, and that last look on Gorman's face, there was no thought of Liam trying to relieve himself as he made his way back to his own cabin. Fortunately his father wasn't in their shared cabin, so Liam finished getting dressed, throwing on the shirt he had worn on the first day when he boarded the Camalain and headed up to the galley.

It turned out that Cook didn't have much for Liam to prepare, because he had not stopped working since he had woken with everyone else in the early hours of the morning. But Crogan did have another tray of food and drink ready to go up to the bridge and sent him there, instructing him to return with the tray and any dirty crockery he had delivered earlier.

Once back Crogan had another tray all set to be delivered to the prince's quarters and sent him on his way again. The prince's cabin was down the corridor from his own, and over the past couple of days, Liam felt he had been fortunate to not have bumped into the man outside his room. Thankfully, today would be no different because neither the prince nor Kael, who was sharing Aerin Manus' room, was there. But a man was standing guard at the prince's door and took the tray from Liam and brought it into the men's quarters.

Upon his return to the galley, there still wasn't any food for Liam to help prepare because Crogan was very efficient, and knowing the crew of the Camalain would be eating on the go, had lain out dry salted meats and bread for the afternoon meal. Because of that Crogan had not done any of the cleaning and directed Liam to the double sinks that were full of pots and pans. So Liam rolled up his sleeves as best he could, walked over to the stove to grab one of the pots of boiling water, filled the sinks and began scrubbing away the refuse of Corgan's hard work.

Crogan continued with his cooking; preparing food that Liam assumed was for dinner. So, for every pan or utensil Liam washed, another one made its way into the sink. There seemed to be no end in sight from the assault of dirty dishes, but their production began to dwindle and eventually stopped over the next hour. Of course, being a staff of one, Liam was now left with the task of drying everything and putting them away.

Once he was done, Crogan dismissed him for the rest of the afternoon, but he expected Liam to be back for the evening meal to help serve and clean up after the crew. Liam was grateful for the short reprieve. He had forgotten to eat breakfast and now found himself famished. Grabbing some meat and bread for himself, Liam headed back to his cabin so he could eat his own lunch.

And this is where Cullen found his son; sitting at the desk with crumbs scattered on its surface as Liam watched Murra's Maze continue to move by the porthole in front of him.

"Hello, Liam." Cullen said as he entered the room, not bothering to slide the door shut as he too had started to find the room claustrophobic. Though he would never admit this thought to Liam. "What are you doing here?"

Liam slid the stool he was sitting on back so he could see his father, the legs of the stool groaning obnoxiously, leaving more marks on the already worn floor. "The cook, err, what is Crogan's clan name?"

"Yanno." Cullen said as he moved Liam's folded blankets and pillows to the end of the bed so he could sit down.

"Well, Master Yanno gave me some time off before the evening meal so I figured I would relax a little."

"In here?" His father asked, not surprised, just vexed that after almost three days onboard the Camalain, Liam was still hiding in their cabin during his off time.

And Liam, who already had similar conversations with his father, had an answer ready for him. "With all that is going on right now I was afraid of being a bother, so I thought it would be wise if I just stayed out of everyone's way."

"I am sure you could have gone above deck and found a spot that was out of the way to have your lunch. You could have eaten it in the dining hall."

Liam shrugged and began moving the crumbs on the desk into a little pile. "I really didn't think about staying in the dining hall." He said, lying to his father because Liam had given it some thought, but didn't want to look foolish sitting by himself. Even though Gorman said not to worry about the incident in the showers, Liam was still embarrassed by it and thought it best to avoid the man and his friends for a bit. "I just came here."

Cullen couldn't help but frown as he mulled over Liam's response. As a child, and a teenager, Liam had learned to isolate himself from much of what was going on around him. So he knew his son was lying, but doubted calling him on it would make the situation any better. Cullen had hoped being in such a confined community would have changed that. But of course, Liam still found a ways to become invisible to everyone. Maybe Cullen would need to be the one who would have to ask Ibor to find more things for his son to do.

"You know," Cullen said, deciding to push the subject while he had a captured audience. "If you didn't want to be by yourself you could have asked someone on deck if they needed help with what they were doing. I am sure there is plenty of work to do and an extra pair of hands would probably be much appreciated."

"I hadn't thought of that." Liam said as he lied once more. Of course he had thought of asking some of the crewmen if they needed help, but he had been fearful of being told no and, obviously, looking foolish, so he thought it wise not to ask at all.

At that moment, the Camalain must have flown by a part of the Maze where the cliffs were shallower, and lower, because sunlight flooded the cabin, momentarily blinding the two men.

Liam blinked several times, and as the sunspots faded from his eyes he asked his father, "How long do you really think we might be on the flats? I was talking to one of the crewman this morning and he was hesitant about saying that we might be out here for a while and he didn't seem happy about the idea."

Cullen didn't like the question either, although he was as surprised, if not a little happy, that Liam was talking to someone other than himself or Moro Croft.

Cullen sighed heavily before he tried to explain the situation to Liam. "I am also not fond of being out here for too long, because the longer we are out here without finding a trace of Prince Dar, the more of a strain will be put on the king and his son, who need to be focused on ruling Birr."

"Fortunately, Banning's loss would not harm the Aerin clan so much as it would the Dar's. Thankfully the consort is still young enough and of a high ranking family so that he could still have a chance to conceive several more children."

Liam, who was appalled by the statement of his father had made, voiced his opinion.

Tapping his cane on the bedroom floor, Cullen nodded in agreement with his son. "I assure you Liam we are both of the same mind. It is a shame but, Prince Dar Banning can be replaced. Prince Aerin Manus cannot. And I would not want to deal with the turmoil that would follow if it had been Prince Aerin that had been kidnapped or murdered."

Liam knew and understood the distinction between the two; Aerin Manus would one day rule Birr while Dar Banning could not because the only status that came with being the son of a consort was to one day become a consort himself. A matrimonial tradition for most of the Gwerin royalty that dated back to before The Great Rift when kingdoms were much smaller and loyalty meant life or death to the ruling clans.

Still, the tradition didn't seem right to Liam. "But, the Lord Aerin could have more children. Couldn't he?"

"Yes, yes. Lord Aerin Riocard could have more children, but it would not be the same. Manus has already earned a place in the hearts of the people. Most definitely in the hearts of the men who make up the Royal Guard. The king could have another child to become heir to the throne, but Manus could not be replaced."

Liam didn't know what to say. The thought of easily replacing a child still did not sit well with him. He was about to continue the conversation when he saw his father's face go slack and his eyes glazed over. "What is it?"

"Barra." Cullen whispered as he pulled himself onto the bed to lie down. "We are getting close."

"Do you need help with anything?" Liam asked his father as he got up and took the cane from the man's grasp and propped it in the corner near the head of the bed.

"Some solitude would be most appreciated right now." Cullen said as he closed his eyes and clasped his hands across his chest as he tried to relax so he could commune with his god. "Now would be a good time to see if help is needed on deck. And close the door behind you."

Liam looked at his father one more time before leaving. Except for the slight movement of his mouth and the sounds escaping his lips, Cullen looked like he might have fallen asleep. With the flashing pattern of daylight and cast shadows from the mountain walls being thrown into the room, Liam knew he would be sleeping soundly if it was himself lying on that bed. He watched his father for another moment as he fell deeper into his trance, then, without saying a word, Liam shut the door to the cabin.

As he took the stairs down to the main living section, Liam couldn't help but feel a twinge of jealousy at the connection his father had with Barra. A relationship he would have liked to have had with the god. A type of relationship with Barra that he yearned for that he even kept secret from his father.

But being a sagart like his foster-father had not been enticing as a vocation for Liam. He wasn't that thrilled about being a stone carver either, but being in the Stone Mason's Guild would keep him within the temple compounds and he also hoped, within the sight of the god of the earth.

Liam stopped for a moment and frowned as his past welled up within him; memories full of sorrow and loss. But there was one spark of joy, in which he was comforted by the god of the earth. How he wished Barra would make his presence known to him, and hold him, the way he done so long ago.

With thoughts of his childhood on his mind, Liam opened the door to the outside and stepped out onto the main deck. He had to blink several times and shade his eyes from the glare of the afternoon sun beating down on him. When his vision adjusted, he could see that the canyon had widened considerably and even though it still felt ominous, the Maze didn't look so dark and gloomy as it had this morning.

While he was standing in the doorway, several members of the Royal Guard walked by him as they made their rounds of the deck and that is when Liam spotted Aerin Manus. The prince was on a small deck situated above the opposite entrance that led to the bridge with Lieutenant Cahl and several other soldiers standing around him and all seemed to be deep in conversation. Liam didn't catch sight of anyone else on the deck that he recognized, and quite confident that the prince would have something for him to do, reluctantly approached the group, only stopping when he reached the stairs that would lead up to the lookout deck. Liam stood there, not wanting to interrupt the men, and hoped one of them would eventually take notice of him.

After several minutes of waiting for someone to look down at him, which wasn't happening, Liam decided to make the attempt of climbing the short flight of stairs. He had reluctantly placed a foot on the first step and was trying to find the courage to climb the rest of the stairs when he felt someone tapping his back. Startled, Liam turned and found Karam Kael before him.

"Oh, sorry sir." Liam stammered as he moved away from the stairs to let the man get by him. "I didn't mean to be in the way."

"You weren't." Kael said as he put his hands in his pockets and smiled warmly at Liam. "And you can call me Kael. We keep bumping into each other so I don't think there's a need to keep being formal."

Liam only nodded because he didn't know what to say to the friendly request. And, beginning to feel uncomfortable standing next to Kael, he looked up towards the prince and to his men to see if they had been noticed. But the gathering seemed more intent on whatever they were talking about than what was going on below them.

"It's unusual for you to be out on deck." Kael remarked, breaking the silence as he drew Liam's attention back to him. "Is there something you need help with?"

"No, I," Liam stammered. "Barra was in communion my father to let him know that we weren't far from the crash site so my father sent me away so they could commune in peace. I thought it would be wise to tell the prince."

The wind had picked up slightly and Kael ran a hand through his brown hair, pulling it away from his eyes. "Unfortunately you wouldn't be telling the prince something he doesn't already know. Did your father send you with any more information from Barra?"

"No."

"Pity. Then there's no reason to bother Prince Aerin with the obvious. Come." Kael said as he walked over to the railing on the left side of the ship.

With nothing else to do, and this being probably the easiest command he might have all day, Liam followed Karam Kael. Upon reaching the railing, Kael bent forward and propped his elbows on the brass bar while Liam walked over to the man's right and stood next to him, grasping the railing with both of his hands. Without the cabin to block the wind, Liam found it much cooler at the railing and wished he had put on a heavier shirt, or had grabbed his cloak, as he shook a little from the slight chill in the air.

Not noticing Liam's discomfort Kael raised his right arm in front of Liam and pointed to the fore of the ship. "That is why the prince knows just as much as your father does." Following Kael's hand, Liam could see the sloop out in front of them that was acting as their guide. The ship was still signaling them and taking a backwards glance up at the deck the prince was on, Liam could see a man with another lantern sending signals back to the sloop. "They say we're maybe an hour or so away from the wreckage."

"So you understand the patterns?" Liam asked as he looked back towards Kael, whose light brown eyes seemed not to have left him.

Karam Kael smiled warmly, his eyes glittering as they caught some of the sunlight. Kael pulled on the railing; the muscles in his arms bulging as they went taught and arched his back slightly, like some animal waking from a nap.

"I know the basics of the signals." He explained. "Everyone in the Guard needs to have some knowledge of the code that is being used. Though I wouldn't be able to work the lantern as deftly the way Gwion does."

"I don't understand any of it. It just looks like a man holding a swinging lantern."

"Well, looks like we might have something to teach you." Kael said, his smile broadening.

"I guess so." Liam grasped the rail a little tighter as the Camalain, following the lead vessel, banked to the right as the channel's direction shifted. As the ship turned, another one of the sloops came into view behind them. "So the other ships are still back there?"

"Only one of them is keeping pace with us. The other is out there, but it is trailing much further behind. If someone tries to sneak up on us from one of these side channels, they'll end up wedged between us and that oncoming vessel. But, now that we are a larger group, I think we'll be left alone."

Liam nodded. "That's good because I don't think I'll be much help if we do get attacked."

"You've been in the galley so much that I figured Master Yanno would have started training you in dicing and the ways of the meat cleaver by now."

"I don't think Master Yanno barely trusts me with the tea kettle."

Kael laughed at Liam's sarcasm as he stood up, bringing himself shoulder to shoulder with Liam. "Then I guess we'll have to find time for weapons training in between your scullery work!"

"Thank you." Liam said, not really relishing the thought that he might have to eventually use a weapon.

"You're welcome." Kael replied politely. "We all should be able to defend ourselves if the need arises."

Since he couldn't think of anything to say to that, Liam let silence fill the air. And the prince's friend seemed to be just fine with the silence as well because he stood there, their shoulders almost touching, with a smile on his face at some thought he was keeping to himself, as he rocked slightly on his heels.

Liam couldn't help but wonder as to why Kael was being nice to him as he rubbed at some of the grit that had accumulated on the railing, flicking the balls of dirt into the air.

"Have you flown through the Maze before?" Liam finally asked another opening in the channel, its walls broken and its entrance dark, gaped on the side of them.

"No. You?"

"No." Liam said quietly, his voice barely audible over the wind. "This is the first time I've left Kinsale since my father adopted me."

"Ahhh. Not the best reason to leave home, is it?"

"No." Liam replied, their conversation dying down once again, the low moan of the wind filling the air around them, a sad reminder of the missing prince. Out of the corner of his eye Liam could see that Kael was looking just as awkward, so Liam turned to watch the lead ship moving along the channel, giving Kael some space and solitude so he too could collect himself.

But the two men were saved by a voice from above as Kael's name was shouted across the deck.

Looking up, Kael and Liam found the prince looking down at them. "If you are done playing guide, I could use your help up here."

"Aye, Milord!" Kael shouted back. "Well, duty calls." He said to Liam as he began to walk away from him.

"Is there anything I should be doing?" Liam called after the man.

Kael could think of a couple of things he would like Liam to do, but kept those thoughts of yearning to himself. Instead he said, "There's a good chance we're closer to the wreck than I thought. If I were you, I would go and see if your father has any new information for the prince. If not, just make sure you and he are ready for when we land.

As Kael turned and climbed the stairs to the observation deck, Liam headed back into the living quarters and made his way to his cabin, sliding the door open as quietly as he could to take a peek inside. His father still seemed to be in a deep trance so Liam closed the door and sat on the hallway floor, hugging his knees against his chest as he waited for his father to wake. Looking down the hallway, Liam saw the man he had handed the prince's food to earlier, still standing guard over the prince's quarters. The man, whose name Liam didn't know, had been paying attention to what he was doing and nodded to Liam in greetings before going back to staring at the wall across from the prince's quarters. Already getting bored and hoping his father would wake soon, Liam rested his forehead on his knees and began to hum.

At some point, Liam must have dozed off because he was startled by a low thrumming that filled the air. The sound seemed to be coming from everywhere at once as the dull sound filled the air again. Liam stood quickly, a little disoriented by whatever it was and how the wall vibrated against his back. At first he thought they were under attack but down the hallway the guard didn't seem too concerned by the sound so Liam asked him what it meant.

"That's the steersman." He answered. "He's forcing air through the ship. Means we're going to land soon."

"Already? I thought we had an hour or so before we came to the crash?"

"You've been out for over half an hour." The guard said as the air pulsed again. "You might want to hold onto something." The guard instructed as he spread his own legs and rested his back against the prince's door. Liam, who had been fortunate enough to be somewhere where he could sit during the previous landings, copied the man's stance and held onto the door jamb to his cabin as best he could.

But the landing proved to be uneventful as the ship decelerated and slowly descended to the sandy floor of the channel. The ship groaned as it settled its weight on the ground, and shouting could be heard coming from the main deck, while several men were seen running down the stairs.

Liam thought now would be a good time to stir his father from his communing with the god, but upon sliding the door open, he found his father already in a sitting position with his head in his hands.

"Are you alright father?" Liam asked, alarmed at Cullen's peaked complexion.

"Yes." The sagart said hoarsely as he tried to pull himself off the bed. Cullen stopped for a moment and ran a hand through his grey hair as his head began to spin from moving too quickly. "Barra had a lot to share." He mumbled as he reached for his cane that Liam had placed in the corner near his bed.

Liam wasted no time in going to his father's side and held onto his elbow as the man struggled to maintain his balance. Cullen's right leg, the one that was injured long ago, seemed to be giving him problems; something it only did when he was extremely exhausted.

"I hope what he had to say was good."

"Wish I could say that it was." Cullen smiled weakly as he moved his elbow out of Liam's grasp and placed a hand on his son's shoulder as he took several tentative steps.

"Is he dead?"

"Dead? No, the prince is still alive." Cullen said as they stopped in the doorway to their room as a couple of men in armor ran by their room. Liam waited patiently as his father stretched his leg a little more. "No, Barra says the prince is fine. But it looks like darker days might be ahead for us."

"Why? What is wrong?"

Cullen squeezed his son's shoulder, in that fatherly way that usually meant to be a good quiet boy, before letting go so he could stand on his own.

"Do not worry," The sagart said before adding a phrase from one of his sermons. "Even the gods need to unburden their souls once in a while."

"What does that mean?" Liam whispered, although there was no need to because the soldier, who had been standing sentinel at the prince's quarters all day, had left his post to go help the others at the crash site.

"Never mind, I spoke out of turn." Cullen said as he guided the two of them down the stairwell. Trying to change the subject and avoid any more inquisitive questions from his son, Cullen said they were going to head down to the cargo hold, because that would be the only way off the ship, so that they too could help with the search.

But Liam didn't want to back down this time. "Why are we here if you know Prince Dar is alive? And if Barra has told you where he is, why not just get him and head back home? And now you hint that we might have trouble heading our way! No wonder Prince Aerin is frustrated with the gods."

"Mind your tongue!" Cullen snapped, anger contorting his face, catching his son off guard as he painfully thrust the head of his cane into his son's chest. "You don't know, you just don't know!"

"Then tell me father! I thought I was here to help you?"

Cullen lowered his cane so that he and Liam could move over to one side as another man came running down stairs. "Liam," Cullen said as the redness from being angry at his son, drained out of his face, leaving him looking grey and ragged. "Please, no more questions for now." Cullen didn't wait for response from his son as he continued to hobble down the stairs.

It was rare that Liam got his father this angry, but when he did, he knew enough to keep his mouth shut and followed his father in silence. Still, why would the god lead them here knowing that there might be danger? The question lingered on his tongue as they made their way through the rest of the Camalain and walked out onto the channel's floor.

As they began to make their way around the Camalain, Liam couldn't help but gawk at the makeshift camp around the downed barge. On their far right, a large cave could be seen in the canyon wall with a fire built at its entrance. About a half-dozen soldiers were seated on what might have been some wreckage from Prince Dar's barge, talking and polishing their weapons, with several looking up at the newcomers before going back to what they were doing.

The father and son were following members of the Royal Guard who had left their ship, when a flash of light caught Liam's eye. Looking up, he was able to glimpse a small glider flying overhead as sunlight reflected off the metal plates covering the front of the small two man ship. Liam stopped and shaded his eyes with a hand so he could watch the arrow shaped vessel fly around the skiff that had been guarding their rear, which had remained in the air and now seemed to be maintaining a defensive position behind them.

"Impressive, aren't they?" Said a man who happened to be walking by. It was Manton, one of the men he had met while waiting to wash. Liam almost didn't recognize him in the clothing and leather jerkin he was wearing, with a sword belted to his waist. "One of those can swipe a man off a deck if they're not paying attention." Manton explained as he stopped and watched the glider with Liam. "Prince Dar might have fared better if he had several of those in his entourage."

"Liam!"

Liam looked and saw that his father had stopped and was waiting for him near the front of the Camalain.

"Coming!" He shouted back, while Manton gave him a quick pat on the back before he left Liam and headed over to the campfire.

"Sorry." Liam said as he caught up to his father. "I got distracted by the glider. I've never seen one this close before."

"Well, now is not the time for distractions." Cullen said a little too harshly. But Liam knew his father was exhausted and let the comment pass without taking offense. "The prince is already at the damaged barge. Come."

As Liam and his father passed in front of the Camalain, the ship that had acted as their guide came into view. The vessel had landed not far from them and many of its men were climbing down several ladders, mingling with the soldiers from the Camalain. Walking through several groups of men, Liam could see another vessel with several more gliders surrounding it on the ground and the downed ship that was Prince Dar's barge.

The barge was on the far side of the channel and it had been kept in its listing position. Little did Liam know he was walking the same route the pirates of the Shaefra had taken when they had raided the barge and kidnapped Banning.

Cullen stopped a man who was walking away from the wreck site, and inquired to the whereabouts of Prince Manus. The man directed them to the far right hand side of the barge where a small station had been set up outside of the damaged craft. Cullen thanked the man before they proceeded on to their destination.

As they climbed up the piled sand and headed around the barge, Liam couldn't help but notice the heavy breathing coming from his father. Concern etched his face as he watched his father struggle with his lame leg trying to navigate the shifting sand underfoot. Especially since his father's cane was of no use as it kept sinking into the sand.

"Father, do you want to stop for a moment? Do you want me to help you the rest of the way?"

"No, I am fine." Cullen said as he waved his son away. "Besides, I think the prince is right over there." The sagart stopped for a moment and raised his cane to point at a group of men standing around a makeshift table underneath a large overhang in the cliff wall.

They approached the men and Ibor, who was part of the group, spotted Cullen and Liam and hailed them over. Thankfully, Liam thought, the ground here was more stone than sand and walking became more manageable for his father. Prince Manus, who was in the middle of the group, looked up at the approaching figures and asked several of his soldiers to stand aside to make room for the father and son so they could join them. Liam, who had felt he would have nothing to contribute to this meeting, stayed several steps away from the prince and the members of his Royal Guard who seemed to be appraising Prince Manus on their situation. But he did stay close enough to listen to what they were saying to each other.

"Were your men able to find anything Milord?" Cullen asked Manus, as the soldiers around him quieted, deferring reverently to the priest's presence.

"No." Manus replied in annoyance. "By the time help came to aid the crew that were stranded here, any trace of the attackers had already been swept away by the wind."

"And how were those men?" Cullen asked Ibor.

"Aside from some cuts and bruises from the ordeal, Captain Thear's crew seems to be doing fine." Manus explained, jumping in before Ibor had a chance to speak for himself. "They've already been returned to the mainland and should be making their way back to Kinsale by now.

The guards, who were here to protect my brother, have remained behind and will be coming with us. Isn't that right Lieutenant Cahl?"

"Yes, Milord."

Liam could just make out the lieutenant in the group, who was usually as quiet as he was, standing next to the prince.

"There will be room for them on the second ship that will be coming with us." The lieutenant continued. "I also think it would be wise to take the three gliders with us for scouting and defense. The Camalain's main deck is large enough to use as a platform for one of them and the other two can remain on the Marmairn. This way we can keep in touch with you through the beacons and the gliders."

"You'll be staying on the Camalain." Manus interjected, not bothering to look at the man.

"Sorry sir?" The lieutenant asked, his voice faltering slightly.

"It was my father's idea to send you on this mission, not mine. And after you're fiasco with losing my brother, I don't trust you to be in command so I will be keeping you as close to me as possible. Your men will do just fine working under Captain Bres. Is that understood?"

"Yes Milord." Cahl Goban said just as flatly as when he was giving his report, a deadpan expression returning to his face as he did his best to hide his humiliation of being dressed down in front of his peers. He quickly continued with his report like nothing had just happened. "My men have also shored up and reinforced the damaged hull of the barge so it can be flown back to port where it can be repaired or scrapped."

Liam was looking up at the damage that exposed two of the lower decks, just able to see some planks supporting the hull and inner walls when the prince asked his father if he had received any word from Barra

Liam saw that his father was rubbing the back of his neck with his free hand while trying to support most of his weight with his cane. A definite sign of his father's exhaustion because, by now, he would have found a place for the cane, usually Liam's hand, so that he could have stood freely and used his hands expressively while he talked. "Yes. Barra spoke to me while we were flying through the channel.

"And?" Manus asked a little impatiently.

"The god says we need to fly south because that was where your brother has been taken."

"We've been flying north only to find out we now need to go back south?" Manus fumed as his face and neck turned a deep red in anger.

"Are we to head anywhere in particular or just south until Barra tells us it's time to fly in a different direction?"

Cullen took a deep breath, too tired to want to deal with the brunt of Manus' ire. "I am sorry Milord. We are to fly south towards the tip of Birr."

Manus, who wasn't even bothering to hide his anger from the men around him, could not believe they had wasted three days getting here, only to find out they had been going in the wrong direction. What game were the gods playing with them?

"So Banning is in southern Birr?"

The sagart shrugged and said wearily that he did not know. That Barra had only informed them that they needed to fly towards the southern tip of Birr.

"Other than that, I do not know." Cullen reiterated.

Manus was about ready to go into a tirade, frustrated by the amount of time they had wasted on this trip, when he was interrupted by Captain Thear.

"You do not look well my friend." The man said to Cullen. "Are you alright?"

The prince stopped for a moment to look at the priest. Cullen's eyes did seem pinched at the corners and his complexion had a grey cast to it. "Yes Sagart, you do not seem well at all."

Cullen breathed heavily and ran a hand through his grey hair. "I am sorry Prince Aerin. My communing with Barra was quite draining today. I am sorry to say that I am certainly not at my best right now."

Manus could be called many things. But callous was not one of them; at least sometimes. "I see no reason for you to stay here. Unless Barra has given you more information to pass on to me?"

When Cullen shook his head in the negative, Manus continued. "Then why don't you go back to your quarters and try to get some rest. There's no reason to be here while we strike camp."

"Thank you, Milord." Cullen said as Liam approached his father and grasped him by his forearm to help him back to their cabin.

"Liam, I need you to stay." Manus said to Liam, who looked to his father, who gave him a nod of reassurance. And not wanting the old man to walk alone, Manus instructed one of his soldiers to escort the sagart back to the Camalain.

So Liam did as he was told, standing at the edge of the group in silence, while the prince continued to pass out orders to his captains and some of their subordinates. That was when Liam noticed Kael standing several feet behind the prince. The man was paying attention to what Manus was saying, but gave Liam a quick wink when he noticed Liam glancing at him. Liam nodded back to the prince's friend, before dropping his gaze to the ground while he waited for his turn to find out what the prince needed of him.

He didn't wait long because after several minutes the prince called him forward to stand within the group.

"Master Keir, how is your father? I'm a little concerned he might not have the strength to continue on this journey."

"M'lord, my father should be fine once he gets some rest. For some reason the trance he was in while talking to Barra took a lot more out of him than it normally does. He was quite distressed when he came out of it."

"How so?" Manus crossed his arms over his chest and began scrutinizing Liam a little harder.

That's when Liam realized that not only the prince, but his captains were staring at him. It also dawned on Liam that what little he had said might have been too much. "I don't,"

"Master Keir!" Manus snapped. "When my father is not here, I am your liege lord. And I am in charge of this expedition. I need to know anything that will be helpful in finding my brother. Is that understood?"

When Liam finally nodded in agreement, Manus asked, "So what else do I need to know?"

Liam jammed his hands into his pockets as he began to shake nervously. He hesitated one more moment, and then said, "My father said darker days are ahead."

Manus looked perplexed, if not a little angry as he continued to question Liam. "I don't understand. Why wouldn't he tell me if my brother would be in danger?"

"Not Prince Dar, M'lord." Liam said as he tried to explain what his father had said to him. "My father meant us. Barra told him he saw darker days ahead for us."

"Then why didn't he tell me that!" Manus demanded.

"Probably because he let that information slip. I don't even think I was supposed to have heard those words."

Manus swore, not knowing what else to say.

"Prince Aerin, if I may?" One of his captains interjected. Manus waved a hand for him to continue. "Maybe it would be wise if we forget about salvaging the barge and use what ships we have here to defend you and to help you find Prince Dar."

Manus mulled that thought over for a moment before looking at Liam. "Is there anything else you need to tell me?"

"No M'lord." Liam responded in a low voice, sorry he had told the prince anything at all.

Manus continued to look at Liam, searching for some deceit in the sagart's son, and saw none. Manus knew he was making Keir Liam uncomfortable with his questioning, but didn't care because he needed to know the truth of what was awaiting them so that he could protect his men.

"Your advice is sound Captain Lochlor." Manus said to the man who had spoken up. "Unfortunately we cannot leave Portroe unprotected. And I need you to send word to my father as to what is going on so he can figure out what measures will need to be taken to protect Birr. We will stick to the original plan."

"On second thought," Manus said, "I'll take the Marmairn and the gliders. But do leave the barge. The ship is already damaged so I see no reason to try and protect it with a skeleton crew on it. No, salvage what you can from it and then get yourselves back to Birr. Is that understood?"

"Aye, Milord." Captain Lochlor responded.

"Now, if there is anything else?"

"Excuse me M'lord." All heads turned to look at Liam, who had been momentarily forgotten as Manus and his men talked about defenses for their small fleet. Now, they all became quiet as they waited for him to continue. "I was wondering, does my father need to know what I told you? I don't know what would happen if he ever found out that I repeated what Barra had said to him without his permission."

Manus snorted. How dare this commoner make demands of him! He watched Keir Liam's face crumble to his response. "That information is for me to use as I see fit. To be honest with you, I am deeply disturbed that your father failed to give me this information. And I think, once your father is well rested, he and I will be having a conversation on what he should and shouldn't be keeping from me."

Thankfully, Thear Ibor came to Liam's rescue. "Milord, there is no reason to spread word as to what Liam has told us. Granted he has given us some useful information so we can defend ourselves. But why get the boy in trouble with his father? And if Liam has told us something he shouldn't, it would be wise not to tell his father and have the wrath of Barra fall upon us. I for one would like to keep the god's blessings on my shoulders."

Manus watched as all of his captains nodded in agreement with Captain Thear. The blessings of Barra! His ire stewed inside him at their fear of offending the god. Unfortunately, he couldn't lose them over something petty as their faith and the hurt feelings of the priest's son.

"Very well." Manus conceded as he pointed a finger at Liam. "But, you will tell me if you hear anything that will help us to find my brother or to protect us from an attack."

"Yes, M'lord." Liam bowed his head in obedience.

"Very well. Let's finish what needs to get done so we can leave. Captain's Thear, Lochlor and you too, Lieutenant Cahl. You men are with me. The rest of you, make sure the camp is broken down and have the soldiers go over the barge one more time and make sure we won't be leaving anything of value behind."

As the group began to break up, Kael approached Manus. "Excuse me, Milord." Kael always made sure he used his friend's title in front of others. "If I am not needed, and it looks like we are heading into trouble, it might be wise to start him on some weapon's training while we are here." Kael explained as he jerked a thumb at Liam.

Manus' face was expressionless as he conceded to Kael's request before walking away.

"Come with me." Kael said as he began leading them back around the barge towards the rest of the grounded vessels. "I'm thinking, rather than trying to fit you with chain or plate mail that you will be better off with wearing a leather jerkin. You'll find it more comfortable, especially if you've never worn armor before. But we can figure that out later." Kael explained as he steered them towards the small camp that Liam saw when and Cullen had exited the Camalain. "Have you ever used a weapon before?"

Liam had done his best to try and avoid anything that had to do with the military reminded Kael that he had not.

"No sword training? Self-defense?" When Liam shook his head in the negative, Kael said with a smile on his face, "I guess we'll just have to keep it simple then."

Liam noticed that most of the men, including Manton, had already left the camp to get back to their duties, though several men had stayed behind to clear the site and put out the fire. Kael approached a soldier and asked for his hand crossbow. "I want to show my friend here how to use one and I'll get it back to you before we leave."

"I'm on the Camalain with you Master Karam." The soldier said, recognizing the prince's friend and handing over his weapon with a small packet of darts. "You can always return it to me after we are airborne."

"Thank you." Kael said to the man as he began to fit a dart into the weapon. Kael beckoned Liam over. "You ever handle one of these?"

"No."

Kael was holding the weapon by its handle with it pointing away from them. He took a step closer to Liam so he could get a better look. "If made right, the crossbow is a beautiful weapon. Of course, it's not the best weapon to use in a fight."

Liam was confused. "Then why show me how to use it?"

"Because one shot might be the difference between life and death and once you get the knack of handling one, they are pretty easy to use." With that Kael lifted his arm and pressed the trigger of the weapon, sending the small dart into some ruined planking someone had been using as a seat around the fire pit. Kael bent down and grabbed another dart out of the pouch and started to instruct Liam on how to cock the small bowstring while fitting the arrow into place. Liam sucked on the inside of his lip and listened to Kael while he explained on how to sight down the barrel of the bow at his target and how to fire the weapon. Kael aimed the weapon a second time and fired again. The dart smacked into the wood several inches from the first.

"It's natural to want to pull back on the bow when you pull the trigger. Doing that will send the dart way off its mark." Kael handed the weapon to Liam along with another dart. "Your turn."

As Liam fumbled with the crossbow, Kael corrected him on how to lock the dart into place, making sure it was seated on the barrel. Kael even pretended to have a weapon in his own hand so Liam could mimic his stance. Liam's hand shook as he raised the crossbow and squinting, fired the weapon. The bolt flew over its intended target and disappeared into the sandy floor behind it.

"Not bad. Try again." Kael said as he handed Liam another dart.

This time Kael only nodded in approval as Liam correctly loaded the weapon. Liam was still nervous about firing it and jerked the crossbow when he fired the second time. The dart flew higher and hit the canyon wall, snapping as it made impact. "Sorry." he said as he tried to hand the weapon back to Kael.

"That was bound to happen." Kael said and instead of taking the weapon back he handed another dart to Liam. "Try again."

"My friend Croft was on the barge when it was attacked." Liam said as he cocked the weapon for a third time. "He said the men that attacked them used hand crossbows with poisoned darts."

"More likely they used a crossbow that could fit in the palm of their hand, or had barrels on one of these modified to shoot needles." Kael pointed at the dart Liam was fitting into the crossbow. "Most of the men would have bled to death instead of just falling asleep if those pirates who had attacked the barge used standard bolts." Kael pointed at the plank for Liam to fire again.

Liam felt like he was having problems aiming the bow so he brought his left hand up, hoping that using two hands would give him better control of the weapon.

But Kael was quick to jump in. "No, don't do that." Kael corrected as he came behind Liam. "Don't look at me, take aim at the plank." Kael instructed as Liam turned to see what Kael was going to do. Liam didn't have to wait long because he suddenly felt Kael standing behind him and as he tried to take a step away, he felt Kael's left hand wrap around his waist and pull him back.

"Trust me." Kael whispered into Liam's ear, his hot breath brushing against Liam's neck. "Stand up straight. Good. Now aim the crossbow again. Raise the crossbow higher so you can sight down the bolt." As Liam did as he was told, Kael's right hand came up and grasped his right wrist, steadying his arm, but also pulling him closer to Liam. "Fire."

With his head spinning, Liam fired the weapon. The dart flew truer, but just nicked the top of the plank and skipped across the ground.

"Better." Kael said. Both men had dropped their right arms but Kael had moved his left hand up to Liam's abdomen, keeping it flat against his belly.

Kael could feel Liam's heart pounding rapidly and his breathing had gotten heavier while he held him. Why did he have to find Liam so attractive? Kael closed his eyes for a moment and swallowed hard as he fought the urge from squeezing Liam tighter.

"You don't want to get in the habit of using two hands when using a crossbow." Kael continued with his instruction, not letting go of Liam.

"If you're using two hands to use this then you're turning yourself into a stationary target and you will be much easier for someone to hit you instead of you hitting them. Just keep practicing at aiming and firing with one hand. No matter how much it shakes."

"Okay." Liam whispered, realizing that Kael didn't seem to want to remove his hand from his body. Liam could feel himself shaking within the man's grasp as Kael's chin brushed against the back of his neck. And when he inhaled, their bodies pressed closer together. With Kael not moving, Liam didn't know what to do.

But flashes of light caught Liam's eye and he watched as a glider came down to land on the Camalain's deck.

"It looks like they might be getting ready to leave. I think I should go check on my father." Liam said as he grasped Kael's hand for a moment and took a step away from him.

"Right." Kael said, embarrassed that goose bumps had run up his arm from where Liam had touched him.

"The crossbow? Do you want me to return it to the guard for you?"

"No, I can take it back to him." Kael said as he went to the plank and began prying the two bolts out of the wood.

Liam went and grabbed the two that were lying on the ground and picked up the pieces of the broken bolt. He approached Kael and gave him the small missiles.

"I really am sorry about that one." Liam said, noticing that this time, Kael was avoiding his gaze. "Should we plan on practicing later?"

"We'll see." Kael looked briefly at Liam, not wanting to stare too long into his hazel eyes, because at this moment he didn't think he would be able to control himself and would only want to pull Liam back into his embrace. He coughed into the palm of his hand, which had become clammy.

"It might be difficult with their glider on the deck and shooting off the deck of a flying ship is much harder than it looks. With the landscape moving by you, it's not too hard to get nauseous. I couldn't keep my lunch down my first couple of times of practice. So, it might be wise if we just practice when we land."

"Oh, alright." Liam said, unsure if he was relieved or disappointed. He took a halting step towards the Camalain. "Well, I should go."

"Right. I, I'm going to make sure this fire is put out." Kael said as he kicked some sand on embers that had already been thoroughly doused. He gave Liam a quick smile. "You can go now Master Keir. I'll see you later."

Liam stood for a moment and watched as Kael moved around the campfire, kicking sand onto the stones and burned wood. Disappointed when it looked like Kael was going to spend some time at the fire pit Liam turned and headed back to check on his father.

* * *

"Hey, Croft!" Jensen shouted. "Looks like Liam made a new friend!"

Croft, Jensen and several other men were working on the main deck. They were moving crates into storage and sweeping sand that had collected on the deck so the glider could have a stable place to land. Jensen who was over by the railing was hailing Croft to come join him. Looking down to where his fellow steersman was pointing, Croft watched as Kael walked behind Liam and embraced him.

Jensen whistled. "So much for the archery lesson."

"What?"

Jensen pointed just as Kael's right hand came up to grasp Liam's wrist. "Liam has a crossbow in his hand. It did look like Master Karam was teaching him how to use it. For a moment at least."

Another crewman had come over to watch the show. "Well, if that's how Master Karam teaches archery, then he can teach me anytime."

Manus, who was on the observation deck, had heard Jensen's call to Croft, stopped what he was doing to also watch Kael and Liam.

"If you would like Sidri, I can see if he has time to help you hone your weapons skills."

The chuckling that had started at the railing quickly died down as the men turned to look up at Manus and his surly demeanor.

"No Milord." Sidi said as he stood at attention. "I'm quite capable of firing a crossbow."

"You better be." Manus said as a glider began circling overhead. "I wouldn't want to replace you with a more skilled soldier when we get back to Kinsale."

Sidi turned pale. "No sir, that won't be necessary." The soldier replied as the glider came to hover over the deck and began to slowly descend.

"Glad to hear it. Now get ready to lock that ship down when it lands."

A chorus of "Aye Milords" came up from the railing before Sidri and Jensen went to grab some rope to tie the glider down so as to keep it from shifting while it was docked on the Camalain. Croft and Manus had kept their places and watched as Kael let go of Liam and then began to walk, separately, back to the Camalain.

"Think you guys can take care of this?" Croft asked Jensen, who was already wrapping rope around a cleat on one of the glider's wings. "I need to go take care of something."

"Sure, we got this." Jensen said as he began knotting rope.

"Thanks." Croft left his mates to finish securing the glider and headed into the cabin section. Passing several men in the hallway, Croft went to keep watch at the stairwell and he didn't have to wait long for what he was looking for. Soon, Liam came running up the stairs, taking them two at a time.

"Hey, hey! What's the rush?" Croft shouted at Liam as he moved by the steersman.

Liam stopped, a little out of breath. "Going to check on father." He huffed. "Something wrong?"

Croft waved a hand at Liam, shooing him up the stairs. "No. Go see to your father and I'll talk to you later." Liam only shook his head at his friend as he climbed the stairs to the next level. When Liam disappeared from view, Croft headed downstairs so he could make his way to the storage bays.

Croft was not far from the main bay when the other person he wanted to see came walking out of it.

"Kael, do you have a minute to talk?"

Karam Kael looked just as flustered as Liam. His face was flushed and his hair looked damp with sweat. Kael also had a crossbow and its container of bolts dangling from his hand.

"Maybe another time." Kael said as he tried to pass by Croft. "I need to return some gear to its owner before we leave."

"This won't take long." Croft said as he grabbed the man by the forearm to stop him.

Kael frowned at being halted, the packet of bolts slapping against his leg. "Look steersman, I really do need to get some work done."

Croft let go of Kael's arm, raising both his hands in surrender. But he wasn't going to back down. "Sorry sir. But I was just wondering how your target practice went. The one you had with Liam? The two of you did put on quite the show."

A worried look appeared on Kael's face and he stepped closer to Croft as a group of men tried to move by them.

"Croft, I meant no offense." Kael said, jumping to the wrong conclusion. "If I had known you two were together, I never would have helped him with the weapon."

The steersman quickly assuaged his fears. "Don't worry, Kael. Liam and I are not a couple. He and his father are only friends of mine. As a matter of fact, it's nice to see someone take an interest in him. I was just hoping to give you a piece of advice."

Somewhat relieved, Kael asked what that advice happened to be.

"Try to go slow with Liam." When Kael gave Croft a look of annoyance at being told something very common, the steersman continued. "To be honest with you, I think of Liam like a little brother and I'm only looking after him. You see, if you haven't noticed, Liam's a little shy."

"A little?"

"Alright. Liam's very shy." Croft scratched the back of his head, debating about what he wanted to say next. Then he thought again about what he was doing. "It's just that, well. Never mind. Forget I said anything." Croft finished and started to walk away from Kael.

Now it was Kael's turn to stop Croft. "Unh, unh. You can't start something then say never mind. Is there something wrong with him?"

"No. It's just that Liam's a good kid – I know he's older than a kid. I've known him for a long time and, well, he went through a lot as a boy. And it wasn't good. That's why Seb Cullen is his foster-father now."

"What happened?"

Croft shook his head. "That story I'll leave for to him to tell you. Let's just say I wouldn't wish what happened to him on anyone." Croft looked at Kael, knowing that what he had to say next would probably offend the young man. "If anything, I'm more concerned about you."

"Why would you feel a need to be concerned about me?" Kael asked as he defensively crossed his arms over his chest.

"Well, let's just say that your reputation precedes you."

Kael scowled. "And who has been talking about me?"

"Well, no one on board the Camalain." Croft assured Kael. "It's not uncommon to be in a tavern in Kinsale and hear a story about Prince Aerin and his sidekick. A man who fancies almost anything he sees."

"Rumors that are greatly exaggerated."

"I am sure." At that moment, the Camalain shuddered and tilted slightly as it began to rise. Both men held onto the wall until they gained their balance. "The thing is, if he's going to be just a toss in the bed for this journey, then maybe you should find someone else."

"Right." Kael said flatly.

"Right." Croft repeated. He jerked a thumb back towards the stairwell. "Well, my shift is next and I think I should get back to the bridge and see what's going on."

As Croft began to walk away, Kael called out to him. "Does Liam know what a good friend he has in you?"

"Liam?" Croft chuckled as he scratched his chest. "He thinks of me as the old man that won't grow up. I'll see you later Master Karam."

"Take care, Master Moro." Kael replied. He leaned up against the wall, allowing Moro Croft to go off on his own and to give himself some time to think. He could also feel the Camalain turning in midair, so they could fly back the way they had come, and decided to wait until the maneuver was done. After several minutes had passed, Kael pushed himself away from the wall and took the stairs to head towards his quarters.

Croft's words stuck with Kael as he climbed the stairs; a toss in the bed. Kael knew he wouldn't turn down the opportunity to sleep with Liam. And he certainly had had a hard time letting go of Liam during his archery lesson. It was just that Liam seemed different from the other men he had been with.

What was it that had caught his attention several days ago? Granted, Liam was attractive, but that wasn't it. And you couldn't help but notice his awkwardness around the prince; around almost everyone else for that matter. When he saw that lost, uncomfortable look on Liam's face, all Kael wanted to do was take him by the hand and lead him to someplace safe.

The look! Kael realized that was what caught his attention. There was just a sad, lonely look in those hazel eyes. But on those few times he saw Liam smile, his face lit up and the green that seemed to be hidden in those eyes found an opportunity to sparkle. But knowing didn't solve the problem, it just made him want Liam even more.

Kael mumbled a greeting to the man who was standing guard outside the prince's quarters and entered the room he shared with Manus. The room was really a small suite instead of the small compartment Liam and Seb Cullen were sharing. As soon as Kael entered the room, there was a wall with shelves and hooks where he and Manus had stowed their gear. In the other wall there was a small washroom – just a niche with a table, basin and a mirror where Manus and Kael could quickly get cleaned. Then the room opened and took up almost two thirds of the back of the Camalain. This section had a table that was bolted to the floor and covered with maps with several chairs scattered around it with room enough to spare to have a bed for Manus and one for Kael.

Manus was already in the room. He was standing at the bank of windows that made up the far wall of their living quarters. Kael was the only person who came into the room unannounced so Manus didn't even bother to turn at the sound of the sliding door.

Kael ignored Manus too as he walked over to his bed. That's when Kael realized he still had the crossbow and bolts in his hand and had forgotten to return them to the man who had let him borrow them. Swearing under his breath, he tossed them onto the bed before sitting down next to them.

Manus heard the wooden furniture creak as his friend sat down. He didn't want to look at Kael at this very moment so he continued to watch the Marmairn and the skiffs that were flying rearguard for them. They would have the protection of all the ships while they were in the Maze. But once they left, the crews of the Camalain and the Marmairn would be on their own.

The silence was slowly becoming uncomfortable so Manus began to tap one of the leaded window panes with a fingertip. The clinking sound only made the silence more annoying so Manus said the words that were roiling in his head.

"That was quite a show the two of you put on earlier."

"Here we go again." Kael thought, covering his face with his hands, hearing Croft's words repeated by his friend. As he rubbed his face, he could feel the sweat and dirt ball up under his fingertips. Looking at the grit and then wiping it on his pant leg, Kael knew he had secretly hoped the room would have been empty so as to avoid what was about to follow.

But this wasn't the case and Manus' comment only annoyed and frustrated him so Kael stood and went over to the basin and poured water into it from the pitcher that was on the side of the basin. "If you liked it so much you should have thrown us a couple of crowns." He clipped before cupping water with his hands and splashing his face and hair.

Manus was not used to Kael talking back to him and it only made him angrier. Turning, he walked over to one of the chairs and grabbed it by its back. "Sorry. It's not my job to pay for your tramps."

Kael lowered his head and gripped the side of the counter, letting the water drip off his hair and not caring that it was running down his back. Kael sighed, already feeling defeated. "It was an archery lesson. I told you I was going to show him how to start using a weapon."

Manus snorted. "I didn't know cuddling was part of the training."

Kael grabbed a small towel that was on a hook near the basin and began wiping the back of his neck. "He was shaking. All I did was to help him hold the crossbow a little steadier so he could get a better aim with it."

"He's always shaking." Manus sneered. "He shakes in a faint breeze."

"Enough!" Kael shouted as he tossed the washcloth at the wall behind the basin. He turned to look at Manus, his hands balled into fists. "What is it you want from me?"

"I want you to do your job!" Manus screamed, only wanting to tell Kael that it was him that he wanted. "I want you to do your job and to help me find my brother."

"Fine!" Kael said as he grabbed a towel from a shelf. He needed to escape the room and taking a real shower would be a good excuse. "If you would like, I can find someplace else to sleep. Considering there's now no room to spare, I'm sure Crogan wouldn't mind me using one of the galley tables as a bed."

"I'm sure there's enough room on the floor with Master Keir." Manus sniped. Kael was already heading for the door and Manus watched as his friend's back tensed at his barb. "Damn!" he cursed. "Kael. You know I'm worried about Banning and the dangers he might be in. Give me a break. Please?" Manus pleaded as he tried to place most of the blame for this argument on Kael. "Keep your bed. There's no reason to find another place to sleep."

Kael only nodded as he placed a hand on the door to slide it open.

"Oh, and one more thing." Manus said, halting Kael before he escaped into the Camalain. Kael turned to look at his friend, only to see Manus' face flushed with anger. "Once you've showered, I need you to make rounds with that dolt, Lieutenant Cahl. The less I have to deal with him the better. I'll be on the bridge if you need anything."

Kael let the cutting remark about Cahl Goban wash over him. Manus had always been like this and for once he wondered why he had maintained his friendship with someone who could be so arrogant. "Aye Milord." He said and left the room.

Manus kept his place as Kael left the room. But as soon as the door slid shut he let his anger get the best of him. Not caring who heard him, Manus roared loudly and swept the maps and other items off the table's surface. Forgetting that the table was bolted to the floor he grabbed it by its edge to overturn it, but when it wouldn't budge, Manus pounded the table top with his fists until his rage subsided. Looking at the mess he created, Manus kicked at one of the chairs. He kicked at it one more time for good measure, sending across the room, before stooping to pick up the debris from his outburst.

***

Kael dragged out the tour of the Camalain as best he could. He and Lieutenant Cahl started on the main deck, while avoiding the bridge, and worked their way down to the storage bays. Kael made sure he stopped to chat with most of the men who made up the prince's Royal Guard, taking longer with soldiers that he knew personally.

The lieutenant didn't seem to mind. After his dressing down by Manus in front of his captains, Goban was keeping to himself even more. When Kael tried to make small talk with the lieutenant all he got in return were clipped responses. Maybe the attitude he was receiving was because of his friendship with Manus. He didn't know and he didn't feel like asking. And if it came down to it, Kael didn't feel like he would have the energy for another argument. Whatever the case, the lieutenant was fine having Kael leading them around.

Once they had finished one circuit of the Camalain, Kael and Goban made their way back to the main deck. Kael, not wanting to go back to his quarters, told the lieutenant he would be making another round and that he was welcome to come along. Goban mumbled something about having nothing better to do and followed Kael around the ship for a second time.

Thankfully, by the time their second round was done, it was time for the evening meal. Parting company with the lieutenant, Kael went to his quarters and grabbed his guitar. For the past several days, he and Manus had been having their dinner in their quarters. After which Kael would play several tunes on his guitar while he and Manus would share a bottle of wine or some ale.

But tonight he didn't feel like being the only entertainment for Aerin Manus and he certainly didn't feel like being alone.

***

After Liam had checked in on his father and found that he was sleeping soundly, Liam made his way up to the galley to help Master Yanno with the evening meal. Not waiting to be told what to do, Liam immediately went to busying himself at the stove and took over some of the prep work, leaving Crogan time to set the serving table in the dining hall.

One thing about working in the galley was that Crogan was a man of few words and couldn't be bothered with small talk. So, aside from an eyebrow being raised, nothing was said when Liam made a plate for himself out of the pans on the stove and ate his own dinner at one of the counters while he started to clear the kitchen. After the day he had, Liam was more than willing to hide himself away in the corner of the ship and not be noticed.

Crogan and another crewman the cook had probably recruited from the dining room, returned to the galley with their hands loaded with dirty plates and mugs. Already knowing the routine, Liam had set up the sinks and threw the dishes into the soapy water after scraping off the remains of dinner from them.

Liam was scrubbing away at a skillet when the chatter and raucous laughter died down and the sound of guitar strings being plucked echoed from the dining room. He hesitated for a moment to listen to the song that was being played before he continued with the dish washing. A round of applause filled the room as the song ended only to be followed by another song.

Yanno Crogan, who had been standing in the doorway listening to the music, eventually came over and began putting away the clean dishes Liam had been piling up on the counter, giving Liam a place to put more clean ones. As Liam began washing some mugs and stacking them onto the counter, he realized the songs being played had a sad, almost melancholy sound to them. The strings being plucked only emphasized the loneliness and frustration he felt by being on the Camalain. Sighing, Liam began fishing for utensils at the bottom of the sink.

Just as Liam was finishing with the dirty dishes, Manton and the man who had just been helping Crogan came into the galley with two more armfuls of dishes.

"There you are!" Manton said, smiling broadly. "You been in here all night?"

Liam shrugged as he grabbed the stack of dirty dishes from the man. "I guess so. Why?" he asked as he scraped food into a waste barrel.

"Figured we would have seen you at dinner. This here's Dolan." The other man carrying dishes nodded to Liam as he placed them on the counter. "Gorman and I were wondering where you were."

"Trying to get my work done." Liam replied. Another song began to be played. The sound was just as low and somber as the first two.

"It's nice that he is playing for us, but he's going to have us slashing our wrists at the rate he's strumming those strings." Dolan said to the two men. Crogan, who had been listening to the conversation, grunted in agreement as he continued to put more of the dishes away.

Manton chuckled. "Don't worry Dol, no one will miss you over your demise. So what do you say Liam? Come join us in the other room."

Liam hesitated as he started to wash another plate. He had hoped he could have finished his work in the galley and escape to his room without being noticed. "I still need to finish these." He said to Manton. "And whatever else Master Yanno has for me to do."

"Master Yanno!" Manton and Dolan laughed loudly. "Come on Crogan! Let the boy come hang with us. He can finish these later."

"At least the boy has manners and knows responsibility." Crogan grunted. "Go ahead Liam, I can finish these."

"I don't mind sir. I'm almost done." Liam said, somewhat hoping to get out of joining the men in the dining room.

"Nonsense. Go have some fun. Just try and be here a little earlier tomorrow since we now have more mouths to feed with the added crew."

"Yes sir." Liam said as Manton grabbed him by the arm and steered him towards the dining room. "I'll see you tomorrow."

As they entered the room, Liam noticed that almost all the lanterns had been doused, leaving the room in a dusky glow. The only other light flooding the room came from the hallway, galley and the back wall of the dining room. That wall was all windows with a doorway leading to a balcony. The silhouette of a ballista could be seen mounted to the center of the balcony's deck. The dark shapes of the ships escorting them could just be made out by the light flickering from their windows.

Trying not to trip over anyone in the dim light, Manton guided Liam towards a table near the window. Liam could see Gorman and several other men sitting on the table and the long bench in front of it.

Gorman smiled broadly when he recognized Liam and patted the table on the side of him. The two men sitting on the bench shifted so Liam and Manton could climb up and have a seat. Dolan wandered off to another table where he had friends waiting for him.

"Manton figured you were hiding back there." Gorman whispered into Liam's ear. "Didn't think you would join us."

Liam only shrugged and hunched his shoulders in embarrassment at the truth of the statement.

"Don't worry." Gorman said as he patted Liam's shoulder. "We'll turn you into one of us yet. Oh, and this is my partner Heath." Gorman reached out and ran a hand over the cropped hair of the man sitting closely on the bench in front of him. "Heath. This is Liam, the sagart's son."

The man turned to look up at Liam. He held out a hand and smiled, the skin wrinkling on the bridge of his crooked nose. "Nice to meet you."

"And you." Liam said as he grasped Heath's forearm.

Gorman's hand hadn't left Heath's head and he rubbed the back of it while running his fingers behind partner's left ear. "This one keeps me out of trouble." He said with a wink.

"That's a full time job in itself." Heath replied.

"Shhh!" Someone from the table in front of them had turned, annoyed by their conversation. He bobbed his hand in the air, indicating for them to keep it down before turning to listen to the music.

"Excuse us!" Manton whispered into Liam's other ear, but loud enough for the rest of the table to hear, eliciting a round of snickers from the group.

"I didn't know your friend could play guitar." Gorman said to Liam over the chuckling. Liam didn't know whom Gorman was talking about and looked over to the musician. Karam Kael was seated on another table near the galley wall playing the stringed instrument.

Liam wished he had seen Kael as soon as he had stepped out of the galley because he probably would have turned right around and finished his chores. Now he was stuck in the dining hall for this impromptu get together having to look at the one person he wanted to avoid.

And were they friends? Kael was definitely his superior and the prince's closest friend. Other than that he didn't know.

"He only started talking to me today." Liam gave as an answer.

Gorman only nodded as Kael continued to play the slow steady chords on the guitar. The sound filling the room was soft and fine and had no rhythm, the tune seeming to be only in Kael's head. A wayward melody that one would hear echoing down the street on a foggy evening, giving one to hesitate in the closing of their door to the night as they listened to the romantic sound.

Not wanting to hear something sadly romantic, and more interested in being entertained by a song that was rowdy or bawdry, and certainly not a man who was shy, Manton shouted, "Come on Master Karam! Play something happy!" A plea by the Manton, which was followed by more of his comrades, all of whom wanted Kael to play something more upbeat.

Kael looked over the group while they shouted. The soldiers were right. He knew he was in a funk over his fight with Manus and had let it carry into his music. "My apologies. . ." He began to shout to the crowd, but faltered when he saw Liam sitting near the man who had called out. The room was so dimly lit that he hadn't seen him walk in. Kael swallowed hard before asking for any requests.

Another set of strings filled the air as Kael spoke. For, while he had been playing, another of the men had run off to his room and had grabbed his own mandolin.

"Do you know this one?" The man asked Kael as he played several chords.

Kael and most of the men in the room laughed at the bawdy tune being played. "Who doesn't?" he shouted as he moved over so the man could join him on the table. Soon, the two guitarists and many of the men were singing a barroom favorite about a duke's son and daughter as they competed to woo a farmer's son. Clapping and laughter filled the air at the antics that the story's characters performed.

Even Liam knew the song and found himself laughing and tapping his foot to the tune. Good humored groans and louder laughter came from the table as Manton screeched out the lyrics.

Gorman was also tapping out the beat of the song on Heath's shoulders when he leaned over and asked Liam, "So how was the archery lesson?"

Liam turned beet red at the question. "You saw?"

"No." Gorman said as the ditty ended and another song, just as raunchy as the previous one started up. "But word gets around!"

Manton, who had been listening to the conversation, ran a hand behind Liam's back, took hold of his shoulder and gave him a rough squeeze, a gesture that was noticed by Kael.

"Awww! No more of this moping Keir Liam!" He shouted and shook Liam again, who forced a smile on his lips. "When's the next lesson? Would like to make sure I have good seat for your training!"

"Man', leave the boy alone." Heath said as he looked over at his comrade.

Manton gave Liam another squeeze. "Good ol' Heath to the rescue. Looks like you have a champion to protect you Liam."

"Only from your pawing hands." Heath shot back, getting a round of laughter from the table.

Manton raised his hands into the air. "The gods save me! Liam, I am a man of virtue!"

"We didn't know you knew that word." Gorman said as he too took a jibe at his friend. "But seriously Liam, will Master Karam continue training you with the crossbow?"

Liam shrugged. "I'm not sure. He did say training would be difficult with the glider on deck and that the moving ship might make me nauseous." He shrugged again.

Gorman patted Liam's left knee sympathetically. "Well, Heath and I will take over your training." Gorman's partner smiled and nodded in agreement. "I'll talk to Crogan and make sure you have leave from the galley. And I'll let Prince Aerin know you'll be spending time with us in the bays."

Liam balked at the thought of his name being mentioned to the prince. "I don't want you to go through any trouble."

Gorman smiled. "No. No trouble at all. We just won't be training with a crossbow. Okay?"

"Sure."

"Good." Gorman patted Liam's knee again before letting go of him and wrapping his arms around Heath, pulling his partner into a closer embrace. Heath leaned back and wrapped a hand around one of Gorman's.

Liam watched the couple out of the corner of his eye. Heath, with a soft smile on his lips while Gorman who began tapping a foot to the new tune being played. Manton and the man sitting next to him began singing the chords to the song which seemed to be a marching tune dedicated to Cillach, the god of war. Not knowing the song, Liam tapped out an erratic beat with his own foot.

Liam looked around the room as the singing died down and was replaced by a low throaty hum by the men filling the room. Even Crogan was at the galley entrance, listening to the music as he wiped his hands with a towel. And Liam noticed in the dim light that Heath and Gorman weren't the only couple in the hall.

As the humming switched back to lyrics, Liam glanced over at Kael and immediately caught his eye. How long had Kael been looking at him, he wondered. Did it really matter, he thought as he smiled at Kael, who in turn returned the gesture before following the lead of the musician sitting next to him, who began playing another marching tune.

And for the first time since he left home, Liam began to relax. He realized he was beginning to feel safe among these strangers who had gone out of their way to befriend him. Resting his elbows on his knees and clasping his hands, Liam settled in to enjoy the music.

While the merrymaking continued on in the hall none of these men noticed as the Camalain and its small fleet left the confines of Murra's Maze. Nor did they notice when the Marmairn shuttered its windows, blocking out any light as it and the Camalain turned south, leaving the rest of the Birrnian ships behind.

Chapter 5
Kinsale
The High Sagartta's Quarters

Betrys dreamed.

She dreamt of her records. The blurred faces of newborns and of withered men and women on the verge of death filled her head, when Cavanna began to talk to her. Cavanna had much to say to her this night. And when the goddess stopped with her forebodings, Betrys woke with a start.

The high sagartta rolled onto her back, uncomfortable lying between sheets that had collected her sweat. Her head was pounding as she sat up and looked over at her lover, Salvo Caitlyn. Cait continued to sleep on her side, undisturbed by Betrys' movement.

Betrys threw the damp coverings off of herself as she rose and retrieved her shift from the ottoman that was at the foot of the bed. Pulling it over her shoulders, Betrys walked over to a table that had a pitcher of water and glasses on it and poured herself a drink.

Betrys watched her lover move slightly, disturbed by the sound of the pitcher as she placed it back on the table. But Cait didn't wake, which is what Betrys really wanted. So she set the glass down, loudly, on the table and called out Cait's name as she walked over to a sofa on the far side of the room and sat down.

Cait had heard Betrys moving around the room but had thought it was nothing. Not until she heard the clinking sound of glass on marble and her name being called out did she try to rouse herself from her sleep.

"What? Are you alright?" Caitlyn asked blearily.

"No." Betrys said curtly as she ran a hand through her dark brown hair that was still damp with sweat. "I just had a vision from Cavanna. She is bothered by the future."

"Banning? Is he?" Cait asked concern in her voice as she hurriedly got out of bed and threw on a robe.

Betrys snorted as she picked at some gunk at the corner of her left eye. "No, my youngest is quite alive. Although I feel his death would have uncomplicated matters for me."

Caitlyn frowned as she tightened the belt on her robe and walked over to the table with the pitcher. She picked up the half empty glass Betrys had left behind and drank from it to quench her own thirst. Caitlyn had thought Banning was as important as Manus to Betrys' plans. Maybe if she had given birth to a daughter her mood would have softened somewhat. But she doubted it.

"Why would you say such a thing?" She asked as she filled the glass and walked over to Betrys.

Betrys took the glass from Cait and drank from it. "Manus would be here if Banning were dead." She said matter of factly. "Not flying across the flats putting his life in danger."

"Why? What did Cavanna say?"

"Only that Ciaran and his minions are stalking the flats."

Cait was perplexed. "But you already knew that from Riocard. What did the goddess tell you this time that was different?"

"Nothing!" Betrys snapped. "You know the goddess cannot tell me the future. She only gives me hints of things that might come to pass." Betrys stood and walked over to the window that overlooked the women's section of the city.

"Unfortunately she says Ciaran is out to cause trouble for us all."

Flustered, Betrys walked back over to the bed. Running her hand over the sheets, and feeling that they were damp from her sweat, Betrys began stripping the bed of its coverings. "I need you to take care of some things for me." She said to Cait as the woman came over to help her with the bed.

"Of course. Anything." What was Cait supposed to say to Betrys, the high sagartta for all of Kinsale? When Caitlyn entered into this relationship, she knew it would be a lot of work with a lot of bending over backwards for Betrys. But Betrys kept Caitlyn and the shipping company she owned very busy and very profitable. Thankfully for Solvo Caitlyn marriage had never been a requirement for their liaisons. "What do you need me to do?"

"I need you to make a delivery of supplies to Surdail for me."

"Oh? Tomorrow I was heading out for Ardane with supplies and then on to some ports in Wex. I can shorten my trip and just return after Ardane for you."

Betrys fumed slightly. "Sooner would be much better that later." She growled as she shook a pillow out of its casing. "I would have had Manus go but he is heading south after Banning."

"South?" Cait asked as she picked up the bed sheets from the floor.

Betrys frowned. She hadn't meant for that to slip. Manus would be much safer if few people knew in what direction he was flying. She grabbed the other pillow. "I need you to leave for Surdail in the morning." Betrys said, ignoring Cait's questioning look.

"Very well." Cait replied as she walked over to Betrys and took the pillow cases out of her hands. "I will have to rearrange my delivery schedules but that should not be a problem."

"I do not need to know the details of your business." Betrys said sourly. "Just have your ship ready for my supplies."

"Yes Betrys." Cait said, the dirty sheets bundled in her arms.

Betrys looked at her lover, then at the bare bed. "Do you mind taking care of this?" She said as she waved a hand over the bed. "I need to organize what I will need you to take to my citadel."

"Of course." Cait said as Betrys turned from her and left the room. Cait walked over to the hamper and dumped the dirty sheets into it and grabbed a new set from a closet in Betrys' dressing room.

Cait started to make the bed as she tried to remember the schedules for her vessels that were leaving and coming into port. Hopefully this delivery wouldn't disrupt her routes too much.

In any event the trip would be good money. Caitlyn could rely on Betrys to pay double for getting her supplies to the fortress she had in the mountains. And if Betrys did not make any more requirements of Caitlyn then she could disappear for the next several weeks. A much needed break from her lover and her plotting's.

Cait shook out a sheet and let it flutter over the bed before she began tucking it in. She could take the long way to the kingdom of Wex; stopping at a waypoint in the flats and seeing if there was a caravan heading to the northern kingdom or if someone needed a delivery made. Cait smiled. Either way, she would find a reason to avoid Kinsale for a while.

***

And how would Banning feel if he knew how his mother felt about him?

Banning already knew. For Betrys made no secret of her disdain towards her youngest son. She didn't hide her disappointment in the fact that Banning was much more like his father and nothing like her.

Nor did she hide her own displeasure in giving birth to another son and not having a daughter. And she held onto a long, smoldering anger that neither Riocard nor Fionn were willing to mate with her again.

Banning had known this for a long time but for the moment none of it mattered.

The trip to Shandon Farm had been uneventful where rows upon rows of cliff cacti that had been cultivated to grow in fields full of gravel with their red flowers withering before coming to full bloom because of an insect that had invaded the fields.

Banning, along with Mac and Davis (Lhoyt remained sulking on the skiff) spent the afternoon walking aimlessly around the distillery while Gwyn was holed up in the main house, writing reports to her father. Gwyn was not thrilled she would have to tell her father how the crop had been devastated and that a third of the fields would have to be burned to the ground in order to save the rest of the plants. Gwyn had earlier explained to Banning that it was only the flower that was harvested, not the entire plant and the part of the field being raised wouldn't produce a mature, flowering plant for almost three years which would be a terrible blow to her family's personal finances.

The news was very frustrating to Gwyn. And upon their arrival to Inchinver, she decided to stay for a couple of days instead of leaving immediately for her uncle's home in the Lahunne City States. Gwyn thought it best to have an inventory done of the squilla they had in storage from her family's other farms and to maybe reduce the amount of alcohol being exported. With less squilla on the market her family could slowly raise prices and eventually recoup some of the money that would soon be lost from the meager Shandon crop.

Gwyn had planned on flying to Lahunne with her storage bays half empty. But now she thought it wise to see if she could find someone needing deliveries made along the way. Any extra money she could make would be helpful for the time being.

Banning didn't mind the layover in Inchinver. It would give him time to explore one of the largest bazaars in the world, with his troupe of men. Gwyn, who would not be joining them on their daily excursions, suggested they stick to the upper city and the more extravagant marketplaces on their streets. Though she did want him to explore her city in the hopes he would relax and not feel like he was a prisoner, Gwyn hoped to have Banning stick to the upper levels and avoid bumping into a fellow countryman that might frequent the lower districts and recognize him.

And, even though the ordeal was fresh in his memory, Banning didn't feel like a prisoner of Argus Gwyn. As a matter of fact, Banning was enjoying himself.

The prince of Birr did not have to go far before he was overwhelmed by the sights, smells and sounds by the sprawling markets of Inchinver. Even here, where the upper and middle classes lived, a thriving trade was happening around him. For the entire economy of the city was based on the buying and selling of goods. Whether there were selling product pirated by Lord Argus' henchmen or by legitimate means, money was changing hands.

Almost every building in these neighborhoods was built to be three to four stories high. All of them having some sort of shop on their main floors with the proprietors and their families living above. And unlike the bazaars and guilds of Kinsale, there was no organization to the shops. How could anyone find anything when a wine merchant was next to a blacksmith who was adjacent to a silk dealer who was sharing a wall with someone selling poultry? Every street was like this. The randomness of it all was quite confusing. But there in was the adventure and why so many Gwer came to Inchinver and spent days, if not weeks in this massive emporium.

Thankfully Banning had Lhoyt, Mac and Davis as guides to the city or he would have surely gotten lost as soon as he left the large compound Gwyn's father had in Inchinver. Gwyn was also generous enough to let him to keep her marker allowing him to get meals for himself and Daigh's men while they were out.

But at night the men found themselves having dinner with Gwyn. She knew of some private, out of the way inns in the upper districts so there was no pretense of hiding Banning away in her home from people who might recognize him.

And after a day of wandering, it was this time that Banning found he was enjoying the most. As always, since the first day he had met her, Banning would find himself sitting across from Gwyn, mesmerized by her black hair cascading over her shoulders and her green eyes shining in the lamplight. Gwyn looked completely comfortable, not aloof at all, while she chatted with Mac and Davis about absolutely nothing. Banning joined in on the conversations but mostly he sat there, listening to them and occasionally rewarded with a smile from Gwyn as she tore a hunk from the loaf of warm bread on the table or over a forkful of food.

During the dinner on their second night in Iniscarn, which was at an inn where most of its tables were outside in a plaza of a crowded street, Gwyn announced, "It looks like we'll be ready to leave tomorrow. I thought I should give you fair warning so you could pack."

"Oh. No need." Banning replied as he picked at the roasted fowl on his plate. "I never unpacked my kit so I am ready to go when you are."

Gwyn smiled over her soup. "Then dawn it is."

Banning smiled back at her but became distracted by a man hawking jewelry dangling from his outstretched fingers.

Gwyn turned to see what Banning was looking at on the street. The merchant had found an empty space not far from their table to sell his wares, with light from the streetlamps bouncing off gemstones and metal, as he tried to attract people to what he had for sale.

"See something you fancy?" Gwyn asked Banning. When he shook his head in the negative she continued. "Well, be careful. If that vendor catches your eye, he won't think twice about swooping down on us and stay until one of us buys something from him."

"How about it Lhoyt?" Davis asked of the man sitting across from him. "We can call him over and get something pretty to match your eyes."

Lhoyt ignored the jibe and the snickers from the table and stabbed at the meat on his plate.

But the question from Gwyn and Davis' joking made Banning feel guilty about the items he had bought using Gwyn's money. "I do appreciate the use of your marker. I've tried to keep track of my spending, and I do want you to be compensated. So, when this trip is over, we can agree on a total is so you and your father can be reimbursed for your troubles."

Gwyn waved her spoon in the air. "Think nothing of it."

"No. I insist." Banning said as he picked the meat off of one the bird's wings. "Maybe there is work for me to do on your ship."

Gwyn smiled. "Perhaps."

Lhoyt snorted as he cut into more of his meal. "Been doing dock work, have you Prince Dar?"

"No, Master Ormin. But I'll do what I need to so I can pay my way."

"Well." Gwyn said as she tried to stop Lhoyt's ongoing sour mood from ruining the meal. "You are my guest, but if help is needed I won't hesitate to ask for it."

Banning smiled back at Gwyn. "I am your humble servant. Maybe you will need help with loading supplies onto your ship tomorrow?" Banning said, wanting to prove his sincerity in helping Gwyn and her crew.

Gwyn stared back into Banning's dark brown eyes. The lamplight reflecting off of them so they looked like two chips of polished wood. She twirled her spoon in the remains of her meal. "I would take you up on your offer but the ship is being loaded even as we speak. We five just need to show up and we'll be on our way.

Not wanting to be outdone by the prince, Lhoyt chimed in, "Will you have work for us Mistress, or are we expected to continue as Prince Dar's bodyguard?" Both Mac and Davis frowned and rolled their eyes at Lhoyt's question. The men were becoming quite comfortable acting as Banning's chaperon.

"Commander, I'm sure I can find something for you and your men to do. But for now, enjoy the night." Gwyn looked back at Banning who had yet to look away from her. Gwyn blushed slightly. "I hope you left some room for dessert Prince Banning. They make an excellent cheese pie here."

"I think I did." Banning said as he wiped his hands on his napkin.

"Good." Gwyn hailed one of the wait staff over to the table and ordered caff and slices of caise for each of them. When everyone had a cup in their hands, Gwyn raised hers in a toast. "To tomorrow, and the journey ahead of us." Her words were echoed by a round of tomorrows filling the air.

Unfortunately for Banning, the night slipped by very slowly as he tried to sleep and failing miserably for he was very excited over the new journey before him. When his tossing and turning finally became unbearable Banning rose and went to sit at the room's only window and prayed while he waited for the sun to rise.

At dawn, he wearily made his way to the courtyard and met Daigh's men, who looked just as exhausted as he did, and waited for Gwyn. As soon as she came out to meet them she led everyone to a coach that was waiting to take the group to the ship.

Even Gwyn seemed to be too tired for any type of conversation this morning so Banning gazed out one of the coach's windows as they made their way down the cobbled streets. Banning was surprised to see shops and stalls already opened with their vendors preparing for today's traffic of prospective buyers. And as the streets filled with people looking for an early meal or to begin their shopping, the coach had to slow its progress to the wharves.

But once at the docks, which sprawled across the lower half of the city, the coach quickly made its way to where Gwyn's ship was berthed.

"Welcome to the Kasser." Gwyn said, proudly sweeping a hand at the large vessel across from them as she grabbed her own bags from the pile the coachman was making of their belongings.

Banning was in awe, if not a little frightened of what he was seeing. When Gwyn had mentioned she was a captain of a merchant vessel, he pictured a bulky ship, blockish in nature, specifically designed for hauling all sorts of materials. Not unlike the barge he flew on when he travelled to Ardane.

The Kasser was a large vessel; almost twice as large as the barge he had been on. Its prow was plated in a polished, silver metal and the same material ribbed its sides. Cabins, about three stories high, took up most of the fore and the aft of the main deck, and there was room enough to have two smaller ships moored on it. Below the main deck were two rows of shuttered windows, their design suggesting some form of weapons arsenal hidden behind them.

Men and women were racing back and forth across the Kasser's main deck and on the wharf in front of it, preparing for the vessel to leave. Yes, the Kasser looked like a ship of war that was well maintained by its crew.

"It's not what I had pictured." Banning said with a little trepidation as he picked up his own belongings. Thoughts of waking up in a locked room began to overshadow the past several days.

"Oh." Gwyn said, not too concerned by his comment. "The Kasser used to be my mother's ship. When she was a captain in my father's military. Its looks do give one pause if there was a thought to attack us."

Banning only nodded as Gwyn turned to the woman who had approached them. "Lu! Is the ship ready?"

"Just waiting for your arrival, Captain." The woman named Lucilla replied.

Gwyn introduced Banning to her second in command, Tor Lucilla, and to Ilwin Mac and Clune Davis. Lucilla was already familiar with Daigh's second, Ormin Lhoyt.

"Accommodations have been made for everyone?"

"Just as you requested." Lu responded. "I've shuffled the men around so the prince will have a cabin to himself and Captain Emmis' men will be bunking with ours. I have someone waiting to show them to their quarters."

"Very good." Gwyn said as they began to board the Kasser. "And the new cargo arrived without a problem?"

"Yes Captain. We just finished bolting down the shipment for Rathad about an hour ago."

"Rathad?" Banning inquired.

"Do you know where it is Prince Dar?" Gwyn asked.

"Well, yes. It's a waypoint out in the Airgrid Flats. Almost a day or so out from Birr. I've never been there though."

"A first for everything." Gwyn smiled as they walked towards the cabins. "We might even stay for a day or two and see if we can pick up trade for Lahunne."

"Begging your pardon Captain." Lhoyt interrupted with a frown on his face. "But, do you think that is wise?" Lhoyt's concerns were justified because Rathad was considered part of Birr, with a garrison of the Royal Guard stationed to protect the outpost. "With the prince on board it would be much safer to fly straight to Lahunne."

The question and the questioner annoyed Gwyn but she didn't let it show. "Well, I've already taken full payment in good faith for a prompt delivery of food to Rathad. Banning, you don't mind that I made arrangements to stop there instead of going right to Lahunne?"

"Of course not. Make your deliveries. I wouldn't want your reputation tarnished because of me."

"So we'll keep to the route." Gwyn said as she hiked her pack up on her shoulder. Gwyn turned to her second. "Lu, I'm going to go to my cabin and unpack. I see no reason for you to wait for me so head to the bridge and get us going and I'll meet you there as soon as I can."

"Aye Captain." Lu replied, leaving the group as she made her way to the bridge.

As Gwyn and her little band of men drew near to the rear quarters one of her crewman who had been leaning against the cabin's outer wall approached them.

"Good to see you Lyle."

Lyle gave a quick bow to Gwyn before responding. "It's good to have you back on board. The commander sent me to escort your guests to their quarters."

"Of course." Gwyn's cabin was in the same direction as the cabins that Banning and the others would be staying in so she led the way into the cabin section, acknowledging members of her crew they happened to pass by.

At one of the two main stairwells, Gwyn left the men as she made her way upstairs to her quarters while Lyle took the men down to another level. He first showed Lhoyt, Mac and Davis to a cabin they would be sharing with three other men. Next, he went to the door across from theirs and slid it open.

"Here's your room Prince Dar. I apologize if it's lacking but it was all we could muster up in a pinch."

Banning stepped into the empty crew quarters that contained three bunk beds, one on each wall, with an empty locker at the foot of the bed to Banning's left and a small, worn table had been wedged into one corner of the room.

The room was also windowless and with only the one door, Banning had that claustrophobic thought about being locked up again. He pointed out the lack of scenery to Lyle while he tried to keep the fear out of his voice.

Lyle paled slightly. "Sorry Milord. We were concerned for your safety and thought it wise to put you in an inner cabin. We did put you next to your men in case you needed them. But if it's not to your liking, I'm sure the captain would be fine with moving the steersmen in here for the duration of your stay with us. Their cabin is starboard side with a bank of windows in the outer wall.

"No. this is fine. I wouldn't want to impose on your captain's hospitality."

At that moment the air throbbed softly and within moments the Kasser shifted as it began to rise. Lyle held onto the doorjamb while Banning stumbled slightly before regaining his footing.

"I'm sure it would be no imposition Milord." Lyle reiterated.

They could feel the Kasser turning in midair as the ship began to pick up momentum. Banning found the movement and the lack of windows disconcerting and was starting to reconsider staying in this room.

But Lyle interrupted his thoughts. "You do know this is just a sleeping quarter Milord, and you are not expected to stay in here for the duration of the trip? The commander did assign me to help you while onboard so, if you would like, I could now give you a tour of the ship."

"Thank you Master Lyle." Banning threw his pack on one of the beds as he relaxed a little. "But I think I'll stay in for a bit and try to get some sleep."

"Very good Milord. I am bunked with your men if you need anything."

He then raised his left hand and pointed to some unseen location on the ship. "Or you can find me down the hallway working in the weapon's locker on this level. Anyone can get you there if you can't find the room."

Banning thanked the man again before Lyle bowed slightly and left the room, sliding the door shut behind him. Banning didn't even bother to unpack his belongings as he sat down on one of the beds, pulled off his boots and laid down in his clothes. Exhausted from not sleeping that night, Banning slowly dozed off to the sound of muffled voices filling the hallway and as the Kasser bobbed through the air, winding its way through the congested wharves as it made several more turns to leave Inchinver's enclosed bay.

Banning woke several hours later, feeling somewhat refreshed and decided to take Lyle up on his offer for a tour of the ship. No one was in the quarters across from his when he opened its door so he made his way down the corridor in the direction Lyle had pointed. Lyle had been right when he said it would be easy to find him because Lyle, along with Mac and Davis, were in a large storage room at the end of the corridor, cleaning weapons.

"I see you found work." Banning commented to the men whom he found polishing weapons with Lyle. Mac and Davis set Banning and Lyle to snickering as they sarcastically thanked Lhoyt, who was not there, for having the good sense to keep them busy on their trip to Lahunne. The men continued to disparage their second in command, when Lyle left with Banning to help him get his bearings on the Kasser.

Acting as guide, Lyle escorted Banning down two flights of stairs, stopped on a landing, and pointed down the stairwell, explaining how the two lower levels and most of the floor they were now on were dedicated for cargo and storage. Banning was fine with not being shown the storage bays although he couldn't help but be impressed by the ingenuity behind the overhauling of the Kasser and of its sacrifice as a vessel for war.

Banning was definitely caught off guard when several young children raced by them as the two men made their way back up the stairs, Lyle's shouts to be careful ignored as their laughter and feet pounding on the steps drowned out his voice. As Lyle guided Banning onto the deck below their quarters, he explained how several families were in Gwyn's employment and that their children were welcomed on the voyage, pointing out several cabins where these families lived.

Not only was Lyle acting as tour guide he also made sure he went out of his way to introduce Banning to his crewmates they met in the hallways. Even now Banning was making the acquaintance of several more men and women on their way to the prow of the ship. Banning politely returned greetings to the people he was meeting, knowing full well he was going to be hard pressed to remember half, if any, of their names when he would eventually bump into them later on the journey.

Banning was once again being led up another flight of stairs when Lyle said, "The bridge is located on the top of these stairs and the captain should be there by now."

"Why don't we skip seeing the bridge for now? I'm sure your captain has better things to do than be interrupted by us."

"You sure Milord? I know the captain won't mind if we stop in or a minute."

Banning was quite sure. Because, deep down in his gut, he knew he would like to see Gwyn again, even though they had been together several hours ago, and would hate to become a distraction for her. "Let's save the bridge for another time."

"If you insist." Lyle scratched the back of his head looking up then down the stairwell. "Well, not much else to show you over here but the galley and dining hall. And since it's a couple of levels below the bridge, we'll almost get the same view of the flats."

The mentioning of a kitchen reminded Banning that he hadn't eaten since the previous night and that he had probably slept through a morning meal. "Do you think there is anything to eat?" He asked hopefully.

Lyle frowned. "I doubt if the cooks have anything made but, I'm sure we can scrounge something out of the pantry."

"Then lead the way." Banning smiled, feeling the empty pit in his stomach growing larger and murmuring impatiently, as he realized a quick meal was just around the corner.

None of the cooks were present in the galley so Lyle did some searching for something to eat while Banning nervously stood in the middle of the room, a stranger afraid of being caught in middle of doing something wrong.

But Lyle was quick and once he received Banning's approval of the dried fruit and nuts he had found, led them into the dining hall, where they sat for a moment, vaguely paying attention to the stark vastness of the Ganeamha Flats outside the halls large window.

Banning tried not to linger over his food as his stomach pangs slowly subsided for he was concerned about keeping Lyle too long from his duties and he didn't want to look like he was taking advantage of Gwyn's generosity.

Lyle only brushed Banning's concerns aside, telling Lyle not to worry because Mac and Davis had taken up most of his duties while Lyle was showing him around. Mentioning the Scarnians made Banning feel a little guilty for leaving his companions of the past several days behind to work, so he offered to go back with Lyle and help him and them with whatever they were doing.

"No reason to Milord." Lyle said as he ran a couple of fingers over his lips, wiping away the thin skin of a nut that had stuck to them. "We're just cleaning and double checking our back stock of weapons. You know, it's never safe out on the flats and a second weapon always comes in handy in a fight. And, if we have to, the captain might use the surplus for a quick trade."

"Well, I'm familiar with how to use a whetstone. My foster-father made sure my brother and I could clean and sharpen our own weapons so I don't mind helping you out. That is, if you could use another pair of hands."

Truth be told Banning really didn't want to spend the afternoon alone and the thought of unpacking his belongings or wandering around the Kasser just wasn't appealing to him right now, so he was relieved when Lyle acquiesced and led the way back to the weapons locker. When they arrived at the room they found that Mac and Davis had finished cleaning a handful of swords stored in the room and were now oiling and tightening straps on some small wooden bucklers that had been hanging from some pegs in the room. The two men made room for

Lyle and Banning to work with them. Which wasn't really necessary because the room was large enough to have about a half dozen lockers and drawers for weapons with a counter for Lyle to work at with plenty of room for about another dozen people to stand around while waiting for their acquisitions.

Mac, whose hand was still bandaged, hopped off of the counter where he had been sitting with a wooden shield cradled in his lap. A position he had found convenient to oil its oaken panels, the shield wedged in the crook of his elbow, his wrapped fingers holding it in place, but gestured Banning over, grabbed another buckler that needed some cleaning and handed it to the prince and began explaining what he had been doing. Not wanting to be rude to the man, Banning nodded to Mac's instruction, already understanding the maintenance of the weapon.

The four men spent the next couple of hours oblivious to what was going on in the rest of the ship as Mac and Banning continued to clean and polish more shields while Lyle had Davis help him fix the fletching on some new arrows they had received in last night's delivery of supplies. With three other men helping him with his work, Lyle kept their pace leisurely and the men chatted idly, mostly asking Banning about life in Kinsale, who was all too willing to tell them about the mundane intrigues of the court.

When the men took a break, wiping oil and pitch from their hands with rags that were just as oil stained, Lyle discovered that Banning had come on board with neither weapons nor armor of his own.

"You should have something Milord." Lyle said apologetically, embarrassed he had not noticed the prince lacking any type of armament upon his boarding.

For his part, Banning only shrugged, more concerned about picking at the dirt and oil collecting underneath the fingernails of his right hand with an equally dirty thumbnail on his left hand. "Sorry, I hadn't given it much thought."

"Well, we can remedy that." Lyle said, and then asked Banning what type of weapons experience he had before rummaging through his store of lockers and drawers, equipping Banning with a short sword, dagger and scabbards for the two weapons. Lyle then excused himself from the room, returning with several leather jerkins and some bracers. Once they found a set that fit Banning's chest and wrists properly, Lyle returned the unused items back to their storage, a spare locker housed in his own room, before finding a piece of parchment and logging all the items Banning had been given.

"Usually you would return the weapons once the trip is over, so they are here for the next trip." Lyle explained as he jotted down some notes before turning the parchment around for Banning to sign. "But I'll let the captain know you have them and see what she would like to do."

Davis, who had been tightening the bandages that had loosened on Mac's hand, smiled wickedly and chimed in, "You still have the captain's marker. Why don't you just buy them?"

The gibe, however friendly that it was, did not go over well. Lyle seemed a little confused by the remark whereas Mac frowned when Banning reddened in embarrassment.

"Thank you Lyle." Banning said as he unbuckled the belts holding the sword to his waist. "As soon as we make port, upon our return to Inchinver, I will properly return these back to you."

"Very good, Milord." Lyle said as Banning turned and left the room with his bundle of armor and weapons. Once Banning had his back to them, Mac used his good hand to hit Davis squarely on the chest, who looked affronted by the assault from his partner, wondering what he had done wrong.

Upon entering his room, Banning dropped the weapons and jerkin onto the bed next to his kit and sat on the bed he had slept in earlier that morning. He began to unstrap one of the bracers from his wrist and tossed it onto the bed opposite him, mortified that he did not have his own money and that he was wholly reliant on the generosity of Argus Gwyn. He unstrapped the other bracer, flexing the leather in his hands. The lack of money couldn't be helped, not now anyway, but he wasn't going to be seen as someone taking advantage of the Argus' goodwill.

So, standing and tossing the second bracer after the first, Banning headed back to the storage room to continue with helping the others. The three men had been talking softly but quickly quieted as Banning entered the room. He once again joined Mac at the counter and grabbed one of the rags from the counter and began wadding it into a ball, searching for the cleanest section so he could begin polishing another weapon.

The quiet lasted for another moment before Davis, who looked ill at ease, made a coughing sound, getting everyone's attention. "I'm sorry for the insult sir. I only meant the comment in jest."

Banning forced a smile onto his face, for once feeling like he was back home, at court, playacting the way he did around his mother and the dukes, governors and sagarts who ruled over the districts and provinces of Birr, who came to court to ingratiate themselves with his brother and parents.

"I know Davis. Though I did not expect to be travelling the world without a crown or copper to my name."

"Milord. Don't hesitate to ask for anything you need." Lyle said reassuringly.

"Well, I think I should somehow be paying back my fair share and if it's okay with your captain, I'll see if she won't mind you having an extra pair of hands in here. And Lyle, call me Banning."

"Very good Milor, err, Banning."

Mac had finished cleaning the last of the bucklers and both Lyle and Davis had gotten tired of fletching arrows, so Lyle went back to his room retrieved an armful of jerkins and began to inspect the stitching on them. He stacked most of them on the counter, except for two that he put aside because the padding underneath the hardened leather had come undone in several places. Lyle grabbed a tin of a pungent oily paste and handed it to Mac who, somewhat awkwardly, explained to Banning how they would be wiping the paste on and off the leather vests to prevent them from cracking while Lyle found himself a needle and thread to fix the other two jerkins. The group continued cleaning in silence but, as is the case with men who had become comfortable with each other, resumed talking after a while.

Banning was thankful when Lyle said it was time to pack it up and headed back to their quarters to get ready for dinner. Lyle offered to take him to one of the washrooms on the deck below them so he could get cleaned, but Banning thanked Lyle, saying he wanted to rest for a bit before getting ready and closed the door to his room.

The lack of funds was still bothering Banning while he paced in his room, rubbing at the mixture of grit and oil on the palms of his hands, smearing the dirt into a larger mess. Not wanting to ruin any of the clothing he had purchased with Gwyn's money, he upturned his kit until he found the shirt he had worn on his trip to Ardane and wiped his hands on it. But there wasn't much he could do about his finances at this time. So tossing his ruined shirt on the floor out of frustration Banning grabbed a clean shirt and left his room in search of the washroom.

After washing and dropping off his dirty clothing in his room, Banning made his way to the dining hall. There he found Lyle, Mac and Davis already at a table eating with a group of men and women. Gwyn was sitting at another table, with Lhoyt amongst their number. It seemed that Gwyn was obviously waiting for Banning because she immediately waved him over as soon as she spotted him, having people shuffle on one of the benches to make room for their guest.

Even though Gwyn was their captain and the daughter of their liege lord, there was no formality, nor pretentiousness to the group eating at her table, because not all of them were officers, just men and women who happened to find an empty seat at her table in the crowded room.

Banning once again found having a meal with her quite enjoyable and more than once caught himself staring at Gwyn while she talked to her crew about their families or what type of work needed to be done on the Kasser. Banning couldn't help but smile and felt his face grow warm from blushing when she turned her attention to him.

Unfortunately the meal ended all too quickly for Banning when Gwyn excused herself from the table so that she could finish paperwork and to have an early start in the morning. Banning stayed a little longer chatting with several of the crew at the table and with Lhoyt, who seemed more amiable, no surly frown crossing his face while he talked to the prince. After a while, Banning also left the table, missing the attractive captain of the Kasser, and went back to his quarters to maybe unpack his belongings and sleep.

When Banning awoke the next day he realized he had forgotten to ask Gwyn about doing work on her vessel and, not wanting to be bothersome, got cleaned up, grabbed a quick meal of some dried fruit from the galley and made his way to the storage locker in hopes of finding Lyle there and maybe with some work for him to do.

Lyle was at his post, as were Mac and Davis, but the man in charge of the room frowned when Banning asked if he could be of some help.

"Don't know if I have anything for you to do Milord, err, Banning." Lyle said to the prince. "Just going to fletch more arrows this morning. Not much fun in that."

Davis, who was helping Lyle with the fletching, wholeheartedly agreed with the man, but Mac, who seemed to be leaving the room with a folded paper in his hand said that Banning could help him with the requisition list he had been given. That way the injured man would not have to make as many trips with the supplies he would be retrieving.

"I don't mind helping Mac." Banning said, hoping to have something to do and not have to spend the day alone wondering the hallways of the Kasser.

Not one to turn down the extra help, especially while he was trying to get other work done and organized, Lyle thanked Banning and sent them on their way.

Mac and Banning eventually made several trips to and from the storage bays, carrying wooden boxes back up to the storage lockers where Lyle directed them to a weapons room down the hallway.

"These boxes contain firing mechanisms for our ballistae." Lyle said to the two men. They had finished carrying the boxes up to the room and Lyle had cracked open the lid of one of the boxes and dug through the wood shavings to show them its contents. Lyle gingerly held a gadget made up of gears, screws and springs in the palms of his hand, explaining where and how they needed to be stored. "Let me know when you're done so I can replace the firing mechanism on this one." He said pointing to one of the weapons sitting in the room.

"I can change it for you." Mac said to Lyle before he left the room. "I maintained the ballistae on the Shaefra. So if you have tools that I can use, I can fix this for you."

"What about your hand?"

"Don't worry, Banning can help me and I'll let you know when we're done so you can check our work."

Lyle shrugged, not too worried if he had to fix one weapon. He showed Mac where the tools were kept and left the room.

Although he was nervous about this new job, Banning listened to Mac as he instructed Banning, whose hands were shaking slightly, on how to slacken the weapons bowstring before having him unscrew the firing mechanism so they could separate it from the main body of the weapon. And when Banning was ready, Mac gave him a new, well-oiled trigger to put back into the stock. When Banning had completed that task, Mac set off the release on the weapon, a sharp metallic clicking sound filling the room, so he could see how the springs were working.

"Just wanted to see if everything was screwed in tightly. I'll let Lyle fire it properly later." Mac told Banning as he reset the thick bowstring back into place.

Mac picked up the firing mechanism they had just replaced, turning it with both hands as he inspected it for damage. Though he had tried to be careful while he and Banning were working, Mac's bandaged hand still got dirty so he wasn't bothered as more oil and grit were smeared on it.

"See here." Mac sat down, with his back against the weapon they had just fixed, with the broken mechanism in his left hand, waving it at Banning as a beacon to come join him on the floor. "This spring is busted, torn in two pieces." Mac rolled the amalgamation of iron and brass parts in his left hand while trying to point at the ruined spring with the mass of wrapped fingers on his right, the tips twitching involuntarily underneath the tightly wrapped cloth.

Mac handed the mechanism to Banning while he stretched and grabbed a screwdriver off the floor, and after handing the tool to Banning, Mac guided his hand so he could get at the main screw holding most of the contraption together and in his soft spoken voice explained to Banning what he needed done by having him remove several more screws, then having Banning pull apart the cogs, before he was able to get at the broken spring.

Mac had Banning finish taking apart the rest of the mechanism before laying out all the intact pieces in front of them, placing all the parts into neat little rows. Now strewn out on the floor like that, Banning couldn't comprehend how all those small pieces would fit back together into one working unit.

But Mac didn't seem too concerned about fixing the mechanism. Instead he picked up the largest gear, its teeth coated in grease and handed Banning one of the rags from the ground and explained how to clean it.

"No reason to rush onto another project." Mac added with a smile.

So the two men sat there, quietly, not really worrying about anything, the wind moaning persistently against the shuttered windows as they cleaned and polished the small parts in front of them.

Mac was in the middle of cleaning the threads on a screw, the part grasped in his left hand while he ran his thumbnail into the thread, forcing the dirt out, most of it now embedded underneath said thumbnail when the screw slipped in his grasp. He fumbled with the part before catching it with his right hand and hugging it to his chest. Not wanting to drop the part again, Mac slowly pried the screw from between his right hand and chest with his left hand and rolled the screw in his rag trying to get more of the dirt off of it in a more mundane fashion.

"How did you hurt your hand?" Banning asked the man, realizing that, other than Davis cleaning and rewrapping the wound, no one had mentioned his injury for the entire time he had been with them.

Mac went pale; his fair skin turning a shade whiter, the sunburn on his cheeks and on the bridge of his nose turning a deep red, almost looking bruised as he silently cursed Sioda, the god of guile and treachery, for the bad luck the god had bestowed upon him.

"We had an accident on board the Shaefra when a ballista came loose of its moorings. I was in the way and my hand got pinned between the weapon and the ship's hull. My palm is all stitched up and there are cuts all over my fingers so, the gods willing, I'll still have full use of my hand when it's healed." He said somewhat truthfully to Banning.

"Well, I hope it heals properly." Banning said sympathetically.

"Thank you." Mac was rotating his right hand, looking at it as if he could see through the dirtied bandages at the black stitches now crisscrossing the palm of his hand and the bruises that marked his wrist. He and Davis had become quite friendly with Banning over the past week and Mac couldn't help but feel guilty about the prince's kidnapping. And even though it was his job to raid other vessels, he now regretted the attack on Banning's ship. If only Captain Emmis had left well enough alone, followed the rules and had not taken this Gwer as prisoner and not given a face to their prey.

If only. How Mac wished Davis was working with them right now. His partner was quick witted and had a knack for creating a distraction with his humor and his sometimes nonsensical chatter.

"I should go." Mac finally said when he realized Banning was watching him while he stared at his hand. Mac had been using his wrapped hand as a brace to hold onto objects while he was working and the wrappings on his hand looked to be soaked in oil and the linen was torn in several places. As a matter of fact, the bandages now looked like the rags he and Mac had been using to clean the small parts. "I should have Davis check the stitches and rewrap my hand."

"Oh. If you would like, I could probably help you change them."

"No, thank you though." Mac said as he stood, tossing his rag and the half-finished screw to the floor. "There's a salve that needs to get rubbed into my hand to keep the skin stretched and I'd be more comfortable if Davis took care of it for me."

"Sure, no problem." Banning said, shrugging as he picked at some dirt that seemed to be embedded in a crack in the wooden cog he was working on.

As he was heading towards the door, Mac swept his left hand in the direction of the parts on the floor. "Why don't you keep working on these, put aside the ones you have problems with and I'll get back as soon as I can."

Before Banning could respond, Mac had turned and quickly left the room, unspoken words of good luck left on the prince's lips. Although Banning had found Mac's behavior odd, he just brushed it off as something to do with his status above them.

So Banning continued cleaning the broken down mechanism, finishing the screw Mac had made it half-way through, before wiping grease and dirt off several more parts. Not a long stretch of time went by before Mac and Lyle returned to the room, Mac smiling and waving his right hand with its clean, white linen wrappings, like some prize won from some child's chance game found on the side streets of Kinsale's bazaar.

"It's wrapped differently." Banning said to Mac when he noticed the man's index and middle finger wrapped together but separate from his ring finger and pinky, which were similarly wrapped together. Mac's thumb was free of any covering and Banning could see how his thumbnail was cracked and that it had been blackened by blood from the accident that had damaged his hand.

Mac's grin broadened, lips stretched widely with his teeth clenched tightly in exaggerated happiness, while he wiggled his hand again, a three fingered monstrosity, wrapped in an odd white glove.

"Should be easier to work now." Mac explained to Banning, happy to have had a break from Banning's questions. "Most of the redness and swelling is gone and Davis thinks the ships cook might be able to remove the stitches soon."

Banning nodded approvingly, but grimaced slightly at the thought of not having a physician on the ship, though it was quite common for the cooks to take over the duties of doctoring its crew. Whether the cook was going to dress food or dress a wound, it could all be done in the same place.

"So how did you make out on your own?" Lyle said, interrupting the two men as he squatted to inspect Banning's work.

"Almost finished." Banning replied as he and Mac joined Lyle on the floor. Banning picked up another dirtied gear and began wiping it down with his rag.

While Banning continued with the cleaning, Mac handed Lyle the broken spring, who pocketed it to later toss it in a scrap bin of material that would be sold to a smelter on their return home. Lyle then picked up some of the cleaned parts and showed Mac a shelf with wooden boxes on it, containing gears, screws, all sorted by type and size, that Lyle used as back up parts when needed. Sorting them was self-explanatory so, while Lyle went to help Banning clean the rest of the parts, Mac stored the parts they cleaned, a chore which also avoided getting his new bandages dirty.

"Well, I think we can be done for the day." Lyle stood with the last gear, its brass all shiny from being polished and stashed it in a box while Banning was helping Mac with cleaning the room and putting away the tools they had used.

"Don't you have more work to do?" Banning asked.

Lyle shrugged. "Of course. But at the rate we're going we'll soon need to ask the second for more work to take on. No, take the rest of the day off."

"Wouldn't mind lying down for a spell." Mac said, stretching his arms over his head and arching his back as he tried to loosen the muscles that had tightened up in his lower back. Mac was still feeling remorseful over the reminder of Banning's kidnapping and wanted to avoid the prince for a while. "Go explore the ship Banning; get your bearings. You can always visit Davis who went down to go work in the lower storage bays."

"Maybe I'll do that." Banning said as he and the others left the room.

But before Banning could get away, Lyle took a couple of quick steps to catch up to the prince and placed a hand on his shoulder. "I almost forgot, the captain sent word that you would be having dinner in her quarters. Said she would send someone for you around six bells to get you." Lyle gave him another quick pat on the back and turned around to catch up with Mac who was heading in the opposite direction.

It was just past noon and Banning was feeling hungry so, after going to the washroom to get cleaned, he made his way over to the galley where two cooks were preparing food for the evening meal, grateful at receiving the heels from a loaf of dark bread and some salted meat from them, and headed into the dining hall to eat his meal. Several other men and women were spending time in the room, either eating or using the room to relax, and greeted the prince warmly as he passed by them and took a seat near the window.

Of course there was not much to see. The ship was flying out in the open desert, no land masses on the horizon with the sun brilliantly reflecting off the desert's floor. With no points of reference to go by, Banning wouldn't even know if or when they passed from the Ganeamha to the Airgrid Flats until they reached Rathad.

Once he was done, Banning took Mac's advice and wandered around the Shaefra, eventually making his way down to the storage bays in search of Davis. Mac's partner wasn't hard to find because he was right where Mac said he would be; on the lowest level of the ship, in the largest of the storage rooms, working with a half-dozen other men. With the exception of their overseer, a woman, who was reading labels off of crates and jotting notes on a manifest in her hands, all the men were shirtless, sweating from exertion as they moved crates and barrels across or out of the storage bay. Davis, who was helping another man carry a large crate across the room, noticed Banning and nodded to the young man.

"They're keeping me busy down here." Davis huffed when he walked over to Banning. Davis and the other man had lifted the crate onto several others and Davis was using Banning's arrival as a reprieve from the work he was doing. Davis' tanned olive skin was glistening with perspiration and his stomach tightened several times as he tried to catch his breath. He had a rag wrapped around the top of his head, to keep the sweat from dripping into his eyes, and he took that off to wipe down his face and shoulders.

"Master Clune!" Davis and Banning turned to look at his boss, at least for this afternoon. The woman had rolled the sheets of parchment that made up the manifest, into a hollow baton that she was tapping against her thigh. "These crates aren't going to move on their own. So if your friend isn't here to work he can visit with you during your break at the next bell."

"Sorry." Banning said in a hushed voice to Davis, who only shrugged casually, before he rewrapped and knotted the rag around his head and walked over to the man he had been helping, who was already standing near another large crate, grateful that he too had a slight break.

Banning had to quickly move out of the way as several men carrying smaller boxes in their hands tried to walk by him as they left the room, taking their burdens to other facilities within the Kasser. Not wanting to be in the way or to become an annoyance, Banning left the entrance to the storage bay and headed back to his room.

There in his quarters the wind was only a soft dull moan as the Kasser flew through the air on its way to Rathad. Banning found the time begin to drag as he waited for six o'clock to roll along. Once he had laid out the clothing he had decided to wear for dinner, Banning decided to rest, hoping to fall asleep, which is exactly what happened, Banning only waking when he heard the knocking on his door.

After giving his apologies to the woman waiting for him outside the door, Banning quickly changed his clothing, dragged his hands through his blondish brown hair, hoping that he looked presentable, for he had no mirror in the room to look at himself in, and left the room to follow the crewman to Gwyn's cabin.

Upon reaching Gwyn's quarters Banning's guide knocked on her door and, not waiting for a response, slid the door open for Banning to enter. Gwyn, who was standing at a table in the middle of the room, greeted him with a smile. A smile that was readily returned by Banning who took several steps into the room so he could admire Gwyn's beauty.

For this evening, Gwyn was wearing a bustier of a brocaded paisley done in shades of a dark blue and stitched with a gold thread pattern swirling around her slender torso; an article of clothing she seemed to wear whenever she was around Banning. The dark gold buttons, that started just below the dark fabric covering most of her shapely body, trailed down to her waist where Gwyn had left two of them undone, leaving the flesh above her belted, midnight blue trousers, somewhat exposed when Gwyn moved slightly. The only adornment Gwyn wore was her black hair that had been combed out and oiled for it glistened in the lamplight as it draped over her bare shoulders while leaving the tanned skin of her neck exposed.

Then again, a woman such as Argus Gwyn didn't need jewels when her green eyes glistened like two pieces of polished jade.

Banning had forgotten how attractive he had found Argus Berach's daughter and could feel himself growing flush, his palms becoming clammy, and his throat dry by being in her presence. But these things could not be helped when one was in the company of such an enticing woman.

Gwyn's smile also broadened, her cheeks becoming rosy, as she tilted her head to one side, while rubbing the palms of her hands on the thighs of her dark trousers, for Banning's intense gaze could not go unnoticed. "Thank you, Meryl, you may go now."

Banning, who had forgotten that someone was standing behind him, looked over his shoulder to see the woman nod, before closing the door, leaving the two of them alone in the room.

"Uhmm." Banning coughed to clear his throat. "Will anyone else be joining us?"

Gwyn laughed. A sound that did not seem to fit the captain's short lithe frame because it was hearty and strong and full of warmth and was more suited for a bar room with friends. "Not unless they wish to sit on the floor." She chuckled again as she went over to Banning and took him by the elbow, escorting him to one of the two chairs at the table.

Although they were seated in the middle of the room, Banning had a clear view of the night sky from his seat, all blue back, sprinkled with stars, like diamonds on a dark blanket. And when she sat down, the starkness behind her accentuated her beauty even more.

"Some wine?" Gwyn asked as she reached over to a cart that was off to one side of the table and lifted a glass carafe and poured some of the drink into a silver cup in front of him.

"Thank you." Banning replied while Gwyn poured some wine for herself.

When both glasses were filled, Gwyn placed the carafe to one side of their table and began to remove lids off of several bowls that were still on the cart.

"Smells good." Banning said in appreciation of the spices wafting through the air.

Gwyn, a large spoon in her hand pointed at the contents in the silver and enameled bowls. "We have a long grain, brown rice. This is a stew of wild gabhar and vegetables and we have brown bread. Fresh out of the oven of course."

"You shouldn't have gone to all this trouble." Banning said as Gwyn picked up the bowl in front of him.

"Same meal that the rest of the crew is eating tonight." Gwyn smiled as she ladled a large clump of the sticky rice into his bowl and then ladled some stew over that. "Might even be dinner for tomorrow.

The only thing fancy are the bowls it's in." Gwyn picked up the bread and tore a hunk for herself before handing the loaf to Banning for him to do the same.

They both sat in silence for a while, this being the first full meal Gwyn had since the night before, and she was much hungrier for food than conversation at the moment. This gave Banning a minute to look around her room where he noticed a large sofa sat in front of the window, a unit of shelves and cubby holes stocked with books and various sundries, a bed over to his left, somewhat neatened with a large chest at its foot with clothing draped over it and a pile of tubes and parchments over to one corner piled unceremoniously in one heap.

"Sorry." Gwyn said between mouthfuls of food at Banning's perusal of her quarters. "I pretty much sleep here and the maps and paperwork usually live on this table but had to go somewhere for us to eat." Gwyn shrugged, not too concerned about the mess, as she dipped some bread into her stew before eating it.

"No need to apologize." Banning replied, savoring the spiciness of the stew. "I haven't unpacked myself."

Gwyn nodded while she swallowed the bread in her mouth. "Heard you've been working with Lyle and Daigh's crewman in the weapons locker." She pointed her spoon at Banning's left hand which he had been resting on the table. "And it looks like he's been working you hard too."

Banning squeezed his hand into a fist, hiding the cracked and oil stained fingernails that, try as he might, he couldn't get cleaned. Even his signet ring that bonded him to the clan of his foster- father, Aerin Riocard, had dirt embedded within its carvings. Banning frowned. "Sorry. I did try to get them clean."

Gwyn placed her spoon down and reached over and grasped his left hand, and slowly opened it, running her fingers over his once manicured hand.

"Don't worry, we'll make a Scarnian out of you yet." Gwyn said as a devilish laugh escaped her lips. "With three pairs of hands, Lyle should be able to handle the extra work I'll be sending his way."

"I did not mean to be a burden to him." Banning said as he reluctantly pulled his hand out of Gwyn's grasp. "If there is some other work you can find for me, then I'll gladly do that for you."

Gwyn laughed even harder at the look of dismay on Banning's face, as she waved a hand in the air to hush the prince. "It won't be much more work than you already have. Besides, it was nice of Lyle to take the three of you under his wing. And I now know where you are if I ever have a need of you."

Banning spooned another scoop of rice and stew into his mouth, flustered over the fact that he had turned red in embarrassment from her remark.

But after regaining his composure Banning asked after the whereabouts of Lhoyt, finding out that the man was working with Gwyn's second, Lucilla, and had been given charge of maintaining the storage bays, leaving time for Lucilla to spend with her mate and child that were also onboard the Kasser.

Talk then turned to their travel time with Gwyn explaining how they were another three to four days out from the waypoint and their first delivery, informing Banning that she wanted to stay in Rathad for a couple of days to try and pick up some deliveries that could be taken south.

"I'm in no rush." Banning said around another mouthful of stew. Knowing that his own family would be worried about him, even though Emmis Daigh had gone to reassure his family about his well- being, Banning found himself enjoying his liberty and the thought of going home sat in his stomach like a heavy rock. "We can stay longer in Rathad if it will help you to find work."

"We'll see." Gwyn had picked up her cup of wine to take a drink and found herself watching Banning over the rim of her cup, who was scraping the inside of his bowl with his spoon. He looked up at her and then looked down again, his lips moving from left to right as if he was rolling something in his mouth.

"What?" Gwyn asked, noticing he seemed to be frustrated over something.

Banning poked his spoon into the remains of his meal before responding. "Well, I don't, I. Could you ask your crew to forget about my title and to either call me by my clan or my proper name?"

Gwyn placed her cup down, a little taken aback by the request. "Don't feel like being a prince anymore?"

"No. At least, not for this trip."

Gwyn smiled warmly at him, charmed by his awkwardness over the question and his sincerity. "I'll pass the word that the prince of Birr has left the Kasser and that we have taken on Master Dar Banning in his stead."

Banning chuckled at Gwyn's jest as the two continued to eat, Banning accepting Gwyn's offer of more rice and stew. Banning plied Gwyn with more questions as they ate, wondering how large of a crew she had and what type of cargo she was carrying with Gwyn answering readily and honestly to her charming companion.

And as dinner waned and bowls were pushed away as appetites were satiated, Gwyn asked Banning if he knew how to play tables.

Banning smiled. "Among other games. Mac and Davis can tell you how badly I lost to them at Forte Five. Although I can hold my own at King's Men." Banning knew he was starting to babble, but he was now happy to have a reason not to leave.

"Unfortunately I don't have a set for King's Men. Too many pieces. But I do have a deck or two of cards and a set of Tables lying around." Gwyn had refilled their cups of wine and picking them up walked over to the sofa near the window. Placing the cups on the floor, there being no tables nearby, Gwyn patted one of the cushions for Banning to have a seat while she picked up a large, flat, dark stained wooden board, from the side of the sofa, then walked over to her stack of shelves and pulled a long cylindrical tube out of a wooden box that was bolted to the shelving and walked back over to the sofa to take a seat opposite of Banning.

As Gwyn unscrewed one end of the cylinder, Banning noticed the intricate detailing on the objects rounded side. Small images of figures, all paired off, were seated and hunched over small tables between them. Usually such icons were of the gods, playing games at their leisure and these were painted intricately in colored enamels on the brass tube.

Gwyn upended the tube and a rolled cloth about arm's length slipped out. She handed this to Banning while she unscrewed the center of the tube and carefully let fifteen grey and fifteen red checkers, along with two ivory dice, slide out onto the sofa.

And while she sorted the playing pieces into two piles of color, Gwyn asked Banning to unwrap the cloth onto the board she had placed between them. The cloth turned out to be the playing board, intricately woven with two rows of twelve elongated triangles in alternating colors of black and greenish silver. And instead of the traditional "bar" in the center of the board, a circular symbol representing Dubhas, the god of death, had been woven into the center of the cloth, the home for all "hit" pieces during play. Capping off the point of play were symbols of Aodhagan, the sun god, creator of worlds, woven too in black and greenish silver which were the homes for the checkers as they left the board.

Gwyn kept the enameled red checkers in her lap and handed the dark grey checkers to Banning. They seemed heavy for their size and when he held one in each hand, he felt a faint vibration run through his body.

"Are these lodestones?" He asked.

"A gift from my mother." Gwyn smiled mischievously at the secret, which really wasn't one. "All thirty pieces are lodestones. My checkers have been painted in red. The stones are not much use without wood to bind them to use for flight but we have them in a pinch."

Banning could only nod in appreciation as he set up his pieces on the elaborate and extravagant board.

Gwyn showed her expertise, and luck with the dice, when she landed on several of Banning's single pieces and placed them on Dubhas' symbol in the center of the board. Banning quickly got two of his checkers back into play but struggled with the third one because Gwyn had most of her home points doubled, leaving no way for Banning to get off the bar. Needless to say the first game ended quickly as it went to Gwyn.

As they were setting the board for a second game, Banning commented, "It looks like a lot of your people still follow the old ways."

"The old ways?" Gwyn knew what Banning was talking about but decided to play coy as she handed the dice to him. Since she had won the first game, he would start off the second.

"It just seems like a lot men and women are following the old teachings of Cavanna, from before The Great Rift, and seem to be married."

Gwyn took her turn, rolling the dice and moved one checker twice, leaving only one checker open to Banning's two.

"It's why my great grandfather and his followers left mainland Birr in the first place. To continue to follow the old ways."

"But it was Cavanna who brought change so there would be a stronger peace for us all." Banning rebutted.

"True. But Cavanna never said we couldn't follow the old ways. And when we get to Lahunne you'll see teachings still in practice that are much older than the ones we use. Besides, if Cavanna was displeased with us and how we worshipped her, would she not wipe us from the land?"

"I would not want that." Banning said as he took his turn, not paying attention what he just cast as continued to looking into Gwyn's eyes.

Gwyn couldn't help but blush at the compliment before pointing out that Banning had rolled double fours and suggested that he move his pieces.

"What? Oh!"

"So your family would not allow you to marry a woman?" Gwyn asked while Banning moved checkers for his two extra turns.

Banning laughed sarcastically at the comment while Gwyn took her turn. "Not likely. On my return home I am to travel to Tuame where its lord has three sons that are all of marrying. And there are plenty of governors in Birr who would gladly see a joining between me and one of their own sons."

"No, my life has been planned for me exactly the way my father's life was planned for him." Banning smirked. "So you can understand why I am in no rush to get home. And it would be a boon to me if you took your time getting me back to Kinsale."

As Banning picked up the dice, Gwyn grasped his hand, squeezing the dice into his palm. "I think that can be arranged."

Banning could not only feel but heard the blood pumping, no racing, through his body. He felt himself grow warm with the dice in his hand become moist as his own hands became clammy, all elicited from Gwyn's touch. Banning shifted uncomfortably in his seat which sent the wooden board, with the game on it, sliding towards the floor with both participants letting go of each other so they could stop the landslide of playing pieces. The board was saved but most of the checkers shifted and since neither of the two had been paying attention to their locations, called the second game a draw.

"I take it your mother lives with your father?" Banning asked, hoping to change the subject while they set the board for a third game.

"She did." Gwyn said as she set her pieces on the board while not bothering to look at Banning. "My mother died almost four years ago."

Banning looked over at Gwyn who continued to set her checkers, her hand trembling slightly and her lips pursed into a tight, thin line.

"I'm sorry. Do you mind me asking how it happened?"

Gwyn did mind. Although a good deal of time had passed, there were days, moments, when her mother's death felt like it had just happened. A brutal death she hated to be reminded of and for some reason, Banning asking the question made it feel like a fresh wound all over again. Sighing softly, a sound full of pain, regret, loss, Gwyn somberly answered the question.

"A portion of our docks in Maum extend into some large underground caverns that we have used to protect our fleets from the storms that travel across the desert. Well, we had a ceiling collapse in one of the secondary caverns." Gwyn stopped and swallowed hard for a moment, fighting back tears at the memory of the disaster. "We lost my mother and over a hundred men and women who were out in the open when the ceiling feel on them. It took us weeks to clean out the debris and find all of our dead."

Banning didn't know what to say except to apologize for a second time, wishing to only reach across and pull Gwyn into an embrace and comfort her. An act of affection that would have been highly inappropriate for the amount of time they had known each other and for their status within their families.

"At least I got the Kasser." Gwyn shrugged and laughed a sound that came out flat and stilted.

Not knowing what to say and feeling like he should not be here to watch Gwyn's grief, Banning offered to leave so that she could be alone.

"No, don't go!" Gwyn said a little too sharply, as she laid a hand on Banning's thigh so he wouldn't rise. "I don't really feel like being alone." She whispered.

"As you wish M'lady." Banning said as he forced a smile onto his face and, trying to lighten the mood, he added, "Besides, I don't have far to walk home."

Gwyn relaxed a little and leaned into the corner of the sofa, resting her head onto its back. "You can go first this time."

"Right." Banning rolled the dice and cursed at the ill numbered cast, a one and two. "Here we go again."

Gwyn watched Banning with his mock frustration and smiled as she rolled the dice, happy for the company and the handsome distraction that was in the room.

***

The rest of the trip across the flats proved to be uneventful as they made their way to Rathad. Gwyn had asked her steersmen to take their time, no need to hurry she said, and the flight lasted almost six days instead of the four that it normally could have taken to reach the waypoint.

Banning continued to work for Lyle, alongside Mac and Davis, sometimes in the weapons armory down the hallway from their sleeping quarters or they ended up in some other section of the Kasser where some weapon or other part of the ship needed to be serviced. And with the help of Davis, who had the use of both his hands, Banning even learned how to build a fully functional firing mechanism for one of the large ballista on the Kasser out of the spare parts Lyle kept in his little wooden boxes scattered in his workrooms.

And with the slowing of the Kasser's flight a relaxed atmosphere filled the vessel while Gwyn, with the help of Lucilla and Lhoyt who continued to maintain order and an ever watchful eye on the horizon, the crew couldn't help but enjoy this trip, a rarity on any merchant vessel and one luxury the crew knew they shouldn't get used to.

Unfortunately for Banning, one of the indulgences he would have liked to have enjoyed more of was dinner alone with Gwyn. Even with talk turning to the passing of Gwyn's mother, that one night had been pleasurable and the prince of Birr had hoped for more nights like it. Instead he and Gwyn shared their meals in the dining hall with the rest of her crew, sometimes together, sometimes not, but always casting glances in the others' direction, hoping to catch their eye. What Banning didn't realize was that Gwyn would have liked her dinners alone with him too, but it was an indulgence she was just not ready to give in to.

And Banning, who was starting to appreciate his freedom on the Kasser, would have liked the days on the ship to roll on as they were; days with no stress or demands, with the Kasser only stopping in a port if or when supplies were needed, a small little world where Banning would be considered just as unimportant as the next person and where he could live his life in peace and not worry about duty to family.

But his reverie, if you could call daydreaming while fletching arrows that, was broken one day by the shouts of Lucilla's ten year old son, Micah, as he entered the locker room where Banning was working.

"Master B! We're here! We're here!" The child shouted exuberantly while dancing on his toes, his hands raised in the air, small fingers clutching at nothing, eyes sparkling with the news he brought to Banning.

"We're where?" Banning asked Micah, already knowing there was only place that they had to be.

"Rathad!" Micah tensed his body for a moment and a shocked look crossed his face at the sound of his own high pitched voice bouncing around the room.

"The captain and momma said you should come and see." Micah explained a little more quietly.

Banning chuckled at the child's excitement as he placed the unfinished arrow on the table. As he stood, he blew out the candle underneath the pitch pot he was using, allowing the tar within to cool and replaced the lid on the pot. Banning poked at his fingers for a moment for even though he had used a thin blade to lay the sticky substance, Banning couldn't help but have hardened tar covering his fingertips.

"Let me go clean and I'll be right there." Banning explained as he displayed is tacky fingers to Micah.

"No, you must come now! Now!" Micah shouted with only the urgency that a child could find in something mundane as flying into port. Micah reached up and tugged at one of Banning's forearms. "Please."

Banning was not so old to have forgotten the small pleasures found in the least significant of things and allowed the child's enthusiasm to overtake him. "Well then, Master Micah, do your job and lead on!

Micah willingly led the way to the bridge, flitting around Banning, like a puppy excited to be with its master, while he chattered almost incoherently about the things he had seen on previous trips to Rathad. Of course these adventures weren't many and anything perceived as exotic might have seemed mundane to an adult because Micah's parents never took him past Rathad's market district into the upper parts of the city; if he got off the ship at all.

Throughout all of Micah's animated discourse, Banning smiled and nodded, adding an ooh and an ahh or an "how exciting" as he tried to make some understanding of the child's babble, all the while attempting to remove more of the crusted tar from his fingers.

But as soon as they entered the bridge Banning couldn't help but stop and stare and finally understood some of Micah's excitement as Rathad slowly grew larger in front of them.

Now that his job was done Micah quickly forgot about his charge and ran over to stand by his mother to watch their approach to the waypoint while Gwyn walked over to stand at Banning's side.

"Impressive?" Gwyn asked Banning

The prince only nodded before explaining to her that he had known of Rathad, it being under the jurisdiction of Birr, though he had never been to the city, as it was isolated in the middle of the Airgrid Flats.

As they made their approach to the city, Gwyn pointed out how Rathad was built upon several enormous stone spires, reaching into the sky, and how at one time only the top of the furthest spike of rock could be seen above the ocean that had once covered this area and how even then sailors used it as a place to anchor their ships on their journeys between the smaller kingdoms that once made up Birr and the nations of Wex.

Gwyn continued to describe how, by the grace of Murra, several wells of water had been discovered in these towering rocks, allowing Rathad's first settlers to survive out in the middle of nowhere. But as the waypoint grew, water would eventually be shipped in from Birr and stored in aquifers to help maintain the population, its merchants and the military who continued to use Rathad as a stopping off point during their journeys across the northern hemisphere.

"Do you know who founded Rathad?" Gwyn asked Banning who only shook his head in the negative even though the prince knew the history of Rathad for he had been educated in Birr's history of expansion. Banning chose to feign this ignorance because he was enjoying listening to the sound of Gwyn's voice and felt no need to stop her.

"Well," Gwyn continued. "Rathad was founded by an offshoot of followers worshipping Cillach, the god of war. All of them being women who wanted to live without any male influences, with the exception being Cillach of course, and to raise their daughters in the warrior ways. The Rathadians did not want to displease Cavanna either so, in the beginning, they either went to the mainland to mate or they brought men here for that purpose. So, aside from the larger temple to Cillach that had been originally built, the Rathadians built two smaller temples. One temple to Cillach which was for the growing male population and the other was built for Cavanna to help record the births and legitimate fathers of the children born to these warrior women."

"A whole city ruled by women." Banning replied as the docks and wharves that branched out across the desert like veins on the skin of a giant as Rathad came into view. "I think it's more unusual than impressive, although these women do make up most of the Royal Guard for the garrisons in this area."

"I guess. But Rathad is not as unusual as a kingdom where men and women still marry." Gwyn said teasingly. "And this town is very similar to Lahunne. Although they're not as refined as the Lahunnans."

Banning shrugged. He was only vaguely familiar with the Lahunne City Sates because there wasn't any prospect of him being paired with a prince from that area of the world. He did ask Gwyn where they were going as her steersman continued by several empty spots at the docks they were passing.

"My kingdom rents a stretch of dock on the far side if Rathad." Gwyn replied as she watched two skiffs with markings of the Royal Guard on their hulls fly by them on their starboard side. "And we'll be much closer to the town than these docks are."

But their conversation was interrupted by Micah who had turned towards them while bouncing on the toes of his feet and pointing out the window. "Master Banning! Look, look! The bridges!"

Now Banning had to admit being impressed at the sight he saw spreading out before him as the Kasser flew around the base of the first large monolithic spire and the space between the three columns came into view. A space filled with bridges.

In its early years, what had started off as aqueducts and walkways to get water and people around Rathad soon became, with the ingenuity of its people, the foundations for a city. For as Rathad grew from a village of Gwer huddled in caves or tents and into a proper city, it was decided to construct buildings on these causeways with more stone bridges and walkways stacked on top of those structures for more buildings. All of which soon went off at odd directions from the ones they were built on with some of these new paths trailing off to or becoming some of the docks they were now passing.

"You should see it at night from above." Gwyn said to the gaping Banning, who was still looking in awe at the stacked structures that rose about a quarter of the way up and across the three mountains. "The bridges are wide enough for homes and shops to have been built across the expanse of them. So wide that they left room for carts and people to get by and you soon forget that you are out in the middle of nowhere. The whole of the lower levels are riddled with shops and taverns where you can spend days looking at Rathad's wares. They come close to the variety in Inchinver's bazaars, but not too close.

Since most of the city was one big market, Banning could understand why Micah never made it out of Rathad's market district, when he felt fingers gingerly pressing into the side of his waist. He looked at Gwyn who was blushing slightly at wrapping an arm around him. Her embarrassment though didn't stop her from pulling him a little closer and pointing at Rathad's peaks with her free hand. "Most of the elite and the ruling clans live in the upper levels on the spires. Our first delivery will be going to someone who lives on the peak we just passed."

"Will we be going up there today?" Banning asked. Resisting the urge to place his own arm around Gwyn's waist, Banning remained where he was, leaving his arm dangling by his side, only allowing his body to slightly rest against hers.

"Probably not." Gwyn had started to gently rub Banning's side as she explained they were coming into port late in the day and that she would be first sending a messenger to let her contact here know of their arrival.

"Lu, does it look like the inner gates are open?" Gwyn asked her commander.

"Seems so Captain." Her second answered, a faint smile on her face, as she caught a glimpse of Gwyn's and Banning's interaction.

"Then let's give our guest a tour of Rathad he'll never forget."

Immediately Micah started clapping, his hands never really touching, only moving back and forth, while he bounced on his heals again, eliciting chuckles from some of the bridges crew at the child's exuberance. Lucilla laid a hand on Micah's shoulder to quiet her son before ordering the steersman to turn the Kasser and fly towards Rathad. Lu then ordered one of the lookouts to grab a lantern.

"Where are we going?" Banning asked as the Kasser made its way down a wide aisle between the docks.

"You'll see." Gwyn said as she removed her hand from Banning's waist. "The way will be slow going but well worth the view."

Banning only nodded as the Kasser approached one of the large bridges that traversed the landscape. Most of the arches of this bridge had been filled in, either with stonework for walls or what looked like buildings that might be warehouses and or fortifications. The exception to this construction was the arch they were heading for which seemed to have gates attached to it. And as they approached the gate, a series of flashing lights appeared from a large window above it. The code were signals used by the Royal Guard, which Banning understood, and knew that whoever was using the light was asking who they were.

Of course, Gwyn had been trained to use the code of the Royal Guards and immediately, yet casually, ordered her man to respond who they were, that she was onboard and that they wanted to cross the Bowl to get to their dock near the southern gate. And as the Kasser slowed, a response in the affirmative came flashing back.

Lucilla wasted no time in giving several orders to the Kasser's steersman, which were to pick up speed and to fly under the arch. Lucilla also gave her son permission to go find his father, who was probably working out in the open on the main deck, so that the child could have a better view of Rathad as they entered the city.

"Shall we join him?" Gwyn asked Banning as Micah raced by them and left the bridge to make his way to the main deck.

"No." Banning said as the bridge darkened, the only light coming from the open lantern the crewman at the window was holding and the opposite end of the tunnel they were now in. "Don't want to miss any of it."

Gwyn knew that Banning could get a better view if he wasn't standing in the middle of the bridge so she grasped a couple of his fingers. "Come." She said as she began walking towards the window at the front of the bridge.

Banning all too willingly allowed Gwyn to be led him by the hand, only sorry that she let go of him when they reached the window. Gwyn's crewman, who was standing at the window, nodded politely to them as he moved over so they could have more room to look out of it, shuttering the lantern so it would not be a distraction from the view outside.

Banning watched as they left the arched tunnel, a gasp of surprise escaping his lips as they flew into a large, almost round open space that was completely surrounded by Rathad. Although the sandy plain was flat, with the occasional splinter of rock breaking the surface, it had been nicknamed the Bowl by the Rathadians because of its likeness to said piece of dinnerware as the city swooped upwards around the enormously large flat plain.

Lucilla ordered the ship to be slowed as it made its way across the plain so Banning, who almost had his face plastered against the leaded glass of the main window, could examine the city.

On the inside of Rathad the bridges seemed to be much more orderly, staggering back towards the outer walls as they rose up into the air. Stone walls wrapped sporadically around the bases of the three towering pillars of rock, looking more like defensive structures instead of bridges. But everywhere Banning looked there were dwellings built over, across, and on top of these walls and bridges. Some of the buildings had been placed neatly in a row, as if they were planned, all painted in clean vibrant colors, while their terra cotta roofs were all uniform in that single orange clay color. While the lower levels, which were much older, were more of a jumble of buildings, afterthoughts, as they were stacked one on top of the other; though they were as well maintained as the newer upper levels of the city.

"The Bowl was designed to protect any ships if the waypoint was attacked." Gwyn explained to Banning who caught glimpses of pale wisps of smoke slowly billowing from chimneys and occasionally someone's laundry, stretched across a line between two homes, drying in the afternoon sun. "I heard that almost fifty ships could fit in here without a problem. Now it's mostly used for festivals to honor Cillach, with tents and arenas spreading across the bowl when they honor him."

"I didn't know that." Banning replied, still in awe of the sight outside of Kasser's window.

"My parents took me once when I was much younger. We were here for almost a week watching duels and mock glider fights that took place over our heads."

"I would much like to see one of their festivals." Banning said wistfully as he thought of the things he might not have a chance to see because of his duty to his family.

But before Gwyn could answer, they were interrupted by her steersman who spoke a single word. "Glider."

Sure enough, one of several gliders that guarded the Bowl had flown over to meet them and was now only about a hundred yards in front of them flashing the questions of who they were and why they were slowing down.

Gwyn had her crewman reply with the same answer they used to get into the Bowl, watching Banning out of the corner of her eye as he took a step back into the shadows of the bridge.

"That's fine." Gwyn said out loud, acknowledging the glider's response and telling her own steersman to increase their speed and to head for the southern gate.

The rest of the short trip was uneventful as they traversed the Bowl and eventually made their way out to the piers on the opposite side of the city.

The wharves on this side of Rathad seemed to be even more crowded than the other side had been. With ships of all shapes and sizes flying banners from many lands. But they did not have to fly far through this menagerie of vessels as the Kasser's steersman flew the ship toward a dock near the outer walls of the city.

But Gwyn huffed softly in annoyance at seeing all the berths filled with ships flying the colors of Iniscarn across their prows.

"Try to get their attention and let them know who we are." Gwyn ordered her crewman. "Let them know we'll be docking alongside one of them."

The man started working the shutter of the lantern, flashing out code to let the other ships know that the daughter of Lord Argus Berach was here; hoping his signaling and the hovering bulk of the Kasser would at some point get someone's attention.

As the crewman repeated his signal, Banning intently watched the flashing lights, not knowing a single word of the Scarnian's code being used. Banning had known that every kingdom had its own unique code but one usually found a word or two that was translatable. Why, not even a word from the code used by traveling merchants, which he had been part of his education, seemed to be part of the vocabulary Gwyn and her people had created.

And while Gwyn's crewman was beginning to send the request for a third time, and Banning was thinking of having Gwyn show him the code they were using, responses began flickering from two of the vessels, followed by a third ship sending its own response of greetings.

Fortunately Gwyn's crewman wasn't disoriented by the babble. "Captain, the Ogham says they are to leave in two days." Her man said pointing to one of the middle ships on their starboard side. "Most of the others are saying they got here over the past day, but won't be leaving for a while. All are saying they will move for you and the Kasser."

Gwyn wasn't willing to put her people through all that trouble just for herself right now. "Tell the Ogham we'll berth next to it for the night and we'll have the ships switch places in the morning."

While the crewman flashed Gwyn's reply, the captain of the Kasser walked over to her steersman, giving precise orders where to park the ship. The steersman didn't even reply, only turning the ships prow to starboard as the Kasser began a very slowed descent.

"You might want to hold onto that rail next you Master Dar." Gwyn's crewman said to Banning, distracting him from the events unfolding outside the bridge window. Banning looked over to the man to see that he was holding a wooden rail bolted to the side of the window with his right hand, the shuttered lantern still held in his left. The man nodded towards Banning's left side, grasped the rail he was holding a little tighter, the muscles in his wrist and forearm contracting as he once again suggested for Banning to grasp the rail.

Banning took the man's advice and just in time too because when he looked out the window again he couldn't help but turn pale as the Kasser descended, rather quickly Banning thought, with the Ogham coming up to meet them on their left. The prince of Birr couldn't help but hiss in surprise, rather loudly, as it looked like both ships would slam into each other. But the Kasser stopped just above the desert floor, before moving slightly to the left and landing, leaving only a fraction of space between the two crafts. Unfortunately, the main deck was almost a full level higher than the Ogham's and ladders would be needed to get back and forth between the ships for now.

But Banning wasn't thinking about that, nor how the crews would be boarding each vessel because he was busy silently thanking the gods for having the ship land in one piece. Giggling from behind did get his attention and turning he found Gwyn standing next to him grinning broadly, admiring the whitish tone his complexion had taken. Banning only shrugged, smiling crookedly, as he tried to make light of the fear he felt from the landing.

"Shall we go and meet the captain of the Ogham?"

Banning, who felt that some fresh air might settle his nerves, nodded to Gwyn and followed her off the bridge.

As they made their way out onto the main deck, Gwyn came across one of her runners and gave the woman instructions that included a message she wanted sent to their employer who lived up in Rathad. And while Gwyn had her crewman repeat the message, making sure no important detail was omitted, Banning walked over to the railing to get a better look at the ship they had landed next to and the surrounding area. He saw Micah off a ways and when the little boy saw Banning he tugged at the tunic to the man he was standing next to, his father, Tor Varin, who turned and quickly waved to the prince before returning to what he was doing which was helping several Gwerin onto the main deck as they climbed up a ladder from the Ogham.

Gwyn immediately recognized Mandor Eshyn, captain of the Ogham, and went to greet him and his crew. Gwyn knew the older man from home and they talked jovially for a moment before discussing arrangements to have their ships swap places in the morning.

"What will you be doing in the meantime?" Eshyn asked her.

When Gwyn told him that she would be keeping her crew onboard to get her ship ready to be unloaded in the morning, Eshyn suggested she have dinner with him.

"Not just you, but your entire crew!" Eshyn said to Banning's relief, fearful that he might have been omitted from the invitation. "We can rig tables on the main deck and have both our crews mingle for the night. And I know the other captains here would be happy to see you, Lady Argus."

Knowing that her crew would be working hard over the next several days, Gwyn readily gave in, offering her cooks, kitchen and stores of food to help in the preparation of this impromptu feast. Mandor Eshyn willingly accepted his mistress's offerings and parted company so they could have their crews prepare the decks of both ships for the upcoming dinner.

In the end, with so many of the Scarnians wanting to see the daughter of their liege lord, the dinner took on a festival like quality, the celebration spreading out onto the wharves, with lanterns clustered together on empty crates or barrels, keeping the night at bay as casks of ale were brought out from the other vessels with the revelry lasting well into the early hours of the next morning.

Needless to say, with men and women scattered across the decks of the Kasser and Ogham, asleep in drunken stupors who needed to be woken and sent back to their respective vessels, Gwyn didn't get the Kasser sorted and moved into its new position well until midday, giving her own crew a slight reprieve to recover from the nights festivities before beginning to unload their ship.

While her crew were left to do their jobs, Gwyn, along with Banning, his little escort of Daigh's men and her own second in command, made their way to the home of their employer to receive payment for this transaction and to hopefully find more work on their journey south.

Gwyn had them go on foot so Banning could enjoy the sights of Rathad and because it gave Gwyn an excuse to hold his hand so he wouldn't get lost in the crush of people. Of course Banning was all too willing to be led through the sprawling market district, relishing in their closeness, the faint spicy scent she was wearing enticing him to stay by her side, more interested in her than in the places she was pointing out to him as they made their way to the eastern spire of the city.

Eventually they left the throng of people behind, ascending into a much quieter district of the city. Here a broad street ran between the dwellings, all brightly painted, with each very different from its neighbor, with the home on the left side of the road only facades as they led back into the mountain side while the ones on the right side of the street stood like sentinels, on the mountains rocky precipices, overlooking the city below them.

It was here that it became obvious that Rathad was a city ruled by woman as they passed female couples arm in arm, or watched a lady sweeping the threshold of her home, minding her daughters who were playing in the street. They did pass a man or two coming down the street but they seemed to be a rarity in this affluent district of Rathad.

They eventually rounded a corner of two and three storied homes clustered together on their left where the voices of many women could be heard filling the afternoon air. Here the street had become a plateau with several large buildings connected by walkways overhead, dwarfing a number of stalls where the upper classes of Rathad came to do some of their shopping. And it was here that Gwyn finally let go of Banning's hand and suggested they take a short break as she and Lucilla walked away and headed towards a stall where a woman was selling an assortment of brightly colored fabrics. The men shrugged to each other with Lhoyt and Davis trailing over to another woman selling sweetmeats while Banning and Mac decided to head over to the tavern on the opposite side of the plaza and find a table that was outside so they could wait for the others to be finished with their browsing.

The two had just about reached the tavern when Banning thought he recognized one of two women sitting at a table not far from them.

"No. It couldn't be!" He mumbled softly. But turned pale as he realized the woman was whom he thought she was and quickly grabbed Mac, who protested loudly in surprise, attracting some attention from the tavern's patrons, as Banning pulled Mac between two stalls they were near and tried to hide from the woman's view.

"What's wrong?" Mac asked, concerned over Banning's sudden odd behavior, while having to remind himself that even though they had become friendly over the past couple of weeks, it was Captain Emmis who had kidnapped the prince and Mac now feared this maneuver might be some trick for a planned escape.

"We need to leave!" Banning hissed as he pulled at Mac's arm again, who held his ground this time so that Banning let go and began walking further into the space between the two tented stalls, only to find them butting up against a stone wall. The sense of fear was beginning to overwhelm Banning and he felt like he was going to cry out of frustration as he walked back to Mac, noticing the shop owners over the man's shoulders, who were watching them suspiciously. One of them even looked like she was debating about kicking them back out into the plaza, only enhancing Banning's fear.

Again, Banning reached out a shaky hand towards the man he had started to consider as a friend and grabbed him by the shirt. "Please! We," Then, "Give me your shirt!"

The demand caught Mac off guard and he was even more surprised when Banning pulled off his own blue shirt, his clan's signet ring that he had strung around his neck on a leather cord to protect it from getting dirty, thudding flatly as it slapped against the prince's chest.

"But?"

But Banning only stood there, the entire frame of his body shaking, his left arm outstretched towards Mac with the shirt grasped in his hand, a slight tremor to his pursed lips with tears that he seemed to be fighting back welling up in the corners of his eyes.

How could Mac say no to such a pathetic sight? "Oh, very well." Mac grumbled as he pulled off his own clothing; a dun colored shirt made of coarse cotton that was sleeveless and having a deep hood on it.

Banning wasted no time in putting on the shirt and had his head down, adjusting the hood over it, when he heard Mac give a yelp of surprise. Looking up he saw Mac's partner, Davis, standing behind him, pinching a nipple on Mac's bare chest.

"Mmm. What do we have here?" Davis said, smiling wickedly.

"Stop it!" Mac replied a little too loudly as he slapped Davis' hand away from his chest before quickly putting on the prince's shirt.

"What's going on?" Lhoyt asked over the shoulders of the two shop owners who had now blocked his way into the narrow space, stopping him from joining the other men in this makeshift alley.

"Are these yours?" One of the women snapped at Lhoyt, her hands balled into fists that were resting on her waist, ready for a fight. And since Lhoyt was obviously the oldest one out of the group the shop owners assumed he was the one in charge of them. "What is the meaning of this?"

"Apologies, Mistress. That is what I would like to know myself." Lhoyt said as he squeezed by the two women, who were refusing to budge, grumbling about the poor behavior of men in public as he inched by them.

"Alright. Can any of you tell me what's going on?" Lhoyt looked to Davis who shrugged and shook his head while Mac mumbled that something was wrong with Banning.

Of course Lhoyt could tell there was something wrong with the prince who was standing with his arms crossed over his chest, the hood of Mac's sleeveless shirt pulled tightly over his head, hiding most of his face that had gone pale, only leaving his trembling lips exposed, making Banning look more like a boy in his early teens instead of the confident twenty-two year old he had gotten to know over the past couple of weeks.

"Banning, you okay?"

Banning's voice trembled, the words tripping out of his mouth as he told them that he needed to leave and that he wanted to go back to the Kasser.

Lhoyt ordered Davis to go find the captain, giving the rest of them a little room to move about, while the two women at the entrance demanded they get themselves in order or they would call for the guard to do it for them as Davis quickly pushed by them.

"For gods' sake, just give us one more moment!" Lhoyt snapped at the women, who were taken aback by his outburst. Focusing his attention back on Banning, who begged the man once again to take them back to the Kasser.

"Now you know we can't leave." Lhoyt wrapped an arm around the prince's shoulders, pulling him in close, their heads almost touching, as if he was consoling a small child. "We just got here and we're not far from our destination. If you're ill we can find you a table at the tavern and leave Mac and Davis with you until the transaction is done."

Banning tried to pull out of Lhoyt's embrace as fear began to overwhelm him. But the man would not let him budge.

"Please." The word escaped Banning's lips, sounding like a whimper, as he looked at the man. "I just want to go back to the ship."

"But Banning?"

"There you are! What kind of trouble are you boys causing?" The three men turned to see Gwyn talking to the two shop owners, handing them several coppers each as she explained who she was and these were crew from her ship. She also handed Lucilla, who had been shopping with her captain, a couple of gold coins while telling her to go buy some wares from the two ladies. Upon hearing this and being coddled with money the women became quite friendly, each tugging on one of Lucilla's elbows as they tried to direct Gwyn's second in command into their adjacent shops.

Gwyn also left Davis at the entrance to the alley, ordering him not to let anyone in. "Is everything alright Master Ormin?" Gwyn asked the man, noticing for the first time that Banning and Mac had changed shirts, not to mention the pathetic look on Banning's face.

"That's what I'm trying to find out Captain. Seems Banning wants to go back to the ship."

Concern crossed Gwyn's face as she stepped a little closer to Banning and Lhoyt, who still maintained his fatherly embrace around the prince.

"Are you ill?" Gwyn asked as she placed a hand on his bare forearms that he had yet to unfold from over his chest.

Banning didn't say a word as he looked at her, almost embarrassed at his own outburst and now not knowing what to do.

Lhoyt misread Banning's quietness and assumed just as Mac had that Banning was planning an escape. An escape they had probably foiled. "Come on lad," He said squeezing Banning's shoulder and slightly rocking him. "You can trust us."

"I know." Banning said, comforted a little by the warmth from the man holding him. "It's just that my mother's lover is sitting at one of the tables at the tavern."

Lhoyt's hand tightened on Banning's shoulder with a shocked look on his and Mac's face at the revelation. Gwyn looked over her shoulder at Davis who, at the moment, had his back to them, giving herself time to think about what Banning had said.

"Are you sure?"

"Yes it's her. Her name is Solvo Caitlyn. And thanks to my mother she is one of the biggest and most powerful merchants working for the temple. She's sitting at a table with a red headed woman just to the left of us."

Gwyn didn't doubt Banning's sincerity but decided to take a look for herself. Not that she would recognize this Solvo Caitlyn from any other woman sitting in the plaza. Tapping Davis to move aside Gwyn peered around the corner of the stall towards the tavern. Sure enough, the red haired woman was easy to spot, since she was the only red head at the tavern and she was seated with an older woman, maybe late forties, early fifties, with shoulder length brown hair that was slowly turning grey, who momentarily looked in their direction before returning her attention back to her attractive companion.

Gwyn retreated behind the stall's tented walls listening to Lucilla within haggling with the shop owner over some bauble and looked back at Banning. "Well, if it's her, I don't understand why you are hiding here when you could get a ride from your mother's lover and be home all the more quicker instead of tagging around with us."

"I know," Banning sighed, tapping the toe of his left boot against the rocky ground, scuffing it slightly as he debated over what he wanted to say. "But, I'm not ready to go home."

Not knowing what to say to that comment Gwyn watched the sour looking frown form on Lhoyt's face, while Mac, who didn't want to be part of this conversation, hunched his shoulders, stuck his hands in his pants pockets and shuffled behind Lhoyt, hoping to be out of Gwyn's view.

From Lhoyt's embrace Banning watched as Gwyn brought a thumb to her mouth and began chewing on its nail while she looked at him thoughtfully. Even though she looked frustrated over the mess he was causing, Banning couldn't help but still find her attractive, only wanting to tell her that. Instead he said, "I just don't want to be an inconvenience to you."

"You're not an inconvenience." She said truthfully as she took a step forward, reached out and pulled Banning out of Lhoyt's embrace. "I invited you on this trip and you're welcome to stay with us if you like."

"I would."

"Well then, let's go."

Banning blanched at the idea. "What about Solvo?"

"Davis," Gwyn said over her shoulder to get the man's attention. "Mac, there's a tram just after the arch on the far side of the tavern. I want you two to take Banning there. Lhoyt, Lucilla and I will follow a little behind to make sure there is no trouble."

"But what if she stops us?" Banning asked. Unsure of how sound Gwyn's plan was.

"Well, you are the prince. So, if she tries to stop us, just tell her you're going with us. You'll get home when you get home." And before Banning could mull that thought over, Gwyn sent the three men on their way, ordering them to take their time crossing the plaza, while she and Lhoyt entered the stall Lucilla was in as they occasionally cast guarded looks towards the tavern.

"You know we could just be rid of him and then be on our way." Lhoyt whispered to Gwyn as she gestured for Lucilla to finish up her transaction. "Having him leave now would be best for all parties. Especially where for your is father concerned."

Gwyn hesitated as she watched Banning and the others reach the arch and pass under it to disappear from view. Gwyn knew Lhoyt was right for it had been he who told his captain not to kidnap Banning in the first place. But now Gwyn was willing to risk the ire of her father because she was not ready to see the prince go.

"I know." She finally answered as they left the stall, making their way across the plaza. Gwyn couldn't help but look at this Solvo Caitlyn and wasn't really surprised to find the woman staring back at her. "But I think the god Sioda has played the same trick on me that he played on Captain Emmis." The woman gave Gwyn a faint smile, like she knew Gwyn's secret before her attention returned to her companion. No, Gwyn thought to herself, momentarily forgetting that she had been talking to Lhoyt. "He can stay with us for as long as he wants."

***

"Found something new already?"

"Mmmm?" Cait turned to look at the questioner, her smile deepening. "I am very sorry Maive, I was distracted by something."

"Well, I could see that!" The red headed Maive said as she too turned to watch the man and two women leave the plaza. "She was attractive."

"Sorry?" Cait had picked up the glass that was in front of her and sipped from the cold drink as she too watched the group leave.

"The young one. Tanned skin, black hair? I saw how you were looking at her." Maive pouted her full lips and shook her head slightly, sending her red curls to dancing about her head. "I hope you don't think she is prettier than I am."

"Of course not." Cait replied, for Maive was quite striking with her fiery mane that surrounded her heart shaped face, with emerald and green enameled earrings dangling from her tapered ears that also complimented her sparkling grey green eyes, while bracelets of citrine dangled on her left wrist, while being wrapped in a dress, that was sleeveless, dyed in shades of deep yellows and soft oranges. "You are like some flaming child of Aodhagan, come down to burn us mortals with your beauty."

"But you could have the night." Maive teased. A flirtatious jest that hinted at Gwyn's features and attire.

"Oh, but I much prefer the day." Cait retorted as she reached out to grasp one of Maive's hands. A public display of affection that Betrys would never have tolerated.

"Actually," Cait purred as she opened Maive's palm and ran a fingernail over the soft skin, thoughts of Betrys, her lover, bubbling to the surface, starting to mar what was turning into an enjoyable afternoon. "I was wondering if they were with those "boys" that were making a commotion near the shops across the way."

"There's always a commotion when you have men around." Maive drawled, her eyes half-lidded as she enjoyed the dance of Cait's fingers on her open hand.

Cait chuckled softly. "This is true. But," But. "I thought I recognized one of them."

"Oh! They seemed kind of young. I hope one of them wasn't yours!" Maive suggested with some distaste, surprised that someone of Solvo Caitlyn's standing would know her sons. That's if she had any and if they were at such a mature age.

Cait laughed harder, more so at the expression on Maive's face than the question. Squeezing Maive's hand she informed her lover that she had not given birth to any man child. Only that one resembled the son of a friend.

"So, did you know him?"

"No." The lie came easily, the word flat as it escaped her lips, knowing full well that it was Banning she had seen hurriedly slip between the shop tents, and watched with some intrigue as the troupe began to gather around him, surprised that the one whom she thought was Banning emerged from hiding only to be hooded, with the two older men trying to block her view of him.

But it was Banning and he knew she was here too for she saw, in that split second when their eyes met, that fear of recognition appear on his face.

So why was he here and not home? Had the attack been a play just to get out of his home? In which case, Cait couldn't blame the boy for running away. Especially with the High Sagartta as his mother for it was she who was helping to plan his life for her benefit.

But what would she tell Betrys? Nothing she decided.

As long as the boy seemed healthy and not in trouble there was no reason to interfere and then there would be no reason to explain what had brought her to Rathad and no reason to explain the lovely Maive to Betrys. Granted, that Betrys knew of her occasional trysts, the High Sagartta just didn't want the stories of Cait's affairs laid bare at her feet. No, it would be better to keep quiet.

"No." Caitlyn said again, reaching out to toy with the bracelets on Maive's wrist, pushing down all thoughts of Betrys and her family. "I thought it was him. But I was mistaken."

Chapter 6
Na Lomahn

Urnin Saul had only arrived at Na Lomahn several days ago and found that the entire construction site was on the verge of slipping into chaos.

Five ships were berthed at the one wharf that had been completed with about fifteen ships docked around those vessels, with rope and planks being used as bridges connecting the stationary fleet together, turning the ravine into a makeshift village and hindering the construction of the second wharf that was needed to berth them. Nine more of Berach's ships couldn't fit into the ravine and Saul had found them grounded as a group outside the mouth to the ravine for Na Lomahn was too rocky and broken for any of those ships to land on.

The problems of cracks within the cistern hadn't been resolved by the time he arrived so Saul was having them build kilns out of the bricks they had brought purposely for the wells. Saul knew it would hamper the solution to their eventual water troubles by lining the large well with them but the kilns would be a resource for material to build much needed barracks and warehouses for Argus Berach's people because there would never be enough lose stone to construct all the buildings they would eventually need.

So the lack of a storage facility for water meant that conservation would be necessary, as it always would be in this barren wasteland, which also meant Saul would be sending ships back to Iniscarn more frequently than was expected. Fortunately the Scarnians were a resourceful people and barrels of ale and wine had made the voyage to Na Lomahn, giving many crewmen a substitute for the precious liquid and the opportunity of drinking themselves to sleep at night during their forced exodus.

But having water would not be an issue, at least for now, for Saul had already emptied several ships of their supplies and would be sending them back to the port of Maum for restocking where they could pick up more barrels of water for this outpost. Hopefully by the time they returned more ships would be emptied, giving Saul another opportunity of sending them to be refilled before curtailing all flights to and from Iniscarn.

Now the crew, especially the dockworkers who had been ordered to come along on this venture, was a different story. For many of them had left families behind, knowing full well there was no guarantee of them returning home any time soon, and the shared living arrangements with many still sleeping among the crates, barrels and sacks in the storage bays of the ships, had become so unbearable that many men and women had taken it upon themselves to camp within the small caves and crags surrounding the two worksites. Fortunately, though many were disgruntled about their predicament, cursing Emmis Daigh under their breath (Saul had made sure to let it slip why they were all on this rock) they had remained professional and regimented while working. For all citizens of Iniscarn had to spend at least two years in the Scarnian military, so they unquestioningly obeyed Saul's commands of camping close to the area while only using shuttered lanterns and prohibiting campfires.

Yes, a subtle chaos ruled over Na Lomahn, with the name of Ciaran, the god of chaos, voiced at every stubbed toe, shattered piece of pottery, miscalculated measurements and the occasional bad card deal that happened in the area. And Saul had no interest in quelling the disruptions because it gave him the opportunity to sneak twenty of his own men into the camp from the Menden's hideout on the far side of the island, installing most of them as dockworkers or steersman who were supposedly newly hired before the mass exodus to this new outpost for Argus Berach's raiders.

Not all the Mendens had been emptied from the secret campsite into Berach's because their overly thick accents would have definitely given away their heritage. Saul also kept one man behind with him, who did have a passable dialect, to act as runner for messages that might need to be passed between him and the camp as was the case almost two weeks after his arrival to the island.

Villis Dane, captain of the Dotain and commander of the Menden marauders harrying the north had arrived at their hidden camp on the northern side of the island and wanted a meeting with Urnin Saul.

And as overseer of Na Lomahn, Urnin Saul knew he would have a difficult time of getting away from the site, quite confident that he would be missed almost immediately. Unfortunately Villis Dane was not a man to be ignored and Saul knew he would need to chance it and leave for a while.

Two days had to go by before Saul could break himself away from the demands of Argus' people and his projects, having to finally tell his underlings that he wanted to take a glider pilot (one of the secreted Mendens) and survey the land around their camp so that he could make his rendezvous at the camp on the far side of the island.

Needless to say, when he debarked from his glider, Saul watched Villis Dane apprehensively, for it well known that the man had very little patience, as the man stalked over to him.

"I am sorry Captain. This was the earliest I could leave." Saul said to Dane as he tried to meet the captain halfway. And though they were the same height and Saul was broader than the captain, he still hoped his tone was subservient enough to assuage the captain's anger for having been made to wait.

But determining the captain's mood was always risky at best. For Villis Dane was a dark man to begin with, as thick black hair that curled around the olive skin of his face and the nape of his neck, writhing about like snakes wanting to strike.

Saul also couldn't see the captain's eyes in the dim light of the corridor to determine his mood. But that didn't matter for they were black; two orbs as deep as the midnight sky, with no difference between iris nor pupil, embedded in the man's head; two identical, menacing voids that many men and women did their best to avoid looking into. And Dane walked, always walked with a purpose; sleekly, silently on his black booted feet, as if he was some virile carnivore stalking prey amongst some unprotected herd.

Thankfully, Cabot, Saul's lover and his liaison to the captain, was there waiting in the main chamber, the living quarters for the Mendens that were holed up here, with more of their fellow countrymen sitting around, keeping themselves occupied while a sagart was off in one corner of the room mumbling prayers to Ciaran while using a white stick of chalk to scratch runic symbols of the god onto the cavern walls.

Saul relaxed slightly, the tension leaving his shoulders when, in the flickering light of the campfire, he saw a smile appear on Cabot's lips; a smile only for him. And when Saul nodded at Dane's back as the captain walked away from him and his steersman, Cabot silently mouthed and gestured with a hand for Saul to relax.

And relax is what Saul tried to keep on doing as Villis Dane, in his tight fitting clothing, a pair of dark leather pants and a grey linen shirt, moved about the cavern, stopping close to the sagart and waited as the man continued to chant his prayers, listening as if to catch some imperfection in the inflection of the priest's voice.

"You wanted to see me Captain?" Saul somewhat hesitantly asked, drawing the man's attention back to him.

Dane ignored the question for the moment as he walked over to one of the characters the sagart had scratched on the roughhewn wall and flicked away a stray fleck of chalk, obliterating it as if it was something obscene in the sagart's work and to his eyes.

"We were almost spotted coming here." Dane said in his thick Menden accent. His r's sounding like heavy rocks tumbling across the ground, his t's like two pieces of flint striking each other in their quest to make fire and his d's sounded like a large block of marble closing the tomb in a mausoleum; a deep dull thud to echo in the middle of the night.

"I will be sending more priests here to keep these caves hidden from prying eyes." Dane turned to look at Saul, several fingers on his left hand trailed seductively across the stone wall. "Try to keep your ships away from this area."

Saul blanched a little, for "try" really meant to do. And what story could he possibly devise to devise to have his patrols avoid the northern side of Na Lomahn?

But, to his relief, Saul was spared by the sagart, who stopped praying for a moment to answer for him in a voice whose accent was as deep, if not thicker than Villis Dane's. "Not to worry Captain. Ciaran's presence will soon fill this place and it will be He who will dissuade and distract our enemies when we need to reach these caves."

Dane nodded, accepting the sagart's words as truth and quickly mouthed a silent prayer to his god, Ciaran, the god of chaos.

Dane then proceeded to pointedly ask questions as to the construction of the facilities on Na Lomahn, its timeline of completion, the amount of manpower and military regiments, if any, Saul had been given and an idea for flight schedules and routes they would take to and from Iniscarn.

"And how about supplies? Are you able to supply us with what we need?" Dane asked over the voice of the sagart who had begun chanting again as he continued to scribe on the wall.

"I do not know Captain. We are keeping an accounting of all food and water, especially the water. I don't know how much I will be able to sneak away."

"Find a way!" The captain said matter of factly as he stalked around the campfire.

Saul knew he couldn't say no to the captain but how would he be able to get supplies here? Maybe he could probably have one of his men hike across the island with them. But that would take almost two days to cross the terrain and would be a wasteful way to deliver one pack of food.

"I might be able to have some, if not all, of the infiltrated men get on the rotation for scouting the island and have them drop supplies. We can skim from storage, as close to here as possible."

"And when are the raids supposed to start up again?" Dane asked while continuing on his trek across the cavern.

"Not for a while Captain. Berach wants us to focus all of our energy on building his hideout. By my estimate it might be a year and a half, two years, before the raids resume."

Dane cursed silently at the apparent delay to his own plans. Because the captain would have no way of camouflaging his own attacks, if Berach was going to halt his own pirating operations. Especially when this spit of land was as far north as he could safely fly which meant he might need to keep his raids isolated to the southern lands for a while longer. Dane watched the sagart as the man made his slow, incoherent journey along the cavern wall.

"We must make sure these holes are well hidden from the eyes of our enemies." Dane said to no one in particular, only voicing an idea out loud.

"And Cabot says you have a ship for me?" Dane purred as thoughts of attacking their neighbors reminding him about the vessel called the Shaefra.

Saul, happy that he had something positive to tell the captain, began to recount the tale Berach had told him about Emmis Daigh but Dane interrupted him with a wave of his hand.

"I do not need your stories about these weak people! Just get me that ship." Dane commanded as he walked over to his own pack that was lying on the ground, pulled out a black tube from one of its side pockets, and shook out a rolled piece of leather with a map of the area inked on it.

While Dane explained to the men when and where he wanted the Shaefra dumped, Saul frowned at the idea of having to move all of those people who were now using the ship as a home into new housing. But then again, the reshuffling of people would cause further disruption, hopefully making it more convenient for his own people to further blend into this small community.

Dane had Saul repeat his instructions, several times as to when and where he wanted Daigh's ship left, and once he was sure Saul knew where to abandon the ship for him, he rerolled the map, stroking its soft, supple skin.

"We're done here for now." Dane said to Saul as he slid the map back into its case. "You should get back before you are missed."

"Yes Captain." Saul said to the man, his reply polite, monotone and sterile from any emotion, hiding all personal disappointment at this curt dismissal.

A disappointment Saul refused to hide as he, Cabot and his steersman headed back towards the outer cave containing their vessels. And not caring that the steersman was walking several steps behind them, Saul took Cabot by the hand and pulled him against his own body, the two stumbling against the wall with Cabot's full weight pressing against him while wrapping one arm around Cabot's waist and the other grasping Cabot by the back of the head, drawing his lover into an impassioned kiss.

A kiss that was short-lived for Saul, who licked at their mingled saliva glistening on his lips, their bodies warm, throbbing against each other as Saul looked wantonly into Cabot's own half lidded eyes.

"I know, I know." Cabot whispered huskily to the unspoken plea from Saul, kissing the man again, nipping at Saul's lower lip upon their release. "You do know we are not alone?"

Remembering the man who had flown the glider for him, Saul turned to see that the steersman had moved maybe twenty feet back up the corridor, his back to them as he seemed to be fidgeting awkwardly as he did his best to ignore their affections.

The thought that they were being watched only aroused Saul even more, sending him into a fit of snickering. A sound full of impish mirth that was so infectious that Cabot echoed his lover's laughter, which bounced roughly off the tunnel's walls, at the absurdity of their predicament.

"I've missed you." Saul growled as he tightened his grasp around Cabot's waist.

Cabot leaned back in his lover's grasp, their groins digging, struggling against the confines of their clothing as he threw a playful punch against Saul's solid chest. "And I you."

Cabot's closeness was maddening to Saul. Especially when he could feel Cabot's body throbbing against his own. Standing this way Saul did not know how much longer he could last.

"Will you be staying here?" Saul asked as an impulsive thought came to him. "Maybe, after the captain leaves I can sneak back and. . ."

"No. He has me leaving with him so I can get back to Iniscarn as soon as possible."

Saul couldn't help but groan in frustration, burying his head against Cabot's neck, inhaling deeply, doing his best to memorize the musky scent of his body with the coarseness of his unshaven neck rubbing against his own face while the salty tang of his sweat coated Saul's tongue as he ran it across Cabot's collarbone. All things that did nothing to abate the lust that pounded like a heavy hammer on the inside of his body.

Cabot smiled lasciviously at having such a beast of a man crumble like a weathered piece of rock leaning up against him. Squeezing a hand between their bodies he grasped one of Saul's nipples, eliciting a hiss of surprise followed by a low growl as Saul raised his head to look at him.

"You need to go." Cabot said huskily, knowing that Captain Villis wanted to also soon leave which meant that their time was limited in this rocky corridor.

Urnin Saul wasn't a stupid man and understanding their predicament let go of his lover, but not before grasping him by the chin and planting another kiss heavily on Cabot's lips. "Soon?"

"Soon." Cabot promised as he stepped away from Saul, watching the man's body heave from their unspent passion. "Go." He growled to the man. "Let me watch your backside so I have something to remind me later of what I have missed."

Saul ignored the request and went to grasp Cabot by the hand, only wanting to drag him along, hoping for a couple more stolen minutes together at the glider.

But Cabot resisted, pulling his hand out of Saul's grasp. "No, go."

Saul knew he had been defeated, that Cabot was right to not continue on with him, that Cabot had to get back to his own job. Taking one last look at Cabot and growling again in appreciation at what he was leaving behind, Saul called out to Kellim, his glider pilot who had remained further up the corridor, and ordered him to follow him before turning his back on Cabot, giving his lover the view that he so hungrily wanted.

And as Kellim passed Durdst Cabot, the man hissed the pilot's name, halting him in his tracks.

"Sir?"

"I need you to take care of something for me." Cabot watched the man who was unsure of what he wanted, especially after listening to Cabot's and Saul's interaction. "I need you to take care of your commander for me."

Kellim's tanned skin turned pale while the befuddled look remained on his face at the request. "I don't understand?"

"What I mean is this. Your commander has needs. I cannot be there nor do I know when we will see each other again so I want you to take care of those needs for me."

Kellim definitely understood what Cabot was requesting, but was halted again by Cabot as the glider pilot tried to voice his skepticism.

"Look! We don't have time for this! You heard us and I can tell you enjoyed it!" Cabot pressed a hand against the front of Kellim's trousers feeling the man's erection, something Kellim had hoped Cabot would have overlooked. "Just land the glider before you get back to camp and finish what I started. And if the commander balks at the idea, tell him I gave my consent and that the two of you leaving to find someplace secluded makes much more sense than the commander just wanting to personally survey the lay of the land. You need to do this!"

"Yes sir." Kellim replied.

But Cabot could tell the man was still unsure of his plan.

"One more thing," Cabot said as he grabbed Kellim by his belt buckle, pulling him closer so that their bodies were almost touching, loosening his shirt and running a hand over the man's flat abdomen to let him know he was serious about the request. "You are not replacing me." Cabot began to explain as he turned his hand and moved his fingers past the man's belt, trailing across the damp, sticky flesh he found there. "If the commander chooses to be with you then so be it. Other than this one time you are not to instigate anything on your own. Mark my words, if you cross this line I will make sure you are reduced to the status of a Sothair Dor and I will do my best to make sure you end up in the breeding pens of the lowliest clan on Mendes. Is that understood?"

"Yes sir." Kellim stuttered, fearful of the words spoken by Cabot while his body continued to respond uncontrollably to the man's ministrations.

"Good! Now go after him and get out of here!"

Kellim didn't think he could keep his voice from shaking so he only nodded and moved away, Cabot's hand slipping from his pants, and turned, running to catch up with his commander.

Thankfully the man was attractive, not as tall as himself, but passable, Cabot thought as he sniffed at the mixture of fluids on his hand before licking the tang off two of them. Cabot knew that with the mood those men were both in, the seduction of Saul should be easy enough and hopefully his partner would find some relief from the frustration he was in so that he could keep himself focused on his job and protecting their men hidden away in Na Lomahn.

The voices of Villis Dane and the sagart reached Cabot's ears so the man wiped the rest of his damp hand on the side of his pants leg and straightened himself up by tucking in his shirt where it had come undone and fixing his belt.

And as Cabot fell in behind Dane and the sagart with their pilot, allowing the two superiors to continue with their conversation, he couldn't help but be thankful he had been given his own private cabin during his stay on the Dotain where he hoped he could find time to relieve himself before being sent back to Iniscarn. Cabot knew he would not go looking for another body to share his bed upon his arrival to Iniscarn. Not the way he pushed Kellim on Saul for that was a gift freely given.

Durdst Cabot couldn't help but smile contentedly as they entered the main cave and noticed that Saul's glider had already left. No, he could wait until his and Saul's next reunion, for Cabot would make sure it was quite memorable for the two of them. Maybe, just maybe he thought, as they boarded the remaining glider, he could get Saul to talk about his encounter with Kellim. And just maybe, he thought salaciously as he sat down, waiting for the pilot to connect with the lodestones so the glider could start its ascent, if Kellim was still around, he might be able to persuade Saul into a reenactment for his own benefit, so that he too knew that Kellim took proper care of Saul.

***

Sand; millions upon millions of those quartz filled the air. The sky was darkened by the tiny particles as they swirled around the Dotain, peppering its metal plated hull, scarring the ship with tiny abrasions on its already dull finish, briefly collecting in the crevices between the ships armored plating, only to be swept away by the fierce winds keeping the sand up in the air, obliterating from sight the Dotain and the other two ships that were part of its retinue, hiding them from the view of their enemies.

Usually the sound of sand and its faint serpentine hiss as it scraped against the metallic skin of his ship did not bother Villis Dane. Usually.

Today, that persistent irregular pattering was a loud cacophony scraping against his ears.

Dane shifted in his seat on the bridge, drumming his fingers on the arms of his chair, listening to the two sagarts chanting their charms of protection for the ship from their own seats that were situated behind him.

Maybe it was the absent sound of that third voice, now lacking because he had sent one of his sagarts, one from each ship, to protect their foothold on Na Lomahn, which was the root of his annoyance. A missing voice that seemed to have been a counterbalance to the other two as they softly sang their prayers of protection and devotion to Ciaran. A third voice to help drown out the elements and one that he found melodic and soothing. A third voice combining with the two other voices to create a gentle hum in the back of his head. A third voice he yearned to have back on his bridge singing praises to Ciaran.

That lack of a third voice also meant that there was one less priest to protect his ship was the thing that bothered Dane the most.

Dane continued to shift in his seat. A noticeable contrast compared to the unmoving, almost stagnant, air that was making the bridge feel warm and humid. And with the entire ship sealed against the onslaught of the sandstorms, the air would continue to be stuffy and thick until the sagarts tired from their labors of controlling the elements when windows could then be unshuttered without fear of glass being abraded and vents could be opened so that fresh air could be allowed into the Dotain and fill the inside of the ship with sand.

Now perturbed at realizing what was bothering him Dane turned in his seat hoping for a distraction as he looked at the rest of his crew in the faint glow of some half shuttered lanterns. Two guards in hardened, black leather armor stood at attention at the bridge's entrance, one wiping away the sweat on his brow while the other continued to stare off into space, ignoring his own discomfiture in the stuffy room. Several other crewmen, two lookouts and another man, who served as a secondary steersman, their shirts as opened as decorum would dictate, sat as silently as they could, while one of them mouthed the words to a prayer and toyed with a small charm of Ciaran in his hands while they all waited for their shifts to end.

And the man who was actually steering the Dotain? The man sitting directly in front of Dane? The only man on this entire ship that could see what was going on outside? The steersman was impassive, immobile like a piece of stone, his skin cool and dry for he was unaware of the stifling heat of the ship in his trance like state as he did his job and guided the Dotain to its rendezvous with the abandoned Shaefra.

Finally, standing just behind the right side of his chair was his own personal servant, Cremin Vokes; a man who had come from the Menden leader's clan and had been a gift from their leader himself, Lyro Stowe.

Vokes was third generation born and as such had been given the liberty to leave the confines of Mendes. Not that there were any concerns of escape from a ship that would never see the mainland until they returned to Mendes. And even if it was a thought that did cross Voke's mind there was no way he could not be noticed trying to escape from a ship that was always had its crew on alert.

So Vokes stood behind Dane's chair, like he had been trained to do when they had left Mendes for a new series of raids that had started a little over three months ago, and waited patiently, his athletic torso bare, a luxury awarded to only the servants in the stifling warmth of the ship. A visual distraction for the rest of the crew who had to remain fully clothed and armored during this part of the trip. And in his hands a towel held solely for the captain's convenience.

A towel Villis Dane readily reached for to wipe his own face and neck. Returning the towel to Vokes, Dane watched the man as he refolded the towel, whose own gaze never met Dane's, and just returned to looking blankly at the shuttered main window, waiting for Dane's next command.

But Dane's only thought at the moment was to continue looking at the man. His man, whose presence seemed to be the distraction he needed to relieve his agitation because, naked from the waist up as he was, Vokes still had a thin sheen of sweat covering his body, the shuttered lamplight casting a flickering reddish, almost coppery glow across his tanned glistening skin.

Dane was thinking of what he would like to do to Vokes' tight glistening body when his licentious thoughts were interrupted by the sound of one of the sagart's upraised voices. "There are ships."

"Excuse me?" Dane stood and turned to look at both of his priests who were also standing. He demanded them to speak, unsure of which man had spoken.

"There are ships." The sagarts now spoke in unison. Their voices deepening as they lowered an octave, the same tone emanating out of both of their mouths as their words echoed around the room.

"Ciaran? My Lord?" Dane asked the question but already knew its answer. The captain made the sign of the god across the center of his breast as he looked at Vokes out of the corner of his eye, who had kept his gaze focused ahead of him even though his skin had turned pale from fright, the once enticing light now a sickly pink scrawling across his body.

"There are ships." The sagarts repeated, looking just as blankly as Cremin Vokes was trying to be. The muscles in their face slack, their jaws opened like miniature caves, with only the whites of their eyes exposed because their irises had rolled up into their heads. "They are full of Sothair Dor. You must fly southwest!"

Dane stepped confidently towards the priests and motioned for everyone, with the exception being the man flying the Dotain, to get down on one knee to pay respect to their god.

"But we go to retrieve a ship." Dane said with the surety of a man who was talking to an equal. "We are but a day away from it."

The god did consider Dane as a favored pet, for the time being, and Ciaran reminded the captain of this by sending a rumble through the ship, its timbers creaking in distress, while the sagarts hissed in pain as the god did some unseen thing to their psyche, for the captain's forwardness.

But Dain knew the god needed him. That Ciaran reveled in Dane's adherence to the ancient ways. Just the same Dane supplicated by lowering himself to one knee, his arms outstretched in worshipful devotion.

"Please Lord!" Dane said over the voices of his men which were raised in prayer. "The ship comes from a land that has been treacherous to its neighbors. Can we not retrieve the ship and still have time to go after the Sothair that you so willingly offer us?"

The bridge went silent, the wind the only sound as it howled menacingly around the Dotain as everyone waited for the god's decree.

"Three days." Were the words that finally escaped the mouths of the sagarts, the two men oblivious to any affliction that was being inflicted upon them by their god. "You have three days before they will be out of your reach. Do not disappoint me."

"Yes Lord." Dane replied, bowing his head as he waited on more information from the god.

But none was forthcoming and Dane only raised his head when the sounds of pain from the sagarts filled the bridge. Moaning, drained by the possession of their god, the two men all but forgot their chants and slumped back into their chairs as the conjured winds and sand died away, allowing the Dotain to buck forward as the force of nature dissipated from around it.

Dane stood, maintaining his footing while his steersman regained control of the ship, and shouted out orders to have the main window's shutters rolled back and commanded one of the guards to have the rest of the ship opened and for Vokes to go tend to the priests.

As the shutters were pulled back from the glass windows, Dain could see that storms still brewed around the other two ships which were still heading for their destination; a sign that Ciaran had only spoken to him and not the entire assault group. So Dane ordered his steersman to halt the Dotain and to have it list from port to starboard several times. A signal that only the other steersmen of the other ships could discern while the crews of the other ships was blinded by this weather. A signal Dane had created for any of them to use if one of them was in trouble or if their plans needed to change. And now their plans needed to change.

Dane scratched at his collarbone, rubbing away some of the sweat that had collected in his chest hairs and ordered one of his men to get the signal lantern ready as he watched the other two ships appear out of the sandstorms that had surrounded them which were slowly dwindling into a cluster of dust devils that spun off along their own paths across the flats.

Once Dane had explained to his other captains what had occurred on the Dotain and of the Sothair Dor that were within their grasp, the captain ordered all of his ships to fly as quickly as possible, forgoing any protection for speed so they could reach the abandoned Shaefra as soon as possible.

Even though the ship had been vented and fresh air was seeping into all of its corners Dane remained in a foul mood. The man refused to leave the bridge until they reached the Shaefra, his gruff attitude a dark cloud that filled the bridge, setting his own crew on edge as they awaited his orders.

Still, their flight took them the better part of a day to reach the drop off point. And upon reaching the ship Dane's mood did not improve, for while his crew secured the ship, they had found that it not only had been stripped of all its weapons, something Dane had assumed, but there was some extensive damage to the hull in one of its weapon's rooms. Something Saul or Cabot had not known or had just failed to mention which left Dane with only two options for the ship which was useless to him in its current condition; to leave the ship along with any value it might have or to send it back home and have it overhauled and returned to him to be used as part as his clan's fleet.

Dane already knew he did not want to leave the ship behind so Dane sacrificed one steersman and skimmed half a dozen other men from all three of his ships to protect the stolen vessel, an inadequate amount of men to protect an unarmed and damaged ship, and sent it on its way to limp back to Mendes.

The loss of seven men did not improve his mood as they flew southwest towards their goal, Dane's sagarts once again praying behind him, their rhythmic chants echoing throughout the bridge. This time their prayers and incantations were not for protection from their enemies but bequeaths to Ciaran for help in finding those Sothair Dor who were out on the flats.

Eventually even a man as strong willed as Villis Dane tired. For the man had forced himself to stay awake for almost two days. And as exhaustion finally overtook him he relinquished control to his second in command so he could get some much needed sleep while his men searched for their prey.

Dane was so worn out from his stint on the bridge that as he entered his room he unbuckled the dagger he carried while on board his ship and heedlessly allowed the weapon and its belt to fall to the floor and did the same with the sweat soaked shirt he had worn for the past several days.

And Cremin Vokes, who had been given the luxury of sleep, obediently picked up the discarded items, hanging the dagger on its peg near Dane's sword and threw his shirt, still damp and reeking with body odor, into a hamper so he could launder it later.

Vokes watched as the man undid his belt and tossed it onto the bed before sitting beside it and beckoned for the man to approach so that Dane could raise one of his legs whereupon Vokes instinctually went to his knees and began to pull the black leather boot off his foot followed by the woolen sock, also drenched in sweat, before doing the same to Dane's other foot.

Instead of lying down Dane stood once more and watched as Vokes flinched instinctually as Dane's hand approached his face as he patted the kneeling man's shoulder. Dane left his hand where it was for the moment so he could regain his balance before padding across to a low chest of drawers directly across from where he slept.

On top of the chest of drawers sat a box. A wooden box, that was as tall as a man's head, was stained a deep black with gold scrollwork snaking around its surface. The entire object had also been heavily waxed so that the light in the room reflected brightly off of its sides. The box had two doors on the front of it, with a latch made of gold that kept it shut and hinges that were also made of gold.

Mumbling softly, Dane unhooked the latch and opened the doors, which was like cutting into flesh, because the wood that was revealed had retained its natural color, a deep reddish brown, while a rich spicy odor exuded from its woody interior.

Dane immediately made the sign of Ciaran across his breast for the box was home to an idol of the god, a family heirloom that had been cast in bronze with a thin skin of gold covering its surface. An icon of Ciaran in one of his more feral states; naked, the god's head was horned like a goats, his feet cloven like some wild animal, its body muscular and well-proportioned, the statue's arms at its sides with the palms of its hands facing outwards. And it was naked. Everything about the statue said worship me, for I deserve to be worshiped by you.

Which is what Dane did because he took out a candle that was also inside the box and lit it, the candle giving off a musky odor, for its wax had been mixed with the scent glands of a male jackal, the scent mingling with that of the wooden box, the room taking on the feeling of a stony den hidden in the midst of forgotten forest.

Vokes watched as Dane went to his knees with his arms outstretched; palms flat to the sky, and began to pray to the god of chaos. Vokes also knelt, mirroring Dane's words, for he too knew the litany of vanquishing that the captain was chanting. But Vokes did not look to the statue as he said his devotions. Instead, he watched Dane as slight tremors ran through the man's back and shoulders due to his exhaustion from lack of sleep.

The tattoos that ran across Dane's back were glistening with sweat. The mark of Ciaran that was on his left shoulder blade, a black rune that was inked on the shoulder of every Menden, a mark that claimed every man and woman as servants and as property to Ciaran, seemed to have a life of its own. That mark and the remainder of tattoos that represented his clan and family writhed like snakes while Dane flexed involuntarily while in prayer to his god.

Vokes eyes then trailed down his captain's back until they came to rest on the two streaks of white ruined flesh that were just above the waistline of his trousers. Scars that marred Dane's olive skin. Long marks inflicted by an enemy upon a much younger Dane, when the crew he was with raided one of the small villages that had once hugged the southern coast of Birr.

But his eyes didn't linger long on Dane's disfigurement. Looking up Vokes saw that Dane's hands had turned, the palms rolling forward and exposing on his right hand a large steel ring that fit over the knuckles of his index and middle finger. The ring's only adornment being the flat polished surface on the quarter inch solid piece of metal as the lamplight from the room reflected off of it.

The ring was an odd piece of jewelry. More like a weapon, Vokes thought, as he not only remembered the punch to his left shoulder for some discrepancy during that first week he was on the Dotain, but how he was made to watch Dane use the ring to brutally beat a man they had just captured from Belmar during a raid. A Sothair Dor who had demanded to have his two sons returned to him because the children had been separated from their parents during their trip back to Mendes.

The Sothair male eventually stopped pleading. Not from the multiple cuts and bruises across his face and chest or from the cracked and missing teeth inflicted upon him by Dane's ring. No, the man stopped talking because Dane eventually tired of his toying with him and upon looking at the wreckage before him proclaimed that the man was now nothing more than damaged goods and ordered him unceremoniously tossed off the Dotain while they continued on their flight back to Mendes.

Vokes, who couldn't help but remember how the man's tone changed to pleas for forgiveness when he realized his fate, began rubbing at the spot where Dain had also hit him, the skin already healed and thanked the gods that he had been luckier than that Sothair Dor.

But Vokes didn't have long to reminisce on his fortunes because Dane had stopped praying, his arms lowered to his sides and had turned to look at his servant.

"You cannot tell me that you are still in pain?" Dane asked, incredulously, unsympathetically.

"No sir." Vokes replied. And as Dain stood, Vokes did likewise.

Dane approached the man and ran a hand over Vokes' shoulder before inspecting the faint callouses. "Why there's barely a mark." Dane held the man's gaze, looking for any trace of fear in his grey eyes. "You should think of it as a battle wound."

"Yes sir." Vokes answered as Dane gave his arm a squeeze, muscles rubbing uncomfortably against bone, before Dane removed the rest of his clothing, dropping his pants and undershorts to the ground before sitting on the edge of his bed and leaned forward as he tried to stretch the stiffness out of his back.

"After all this time does Sothair blood still run through your veins?" Dane teased, smiling as he watched the tremor of fear run down Vokes' spine.

Vokes knew he should be fearful because he was unsure of where the captains toying would lead and taking a deep breath he turned to look down at Dane who was watching him intently. "No sir. No mongrel slave blood runs through my veins."

"Good." Dane said as he pulled the covers and sheets back from the bed to crawl under them. "The men and women of clan Lyro, and their cousins, have always been made of sterner mettle. I would hate to think that Lord Lyro had given me a gift that was of inferior stock. Tainted."

"No sir." Was all that Vokes could think of as a reply as he began to pick up the rest of Dane's belongings from the floor and put them away before turning back to Dane who was lying on his back, staring blankly at the ceiling, and shuttered the windows in the room to block out the mid afternoon light.

Vokes blew out one lantern and shuttered the second, allowing a faint light to illuminate one corner of the room, then walked over to Dane's shrine and blew out the candle before putting it back in the box.

But Dane, who hadn't bothered to watch Vokes as he tidied his quarters, ordered the man to leave the box open. Let the god's presence fill the room for now, the captain said in his deep gravelly voice.

Vokes took one more look around the room in the dim light to make sure he hadn't missed anything and was about to leave and go to his own small room, a cabin that was slightly larger than a closet that he stayed in when he was not at Dane's side when the captain ordered him to stay.

Vokes hesitated, surprised by the request to remain because Dane only asked him to share his bed for only one reason and Vokes assumed that after two days of keeping himself awake the man would be too exhausted for any type of encounter. Not that Vokes minded, for in this one thing he and Dane had similar appetites. Although Vokes could do without the pain and abuse Dane seemed to want to inflict upon him when he was angry with the other subordinates.

Dane had raised himself onto his right arm and side and pulled the covers away, exposing his nakedness as he watched Vokes in his hesitancy. "Well, are you just going to stand there like an oaf or are you going to join me?"

"Yes sir." Vokes replied, an idiotic response he knew, to the question he was asked before he quickly undressed, placing his clothing over a chair in the room, before joining Daigh in his bed. As he pulled himself near Dane, his own body responding to their closeness, the man told Vokes to turn around.

"Go to sleep." Dane whispered into Vokes' ear and draped an arm over Vokes' body, pulling the man in closely as Dane dropped into a deep slumber.

Vokes was surprised by the act, Dane's arm relaxing around him and his warm breath brushing against the fine hairs on the back of his neck. For up until now Dane had not been affectionate, only looking to have his needs met before sending Vokes back to his own cabin.

Ironically, Vokes who had been allowed to rest couldn't sleep and found the position he was in uncomfortable because he had gotten used to not having to share his bed and did not want to move into a more comfortable position for fear of disturbing Dane.

So he lay there, counting numbers, telling himself to go to sleep, anything that would help him follow Dane in his pursuit of undisturbed oblivion. But sleep had become allusive so Vokes did the only thing he could do and let his eyes wander across the dimly lit room until they came to rest on the statue of Ciaran, the slightly shuttered lamp, on one of the tables, reflecting off the statue's golden skin. All reds and coppers, giving an ominous life to the icon, as if the god was down some long corridor unabashedly looking into the room on them.

Ciaran, a naked, uninvited guest was looking, no leering at them. Or maybe it was more like the master checking in on its pet feline, making sure it was doing its job of stalking the premises, only to discover that it had caught some vermin and was content to let it keep its prize alive for now.

Trapped under paw. That's how Vokes felt; trapped like a slave. For all intent, and since all status of family and clan had been lost to him in this offering to Villis Dane, Vokes was a slave. A man forced into servitude by his cousin. All because of one indiscretion on Vokes' part, until Lyro Stowe changed his mind or said otherwise.

And that's how Vokes finally fell asleep next to a man who seemed to have so little use for him; trapped and alone on a ship full of fellow countryman who were making sure to have as little interaction with him as possible. Aware of where Vokes came from, understanding his service to their captain, fearful of falling as low as he had in his clan.

Although Vokes slept fitfully, waking every so often, moving as little as possible, Dane slept as if he had succumbed to death, unmoving in his exhaustion, only mumbling incoherently into Vokes' ear over some dream or other that filled his mind.

Dane's crew had been told not to disturb the man unless their need was great so almost a full ten hours went by before a knock was heard on the captain's bedroom door. Dane woke immediately, like he had never gone to sleep and climbed over Vokes' body to open the lantern the man had closed earlier.

"Yes! What is it?" The captain shouted while he grabbed the pants that Vokes had left out to put back on and watched as servant, who had also risen, began making the bed, knowing full well that Dane would not be going back to sleep anytime soon.

"Sir, the sagarts have found the Sothair Dor!" The crewman shouted through the closed door. "The priests say they have turned and are now flying southeast!"

A course correction this far out in the open desert meant those ships were now heading towards either Tuame or Belmar and were about two, possibly three days away from either of the kingdoms' mainland.

"How far are we from them?"

"It will take us a little less than a full day to reach them!"

"And what time is it now?" Dane asked as he watched the naked form of Vokes walk over to the second lantern to relight it, feeding more wick to the fire and brightening the room.

"It is one bell past midnight, sir!"

Damn! That meant they would cross paths with those ships in the middle of the night. Not a bad time for an attack but the cover of night would give the Sothair Dor the opportunity to escape from them.

Dane opened the door to his quarters so he could speak to his man directly. The crewman was momentarily caught off guard by the sudden movement but quickly came to attention, a stony look of indifference on his face as he tried to ignore the fact that his captain was standing in front of him, bare-chested, his pants on but still unbuttoned, and that his servant was walking about the room without a stitch of clothing on as he tidied up the captain's quarters.

"Have the commander try to increase our speed so we will be within attacking distance as soon as possible. But let him know we will pace them until dawn and that is when our attack will come. I'll be there shortly to take over."

"Yes Captain." The crewman replied, but it was an unnecessary formality because Dane had already closed the door on the man, not bothering to dismiss him.

Turning, Dane found Vokes with his back to him as he began to get dressed. Taking several quick steps Dane walked up behind Vokes and grabbed a handful of brown hair growing at the nape of the man's neck with a loud hiss, more from surprise than from pain, escaping from his lips as he let go of his own pants, allowing them to fall around his ankles while he was guided back into a standing position by Dane's brutal hand.

Dane continued to pull Vokes' head back until it was almost resting up against Dane's left shoulder, the captain's body once again rubbing up against his, supporting the full weight of Vokes' body while he struggled to keep his balance. From this position Vokes couldn't help but look at Dane and watch the gleam of pleasure emanating from his eyes.

"I'm going to go and get myself cleaned. Have clothing prepared for me so I can go right to the bridge. Then go wash yourself before having food brought to me on the bridge."

"Yes sir."

Dane let go of Vokes and allowed the man to stagger a little as he tried to keep his balance, his pants still forgotten on the floor, wrapped around his ankles and underfoot while he expected more attention from Dane. But none was forthcoming because the captain was buttoning his pants so that he could leave.

"And make sure my armament is brought to the bridge as well."

"Yes sir." Vokes replied once again as Dane, who could care less if Vokes responded to him or not, left the room.

Vokes dressed quickly, knowing that Dane would want him by his side, at his beck and call, for the remainder of the day, until their attack started. And since he was not really trusted enough to join the rest of the men away from the ship, Vokes would be expected to remain behind and defend the Dotain from any possible attack.

Going to the drawer, the one where Dane's clean clothing was stored, the one with Dane's shrine on top of it, Vokes stared at the statue and shuddered. For it seemed as of the golden icon of Ciaran was still looking at him lasciviously. More so now that he was alone in the room. Forcing his hands to move Vokes closed the doors to the box to hide the icon, the mark of the deity that was on his left shoulder itching slightly as he opened drawers to retrieve the clothing Dane had asked for before continuing on with the rest of his duties.

***

So, with Dane's expertise as a leader, and the god Ciaran guiding and protecting them during their flight, the three slave ships eventually caught up with the their prey in the middle of the night.

Dane gave his crew a slight respite, putting a fresh steersman in the chair and allowing most of his men a couple of hours of sleep before the attack. And knowing that he was down one sagart, Dane took a chance and allowed one of his priests to sleep as well. For he would need a well-rested sagart for the battle ahead, knowing full well that Ciaran would do all in his power to not let these Sothair Dor slip from their grasps.

Unlike his earlier agitation that had filled the bridge for the past couple of days, Dane was now calm, his entire being completely focused on their goal as they inched towards them, making sure that the two vessels always stayed just within their grasp.

This calmness, this confidence that fell upon Dane while stalking foreign Gwer across the flats, was one of the things that Vokes admired in the man. Of course Vokes was also grateful that Dane's predatory urges were directed towards something other than himself.

Vokes shifted slightly, his booted feet pressing firmly to the bridge's floorboards as the Dotain, and the two other vessels that made up Dane's fleet increased speed to once again keep pace with the unsuspecting vessels ahead of them.

So this is how it went from midnight through the early hours of morning. This sporadic flight over the flats until dawn began to creep across the brittle landscape, casting a pink glow across the shifting sands of the desert, the sign Dane had been waiting for so he could set his plan in motion.

Turning neither to the left or the right, blinking away the spots dancing across the irises of his eyes from the sun as it flooded the bridge with its glorious light, Dane called out the name of his steersman to let him know that it was time to strike.

The increase in speed and the low thumping sound the steersman sent through the Dotain was all that Dane's well trained crew needed to prepare for the attack. The captain watched as his bridge crew, including Vokes, adjusted their leather armor and loosened straps so that weapons were readily available. All this happened while the sagart who had rested, and with the help of Ciaran, conjured up a new sandstorm. The god using his will to force the storm to move in front of the Dotain.

That accelerated movement and the conjugation were all the other two ships needed as signals from their captain and followed suit. The two slave ships making sure they flanked the Dotain defensively, while their own sagarts created more storms to push in front of their group so that they were all blotted from view of their enemies.

Of course the Sothair were also now hidden from their eyes, the captains of the three vessels relying on their steersmen and sagarts to keep track of their prize inside the mystical storm. So Dane was not too surprised when one of his sagarts informed him that their prey had changed directions and that they were now flying south. But this was to be expected, especially if the steersmen on the fleeing vessels sensed the storms and only wanted to get out of their way.

Next the sagart informed Dane that the ships were also picking up speed. Something else to be expected as those ships tried to avoid the storm. But Dane knew that his own ships would follow suit, slowly increasing their own speed so that they would not be left behind. And as they began to overtake the fleeing ships Dane could just make out that one was a frigate, not too large and slightly plated, while the other vessel looked to have seen better days; a smaller vessel, worn and ravaged from its time traversing the flats. A ship that Dane would have had dismantled years ago. Two ships that Dane knew that he and his men could easily overwhelm if they could just catch them.

What Dane wasn't expecting to hear were the slight gasps of pain coming from behind his chair. Turning he found his two priests with their heads in their hands and then having his crew before him shout in surprise as they watched the sandstorms die away and billow around them as they passed through their remains.

Dane angrily growled and ordered his own steersman to try and overtake the two vessels, hoping that his other two ships were able to keep pace.

"Do something!" Dane yelled to no one in particular, Vokes taking a step away from the man as his composure crumbled, the beast living within him quickly rising to the surface. "Stop them!"

"We're trying Captain!" One of sagarts said as they made several attempts to create another storm with their reward being failure as the lifted sand was hurled back at them.

"There is another presence." The sagart continued, his head tilting down to one side, his eyes closed tightly as if he was trying to hear the words of someone that were being mumbled from far away.

"Barra!" The man shouted, his eyes snapping open in surprise, the god's name setting Dane's crew to mumble in concern. "It is Barra who trying to prevent us from reaching those ships."

And those were the last words spoken before shouts of surprise filled the bridge, Dane grasping the arms of his chair tightly as the Dotain and his other two slave ships seemed to lighten, and almost becoming ethereal as they suddenly hurtled towards the fleeing vessels.

***

Yes Barra was out there.

For as Dane spat the god's name out with vitriol and disgust at his interference, the crews of the ships before them were praying to Barra as well as the rest of the pantheon in the hopes that one of them would take heed to their plight.

Yes, it was Barra who heeded their calls and disrupted the concentration of the Menden sagarts on the attacking ships, hoping to thwart the attack from Ciaran's disciples. And it was Barra who urged and guided the escaping Gwer to an outcropping of rock not far away as Ciaran used his own will to hurtle the slavers closer to their prey.

Barra's voice echoed in the heads of every man and woman on those ships, asking them to remain calm, while the god directed their steersmen to a safe place to land.

But remaining calm was a hard thing to do when all were transfixed with fear as the three Menden vessels, sunlight sporadically reflecting off the few polished pieces of metal, looked as if life was trying to be breathed back into three lumps of dark coal.

The Gwer remained frozen with fear as the Menden flagship flew overhead to pass them while the sound of metal and wood grinding together filled the air as one of the other attacking ships plowed into the side of the frigate. A multitude of debris, including a handful of bodies scattered across the winds while the frigate dropped, like some wounded bird, to the ground as the Menden's advanced on the smaller vessel that safely made its landing.

Men and women were already evacuating the downed frigate as the Mendens landed their vessels. The Gwerin doing their best to make for the highest of the splinter of rocks they had crashed next to while the crewman of the intact ship began to also abandon their vessel, escaping through the storage bay doors or chancing a jump from the main deck onto the sandy floor where they were being chased by the men from the three Menden ships. The slavers, all clad in black leather, screaming in heavily accented voices, with clubs and nets in their hands as they tried to subdue them.

But the Gwerin had always been a warrior people. A people encouraged by their gods to fight the wars they had once instigated. So that even in this time of peace, that aggression still ran true in the veins of the people the Mendens called the Sothair Dor, the slave labor, who willingly fought, with bare-hands or the simplest of weapons, against their aggressors.

Fortunately the captain of the smaller of the fleeing ships, at the cost of losing his steersman and several other crew members he had known for years, fought courageously and was able to break through the attacking line with a handful of his younger charges.

With the Mendens already nipping at their heels the captain, and his small group started to climb up into the hills following some of their countrymen who had already climbed among the ledges and tumbled stone to hide. The captain was helping one of his crew off the ground, the boy stumbling and spraining his ankle, when a voice called out to them.

"Here!" Someone shouted out to them again.

The captain was trying to quiet his injured crewman, who was pushing at him and begging to be left behind so the rest of them wouldn't be captured, wondering where the call had come from, when an unfamiliar Gwer appeared in front of the fleeing group.

The group was ready to push by the man, the screams of the Mendens growing louder behind them, when the newcomer smiled, trying to assuage their fears as the voice they had just heard called out once again, the man's lips unmoving, and the deep accented sound of his voice echoing within their heads. "You will be safe in here."

Gasps and the mumbled name of Barra escaped the lips of the Gwer as they watched the man in front of them place a hand on the rocky wall so that the granite flowed away like sheer curtains on a breeze, exposing a dark cavern beyond.

"Now hurry, you will be safe inside." The voice commanded.

As the group stumbled into the cave, the captain handed the injured boy off to another man, helping the rest of his crew into the hole before turning to look at Barra, the god of the earth. The captain couldn't help but stop to stare in awe at the god for Barra looked no older than someone in his late thirties, with a warm glow emanating from his tanned skin and golden brown hair. No wrinkle from joy or worry, nor from any care of this world, marred the handsome face of this immortal that had come to save them.

"Thank you." The captain said, pushing his last man into the cave and following him through the portal as the shouts of the Mendens grew louder as they clamored up the path.

Barra only nodded as the captain noticed the god's eyes, for they were iron grey, a color not unlike the lodestones themselves. But their color seemed to be flat, as if they held all the regrets and sorrows, all the burdens of the world.

"I wish I could have saved you all." The god's voice sounded forlorn as it echoed in the captain's head, the god once again placing a hand on the wall, the stone reflowing back over the entrance, blotting out the day, sealing in the fugitives from the chaos of the morning.

Left alone, Barra stood against the rush of the Menden marauders as they made their way up the slope.

So used to the fear that their numbers, aggression, and the grace of Ciaran caused, the Mendens were surprised to come across a lone man blocking their path. A man who simply asked what they wanted out here so far away from their home.

At first the men were startled to hear the thick accent, so native to their homeland, come from this man who was not obviously one of their number for he was not armored nor carrying a weapon as they were; a man simply dressed in his best, as if he was out for a stroll across the country.

The leader of this slave party quickly got over the surprise of finding this lone man who asked such an odd question and laughed harshly. His men followed suit, their laughter filling the air with mockery and a lust for the attack, as they were reminded of what they were here to do.

"What do we want?" The Menden mimicked. "Why do you think we are here?"

The man took the leather wrapped truncheon in his right hand and pointed down the slope where the rest of the Mendens could be seen, scurrying about like black insects collecting food, herding Gwerin prisoners back to their ships.

"We're here for you." The leader leered, slapping the head of his weapon in his left hand. "Now come nicely please. Don't want to mark you too much 'cause it looks like you could fetch a handsome price in the breeding markets."

Barra simply said no.

No, they laughed back, the tone of their voices taking on sarcastic, feminine qualities as they raised their weapons, one man wrapping some chording between his hands as they moved to subdue Barra.

Raising his right hand, halting the advancing men, Barra sent a ripple of energy through the air. The Mendens stopped in surprise, not by the slight breeze that passed by them, but by the faint vibration in the stone under their feet. The sound of groaning rock growing louder as it traveled down the cliff until it hit the desert floor where sand and crusting salt undulated under the will of Barra, like a rock hitting the smooth surface of a pond, sending both hunter and hunted to stumbling, as it moved across the land. The force passing over the Menden ships where the sand began to move away from the vessels, allowing them to slowly sink, only to have the sand come crashing back against their sides, covering their main decks, bogging them down like some long forgotten derelicts.

Villis Dane, who had remained on the dessert floor to help collect the Sothair had been able to keep his footing, scowling and cursing out loud at the predicament his ships were now in as a single word hissed through his head and the head of every other person on this spit of land. Barra.

"Barra!" Dane cursed as he grabbed at the fleeing man who had slipped from his grasp while he struggled to keep from falling.

The god's name echoed off the lips of everyone; with hate and fear on those of the Menden's and hopefulness from men and women who worshipped the god.

Barra, they said.

Barra, the group standing near the god mumbled in trepidation.

"Barra, you go too far!" The group leader shouted, his voice deepening as it bounced off the cliff sides, as the man took several steps towards Barra, the truncheon falling uselessly from his hand.

"Ahh, cousin. Leave this man and show yourself." Barra said to the man when he stood only inches from him.

"Why? When I have this vessel? " Ciaran shouted with the borrowed voice of his disciple, his arms raised and spread wide at his sides.

The Mendens on the landing bowed and made the sign of Ciaran while the chosen one's eyes rolled into the back of his head, revealing only their whites, his cheekbones, chin and forehead flattened or became more angular, while he grew taller, the disks in the man's spine popping to accommodate is new height.

"Your interference in these matters is finally being noticed." Ciaran reiterated, the fingers of the body he was in twitching involuntarily, as if the owner of it was struggling as he tried to regain control of himself.

"As is yours."

"Not so." Ciaran said, his hand sweeping to show the Mendens standing behind him. "I only aid in the survival of my people who have chosen not to have forgotten the old ways."

"Then you should have gone into banishment with the others." Barra said as he watched Ciaran walk around in his stolen form as he gained more control over it.

"Then who would have reminded you of the past?" Ciaran laughed.

"We would have remembered. Let the Gwer forget!"

"I do not think so." Ciaran said, his borrowed fingers moving deftly in the air, silently commanding the rock to move away from the hidden cave, shouts of surprise emerging from it as the men's eyes adjusted to the morning light that was now flowing into it. "They are yours my children." Ciaran said, urging the Mendens behind him to apprehend the cornered men.

But Barra was quicker and shouting no, a word that crashed around them like lightening, grabbed Ciaran by his wrists and commanded the cave to seal itself shut again.

"Let go." Ciaran growled, the whites of his eyeballs turning black, a flat colored black, now dead of any mortality. "Let go or I will wipe every living thing off of this hill."

"Including your own people?"

"Of course!" Ciaran laughed harshly. "These men have served me well and shall be welcome in my halls."

With that, Ciaran expelled a wave of force to strike all the living from this piece of land. But Barra used his own will to keep the attack in check, forcing the energy to crash back onto the two gods.

Barra grimaced at the assault he forced upon himself while Ciaran screamed in pain as bones snapped in his stolen body.

"You dare!" Ciaran shouted. A sound that grated on the ears of everyone there and forcing many to drop their weapons as the pain it caused racked their bodies.

Ciaran then used his will to violently shake the land they were on. Sending cracks across the rocky floor, before sending a blast of energy at Barra that engulfed him in light, colors of which that could not be distinguished nor described, Barra's corporeal form melting like wax, bleeding away on the winds, flickering, disrupting his presence in this world.

Although his visage wavered and the air filled with sound of a man moaning in pain, Barra not only held onto his grasp in this reality but maintained his grip on Ciaran as the gods continued to struggle. As Ciaran sent another wave of disruptive energy to surround and pass through his rival, Barra summoned all of his own strength to call forth sharp pieces of rock from the ground.

A roar of pain cracked the stone about them, sending rocks tumbling down the slopes, as the razor like fingers of rock tore through Ciaran's borrowed host, piercing both body and spirit as Barra did his best to anchor Ciaran to the ground.

Ciaran struggled against his imprisonment, a ghost of a form fighting to pull away from the body it inhabited, the Menden slowly beginning to bleed to death from the many stabbings he had received. But Barra would not let go of neither the man nor the god in this battle.

"You dare!" Ciaran shouted incredulously as he felt his own life force begin to ebb through the veins of his worshiper. Though his life would not end as quickly as the man's, it would end painfully just the same.

Barra did not answer, ignoring the remark and focusing all of his strength to hold Ciaran in place.

Ciaran roared, the sound of a thousand beasts unjustly being brought to slaughter, while a look of remorse filled Barra's eyes. Not for the deliberate murder of his nemesis who was also his uncle, but for the sacrifice of the man Ciaran had chosen to reside in.

While Ciaran's voice continued to fill the air, the god's screams and vile remarks dwindling to a pitiful mewling with pleas for mercy from his nephew, lightening, not created by either god, filled the air. The blue white pulsing light blotting out the morning sun while peals of thunder vibrated through the land, blinding and deafening every man and woman who had been watching the gods' struggle as they too became dazed by the cacophony of the elements, momentarily forgetting their struggles with each other.

The torrent of noise increased in intensity and forced the men in the cave, who now felt as if they were inside the shell of a clanging bell, to cower in fear at being destroyed while the Mendens, who had been sharing the ledge with the gods, blindly struggled to find their way back down the mountain path, left Ciaran and Barra to be overwhelmed by the white hot light. As the storm dissipated, the shifting silhouette of a man took shape, until Cillach, the god of war stood before his brethren.

The god of war came caparisoned for battle, as was his wont, garbed in leather armor dyed in a deep dark red; the blood of his vanquished.

In his right hand Cillach carried a javelin only a foot long and polished so brightly that it reflected the land around it, a weapon that when it was thrown by the god of war always struck its mark. At Cillach's waist hung a vicious looking mace that was made of the same metal as the javelin and swung just as true as the javelin. Cillach also held a shield in his left hand that was round and half as wide as a man is tall. The shield was just a reflective as the god's other weapons and always reflected the light of the sun, or the moon if seen at night, so that Cillach's opponents were always blinded when attacked.

Aside from his armor and weapons the god's head remained bare. No helm covered his silvery gray beard or hair, both of which were braided and plated with wire, and seemed to be made of the same material as his weapons. All of which was in contrast to his dark skinned complexion.

"Hold!" Cillach shouted, his voice rocking the land and sending lose shale and gravel sliding, for the conflict between Barra and Ciaran continued unabated.

Cillach strode to the two and raising his javelin pierced the underside of Barra's chin with its tip and turned Barra's head so that he faced Cillach.

"Cousin! What have you done here?"

"Stopped the abuse of the people doled out by the hands of Ciaran!" Barra shouted, unwilling to let go of Ciaran who only wanted to escape from the dead man in front of them.

"Lies!" Ciaran retorted in a voice full of agony over his situation. "It was he who attacked the Mendens!"

"Because of your coercion, they attacked these others!"

Ciaran ignored the accusation, turning the dead man's head, so that he too could look at Cillach. "Please Cillach! It is Barra who has interfered in these small lives and has become judge, jury and executioner over me. It is he who must be punished."

As if to confirm the dying god's accusation, Barra squeezed Ciaran harder so his borrowed flesh and bones scraped against the rock running through his body, eliciting another shout of pain from the god.

"Barra, you must stop this nonsense!" Cillach commanded.

"Only if he will let these people go."

"It is not my place to tell my followers what to do!" Ciaran whined.

"Liar!" Barra called forth more stony spikes from behind Ciaran which embedded themselves into the god. One of which punched through the back of Ciaran's right knee and shattering his knee cap as it passed through the front of his leg. Ciaran roared in anger as he dangled on the spikes like some obscene scarecrow.

"Enough!" Cillach roared, his dark eyes flashing white as lightning struck the land about them.

"Cease this assault!" Cillach once again commanded as the tone of his voice echoed with the sound of several different octaves.

"Cavanna," Barra shouted at Cillach, for it was not only Cavanna, but all of the gods who were now speaking as one through the god of war. "I will end this when these people are allowed to go on their way!"

The heavens rumbled with thunder once more as Cillach and Barra held each other's gaze while Ciaran continued to mewl in pain over his imprisonment.

"Very well!" Cillach shouted in his combined voice of his brethren. Raising his shield, the sun burning brightly off of it as if dawn was bursting across the land, looking for a reprieve to start over, Cillach commanded for all the Gwer to put down their weapons in peace and to go home.

"And their slaves." Barra added. "Give them liberty."

"Very well." The gods acquiesced.

As the decree of the pantheon thundered across the land, the men and women who had been attacked by the Mendens scurried back to the one undamaged ship to make their escape back to their homeland while Villis Dane and many of his men seethed impotently as they watched their prey escape from their grasp.

Cremin Vokes, who had stood with several other men outside of the now partially submerged Dotain, who had been awaiting the intake of prisoners at the hands of his comrades, watched as men they had abducted several weeks ago now emerged from the slave ship and made a quick dash over to the awaiting vessel.

"What say you, Master Cremin?"

Stunned at what he was seeing, Vokes took a moment to realize that one of the men had stopped and had called out to him. A man he finally recognized as one of the servants who belonged to the sagarts.

"Sorry?"

"You heard the gods!" The servant said, taking several more nervous steps away from Vokes, as he watched the group he had been running with begin to leave him behind. "Now is our chance to be free!"

Maybe it was the shock of what was going on around them because Vokes didn't quite comprehend what the man was saying. But when he did, Vokes blanched and walked back towards the sunken ship. "Are you mad?" He asked the servant.

"I would be mad to stay here!" The servant shouted before running, unheeded, towards his one and only hope of escape from Mendes.

He couldn't blame the man, Vokes thought as he moved up the slope of sand that now led to the main deck of the Dotain, as more of Dane's men began to file back onto the ship. He remembered the servant saying his father was in thrall to the temple of Ciaran and himself only being first generation still received a difficult time from the priests around him. Vokes hurried across the deck so that he could make his way to the captain's quarters, hoping to avoid Dane for a while, and thanked the gods, thanked Ciaran to be specific, that he had been third generation born and, no matter what his station now may be, to have been born into the leading clan of Mendes.

As these thoughts raced through Voke's mind the gods watched as the ship with its escaping Gwer finally lifted off the ground and flew off, leaving the Mendens and their still grounded vessels behind.

"Are you satisfied?" The gods asked of Barra.

"Yes." Barra replied as he watched the ship disappear over the horizon before pulling the sands back from the Menden ships, lifting them into the air so they could also go on their own way.

"Now me, nephew." Ciaran said, his head tilting oddly to the right, as he pulled the dead man's lips into a grotesque smile.

No nod in agreement, no wave of a hand came from Barra, as the bonds he created for Ciaran disappeared, the rock flowing back into the ground, allowing Ciaran in his broken body to fall where it may.

Neither Barra nor Cillach moved to help Ciaran as the god began to crawl on the ground before regaining his footing.

"It is time to come home." Cillach informed Barra.

"I understand." Barra replied before vanishing and leaving Cillach and Ciaran alone on the ledge.

Cillach's communion had also ended with the others, his voice returning to normal as he spoke to Ciaran, "Bother, you could have bested him."

Ciaran only chuckled, the shattered bone of the man's right knee a bloody mess on the ground as the god forced veins and sinew to thicken in its place, supporting his broken body.

"Why?" Ciaran laughed louder. a sound that was harsh and manic as it bounced off the cliff walls. "This was much more fun."

"The games you two play." Cillach said in disgust.

"A reminder of the old days when we all played these games. You do miss them, the old days, do you not my brother?" Ciaran said as he dug two fingers into one of the wounds that had been opened up in his torso.

Cillach's expression became cold, unreadable at the reminder of the games, wars, the gods use to wage against each other.

"You are also needed to pass judgment on Barra." The god of war reminded Ciaran before he too dissipated into nothingness.

"Of course." And with a smile on his face, a smile full of self-righteous victory, Ciaran vanished from the Gwerin land.

***

A storm rolled through the corridors of the Dotain; a black thing full of malevolence and violence. With angry shouts barking in the hallways as the crew of the Dotain did their best to get out of its way, their captain, Villis Dane.

Dane, in his maddened state stalked his bridge, ordering the Dotain and the other ships to fly west into the gap that separated Birr and Tuame so they could reach the Olean Flats, where he could decide what their next move should be. Dane then left the bridge to make a round of his ship. Checking its inventories while cursing the loss of the Sothair Dor and the servants, four of them, that had fled his and the other ships, before stomping on to his own quarters.

There he found his own servant, Cremin Vokes, sorting his room which, thanks to Barra's trickery, had been upturned and left in a shambles.

Vokes did his best to avoid Dane, who began pacing the room, and seemed to be purposely aiming for Vokes, the captain's lips moving wordlessly at the thoughts racing through his head.

Their strange dance finally ended when Dane backhanded Vokes, catching him across the face, and sending the man sprawling onto the floor.

"Just go!" Dane shouted in his aggravation. Of course the captain was standing in front of the door, and as Vokes stood to leave, Dane went to strike him again, hoping to release more of the rage, over his defeat, that roiled inside of him.

Maybe it was the constant degradation for the past several months, or watching the gods battle this morning, or maybe it was the reality that the words of the escaping man had truth in them, and that maybe he should have also run, that allowed something to snap in Cremin Vokes.

And as Dane went to take another swing at the approaching man, Vokes threw a punch into the captain's gut before sweeping his right foot across Dane's ankles to send the captain tumbling to the ground.

"You will not take me piece by piece! Like you did that Sothair!" Vokes shouted, a wild look in his eyes as he balled his hands into his fists, widening his stance as he waited to be attacked by the captain. "Finish this now!"

Dane was certainly caught off guard by the assault and by Vokes' outburst. Looking upon the man with a new interest the captain climbed to his feet where he winced in pain as the muscles in his abdomen contracted from where Vokes' blow had landed.

"You are bleeding. Sit."

Now it was Vokes' turn to be confused before he realized that there was something wet on his right cheek. He went to dab at it but was once again ordered to sit down by Dane.

Vokes did as he was told whereupon the captain came to stand in front of him and raised the man's head. Dane then used his left thumb to wipe away the red droplets of blood that had formed on the Vokes' cheek.

"There is the Menden blood." Dane said nonchalantly as he wiped his thumb on the thigh of his pants, before wetting his thumb with his tongue and repeating the gesture.

"Your cousin and I had a bet as to when your true nature would show itself again. Lord Lyro thought you had been tainted too much by that tryst with the Sothair in his household and might need to be disposed of. While I on the other hand, I hoped you would see the light and once again find the Menden warrior within you."

Although he was not happy to hear that his living or dying had been part of some wager, Vokes found himself very confused by Dane's gentle ministrations. As the man before him wiped away more blood from his cheek, Vokes did his best to avoid Dane's eye, expecting his captain's mood to turn once again, and to exact some form of retribution on him.

But none was forthcoming.

"So, are you ready to stand by my side?"

"If you are ready to go to the bridge, sir, I would just like to go to and get cleaned and. . ."

Dane hushed Vokes as he stood and went to find a towel to wipe his hand on.

"Not as my servant," Dane explained. "But as my partner. Or do you wish to go back to Mendes to live with your clan? These were the options Lord Lyro gave to me for your liberty."

Vokes had to think for a moment because he didn't know what to say for he had not expected his freedom.

"I will stay here."

Dane smiled; a rare thing on his lips that lacked any of its usual vicious intent. "Good." Because Vokes answer was good for Dane, who now had a way into the Lyro clan.

And just like that the matter between the two men was settled since Dane did have more pressing matters that he needed to attend to.

"Go have the sagarts look after that cut. Don't want it to leave too much of a scar. Also, from now on you will be living in here with me so, once you are done with the priests, go to your room and retrieve what little belongings you have in there. "

"Yes sir." Vokes said as he could feel his wound begin to bleed again.

Dane gave Vokes a look that stopped the man as he went to reach for the door. "On the bridge, or the rest of the ship for that matter, it is captain or sir. But if we are alone or within these walls, it is Dane."

Vokes could only nod, for after using the man's title for so long his name felt heavy and foreign on his tongue. So, without saying a word, Vokes quickly left the room.

Chapter 7
Garradh dhe Dia

Garradh dhe Dia; the Garden of the Gods was home to the immortal, the almighty, deities of the Gwerin people.

Although the garden outside the Temple to Cavanna in Kinsale was similarly named, it was not the home of the gods. That park was more of a reflection, some might even say a more palatable locale, than the actual realm itself.

The plane itself was expansive and though its entirety was named the Garden of the Gods, the actual garden stood in the center of this realm.

Here, in the very center of the Garradh dhe Dia, a plinth of black stone, a little over three feet wide in diameter with veins of silver and gold running through, was embedded in the ground that was surrounded by a sward of grass. The vegetation only high enough for one's bare foot to rest comfortably on, never growing but extending in all directions, for as far as the eye could see, until it met the tree line off in the very far distance, an eternity, which encircled the garden.

Surrounding the plinth were seventeen columns of a grayish white marble, smooth to the touch, no embellishments marring their surface, each a little over two and half feet high. Not a shadow was cast by these columns because no sun could be seen crossing the sky which was a vast region of cobalt blue, uninterrupted by clouds and vacant of birds.

For over a thousand years this place had stayed empty, this garden, this place of judgment quiet, content in its own sterility.

Until today, for Cavanna had called for the nine other gods who had not been banished during the Great Rift to return to the garden.

So here in Garradh dhe Dia was Cavanna, the earth mother, the mother of all, her long auburn hair shimmering of a light all of its own. As was her brother, Aodhagan, the guardian of the sun, the fire god, who was bald, whose eyeballs were cobalt blue to match the sky, heavily built, with his torso bare of clothing or armament, exposing a body covered in perfectly round freckles scattered across his skin, each freckle representing some world that this pantheon had created and ruled.

Although Cavanna's husband had been cast out at the end of the god's war his sisters Murra and Maat had remained behind and now heeded their sister-in-law's calling.

Murra, the goddess of water, her skin a bluish green with a seductively subtle hint of scales dancing across her body as if waves lapped across her form; Murra caretaker of the waters, who had drained the oceans and seas to save the people from killing each other, and who now kept all of these waters of the world held within the Well of Tears, awaiting for the command to release them back upon Gwer.

Maat, Murra's sister, was goddess of the winds. Large wings with feathers as black as a crow's to match the color of her hair grew from her back. Maat, whose feet were clawed like a bird's, their skin all silver and gold, waited silently for the judgment to start.

Ennaya, daughter to Cavanna, twin sister to Barra, had arrived. The huntress, goddess to the lesser creatures, was garbed in tight fitting clothing in shades of russet and browns. Her brown hair was short and wild. And a stoic look was upon on her face as she sat down on one of the white stones.

The god Sioda followed the huntress into this realm. Sioda, the trickster and the seducer, the maker of good luck, an attractive god who was worshipped by merchants seeking good fortune, gamblers wanting coin, and the forlorn, all hoping for the god to turn love's and luck's eye their way.

Dubhas appeared; god of judgment and the keeper to the halls of the dead, youthful in form, dressed in the robes of a sagart. His only weapon being a round mirror framed in ivory. The god's looking glass, a window for the dying to see the true nature of their souls and to be judged before passing on to the next realm.

Cillach also arrived in the garden, a silent communion passing between himself and his niece Ennaya.

As the god of war sat down, his hands planted firmly on his knees, his nephew, the god of the earth materialized on the black plinth, the navel, of this world. Ennaya frowned, a pained look clouding her face as her brother stood there, a faint golden light emanating from his entire being, bringing dawn to this flat world.

Ciaran on the other hand, who loved to make a scene, was the last to arrive the summons.

Still garbed in the dead man's body, his clothing torn, bones shattered and wounds still weeping blood, Ciaran materialized close to Barra. Just close enough to the plinth so as to allow his nephew's handsomeness to accentuate his grotesque form.

A wave of revulsion filled the garden at Ciaran's appearance; except from Sioda who chuckled wickedly, appreciating the jest.

"You disgust us." Cavanna said out loud, neither liking Ciaran's attire nor appreciating Sioda's laughter.

"Merely an example of the atrocity Barra has gone to this day."

But Cavanna was in no mood for this tableau. With a wave of her hand, Ciaran's body burned away, gathering into a single speck of dust in the air, leaving the god standing there in his true form; muscled like an athlete, his ruddy complexion glistening darkly with vitality, his hair dark and curly, a smile escaping from between his mustache and goatee.

While Ciaran begged forgiveness from his sister, that speck, that remnant of the man whose body Ciaran had worn as his own, grew into a seed, a multitude of fine hair-like tendrils grasping at the air and keeping it aloft as it danced its way over to Dubhas, only to land on the god's mirror, a faint ripple crossing the mirror's surface, like a rock splashing into the water, as the tortured soul of the Menden moved on to the next realm.

"But I was not done with him." Ciaran whined like a child bereft of a toy.

"You can retrieve it later, if you must!" Ciaran's sister retorted. "Now we are here for Barra."

All eyes turned to Cavanna's son who stood on the stone of judgment, who without a word, waited patiently, some would say serenely, on the will of the others.

"So what say you?" Maat asked, her black wings stretching, blotting out the blue sky and sending a faint warm breeze filled with the scent of rosemary across the garden.

Barra smiled warmly at his father's sister. "What is there to say? You all have seen what there is to see."

"We have watched you interfere in the affairs of these people!" Ciaran spat, content to see Sioda nod in agreement with him. "You, who have been content to disobey our laws."

"Unlike you uncle?"

Ciaran walked around the plinth, moving behind Barra, as he feigned shock over the accusation. "Not once, until this day, have I appeared to lay a hand on any of my people."

"But you commune with your sagarts!"

"We all commune with our sagarts." Sioda interrupted, obtaining murmurs of agreement from the sisters Maat and Murra.

"But not as a hand to guide in the misery of others." Barra retorted.

"They would not be miserable if they went with the Mendens willingly." Ciaran quipped.

"They would not be miserable if your worshippers just left the rest of the people alone. And I do what the rest of you have chosen not to do. To protect the Gwer from the claws of my uncle."

"But it is their seed that keeps my people from dying off and becoming mongrels. The chase and the battle keep the blood hot and their bodies strong as they once use to be." Ciaran retorted defensively.

Barra could not help but frown while Ciaran smiled smugly as a faint rumble of agreement moved throughout the garden as all the gods remembered a time when any of the Gwer would have laid their lives down for them. A time that only seemed like yesterday to all of them. A time of continuous conflict that was still missed by many of the gods in this garden who now sat in judgment over Barra.

"The people would still be strong if you were not around." Barra said as a faint frown crossed his face.

Ciaran laughed. "But conflict makes it is easier for them to remember their strengths."

Once again murmurs of agreement with Ciaran's words filled the garden.

"Then we are at an impasse." Barra said, his voice filled with resignation, as no one, not even his sister, came to his aid. "And things will continue on unchanged."

"No they will not!" Ciaran spat and pointed an accusatory finger at his nephew. "It was you who laid hands on me! Not since the banishment have we accosted each other. I demand retribution for this atrocity!"

Ciaran couldn't help but gloat as Sioda, Maat and Murra once again voiced agreement with him.

"So what would you like brother? What would appease your wounded spirit?" Cavanna, her voice flat and aloof, asked, ready to pass judgment on her own son.

"He should be banished. Just like the others have been for their crimes."

"But not with them." Ennaya interjected, finally coming to the defense of her brother.

"No, not with them." Cillach agreed. "His spirit would not survive being around them again for he is too much changed."

"Then send him on to one of the barren worlds!" Ciaran shouted as he sprinted over to his brother Aodhagan, who had not sat down, and laid a hand on the god's bare chest.

"Why not here?" Ciaran pointed to one of the freckles, one of their worlds, on Aodhagan's chest. "Or here." His finger trailed to another spot on the Aodhagan's shoulder. "Or here." Ciaran continued as he walked around Aodhagan, his finger stopping on a freckle in the middle of his brother's back. "Where he can do no harm."

But Ennaya and Cillach were adamantly against the idea of this banishment. As was Sioda, the god enjoying the discord about him and looking to prolong it, bringing a frown to Ciaran's face at his reversal of support.

"But I demand retribution!" Ciaran shouted, taking a step towards his sister, as he felt the judgment he wanted for Barra beginning to slip from his grasp.

"There is another way." Dubhas said, the mirror held loosely in his hand, its surface reflecting only the blue of the sky as he moved around.

"Yes." Cavanna agreed, for she knew the thoughts of Dubhas on this matter.

As did the rest of the pantheon, with each nodding in agreement with the Dubhas, until only Ciaran was left to cast his lot.

"Very well!" Ciaran acquiesced, his face clouding over like a black storm on the horizon, hoping his brethren believed he truly was disgruntled over this decision.

No words passed between mother and son for Cavanna's face was smooth and impassive. Perfect. As if it had been carved in stone and polished by the finest craftsmen. The exception to this being her eyes that now only held sadness and disappointment for her son.

Barra remained silent, lowering his head, as he waited for the finality of this day.

He did not wait long because the black rock he was standing on came to life with a dull, low hum, with its veins of silver and gold shining brightly. A light as bright as the sun and the moon blending together, and as fine as well-honed blades, the light shot up and into Barra's body, the god screaming in agonizing pain as he collapsed to his knees, leaving a reddish gold ball of light floating in the air where he once stood.

Cavanna summoned the ball of energy to her, while Barra struggled to his feet, his essence, his godliness, floating above the open palms of his mother's hands.

For once, Cavanna looked lovingly at the glowing, swirling ball hovering above her open palms, while Ciaran looked at it hungrily, wishing that he could devour the spirit that was once his nephew as retribution for his slights.

But Cavanna had other plans for Barra's spirit and summoned Ennaya forward.

"This is for you and your safe keeping." The goddess told her daughter, as the ball then moved over to the huntress and teasingly danced about her before coming to rest against her bosom, slowly fading as her body absorbed Barra's essence into her own.

Cavanna turned back to look upon the mortal that now stood before them; a husk of the being Barra once use to be.

"What shall we now do with you?" She asked her son.

"I will surely die here, in this place of solitude."

Cavanna agreed.

"Then a boon I ask. One last request as your son."

Cavanna beckoned her son forward, who whispered his favor into her ear. Finally a smile, faint, small and sad, crept across her exquisite face as she ran a hand through Barra's once golden brown hair, now dull and flat in her eyes, as she looked upon his diminishment.

"This request you shall have."

Chapter 8
Kinsale

Daigh stood on the balcony to his room at the inn where he was staying while in the capitol of Birr nursing a drink in his hand as he watched the throngs of people crowding the street below.

No festivities brought the people of Kinsale out of their homes to wander through the markets, neighborhood districts, or down near the wharves, where he was hold up this night; nor the night before.

Daigh watched as groups of men gathered together, some under street lamps looking up towards the heavens, some holding lanterns with their heads close together as if in some secretive conversation, the occasional sound of the word why, floating up to his ears, as they chattered over the portents of the past days' events.

Why was a good question to ask, Daigh thought sourly as he sipped from his drink, thankful the crowds below had remained calm and had not turned into a chaotic mob. Thankful that clusters of the Royal Guard and sagarts from every temple in the city could be seen doing their best to quell any hysteria that was slowly building within the citizenry since yesterday.

Why had the lodestones, the gods' gift they had all come to depend on, suddenly stopped working, leaving ships stranded in their berths and trams dead on their rails. Leaving men and women wondering how they were supposed to continue on with their daily routines without transportation.

How was he about to get home with his ship not capable of flying, with he and his crew stranded in this foreign land, Daigh wondered.

"Well, I won't be going back up to the castle for help." Daigh said out loud as his eyes wandered across the bay to Old Kinsale and the castle sitting in the middle of it, lights shining brightly from all of its windows, like a beacon of hope for its panicked people.

"If I have to cross the flats on foot, then that's what I'll do." Daigh mumbled bitterly while his eyes tried to make out the dark shape of the castle against the night sky. "I am done with you Dar Fionn. I am done with you."

***

Daigh had arrived in Kinsale several days ago on his small yacht, berthing it on the mainland side of the city.

Wanting some solitude away from his crew for the time being, Daigh searched for an inn for himself before his trek up to the castle. As was his want to continue his self-abuse, Daigh first went to the inn he had stayed in on his first search for Fionn almost twenty-five years ago. But the inn lacked any vacancies so he had no choice but to rent a room from an inn further up the hill. Fortunately for Daigh, at least he thought so, it had almost the same view as the last room he was in and spent his first night in Kinsale on the room's balcony, staring up at the indistinct silhouette of the home of his old lover.

Dawn found Daigh slumped in a chair on the balcony, cold and bleary eyed from his vigil over Old Kinsale, as he waited for the castle to finally come to life in the morning light.

Finally surrendering to what needed to get done, Daigh pulled himself out of the chair so that he could get dressed. Putting on a pair of dark green woolen pants and a cream cotton shirt embroidered with a vine native to Talamh Shar, which was stitched in the same colored thread as the shirt with the vine running across the shirt's shoulders, arms and down its back. And over that he threw on a vest dyed of a green that was a shade or two lighter than his pants and brocaded with the same vine as his shirt, its buttons enameled in a deep coppery red.

And as the sounds of the city coming to life made their way into his room through the opened doors of the balcony, Daigh took his time trimming some stray hairs on his beard and moustache, until he realized he was procrastinating once again and reluctantly set his small scissors down on his grooming kit and left his room.

Thankfully the men of Kinsale were of the friendly sort and one man, when asked, directed Daigh to the nearest tram station, even walking to the nearest corner with Daigh to make sure he would be able to find his way. Daigh was even able to get news, mostly rumors that were running rampant on the streets about Fionn's son's disappearance.

He also learned that Banning's older brother had set out for Murra's Maze to begin searching for him, which made Daigh grateful that he, only wanting to avoid the crash site at all costs, had decided to skirt the Maze on his trip to Birr's capitol.

As Daigh walked from the tram to the castle he couldn't help but feel uneasy noticing that a majority of men on the streets in this district were dressed as members of the Royal Guard. Daigh quelled his feeling of guilt for the moment and, maintaining his swagger, did his best to avoid the eyes of many of the men as he continued on his way.

Of course, for a city that was so well defended, the gates to Kinsale's castle were open, with four guards, two on each side of the gate, standing watch as men and some women passed into the courtyard of the castle as they went about their business.

Not knowing what to do, and with all the flair he could muster, Daigh approached one of the men standing vigil and inquired about talking to the consort. The soldier directed him to a man standing on the far end of the castle's courtyard where Daigh repeated his question with the new man also listening to Daigh's explanation about being an old family friend of the consort's from Seruth, the capital of Talamh Shar.

Begging patience from Daigh, the guard called out to a third man and once again repeated Daigh's story, before sending the man on his way to find the consort to see if he would grant Daigh's request for a visitation with him.

While he waited, Daigh tried to make small talk with the guard. But the man proved to be very reserved and tight lipped, very different from the men he met in the lower districts, and Daigh found himself quietly watching the traffic move in and out of the castle proper.

After what seemed like an eternity, maybe about half an hour, the man who had been sent on the errand returned saying that Dar Fionn had accepted his request for an audience and offered to escort Daigh to him.

Once they entered the castle the guard seemed to take a circuitous route, avoiding the main halls, walking through hallways and climbing stairwells, passing a multitude of armored men, as they made their way to the consort's private library. There they found Fionn pacing the room, hands behind his back, moving back and forth in front of a cold fireplace, the consort only turning towards the open door when he caught the movement of the two men out of the corner of his eye.

Both Fionn and Daigh stood transfixed as they stared at each other, momentarily forgetting that a guard was standing within the room as well.

But the moment was short lived because the loss of his son weighed more heavily on Fionn than having a ghost walk out of the past and invited Daigh to have a seat in one of the chairs in front of the fireplace.

"You may leave the door open." Fionn said to the guard who had been reaching in to close the door, assuming the men had wanted privacy. Giving a curt nod to the consort, the guard did as he was told before disappearing from view.

"Well, this is a surprise!" Fionn said as he took the chair across from Daigh.

"I suppose." Daigh forced a smile that he really didn't feel onto his face, lost in the moment because, even though his blond hair was beginning to silver, and dark circles and wrinkles framed his eyes, Daigh could only see the youth of the man he had begged to leave with him to steal away on their own adventure over twenty-five years ago.

As the silence lengthened and became awkward, with Daigh staring intently at Fionn, who began to fidget in his seat, the consort to Aerin Riocard finally asked what brought him to Kinsale.

Daigh blinked as reality reasserted itself on his thoughts of the past, the what ifs of his life blowing away, as the reason for his flight here moved painfully forward in his mind.

"I found Banning."

"What?"

"I found your son." Daigh said once more, looking down at his fingers as he picked at his nails, unable to look at Fionn. "I found Banning."

"Well that's wonderful!" Fionn said as he stood, the shock of what he heard wearing off, relieved that his son was alive. "But why didn't the guard say anything? Where is he? Did he go to his room?"

Daigh's face turned red and he wiped sweat from his forehead, his voice faltering as he explained how he had left Banning back at his home in Carnuaimh.

"I do not understand."

Daigh was devastated at how crestfallen Fionn now looked, but did not feel sympathetic enough to not lie. "I did not know the boy was yours until I got him home."

"We happened to be travelling through Murra's Maze when my men spotted him stumbling through the Maze's main channel. Banning was quite disoriented and exhausted and he wasn't able to tell us who he was or where he was from until we reached Iniscarn. And when he explained what had happened to him, and that he was your son, I thought it prudent to leave him behind so that he could continue to regain his strength and for an armed escort could retrieve him."

"A most wise decision."

Both men looked towards the room's entrance to see Fionn's partner, Aerin Riocard, the ruler of Birr, standing in the doorway. His towering presence and piercing blue eyes made Daigh even more uncomfortable than he already felt with Daigh regretting that he had left Banning behind because if he had brought the boy he could have already been done with all of these people by now.

Fionn walked over to his Riocard, and placing a hand on the man's forearm, pulled him into the room and introduced the two men to each other, excited over the news about his son, oblivious to the tension that was building in the room and the look of recognition that appeared on Riocard's face at the mention of Daigh's name.

"Ah! You are from Seruth?" And when Daigh admitted that he was correct, Riocard said politely, "Then I have met your father, whom I thought was a very honorable man. Our son is safe with him?"

"No." Now miffed at the reminder that he had seen his aging father only twice within the twenty-five years since he had left home, Daigh once again explained how he had found Banning and that he was safe at his own villa in Carnuaimh.

"Iniscarn? How long have you been there?" Fionn asked, because he had not heard that the first time Daigh had mentioned it, his thoughts and concerns being only for his son.

Daigh was peeved by the question and silently cursed the gods for the situation he was now in and explained that he had been living in Iniscarn and working for the Lord Argus Berach for over twenty years.

Riocard nodded as he listened to the man's story, recalling what Goban and Ibor had told him about the attack, wishing they were now here, watching a faint frown form on Fionn's face.

"Was our son injured?" The ruler asked.

"No." Daigh said, trying not to be curt with the lord of Birr, who was making Daigh feel like he should be on the rack to be interrogated. "Like I said, other than being exhausted and sleeping soundly for several days, he is quite well. Not a scratch on him."

"The flats are not as safe as they use to be." Fionn said, still disturbed by the attack on his son and the increasing attacks by the Mendens. "We should have never let him go."

"He is a young man." Riocard corrected his partner. "And just like Manus, he has a duty to his family and our kingdom."

Daigh watched as a discussion ensued between the couple about what was best for Banning, chagrined that he was privy to this conversation, yet wishing, as he watched Fionn redden as he seemed to be in a losing battle with Riocard, that it was he who was having this debate with his old lover.

But Daigh finally coughed into his hand, interrupting the two men, reminding them that they were not alone in the room.

"Banning is not the only one of the reasons why I am here." Daigh then explained that he was not only here to tell them the good news about Banning, but to put forward a business proposition where the Lord Argus' fleet would act as protection for Birrnian merchants flying through Murra's Maze. "Of course, we would hope to be able to keep several ships berthed in one or two of your eastern towns so that traveling and trading would be convenient for us as well."

"And we do not have to only fly to Iniscarn. We would be willing to travel to Ardane, Wex, and of course the smaller kingdom of Wexlan. And, because there is always strength in numbers when one crosses the open desert, we would be willing to brave the flats and travel to Amarra with you."

"For a price." Riocard said as he crossed his arms over his chest, intrigued by the proposal.

"Of course." Daigh said, a smile finally appearing on his face as he mimicked Riocard's stance. "But, whether you pay or the merchant's do, it's entirely up to you and your people. We can send a representative here or set up a meeting in Inchinver with Lord Argus to hammer out any trade details when you come to retrieve your son."

"I will send someone from the merchant's guild who can talk further about this venture with your lord."

"Very good Milord. Do you have some writing materials I could use?"

Fionn directed Daigh to his desk, and pulled out some parchment, quill and ink, and a stick of red colored wax. And as Fionn reached across the desk to retrieve a lit candle from the desk's edge, their eyes met, and Fionn couldn't help but smile at the man, as Daigh's presence and closeness finally brought up fond memories of their past.

A smile that did not go unnoticed by Riocard, who decided to walk over to the desk, joining the two men and watched as Daigh wrote out two letters and folding them into thirds before taking the wax and using the candle to melt drops onto each. As the letters were sealed shut Daigh pulled out an object from his vest that looked like a small, carved rolling pin and, placing it between his thumb and forefinger, rolled it over the cooling wax, leaving the impression of his household's mark from the wheel; hieroglyphs for his family's clan name and a very archaic symbol for the word maverick.

"Give this one to the dock master in Inchinver." Daigh explained to Riocard as he marked the outside of one of the letters with some names, while leaving it on the table so the wax seal could cool properly. "The letter will get you an escort and passage to my villa in Carnuaimh where Banning will be residing. The second one is for your guild representative and will give him access to our court at Inchinver and an audience with Lord Argus."

"You will not be escorting us?" Fionn said, unable to hide the disappointment from his voice.

"No." Daigh said flatly as he tried to keep his own emotions, at seeing Fionn, in check. "I should get back as soon as possible to make sure everything is ready for your arrival."

Fionn nodded, toying with one of the letters on his desk, while Riocard thanked the man for finding and caring for his foster-son and for the audience with the ruler of Iniscarn.

"Think nothing of it Lord Aerin. I would like to think that someone would take proper care of my son, if I had one, if he was lost. Hopefully we can agree upon some venture that will be profitable for our two kingdoms." Daigh said as he bowed to the couple.

"A guard is waiting outside of this room and will escort you back to the courtyard." Riocard explained.

Daigh, understanding that his services were no longer needed, and that he was being dismissed, nodded one more time to the ruler of Birr before leaving the room.

"Thank the gods that Banning is safe and well and has been in good hands." Fionn said, relieved by the news of his son's rescue, rubbing at the muscles on the back of his neck that had been knotted since being told of his son's abduction.

Riocard only mumbled something incoherently while he toyed with one of Daigh's letters, turning it so that he could get a better look at Daigh's mark in the cooling wax.

"Well, I should go prepare to leave. Who do you think it would be wise to take with me and how many ships should go?" Fionn went to grab the letter Riocard had been moving about the table, but was caught off guard when his partner put a couple of fingers on it to hold it in place.

"I do not think it would be wise for you to go." Riocard told him bluntly, a blank expression on his face as he looked at Fionn. "You should remain here until Banning returns and we can retrieve Manus from wherever his searching has sent him."

"But I do not want to stay!" Fionn said angrily, not wanting to let go of the letter. "I want my son back and I want to be the one who gets him."

"Was it nice to see him?"

"What?" Fionn asked, confused by the question.

"Was it nice to see Emmis Daigh again?" Riocard repeated, his blue eyes darkening while the muscles in his jaw clenched tightly. Both signs that meant Riocard was angry; both signs for a mood that had always been a rarity in their household.

Fionn's voice faltered, a response dying on his lips, stunned by the question and its implications, and couldn't help but remember how happy he had felt at seeing Daigh. Although, his red beard and moustache showed signs of graying and there had seemed to be a multitude of wrinkles at the corners of his eyes, Fionn couldn't help but remember the boy he had fallen in love, the man, who still had a place in his heart.

After his brief moment of reminiscing, Fionn finally said, "Yes, it was nice to see an old friend from Seruth."

But the pause said more to Riocard than any word that came out of Fionn's mouth.

"I know."

"Know what?" Fionn asked, somewhat confused by the statement and by the direction their conversation had taken.

"About the last time your old friend Emmis Daigh was here. My father and I knew about the rendezvous the two of you had before our marriage."

"Rendezvous?" Then it dawned on Fionn what Riocard was talking about with a mixture of fear and anger welling up inside of him over the unspoken implication.

But his anger won out, and Fionn shouted, "But that was so long ago! And I sent him away!"

"I know how you sent him away!" Riocard shouted back at him, his face reddening to match Fionn's, as his left hand gripped the edge of Fionn's desk, his knuckles turning white from his grasp on it as if he wanted to use all of his force so that he might snap the edge off the wooden desk. "You do not think your escorts kept secret of what they came upon in the alleyway?"

A slightly cynical laugh escaped Riocard's lips as he watched Fionn's face, whose resolve in defending himself crumbled away as the truth of that night came into the light.

"You did!" Riocard repeated, confirming his allegation, slapping the top of the desk with the open palm of his hand, the sickly sound of it filling the room as Riocard chuckled a little louder, shaking his head in disappointment.

"My father was livid." Riocard said as he sobered a little, for he too was angry at having to relive a past that he assumed had been forgotten. "How my father wanted to stop our ceremony and send you back to Talamh Shar. He was willing to give up on the unification with your father's kingdom to save me from any embarrassment of your indiscretion before our ceremony was ever found out."

Fionn wished that Riocard's father had cancelled their contract in marriage as he realized that there was a time when he could have escaped with Daigh. But his thoughts of self-pity were interrupted as Riocard continued.

"And then there was Cavanna who was already a member of the current high sagartta's inner circle whom your guards felt obligated to tell about your encounter."

"She knew too?" Fionn whispered, mortified that everyone had known about his secret for all these years.

"Yes she knew, and she was far from thrilled about coupling with you! Father had to give her and the temple a large sum of gold crowns just to make sure your union happened. Why do you think she would never bed with you again to produce more children?"

Riocard couldn't help but shake his head in disgust as he once again thought about the argument his father had with the old high sagartta to Cavanna. "All that money spent for one child."

My child, Fionn thought, while doing the only thing he could think of and apologized for an indiscretion that happened twenty-five years ago.

"You should have sent him away before anything happened."

"Yes, you are right." Fionn whispered, feeling as if he had been defeated once more. "I am sorry and will do as you say. I will stay here and wait for Banning."

Riocard retrieved the letters and looked at his partner, who was now doing his best to not look back at him, his gaze falling on almost every other object in the room, but at him.

"I will get these to the Royal Guard and will have several ships sent to retrieve Banning." Riocard almost slipped and said "our son" but that didn't seem appropriate because Banning didn't feel like his right now, especially after his condemnation of his father. "I will understand if you do not feel up to having dinner with the governors from the northern province tonight."

"No, I will be there." Fionn said, maybe a little too sardonically. "I would not want to let you down again."

Riocard ignored the jibe, knowing full well he deserved it, yet still unhappy that he once again had to be reminded of Emmis Daigh, and left the room.

Grateful for the solitude, Fionn silently cursed the gods. Not that it mattered because he knew that Riocard would not turn around if he had heard him. So Fionn paced his library like a caged animal, and cursed in frustration at not being able to retrieve his son, and he cursed his own stupidity at not knowing what had been going on around him for his entire married life. He cursed Daigh for being the catalyst in revealing his naiveté and the deception within his own household, and he cursed Riocard for what now seemed like a failed union.

But it had not always been that way. At least, so Fionn thought, there had been a time when they were happy. They seemed happy, those early years they were together, until Aerin Broll's premature death. Riocard's father's passing had left a vacuum in leadership that his son had to quickly fill, especially when it came to maintaining the unification of one of the largest kingdoms in the world.

So their relationship became secondary, with Fionn left behind in Kinsale as Riocard spent weeks which turned into months traveling across the continent, acting as monarch, assuring his people that he would continue on with the peace and prosperity that his family had established.

When Riocard was at home in the capitol, most of his time was spent in court, with Fionn at his side, listening to the mass of petitioners awaiting a royal review. Or he would hole himself up with the officers of his guard in the secondary fortress that had been built in the newer section of Kinsale.

Maybe, Fionn thought, he should have tried harder and accompanied Riocard on his trips. Or, now that he knew everyone in his household had known his secret, maybe the travelling had been an excuse to escape him. Or maybe, Riocard would have been better off marrying a warrior, rather than him.

Fionn just didn't know what the answers were to his questions while he sat in the chair Daigh had vacated, wishing not for the first time, as he closed his eyes and squeezed the arms of the chair, inhaling deeply and fantasizing that Daigh's scent still lingered on the fabric of the chair, that he should have run away with his old lover when had the chance.

Fionn sighed heavily because he knew that any dreams of escape he had were not going to happen; especially now, so late in his life.

Opening his eyes, feeling emotionally drained and lonely, Fionn stared off into space focusing on nothing in the room, telling himself he should get up and go get ready for tonight's dinner. But his body felt as if it was made of lead, like he was a burden even unto himself, and remained in the chair, wishing to be forgotten.

That's how members of the Royal Guard found Fionn, looking as if he must have fallen asleep as they mobilized the inhabitants of the castle to deal with the unexplainable phenomenon and uncertainty that was beginning to unfold out in the city.

Because, while Fionn was feeling sorry for himself, and Riocard was angry at having to relive the embarrassment of Fionn's perceived infidelity before their union, and Daigh wandered the streets of Kinsale, bitter over not being able to move on and forget his feelings for Fionn, trams halted on their tracks, barges and warcraft slowly fell to the ground, and any manner of vehicle powered by the lodestones, died.

Not only in Kinsale, but all over the world steersman lost their connections to the lodestones, unable to power their vehicles, sending crowds of people out onto the streets and to the temples, wanting to know what this loss of mobility meant to them.

But the gods were quiet, and had been for several days as the judgment of Barra began and his punishment was exacted.

Mair Mihra, the oracle to the gods who resided in Kinsale, sat on her chair in the Garradh dhe Dia outside of the temple to Cavanna quietly imploring to the gods to call out to her. While Mihra's sister Betrys and many of the sagarts and sagarttas from other temples milled about her and prayed to their own deities. Their own frustrations at being ignored by their gods slowly building, and filling the ceremonial glade as if it was a tub, threatening to drown the blind woman in their fears of abandonment.

And just when their anxieties were about to boil over into panic, with many families beginning to board up their homes while scurrying about for supplies they deemed necessary to survive this impending doom, the pantheon returned, their voices filled with words of reassurance and peace to their followers.

Also the lodestones, which many steersmen now said had a different, feminine quality to them, began to work once again.

Sadly, not all the priests heard from their gods. For at the temple of Barra, the sagarts and sagarttas who worshiped the god of the earth began to question the portent of his silence and of the emptiness they now felt in their hearts.

A portent that many began to contemplate, wondering what doom had befallen the god of the earth as daily life resumed about the city with Daigh all but forgetting Fionn as he planned on getting himself and his crew home as soon as possible. With Riocard postponing the retrieval of his foster-son while he worked on re-establishing order in the city and outlying countryside, sending out envoys to make sure that the rest of his kingdom had fared well.

And Fionn? Fionn went back to his life of solitude within the castle, forgotten once again by Riocard who went back to ruling his kingdom. Fionn, who was also ignored by Betrys, the woman told of Fionn's knowledge of the past and the price that had been paid for his child, as she focused on whatever spiritual endeavors kept her busy. Fionn, who cursed his own lot in life, praying hopelessly to truly be forgotten out of the memories of his partner, his family, and the people around him, so that he might have a chance of having some semblance of a life that he could call his own.

Chapter 9
The Camalain

"Better, much better Liam! Now, step left, left! Punch with your right fist! Now a hook with your left! No Liam, hold, hold!"

Liam stopped as he was told and bent over, grateful for the break as he lowered his hands to his knees to catch his breath.

The crew of the Camalain had left Murra's Maze four days ago and had been traveling towards the southern tip of Birr for the entire time, and as soon as they had left the canyons, Manus had made sure Liam was scheduled to start weapon's training by someone other than Karam Kael.

No, most certainly not by Kael who Manus kept busy by doubling his rounds of the ship, making sure everyone on duty was alert, prepared in case of an attack. Or Manus did his best to have Kael at his side while he was on the bridge just in case an emergency arose.

Thankfully, Gorman, who along with his mates, had befriended Liam and had volunteered to train him during their breaks in the afternoon, for the prince. When Gorman realized the only training Liam had was the show he had put on with Kael and the crossbow, he decided to start Liam off with a much simpler weapon; punching daggers.

Simple they were not, Liam thought, still doubled over, his breathing starting to slow down as Gorman walked over to him. They were practicing in one of the storage bays with sacks of grain and other dried goods piled against the walls, leaving the center of the room empty where Liam, along with Manton, who had volunteered to help with his training, stood waiting for Gorman to correct Liam's mistakes.

Yarrow was at the practice session as well. But he was off to one side sitting on some sacks watching the show, giving his own criticism of Liam's performance. As was Kael, who had in between his rounds today, found time to sneak away from Manus' watchful eye and hang out with the group.

"Here." Gorman said as he instructed Liam to get back into a defensive stance.

Liam did as he was told, the muscles in his arms shaking from the workout and from the added weight placed upon them, as he put his fists up to block his face, because, instead of actual daggers, Liam had thick rounded pieces of wood, about five pounds each, strapped to his knuckles with a thick leather strap that wrapped around the palms of his hands and wrists with leather finger guards to keep the practice weapons in place. Gorman also had Liam wearing a rounded buckler on his left forearm, so he would get used to his weight being unbalanced during combat.

"Your left hook is wide. Looks like you're trying to fly, which means you're leaving your armpit exposed. Get cut under there and you'll bleed to death." Gorman explained as he pushed Liam's elbow closer to his body where Gorman wanted Liam's arm to be and then had him watch Manton recreate the maneuver.

Liam did his best to watch Manton's arm, mimicking the hook. But, because the storage bay was warm and unventilated, both he and Manton were bare-chested, and Liam found it hard to concentrate on he was being told by the combination of being exhausted and a little distracted by Manton's hairy chest glistening with sweat as his muscled torso flexed to the movement of his arm.

"And your right arm seems to be going a little wide as well." Gorman said, interrupting Liam's thoughts. "Keep your arms close to your body and jab quickly with your right. If the weight is feeling awkward on your knuckles, try twisting your hand as it shoots out. You'll have more control over the weight of your weapon and a slightly better chance of hitting something vital in your opponent."

Liam only nodded as he used his right forearm to wipe the sweat away on his forehead as he watched Manton alternate from left hook to right punch, instinctually shuffling his feet before ending his routine with a flurry of quick underhanded punches meant for his imaginary opponent's abdomen.

"Show off!" Yarrow yelled while Manton raised an arm in mock victory, eliciting chuckles from everyone in the room before clapping the solid wooden blocks together.

"Gorman. Maybe you should have Liam go a couple of rounds with someone else." Kael suggested as Manton went to stand by Liam's side as he too wiped the sweat from his face in the crook of his arm before nodding to Liam to once again copy his stance.

Gorman, who had been doing weapon's training for well over ten years, told Manton and Liam to lower their arms and rest for a moment and turned to Kael. Gorman, as well as everyone else in the room, knew that he was here to see Liam and was willing to humor the young man and give him some leeway when it came to telling him how to do his job.

"What do you have in mind?"

"Two teams of course. The attacking men with swords, and. . ."

Kael faltered with his plan of action when Liam groaned in agony at the possibility of being thrown into a competition when he could just barely hold the mock weapons without his arms shaking. Of course, Liam only got snickers from the other men, with Manton giving him a "poor baby" as he patted him on the back while Gorman asked Kael to continue with his idea.

Kael shrugged and mouthed an apology to Liam who sarcastically returned the shrug before Kael resumed with what he was saying. "Well, you're training Liam with defensive weapons, usually used to help protect the back of a swords man. So why not have two men with swords go a couple of rounds with Liam so he can get used to being in a defensive position and to get a feel for what he should be doing?"

The sword bout wasn't a bad idea and Gorman was about to thank Kael for it and to ask him to join them for the next session when a shudder ran through the Camalain right before the ship suddenly dipped in the air, sending Gorman, Manton and Liam stumbling as they tried to maintain their balance while Yarrow and Kael held onto the sacks they were sitting on.

Then the sound that they were going to land filled the air just, as the Camalain dipped again, as it began its slow descent.

"What's going on?" Liam asked to no one in particular as Kael and Yarrow slid off of their seats following Gorman who had already headed out into the hallway to try and find out what was happening.

"Don't know." Kael replied as he toyed with the pommel of his short sword and suggested that Liam should stay behind for now for his own safety before he headed out the door.

But Liam wasn't going to be deterred and followed the men out of the storage bay, shirtless, just like Manton was, because he had no idea how he would have thrown his shirt on while having the blocks of wood and the buckler strapped to his knuckles and arm.

"Just keep your head down if there's trouble." Yarrow whispered into Liam's ear as he pushed the young man in front of him and, just as weaponless as the others with his hands flexing into fists, took up the rear guard.

The group had joined several other men heading up the stairs to the main deck when they felt the Camalain shudder one more time before the ship landed a little too roughly, the men reaching out to brace themselves between the walls of the stairwell to avoid from falling.

"Do you think it's just an early shift change?" Liam asked Yarrow.

"We'll find out when we get above deck." The man replied before nodding for Liam to follow the rest of the men as they continued up the stairs.

Upon exiting the cabin they found that they weren't the only ones out on deck for most of the crew, some of the men with weapons at their sides, were at the railings of the ship trying to find out from their neighbor what was happening.

Kael immediately left the group when he spotted Manus, Liam's father, and several other men on the upper deck and decided to see if he could get some information from his friend, leaving the others to fend for themselves as they too added their questions to the volley that was being tossed as made their way to a railing.

What they saw left them even more confused because the Marmairn had landed almost a mile away with two of the three gliders grounded and within walking distance of either vessel while the third, the one that had been berthed on the Camalain, was nowhere to be seen.

One of the glider pilots already exited his ship and, using a piece of polished metal, started to reflect the sun off of it, as he tried to contact the Camalain, then the Marmairn.

"Says his ship won't fly." Gorman said out loud, a hand shading his eyes as he interpreted the signaling.

"Same goes for the other." Manton added as he pointed to the other glider whose pilot was signaling to both vessels. "He says he can't connect with the stones."

Gorman frowned. "This isn't good. Manton, why don't you and Liam go get dressed, then take him to the armory and grab some weapons for all of us."

Manton grunted in agreement and left with Liam in tow as Gorman gave similar orders to some of the other men who were milling about around him.

"Do you think the same thing happened to us?" Liam asked Manton as he followed the man's lead and began unstrapping the practice weapons from their hands as they made their way to the storage bay where they had left their belongings.

"I hope not because if we can't fly we're screwed."

Liam let Manton's words sink in, wondering what they would do if they were stranded out here as they threw on their shirts before heading to Manton's cabin, a cabin that he shared with a half dozen other men, where he grabbed his and Yarrow's gear.

Once they reached the armory Manton found some leather armor, with a left shoulder guard, also of hardened leather for Liam to wear. Instead of explaining to Liam how to wear the armor, Manton had Liam raise his arms high so he could belt the side straps for the protective gear and shoulder guard for him.

Manton also re-strapped the buckler Liam had been wearing back on to his left forearm before searching for a suitable weapon for him to wield.

"I can handle this one." Liam said, noticing a hammer hanging from the wall. The hammer was slightly larger than the mallets he used while stone carving and was much heavier because its square head was made of solid iron while its wooden handle was covered in leather so the weapon wouldn't slip from its wielder's grasp.

Manton had Liam adjust his grasp on it, having him slip his hand through the thong on the end of the hammer so he would have a harder time losing the weapon if he dropped it.

"And take this." Manton said as he gave Liam a belt with a dagger in it. "Put it on later." He added as he grabbed some gear for Gorman before they headed out the door.

Once topside they passed many of the Royal Guard, now armored, just as the they now were, and made their way back to their group of friends, seeing that Verrim Heath, Gorman's partner, had now joined them.

Heath, who was also wearing leather armor with a longbow strapped across his back, the bowstring resting against a quiver of arrows and a sword belted at his side, greeted Liam and Manton as he took the bundle Liam extended to him and helped Gorman don the armor brought for his partner, before also handing him his weapons.

Once his hands were free Liam buckled the belt to his waist, fumbling with it as he tried to get the dagger to rest comfortably on his right hip and watched as Manton helped Yarrow with his own equipment, wishing he had brought a second belt or something else to strap the hammer to his waist.

So Liam waited quietly, listening with half an ear as Manton interrogated the others for new information, only to find out they were still in the dark as before. He watched as the men on deck sorted themselves into groups of sixes and eights, fighting squads he, as Manton's friend Dolan came to join their group.

That's when Liam spotted Yanno Crogan on deck. The cook was standing in front of the flight of stairs leading to the upper deck where the prince and his officers were still in a deep discussion. Not only was the burly man's body blocking the stairs, he also had a large vicious looking cleaver in his hand; a cleaver Liam had not seen lying around the kitchen and something he would choose to avoid at all possible because the polished weapon looked like it could slice through muscle and bone with a single swing.

With his legs wide, feet planted firmly on the planking, his arms crossed with the cleaver reflecting sunlight, Crogan looked like he was not going to allow friend or foe pass by him. But he did move out of the way as several officers descended the stairs and began giving out orders to the groups of men.

One of them was Lieutenant Cahl, who was followed by Sidri, another man whom Liam had seen in the company of Gorman and Manton, approached their group.

Sidri, who also carried a longbow similar to Heath's, with two short swords at his waist, fell in with the group as the lieutenant informed them they would be going out to retrieve the two downed men.

"We are still not sure what is going on and the prince does not want those men wandering the flats alone." Cahl Goban explained.

"What about Vohr?" Gorman asked, wondering about the third glider pilot who was stationed on the Camalain.

"The steersman says he was somewhere north of us when we went down. We have yet to see a signal from him so he might be a ways back. We will get these two back on board, then plan on fetching him."

"Oh, and Liam, you will be staying onboard." The lieutenant said to the group's adopted member. "I want you to stand watch with Master Yanno until Gorman and his crew returns."

"Aye, sir." Liam replied, somewhat relieved he did not have to go out onto the flats, while also feeling guilty because it seemed like he was letting the others down.

Nevertheless, Liam parted company with the group and made his way over to Yanno Crogan, the old cook grunting a welcome and using the cleaver to point at a place where Liam could stand.

From his new position, Liam could hear the prince and the others deep in discussion. Unfortunately the men weren't talking loud enough for him to make out what they were saying. And when he looked up he only caught a glimpse of his father, who had wandered over to the railing, a worried look on his face, which he did his best to hide when he noticed his son looking at him before turning away to rejoin the others.

But that fleeting look only made Liam more concerned for his friends on the flats so, with Master Yanno's permission, promising the man to keep his head down, hurried back over to the railing to see how they were faring.

The group of men had already made it to the halfway mark to the first downed glider and had left Heath and Sidri behind, their longbows in hand and knocked with arrows. Yarrow had also remained with Heath and Sidri. With weapons in hand, the three soldiers acted as a rear guard in case their friends needed to make a quick retreat back towards the ship.

The Marmairn had also sent out a group of its own soldiers to help defend the rescuers and Liam watched as Gorman and his crew, along with the first glider pilot, scurried over to the second glider to retrieve its man while Heath and the others followed them with their weapons.

Fortunately the rescues went without a hitch and as everyone regrouped and began heading back to the Camalain, Liam turned at some commotion and watched as Captain Thear and one of his steersman passed Yanno Crogan and headed up to the prince where the only thing that could be clearly heard was Manus swearing in frustration over the new information he just received.

The steersman didn't stay topside long and quickly came back down so he could return to the bridge where Moro Croft and Jensen, the other steersman, were still trying to get the Camalain to fly.

Soon thereafter Kael left the upper deck, a solemn look on his face; a look that did not seem to sit comfortably on the young man's face.

Liam watched as Kael stopped to talk to Crogan, the two men's heads close together as Kael left him with some unknown instructions before walking over to another group of men and ordering them to follow him below deck.

Liam found himself disappointed that Kael didn't come over to talk to him because they had become quite friendly over the past couple of days. If only Liam knew that it was the one thing Kael had wanted to do and chose not to do because Kael did not want to have to explain to Liam what Manus had now ordered him to do.

Although Liam soon found out what it was as Gorman and his men, who had disappeared behind the Camalain, reappeared with Kael and the men he had gathered and headed north out onto the flats.

"Where are they going, Master Yanno?" Liam called across the deck to the cook.

"To fetch Vohr by the looks of it. God's willing."

"Will they be long?"

"One can only hope not." Crogan replied sourly, not a single one of those words sounding positive from the man's mouth.

So Liam turned back to watch his friends make their trek across the flats, his hand trailing across the railing as he followed them across the deck, until they vanished from view behind some low hills that they had flown over earlier that day.

And as the winds seemed to pick up around them, and the sun began to make its way towards the horizon, orders were given for men who were not on duty to get below deck until further notice.

"That goes for you too, Master Keir!" The cook shouted to the young man, who had yet to pull himself away from the railing, hoping like many of the other men to catch sight of the returning crew.

Liam walked back over to the cook wishing that his father would head down the stairs so that they could talk. But Cullen, the prince and whoever had remained on that observation deck were still having an intense conversation while one of their number continued to communicate with the Marmairn.

"What about you? Liam asked the cook.

"I am right where I need to be. You need to be in your room. Now go!" Crogan ordered, using his wickedly sharp cleaver to point Liam towards the cabin door, the withering look on the man's face telling Liam not to disobey the man.

So, as the wind whipped up again, sending sand pattering across the deck, Liam did as he was told, falling in line with many of the Royal Guard who were heading inside and made his way back to his quarters.

But, for the first time since this unwelcome journey began, sitting in the cabin was the last place Liam wanted to be right now.

Liam listened to the wind howling and watched through the cabin window as the sun began to set, turning the sky a blood red, when he decided he could not stay in this confined space, his one-time sanctuary, and made his way to the only other place he knew he would not get kicked out; the galley.

Upon his arrival to the galley Liam noticed that Crogan, who was still acting as body guard over the prince, and who had yet to return, had left in the middle of preparing the next meal when the Camalain went down. Unfortunately Liam had no idea what the man was preparing, nor how to make anything elaborate, so Liam decided to make what he knew best and stoked the coals in the stove so he could heat water for caff.

While the water boiled Liam grabbed stacks of cups and plates and took them into the dining hall to set up a buffet style for the crew to know that food would be forthcoming if anyone happened into the room.

Returning to the pantry Liam found some dried fruits and cheeses and brought those out to also put on the table where he couldn't help but look out the window and watch how the storm outside had increased in intensity with the flying sand turning what could have been a lovely dusk into a sickly, bruised, coppery colored sky.

Liam went back into the galley to the cupboards where Crogan kept his baked goods and found some loaves of bread that he began slicing when he heard a commotion in the dining hall.

Rushing out, with the serrated bread knife in hand, Liam came upon two of the ship's men sliding the metal apron across the large glass window so as to protect the room from the sandstorm that was now swirling around them.

"Any word from Praish Gorman or Master Karam?" Liam asked the two, hoping that his friends and Karam Kael, whom he also thought of as a friend and had yet to admit to himself that he had become overly fond of, had made it back aboard.

"Not yet, Master Keir." One of the two informed Liam as they took some food for themselves.

"Word is your father can't hear Barra. And it's the god's silence that is keeping the ships from flying." The other said before biting into some fruit.

"I, I don't, I haven't spoken to him." Liam stuttered, concern for his father filling his eyes. "Is he around? My father?"

"Probably on the bridge right now with the prince and the captain." The first man replied before nudging his companion so they could leave and finish their duties.

Liam was beside himself as he watched the men leave the room, tentatively taking several steps to follow them, and then thinking better of it, before changing his mind and took a step back towards the door.

Then Liam changed his mind one more time as he forced himself to go back into the galley to finish what he was doing, knowing full well that if he stormed onto the bridge to see how his father was doing, and to ask him questions, he would look like the little boy who could not take care of himself; the little boy that Prince Manus perceived and wanted him to be.

So Liam went back to brewing the caff and setting it and the bread out as several more men came in to grab some food, all with muted worries about their predicament on the tips of their tongues. Not wanting to get more agitated by their musings or the howling winds outside, Liam headed back into the galley and began to put away the food Crogan had left out so it wouldn't spoil, and began to clean up his and the cook's mess.

Liam was searching for a container for whatever Crogan had been mixing when the cook finally returned. Crogan still had his weapon in hand and placed it within reach on one of the cleaned counters and joined Liam with cleaning the rest of the galley.

"Sorry, Master Yanno." Liam said feeling the need to apologize for his meager attempt at the evening meal. "I wasn't really sure what to do with what you were making. I didn't want to ruin it."

Crogan's reply was to grunt his appreciation for the work that Liam had done for him.

"Doesn't matter." The cook finally said. "We'll need to go sparingly on the food and water for a while. Who knows when we will be moving again."

"Some of the men are saying the Barra has stopped talking to my father." Liam tried to say offhandedly, though his voice shook slightly, as he wiped down a counter.

Thankfully Crogan didn't have to answer this question. "Why don't you go ask him yourself? He followed me down from the bridge and should be in the dining hall."

Taking the dismissal for what it was, a chance for a break, and a chance to see his father, Liam left the job he was doing and headed out into the dining hall, spotting his father sitting alone at one of the far tables. He also noticed that his father had not taken any food for himself so Liam made a small plate for the two of them and poured himself a cup of caff before heading over to him.

But Liam's father did not notice his son's approach, nor did he look up while Liam stood there, who couldn't help but notice the father's haggard appearance. A look he seemed to have whenever Aerin Manus was finished with him.

"Father?"

"Ah, my boy." Cullen said, looking to his son as he sat down, placing the plate of food between them. "Staying out of trouble?"

"I guess. And how about you? You don't look so good."

"No, I am fine." Cullen replied, forcing a smile on his face.

Liam was doubtful at the sincerity of the response. "Are you sure? The men are saying Barra has gone quiet. Is this true?"

At those questions, the frown returned to Cullen's face, the confidence Liam was so used to seeing in him draining away and leaving an old, frail man sitting across from him.

"You should eat something." Liam said, pushing the plate closer towards his father, hoping to get his attention back on their conversation.

"Mmm?" Cullen looked at his son for a moment before picking up a piece of sliced fruit from the plate. But the food never reached Cullen's mouth for he seemed to already forgotten he had picked it up.

"And what about Gorman and the others?" Liam asked, forgetting himself and blurting out the question as the wind howled loudly, setting the metal shutter covering the window to rattling. "Have they returned or have they been heard from? And how soon before we can start flying again?"

As the frantic questions spilled from his mouth, Liam knew they had been a mistake to ask; especially when the queries about the welfare of his friends seemed to tire his father even more.

Cullen did find his son's simple questions exhausting. But not because they were being asked but that his father just didn't have the heart to answer Liam truthfully when he had nothing positive to say about the situation they were in. So Cullen just decided to excuse himself from the table, smiling wanly at his son, and headed back to their cabin, hoping for some solitude of his own.

So Liam, his questions unanswered, and coming to the conclusion that Gorman, Kael and the others were still out in this brutal storm, half-heartedly picked at the food on his plate before heading back into the galley to help Crogan finish with the cleaning.

The two continued on with their chores in silence, with Liam not bothering to ask after the rescue party and Crogan, who assumed the boy's father had already told him he might need to expect the worst about his friends, was grateful that the only sounds filling the air were those of squeaking hinges as cabinet doors were opened and the clinking sounds of metal pots and porcelain dishes were put away.

And when they were done Crogan ordered Liam to get some rest, just as he was about to do as he picked up his weapon, and told Liam to leave whatever food was left out in the dining hall until the morning.

Just the same, Liam, who didn't feel like going back to his cabin and disturbing his father, made his way back out into the dining hall and retrieved some stray dirty dishes before returning and organizing the remainder of the food before plopping himself down in the far corner of the room, hidden from view of anyone who might enter.

There Liam sat in the semi-dark room as the storm carried on unabated, sand scraping against the wooden hull of the Camalain, his eyes closed, his mouth moving silently in prayer to the gods as he thought of the missing men. Prayer's that Liam unknowingly started off with the protection of Kael.

Eventually Liam dozed off where he sat with his arms wrapped around his knees, his head propped up between two walls where they formed a corner, the storm slowly dying outside, its dwindling moans sending Liam into a deeper sleep.

At some point Liam was awoken by the shuffling of benches and loud talking that began to fill the room. And as he stood, thinking that only several minutes had gone by, Liam was startled to find that someone had made an attempt to drape a blanket over him, which he now grasped in one hand, fearful as he watched many of the crew filling the room.

When Liam saw that Yarrow was being lead in, dust and sand caking his face, hair and clothing, with his left eye closed shut, Liam rushed over to help them. That's when he also noticed Gorman, as well as Heath and Manton entering the room, with Kael in tow. All of whom were covered with sand, all with what looked like abrasions or burns on their faces or some other portion of skin that had been exposed to the elements.

The dining hall quickly filled with the injured search party and crew who wanted to help out, with Yanno Crogan, followed by Manus and his father, who looked like he might have slept very little, taking up the rear of this gathering.

Crogan immediately took over and began barking out orders, sending Liam and several others into the galley to retrieve fresh water, clean linens and some special jars Crogan had put aside for medicinal purposes.

And not one to be outdone by a subordinate, Manus jumped in with his commands. Ordering the shutter to be opened, flooding the dining hall with the pale cerulean light of early morning, and sending away the men who had begun gathering uselessly at the hall's entrance.

So, after many of the men having their first drink of water in over a day the search party, some with the help of the remaining crew, began to remove armor, weapons and shirts, sending the dust and sand from their ordeal into the air so that it began to coat the tables and benches in the room with a thin layer of grit.

Fortunately most of the wounds seemed superficial, with only a deep gash here or there. Yarrow being the exception, who still couldn't open his left eye, the man complaining of having sand inside of it while his hands twitched in frustration as he resisted the urge to raise them to rub his eye with the possibility of scratching himself into blindness.

So Yarrow became Crogan's first patient. The soldier being told to sit and to tilt his head back and to the side, with Crogan using two fingers of one hand to pry the lids of his eye open while pouring water into it from a cup held in his other.

"What happened out there?" Manus asked Kael, ignoring Yarrow's mumbled curses and the sound of water splashing against the floor.

"Vohr was further out on the flats than we thought." Kael said of the glider pilot, who was sitting a few tables down from them, his head bent as he tried to shake the sand out of his hair.

"And he was heading too far east. Walking away from us." Kael continued. "If we hadn't seen the mirror in his hand reflecting the sun, we never would have found him."

"And the glider?" Manus asked as Kael began to wipe sand off of a long cut on his right forearm.

"Sorry. The winds started to pick up by the time we found Vohr. Damn!" Kael's arm began to bleed again from where he had scraped away the sand off. Fortunately it didn't look deep. "I thought it wise for us to head back and collect the others."

"We were lucky to reach those hills we passed earlier. We huddled together as best we could until the storm finally died down and waited until morning so we could find you once again. Liam can you help me?"

With water and linen in his hands, Liam excused himself as he passed the prince to sit next to Kael. What Liam missed in the exchange was the withering look that Manus gave him. A look that all on its own could have blown out the storm they endured during the night.

"Does it hurt?" Liam asked, his hands trembling slightly, as Kael extended his forearm for Liam to take it.

"No. Just looks messy I think."

The man was right. For as Liam used water and a cloth to wipe away the dirt from the wound, Liam could tell that the cut that ran down the length of his arm was not too deep. Liam continued to clean the wound, his head bent low, only catching the rise and fall of Kael's abdomen as he breathed. Liam felt a twinge of guilt at what he was doing, yet knowing all he wanted to do was look at and to touch the man's naked torso.

Once Liam was sure that he had cleaned the wound thoroughly, he asked his father to help him staunch the flow of blood and to seal the wound. Because it was known that all sagarts and sagarttas had the gift of healing bestowed upon them by the gods.

"Sorry Liam, Master Karam." Cullen said with a frown crossing his lips and the sound of disappointment in his voice. "That power seems to have failed me."

"Nothing yet!" Manus snapped.

"No, nothing yet!" Cullen snapped back, too tired to care that he was not showing respect to the prince. "I am sure we would be far from here if Barra was still among us."

"Uh, my arm." Kael interjected, hoping to diffuse the tension that was starting to fill the room.

"And what about my eye?" Yarrow whined.

"Your eye is fine!" Crogan said, slapping the back of the men's head when he caught Yarrow blinking several times without any problems. "Be useful and move aside so I can help someone else!"

While Yarrow collected his things so that he could vacate the space, Crogan pointed at two jars for Liam to get to help with Kael's wound.

"Stay there." Cullen also wanted to be useful, so propping his cane up against a table, grabbed both jars and hobbled over to where his son was sitting.

Liam couldn't help but use that very short moment to look at Kael. The man's cheeks were red from wind burn and sand still clung to his brown hair and long sideburns. There was sand still plastered to the top of Kael's chest and clavicle and Liam bit his lip as he thought of what it would be like to wipe the sand away from them.

Kael must have known what he was thinking because a smirk, or was it a smile, formed on his lips.

But the moment and their thoughts were fleeting as Liam's father's arm extended between them to place the jars on the table.

"Use the one with the red stopper first." Crogan explained as he began to clean the wounds on the neck of another man.

"What is it?" Liam asked, his eyes watering and nose burning from the smell emanating from the jar as he un-stoppered it.

"Alcohol." Crogan said matter of factly. "Will clean that wound much better than water ever will."

Doing his best to keep Kael's arm steady with his left hand, the man's forearm resting on top of his, Liam tried to gingerly pour the strong alcohol over Kael's cut. Nevertheless, Kael couldn't help but hiss in a mixture of surprise and pain as the clear liquid ran over his wound.

"Sorry." Liam said quietly, hesitating with what he was doing, his face scrunching up in pain, as if he was pouring it over his own arm.

"Just put some in a cup for me later." Kael chattered through clenched teeth and nodded for Liam to continue with what he was doing.

"And I want to apologize to you too, Milord. I should not have spoken so harshly." Cullen said to Manus as the two men continued to watch Liam who was now patting Kael's arm dry.

"As am I." Manus replied somewhat sourly. A tone he failed to hide because the prince was unwilling to remove his eyes from Liam and Kael as the dislike for the sagart's son continued to grow.

"What do I do now?" Liam asked while he had Kael's arm wrapped in a towel, his gaze moving from his father to the cook for an answer, oblivious to the animosity of the prince behind him.

Even his voice grated on his nerves, Manus thought as Crogan explained to Liam that the other jar was honey and that he needed to use a finger to spread a thin layer of the golden, viscous liquid over Kael's cut.

"Will keep his arm from getting infected." The cook explained as he did the same to the neck of the man who was still sitting in front of him. "It'll need to dry a little before it can be wrapped."

Liam simply nodded as he dipped a finger into the honey and began to run a finger over Kael's cut. Liam did his best to focus on what he was doing, ignoring the sound of his heart beating and the goose bumps that were quickly appearing on Kael's arm from his touch.

The application of honey only took a moment, with Liam only stopping to dab at some fresh blood that continued to seep from the cut. But when he was done, Liam sat there with Kael's arm still resting against his, his thumb reflexively rubbing the side of Kael's forearm: a movement that Kael was not objecting to.

So to distract himself with what he was doing, Liam focused on Gorman and Heath and watched as they cleaned the other's wounds that covered their faces and arms. But watching the partners and their ministrations only brought a pang of loneliness to Liam.

Ironically, while Liam was feeling melancholy, almost sorry for himself, Manus couldn't help but become angry over the familiarity that seemed to be growing between Kael and the sagart's son.

"I think you can let go of his arm, Keir Liam." Manus finally said, enjoying how Liam jumped at the sound of his voice and how he quickly pulled his hand away from Kael. "Holding his arm will not make it heal any faster."

"Sorry, M'lord." Liam stood, now embarrassed that many of the men had turned to look at them.

"I didn't mind." Kael chimed in, smiling warmly at Liam, while giving him a friendly an almost flirtatious wink of the eye.

"Well I do!" Manus snapped at his friend, who sat there helplessly, exhausted from the night's ordeal, his wounded arm glistening like it was covered in amber in the morning light. And not feeling the need, nor wanting to explain himself to Kael, who now looked crestfallen at the rebuke, ordered Liam and several of the other men to follow him as he left the dining hall.

"Oh, and Master Yanno." Manus said to the cook who had now moved on to another wounded man. "Begin rationing the food and water. No more midday meals for now. Only the gods know how long we will be sitting out here."

Many of the men frowned or stifled moans of disappointment at this news while Crogan acknowledged Manus' command as the prince left the room with Liam and the others in tow.

Liam did his best to shuffle to the back of the group, wanting to have some distance between himself and the prince, as they made their way to the main deck.

And as soon as they made it out into the open, Liam moved out of the way of the men still behind him so they and the others could better defend the prince, if need be, as they made their way to the observation deck. Once there Manus shouted for Lieutenant Cahl, who had been standing watch to come down and join them.

The men stood patiently, with several of them, including Liam, wrapping their arms around themselves as they tried to stay warm in the cool morning air while Manus listened to Cahl Goban's report.

"And the gliders?" Manus added, already knowing the answer to this question.

"Buried by the storm. But they should be easy enough to find." Goban replied in a tone of voice that was void of any emotion. A stoic voice Goban had started using since Manus' reprimand while they had been searching Murra's Maze.

"Good. Take these men and whoever else you need to go and uncover them. I will take over the watch and have the Marmairn send some men to help you."

It was not the safest thing to be doing. To send men back out onto the flats. But Manus needed to keep his men occupied as much as possible, hoping there might be a chance all his ships would fly once again. And sending Liam along with this crew would keep the sagart's son out of eyesight and earshot for a while.

No matter what Manus' impressions were of the man, Cahl Goban was a good soldier and wasted no time in collecting another dozen men to help with digging as they made their way to the storage bays so they could exit the Camalain. But with only a half dozen shovels on the ship the men would either be taking turns shoveling or using their shields to uncover the buried gliders.

But as they were about to move out, the lieutenant noticed that the only thing Liam was carrying were shovels; one in each hand.

"Where's your weapon?" Goban asked the young man who was waiting patiently for someone to tell him the next thing that he should be doing.

"In my room, Sir." Liam's face turned a bright red at his mistake, cursing silently at the realization that he probably should have not put aside his armor and hammer during this crisis. "I can go get them."

"We don't have the time." Goban looked around and scratched at the back of his head. The subtle signs of frustration that showed he was annoyed. Though, Goban was frustrated at having Liam in his troupe, but at the situation that sagart's untrained son was being put in.

For Cahl Goban was not fond of sending an untrained citizen of Birr out onto the flats. And Goban had half a mind to send Liam to his quarters or to stay here and await their return. Unfortunately the lieutenant did not want to fall further out of favor with the prince and saw no solution but to take Keir Liam with them. Thankfully the lieutenant was spared his dilemma by one of the other men in the group.

"Lieutenant. I'll keep him out of trouble." Aurello Munson chimed in. "Me and the men will, that is."

Goban watched as several of the men closest to Munson nodded in agreement with him. They did so because Gorman, who had taken the sagart's son under his wing, had spread the word amongst the men to watch over Liam. None hesitated in helping out because many of them, who had come from humble beginnings like Liam, quietly watched at how the prince had been treating him since he had boarded the Camalain and were not happy with what many perceived as the abuse of someone for being just a commoner.

Goban cracked a smile, rarity even under good conditions, grateful for the protection these men would afford Liam.

"Yes, we all will. Stick close to Master Aurello." Goban said to Liam and simply patted Munson's shoulder in gratitude as he moved forward and ordered everyone out of the ship.

"You heard the lieutenant." Munson said to Liam, a reassuring smile on his face while he moved into the middle of the group of men, forcing Liam to follow him as they made their way out onto the desert. "If things do get sketchy, use one of those shovels as a weapon and cover my back."

Liam said that he would and as they left the shadows of the Camalain, looked back to the ship only to see the hanger doors closed by several men who would remain outside to stand guard over the lower entrance into the ship.

When they made it to the halfway point, Goban ordered four men to stay behind, just like Gorman had the day before, to cover their tracks in case of an attack, and ordered the rest of the men on to the first glider.

The lieutenant had been right that the gliders would be easy to find because a large mound of sand loomed in front of them while a second dune could be seen on the horizon off to their right.

But shouts of surprise ran through the group and weapons were drawn as dark shapes, created by the eastern sun rising over them, climbed over the buried glider.

Just as quickly, everyone relaxed as they were hailed from those men who happened to be from the Marmairn.

The man leading the Marmairn's crew, came out to meet the Camalain's and introduced himself as Darius Fallon and fell in with Cahl Goban and made their way to the buried craft where Fallon's men had already begun removing sand from the glider. Liam and five other men from the Camalain soon joined them to help in uncovering the glider while the rest of the Royal Guard set up a perimeter of defense to protect those who would be working.

Unfortunately the men hadn't expected the amount of sand that had been dumped during the storm and were just beginning to uncover the glider after an hour's worth of work.

"Let somebody else jump in." Munson finally said to Liam who had only stopped to once relieve himself while they had been working.

"I'm fine." Liam replied, knowing that this was the only useful thing he could do while they were out here.

"Nonsense!" Munson responded as he watched Liam use one of the sleeves of his shirt to wipe the sweat from his face. "I said I'd look after you. Not drag your limp ass back to the ship."

Munson took Liam's shovel and handed him his sword and a water skin and good-naturedly ordered him to sit in the shade of the ever growing pile of sand.

"Besides," Munson explained as he watched Liam take several sips from the skin. "You still need to help uncover the other one."

Although he was grateful for this reprieve and watched as Munson and the others cleared away more sand, Liam found it more uncomfortable sitting there with several of the other men who were also taking a break and soon wandered back over to the group of men that had just uncovered the entrance to the glider.

Moans and curses filled the air when the soldiers realized that the hatch had not been closed properly and that the inside of the glider was also full of sand. With room for only one shovel to be used while the others were used to clear away its hull, the men, along with Liam who had joined them, began scraping the sand away with their bare hands.

Eventually, while the sun climbed overhead in the cloudless sky, several of the men took off their shirts and began using them as buckets to carry away the accumulated sand.

But the job got done and Liam found himself seated next to Munson once again while the group as a whole took a much needed break. Thankfully the Marmairn sent out a handful of fresh men who also brought food and more water for the others to tide themselves over before they all got up and made their way to the other glider.

The second ship was just as buried as the first had been, so the group did their best to make quick work of clearing the sand away from it. This time they were fortunate to find that the hatch to this one had remained somewhat closed and that there was very little sand to be removed from within its interior.

The sun was well past its zenith before the men finished what they were doing and disbanded, with Darius Fallon and his men heading back to the Marmairn, while Cahl Goban and the others trudged back to the Camalain.

Of course hopes were dashed when Goban's crew found out that showering had been restricted until further notice to conserve water, and that many only had a couple of hours of rest before their shifts on the Camalain began. Liam was one of those men. And since it was well close to the third bell, he would be expected to be in the galley to help with preparing dinner. That meant Liam had maybe an hour to relax for a bit and to get cleaned as best as he possibly could.

Again, his father was not in their room, which worried Liam because it meant he was probably in the company of the prince, who would be haranguing the old man for the predicament they were in.

How Liam wished the prince would treat his father with a little more respect that a sagart of his standing should have, he thought as he got out of his sweaty and sand covered clothing.

"But what can I do?" Liam mumbled as he grabbed one of his blankets and stood on it as he began wiping the sand off of his body with his dirty shirt. Watching the tiny grains rain down upon the woolen blanket and bounce across its dark colored surface.

Liam continued to brood on these thoughts while he tried to clean the sand out of his hair. He spent a while with his head tipped over as he raked his hands through his black locks, using his fingernails to pick at the tiny grains that were refusing to give up their resting places against his scalp.

Sadly these thoughts of how small he was and what he could accomplish only made him feel more tired than what he really was and tried to forget them as he rolled up the blanket to keep the sand from scattering across the floor.

Once dressed, with his soiled clothing tossed on top of the blanket, Liam left his room, remembering to take his weapon and shield this time. And in the hopes of bumping into his father, Liam took his time walking the halls as he made his way to the galley.

Of course no sign of Seb Cullen was to be had. The man was most likely on the bridge with the prince, Liam thought as he made his way into the galley and found the cook almost finished preparing the sparse evening meal.

"Anything I can do Master Yanno?" Liam asked, noticing that there were no pots or pans to clean and very few utensils to wash too. "Does the hall need to be cleaned?"

"Had help with that earlier." Crogan grunted as he finished with what he was doing and wiped his hands on the apron wrapped about his waist. "Everyone is staying on duty and just grabbing what they need. So I don't think there'll be much for you to do. Take this tray out and grab something for yourself. Looks like you could use something to eat."

Leaving the hammer and buckler behind, Liam took the tray of salted meats and brought them out into the hall, placing them on the long table with the food that was already there. Liam still felt the need to do something, so he tidied the table, stacking some dirty forks, knives and plates at the end of it before serving himself and looking for a seat in the empty room.

To protect the ship from invaders, the hall's window had once again been shuttered for the night. A disappointment to Liam because he would have liked to have stared off into the evening sky. And with the hall being dimly lit to conserve lamp oil, Liam sat where he could see the yellow light from the galley emanating into the room.

But Liam didn't sit long for he was finding the silence in the hall quite discomforting and quickly ate his meal before returning to the galley to help Yanno Crogan.

The cook, who still had nothing for Liam to do, and having noticed his sunburned cheeks and the dark circles marking his eyes with exhaustion, told Liam he wasn't needed and ordered the young man to return to his quarters to get some much needed rest.

Liam, who did not want to contradict Crogan, obliged the man by thanking him before collecting his belongings so he could head back to his cabin.

Thoughts of stretching out on the floor under his blankets and sleeping until he was needed in the galley for the morning shift did bring a sense of relief to Liam as he slid the door open to the cabin, only to find his father already in the room. Seb Cullen must have had the same idea as his son because he was already in bed, a blanket pulled up to his shoulders, with his back to the entrance to the room.

At first, Liam thought that he was still awake because he thought his father had spoken and moved slightly. But then he realized his father was talking in his sleep. The only things audible in his garbled, one-sided conversation were the words "where" and " help". And of course, the name of their missing god: Barra.

"Father?" Liam whispered, not wanting to disturb his father, yet hoping he would awaken. When his second attempt in a slightly louder voice failed, Liam left the room and slid the door shut, unwilling to disturb his father.

But what was he to do?

Looking in the direction of the prince's quarters, Liam saw that a guard was standing outside its door. A sign that meant either the prince, or Kael, or both had gone back to their room.

How he wished Kael was around right now to talk to, Liam thought as he walked away from his quarters and headed down the flight of stairs. Not that Liam said much when they did converse because Kael did much of the talking while he listened. Liam was just dumbfounded by the fact that the prince's friend wanted to be around him during his time away from Prince Manus. Especially an attractive man like Kael who could probably have anyone he wanted on the Camalain.

Liam was thinking about Kael's light brown eyes and how they seemed to sparkle when they turned his way, with the faintly sweet smell of honey from when he had nursed Kael, still lingering in his nostrils, when he found himself standing outside the quarters of Gorman, Heath and some of the other members of the Royal Guard. Liam could hear several voices from behind the closed door and only hesitated momentarily before knocking and calling out Gorman's name.

All conversation stopped within the room as the door quickly slid open, with Gorman's muscular body, covered only in a pair of breeches, and a dagger in his hand, filled its frame.

"Liam! Is everything alright?" A look of concern was on the man's face as he peered out into the hallway to see if any of the other soldiers were being mobilized.

Liam could see Heath, Yarrow and Dolan behind Gorman. All of them were standing, holding weapons, and just as scantily clad as the man in front of him.

"Everything's fine. Sorry." Liam said. His face turning a deep red, accentuating his sunburn as he was now embarrassed that he had bothered the men. "Sorry, I, could I sleep here tonight?"

"Is something wrong with your pa?" Gorman asked, lowering his weapon, the look of concern still etched on his face.

"I don't think so. It's just that he was already asleep when I got to our room and I just didn't want to bother waking him."

"Sure. We can make room for you." Gorman said as he stepped aside to let Liam into the room before taking the hammer and buckler out of his hands and offering him a seat on one of the bunk beds.

Liam obliged the man and sat down on one of the lower beds. The others relaxed and returned to where they had been sitting, placing their weapons down within reach if they were needed once again.

All the men remained quiet as Liam looked about the room that the men were sharing. The cabin was almost as big as his room back home with four sets of bunk beds and several footlockers lining its walls. A single porthole was on the outer wall where the purplish remains of dusk were pouring through it. The middle of the cabin was empty, a worn rug covering the floor, leaving enough room for the men to move freely about the room.

"If you can spare a blanket or two I can curl up in one of the corners." Liam said to the men, who all seemed to be looking at him.

"Nonsense!" Verrim Heath said as his partner came to sit on the floor at his feet. "You can have my bunk."

"I don't want to be a bother."

"No bother." Heath chuckled and pointed to the bunk Liam was sitting under and told him to climb up and to try it out. "Duwain and Rhyne are on duty and I can use one of their beds for now."

And as the men went back to their idle chatter, Liam took off his boots and climbed into the offered bunk. Liam felt himself sink into the straw filled mattress and ran a hand over its linens and blanket which smelled like they hadn't been changed in a while, and smiled at not having to sleep on a wooden floor this night.

"You sure?" Liam asked one more time. "I don't want the others to get angry with you on account of me."

"If they come back early I'll just crawl into bed with this one." Heath replied, playfully kicking his partner with his foot.

"That's all we need!" Yarrow shouted in mock disgust. "The two of you curled up, rutting around while the rest of us try to sleep."

"I thought you liked our rutting around." Gorman shot back at his friend.

"Only because it keeps the two of you from sniping with each other." Yarrow sneered as he looked at Liam. "You can always tell when these two haven't had it in a while."

"And who wants to listen to you two when the rest of us aren't getting any." Dolan added while he tried to scratch an itch in the middle of his back.

"Well, if you knew how to treat a man you might be getting some regularly." Heath shot back.

"I know how to treat my men just fine!" Dolan said smugly as he crossed his arms over his bare chest.

The others just laughed and began to list Dolan's multiple failed attempts at romance.

Dolan finally relented and begged for his friends to stop with their barbs. The group did and laughed in good humor with Liam joining at the sexual innuendoes being tossed about the room.

And as the men continued to talk Liam got undressed, leaving his undershorts on, tossing his shirt and breeches to the foot of the bunk bed, before crawling under its warm covers.

Liam had to admit that it felt good to be out of his clothes, especially since they felt uncomfortable against his grimy skin. And he tried not to think of how dirty he was or when he or the others would be able to shower again as he lay on his back and adjusted Heath's pillow under his head, all the while listening to his friend's voices drone on about the day's events.

Eventually their talk turned back to their lack of flight and being prepared for whatever the prince would have in store for them.

"So, Liam. How is your father?" Gorman asked. "Liam?"

When Liam didn't respond Gorman stood, calling out to Liam one more time, only to find his new recruit with his eyes closed, mouth open and head tilted to one side, his breathing soft and regular as he slept.

"Out cold." Gorman said softly to the others as he dimmed a lantern closest to the bunk bed. Yarrow followed suit and shuttered another one near him, leaving the room in the faint glow of a solitary lantern that was resting on one of the footlockers.

"Poor lad." Heath said in a low voice as his partner came to sit next to him. "Best not to worry him."

"I know." Gorman said as he rubbed his face with both hands. Even though he had slept most of the afternoon, Gorman was once again felt tired.

"But he has to be told." Gorman continued. "If the prince decides to make the journey to the mainland then Liam should have his father ready."

"I would think the sagart is more prepared than his son." Heath replied as he rubbed Gorman's back. "Considering the sagart hasn't left the prince's side these past couple of days."

"Just the same, the sagart's the one who's lame. And they're saying a trek back to the mainland would take at least two weeks. Ten days if we are lucky." Gorman replied.

"Well, we won't know for a couple more days if we're going or not." Dolan added. "I agree with Heath, Gor. Best not to worry the lad for now."

Yarrow also agreed with his friends. "I just don't like how the prince treats him." He said, frowning slightly. "Working him just as hard as, if not harder, than the rest of us. With no training as a Guard at all."

"Rhyne found him in the dining hall, curled up in one of the corners sleeping. Said he went to one of the larders and got him a blanket just to make sure he stayed warm through the night."

"When was this?" Gorman asked, annoyed that he had not heard this piece of gossip.

"Last night. While we were out on the flats."

"Be that as it may, Liam is at least holding his own. Think even old Crogan is taking a liking to him." Gorman chuckled softly. "But if and when the time comes, we'll all make sure Liam's father makes it across the flats."

The others agreed with Gorman, knowing that leaving the kindly priest behind would be like leaving one of their own fathers behind.

"Well, I think Liam has the right idea." Gorman said as the conversation died down. And kissing Heath goodnight got up and undressed and crawled into the bunk below Liam's.

The others did likewise, with Yarrow extinguishing the last of the lanterns, sending the room into darkness, before crawling into his own bunk above Dolan's. He and Yarrow were still wide awake and continued to talk for a while. And that's how Gorman and Heath finally fell asleep; listening to the sonorous voices of their friends.

***

The grating sound of wood against wood filled the air. A quick flash of light crossed the room before it receded as the door to the cabin was once again closed.

Liam, disturbed by both, turned in his bed to face the wall, pulling the blankets over his head.

Time went by. Five minutes, half an hour, an hour. Who knows, but Liam quickly sat up in the bunk in surprise, as is the case when one remembers something important, and looked around as he tried to get his bearings.

The lanterns were still doused in the room when he realized he had spent the night in one of the crews' quarters with the early light of dawn, from the one porthole, sending a bluish glow into the center of the room, leaving the quiet room in deep shadows.

Liam listened to the heavy breathing of several men sleeping before he climbed out of bed, doing his best to make as little sound as possible so as not to disturb the others.

But he failed.

"Where do you think you're going?" Gorman asked hoarsely, raising himself on one elbow, as Liam was about to gather his belongings.

"I'm late to my shift in the galley." Liam whispered, afraid of waking the others. "Master Yanno will have my hide if I don't show."

"Don't worry. Dolan got up a while ago. Said he couldn't sleep and was going to take your shift this morning."

"You sure?" Liam asked, hesitating as he was putting on his breeches. "I really don't want anyone to get into trouble on account of me."

"Go back to bed Liam." Gorman said as he rolled onto his back and threw an arm over his eyes, too tired to coddle Liam this morning. "Dolan'll do your job just fine. Now you got an hour before you'll be making the rounds with us, so make the most of it and try to relax a little. That's an order."

"Aye Sir." Liam climbed back up into his bunk and got comfortable, also lying on his back as he stared at the ceiling, the planks and beams slowly emerging as the light grew in the room.

"And Liam." Gorman said from below him. "We help each other. Remember that."

"Aye Sir."

Liam must have dozed off again because he was awoken by the creaking bed frames and the sound of voices as the men began to get up and move about the room as they got ready for the day.

Two other men were in the room and Liam was introduced to Rhyne and Duwain who were getting undressed to sleep just as Liam joined the others on the floor to get ready for the day.

"Here." Yarrow said to Liam, handing him a dry towel with another over his shoulder. "Only washing we'll be doing today. Leave it on that trunk when you're done."

Liam watched as Yarrow began to wipe himself down with the towel in his own hand and followed suit by wiping his own face and body with the one he had been given. Doing his best to ignore the smell that said this towel had been used for the same thing on more than one man on one more than occasion.

Once they were dressed, covering themselves in their armor and strapping on weapons, Gorman herded his men out into the hallway, leaving Rhyne and Duwain alone in the room to get some much needed rest.

"So use the facilities if you need to and we'll meet in the dining hall." Gorman told his crew, only explaining something that was routine, mundane, for Liam's benefit.

"Oh, and Liam." Gorman stopped him from leaving as the rest of the men made their way down the hallway. "You'll be moving in with us. So after our rounds tonight get your belongings and we'll find someplace to stash them in the cabin."

"But what about the prince? He told me I had to share a room with my father and I don't want to get you in trouble!" Liam blurted out, feeling awkward by the man's generosity.

"Prince Manus has enough on his plate to worry about and what he doesn't know won't hurt him. Besides, what's one more? Right?"

Liam didn't know what to say. "Thank you, Sir."

"Now don't start up with the formalities! Nothing has changed over the past couple of days. Gorman's fine. Now run along and get what you need for the day."

Liam stuttered over a handful of sir's and Gorman's, a mixture of nervousness and excitement coursing through his veins at the fortunate turn of events for himself as he headed towards his own cabin.

And if he was expecting to find his father in their room, then Liam was to be disappointed. For his father had already risen and made his way to be by the prince's side, leaving the bed and tiny cabin disheveled in his haste.

Liam took a minute to clean up after his father by making the bed and folding the man's clothing, stacking them on the bed before grabbing his leather armor and rushed up to the dining hall.

But first he stopped in the galley to apologize to Crogan for missing his morning shift. Unsure if Crogan would be angry that he had not shown to begin with or because he would be bothered while he was now working.

"Well don't let it happen again." Crogan grunted as he pressed his palms into the pasty mass and rolled it across the floured surface of the counter. "That Dolan has a need to babble on about nothing. Grates on one's nerves. Just show up from now on when you're supposed to."

Liam thought he had received a compliment, but wasn't sure because the cook had in his own way, dismissed him, and had returned to methodically dividing the dough in front of him and slapping them into smaller mounds to be cooked.

Making his way into the dining hall, Liam grabbed some food for himself before finding Gorman and the others in the crowded room. Manton and Sidri were also at the table and greeted Liam as he joined them.

Gorman had waited for Liam to show before informing them that they would be one of several groups acting as lookouts on the main deck for the morning, and that Lieutenant Cahl would eventually let them know what they would be doing for the afternoon.

"Just make sure we have enough water while we're up there." Gorman ordered, directing the statement at Manton and Dolan, who only nodded as they ate their meals. "Liam, grab some fruit or bread for yourself to hold you over for lunch."

Gorman allowed his men a little more time at the table before finally sending them up on deck.

As they moved along, Liam threw on his leather armor, hoping to have it strapped on properly before they reached the main deck, when he caught up with Dolan and thanked the man for covering his shift.

Dolan laughed. "Won't be doing that again. Forgot that man has the personality of curdled milk. He's all yours from now on."

Liam chuckled at the description of Yanno Crogan and when Manton added his own off color opinion about the dour moods of the cook as they made their way out onto the main deck.

Liam had to blink several times as his eyes adjusted to the light, for it looked like it was going to be another cloudless day on the flats. But then again, the skies were always void of clouds when one was this far out from land.

And Liam watched as a couple of men with canvases and poles, placed the poles into holes in the deck designed to hold them, with a corner of the canvas being attached to the poles and then attached to rungs in the wall, creating shaded lean-tos: one lean-to constructed near the entrance to the living quarters of the Camalain while the other went directly across the entrance to the bridge.

"Now that's the job we should be getting." Manton said to the group as two other crewmen, with shields strapped to their backs and swords at their sides, took up position as sentries under the canopy that led to the bridge.

"Just thank the gods we're not out there." Gorman replied, pointing to a team of men who were out on the flats and were clearing away sand that had collected on the gliders during the night.

Gorman's squad was to take up position on the starboard side of the deck, and he divided his men into two groups, sending Heath and Yarrow to guard the stern of the Camalain and Dolan, Manton and Sidri towards the prow.

Liam he kept by his side and, standing between the two groups, explained how he divided them with an archer in each group and an extra man towards the front to help defend the bridge if they did get attacked.

Gorman, who was fearful of losing his most novice man in a raid, spent the morning training Liam. Describing the types of movement he should watch out for on the dunes so that Liam would know if they were being attacked. He also emphasized to Liam the importance of keeping the soldiers in view if he needed help. Gorman also took the time to guide Liam over to the port side of the ship and made sure Liam knew the names of the Royal Guard on that side.

So the morning wore on, with the sun climbing higher into the sky and the air becoming warmer, as Gorman and Liam alternated positions with the men standing guard so everyone had a chance to take a break and cool off underneath the shaded confines of the lean-to.

Midday, which was slowly passing, saw Liam up front with Dolan, Manton and Sidri, as the men watched over the flats to their west. The men who had been sent out to clean the gliders had finished their job hours ago and had retreated back to their ships, leaving the flats barren. And the desert would have been void of any movement were it not for the sun reflecting off the glass and metallic parts of the gliders and the occasional communique coming from the Marmairn.

Liam was listening to Manton grumble about their predicament, a sentiment heard all over the ship for the past several days, when the door that lead into the bow section of the Camalain opened, with the prince, his father and Kael, and six soldiers exiting onto the main deck.

It looked like the group was making their way to the upper deck when Seb Cullen excused himself from their number and hobbled over to his son.

"Are you alright?" The sagart asked his son, acknowledging the other three soldiers who were doing their best to ignore the two.

"Yes." And Liam explained he had wanted to ask his father the same thing as he noticed the dark circles under his eyes and heard the raspiness in his father's voice.

"I am tired." Cullen said, rubbing a slightly shaky hand over his mouth. "And lonely."

"Lonely?" Liam found that hard to believe because his step-father was very social within the temple and, with the exception of the prince, he seemed to be getting on quite well with the Camalain's crew.

"Maybe lonely is not the right word. Empty would be more like it."

Cullen then proceeded to explain to Liam how the loss of Barra's presence and of the lack of the god's voice during prayer and his dreams was affecting him.

"It is as if I have lost a limb. Or a very good friend has passed away." Cullen placed both his hands on his cane to steady himself as he spoke. "Barra has been in my life for so long that the emptiness is unbearable right now."

"Is there anything I can do?" Liam explained how he had been hesitant to disturb his father's sleep and had spent the night in Gorman's cabin. "Master Praish said that I could stay there for the rest of the journey but I can stay with you if you need my help."

"No, spend the time with your friends. I am not yet feeble enough where I cannot take care of myself."

Cullen had more to say to his foster-son. He especially wanted to apologize to his son for he had not expected the trip to end this way when he noticed that Liam's attention had begun to wander.

Turning to see what had distracted Liam, Cullen saw that Kael had stayed behind and had been watching them from the stairs that lead to the upper deck. When Kael saw that the two were looking at him, he raised his right arm, his forearm wrapped in a white bandage, and waved. Cullen nodded back to the young man while Liam blushed; embarrassed that he had been caught looking at the man.

"He is a good boy." Cullen said, smiling at the flushing of Liam's face, happy to have something else to talk about other than their current predicament. "He has been very attentive to me these past couple of days. And I think he likes you."

"Father!" Liam hissed, his face turning a deeper red.

"And I think you like him too." Cullen said as he stood a little straighter, a mischievous look of "I know my son better than he knows himself" lighting up his eyes.

Liam didn't know what to say. Because he was not only mortified by what his father had said, he was mortified that he had said it loud enough for Manton, Sidri and Dolan to hear, who were now snickering like little boys at the remark, all the while with Kael curiously watching them.

"Well, I think I have teased you enough." Cullen said as he took a step away from his son.

Liam found his voice and told his father he would be stopping by tonight to retrieve his things and his father promised to be awake, hoping that he could visit for a while, as he made his way back over to where Kael was waiting patiently for him.

Liam watched as the handsome Karam Kael helped his father up the stairs. The two talking amicably, with Kael's left hand on his father's back to steady the man as he reached the top of the stairs. All the while turning back to catch little glimpses of Liam as the two made their way to where Manus stood.

Liam returned to his duty and continued to be embarrassed by his father's remarks as he was pelted with the friendly jibes and catcalls from the others about his not so secret infatuation with Karam Kael.

Their shift didn't last much longer because Cahl Goban, who had been standing watch on the upper deck, came down with another soldier by his side, and talked to Gorman and the other squad leader before the lieutenant and his man headed into the living quarters of the Camalain.

Gorman made his way to Heath and Yarrow to talk to them before making his way forward to Liam and the others.

"You know the drill." Gorman said as several squads came out to replace them. "Let's head in and we'll regroup in the storage bays."

Of course knowing the drill was for everyone making a dash to the water-closet before some of them headed back to their cabin to wipe off the day's grime with the cleanest towels they knew they had around.

When they had regrouped in the lower level, Gorman gave them time to eat the meager meal he had ordered them to stash; slices of bread and dried fruit, all washed down with tepid water from the sacks they had stored under the lean-tos while they were on guard duty.

"Wish I could let you slack the rest of the afternoon," Gorman said as he stood to address his men. "But the lieutenant says we'll be abandoning the ship tomorrow and be making for the mainland.

Gorman let the men grumble about this information for a bit, while Liam just sat there with a confused look on his face before Gorman raised a hand to silence them.

"I know, I know. But we knew this was coming (with the exception of maybe Liam). And with the ships not flying it can't be helped. So it's either stay, let the stores run out and die. Or use what we got and try to get home."

The men knew that Gorman was right and several voiced their agreement with the unfavorable decision.

"Right! So the lieutenant wants us to be prepared and has given us the job of getting what we need for the journey. We'll be looking for extra bedrolls, blankets and backpacks to carry our food in. And if we're lucky we might come across a tent or two to use as shelter."

Cracking the knuckles in his hands to relieve some of the tension that he was feeling, Gorman divided up his squad to scrounge through the stacked crates and sacks to find whatever they would need.

Liam, who had remained quiet, fidgeting with his hands, while Gorman talked, did his best to push down the fear he was feeling over having to traverse the flats and what an ordeal it would be over the upcoming days as he and Sidri went to pry open some crates in one corner of the bay. Thankfully Sidri was the least talkative of the group and left Liam alone with his own thoughts while they worked.

But what was he to do? Liam thought as he and Sidri moved the first crate they touched over to one side, the stamps on the outside of it indicating that it had nothing of value for their journey.

These men had gone out of their way to be friendly to him and the last thing they needed was for him to be a burden to them.

"I just can't let them down." Liam thought as he watched Gorman walk over to them while he and Sidri pulled the lid off the third crate they had found so that they could get the items they could use.

"Just want to make sure you're okay with all of this." Liam's squad leader said as he and Sidri continued to work.

Liam stopped for a moment, his hands deep in wood shavings, and looked at the man, for he could hear hesitancy in Gorman's voice and a look of concern on his face that he had never seen before.

Liam forced a smile of his face that he didn't feel as he pulled a sealed clay jar containing oil out of the crate. "Got no choice in the matter. But I do make a better pack animal than a soldier, so I'll carry as much as possible. Especially for my father. He already seems to be burdened by much."

"And don't worry Gor," Liam said as he went back to work, not even sure if he believed in what he was saying. "I won't be a burden to you."

Gorman watched Liam's back as he returned to stacking more clay jars of oil off to one side when Sidri got his leader's attention and gestured for him to leave.

Gorman knew he should do what he was being told and went back to helping Heath, who was pulling some large packs out of another crate. But he couldn't help but worry about the boy. For Liam was greener than any recruit he had ever been given and Gorman never would have subjected one of them to what was about to come their way over the next couple of weeks.

"He's strong and in good company." Heath whispered into his partner's ear when Gorman began helping him. "He'll be fine."

Gorman knew that he was not going to stop worrying about Liam and responded to Heath's words with a shrug and a barely audible grunt.

Heath also knew Gorman's moods enough to know that talking to him would not comfort him and his apprehensions so tried a different route. "You would have made a good father."

Gorman scoffed at the idea, sweeping a hand to encompass the bay. "These misfits are handful enough! How would we have time for a child?"

Heath pulled the last of the large packs out of the crate before stealing a kiss from his partner. "I love you."

Gorman smiled, repeating the sentiment.

And as the two were moving the half empty crate so that they could get at another to search its contents, the room shifted, tilting to one side before quickly righting itself as the Camalain lifted from the ground. The warning that usually preceded a launch finally echoing through the ship just as it began to right itself in the air.

Heath and Gorman let the crate fall back on top of the one it had been resting on as they maintained their balance. But someone else was less fortunate as the sound of shattering clay and cursing filled the air.

Liam had fallen to the ground, still not comfortable with the quick movements of the Camalain, and had dropped the pots he was carrying, oil now spreading across floor. Sidri, who had held the crate in place that held more oil jars, helped Liam off the ground, who apologized profusely for letting them fall.

"And who taught you those words?" Manton asked as he hurried over with a bucket of sand that was kept in the room for such emergencies and began tossing the sand on the puddle of oil.

Liam mumbled incoherently, somewhat annoyed he had sworn like that and began picking shards of clay off of the floor.

"Think I was more surprised by your foul mouth than by the ship flying again!" Manton laughed.

The others joined in on the joke, including Liam, as they relaxed a little, realizing they weren't falling out of the sky.

Gorman, who was just as happy as the rest, was still apprehensive about this turn of events. Silently thanking the gods, he ordered Sidri to look for Lieutenant Cahl and to see if he could find out what was going on outside. And as Sidri was about to leave the room, the Camalain began to dip in the air, everyone's stomach rolling slightly as it seemed like the Camalain was once again going to resume its position on the flats. Sidri looked questioningly at Gorman who only told the man to hurry up.

Sidri wasn't gone long before he returned to inform the rest of them that the Marmairn was also aloft and that they were landing for the men who had been put on guard duty outside before retrieving the gliders.

"The lieutenant wants us on deck to help secure the glider when it lands." Sidri said as the Camalain began to move once again.

Leaving Liam and Manton behind to finish cleaning the spill, Gorman had everyone else head topside and for the other two to join them as soon as possible.

When they did make it to the main deck, Liam and Manton were just in time to watch as one glider came in to land on the Camalain while the second made its way back to roost on the Marmairn.

And as the men strapped the glider down to the deck, Liam listened to several other men talk of how the third glider was being left behind.

"We lost too much time sitting here." They said. "And who knows how long it would take to find the glider after that storm we had the night before."

The men were securing the last of the leather straps for the glider when the Camalain pivoted and flew to be alongside the Marmairn, with both crews finally cheering at their good fortune before they continued on their south-easterly direction.

The rest of the afternoon flew by with Gorman sending his men back to reorganize the mess they had made, who chatted cheerfully while they worked. The hallways were also filled with men as Manus had the Camalain and Marmairn fly as fast as they could go, because no one wanted to be on the main deck, especially at the pace the Camalain was now moving, for fear of being blasted by sand or being tossed over the side by a strong gust of wind.

Once again, dinner was meager, and when Liam left his duties with Crogan to eat his own meal, he found many of the men sitting quietly, praying to their gods, hoping that their words would continue to keep them aloft on the rest of their journey.

Which is how he found his father when he returned to his room when he went to fetch his belongings: sitting at the desk, his hands resting on its surface fidgeting with nothing, while he stared blankly out the porthole in front of him.

"Father? You alright?"

Cullen, who had been lost in his own thoughts, turned at the sound of his son's voice.

"Ah, my boy." Cullen said as he forced a smile on his face. "Sit. Can you stay a while?"

"For a bit." Liam said as he sat on the edge of the bed. "It is good to be flying again."

Cullen agreed with his son, saying that he had dreaded the idea of having to walk across the flats to make it back to Birr.

Liam seconded his father's sentiment. "Thankfully Barra did not abandon us completely. Has Barra told you where we should be looking for the prince?"

"No. The god is still silent to me." Cullen frowned, his grey-blue eyes clouded by the disappointment of the god's absence. "Maybe we are meant to be blinded for a while."

Liam watched his father as the man momentarily looked about the room as he tried to regain his composure, the fingers of his left hand sliding aimlessly across the top of the desk. How he wished he knew the right words to say to his father that would make him feel better. But anything that came to mind only seemed flat and unhelpful.

When Cullen looked back at his son, he saw the concern for his well-being clearly etched on the young man's face.

"But look at you." Cullen said as he reached over and patted Liam's knee. "You, look awful!"

Both men could not help but laugh at the absurdity of the remark. A laugh that started off as a chuckle until the sounds of their voices boisterously filled the room.

Liam knew he was quite a sight. With his black curly hair matted from sweat and his face sunburned from spending the past several days outside. Although several of his nails were cracked or broken from the work he had done since the Camalain had stopped flying, his hands were the cleanest things on his body; especially since he had to continue with his cooking duties in the galley.

The mood somewhat lightened, Liam went on to tell his father about the work and training he had done with Praish Gorman and his squad. Doing his best to remember the tiniest bits of details as he noticed a genuine smile cross his father's face as the man listened to his ramblings.

Liam asked after Moro Croft, who along with the other two steersmen, had been ordered to remain on the bridge while the prince hoped for a way out of this situation.

"Give him my best." Liam said. "And how is Kael?"

Cullen's smile broadened at his son's hesitant question, explaining how Karam Kael was doing just fine. And that the scratch on his arm had not been deep at all and was now only covered so it would not get infected. Cullen's smile also hid the fact that Kael had been asking Seb Cullen about his son whenever the two were out of earshot of the prince.

Cullen did not bring up the obvious interest Kael had in his foster-son. For it was there for all to see, who wanted to see, how Kael had been hounding Liam's every step since his arrival on the Camalain.

And if Liam had noticed the attention, he was not saying a word, keeping his own thoughts secret on the matter. Now seeing that his father seemed to be in much better spirits, Liam took his leave so he could get some rest before his own early day started tomorrow morning.

Thankfully the next day brought a sense of normalcy to the Camalain, with Crogan stirring up a breakfast that looked like a banquet after the sparse meals the crew had been served for the past several days.

Crogan also informed Liam that the prince had doled out some water for everyone to wash. And Liam, along with everyone else with shift duty that morning, took advantage of a much needed sponge bath before returning to the dining hall to have his own breakfast.

Liam was making his way across the dining hall towards Gorman and the others, his plate stacked with griddle cakes covered with butter and syrup, when he spotted Croft and Jensen, one of the other steersmen for the Camalain.

Liam had not seen his friend in a while and both steersmen greeted him warmly when he took the seat across from them.

Although the two were very animated and obviously hungry by the way they dug into their meals, Liam could not help but notice that the they looked just as haggard as his father had the day before.

"So any problems during the night?" Liam asked as he cut into his own breakfast.

"If there was trouble the entire ship would have known about it." Croft said, a steaming cup of caff in his hands, while Jensen nodded in agreement as he chewed on some sausage.

"Well, thank Barra." Liam said, offering a whispered prayer to the god of the earth.

"Barra nothing!" Jensen scoffed, interrupting Liam's prayer, before shoveling more food into his mouth.

Croft hissed at the man to say nothing else before drinking from his mug.

"What? What do you mean?" Liam asked, concerned by the quick exchange.

Liam asked the question one more time while Croft drank some more of his caff, doing his best to ignore Liam's demand.

"You might as well tell him." Jensen said, ignoring the looks from some of the other men seated next to them who had been intrigued by the exchange. "He is the sagart's son and will hear about it soon enough."

"What? Tell me!" Liam whispered sharply as he leaned across the table.

Croft looked at his young friend and frowned because the prince had told them that a secret like this one would not keep long on the Camalain. And who knew what was being said on the Marmairn.

Croft turned to Jensen for help, but the steersman reminded Croft that Liam was his friend and that it was he who should continue.

Dragging a hand through his wavy brown hair, pulling it away from his bloodshot eyes, Croft leaned forward to join Liam in the center of the table. "Barra is not helping in guiding the ship."

"I don't understand." Liam said as he pulled a little away from Croft.

But Liam did understand, for everyone knew that the gift of flight came from Barra and the lodestones that the Gwerin mined from the land. That it was through these stones that Barra's will flowed into the men and women holding the stones, giving them the power to move the object they were attached to.

"I don't either." Croft agreed. "I know we're flying, but the energy from the stones just feels different. Not like what I'm accustomed to at all."

"How so?"

Croft only shrugged at Liam's question. He knew how he felt when he sat in the chair. That sense of control over the world around him as he flew the ship. But now, to describe the subtle changes that happened when he was away from the mystical orbs only left him frustrated.

"They feeling I get using them is different. Softer. Not the energy I'm accustomed to when I know Barra is directing my vision." Jensen added for his friend.

"And my father hasn't heard from Barra during his prayers since we stopped flying."

"Maybe they're connected." Jensen mused as he used his fork to cut into more of his breakfast.

"Maybe you should all shut up!" The crewman sitting by Jensen said, a mixture of fear and anger at having to listen to their conversation covering the man's face.

Of course Liam did as he was told and pulled away from the other two men and went back to quietly eating his own breakfast, while Jensen turned to the man.

"Aaron, maybe you should mind your own business!" Jensen quipped, knowing that the older man, who also worked on the bridge, was more superstitious than he was religious, and that Aaron also had a tendency to be very nosey.

"And you should mind what the prince says!" Aaron, who was a devout loyalist, reminded Jensen, as he waved his fork at the steersman, sending bits of his own meal onto the table and into the Jensen's plate.

Revolted by the assault, Jensen pushed his half-finished meal away and proceeded to tell Aaron, and not too politely, that he was not only disgusting but old and foolish and better suited to be hovering over a washboard instead of being a soldier.

Quite offended by the remark concerning his age, Aaron shot back that only a half-wit could fly a ship for how else could Barra fill his mind with the power of a god to keep a ship aloft? Aaron also informed Jensen that he would be informing the captain and the prince about the abuse he was receiving.

As the tirade got heated, with Jensen mimicking Aaron's remarks in a childish voice, stirring laughter from the rest of the men seated around them, Manton appeared at the table. Liam's squad mate didn't bother to interrupt the two haranguing each other because everyone knew how much of a gossip Aaron was, and just patted Liam's shoulder and said it was time to go.

Picking up his own plate as he stood, Liam asked Croft to say hello to his father if and when he saw him today.

"Well, we're going to bed once this show is over. But I'll pass your message along when I do see him."

Without missing a beat, Jensen also said goodbye to Liam before tearing back into Aaron.

The verbal assault between Jensen and Aaron was the most exciting thing that happened on the ship this morning, as Liam ended up with the others in the storage bay they were in yesterday and continued to sort the supplies. In case an emergency did arise, Gorman said.

In the afternoon, they went back to training with weapons. This time Gorman had him acting as back-up for Manton who fought against Sidri, forcing Liam to maintain his guard over Manton's back as the other two men danced across the floor.

The next day's routine was the same as the day before. The same as the day's had been before the ships had stopped flying.

Although the work he was doing was strenuous, especially his weapon's training, Liam began to enjoy it and the camaraderie he was sharing with the others. Liam also had a hard time keeping the smile from his face when Kael reappeared that afternoon to once again join in on the mock fighting.

A smile that Kael also mirrored when he too saw Liam.

A smile that reappeared on Kael's face when Gorman had the two spar against each other, having Liam use his fake punching daggers and bucklers against Kael who would be wielding a blunted short sword and shield. Gorman hoped this would get Liam used to blocking and parrying a longer weapon while trying to push his own attack with his much smaller weapons. Gorman also had Yarrow, Dolan, Manton and Sidri sparring in pairs, on either side of them, so that Liam could get used to the distracting sounds of battle around him.

But Liam seemed to be tolerating the sounds of wooden weapons clacking against each other, and the catcalls the men were making.

No, what Liam was finding distracting was Kael's smile. For there was a gleefulness to it and his eyes sparkled mischievously while he skillfully thrust his sword past Liam's guard, getting in close enough to feel Kael's hot breath on his sweat soaked skin.

Gorman on the other hand, who had been hovering around the group and doling out pointers, found Kael's smile not only distracting but quite annoying. Passing behind the man, Gorman waited for Kael to dance away from another one of Liam's failed attacks and kicked at his feet.

The move definitely surprised Kael, who lost his footing and stumbled to his right, falling into Yarrow who used his own shield to push Kael in the opposite direction.

Manton, who had been on Kael's left, saw the commotion out of the corner of his eye and sidestepped out of Kael's stumbling way. Of course Manton couldn't resist tripping the younger soldier and bringing his own wooden sword down on his back, sending the man sprawling across the floor amidst the jeering and heckles of the others.

Gorman strode over to Kael, the burly man extending a hand to help him off the floor. But before the Kael could find his footing, Gorman pulled him in close enough so that their bodies were touching.

"On your time, if you want to make lovey, dovey eyes at Liam that's fine with me." Gorman growled into Kael's ear. "But on my time, it's my job to keep him alive, and you flirting with him like this isn't helping me with that right now!"

Kael knew that the squad leader was right and the thought of Liam getting killed because of him was quite sobering. So Kael quickly apologized and said it wouldn't happen again. For Kael was not only enjoying Liam's company, but the company of the others, happy to have a break from Manus' perpetual sour mood.

With a pat on the back and squeezing Kael's hand tighter, Gorman accepted his apology before steering Kael towards the others.

"Think we've had enough for today!" Gorman informed the group as he grabbed a towel that was resting on a crate and tossed it to Dolan.

Heath, who also had watched the bouts from the sidelines, handed out several water skins to the exhausted men as they gathered around him.

Kael, whose smile had finally left his face, approached Liam, who handed him a water skin while Liam used one of the now damp towels that was also making its rounds through the group to wipe his sweat soaked face and hair.

"What did he say to you?" Liam asked Kael as he traded the towel for the waterskin in Kael's hand. Liam couldn't help but be curious about what Gorman had said to Kael.

Kael shrugged as he unstrapped his leather vest and began to take off his shirt.

"Just pointed out a move that was in bad form." Kael replied, his voice muffled by the shirt he was pulling over his head.

Liam accepted the statement as truth as he too took off his own vest and shirt, just like everyone else in the storage bay, for the men's clothing had become uncomfortable against their sweat covered skin. And Liam, who had been wearing the same shirt for the past several days so he wouldn't ruin his other slightly less dirty shirts, thought that a couple more days of this and their clothing would be able to stand up on their own.

Kael had turned to go sit on some crates, beckoning for Liam to join him and that's when Liam noticed the tattoos running across Kael's muscled back.

As the two sat down Kael bent forward as he ran his hands through his brown hair that had become matted to his head, freeing it so it fell in front of his eyes and sending drops of sweat to the ground.

Of course his back was again exposed for Liam's perusal and that gave him a better chance to scrutinize the detailed work inked across Kael's upper back, for they had been done using the traditional technique of running from his left shoulder blade and flowing towards his right. Liam could easily tell that the three in the middle of his back were the symbols for the gods Barra, Aodhagan and Cillach.

But the first one he wasn't so sure about and was about to ask Kael when he noticed the man had raised his head and was staring at him.

"It's my family's clan name. In the old dialect." Kael said, twisting and exposing more of his back to Liam, reaching under his left armpit with his right hand as he tried to stretch the design the design for Liam's perusal.

Liam's mouth went dry and his hands trembled slightly as he watched Kael's skin that still glistened with sweat, as it tightened over his muscles. His eyes followed the black swirls, like they were streets to a town on some fanciful map, wishing that it were his fingers moving across Kael's body.

"How about you?" Kael asked as he raised himself into a sitting position. "Got anything on your back?"

Liam turned exposing his own back, bare of any markings, to Kael. Bare because his foster-father had never encouraged Liam to get one.

"Keir isn't it?"

Liam's response of yes faltered on his lips when he felt Kael's finger, who seemed to have no qualms about touching Liam, began to move across his back. Liam closed his eyes and held his breath as Kael drew the characters for what he assumed were the runes for his own clan name.

Enjoying the sensation of being touched, Liam was also oblivious to the looks that his friends were giving each other.

 Kael could not miss the look of rebuke he was receiving from the squad leader as his fingers trailed down Liam's spine. He smiled wickedly and winked at Gorman before mouthing the words "my time" at the man.

But two could play this game, Gorman thought as he returned Kael's smile. He was not going to deter Kael's advances towards Liam, especially since Liam also seemed just as interested in Kael. He just did not have to make it easy for the man.

"Did you bring them?" Gorman quietly asked his partner, who was watching him, waiting to see what he now had in store for Kael.

Heath nodded and lifted a wooden box that had been sitting off to one side on the storage bay floor. The case, which was crafted of a dark polished wood, with its corners wrapped in a tarnished bronze as were the cases handles, covered in scuffs and nicks from its many travels with its owner.

"Liam? You busy?" Gorman asked, startling the young man who had forgotten where he was, a round of low chuckles coming from the squad as Gorman approached Liam and Kael with the case Heath had given him.

Liam only blushed with Kael's hand slowly withdrawing from Liam's back as he took the heavy case from Gorman and placed it across his lap, thankful that he had something to cover his arousal.

Liam was running his hand over the carved runes that represented Praish Gorman's household, the runes that had been painted in a deep red now a rusted brown from age, when the others urged him to open the box.

Moving the case over onto the crate he was sitting on to do what he was told, Liam undid the bronze latches to reveal what was inside.

Kael whistled from behind him, impressed by what he saw. "They're beautiful." He said. Words spoken like a true soldier.

Liam on the other hand, was filled with dread and intimidation by what he saw.

For resting in the auburn colored velvet, a little threadbare where its edges met the wooden case, were a set of steel punching daggers.

More like short swords than daggers, Liam thought, for the shiny, well-polished blades were almost a foot long. Each blade being attached to a steel gauntlet and instead of having a short cuff, the gauntlets were attached to an ornately carved plate that would cover the wearers forearm.

"My father gave me these when I was sixteen. Right before I joined the Royal Guard." Gorman said as he removed one of the weapons from the case, its segmented knuckle guards clinking dully.

Moving the case aside, Gorman sat down next to Liam and had him extend his right hand so he could fit the dagger onto him. The weapon was designed more like a piece of armor rather than a glove and Liam easily slipped his fingertips into the thimble-like guards as Gorman fitted the straps to the padded weapon across the palm of his hand and his arm.

Gorman then turned Liam's arm over, explaining how to put the weapon on and told him that he should find some scrap clothing to wedge underneath the straps so that his skin would not get too cut up by the leather.

They stood so that Liam could get a feel for how the weapon moved, the men giving Liam a wide berth, fearful of getting unintentionally nicked by the dagger.

Liam already knew he would have to get used to the weight of the thing because the punching dagger was much heavier than the block of wood he had been practicing with and that he would certainly need to learn to control its movements, for the blade did not want to stop once he got it moving.

"The daggers also come with bucklers." Gorman informed Liam as he pointed out on the arm plate where the shields would get snapped and strapped into place.

Kael watched Liam, and found himself growing more attracted to him as he stood there, bare chested, his body glistening with a new sheen of sweat, his pants riding low on his waist from the dampness of his skin and from moving around as he awkwardly swung the dagger, its blade a reddish yellow as it reflected the lamplight in the room.

"We'll make a soldier out of you yet." He said, coughing slightly as he tried to hide the huskiness that had entered his voice.

Fortunately the voices of the others drowned out any emotion that might have escaped from Kael as they too agreed with him and joked how Liam looked like a warrior of old going to fight in one of the clan wars.

Liam smiled politely and laughed along with the others as the dagger dangled off of his hand. Liam also knew that practicing was one thing and that truly fighting was another and that he was so unsure of himself right now that he did not know if he would ever be of any use to these men if trouble ever did arise.

"But won't you need these in case we get into a skirmish or something?" Liam asked Gorman as he raised the dagger, sending Manton and Yarrow, who had gotten a little too close to Liam, skipping away as the blade flashed upward.

"No, no," Gorman laughed as he watched his men's foolishness. "I haven't used them in a long time. Nowadays I keep them around as good luck charms more than anything else."

"Gor can be very superstitious." Heath said, finishing the sentence for his partner.

Gorman watched as Liam, whose arm and shoulder had begun to throb from the weight on it, had gone back to the crate to take the weapon off. Of course Kael was right there to help him with unstrapping it from his arm.

"I'll show you how to oil and clean them after your shift in the galley tonight." Gorman walked over to the two and noticed the long red welts running across Liam's arm from where the leather straps had wrapped across his arm. "Make sure you find something soft to put under those straps so you don't get scarred. I'm sure Crogan has something you can use."

"You should get some salve for those too!" Gorman added as he also noticed more redness and a slight cut on the palm of Liam's hand.

"I can help you with that." Kael piped in, seeing an opportunity to spend more time with Liam interrupting Gorman before he could finish with anything else he was about to say.

Liam simply blushed at the comment. His face, shoulders and the upper part of his chest turning a bright red as he heard snickers escape from some of the others and watched as knowing smiles appeared on their faces.

Gorman only shrugged and gave Kael a conspiratorial wink. "Wouldn't hurt. Liam did help you with that cut on your arm and one good turn deserves another."

"And be prepared to work with these tomorrow. No more slacking." Gorman said to Liam, his voice deepening and his eyes lidded; a stern look that was only belied by the smile on his face.

But weapon's practice did not happen the next day.

For when Liam made his way to the galley the next morning, he was surprised to find that Crogan had already prepared all of the day's breakfast. A simple meal of the ships remaining dried fruit and bread he had baked the other day with butter and preserves.

"I won't be needing your help today." Crogan said as he handed Liam a tray of mugs to take out into the galley while he began to brew some caff.

"How come?"

"We're making landfall." Crogan replied. "Got word we'll be flying into port within the hour. So you'll be needed to do dock work with the others for the rest of the day."

"Where are we landing?" Liam asked as he grabbed another tray to take out into the galley.

"Fomor. A small military outpost of sorts on the southern tip of Birr."

Liam froze in his tracks when he heard the name of the village, setting the clay mugs to clinking slightly. A fear he had not felt in a very long time gripped him as old nightmares of his last time in Fomor took a hold of him.

"We're only a day and night's journey from Tuame." Crogan had been wiping a counter and assumed Liam had stopped because he was interested in more information as to where they were going. "Lieutenant Cahl said we would be staying here for a couple of days so we can restock the ships."

Crogan's voice snapped Liam out of his terror, and Liam left the room to finish what he was doing.

After that, Liam made his way out onto the main deck and to the railing to watch as the Camalain and the Marmairn headed for the coast of Birr.

Crogan was right, Liam thought as a strong wind whipped across the deck, forcing him to momentarily close his eyes and grip the railing a little tighter: they were not far from Fomor.

Their destination was close enough for Liam to see the stone walls and towers that were protecting its port and lights flickered sporadically from windows of the walled town that rose from the sloping landscape behind it. Fomor looked peaceful; all pinks and yellows in the morning light, a sleepy little village at the end of the world. A sharp contrast to Liam's own memories of a Fomor filled with black smoke and the cries of many voices long unforgotten morning.

Liam's grip on the rail tightened once more as both ships banked to the left, correcting their path to make for the port's entrance. Several vessels appeared leaving Fomor and as they got closer, signal lights began flashing from the lead ship.

Liam listened to the activity building around him as the Camalain's crew came to life, leaving him several more minutes of quiet contemplation before he felt a presence to the side of him. Liam didn't bother to look at who it was. The light tapping of wood on wood easily gave the person away.

"I went looking for you in the galley this morning." Cullen said to his son, his voice just audible over the shouting of other crewmen that was building around them. "But you had already left and Crogan thought something might be wrong with you. He said you had an odd look on your face and found it unusual that you did not come back and ask if he needed help with anything else."

Liam knew why his father would have been looking for him today and Liam knew there was no reason to explain why he was out on deck.

"It's much bigger than I remember." Liam finally said as the walls of the village began to loom over them.

His father agreed. "Fomor has grown much in twenty years. At that time there were only several hundred men and their children living here. And the village had no defenses whatsoever to speak of."

"That would have helped." Liam had a hard time keeping the bitterness from his voice.

Cullen agreed, but didn't bother to express his opinion on Liam's comment.

The silence returned between father and son as the Camalain and then the Marmairn entered the small military port. But their reverie was finally interrupted by a cough from behind them.

"Excuse me Sagart." Gorman said to the two. "I just came to reclaim your son to help with loading the ship with new supplies." But his smile faltered as he watched Liam quickly drop his head and looked to be wiping at tears in his eyes.

"Maybe I'll see you tonight?" Liam asked his father before he left the railing and walked past Gorman to join the rest of the squad who had just come out on deck, halting Gorman from asking any questions that he just did not feel like answering.

That didn't stop Gorman from looking to Liam's father for those answers, who only closed his eyes and shook his head in the negative. A gesture full of its own pain that informed Gorman that the boy had gone through a lot and that it was something he did not want to talk about. Still, that did not stop Gorman from trying to ask Liam's father how he was fairing, who was only listening to the squad leader with half an ear as he continued to watch his foster-son and the rest of Gorman's crew make their way to Fomor's docks.

While the group joined several other squads already on the docks and waited for Gorman, who was stalled by the glider leaving Camalain's deck, Manton told Liam how Lieutenant Cahl informed the squad leaders there might be a good chance they would be here for several days.

These were not words Liam wanted to hear and for the first time since this flight began he wished they were back in the skies over the flats.

"It will be nice to be off the ship for a while and to look at some faces other than this sorry group." Manton said as he stretched and looked around.

"Do you mean faces? Or asses?" Sidri retorted as several dock workers walked by them, with one of them turning to shoot a smile at the group before disappearing into the crowd of men that had gathered on the wharves.

The Fomoran's open flirtation set the group to laughing, with Manton and Dolan joking that the smile was solely for one of them.

"I think he was smiling at Liam!" Yarrow said as he gave the young man a nudge. "Who in their right mind would be interested in either of you two cows?"

Liam only blushed and took the ribbing that followed. Especially when Manton and Dolan jokingly tried to talk him into going into town and cruising with them, promising not to tell Master Karam of their wicked adventure.

Finally joining in and chuckling at the absurdity of the remark, Liam couldn't help but thank the gods that these men and their foolishness and good humor would be around him to help buoy his spirits during their stay in this town.

When Gorman finally joined them, Liam was grateful that the man acted like he had not seen his earlier display of emotion. Or maybe he didn't, Liam thought as he listened to Gorman explain how they would be part of a chain gang helping to unload the Camalain of its empty crates and barrels to make room for the fresh supplies they would be taking on.

The soldiers did not have to wait long before a foreman and several dockworkers came over to help them and directed where they would be able to put the empty containers. While Gorman asked several questions of his own for the foreman, Liam watched as his father, Prince Manus, and Captain Thear and Kael left the ship. Kael waved at Liam, who returned the greeting, while Manus talked to Lieutenant Cahl, who had followed them off the Camalain, before making their way towards the town, leaving Cahl Goban behind.

The lieutenant, who was only dressed like one of the laborers came over to join them. Goban nodded to a man that had remained on the Camalain who pulled the planks away from the docks where the ship was berthed.

"Hope you don't mind an extra pair of hands Master Praish?" Goban asked the squad leader while they waited for the Camalain to lift off and turn so they could get into the storage bays on the lower decks.

"The more the merrier!" Gorman replied, smiling at his superior.

All the men were quite surprised to see a smile creep onto the tight lipped, stoic face of the lieutenant. A smile, that if the men only knew, was one of relief at not having to be in the presence of the prince and an escape from the man's ongoing demeaning attitude towards him.

Soon though, all thoughts were turned to the work that needed to get done as empty barrels came through the bay doors and rolled their way.

"Wished they had started with the empty crates." Yarrow said, receiving grunts of agreement from several of the others as he rolled a barrel by Liam.

"Why?" Liam asked as he joined Yarrow to push the barrel to some dockworkers waiting to take it from them.

"This is easy." He said as they moved out of the way as the lieutenant and Dolan came along with another barrel. "Would have liked to have done the heavier stuff first, not later."

In the end, removing the heavier or lighter crates didn't matter because it wasn't long before more men from Fomor came to help them and the men of the Marmairn, which had also risen into the air so it could be cleared of its own empty containers.

Of course with the men gathering, most of who belonged to the Royal Guard stationed here, talk soon blossomed. The Gwerin were gregarious by nature and would strike up a conversation over the simplest of things with their neighbors.

So questions were asked as to why they were here, with shocks of dismay over the missing prince and concern over his whereabouts, because news of banning's disappearance had yet to reach this far south.

Everyone also talked about how all the ships and trams, anything that happened to be powered by lodestones for that matter, had stopped working for several days.

The conversations were also peppered with how all the gods had gone silent for those same three days; something the men on the ship had not known.

They did know about Barra's silence. Although the prince had ordered the bridge crew not to talk about it, word of the god's absence still spread throughout the Camalain. Speculation soon filled the air when the men of Fomor told of how Barra had yet to commune with any of their sagarts in the town's small temple.

Liam, of all the people, was relieved to hear that it was not only his foster-father that Barra had abandoned.

By noon almost all the bays had been emptied out, with the lieutenant finally calling for a much needed, and extended, lunch break before they finished clearing out the ship.

But their work was far from done. And the rest of the afternoon and the early evening saw the men laboring away, with Cahl Goban still working by their side and looking just as sweaty and tired as the rest of them, as they consolidated what remained in the bays, cleaning the rooms of any debris and taking inventories for new supplies.

By the end of that strenuous shift, Liam was so exhausted that he did not argue with Heath, who offered him his own bed that night, so that the man could sleep with his partner. For Duwain and Rhyne had also helped with the cleaning and wanted their beds to sleep in.

The next day brought a reprieve for both crews as Prince Manus, although somewhat reluctantly, gave all the men a day of shore leave while the supplies they needed for their ongoing quest for his brother were gathered. Even Yanno Crogan was given a break from the galley that morning as the prince had breakfast prepared by the canteen run by the soldiers in Fomor.

So, while the water tanks of the Camalain and Marmairn were filled with fresh water, the first thing everyone did was to use the showers and baths housed in the barracks of the Royal Guard in Fomor. Even Liam overcame his modesty, grateful to wash what felt like a weeks' worth of grime and sweat off of his body.

But when Liam thought that he might be able to wander around the Camalain and hide from the stone walls and cobbled streets that made up this southern town, Gorman invited Liam to join him and the rest of the squad as they spent the day in Fomor's small market district.

"I could use a new shirt or two." Liam said out loud, realizing that even the cleanest of his shirts that he was now wearing stank a little.

"Then you'll be needing these!" Gorman laughed as he handed Liam seven silver pieces.

"But I have a marker from my father. From the temple." Liam looked down at the coins; dulled and tarnished by their passage through many hands, before trying to hand them back to Gorman.

"No, no! You've earned those." Gorman said, still chuckling over the surprise. "You've been working just as hard as the rest of us so I asked the lieutenant to put you on the books. He agreed with me so you'll be getting paid just like the rest of us. These are out of my pocket for now until Lieutenant Cahl or the captain can pay me back later."

"Oh! I can't take your money. I can wait until. . ."

"Well if you wanted a pet then you should have brought one of your hounds with you instead of me!" Kael snapped, as he and Manus stepped out of the Fomoran barracks, drawing the attention of everyone around them as the conversation he was having with Manus became heated.

"You don't need me for your war meeting." Kael whispered when he realized that many of the men were now overtly watching their tirade.

"You're right, I don't. I just wanted a friend by my side!" Manus shot back.

Kael knew that Manus was trying to guilt him into going with him and it usually worked. But today he did not want to back down. "Please, just one day for myself?"

"Your afternoons aren't enough?" Manus sneered. "Fine!" he snapped, rapping the back of his knuckles against Kael's chest. "Go play with your new friends. Go play with your new pet!"

Kael, hurt by the remark, simply turned from his best friend and walked over to Liam and the others, unaware of the withering look that Manus shot their way. A look primarily directed at Liam.

"So where are we going?" Kael asked of no one in particular as he forced a smile onto his face.

"To the market." Gorman replied as he and his men did their best to ignore the prince. But after a moment Manus, with Captain Ibor, Lieutenant Cahl and Liam's father following in his wake, stormed off to talk with Fomor's military and religious leaders.

Not wanting to be right on the prince's heels, Gorman and his squad, along with Croft who decided to join them, took a leisurely pace as they left the barracks that abutted the wharves and took a circuitous route into the town proper.

As they walked the narrow, shadowed streets of Fomor's lower district, Kael's sour mood finally began to ebb; slowly rolling away like the tides of old that used to lap on the now dry shores of the Gwerin lands.

Kael finally relaxed, his smile becoming genuine, although his eyes still seemed pained, as the group took in the sights of the town.

By the time they reached the small market district, many of the men from the two ships had already made their way to the plazas that made up this area, where a cacophony of talking and laughter filled the morning air.

It was rare for the men of Fomor to see such a large influx of travelers, so the mood in the markets was very festive. With many of the shop owners at their doors or stalls, some dressed enticingly, as they hawked their various wares to these newcomers.

Eventually the squad began to disperse as different things began to pique their interest. Since the lieutenant had given them a chit to cover meals, Gorman ordered his men to try and meet for lunch in a couple of hours.

With the thought of lunch already taken care for them, Liam, Kael and Croft wandered off into one of the smaller squares that made up the town's market district. Of course hanging around with Croft, who liked to talk to everyone, meant that Liam had to patiently wait as they hunted for a shop that sold clothing.

Kael on the other hand, who was just as sociable as Croft, was grateful that the steersman was dragging his feet because it gave him time to spend with Liam. But now, Kael was finding Liam's shyness somewhat odd, not as Liam deflected questions about his personal life which left Kael to talk mostly about himself.

Luckily, as their one sided conversation dwindled to a somewhat awkward silence, the trio finally came across some shops that contained clothing. After browsing through several of them, Liam bought two rough spun, plain cotton shirts to work in. And at Croft's insistence, he bought a nicer shirt, dyed a deep burgundy, with long sleeves that were slit at the wrists. Kael had to admit, as Liam took off the shirt to purchase it, that it was a nice color on Liam and not only did the shirt fit him well, Kael liked how the neck line cut in a v with a woven string to close it, exposed some of Liam's dark chest hair.

Once Liam was done with his transaction, they continued on with their window shopping until they came across a leather smith, selling a variety of vests, jerkins and aprons.

The man also had a selection of ornately carved armguards and wristbands. One of which caught Liam's eye for the wristband was of supple leather, dyed a dark walnut brown, with the symbol of Barra and the constellation that represented him carved into it with both icons dyed a rich black. The bindings, which would sit on the inside of the arm were also of leather, with charms painted with the symbols of Barra, labor and good luck on them which would dangle into the wearers palm so they could be rubbed for good luck.

"How much is this one?" Liam asked the shop owner, who had walked over to see which item he was asking about.

"Four silver pieces." The man said when he saw which item he had in his hand.

Croft couldn't help but whistle, while Liam only stood there, stunned by the price. Why, the shirts that were all wrapped in a neat package only cost him a total of two silver pieces. Buying this would only leave Liam with only one coin of his own money, and he did not want to spend the temple's money on something so frivolous.

"Can you do any better?" Kael asked the man as he watched the disappointed look appear on Liam's face.

"Well, I could do three silvers for it. But not a copper less – I did do all the work on it."

Liam still thought that was too much money, and ignoring Croft and Kael who were trying to goad him into buying it, handed the wristband back to the leather smith who returned the item back to its place on the table.

Taking their time to stop at several more shops, the trio eventually made it back to the plaza and found Gorman, Heath, Yarrow and Sidri standing underneath the awning of one of the shops, waiting for them. As Gorman lead them to a tavern he and Heath had found further into the town, Sidri informed them that Dolan and Manton had befriended some of Fomor's residents and had made plans for the rest of the day and would not be joining them for lunch.

The group joked that it would be nice to have a meal free of Dolan and Manton's antics when they arrived at the tavern, its tables crowded mostly by the residents of Fomor.

"Wasn't like this when we first found this place." Heath said. "We thought it would be out of the way and quiet."

"Well we have taken over the rest of the town." Croft replied as he dodged out of the way of one of the barmen whose hands each grasped several tankards of foaming ale.

The group finally found a table and scavenging for two lone chairs squeezed themselves into a spot that was certainly meant for four.

Fortunately they were spared the trouble of trying to flag a barman down when a boy, who looked to be in his late teens, wearing a stained apron and carrying a stack of dirty plates and looking very harried, told them someone would be over to see what they wanted as soon as possible.

Liam and the others didn't mind the wait for it gave them some time to relax, happy to be away from the confines of the Camalain, and it wasn't too long, maybe twenty minutes, before someone did come to take their orders. Of course Gorman took charge and kept the meal simple by ordering a round of ale for everyone and some platters of cooked meat and vegetables that they could all pick from.

When their meal arrived, the meat and vegetables looked very tasty sitting in a bowl with gravy that was quite aromatic, reminding the men of how hungry they really were, their stomachs urging them to dig in and load up their plates with a lunch that would once be void of dried fruits and day old bread.

Talk at the table died down to nothing as the men enjoyed their meal, with several of them already helping themselves to a second helping of meat. But after a while Liam began to fidget, shuffling his chair closer to Croft, who was on his left, and bumping the table, setting all the plates and mugs to rattling.

"Do you mind?" Croft said around a mouth full of food. "I like you and all but I barely have enough room to hold my utensils."

"Sorry, but that man over there keeps looking at me."

"Where?" Kael asked.

"There. The one sitting at that table behind Sidri."

Of course all heads turned to see whom Liam was talking about, making the situation worse by definitely drawing the man's attention to them. A man who looked to be in his early fifties and who raised his mug in greetings to the group when he noticed them looking back at him.

"Seems to be winking at you." Croft said as they all turned back to their meals. "Maybe he's got a thing for younger men."

"Gross."

Heath turned back to look at the man, while his partner jokingly reminded Liam he was at a table full of older men.

"No, I think there's something wrong with his eye." Heath informed them. "But you're about to find out because I think he is heading over here."

Heath was right, because Liam watched the man, who was very tall and had the muscled arms and shoulders of a blacksmith excuse himself from the table of men he was eating with before making his way to their table.

"Excuse me sirs." The man said in a deep southern accent. "But did you arrive in one of the prince's ships?"

Gorman took the initiative and spoke for the group, saying that they had.

The man, whose left eye was slightly closed from a scar with several more old wounds on his left cheek apologized once again for bothering them while continuing to stare at, almost like he was scrutinizing, Liam.

"I'm Cosaur Eli." The man said as he introduced himself to the group. "I'm sorry for staring young man, but you look so familiar. Do you mind telling me your clan name?"

Damn! Liam thought as he turned a little pale. He did not want to answer the question and thought of telling this man that his clan name was that of his foster-father. But what would his friends think and how would he explain the lie to them?

"K, Ki," Liam coughed, doing his best to clear his throat before starting again. "My clan's name is Keir."

"Keir." Eli repeated, the clan name stirring up old memories for the man. "Liam? Is it you?"

All the men, save for Croft who was watching this man over his mug of ale, stared at Liam, curious with questions of their own as to why this person knew his name.

Dread and memories that had always haunted Liam threatened to overwhelm him as he silently shook his head in the affirmative and left it hanging, trying to do his best to blot out the vision of Cosaur Eli from his sight.

"By the gods!" Surprised by the admission, Eli involuntarily grasped the back of Sidri's chair to steady himself. "Liam! You're the last person I thought I'd ever see. When your father. What! Oh Liam!"

The stress of being in Fomor and what this man would have to say were just too much for Liam and he quickly got out his seat, batting away Croft's hand as his friend tried to stop him, so he could escape from the meal that was becoming a nightmare.

"What was that all about?" Kael asked, shocked by Liam's outburst.

"Maybe you should go after him." Croft suggested to Kael, the face of the jovial man now marred with sadness.

"But?"

"Go after him Kael." Gorman seconded. "I don't think he should be alone right now."

"I'm sorry, I didn't mean for this to happen." Cosaur Eli said. Regret filled his eyes and his voice choked with pain. "Maybe I should have not said anything."

"Well, Master Cosaur?" Gorman looked at the older man, whose face told of a painful story all of its own, and asked him how he knew Liam.

"You don't know?" Eli asked.

All the men shook their heads, looking just as bewildered as Eli. Save for Croft, whose stony expression met Gorman's curious one.

"I know." Croft said before taking another pull of his ale. "But I've known Liam since he was in his teens and I will not betray his confidence."

"But I won't stop you Master Cosaur from telling your story. For it is a sad one that is worth the telling."

"Do you mind?" Gorman offered Eli one of the vacant seats. "Let me buy you an ale?"

Eli took one of the seats and looked at the table of strangers surrounding him. "Thank you. But something stronger if you don't mind. And you might want something stronger for yourselves if you truly want to listen to what I have to say."

***

"Liam! Wait!"

Kael called out again to Liam who was heading north into the town, walking at a quick pace away from the market district and in the wrong direction to go back to the wharves.

Liam not only ignored Kael's calls to stop, but carelessly bumped into a man he was walking by, the man losing his grasp on a basket he was carrying and sent its contents of fruit tumbling down onto the street.

Kael quickly apologized to the Fomoran, who was cursing Liam's back as he hurried down a side street, and helped him to retrieve his produce before hurrying after his distraught friend.

But Liam was nowhere to be seen when Kael turned the corner and he scanned several side streets before asking passing pedestrians if they had seen someone fitting Liam's description.

Fortunately the gods were with Kael that day and a group of soldiers pointed to a far street at the end of the one they were on and said they had passed someone who looked very upset and who was heading up into the town.

Kael quickly thanked them before running to the street they had pointed at. Though this new street he turned onto seemed more like an alley with a solid twelve foot wall that protected the town on his left and the only openings on the structures to his right being the windows that appeared on their second and third levels.

At the top of the street it branched off into three directions and after making some inquiries, found that Liam had continued on the street that paralleled the town wall.

Running and hoping to finally catch up with Liam, Kael came across an opening in the wall. An arch big enough to let a cart through, with its gates wide open for the day. A group of children were playing with a sewn cloth ball filled with sand while several soldiers, who were standing guard at the gate, watched them run about in the middle of the street.

When asked, the boys pointed towards the gate and said that Liam had left the town.

"We close this gate at dusk!" One of the soldiers called out as Kael ran past them and up the stony road before him.

But Kael's concern wasn't getting back in before the town was locked up for the night but finding Liam who seemed to be running away.

Kael ran up the road that was climbing into the rocky hills surrounding Fomor and had gone less than a mile when he found Liam sitting on the ground with his head resting on his knees with his arms wrapped around them.

Liam did raise his head when he heard the sound of Kael's booted feet on the road. But put it back down when he saw Kael making his way towards him.

"Are you okay?" Kael asked as he scanned for traffic on the round.

Liam didn't even bother to raise his head when he mumbled that he wasn't.

"Do you want to talk about it?" Kael asked as he sat down beside Liam.

"No."

So Liam and Kael sat on the ground in silence. The only sound coming from a hawk flying above them as it called out, its screams bouncing off the stony landscape, while circling overhead in its search for food.

Kael wanted to ask Liam if he wanted to head back to town, hoping that his father or Gorman might have a better chance of finding out what was wrong with him when Liam finally raised his head whereupon Kael couldn't help but notice how puffy and bloodshot Liam's eyes looked from crying.

"Sorry." Liam sniffed, choking on the word as he wiped his eyes with the palms of his hands and his nose before wiping it on the sleeve of his shirt. "I just wanted to get away but ended up here."

"Does this have something to do with the man back at the tavern?" Kael asked, unsure of what Liam meant.

"Sort of." Liam said as he looked at Kael. "You see, I'm from Fomor. Or at least, I was born in a temple not far from here."

"So your father, the sagart, is from here?"

"No, but my real father was. Well he settled here from a town further east when Fomor was just a small village."

Kael, who was happy that Liam was at least talking, listened to his friend and the fragmented story he was telling.

"I think I was four when my father retrieved me from the temple and brought me here. And from what my foster-father had once told me, Fomor was more of an outpost than a village back then."

"So your father and the sagart were married?" Kael asked as he tried to piece the story together.

"No." Liam snorted at the absurdity of the remark.

"Liam, I don't understand."

"I'm sorry." And with a heavy sigh that shook Liam's entire body, as if he was unloading himself with a heavy burden, made a second attempt at his story.

"Fomor was only a small outpost when my father came here to start a new life. He was single when he had me. And a year after he had brought me home, Fomor was attacked by Mendens. At least, that's who I was told attacked us by Seb Cullen when I was older and able to understand what had happened to us."

Now it was Kael's turn to lower his head as he listened to what Liam had to say.

"I remember that night as if was yesterday; the shouting, the cries for help, the harsh laughter as the Mendens did their best to collect us alive."

"The Mendens had set the ships and many of the buildings closest to the wharves on fire, and a thick smoke filled the air."

"My father did his best to keep us hidden that night. I remember his hand over my mouth as he did his best to keep me from coughing from all the smoke that filled the air. And I remember his voice in my ear, drowning out the cries of the other villagers as they were captured or murdered, telling me not to cry so we wouldn't be found."

"I thought everything was going to be okay because he was able to keep us hidden among the ruined buildings while the Mendens went about their killing and gathering up the wounded or undefended."

Here, Liam grew very quiet as he found it difficult reliving and talking about his past, the now mournful sounding call of the hawk being the only thing filling the air.

Kael, surprised at the story Liam was telling him, put a hand on Liam's back in sympathy, and scooted closer to him so that their bodies were almost touching, and waited quietly while Liam struggled with his emotions.

"We don't have to talk about this." Kael finally said when their silence began to become uncomfortable.

"No, I'm fine." Liam replied. But another minute or two went by before he continued.

"In the morning we tried to make a run for it." Here Liam shuddered at remembering the corpses of men and children they came across, that had been left to rot where they lay, as he and his father attempted their escape. "There was no wall surrounding the village at the time and my father thought we'd be able to make it into the highlands and hide."

"This is even the path we took when we tried to make our escape." Liam looked up and pointed to some large outcroppings further up on the road. "I'll never forget that view because my father kept pointing at them and said, "Just past those hills Liam. Just past those hills and we'll be safe."

But we hadn't gone too far before we heard shouting from behind us. Four, five, seven, I don't remember how many Mendens there were, but I remember their wild shouts that echoed off the rocks and the morning light that reflected on their weapons."

Once again Liam grew quiet and Kael wrapped his arm around Liam's shoulder and gave him a comforting squeeze.

"My father had a dagger, the only weapon he could get his hands on during the attack, and he pulled it out of his belt as we ran."

"Then, then. . ." Liam choked. "Then he suddenly stopped and pushed me forward, telling me to run. I didn't understand at first, but he pushed me again and told me to run."

"So I did, thinking he was going to be behind me. But when I got behind a large boulder I turned back to see that my father had stayed behind. He looked at me and mouthed "Go on" before he turned to meet the men coming for us."

"I should have run, but I was afraid of leaving him and watched as he thought he was defending my escape. But it wasn't much of a fight with his dagger against their weapons and he went down quickly."

"His blood was everywhere as he fell to the ground with the Mendens laughing all about him. Then I watched as his head rolled my way and it looked like he saw me and mouthed my name."

"Or maybe he said it out loud because that's when the Mendens turned and saw me because I guess I had stepped away from my hiding place."

"Their laughter was wicked and their speech was taunting as they walked towards me. I knew I had to get away so I turned and ran in the direction my father had been taking us. Their calls from behind me even became rowdier at the sport I was giving them."

"At one point I fell and knew they would soon be upon me when I spotted a little hole under some large rocks. Thinking I might be able to hide in it, I began to scramble to it when arms wrapped around me and picked me up."

Here Liam stopped and looked at Kael.

"I think I cried out at the sight of him. But he just smiled at me and held onto me while I squirmed in his embrace, thinking that I was going to die."

"But his smile." At this point Kael could feel Liam relax a little under his embrace as he continued with his story.

"His smile wasn't wicked. And his skin on his arms glowed as if the sun was shining from within him and he spoke softly so that I finally stopped struggling in his arms. "Do not worry little Liam," he said, though I don't recall seeing his mouth move. "You are safe."

"With we walked over to a stony outcropping on the side of the road and I don't know if we walked into it or if the rock flowed around us. I just know we somehow became one with the rock."

"That was a strange feeling; being able to breathe and see, yet encased by stone. Although I found the smell of him comforting. A smell of salt on rocks that had been heated in the noonday sun."

"And while we stood there, that man," Liam couldn't help but laugh cynically at his description. "That man told me his name was Barra and that he would protect me."

"Barra?" Kael asked skeptically as he pulled a little away from Liam.

"Yes it was Barra. Although I don't really think I knew what that meant at the time. Anyway, Barra apologized for not saving my father and he continued to tell me I would be fine, his thoughts whispering in my head as we watched the Mendens pass us, unseen, as they continued on with their search for me."

"I don't know how much time passed, maybe an hour, or maybe it was a day, but after a while the Mendens disappeared and Barra finally pulled away from the rock wall and put me down so that we could walk back in the direction of the village. And my father."

Liam had to stop as fresh tears ran down his cheeks.

"My father's body was still there and lay exactly how the Mendens had let him fall. All twisted, his blood that had pooled around him blackening the sand and rock. His eyes were missing and it looked like his face and hands had already been picked by birds."

"I'm so sorry Liam!" Kael blurted as his grasp on Liam tightened.

"That's what Barra said as I pulled my hand from his grasp and ran to my father, shaking him because I stupidly thought that there might be a chance that he was still alive and was just waiting for me to return to him."

"But he wasn't. Barra knelt beside me and wiped away my tears before straightening out my father's ruined body, passing a hand over him while he mouthed a prayer, healing his face and wounds, so that it only looked like he was asleep."

"And while I stood there, watching Barra continuing to pray over my father, we heard voices coming up the road and heading in our direction. I grew fearful and grasped one of Barra's hands, but he whispered for me not to worry, that the men were good, that they would take care of me. And as I watched the group of men who, as it turned out, were led by Seb Cullen, approach us, Barra faded away."

"After that Sagart Seb took me back to Kinsale, where he lived, and adopted me. You know the rest."

Kael was at a loss for words and could only bring himself to repeat the words "I'm sorry".

Liam only shrugged before wiping his face again. "This is why I didn't want to come on this adventure. Why I didn't want to leave Kinsale. With the exception to Cullen, I promised myself I would never get attached to anyone because I would be afraid of losing them. I even joined the Stonemason's Guild so I wouldn't have to leave the temple complex."

Kael was shocked by the admission, although it now explained Liam's shyness. "At least you like being in the Guild."

"I hate it!" Liam laughed. "I hate the sound of the hammer and chisel on stone. How my hands vibrate on the tools all the time. The stone dust that covers everything after polishing out imperfections in a statue. I hate it all!"

Kael laughed along with Liam, surprised by the confession, yet happy that Liam was willing to tell him this.

"But it's no way to live. Hiding behind walls." Kael said as he sobered.

"I know." Liam replied as he stared at the rocks on the far side of the road.

Kael had not removed his hand from Liam's back during this time and found himself running his fingers across Liam's shoulder blades and down his spine.

"I like you Liam." Kael said, his throat parched from nervousness and of his own admission. "I like you a lot."

Liam turned to look at Kael, whose cheeks were flushed from embarrassment while a thin sheen of sweat covered his brow from sitting out in the sun. And there seemed to be a look of worry, as if he had said too much, in his light brown eyes.

"I like you too." Liam replied as he dropped his left hand from his knee and placed it on Kael's calf, and pulled himself closer to the man who had haunted his dreams for the past week.

Kael relaxed a little, happy to hear those words come from Liam and brought his left hand up to Liam's cheek, and watched as Liam closed his eyes, enjoying the sensation, while he wiped away some dried salt from Liam's earlier tears, before pulling Liam's face towards his.

Kael watched as Liam opened his eyes, the two transfixed by each other over this moment, a faint smile tugging at Kael's lips in anticipation at what was to come next.

But the two were startled by the sound of rocks tumbling somewhere further up the road. Kael quickly got to his feet when the sound came again and cursed when he saw that the hawk that had been flying overhead had now circled away to the east instead of towards the maker of the noises.

Kael cursed once again as Liam also stood, for he had not brought a weapon with him because Kael had thought they would be safe in the confines of the town. But after hearing Liam's story, Kael was not so sure that that had been the right choice.

Quickly picking up some large stones, one for each hand, Kael had Liam do the same. That way they could at least have a weapon to throw at any would be attacker or some wild animal that had made its way onto the road.

"What do we do now?" Liam whispered.

Kael was going to suggest that Liam head back to town and alert the sentries at the gate, but both men quieted at the sound of more rocks shifting on the road. Kael had the two of them hold their ground as whatever was out there sounded as if it had gotten closer.

Instinctively Kael raised his right hand above his ear and arched his body as if he was going to throw the rock he had in it at whatever was about to come into view, but both men were completely taken by surprise at the sight of a naked man stumbling from around the bend.

Kael lowered his arm as he and Liam watched the man take a few more hobbling steps, his bare feet slipping on the large rounded rocks that covered the road, before stopping because he seemed to be struggling to catch his breath.

"Hello!" Kael called out to the man when he realized that this unclothed traveler had yet to notice them.

The man took several steps backward as he raised a trembling hand to shade his eyes to see where the call came from. Finally focusing on the Kael and Liam who were not far from where he stood, and unsure if they were real or not, and not caring, struggled to call out for help before slumping to the ground.

Dropping his makeshift weapons, Liam hurried over to the man, with Kael quickly following and hissing for Liam to hold back.

Kael eventually dropped his rocks when they reached the man, who too exhausted and injured to be a threat to either he or Liam because, from where they stood, Kael and Liam could see that the stranger's knees and elbows were covered with a multitude of cuts and friction burns from the numerous times he must have fallen. And the only thing that came close to even clothing on the man were the dark bruises on his legs and arms with a grey layer of dust caking his body and matting his hair.

Kael asked the man if he could stand. Whereupon the man nodded that he could and ignoring his nudity, Kael gave the stranger a hand getting to his feet, before helping him to a large flattened boulder where he could sit a little more comfortably.

"What is your name?" Kael asked while he took off his own shirt and handed it to the man, who only looked at it uncomprehendingly before Kael pointed to the man's groin.

"Your name?" Kael asked again as the man covered himself.

But the stranger either seemed to be having trouble remembering his name or he was just too tired from exposure because it took him a moment before he uttered a word from his parched lips.

"My name is Caittle Anam." The seated man replied while absentmindedly picking loose sand out of his tapered ears. "And yours?"

Kael gave his own name while he and Liam watched Caittle Anam come to some semblance of life as he did his best to shake the dirt out of his hair and to wipe some of the grime off of his face.

"And yours?" Anam asked Liam, who had remained quiet and had allowed Kael to take charge of the situation.

Liam gave his and received greetings in return, finally starting to hear the thick agrarian accent as the man's throat cleared while he spoke. A pleasant sounding drawled that seemed to fit with the man's almost archaic sounding name.

"How did you get to be like this?" Kael asked, concerned about being out here too long now that he had two helpless men in his care.

Anam tilted his head to one side, then to the other, as if he was looking for the answers to be written in the sky.

"Sorry," Anam started. "I seem to remember having a falling out with some friends. But I think that was days ago."

"And since then you've been wondering around like this?" Kael frowned, his hand sweeping up and down, emphasizing Anam's nakedness. Kael had to admit that, though his body was marred by days' of hardship, Anam did seem well formed, and only one type of man, a courtesan, would be abandoned by his friends to wander naked through the hills.

Caittle Anam only shrugged, leaving Kael's unspoken question to linger in the air. "Where are we?"

"We're outside of Fomor." Liam answered as Kael crossed his arms over his chest as he wondered what type of trouble he and Liam were getting into.

Anam smiled, as if he was remembering something fondly. "Fomor. I think I have visited the town once or twice before. Do either of you happen to have any water?"

"No." Kael apologized. "But we are not far from town and can get you some once we get there. Are you able to walk?"

"I think so." Anam stood, towering over Kael and Liam by several inches, and did his best to wrap Kael's shirt around his midsection. The shirt wasn't quite long enough to overlap itself and be knotted, so Anam had to hold the ends together with his left hand. "Lead the way."

The momentary respite seemed to have helped because Anam was able to stand on his own and walked between Kael and Liam as they slowly made their way over the gravely road towards Fomor.

"By any chance," Anam asked Liam as the tops of the town walls came into view. "Do you know a sagart?"

Kael only shook his head, thinking that Anam probably needed to confess his sins as to how he got in his predicament while Liam told Anam that his father was a priest.

"A sagart to Barra. Visiting Fomor for the next couple of days." Liam added, already dispensing too much information for Kael's liking.

"Even better!" Anam smiled. At least he tried to smile without cracking his parched lips. "I follow the teachings of Barra and would appreciate talking to your father."

Liam smiled back at Anam finding the clearness of the filthy man's grey eyes that were still directed at him somewhat disconcerting.

That moment of being lost in Anam's eyes was fleeting as the man stumbled on some lose rocks in the road. Fortunately Liam caught the man and kept a hand on Anam's back while Anam regained his footing and adjusted Kael's shirt around his waist.

The smile returned and Anam's eyes glittered, thanking Liam, while Kael only frowned, thinking that Caittle Anam had just found a new mark to hit upon.

But Liam was oblivious to the expressions, finding himself confused that Anam didn't stink like someone who had been out in the wild for days would have. Maybe, Liam thought as he got frustrated, that the smells of the past were still imposing themselves upon him; smells of salt and rocks heated by the sun. A strong clean smell, Liam realized, of a freshly washed man.

Thankfully Fomor's gate came into view and Liam couldn't help but thank the gods as he slowly picked up his pace to be safe within its walls and to be grateful that he would finally be off the road his father had been killed on, hoping for once that he might be able to leave many of his old bloody memories behind.

***

Not only did Fomor's side gate have three guards stationed at it, there were soldiers walking the town's perimeter on the wall's parapet. So men watched as Liam and Kael made their way back to town, with the barely clothed Anam between them, and ordered some of their own to go out and investigate the odd scenario.

Once it was determined that the trio was of no threat to the inhabitants of Fomor, one of the guards gave Anam the cloak off his back so Anam could cover himself, and more importantly, the guard handed over his water skin, giving Anam the first drink of water he had had in days.

Anam was also appreciative for the short rest while Kael, his returned shirt held in one hand, explained how they had come across the man.

The group eventually made their way into town, gathering a score of onlookers consisting mostly of the children who had been playing at the gates entrance, the older ones doing their best to question the Royal Guard as to what was going on. The only response the children received was to be shooed away, although the youngsters could not help but cast speculations about the stranger among themselves as they trailed behind the men in hopes of having an interesting tale to tell their fathers.

Once the throng reached the Temple to Barra, one of the only two temples in town, and their story was retold to a sagart who happened to be outside the temple, Anam, Liam and Kael were ushered into the temple's courtyard, while one of the guards went to fetch Liam's father (who was not within the temple compounds) and the other stood at the temple's entrance, and for the first time since its construction, forbade the children from entering.

Not only was Barra the god of the earth, but his teachings spoke of generosity and charity, so the sagarts who were on the premises promptly escorted Anam into the temple complex where he could get cleaned and fed while Kael and Liam waited in the courtyard for Seb Cullen's arrival.

"It's more like a fort than a temple." Kael said to Liam as he inspected their surroundings, happy to be relieved of their wayward guest.

Liam had to agree with Kael for this temple was like none of the temple compounds that had been built in Kinsale. Save for Cillach's, the god of war.

The courtyard, which looked like it might hold maybe two hundred people, seemed to be the main area of worship for the temple itself, with a short flight of five stairs running back into the complex where Liam assumed that the sagarts would preach from the top step to the men below them.

Surrounding the courtyard on three sides were walls about three stories high, with the temple's entrance in one of them. A set of solid, wooden double doors, mounted on enormous and ornate, well-oiled hinges, flanked the entrance; doors that had never been closed since the temples construction. Doors that would be closed if the city was ever attacked again and the temple needed as a place of defense for its people.

The fourth wall, which was the side of a cliff face, was riddled with the living quarters, offices, storage areas and work rooms of the temple. A series of balconies overlooked the courtyard from some of these rooms and above those, small slits suitable for arrows to be shot through, crowned off the cliff face.

A small defensive stronghold that only reminded Liam of Fomor's failed past.

"All this for a courtesan." Kael said out loud, interrupting Liam's thoughts, as he walked into a shadowed area cast by some stairs leading to the ramparts above them. Kael, who had refused to put back on the shirt that Anam had wrapped around his body, only now wanted a break from the heat while they waited for Liam's father.

"You sure?" Liam, who had followed Kael into the shade and rested his back against the cool granite blocks of the stairs, assumed he could only be talking about Caittle Anam.

"Of course! Who else gets left the way he was? We could have just dropped him off at a hostel and have been on our way."

"But he wanted help from the temple." Liam reminded Kael. "And if it wasn't for Seb Cullen, and the kindness of Barra's other sagarts, I don't know what would have happened to me if I just got dumped in a hostel."

Mollified by Liam's remark, and embarrassed at being reminded of his friend's dreadful past, Kael quieted and the two remained that way until Liam's foster-father arrived. They did not have to wait long before Seb Cullen, who had been at Fomor's forum with Manus and the leaders of the town, walked through the temple's entrance, escorted only by the soldier who had gone to fetch him.

The two retold their story of finding Caittle Anam outside of Fomor and of how he had wanted to be brought here to speak with one of Barra's sagarts. Kael, who was also a well-trained soldier of the Royal Guard, saw Liam's father as a leader in this mission for Banning, Manus' brother, and gave his assessment of what he thought of Master Caittle and his situation. Something he would have certainly done if he was standing before the prince.

"No matter what their circumstances, or professions, all are welcome here." Cullen said, repeating what Liam had said earlier, thanking the young man for his report. "Why are you not wearing your shirt?"

His cheeks burning a little as he realized how he must look to the sagart, Kael explained how he had given his shirt to Anam to wear. That's when Liam realized he had forgotten his package of shirts back at the tavern. But Kael quickly eased Liam's fears of possibly losing his purchases, and his money, by letting him know that either Croft of Gorman would have taken them back to the Camalain for safe keeping.

From their behavior, and some of their stilted responses to some questions, mainly those pertaining to them being outside the village's wall, there seemed to be more to Liam and Kael's story that they had not told Cullen. But out of frustration at current events, and still with no idea where Banning was, and with Manus setting some plans of his own into motion, giving Cullen very little time to tidy things up with this injured wanderer, Cullen was left to wonder what information had been omitted out of their story, hoping that if there was anything else of importance, that his son would relate it to him later.

"Also, the prince is looking you." The sagart told Kael. "He has learned that the Mendens have attacked some towns on the Tuame coastline. Rumors have also come down from the east about several ships that were attacked by more Mendens."

"The prince wanted me to tell you, if I saw you, that he could use your help with organizing our departure. I am sure he will fill you in with the details of those events."

"Then I must go." Kael said, mumbling about going to the Camalain to get a clean shirt before finding Manus.

Liam realized that if the prince was preparing the ships to leave, then his help would be needed loading the new supplies onto the Camalain, and headed back to the ship with Kael.

So Liam and Kael left Cullen and the guard to interrogate Caittle Anam. And as they headed back to the docks they were joined by men from the Camalain and the Marmairn, who were also walking back to their ships, for word had spread throughout the town to the prince's crew that they would be leaving soon, with Manus commanding that he wanted everyone back on board the vessels as soon as possible.

The two didn't even make it onboard the Camalain when they spotted Gorman, Heath, and about a half dozen other squad leaders from both vessels, talking to Fomor's dock master about loading fresh supplies onto the ships. Heath, who had been towards the back of the crowd, spotted the two as they drew closer and hailed them over to where he was standing.

Heath, along with every other man on the wharf, could not help but notice that Kael was bare-chested and naturally inquired why.

"I'll tell you later." Was Kael's curt reply, for it was a question he had endured from his shipmates as they made their way back to the Camalain. "Or better yet, ask Liam. He can fill you in about our afternoon. Right now I have to change and go find Manus."

"The prince is still up at the forum. Might be for a while." Heath informed him.

Kael excused himself and quickly boarded the Camalain while Heath asked Liam to remain for a minute. The older man's face had softened and a crooked smile crossed his lips as he looked at Liam while the two waited for Gorman to finish with the dock master.

When he was done with his business, Gorman called Liam and his partner over to one side of the dock.

"Liam," Gorman started, a slight hesitancy to his voice. "We're all very sorry about what happened to your real father."

"All?"

Gorman couldn't help but place both his hands on Liam's shoulders, as if to steady the dejected youth, hoping that his touch reminded Liam that he was now part of a team where the men considered him a friend, while he mentioned how Cosaur Eli recounted them with his own horrible memories of the razing of Fomor.

"Master Cosaur seemed very distraught over the fact that he chased you away." Gorman explained. "Especially when he explained how he and your father had been good friends and had come down to Fomor when they were about your age to make their own fortunes."

Liam didn't trust himself to talk for fear that he would not be able to keep his emotions in check, so he only listened to Gorman as he related how Cosaur Eli still hoped to have a talk with Liam before their departure.

"But, but," Liam coughed, not sure he wanted to meet with man and to once again relive memories he wished would just finally fade into the past. "Aren't we leaving soon?"

"With what we need "soon" won't be until tomorrow morning."

"I still have my duties in the galley."

"I can't let you go this afternoon because we have too much to do. But I did speak to Crogan about this and he's willing to let you have the evening meal off to talk to Master Cosaur."

"Oh." Liam couldn't help but wonder how many of the crew now knew about the sad story of his life.

Gorman on the other hand, saw someone who was hiding from his past, a past he had no reason to be ashamed of, and who was doing his best to whittle his way out of meeting with Cosaur Eli.

"Liam, this was such a chance happenstance." Gorman's voice had taken on a softer, almost taking on a fatherly tone while he talked. "The gods must have planned for you two to meet. Don't let this opportunity slip away. Because who knows when you will be back this way. Why live with the regret of missing out on finding out more about your father and where you came from?"

"One of us would be willing to go with you if that would help." Heath added.

Liam yielded to the kindly couple, who were only looking out for his best interest, and said that he would think about going to see the man.

"That's all one can ask for." Gorman said before telling him to head down to the storage bays, where he could find Sidri, the rest of the squad, and most of the crew already loading fresh supplies onto the Camalain.

Liam took his leave, but instead of going down to help his friends, he detoured up through the cabin section, just in time to bump into Kael who was running down the stairs on his way to meet Manus. Thrilled at finding Kael before he had left the ship, and only wanting to talk about what had happened between the two of them, yet knowing this was not the right time for such a thing, Liam explained what had happened after they had left the tavern and of how Cosaur Eli wanted to meet with him.

"I agree with Gorman." Kael said as the two of them moved out of the way of some men heading down the stairs. "I think you should go."

"I know. Gorman said that he or Heath would go with me if I wanted the company. But I was hoping that it could be you."

Kael, who truly wanted to spend more time with Liam, and also curious about Liam's past, was flattered to be asked.

"The only chance I would have would be tonight during the evening meal." Liam explained.

"I would just have to tell Manus why I need to take off tonight." Kael replied as the two headed down the stairs so that Kael could leave. Kael also knew that for some reason, Manus did not particularly like Liam, and telling the prince the truth might make him a little more sympathetic towards Liam and to let him get away for several hours with the sagart's son.

"What's one more?" Liam mumbled, wondering how long it would take for the entire ship to learn about his past.

"What?"

"That's fine." Liam said a little more loudly, ignoring Kael's question as they made the landing to the hallway that would lead to the main deck.

"Then I'll see you tonight." Impulsively Kael grabbed Liam's left hand with his right, and squeezed it while looking into his dark, hazel eyes; a greenish brown that reminded Kael of dusk settling on a bower of leaves, and let out a soft moan of frustration, longing for that interrupted kiss, before letting go and quickly heading out onto the main deck.

Liam stood there for several more moments, his right hand squeezed into a fist as he tried to hold onto that feeling of Kael touching him, before making his own way into the bowels of the Camalain.

***

Kael had been right about Manus. The prince was not fond of Liam. As a matter of fact, Manus detested the sagart's son.

But after being told how Liam had been orphaned when he was quite young, a chink formed in that cold, calculating, politic heart of Manus', grudgingly giving Kael leave to join Liam on his quest for information about his past.

Sometimes a small chink, a crack, can lead to a bigger disruption in one's guard. Sometimes that chink will ice back over, once again creating an icy fortress against the outside world.

For Manus yearned to be more than just "close friends" with Kael. Unfortunately his station and his parents would not allow him to pursue such a desire. So jealousy and hatred became Manus' new companions, always taunting the prince, while he wished in vain that he and Kael could have more than what they had now.

***

Gorman had told Liam that Cosaur Eli's home would be easy enough to find. Go back to the tavern where they had lunch, follow the street and take the second right and the man's home would be on the far left corner on that short street.

The home was exactly where Gorman told Liam it would be. What the squad leader failed to tell him, or Gorman wasn't told himself, was that the home took up most of the block.

Cosaur Eli's home was squat, two stories high, with a large smithy attached to it on the right hand side. There was a stone wall with two gates built into it; one for the home and a double door gate for the shop, wrapped around the well-maintained structure, leaving a small yard between wall and home.

Four young boys were playing in the yard with a black fox scampering about them while a fifth older boy, who looked to be in his teens, and somewhat resembling Cosaur Eli in looks and build, watched over the group in the day's fading light.

Liam stopped to take in the scene, for he was still somewhat fearful of what Master Cosaur would have to say, and he looked on wondering if this little slice of domesticity was how his life could have been.

"You okay?" Kael asked in a whispered voice, concern coloring his eyes.

"Yeah, just nervous I guess." Liam said as the teenager noticed the two of them staring at his family. Liam met the boy's gaze, knowing that it was going to be now or never, though he was finding it hard to take the next step forward. A step he was finding difficult to take even with Kael standing by his side.

The spell of Liam's hesitancy was broken when he saw the door to the home open, allowing a warm golden light to escape its interior, as Cosaur Eli stepped outside to take in the evening air.

The blacksmith instantly recognized Liam and Kael as they walked along the sidewalk towards his home's gate and waved at the two in greeting before saying something to his eldest son, who ran inside, before walking over to the gate and opening it to allow the two into his yard.

Eli's eldest son returned, followed by another gentleman who seemed to be similar in age to the blacksmith and was introduced as Eli's partner, who also welcomed the two to their home.

Watching Eli's family gather around them reminded Kael of his own family, especially when he and his father returned to their own village to visit his grandfather, uncles and cousins, and feeling like he had suddenly become an intruder into this reunion, and took a step back out into the street.

"You should go on your own." Kael said when Liam, along with the other adults, looked at him questioningly.

"You sure?" Liam asked as the group made their way towards the home.

Kael watched as the youngest of the children wondered out loud who Liam could be while the fox jammed it's wet black nose against Liam's hands and stood on its back legs so it could place its fore paws on Liam's body, offended that this stranger was being allowed through its defenses.

"Take your time." Kael called out to him. "I'll be waiting for you at that tavern where we had lunch."

Liam acknowledged Kael's remark before disappearing into the home with Eli's partner, while the blacksmith held back and picked up his youngest son who had fallen behind the rest of them and mouthed the words "thank you" to Kael.

A smile crossed Kael's face, a smile to match the one that had blossomed on Eli's lips, a smile of gratitude, and waited as the door closed behind the blacksmith, muffling the voices of Eli's clan and the yipping of animals, before turning and heading towards the merchant's district, taking the leisurely, long way back to the tavern.

***

While Liam and Kael were off meeting with Cosaur Eli and his family, Seb Cullen, along with Caittle Anam were boarding the Camalain.

The ministrations, confessional, whatever you would like to call the gathering of Barra's sagarts with the naked man who had wandered out of the hills, took much longer than any of the priests had expected. And at the end of the day, Seb Cullen found himself burdened with yet another charge in his care.

Burdened he looked, the crewman he passed assumed. For Cullen's complexion was ashen, and the arch of his back was more pronounced while he stooped over his cane, looking diminutive for a once tall man. His breathing also seemed to be coming in loud ragged gasps as he hobbled along the deck.

His ailments and age were only pronounced more so by the man who accompanied him. A man, who with sunburned skin and dark circles under his eyes from sleepless nights while wandering the mountains, was clean, well-groomed and clothed, still looked quite attractive; a muscular man in his late thirties, maybe early forties, who stood quietly, a soft smile on his lips, while the sagart asked for the whereabouts of the prince.

The crew of the Camalain did their best to keep the pity they felt for the kindly priest off their faces, many assuming that the prince, who had been relentless in his demands on Seb Cullen, had only pushed him harder during their brief sojourn in Fomor and had found new ways to torment the sagart in the hopes of finding Banning, his lost brother.

But Cullen saw none of those looks, for today had indeed been a strain on him. A day Cullen wanted to be done with, he thought, as he made his way into the cabin section with Caittle Anam following quietly behind him, to find the prince, then to find some much needed rest in his own cabin. Thankfully Manus was holed up in his cabin because it meant a quick walk to his own small room once his meeting with the prince was done.

Upon their arrival, the guard gave Caittle Anam a quick pat down to make sure he had no hidden weapons, while Cullen sighed heavily, saying his search was unnecessary, before permitting the two into the prince's domain.

"Just one moment Sagart." Manus said as the soldier slid the door shut behind the two, for the prince was not alone in the room. Captain's Thear and Bres Dorset, of the Marmairn, were with Manus, all with glasses of wine in their hands, all standing around a table littered with maps, the decanter that their drinks had come from being used as a paperweight for several of them.

"I still do not think this is a wise decision." Captain Bres said, repeating a remark he had seemed about to make before the door was opened.

"I know Dorset." Manus said while looking at a ledger with numbers of available soldiers and ships listed on it for the area. "But what we have learned of the Mendens, the Marmairn will be of more use here rather than flying alongside us. Though, I will take the glider as you suggested."

Bres Dorset was wise enough to only nod as he accepted the prince's delegation of orders, knowing that a third contradiction to Manus' plans would not go over well.

"With that settled, how can I help you Sagart Seb? And who is your friend?" Manus asked, taking a sip from his glass of wine.

Cullen quickly introduced Caittle Anam and just as quickly stopped with a question faltering on his own tongue as he watched a smirk form on Manus' face.

"I see Master Karam has already spoken to you of Master Caittle." Cullen said, too tired to deal with Manus' immature behavior, forcing his exhausted body a little straighter, offended that Anam was the brunt of some joke between Manus and Kael.

"Yes well. . ."

"I can assure you that young Kael was quite wrong in his assessment of my guest."

Manus' face reddened. Because Manus knew that by calling Kael young, Cullen was also reminding Manus of his own age.

But he was the prince, not a commoner, and how dare the sagart rebuke him in front of his captains! Manus left the two men standing quietly in front of him while he finished his drink.

"As you can see I am quite busy, so what is it that you want Sagart?"

Cullen swore silently, cursing to a god who no longer listened to his inner thoughts, as he watched the dark look form on Manus' face, and saw how the captains were doing their best to look inconspicuous within the confines of the prince's cabin.

"Yes, well it turns out that Anam is a member of my order, from Sliabh Mianach, who was attacked by some bandits on his way here. I was hoping that Anam might be able to join us on the Camalain and,"

"Not his son all over again." Manus growled in a low voice.

"What about my son Prince Aerin?"

Manus caught himself, not realizing he had spoken out loud, and knew he had crossed a line by the angry expression that was now forming on the sagart's face.

Manus placed his empty glass down and coughed into his hand before once again meeting Cullen's dark gaze and answering. "I was sorry to hear how Liam lost his real father."

The comment caught Cullen off guard. Looking to Thear Ibor for an answer, a man who also knew of how Liam had come into the care of Seb Cullen, the sagart saw that the captain was just as surprised as himself at hearing those words.

What had his son failed to tell him about this day?

Somewhat mollified, Cullen graciously accepted the prince's condolences and was about to once again ask for passage for Anam, when the younger sagart interrupted him.

"If I may be so bold Milord?" Anam took a step forward so he could look squarely at Manus. "Sagart Seb is exhausted from using his healing arts on me and has failed to tell you that I have come to see you."

Manus frowned in annoyance, quite skeptical as to why this stranger would want an audience with him, and did his best to politely ask Anam to explain himself.

Anam, whose smile had not left his face during the entire exchange with the prince, a smile that Manus thought belonged on the face of someone that was dimwitted, explained how he had been visited by Barra in his sleep.

"Anyone can have dreams of the god." Manus said in a matter of fact tone.

"True. But Barra told me that you were looking for your brother." With that Anam started his tale again. Relating how the god had visited him several times and urged him on this quest. Anam had become quite relaxed with the telling of his story and his rustic accent thickened, making it difficult for the others to understand what he was saying, forcing the prince to ask him to slow down and to repeat himself.

"Beg pardon Milord. Barra said you would be in Fomor and that I should get there as soon as possible. So when the trams stopped working I tried to get here on foot because I was fearful of missing you."

"Can you explain why my men found you in the condition that you were in?"

Here a frown formed on Anam's lips and a blank look filled his eyes as he faltered in his story.

"It is as I said earlier Milord." Cullen said, jumping in to help the other sagart out. "We assume that Anam was waylaid on his journey here and was left as he was to fend for himself. Unfortunately he has no memories of the past several days while doing his best to stay focused on finding you."

"I also thought our high sagart in Kinsale might be helpful in healing Anam's mind and that is another one of the reasons I wanted to book passage for him on the Camalain."

Manus ignored the subtle plea from Seb Cullen and asked if Anam remembered anything else.

"Do you have maps of the area?" Anam asked, and when the prince beckoned him forward, sorted through the unrolled charts on the table before he hesitated over one, turning it to face him, then jabbing a finger at a location on it. "There! This is where we need to go."

Manus looked to where Anam was pointing, and then looked at the man himself. For some reason Manus found this location dubious at best and vocalized his misgivings about moving further away from where his brother had been abducted.

"Why can't Barra just tell me where Banning is?" Manus asked as the frustration at being on this quest got the best of him.

"Well, Barra is lost to all of us now." Anam said, stating the obvious to the prince, as if Manus didn't know that the god had been silent for some time. "Barra also told me that he was saddened that you have closed your heart to him and the others."

Manus looked into those deep grey eyes of Anam's, looking for some mockery in them, only finding what he assumed was serenity, before looking to Cullen, assuming that his family's sagart might have said something to this stranger.

Cullen only shook his head in the negative, a look in his eye that said the prince's devotion, or lack thereof, had never been mentioned by him.

"The other reason I would like to have him come with us Milord." Cullen explained. "He is the only other sagart that I know of who has heard from Barra about your quest."

Manus didn't want to be burdened with another priest, and he didn't want Cullen on his ship either. But what was he to do? These were the only men he seemed to be able to rely on to find his brother.

"And where would Master Caittle sleep?" Manus relented, finally pouring himself another glass of wine.

"He can stay in my room Milord." Cullen offered.

"That would be a cozy fit!" Manus snorted as he drank from his glass.

"If I may, Prince Aerin?" Thear Ibor stepped in and suggested that, since Liam was training with Praish Gorman, that maybe the young man should bunk with his squad, suggesting a move that had happened almost a week ago; a move that had gone unnoticed by the prince who had begun to ignore the fact that Liam was on his ship.

"Then make it so." Manus said to Ibor. "Now if the two of you don't mind, the captains and I have some more business to finish before we leave tomorrow."

Cullen and Anam bowed respectfully at the dismissal and left as Manus went back to pouring over the maps in front of them, asking Dorset to meet with the town leaders and to begin searching for bandits that might be hidden around the town.

Sliding the prince's door shut behind them Cullen pointed to their own cabin down the short hallway.

"Liam took his own bedding so I will have to find something for myself to sleep on." The elderly sagart said to his companion.

"Nonsense, friend. You keep the bed. I will be fine on the floor."

"I insist Master Caittle." Cullen said, a tone of deference creeping into his tired voice.

"As do I. Keep the bed, I will find blankets for myself later. And there is no need for formalities between us when we are in your cabin, so call me by my given name."

"As you wish Anam." Cullen said as he opened the door to his own small cabin, offering Anam entrance into it.

"This place I come from? Sliabh Mianach?" Anam asked in a softened voice as he passed Cullen and walked into the cabin.

Cullen couldn't help but look up and down the hallway to see if anyone was near them before answering. "A temple that, by foot, is about a week's journey from here. The sagarts who live there are considered to be very reclusive."

"Ahh, then you will need to explain this place to me."

"I will Anam." Cullen said as he went to sit on his bed, grateful to be off of his sore feet and painfully throbbing legs.

***

"Nice work. Especially with the detailing on something this size."

"Yeah. Master Cosaur said my father liked to make these small trinkets in his spare time."

Almost four hours had gone by for Liam at Cosaur Eli's home before he realized the time and made his goodbyes to the man and his family and hurried to the tavern, hoping that Kael was there to meet him as planned.

Kael had waited for him and smiled broadly at Liam's approach, patting the vacant spot on the bench next to him, asking him how the reunion had turned out.

Kael also must have ordered a drink earlier for him because as soon as Liam sat down a man came over with a pint of ale for him while he was fishing some objects out of his pocket to show Kael.

One of those objects, a three pointed star, was being turned over in Kael's hand as he spoke. The star, which fit into the palm of Kael's hand, had been shaped as a traditional Gwerin knot with an archaic rune for a yew tree in its center; the yew tree being the wood preferred by archers for their arrows and therefore one of several runes used as a ward for protection.

An eyelet had been placed on the back of the star so the amulet could be worn. And below that Liam's name had been carved into the delicate object.

Liam then retold the story of how Cosaur Eli, his partner Brogan Giles, and his father, the three friends all being the youngest sons in their own families, had set out for Fomor, leaving their own prosperous town of Carrach Gleann behind, all hoping to make their riches in the growing frontier town.

"My father and the others had trained as blacksmiths and word had reached Carrach Gleann that Fomor needed smithies, so they decided to take their chances and come here."

Kael handed the amulet back to Liam who turned the object in his hands so that it reflected the candlelight from their table off of its somewhat pitted surface. Kael was right that the amulet had been well-made, although it had barely survived the assault on Fomor, with Eli finding the amulet in a pile of ashes several days after Liam had left with Seb Cullen.

"Master Cosaur felt badly about sending me away with Sagart Seb. Said he and Master Brogan would have adopted me, but Fomor was no place for a child after the attack. So when he found the amulet after I had gone he couldn't bring himself to melt it down for something else and decided to keep it as a memory of my father and myself."

"He could have sent you back to your family in Carrach Gleann." Kael said, somewhat appalled at how Liam had been given away.

"They apologized for that. Said the survivors were fearful of another attack and thought it wise to send all the orphans away as soon as possible."

"But I'm not from Carrach Gleann." Liam continued as he took the second object he had been holding onto, a piece of parchment, and unfolded it.

"Oh?"

"They were passing through Cloras, a town not far from here that had a temple to Cillach in it (everyone knew that blacksmiths usually worshiped the god of war). That's when my father decided to visit the temple in the hopes of starting a family."

"Well, the god was smiling on your father that day." Kael chuckled, raising his mug to Liam in honor of his birth.

Liam remained silent, wishing that Cillach could have smiled one more time and had spared his father's life and those of the other men and boys that were slaughtered or abducted by the Mendens.

"Anyway," Liam sighed. "Master Cosaur said my grandfather and uncle are still alive and still live in Carrach Gleann."

"Well, that's wonderful news!" Kael, who had a large extended family of his own, was truly happy for his friend, and this new found information. "Looks like you have a bigger family than you thought you had!"

Liam didn't reply as he ran a finger over the neat handwriting of Brogan Giles, slowly tracing the black lettering while thinking of the words on the paper, as if he might be able to conjure the faces and see the places that had been written down.

Finally. "Master's Cosaur and Brogan said I was welcome to stay with them if I wanted to."

"For a visit?"

"No. To move here so I could find out more about where I came from and to finally meet the rest of my family."

Kael remained quiet, hoping that Liam would clarify his thoughts, yet dreading what Liam's decision might be.

The silence dragged on and Kael finally commented that the night was getting late and that they should get back to the Camalain, hoping that the further they moved away from Cosaur's home, the better chance there was of Liam possibly staying with the ship. And him.

But Liam had already made his decision. Although the offer had been tempting, Liam had told Eli and Giles that he would be on the Camalain when it left tomorrow.

"How come?" Kael did his best to hide his relief at hearing this as he and Liam walked down the quieting streets of Fomor.

Liam shrugged as he watched the moon rise into the night sky. "My father still needs me and, and the thought of leaving scares me a little."

"Although I'm sure the prince will be disappointed that I didn't pack up and leave."

"Don't worry about Manus." Kael chuckled. "He's coming round to liking you."

Liam doubted that comment, keeping his own opinion of what he thought the prince thought of him to himself.

"They were kind enough to tell me their door was always open if I changed my mind. Even said I could apprentice with them as a blacksmith if I wanted to."

"Looks like you now have an excuse to leave the Stone Mason's Guild." Kael laughed.

Liam laughed as well, saying that he didn't think he would want to change the annoying clashing of hammer and chisel for that of a hammer on anvil.

But Liam's laughter abruptly stopped when he felt something poking at his left hand, quickly pulling it towards his chest, before realizing it had been Kael's hand reaching for his.

"Sorry. Cosaur and Brogan had a pair of black foxes with a litter of kits and they kept poking their noses into my hands and nipping at them."

Liam knew he had screwed up this chance for them while they were alone, as Kael only smiled slightly, his hand now remaining by his side. So Liam did the only thing he could think of; he moved a little closer to Kael until his own fingers brushed against the back of Kael's hand as the man's fingers once again wrapped around Liam's.

The two locked eyes and it felt like a bolt of lightning was coursing through their arms as goose bumps crawled up Liam's arm from the connection. Liam also found that he could not hold Kael's contented gaze for long, and allowed his eyes to wander across the darkened street as he felt himself blush.

"They," Liam stuttered as he felt Kael's hand tighten around his. "They said the vixen was descended from a black fox my father domesticated when he first got to Fomor. It survived the attack, they took it in, and have bred several litters since. Even offered me one of the kits for me to take."

Liam then described how one of the little black creatures had pulled itself up into his lap, curling into a little ball and falling asleep while the group had carried on.

"I didn't think the prince would have appreciated one stray coming on board with another one."

Kael dismissed Liam's comment about calling himself a stray, but did agree with Liam about boarding the ship with a pet. Kael then proceeded to deepen his voice, doing his best to mimic Manus' as he bemoaned the uselessness of a pet and the amount of excrement it would leave around on the main deck.

Of course, both men knew nothing about the second "stray" that was now aboard the Camalain.

Silence once again wrapped around them as their laughter died away, the only sounds now coming from the footfalls of men they happened to pass by and the occasional cricket in some unseen corner.

Liam was happy to remain this way for their entire walk back to the ship. But Kael, who was much more experienced in the ways of romance pulled Liam closer so that the length of their arms were touching and, using his knowledge as a sailor, raised his left hand to the sky as he began to point out the constellations dedicated to the gods.

So, with their eyes pointed upward at the flickering gems scattered across a velvety sky, and the heat of their bodies chasing away the chill that was creeping into the air, Liam did the only thing he could think of and slowed his pace, enjoying the soft cadence of Kael's voice, for once not wanting to return to the Camalain, not wanting this moment to end.

Chapter 10
The Olean Flats

Dane's defeat at the hands of Barra had been humiliating. But then again, who could best a god?

Not only was the fight humiliating, it was devastating spiritually and financially. For Dane had to sacrifice the Sothair Dor, men and women he had collected as slaves, not only for his and his men's freedom, but for his god's as well.

A sacrifice that left him empty handed as he ordered his ships back home for fresh supplies and to report the events that had occurred to Lord Lyro Stowe.

But Dane and his small fleet hadn't flown very far before their lodestones stopped working, with the three ships finding themselves stranded only a day's flight from the southern coast of Tuame. Three ships that now not only lacked flight, but lacked the divine intervention of Ciaran, who had also gone silent with his brethren.

Fortunately, not only for Dane, but also for his crew who would have to deal with their captain's wrath at being abandoned, Ciaran sent one last message through his sagarts, informing them to be patient.

Of course patience was a virtue that Dane had crafted into an art. For how could one not be patient while stalking prey in the vast expanses of the dried Gwerin seas?

So, his mood somewhat mollified, for who could honestly say they would be comfortable being stranded in the middle of nowhere, Dane and his crew continued to remain vigilant, still somewhat apprehensive that they might be discovered, unaware that every other ship across the globe had stopped working.

The only thing to assault Dane's fleet during this time was a sandstorm that blanketed the area. A storm that rolled in during the middle of the first night, sending the guards scurrying for cover below deck, with all the windows on all three vessels shuttered against the maelstrom as it continued unabated during the next day.

For most people, their nerves would have been rattled by a storm of this intensity as it beat down on them. But Villis Dane was unlike "most people" and found the incessant metallic hissing quite relaxing. So being in good spirits with nowhere to go, and his sagarts free for the time being, Dane did the only thing he could do; he married Cremin Vokes.

With his eldest sagart giving rites and his most senior of commanders acting as witnesses, the two men went through with the formalities of the ritual, both men willing to forgo the traditional Knot Ceremony until it could be performed before the eyes of both clans; a quick marriage for the two men that would now help to embed Dane into Vokes' clan, clan Lyro, the ruling family of Mendes.

Dane, who was meticulous about his devotions, meticulous to the point of being obsessive, did make sure the rites that were spoken were precise, acting as if this was the actual ceremony, before spending the rest of the blustering day holed up in his quarters with Vokes, training him on how he wanted his household organized.

"Am I not to go with you on more of your missions?" Vokes could not help but ask.

"Is that what you want Vokes? To be by my side?"

Looking into his partner's unwavering gaze, Vokes couldn't help but swallow hard.

Only days ago Vokes had been indentured to this man by his cousin, only to find out it had been some sort of game between the two men. Until Vokes had stood up for himself, Dane had been all too willing to torment Vokes for his own amusement.

Now, as Vokes sat next to Dane staring into eyes as black as coal, eyes that weren't even reflecting the lamplight from the room, experience told Vokes that a subtle malice was veiled underneath those two pools of darkness. A malice that could just be seen twitching, looking for some release, at the corners of Dane's mouth.

Vokes knew he probably should not have opened his mouth and made a promise to himself to never put himself into a position where he could be harmed by the man.

"Yes," Vokes said to the man he had just married, not backing down from Dane's intense gaze. "I want to be by your side."

A smile blossomed on Dane's face. The man stretched in his chair, raising his arms behind his head while stretching his long legs out in front of him. Dane did not miss the doubt clouding Vokes' face and in his voice and enjoyed this little game. As was evident by the arousal clearly seen underneath the man's tightening clothes.

"That is good. I was not ready to replace the steward of my, our, household."

Vokes heard the sarcasm in that word "our" and knew he would never share in Dane's property. If anything he was now a part of that household. Just a new purchased piece of property.

So Vokes continued to listen to Dane describe the men and women who lived in and ran his villa, and what his personal holdings within his own clan were, while only asking the occasional question that seemed appropriate during his tutelage.

Dane was about to go on about Villis' clan elders when Vokes decided to break the promise he had just made to himself and took the chance of once again interrupting the man. "Excuse me, Dane." Vokes still had a hard time using the man's given name. "There are things about clan Lyro you should know as well."

Vokes was right about interrupting Dane; the man didn't like to be stopped and that hint of anger began to cloud his eyes once more. But Dane was feeling generous, and pulling his chair a little closer to Vokes', closer so that he could strike his partner if what he was about to hear was worthless, told Vokes to proceed with what he had to say.

Swallowing hard and grasping the edge of the table to hide the fact that his hands were shaking, Vokes began to explain to Dane which of his own cousins he should align himself with, and how to curry favor with those elders so Villis Dane could have a better footing within clan Lyro.

Vokes was beginning to explain to Dane who he should also trade with, both inside and out of the clan, when Dane reached out to grasp one of Vokes' hands.

"Why are you telling me these things?" Dane wanted to know.

Vokes was silent for a moment for he had known who Villis Dane was before being handed over to him. A man full of ambition and drive, with a strong touch of sadism, a characteristic common in all Mendens who worshiped Ciaran, who only wanted to further his and his clan's interests. A man that Lyro Stowe chose to watch closely in case Dane's goals began to overreach his station and interfere with Stowe's own enterprises. A man that Vokes had secretly admired. A man he had once been told to avoid.

But now. . .

"You and my cousin are of the same ilk. And he does not trust you, nor does he entirely trust your clan."

"As a matter of fact, Cousin Stowe has you and several of your cousins, along with members of the other major clans being watched."

Dane's grasp of Vokes' hand tightened. "Do you know their names?"

Vokes only knew the name of one Villis elder under surveillance. A man who ran the several of the minor Sothair breeding houses for the clan and who frequented Lord Lyro's court on a regular basis. Unfortunately, Vokes was in the dark as to who the other members were.

"And I am sure that Stowe has the shipwright in clan Ungus being watched."

"Why do you tell me these things?" Dane asked one more time, still unsure of why this information was being revealed to him.

"We are married." Vokes said bluntly. "One misstep from you or one thing that Cousin Stowe finds offensive and you will die, with my cousin claiming everything and everyone that you own. And if you die, then I will surely be put to death for having been married to you."

For survival Dane thought. Now that was a trait he could understand and respect.

"Also, the man that is watching you is on the Dotain."

"Who?"

Dane wasn't surprised to learn that the man shadowing his movements was one of his own commanders, nor that this man also had standing orders to kill him. But how could Dane dispose of this man so his demise looked like an accident? Ah well, something to think about later.

"Vokes, you are a rare find. A rare find indeed." Pulling Vokes towards himself, Dane kissed the man's hand that he still held in his own. "A gift from Ciaran I will not waste."

"I hope not." Vokes shut his mouth, holding back anything else he might have said as he once more broke his vow to keep his own opinions to himself.

But Dane only chuckled, enjoying Vokes' discomfiture at not knowing how to act in front of him. Dane wasn't about to help the man while he stood and pulled Vokes into an embrace, holding the man tightly to him.

"No, you are a gift I will not waste at all." Dane repeated, smiling lasciviously at his partner, before leading Vokes to their bed, where the men spent the rest of the evening and all of the night entwined together.

Dane not only knew how to mete out pain for disobedience, the man also knew how to reward the men who pleased him. And Vokes, who had just given him a trove of information, was rewarded very well.

Eventually dawn arrived, the men only knowing this by the light rapping upon the door. The sound, barely audible over the howling wind of the storm that continued to rage on, quickly woke Dane, who had flitted in and out of sleep for some time, with his movements also startling Vokes into waking.

After listening to reports that there had been no change in the weather and how the lodestones still did not work, Dane ordered food to be brought for him and Vokes.

Once the two were refreshed, Dane requested that a crewman, one Ulak Mose, a cousin and member of his own household, be brought to the cabin.

"Captain?" Mose, a man just as dark haired and swarthy as his lord, for he was as pure of Menden blood as Dane, bowed before the man.

"Mose, I have a new job for you."

Dane promoted the man to Vokes' bodyguard and ordered the man to move into the room that Vokes had just vacated. And not telling Mose, who the assassin was, for Dane did not want word to accidentally reach the assassin's ears, explained that he and possibly Vokes were being watched by another crew member.

"Stay on your guard until we reach home where I can switch out the crew with more of our brethren from clan Villis."

"Aye, Captain."

"And make sure you are by Master Cremin's side at all times."

"As you wish."

Vokes was surprised by the deference of request given to him, for once remaining silent, only nodding in accession when Dane ordered Mose to take him to the ship's armory and to have him fitted with better accoutrements and weaponry.

"Vokes, once you're done, return here and do your best to remember everything you can about what we talked about yesterday."

"Aye Captain, err, Milord."

Calling Dane captain would have been the appropriate title, even in front of another clan member, but Dane didn't bother to correct Vokes, only smiling, a smile that broadened as he watched Vokes flinch as he raised his hand to pat the side of his partner's face, as if he was some favored pet who had performed well at a new trick, before leaving the cabin.

Nothing had changed when Dane arrived on his bridge.

The sandstorm still roiled about them, blotting out any view of his other two ships and any way to communicate with them. One of his steersmen sat impotently in his chair, hands fidgeting on the lodestones, hoping for some connection to be made, while a sagart sat behind them praying to Ciaran for his guidance and blessings.

Almost an hour went by before Dane found that he was growing just as frustrated as the rest of his crew and decided to take a tour of the Dotain to see how the rest of his men were faring.

With several crewman in tow, one being his would be murderer, Dane slowly took a tour of the sleek vessel, thanking the gods that his and the other two ships were heavily plated because it sounded like this storm would have blasted all of his vessels to splinters if they had not been protected.

Dane reminded himself that Ciaran had told him to have patience during this ordeal. But knowing and doing were two totally different things as Dane walked down the dimly lit corridors of his ship, all filled with a stifling, humid air from the ship not being ventilated.

When it looked like the storm wasn't going to relent in its assault on the ships nor that they would be flying anytime soon, Dane gave up command to his second and made his way back to his own quarters.

Vokes stood as soon as Dane entered the room and was about to explain what he had been doing and what he remembered about who his cousin had being watched, was stopped in mid-sentence as Dane rushed the man and pushed him to the bed where he began to forcefully tear at the man's clothes.

"Fight back, fight back!" Dane hissed, a lustful gleam in his eyes as he tried to pull a boot off one of Vokes' feet.

Understanding dawned on Vokes' face at what he was being asked and instead of laying prone on the bed to be pawed by Dane, Vokes struggled to remove his foot from Dane's grasp, only succeeding when his foot shot forward, the heel of his boot hitting Dane squarely on the chin, snapping his partner's head backward.

Stunned by what he had done, Vokes stopped, dropping his foot to the bed as Dane brought his left hand to his chin and moved his jaw around. Vokes, seeing no blood on his mouth or goateed chin, began to apologize when the flat of Dane's right palm struck the exposed skin of his taught abdomen.

Vokes gasped in surprise and flinched in pain as Dane hit him several more times, the skin on his stomach turning a bright red.

"Come on," Dane growled, a crooked, lecherous smile appearing on his lips as he leaned over Vokes, placing a hand on each of Vokes' shoulders, his weight painfully forcing him deeper into the bed. "Are you going to fight back? Or do I have to tie you up and have my way with you?"

Vokes, having been trained in the martial arts of his people and knowing that he did not want to be in a position of immobility with this man, did as he was told.

So, using his anger at being tortured by Dane and his cousin, his frustration at being stranded in the middle of nowhere, and the attraction he did have towards this man, Vokes' legs shot out and wrapped around Dane's torso, squeezing the breath out of him. Grasping the side of the bed, Vokes flipped the two of them onto the wooden floor of the room, landing on top of Dane, fighting with the man to keep his hands away from his own body, ignoring the smile of enjoyment that now covered Dane's face.

While outside, Dane's personal guard and Ulak Mose, who had standing watch over the captain's quarters, gave each other a knowing look as they did their best, and failed, to ignore the shouts and the thumping of furniture as the couple within the room tore at each other's clothing as they fought for dominancy to ravage each other.

Hours went by before the yells and the sounds of pleasure eventually died down, allowing the storm that was still raging around the ship to continue with its own howling unchallenged, giving the two men in the hallway a reprieve until they could take care of their own lustful appetites.

***

Dane stirred out of a heavy slumber; a deep sleep that was quite uncommon for the Menden captain.

There it was again, Dane thought as he struggled with consciousness, realizing that his late afternoon foreplay with Vokes had taken more out of him than he expected.

A moan, soft and muffled, forced him further into waking.

A moan not of pleasure, but one filled with pain.

Dane realized the cries were coming from Vokes, so he rolled over to wake his partner, but raised himself quickly when he found the cabin bathed in a blood red light and a man standing over the two of them.

No, not a man, but a god. Ciaran.

The god, who was only clothed in the dark shadows of the room, had a mischievous glint to his crimson eyes, for it seemed he had been looking upon the sleeping couple for some time.

Dane deferentially lowered his eyes and gave a blessing to the god, while placing a hand on Vokes shoulder to wake the man, who was still asleep on his stomach. Dane stopped shaking Vokes when he realized that the covers had been pulled away from most of his partner's body and that the god was running a finger over Vokes' exposed skin.

No, not running his finger over Vokes' sweat covered skin, but through it. Like any Gwerin would skim his fingers across a still pond, sending soft ripples across its surface, so did Ciaran's finger pass through Vokes' body, the man's flesh and the base of his lower spine breaking and then reforming as Ciaran's finger slowly moved its way up to Vokes' shoulder blades.

Vokes, whose head was turned towards Dane with saliva drooling from his opened mouth and the whites of his eyes barely visible under his fluttering lids, moaned painfully from Ciaran's touch.

Dane watched quietly as Ciaran pulled his finger away from Vokes' body, a bluish green vapor swirling about its tip, and brought the finger to his mouth, eating what Dane assumed was some part of Vokes' essence.

Dane's own thoughts were jumbled as he watched Ciaran repeat the process, Vokes' cries filling the room once again. How he hoped he would not end up with a damaged partner, a valuable tool he might now have to dispose of, all the while wishing that he too had this power over other men.

Ciaran easily read Dane's thoughts and laughed wickedly.

"He will be fine." The god chuckled. "Just some disturbing nightmares for a while."

One long wail of pain emanated from Vokes' mouth as Ciaran pushed two fingers into the man's body, just above his buttocks, his fingers slipping in as far as the first knuckles on them. Ciaran took his time, savoring the pain he was causing to Vokes' body and his soul as the god's fingers began to trail over the man's spine up to the base of his skull before pulling them out.

"Taste." Ciaran said, offering his fingers to Dane while Vokes' body shook between them as his muscles involuntarily tried to relax from the assault upon them.

Dane did not hesitate at the gift being bestowed upon him and enveloped the god's fingers with his mouth, the captain's tongue running along Ciaran's digits, savoring the essence of his partner as his body tasted almost everything that made up Vokes' soul; his hopes, fears and desires warmed Dane's body while flashes of Vokes' own memories danced within Dane's mind.

Villis Dane closed his eyes as he listened to the god's laughter as Ciaran's fingers teased the captain's tongue. His laughter a sound one might hear from a master who was enjoying the antics of a pet as Dane's own body awakened to what he was devouring.

"More?"

Dane inhaled deeply and only nodded a yes for his mouth was still wrapped around Ciaran's fingers. But the captain moaned at the loss as the god removed his fingers from the Dane's mouth.

"There is something I need you to do for me." Ciaran said as he dipped his fingers back into Vokes' spine, a new squeal of pain escaping from the tortured man.

"Anything!" Dane watched hungrily as the god's fingers made their way back up his partner's body.

"I need you to head west to find something for me."

"But, but, we are marooned out here and we are short on supplies."

Ciaran's fingers reached Vokes' skull and the god pushed them so they disappeared as they swirled around in the man's brain. Vokes' squeals became a roar of pain at the assault, with tears rolling down the man's face as he unknowingly whimpered the words, no, no.

The god left his fingers where they were, enjoying the thoughts his ministrations were causing in Vokes' head, as he explained how they would soon be able to fly and that there was a ship not far from them that they could raid for supplies.

"I will keep Sothair Dor from flying until you reach them. And this time, you must not kill any nor take them for prisoners. We need to be as subtle as possible and we do not need the eyes of my brethren turning our way."

"I understand." Dane replied, raising himself to his knees, the covers falling from his body as Ciaran removed his fingers from Vokes, the thick vapors swirling slowly about the tips and held them in front of Dane, like a treat to a hound.

"What is it that I am looking for?" Dane drooled, fearful that Vokes' essence might evaporate into the air before he could taste any more of it.

"I will tell you when you are closer to my prize. And how would you like to be rewarded if you are successful on this hunt."

A frown formed on Dane's lips, afraid to answer, for everyone knew that the gifts of Ciaran always came at a price.

"To serve and worship you is reward enough, Milord." The captain finally replied as he tore his eyes from the bluish green substance that was Vokes, to look into those red orbs of his god.

Ciaran laughed in approval at Dane's response and beckoned him to dine on his fingers once more, the captain crawling over the immobile body of his partner to reach them. Dane moaned and growled in ecstasy, falling into a delirium as his own senses were overwhelmed by the sensation of Vokes' essence mingling with his.

Yet a chill ran down his spine as Ciaran ran his left hand over the naked body of the captain, who had suddenly become fearful that he too would be tortured like Vokes.

Ciaran's laughter softened, content to enjoy the mixture of pleasure and dread flowing from Dane's body.

"No," The god chuckled. "You deserve something. No matter how trivial it might be."

"I know." The god purred. "How would you like to be king? To replace this one's cousin and to become ruler over your people? Or maybe a little kingdom of your own?"

Dane, his mouth still full by the god's fingers, stared into those dark crimson eyes of Ciaran and nodded, his own eyes pleading for the chance to become a ruler over his people and to continue to serve this wicked being.

"Of course you do." Ciaran laughed, removing his saliva coated fingers from Dane's mouth and running his hand over Dane's face, leaving a shiny wet trail across the captain's cheek. "Be ready."

* * *

Dane sat up in his bed, huffing to catch his breath, confused as to where he was for the moment, the sounds of someone pounding heavily on his door and shouts asking if he was alright filled the darkened room.

"Yes, yes!" Dane shouted as he climbed out of bed and padded to the door. "What do you want?"

"I am sorry Captain Villis!" His guard shouted. "But the storm has moved on and we are aloft again. Have been for some time."

Aloft? Yes! Yes they were hovering in the air because Dane could feel the Dotain shifting slightly under his feet.

"The storm? Has it dissipated?" Dane asked as he rested his forehead on the closed door.

"No Captain. It has moved west."

West.

West. The word echoed with the sound of Ciaran's voice within his head.

Dane stood up, doing his best to overcome the exhaustion that his body felt. "Are we able to contact the other ships?"

"Yes, Captain!"

Dane paced slightly, scratching at his abdomen while gathering his thoughts together over what Ciaran had said.

"Inform the bridge we will be following that storm for now and have word sent to the other ships to do so too."

"Yes, Captain."

"I will be there shortly. And have the sagarts report to the bridge!"

"Aye, aye, Captain!" The man shouted before running off on his errands.

"Vokes. Vokes!" Dane called out as he felt his way around the darkened room, painfully bumping into the table with his left thigh that had been moved during their romp last night.

"Vokes?" he called out again as he opened the shutter on a lantern at his desk, bathing the room in a warm light before heading back to the bed to open the lantern at its side.

Vokes, who felt like he was battling a migraine, had heard Dane call out his name, but chose not to answer as he struggled to get out of bed.

"What is wrong?"

"Nothing." Vokes hissed as he swung his feet onto the floor and lowered his head, keeping his eyes closed as he tried to avoid the light that was flooding the room.

"Nonsense." Dane said as he began to pick up his clothing off the floor.

"My head hurts." Vokes lied. Although the remark really wasn't a lie because Vokes' head hurt so much that it felt like someone was scraping the inside of his skull, right above his eyes, with a knife. The headache was so painful that it was making Vokes feel nauseous.

What Vokes didn't want to tell Dane was about the nightmare.

A nightmare where a demon, tall, muscular and ram headed, had plucked him out of bed, only to dangle him off a clawed finger that had pierced into his skull. In the nightmare, the demon had kept Vokes alive by his will alone, jeering at and mocking the man, all the while allowing his minions, ravens as black as night, to land on Vokes' back to tear at his flesh, exposing his spine so that the crows could then peck on its bones.

The horrendous dream felt like it had lasted all night and no, Vokes would not be telling Dane this story, too embarrassed at how it was affecting him.

"I need to go to the bridge!" Dane said, annoyed that he was repeating himself. "And I need you too. . ."

Dane stopped in mid-sentence and dropped his clothing that he had yet to put on when he looked at his partner a little more closely. Vokes had remained slumped over with his back exposed and Dane could see a long red line, more like a birthmark than a welt, crawling over the man's spine.

Dane sat down beside Vokes and ran a finger over the mark, eliciting a whimper of distress from Vokes as the man relived the pain from his nightmare, unaware that he had also been part of a vision with Dane and the god Ciaran. As he reached Vokes' shoulders, Dane was shocked to see the marking for the Stowe clan that had been inked after Vokes' own clan name, fading away. Fading like it had never been there to begin with, just like the weal that was on Vokes' spine was beginning to fade.

"My gift to you and your new empire." A voice whispered in Dane's ear.

Dane left the bed, and squatting in front of Vokes, raised the man's head so the two were looking at each other.

"What?" Vokes asked, not caring to think what now Dane had in store for his tortured body.

A crooked smile formed on Dane's lips as he wiped Vokes' damp hair away from his face.

A smile that Vokes found disconcerting for it was not one that was normally seen on Dane. A smile that was not born out of malice or deviousness, but one that seemed to show a hint of tenderness.

Or maybe it was fondness Vokes thought as he tried to stand to get ready and to get on with his own duties, only to find that Dane was holding him down.

"Vokes, do you stand by my side?"

"What? Yes. We've already talked about this."

Vokes swiped Dane's hand away so that he could stand, but Dane was quicker as his own hand shot out to grab Vokes by his lower jaw, squeezing until the inside of Vokes' mouth rubbed painfully against his teeth.

"I am serious! Do you stand by my side no matter what will come my way, our, way?"

"Yes!" Vokes hissed through his clenched teeth. What was he supposed to say to the man who owned him more so now than he did when he had been the captain's servant?

Dane gazed into Vokes' grey eyes that were dull from exhaustion, searching for some sign of treachery, or better yet, a sense of survival that he knew was there. For how could he not know these things after feasting on the man's soul?

But all he saw on the surface was fear and frustration, with a hint of adoration mingled in there that Dane now knew Vokes had for him.

"Rest." Dane said as he let go of the man's face and grabbed his own clothing so he could dress. "I will have Mose check in on you to see to your needs for I will need you fit for what is to come."

"I do not understand. What is coming?"

Buckling his pants, Dane walked back over to Vokes, pushing the man back down onto the damp linens of the bed.

"I will tell you later." Dane chuckled. A sound that had a sly quality to it that Vokes was more familiar with. "For we are destined for greatness. You and I."

***

With the knowledge of the recent Menden attacks fresh on his mind, and unwilling to risk his life nor those of his crew on the Olean Flats, Manus set out from Fomor heading northwest from the town, hugging the coast of Birr until they were closer to the destination provided by Caittle Anam.

A route that was quite conservative for the brash prince because it tacked on almost five days of flight to their trip.

A trip that Manus felt was taking them in the wrong direction. But with nothing else to go on in the hopes of finding Banning, Manus took the word of Caittle Anam and Seb Cullen, doing his best to keep as much of his fate and that of his people out of the hands of the gods.

The gods! How Manus wished the rest of them would go the way of Barra and to simply disappear from their lives.

Barra gone. That was the one thing they did learn while they were in Fomor: Seb Cullen was not the only sagart Barra had abandoned. It seemed the god had decided to leave all his sagarts and sagarttas to their own devices.

With the loss of the god, his men's frustration seemed to build on their first day out from Fomor.

But they, and almost all of his crew, were finding solace in the voices of Cullen and Anam, who not only read from Barra's sacred text, the Bunusacha, the Fundamentals of Rock and Stone as it was more commonly called, but also from Cavanna's Book of Truths, the Fhirinni, and from any other of the other sacred writs the crew had upon their possession.

How Manus wished his men would turn to him the way they had turned to the two sagarts for solace, Manus thought one afternoon, while sipping some caff in the dining hall and watching a prayer meeting being conducted by Anam with some of the men who were off duty.

"Anam seems to be of a friendly sort." Said Captain Thear to Manus who, had also taken a break and, was sitting next to the prince in the dining hall. "Think he has already learned most of the crew's names."

Manus didn't respond to the captain as he watched Anam pass the well-handled book of scripture he was reading to the man next to him so that each could take a turn reading the sacred words before them.

"And what is wrong with Seb Cullen?" Manus did ask as the elderly priest came into the hall and joined the group seated around Anam. If possible, the man looked more fatigued than he normally did. Almost like he has the grey in him, Manus' long dead grandfather would have said. The grey meaning a person's skin looked ashen, almost unhealthy, like they were on death's door.

"Cullen has taken up weapon's training." Ibor said and described to the prince how Cullen had started practicing using staves with Croft during the steersman's off time.

"Explains his new staff." Manus replied, noticing that the sagart had replaced his cane with a thick oaken staff, shod in iron on both of its ends.

"Like the man doesn't do enough as it is." Ibor replied, admiring the sagart for what he had been trying to accomplish while serving on the Camalain.

Once again Manus did not bother to reply, ignoring the slight sound of recrimination in the captain's voice at how he had a habit of pushing the elderly sagart to find his brother.

Well, Cullen was free to do whatever he wanted to do during his spare time, Manus thought, just as long as the sagart was there to help Manus out when he was called for.

As some men left the group, to either head to their shifts or to a bunk to find some much needed rest, saluting the prince as they passed him and the captain, Manus knew he might not have sway over their spirits, but he did over his men's bodies. Hopefully filling their time with work would help to somewhat distract them from thinking too much about their missing god.

One person he could control, Manus thought as he and Captain Thear left the dining hall to make their way back to the bridge, was his friend Kael.

For Manus couldn't help but notice how Kael was trying to come up with excuses to spend more time with Liam. Time Manus would have spent with Kael, if the two were on land somewhere, or if the sagart's son had never been on board.

A decision Manus now regretted.

Unfortunately it had taken a long time for Manus to realize he was attracted to Kael and the irony to it all being that it had taken Liam's presence to make him realize how he really felt for his best friend.

But his parents foresaw this and had worked on keeping their son from going down that road.

"Kael is a good boy and a fine soldier just like his father." Manus' father once said, the words echoing in his head. "A fine friend who should turn into an excellent advisor as you two mature."

And where his father had done his best to be as subtle as possible, coaxing his son to do the right thing for himself and their kingdom, his mother was much more direct.

"Do not let this boy be a distraction." She would say, especially when Betrys thought he and Kael were spending too much time together. "Remember. He is just a servant and he will need to know his place when your father and I choose a suitable partner for you."

Manus knew all these things and had done his best to listen to the wisdom of his parents. Still, the stress of looking for his brother and watching his friend move towards a relationship that did not look like one of his usual flings only made Manus yearn to keep Kael by his side.

So Manus allowed his selfishness to win out over common sense, and thought of ways to keep Kael and Liam apart.

Having Ibor begin to train Kael on captaining the ship was the easiest distraction Manus could devise for Kael who was flattered at being asked. But their off time was a little more difficult because how many times could you pour over the same maps feigning to look for clues to find Banning or spend meals cooped up in their quarters?

Finally, when even Kael couldn't hide his frustration of being kept away from Liam and having to spend all of his time with Manus, the prince decided to play a hand he had hoped not to use to keep Kael by his side.

"I don't know Kael." Manus said one night from his bed after dinner as he listened to Kael strumming his guitar. "I don't think we'll ever find Banning."

"Nonsense." Kael said, pausing in the middle of his song. "We haven't been steered wrong yet (that they knew of) and with two sagart's on board I think our chances are much better that we'll find Banning."

"You think so?"

"Of course I do. Have faith in the gods!" Kael blurted out before remembering that one was now lost to them.

"Thanks." Manus said as he got comfortable on the bed by lying on his back and propping his head up on his arms so that he could stare up at the ceiling of the room. "You're a good friend, Kael. I'm glad you're here."

Kael watched his friend for a moment, grateful he did not have the burdens that came with being a prince, while wishing he could do more for Manus, doing his best to hide the loneliness he was feeling, before starting a new tune on his guitar.

***

Although he had not spent time with Liam, Kael had searched him out and explained how Manus had slipped into a funk and wanted the two of them to spend more time together.

"I'm sorry." Kael had said to Liam as the two stood outside of the storage room where Liam still trained with Gorman and the others.

"No worries." Liam had said as he wiped sweat from his face. "I understand."

Kael smiled, giving Liam a hug, happy to see that he did understand before heading back down the hallway, knowing full well he would be late in meeting Manus on the bridge.

Liam watched as Kael hurried away, returning the goodbye wave before he disappeared up the stairs.

Making his own way to the washroom before heading up to the galley to help with the evening meal, Liam couldn't help but think how fortunate Manus was to have a friend like Kael.

A friendship he wished he had, somewhat ignorant to the fact that the seed of comradeship had been planted by Gorman, Heath and the others. Men who had warmly welcomed Liam into their group and already thought of him as a friend.

So as the days carried on with Kael either holed up on the bridge or hanging out with the prince in their quarters, Liam began to truly wonder if Kael had already grown tired of him, and the run-in they had the other day just something polite that Kael felt he needed to do.

But that feeling of loss didn't stop Liam from longing to bump into Kael, or to find Kael standing behind him, his brown eyes sparkling in delight, a broad smile on his attractive face, as Liam fantasized about being surprised by the man.

On one such occasion, after finishing his duties of cleaning dishes and cooking pots from that night's dinner, Liam heard laughter coming from the dining hall. Liam was quite confident that one of the voices belonged to Kael, so hurried out into the hall before he could leave.

Liam's heart sank when no sign of Kael could be found and noticed that the sounds of merriment were coming from Caittle Anam and the men seated around him.

"Hail! Liam!" Anam shouted jovially in his heavy accent, with several men turning to look at the young man as the sagart waived him over.

"Sorry, Sagart Caittle," Liam politely said as he took a step backwards to head back into the galley, only wanting to hide his disappointment at not finding Kael. "I didn't mean to interrupt."

"Nonsense! We just finished." Anam beckoned Liam over once again. "Take a break from your work! Come sit. Sit!"

A couple of the men got up to leave, so Liam took one of the vacated seats across from the priest.

Looking into those grey eyes that shined like polished stones, framed by his golden brown hair and tanned skin, qualities that the crew were whispering as handsome and manly, Liam found it hard to believe this was the same man that had suffered any ordeal to reach Fomor, and said just as much to Anam.

"Your father certainly has the healing touch of a sagart!" Anam laughed, his gaze never leaving Liam's. "Thanks be to the gods for him because I was certainly beyond helping myself."

Liam sat quietly as the men still around him nodded and also gave their praises to the gods, for he remembered how his father could not even heal a cut on Gorman and his men during that sandstorm when they were stranded out on the flats.

"How is my father?" Liam asked for he too had heard how his father had taken up a weapon once again, remembering how the elderly sagart frowned as he made some comment about wanting to be ready to fight if necessary, when Liam had had a chance to ask about his new activity.

"Seb Cullen is a hard worker. Just like his son." Anam smiled, this being his only answer to Liam's questions.

Liam didn't feel the need to respond to the compliment because it was common knowledge that the prince, who was concerned that they could be attacked at any moment, had everyone working a little harder.

So Liam, who felt a little daring as some more of the men left or began talking to each other, decided to ask Anam about himself.

"Father said you came from Sliabh Mianach. From up in the mountains?"

"Yes." Anam attested. "And I pray not to have to make that trek on foot again."

Liam had heard stories from his father and from other sagart's in Kinsale that had traveled to the isolated temple and found it interesting that this gregarious man came from a place where the priests were supposed to be reclusive and had chosen to spend most of their time in silence.

"Do all the sagarts work in the mines?" It was also common knowledge that the temple and its extensive complex was built around a lodestone mine and that the priests living there mined the ore, shaping it into its appropriate roundness before selling it in the local markets.

"We all did." Anam agreed. "Down in the dark with only a lantern to light your way with nothing but your thoughts to keep you company while hammering at rock. The mining left plenty of time for contemplation and prayer."

"It makes me so grateful that so many of the men here love to raise their voices to honor the gods." Anam laughed.

"Pray with us Liam. One more time before everyone goes their way."

What could Liam say to the attractive man across from him who had leaned in with his arms stretched across the table, hands open for him to take?

Grasping those smooth, warm hands, Liam closed his eyes and joined the others, his voice blending with the others as Anam lead them in "Prayer of Finding". A chant to Barra that was very old and to this day still used by miners who sought the mystical ore that flew the Gwerin ships. A chant that over time became a prayer commonly used by many people who were looking for good luck in their own affairs.

And these thoughts were on Liam's mind that next evening while he was on deck with his mates, only half listening to Gorman who was explaining what they would be needing to do over the next couple of hours; of Anam's strong tanned hands, unmarred by any sort of work. Hands that were unmarred by mining.

How clunky his own hands felt Liam thought while picking at the callouses on the palm of his hand as he watched a barge pass them on their port side.

But Liam forgot the oddity of Anam's miner's hands when Gorman called out his name, explaining how he would be helping Manton and Dolan when they started taking on new supplies. For the Camalain had flown into a trade route early that day, with all manner of ships passing them, flying in either direction along the Birrnian coast, as they made their way on their own journeys.

Manus, who was refusing to take nothing to chance, had decided to stop in Pallack, the next city along the coast, to replenish their supplies before heading back out onto the Olean Flats.

"Remember," Gorman said as a military skiff came to fly alongside them as escort while the city lights of Pallack flickered on the horizon. "We're not staying for a visit and we'll be working through most of the night. So once we start working try to keep the chatter to a minimum so we can get out of here."

"It's a shame the prince sent a requisition on ahead with that ship that passed us this morning." Manton said as Gorman dismissed the men for the time being. "Might have had at least a couple of hours to see the sights."

Sidri snorted at the man's remark as the group went to stand at the railing and watch the traffic of ships, their lanterns lit against the oncoming night.

"What you really mean is there won't be time for you to sneak in a "hand job" with one of the locals." Sidri chided.

"Hey! I got needs too ya know!" Manton pouted, responding to the jibe while the rest of the group laughed around him.

"Please!" Gorman chuckled, jokingly cuffing the man across the back of his head. "We know way too much about your needs!"

Manton childishly mumbled something incoherently before the group's conversation turned to more mundane topics as a trio of barges, with two armored skiffs as escorts, flew by them as they made their way south.

Liam was standing alongside Heath and Gorman, listening to the two who were now playing a game of guessing what type of cargo the barges could possibly be carrying when someone coughing from behind them interrupted their banter.

Turning, the three found Kael standing behind them, his stance tall, his hands held behind his back, and an odd look of determination set in his light brown eyes.

"Excuse me Master Praish, might I steal Liam for a moment."

Gorman found it odd that after almost two weeks of working together that Kael had suddenly become formal. Gorman did his best to suppress a smile as he replied. "You may Master Karam. But only for a moment. We are expected to be working in the bays."

"Yes sir. We won't be long."

As Liam walked with Kael further along the railing, only slightly out of earshot from the rest of the men, Liam wondered what this was all about.

As a matter of fact, with Kael not showing his face since their talk a couple of days ago, Liam had begun to wonder if Kael had only used Manus as an excuse to finally be done with him; done with a man who had no clan, no family. For a man with no family was usually seen as a man without status.

Maybe Kael finally saw him the way his friend, the prince, did.

And not for the last time over these days that had begun to drag out painfully from a loneliness that Liam had never felt before, he wondered if he should have accepted Cosaur Eli's offer to stay in Fomor and to strike out on his own. Just like his own father had done before him.

"What do you want?" Liam asked, doing his best to keep the tone of his voice as flat as possible and trying to steel himself for what Kael was about to say.

But Liam was caught off guard by the nervousness in Kael's eyes and the thin sheen of sweat on the man's upper lip. Sweat that did not seem to want to dry in the night's cool air and as a soft wind wrapped about them.

"Is something wrong? Are you ill?"

"No. No." Kael repeated, embarrassed at the question, as he brought his right hand to his face to wipe the sweat away before it quickly disappeared behind his back where his left hand had remained.

Taking a step closer to Kael, Liam did his best to ignore the distracting sounds of whispering and soft chuckles that were coming from behind him. "Then what is it?"

"I can't stop thinking about you!" Kael blurted out in a voice that was surely heard by most of the men around them.

"I thought I could wait until we reached home." Kael explained, wiping at his face again. "But I can't. I just can't!"

Liam remained silent, unsure of what to say, as Kael, who was always calm and confident, did his best to compose himself.

"I am serious about you. At least, I want to be." Kael finally said, an odd look of pleading clouding his eyes.

"Me neither." Liam replied.

"What?" Kael pulled back unsure of what that comment meant.

"Me neither. I can't stop thinking about you too."

Kael relaxed at hearing Liam's comment and a smile finally appeared on his face. A smile that made Liam's heart beat faster and his own face begin to flush, embarrassed at having expressed his own feelings.

"So now what?" Liam asked. For now that they had made clear their attraction for each other, Liam was unsure what to do next.

Of course, Kael came to his rescue and revealed what he had been holding behind his back; a bundle wrapped in soft brown leather that Kael placed between them for Liam to take.

"I was going to ask you out to dinner at our next stop and give this to you then, but once I heard we weren't going to stay, I just knew I didn't want to wait for the next opportunity. I know it's not very romantic, but here!"

Kael watched Liam, who seemed to be confused by the present before him, decided to hold his hand, which was slightly clammy and shook from nervousness.

As Liam took the gift, Liam was immediately impressed by the suppleness of the soft leather that encased the object within. Almost like cloth, not like some animal skin, Liam thought.

Liam's breath caught in his throat as he pulled back the folds of leather to reveal the wristband hidden within.

It was not the one they had seen in the leather-smith's shop back in Fomor. But it was quite similar.

This wristband had been dyed a rich, deep burgundy, almost the color of wine, with fine runes to Barra and intricate whorls carved into it, all of which had been painstakingly colored black.

"Turn it over."

Doing so, Liam saw that black leather chords had been woven into it so the wristband could be tightened once in place. With the chords at the wrist end were knotted with charms dedicated to Barra.

But the charms were not of clay or glass. They were of lodestone. Small chips that had holes bored into them so that they could be threaded onto the leather and polished so well that their surfaces easily reflected the moonlight.

"I know you can't see them," Kael said as he stepped closer to place a hand on one of Liam's so he could turn the charms over. "The stones have been marked with the symbols for fortune and good luck."

"I remember how much you liked that other band we saw while we were in the market. So while you were at Master Cosaur's home I went back to the shop but it but it had been sold so got this one for you. I think we can unknot this chord and add your father's charm to it. If you like."

With the detailing and the lodestones attached to it, Liam could only assume the wristband was at least twice as much, if not more, as the one he had seen.

"I can't accept this." Liam whispered. "It's way too much."

As he made to give the gift back to Kael, the man squeezed Liam's hands to stop him.

"Of course you can." Kael said as he continued to stare into Liam's hazel eyes. "It's a gift. Now you're supposed to say thank you."

Liam did so, enjoying the touch of Kael's fingers as they slowly moved along the back of his hand.

"And now it's your turn to give me something." Kael informed Liam.

"But I," Liam stuttered, taking Kael a little too seriously, confused by the fact that Kael had assumed he would have something for him, when Kael, who without hesitation, stepped in and kissed Liam on the lips.

The kiss was quick. An abrupt peck, like the ones teenagers would give each other when they were at play or when they were testing the waters of love.

"That wasn't so bad." Kael said as he watched Liam's expression, dreading that he might have gone too far, too quickly. But when he saw the smile on his face and felt Liam's hand on his own, Kael kissed Liam once more, not rushing to pull away this time.

So caught up in the moment, that sweet taste of something new, especially for Liam, that they had all but forgotten they were surrounded by the crew of the Camalain as it wended its way to Pallack.

Sadly, as is the case with the fantasy of wanting to escape the everyday and to enjoy the moment, reality was there to make itself known.

"Kael!"

Surprised by the coarse bark of Kael's name, the two separated and looked up towards the observation deck from where the shout had come from to see the silhouette, darker than the night sky that surrounded it, of Manus staring down at them.

"I need you up here!" Manus called out as he stood, crossing his arms over his chest, his hair whipped wildly by the wind, Manus' black shape reminding Liam of Dubhas, the god of death, the god of judgment.

"Aye Milord!" Kael shouted over his shoulder, doing his best to keep a frown off of his own face.

"I hope I didn't get you in trouble." Liam whispered. For he was constantly reminded of the disdain that Manus had for him and knew that the prince would most likely blame him for this event.

"Don't be silly." Kael ran a hand up and down Liam's arm to reassure him. "He'll be fine."

To be honest, Kael had reached a point where he didn't care if Manus was going to be fine with the relationship he wanted with Liam.

Kael thought he had done his best to be a good friend over these past couple of weeks. Being here as moral support for Manus and to do his duty to save Banning if need be.

Maybe Kael just realized had been too willing to constantly be at Manus' side and remaining silent about some of the things he wanted for himself while tending to Manus' needs.

Especially, he thought, over these last few days when Manus began to test the waters and to make slight disparaging remarks about Liam. Considering that Manus knew about Liam's past, Kael thought he would have treated the sagart's son a little more gently; a little more respectfully.

But no, the jibes continued.

The final straw came when Manus began to call Liam "Master Misfit". Master Misfit can barely handle a weapon. Master Misfit always stutters when he has to talk to me, and half of what he says doesn't make any sense. Master Misfit is afraid of his own shadow. Master Misfit, Master Misfit.

Kael had heard enough about Master Misfit because those things that Manus was chiding were the qualities that Kael found endearing in Liam.

So, not wanting to have another altercation with Manus, like the one they had in Fomor, Kael decided he couldn't wait any longer and felt that it was time to search out Liam.

Granted, making his feelings known on the main deck, one of the most public of places on the Camalain was not the most romantic way to try to court Liam. But it was the quickest way for word to spread throughout the ship about his interest in Liam. And as he had hoped, Manus was there to catch the public display of affection. How he wished this would stay his friend's rudeness and finally accept his attraction to Liam, but it seemed like he would be dealing with Manus' icy silence and black mood for a while.

"He's still watching." Liam said, recalling Kael from his reverie.

Turning to look over his shoulder, Kael searched to find his friend in that shade of a man that loomed over them, hoping to find some sign of acceptance in his stance, and knowing that the search would be futile at this time of the evening, Kael returned his attention back to Liam.

"Oh well." Kael shrugged before wrapping an arm around Liam's waist to pull him in and kiss him once more. And Kael made sure this kiss lasted longer than the last as he savored the pleasure of being near this man, only wanting to keep this moment as a memory to use as a shield against what he knew what was to come next.

"Believe me," Kael said when he finally pulled away from Liam. "I might not see you over the next few days, I will be thinking about you because all I want is to be with you."

"I'll wait." Liam breathed heavily as Kael pulled out of their embrace and left so that he could make his way up to his friend who had vacated his space at the railing.

Of course, before the moment could fade away, only to remain as a memory to be cherished in later days, faint clapping and lewd whistling filled the air.

"Well boys, looks like another one is off the market!" Manton laughed, good-naturedly.

"You mean one less man to lay your paws on." Dolan rebutted.

Manton slapped his friend playfully. "I wasn't thinking about me! I was thinking about all those other lads, like the ones in Fomor. Liam, you saw how they were looking at you? In Fomor?"

If at all possible Liam's face, that was already a beet red, deepened in color. "No, wasn't paying attention."

"Think you broke a couple o' necks." Dolan agreed with Manton, dramatically mimicking how the Fomorans were turning to look at Liam, Dolan's boyish antics eliciting another round of friendly chuckles from the group.

"So what did you get?" Sidri asked, pointing at the package Liam had grasped with both hands.

Exposing the wristband won him whistles of approval from both Dolan and Manton.

"Nice! That must have set him back several silvers. Maybe a gold." Dolan said as he admired the workmanship of the gift.

Liam remained silent, afraid to think of what the wristband had actually cost Kael.

"All the more reason you gotta be the heartbreaker!" Manton informed Liam. "Learn to flirt with your admirers, let them take you out a couple of times, get some nice things, then dump them and move on to the next guy! Dol' and I can show you some tricks, if you like."

Nodding in agreement Dolan leaned against Manton like a man swooning with love playfully pinching his left cheek. "I can't see you anymore." Dolan crooned. "It's not you, it's me. I hope you understand."

Those comments created a roar of laughter from the group. For what man among them had not heard, or said, those words when, for one reason or another, a man wanted to escape from a lover?

"Two heartbreakers in my troupe happen to be more than I can handle!" Gorman chuckled as he separated the two friends.

"Now don't go listening to these two." Gorman said to Liam as he held onto Dolan and Manton like they were recalcitrant children about to be punished. "If they weren't so old they would still be trying to turn whoring into an art form."

The group, including Liam, chuckled as Dolan and Manton became dramatically exasperated over being called old, because the two men could not deny that they liked to sleep around.

"And you are one to talk about being old!" Manton said to Gorman, reminding the group leader that he had almost ten years on most of them. Twenty on Liam.

"Then your fathers should have raised you to have more respect for your elders!" Gorman laughed, not offended by the remark as he slapped the back of Manton's head.

The friendly barbs would have probably continued on for a while, but Yarrow, who had been looking over the railing at the ever growing lights on the horizon, pointed out that they were not far from Pallack.

"Looks like we will be there within the hour." Heath agreed.

"Well then, I think we've had our fun for now." Gorman said as he stepped over to Liam, tussling his hair in a fatherly way before draping an arm across the young man's shoulders.

"Master Karam is a fine young man and it's nice that he's sweet on you." Gorman said to Liam, saying all the things that Seb Cullen or his biological father, if he were alive, would have said to Liam if they had been around for this moment.

"I'm thinking you should go put Kael's gift in a safe place. Don't want to ruin it while we're working tonight."

"Sure, Gorman." Liam said as Gorman nudged the boy on to run his errand. "Be quick about it and meet us down in the storage bays!"

Liam raised a hand, acknowledging that he heard the squad leader, as he made his way towards the door that lead back into the cabin section.

The group continued to chuckle warmly as they pointed out the bounce in Liam's step, as only friends would notice upon seeing a companion finally showing signs of happiness, while several of them reminisced about their first crushes. Their first loves.

Gorman only nodded, listening to his men's chatter, as he gave a knowing wink to Heath. For Gorman thought he saw more than just happiness in Liam. More in the young man's stance as he walked away and could discern that Liam was standing a little taller, with his head held high. Something he had been trying to instill in Liam since he had joined Gorman's little band of men. Confidence.

And whether it was confidence or happiness over the moment, Liam's emotions were etched across his face and body for all to see.

Liam's friends could certainly see it.

Kael also saw it from his vantage point on the upper deck. Since he was being given the cold shoulder by Manus, something he had predicted to Liam, Kael had gone to the railing to watch Liam with his friends, wishing that he was among them to be a part of their merriment. For once, happy to see that as he left the deck, Liam hurried away without stooping his shoulders or lowering his head.

Manus saw it too, for he had felt Kael's presence turn away from him and his stony silence. Something Kael never would have done in the past because his friend would have tried his best to coax Manus back into a good humor.

So, curious as to why Kael had left his side, Manus also turned, walking to stand behind his friend, his jealousy and anger still seething within him, and watched as Liam strode away from Gorman and his men.

And by the lanterns that peppered the main deck, Manus saw everything that Gorman, Kael and the others could see in Liam. Manus, on the other hand, in a very un-princely manner, could only think of beating what he saw out of the sagart's adopted son, and leaving him beaten and bloodied, forgotten on the desert floor.

Chapter 11
The Airgrid Flats

The trip to Rathad should have been a routine trip for Gwyn and her crew. Fly into the city, deliver the cargo, get receive payment, higher out the Kasser for more deliveries, move on to the next destination. Routine.

But this trip did not turn out to be routine for Gwyn because she had invited Dar Banning, the younger of the two princes of Birr, along for this delivery.

The invitation to Dar Banning had been given for a number of reasons. For starters, one of her father's most trusted of captains, Emmis Daigh, had done one of the most untrustworthy of things and had kidnapped Banning because of an infatuation the captain still had with the prince's father, Dar Fionn.

The other reason she had invited the prince along was to annoy her father, the Lord Argus Berach. For her father had thrust upon her the responsibility of distracting Banning, and what better revenge to have on her father than to disappear with Banning.

Still, being the dutiful daughter, she had done the responsible thing and had left a note about her trip for him.

And now as they were leaving Rathad behind and flying across the sands to their next destination, Gwyn began to second guess her decision of having invited the prince on this voyage.

No, she had not become indecisive about her decision to invite the prince because he would be underfoot. Quite the contrary, Banning had gone out of his way to be very helpful. Her concern was at how quickly she had become infatuated with Banning.

Maybe charmed was a better word.

For she knew this immediately, knew as soon as she met the prince that day on Daigh's terrace, that she was attracted to Banning; a handsome man, only slightly taller than she, with golden brown hair, and eyes to match, who was very courteous, with a smile that she found quite disarming.

Gwyn also thought Banning felt the same way because, during those times they were together, he did not avoid her advances. He did not pull away on those occasions when she had held his hand, and he too seemed to enjoy their closeness.

Because of this Gwyn thought their stay in Rathad would have been fun.

At first it did seem like the trip was going to be pleasurable. But Banning had spotted his mother's lover, Solvo Caitlyn, in one of the cities upper taverns. A well -played coincidence by the gods which sent Banning scurrying back to the Kasser as soon as he could, where he stayed holed up for the rest of their sojourn.

Maybe hiding was a more appropriate word. At least that was Tor Micah's opinion of Banning's behavior. Her commander's ten year old son had latched onto the prince, as if he was befriending a boy his own age, and unabashedly questioned any adult who would listen to him as to why Banning was refusing to leave the lower decks and why he did not want to hang out with him or the others on the wharves or to go into market.

So Micah was frustrated and worried about his friend because no one, not even the prince himself, would explain why he had become so reclusive, the prince only making his way to the storage room at the end of the hallway from his cabin to help Lyle and then back to his cabin when he was done.

Frustration. A sentiment that Gwyn found she had in common with the precocious little boy. For Gwyn, who not only had to spend the next couple of days searching out merchants who needed their products moved to the west, and to have the Kasser replenished with necessary supplies, did not have the time to spend allaying Banning of his fears over the incident in Rathad.

If Gwyn thought she would have the opportunity to see Banning at dinner time than she was sadly mistaken because the prince had gotten either Mac or Lyle to make him his meals and to deliver it to his cabin.

So Gwyn cursed the gods for the games they were playing with her heart and with Banning's life, and kept her distance from him for the time being. For she too had to remind herself that they were in a Birrnian outpost, and that the safest place Banning could be was in his cabin. It was sad that Solvo Caitlyn's appearance had done a better job at detaining Banning than she ever could.

Not that restraining him is what she wanted, at least not that way, because Gwyn wanted to keep this likable man by her side, which meant that Gwyn did everything she could think of at finding work and getting the Kasser underway as quickly as possible, forgoing any enjoyment she or her crew might have found in Rathad, so that Banning would crawl off the deck he was living on.

Half a week went by, a painfully long time Gwyn felt, before she had her ship loaded and on its way to their next destination.

Once they were finally back out on the flats, it wasn't until the next day, a full day after Rathad had vanished on the horizon that Banning left the confines of his forced imprisonment to find Gwyn on her bridge.

Gwyn couldn't help but turn, her face lighting up with excitement, as several of her crewman greeted Banning by name as he went to stand by her.

"You were missed." Gwyn said, a smile warm and inviting, not caring who saw it, plastered on her face.

Banning looked away, feeling somewhat guilty at having become a recluse over the past few days, before turning to look at Gwyn, realizing that he too had missed being in her company.

Banning started to stutter an apology for avoiding everyone while in Rathad, but Gwyn placed a hand on Banning's bare arm, because he was once again wearing the hooded, sleeveless shirt that he had pulled off Mac in the upper district of Rathad, halting him in mid-sentence.

"I understand." Gwyn said, her hand remaining on Banning's forearm as her eyes ran over his body appreciatively. "The shirt looks good on you. More like one of my crew than a lord from Birr."

Banning blushed as a smile tugged at the corners of his lips, taking Gwyn's comment as a compliment, because, unknown to Gwyn, one of his guiltiest secrets was to have not been born into his family.

But Banning did not reveal this thought to Gwyn. "I kind of like the cut of this one and asked to keep it." Banning said as he ran a hand over the soft, somewhat worn fabric of Mac's shirt. "Also, Davis liked how mine fit Mac, so I saw it as an even trade for the two of us."

"Well, make sure not to cover your pretty face with this." Gwyn joked as she grabbed the shirt's hood and gave it a tug.

"Aye, aye, Captain."

The two remained silent for a moment, each secretly enjoying the closeness of the other, as sunlight reflected off the quartz filled sand, creating a kaleidoscope of color, before disappearing underneath the ship.

"How much time before we reach the city-states?" Banning finally asked, curious as to how much longer he had to spend with Gwyn, and as to when he would be returned to his own homeland.

Gwyn pursed her lips as she calculated the days of travel before telling Banning it would be almost two weeks before they reached the southern kingdom.

"But first we need to stop in Farro to deliver some goods we picked up while in Rathad. Farro's another waypoint not far from your family's province, Talamh Shar."

"I know of it." Banning said flatly, disappointed at being reminded of how close to home he really was. "Farro is considered part of the province, so part of Birr."

Gwyn knew this fact as well. "If you would like, once our deliveries are made, we can drop you off on the mainland. I'm sure your grandfather and uncles would be happy to see you."

Banning couldn't stop the sour looking frown that formed on his lips because his mor, his grandfather, the great Dar Seldon, would certainly be pleased to see him and to act as Banning's escort back to

Kinsale, bending his grandson's ear as to what compensation would be most beneficial and appropriate for their family, reminding Banning how they had sacrificed their kingdom for the benefit of Fionn's marriage to Riocard.

"If it's all the same to you, I'd like to remain on board." Banning said to Gwyn. "I feel that I am still indebted to you for your generosity and hospitality, and would like to continue working off what you have given me."

"If you insist, Milord." Gwyn replied to Banning, tilting slightly in a mock bow to the prince, grateful he had not taken her up on her offer, happy in knowing that she would be spending more time with this man.

***

So another full week went by as the Kasser traversed the Airgrid Flats on its way to Farro. A week of flight that proved to be uneventful and void of any contact from the outside world for Gwyn and her crew.

The ship's crew continued on with its routine of work while in flight, with Gwyn and Banning once again settling into some normalcy with each other, their unspoken desires just barely breaking through their relaxed demeanors as they went about their own duties, while spending their meal times together, oblivious to the rest of the crew that surrounded them in the dining hall.

How Banning wished that this could go on forever, he thought one afternoon while cleaning the day's work off of his hands, absentmindedly listening to Lyle chatter about some vendors of scrap materials in Farro where he could always find spare parts, at reasonable prices, for the weapons he maintained on the Kasser.

To not make landfall at all, Banning thought, willing to follow Gwyn wherever she would lead the Kasser and its small kingdom of men and women across the desolate flats of Gwer.

But as is the case with wishful thinking, Banning's fantasies of escaping the world around him scattered on the winds one evening as the Kasser flew into one of the many ports that surrounded the waypoint called Farro.

And this time, Banning chose to remain on board the Kasser when Gwyn and her entourage left the ship.

"Are you sure?" Gwyn asked, standing as close as she could to Banning without being in his arms, with Lucilla, Ormin Lhoyt and one crewman acting as guard, standing only feet away from the two, who were doing their best to ignore the captain's behavior with the prince. "We are only going to the dock master's office and to find out where the benefactors of these deliveries are located."

"I am sure." Banning said. The man was holding a broom in his hands for he had offered to help sweep the main deck clean of any sand or debris that had collected on it while in flight.

"I promise," Banning smiled broadly at Gwyn, only wishing to step in and kiss the lovely Argus Gwyn. "Not to go scurrying into my cabin until after your return."

Gwyn ran a hand through her thick black hair, tucking the tresses behind her pointed right ear as she returned Banning's smile. "Hopefully we can find time for at least one game of tables and a glass of wine before you do disappear for the night."

"I think that can be arranged Captain."

"Until tonight Master Dar." Gwyn said, tipping her head in a bow to Banning, allowing her hair to cascade back over her ear before turning to leave with the waiting members of her crew to go pay her berthing fees and to make arrangements to unload her cargo.

Sadly, all premise of unloading the Kasser being routine that following morning quickly faded as the first sled began to skim away, with its palette of Gwyn's goods, when the sled suddenly dropped several feet to the ground.

Gwyn, her crew, and the dock workers surrounding them, not only watched in astonishment as her delivery man and his sled faltered in its flight, but were astounded as any vessel that had been in the air, stalled and returned to the ground.

"What do you think is happening?" Davis, who had been working on the main deck, asked of Lhoyt, who was standing several feet away from him.

"The hell if I know!" The commander responded before rushing off of the ship to join the bystanders that were quickly gathering around the sled driver.

Gwyn, with Banning by her side, soon appeared on deck, with more of her crew in tow, as confusion and chaos began to slowly build out on the wooden walkways of the docks, as the din of voices from Farro's citizens flowed down from the city like a tide slowly washing the shore.

When the sled operator explained to Gwyn, who had hurried over to assess the problem that he could not reconnect with the lodestones,

Gwyn called over to her crew to begin unloading the sled and to secure the merchandise on Kasser's main deck.

"And that goes for you too, Banning!" Gwyn ordered as she watched the hesitancy of leaving the Kasser cloud the prince's face. Several Farrans shouldered by her, knocking Gwyn to one side, with Lhoyt and another man jumping in front of her to protect her from any other assaults. "A jaunt onto the wharf isn't going to hurt you and I need your help!" She shouted from between her men.

"Aye, aye, Captain." Banning responded, before doing as he was told, joining Davis, Lhoyt, and many others to haul the heavy crates back on board their ship.

The crew, even with some of them acting as buffers against the increase of men and women crowding the docks, had a hard time getting Gwyn's unpaid for merchandise back onto the Kasser, and spent most of the morning doing so.

Once the supplies were securely back on her ship, Gwyn, along with four men acting as bodyguards, headed back out into the fray on the wharf, bypassing the dock master who was under siege by captains from other vessels and his own workers, and made their way into the city so that she could hopefully find answers as to what was happening from the city's elders.

It wasn't until late in the evening, after a horn sounded, its baritone voice echoing throughout the docks and city, with soldiers of the Royal Guard marching down to the docks to announce a curfew was going into effect, forcing frightened and bemused men and women back onto their ships, that Gwyn returned to the Kasser. The woman and her men were grateful to have finally returned to the ship because they were exhausted and in foul moods at having to struggle through throngs of people who had filled the streets of the city.

"So what's the word, Captain?" Gwyn's second in command asked, for Lucilla had remained on deck with the crew who were acting as a defense against anyone who tried to board the ship without permission.

Gwyn and the men who had gone with her were passing a water skin around to slake their thirsts from the unexpected amount of time their trek had taken.

"Nothing good." Gwyn said, finally responding to Lucilla's query, before asking for something a little stronger to drink. "I couldn't even reach the city's leaders. A secretary and some of their soldiers sent us away because they were having a hard enough time dealing with their own population that had crowded the forum looking for their own questions to be answered."

One of the four men that had gone with her grumbled at how rude they were and should have shown more respect for the daughter of Lord Argus Berach.

"Now, now, Artum." Gwyn placed a hand on the shoulder of the man who had spoken out, hoping to calm the man before his anger and agitation spread through her crew. "We would be acting the same way if this was happening at home."

Home. Was this lack of flight, this broken link to Barra happening back home? Gwyn as well as Banning who, had a long staff in his hand and had been helping to guard the main deck, wondered if this calamity was occurring back in their homelands.

"And them down from the city are saying that all the gods have gone quiet!" One of her other crewman blurted out, interrupting Gwyn's thoughts.

"Aye, you heard true." Gwyn replied sourly, passing the skin of wine that was handed to her to Artum, for she had momentarily lost her taste for the drink as the sound of worried mumblings grew around her.

"What are your orders, Captain?" Lucilla asked.

Gwyn breathed heavily, hoping that all the frustration she felt over their predicament would evaporate with her exhale. But it had remained, just as she knew that it would.

"Not much we can do, so we'll do as we're told and stay here. Safest place we can be for the moment."

"So no shore leave for anyone. Only the guards on watch should be on the dock, and for now we'll need to ration the food to two meals a day. That goes for the children too." Gwyn said as she ticked off her instructions to Lucilla.

Gwyn sent the men milling around her back to their duties and gave Lu several more commands before informing her second she would be on the bridge. Although she was tired, Gwyn had decided to go back to work and sit with her steersmen who were still trying to get the ship to fly, and remain on the bridge for as long as she could stay awake.

"Captain, if I could have a minute of your time before you go?" Banning inquired before she could leave.

Gwyn smiled wanly, about to remind Banning that he should call her by her given name, when she recalled her churlishness towards him earlier that day, and found herself apologizing for what she now saw as bad behavior.

"I would have acted the same way." Banning said dismissing the apology as he leaned on the solid wooden staff that was as long as he was tall. "You did the right thing ordering me out there."

Although she was still embarrassed by how she had acted, Gwyn stopped from turning this into another flirtatious scenario, thanked the man and asked how she could help him.

"Well, I thought I could be of help to you." Here Banning fidgeted slightly, then offered to go up to the forum to see if he could find out what was going on.

"Maybe if they were to find out Aerin Riocard's foster-son was here they would be more forthcoming with information on what is happening. I also thought I might be able to get some of the Royal Guard to help defend the Kasser."

For once Gwyn questioned whether or not Banning knew that Emmis Daigh had abducted him over the foolishness of still pining for the man's father. But Gwyn only saw sincerity in Banning's face, especially when he seemed so adamant in avoiding his own people. No, Gwyn's own heart told her that Banning truly wanted to help them.

Gwyn all but forgot what she had just told herself about keeping some space between the two and placed a hand over Banning's own, the bones and knuckles of them feeling solid and warm to her touch as they grasped the staff.

"That is sweet of you." Sweet? Sweet! Did that word just come out of her mouth?

"Banning, I appreciate the thought." Gwyn started over, allowing her hand to trail over one of his wrists and forearm. "But, unless Barra is a personal friend of yours, I see no reason to ask your soldiers for help."

"I don't think you could even reach the forum with the way the streets being as crowded as they are." Gwyn continued as she turned their attention to Farro. Even though a curfew had been implemented, the sound of many voices, and the blaring horns of the Royal Guard continued to echo off the buildings, with the glow of lamplight and torches peppering the streets visible to them as people moved about the city in their search for answers to this catastrophe.

"For now you are safe here with us. But you will be the first person I come to when I am in need of a champion to get us out of this predicament." She winked.

"As you wish." Banning said, accepting Gwyn's assessment of the situation.

Knowing that she was anxious to return to her bridge, Gwyn unwillingly dropped her hand from Banning's arm, and took a step away from the man, suggesting that he could accompany her.

But Banning only smiled and dipped his head in a bow. "I think you might need me out here more than you do by your side. At least, let me have tonight to practice at being your champion."

Gwyn returned the bow, followed by a playful salute. "Aye, aye, Milord. Be safe Banning."

"And you too, Gwyn." The prince replied and remained where he was until he knew that Gwyn had made it safely into the Kasser's interior, before heading back over to where he had been stationed to guard the main deck, doing his best to ignore the worried shouts and rising panic from the town's people.

***

The next morning brought no change to the Kasser's predicament, leaving it and every other ship stranded in Farro's ports.

There was some movement on the wharves, but Gwyn thought it prudent to keep her crew together, as many of the other ship captains were doing, and ordered all of her men and women to remain on board the Kasser. The exception being herself and the small escort she took as far as the dock master's office to see if any more information had trickled down from the city.

The third day continued on as the last two, with everyone's emotions becoming strained over this tense and unusual situation.

***

"By all that's effen' holy!" Gwyn swore as she and her small band of crewman returned from their daily visit to the dock master.

Ormin Lhoyt was acting as shift leader for the main deck that morning and was quick to ask the captain what was wrong as her and her group boarded the ship.

But Gwyn ignored the question as she stomped back and forth on the deck, continuing to swear as she pulled her thoughts together.

"We've been informed that if Farro's state of affairs doesn't change, then our surplus supply of food will be taken possession of to be doled out to the citizens of the city to help maintain its stability." Gwyn said when she finally stopped in front of Lhoyt.

Farro was a large, isolated city out in the Airgrid Flats. By the grace of Murra, the island had plenty of cisterns and fresh water springs. But having very little useable land for agriculture, the majority of its food stuffs were shipped in from the mainland. So, without transportation to Birr, the people of Farro would slowly run out of food and starve.

"So they are going to just take what we have?" Lhoyt asked incredulously. His perception of Birr's royal family was already jaded, so he was not too surprised by what he saw as Birrnian treachery.

"Oh, they offered to pay us for what they would deem as surplus. But only a pittance for what it's worth!" Gwyn sneered. Not only would Gwyn and her crew lose the food they had been rationing off during this emergency, the Kasser would now have to buy back the food if the crew was to survive.

Gwyn was not about to let this happen, so she ordered several of her men to head down to the galley to help the cooks inventory what was in the larders and in the ship's storage bays.

"Let the cooks know we'll be handing the food out to the crew so they can stash it in their rooms for now." Gwyn informed the men. "I will be down to oversee the distribution as soon as I return from the bridge to let Commander Tor know what is happening. I'll have her send up more crewmen to double our watches on deck and around the storage bays."

"Captain, do you think," Lhoyt began before silently cursing, disgusted by what he was about to say. "Do you think we should ask Dar Banning for help? Maybe he can keep the soldiers off our backs and out of our pantries."

Gwyn frowned, somewhat sobered by the question. Although she had to admit that Lhoyt might be correct in asking for Banning to help protect them.

Of course Banning would do it. He had already offered to approach the city elders on their behalf.

But what would happen after he made it known to his people that one of their princes was in their city? Would they allow him to stay on the Kasser or take him up into the city where the Royal Guard could keep him safe? Gwyn already knew the answer to that outcome.

What would happen once he was gone? Chances were the Guard would still confiscate what they deemed as excess food in their pantries.

"No." Gwyn dragged out the word as if she was trying to convince even herself of her own decision as she ran her hands through her hair, pulling her black locks tight against the back of her neck as she looked up to the sky, hoping for a better answer.

"He so much wants to be a part of this crew and to forget where he has come from." Gwyn continued as she met Lhoyt's gaze. "Leave him be for now and we'll use him as a wild card if necessary."

"As you wish, Captain." Lhoyt replied as Gwyn excused herself so that she could head to the bridge.

A wild card? Is that what she thought of Banning as she made her way down the main corridor of her ship. Some token to be played in case of an emergency?

Gwyn chewed on the nail of her right thumb, lost in thought, as she made her way to the bridge. Gwyn found herself caring for the man, but she knew that if they were backed into a corner she would have to sacrifice this one man for the rest of her people.

A thought that did not sit well or make Gwyn feel very proud of herself.

Fortunately the captain of the Kasser never had to find out what her decision would have been because life suddenly returned to normal the next day.

On that fourth day, where the steersmen had been vigilant in remaining at their posts, ships within the port and some of those that had been stranded out on the flats within sight of the city, began to rise off of the ground, amid the cheering and shouts of jubilation from the Gwerin, who were happy to be able to fly once again.

The sagarts and sagarttas of the city were also grateful to feel the comforting presence of their gods returning to their temples with the voices of Cavanna, Maat, Aodhagan and the others whispering words of reassurance that they would remain by the side of their people. All had returned, save for Barra, whose voice had remained silent.

And when the steersmen, who were at time called Barra's Ferryman, we're asked about this oddity, they could only concur with Barra's priests, saying that something seemed different about their connections with the lodestones.

Although many were concerned at the disappearance of Barra, with her people spreading speculations as to the gods silence throughout the Kasser, Gwyn had come here for a purpose; to deliver goods and make some money. And now she felt it was imperative to finish those transactions and to be on her way to Lahunne.

But Sioda, the god of luck, fortunes and chance, and the god Gwyn worshipped, had decided to play his own hand in these events, leaving Gwyn frustrated and angry that two of the buyers had backed out of their sales. The men more concerned about holding onto their money while this crisis settled, not too worried they were leaving Gwyn with a ship full of product she could not unload.

"Damn those bastards!" Gwyn said to Lucilla, adding a few more expletives as they made their way to their third and final destination. "Our broker in Rathad will hear about this outrage!"

"And log their family and business names. I want to make sure we increase their docking fees when we get back to Inchinver."

Lucilla reassured her captain that all would be recorded for their return as they walked the cobbled somewhat crowded streets of Farro.

Their third buyer was only of a slightly better disposition to deal with than the other two merchants. Slightly better because the woman was now trying to haggle over the shipment of dried and candied fruits she had ordered. The fruits being another reason Gwyn had not wanted the Royal Guard snooping through the Kasser's stores, afraid that she would have lost the cargo and the money owed to her, which is what Gwyn saw happen as soon as the meeting began.

"I am sorry Mistress," Gwyn said as she shifted in her seat from across the merchant, doing her best to hide her annoyance and anger as another transaction was about to sour. "But that price is quite unacceptable."

The merchant smiled sympathetically, a look that was not pleasing on her angular face, while toying with one of several bejeweled rings on her fingers.

"I quite understand your predicament Captain." The woman replied from across her desk. "But these are trying times and I cannot see a demand for sweetmeats over the upcoming weeks. Why, it might be months before life returns to normal and I see customers willing to frequent my shops."

"But to now offer forty percent of what you originally offered is laughable. It is insulting." Gwyn replied.

The woman only shrugged, her smile tightening into a thin line so it was almost snake like in appearance. "That is my best offer."

This bantering between the two of them could have gone on forever. But Gwyn was too tired to deal with this cow of a woman and decided to leave. Standing, Gwyn let the merchant know once more that she would sooner hold onto the cargo than give it away.

Turning to Lu, Gwyn gave the woman a quick wink, a cue for a plan they had concocted on the way here.

"You know," Gwyn said, drawing out the words in a slightly sing song voice, as if she just had an idea. "When we get back to the docks, why don't we find that nice general and see if they could use the food."

Lucilla nodded. "As you wish M'lady."

"Lady?" The merchant couldn't help but chuckle, thinking how cute and naive the commander, who was older than her captain, must be to refer to the young captain in such a fashion.

"Yes." Lucilla replied, doing her best to keep a sneer off of her face that would have matched the merchant's. "This is Lady Argus Gwyn. Daughter to the ruler of Iniscarn."

Confusion, then comprehension dawned on the merchant's face as she realized who was standing before her. For many in Farro knew of the princess captain, but few had ever met her, nor had known who she was in their dealings with Gwyn.

An arrangement Gwyn was very happy with. Until now.

"I beg pardon Mistress Argus." The merchant stuttered as she also stood. "If I had known. . ."

"No worries Madam." Gwyn replied as she and Lucilla made for the room's door. "Thank you for your time, but we will be on our way."

"But, but, my offer!" The merchant squeaked, her ringed fingers making dull clinking sounds as her hands grasped the edge of the desk.

"Was quite unacceptable." Gwyn finished as she laid a hand on the doorknob.

"No! My original offer!" The merchant countered out of fear of offending the girl's father, which is what Gwyn had hoped, and explained she had been shortsighted with her investments and now thought the people, who were quite resilient, would bounce back quickly from the ordeal of the past several days.

Gwyn's hand left the doorknob. "Are you sure?" She asked as coyly as she possibly could. "I would hate to leave you financially strapped in this time of uncertainty."

"Do not worry Milady. The fruits have come from a reputable market in Rathad and should be well preserved. And if there is a downturn in the market, I am sure it will be temporary."

"And please," The merchant said as she fumbled with a key to open a drawer in her desk. "Let me pay you now for your troubles."

"If you insist." Gwyn replied as she returned to stand across from the merchant and counted the gold pieces that were given in payment for her services.

"And rest assured Madam," Gwyn said as she pocketed the money. "I want the product off of my ship as much as you want it, so we will work tirelessly to make sure you get the fruit as soon as possible."

"Of course Milady. One could only expect integrity and efficiency from the daughter of Lord Argus Berach."

Once the transaction was completed, Gwyn and Lucilla left the merchant's office so they could get the purchased items ready for delivery.

The two women couldn't help but giggle like little girls over their game and the good fortune at how the scenario had played out in their favor.

"Did you see her face?" Lucilla laughed as they made their way back to the Kasser. "I thought she was going to start crying when she realized who you were."

Gwyn only chuckled along with her second in command for she was not happy she had to use her father's name to tip the scales of trade in her favor. As a matter of fact, she had gone out of her way to have some anonymity when it came to being the successor to Iniscarn while on these trips.

"It's a shame we didn't think of this earlier." Lucilla continued. "Should we go back to the other two merchants and give it a try?"

Gwyn waved her hand in the negative, just wanting to be done with them.

"Forget about them." Gwyn said as they turned onto the street that would lead them to the docks. "We have too much to do and we are behind schedule. We should have left Farro days ago."

"Maybe my uncle can help us unload the surplus when we reach Lahunne." Gwyn's uncle, her father's brother, Argus Rafe, had been a successful merchant in his own right, and not wanting to share Iniscarn or live his life in the shadow of his brother, had struck out on his own and married into one of the wealthiest families in Lahunne. "I'm sure we'll recoup our money once we reach him."

Lucilla accepted Gwyn's word as being final. But she couldn't help but be disappointed that their bonuses would probably be meager from this trip.

The two were going over the best way to unload the preserved fruits as quickly as possible, when they realized that there were more and more people gathering around them the closer they got to port. And that the level of noise, the sound of men and women trying to talk over one another, was getting louder as well.

"What do you think is going on?" Lucilla asked as a man, with several boys of varying ages, all holding the hand of the other, creating a small line, bumped into the commander and apologized before sliding by them.

"Damned if I know." Gwyn replied as they picked up their pace when they realized the rush of Farrans all seemed to be heading towards the port.

When they were within eyesight of the entrance to the port, Lucilla couldn't help but whistle in surprise at the crush of people surrounding it. Movement was almost non-existent as the women could only get as far as the outer group of people, the shouts of adult voices and the crying of the young filling the air when they noticed the large gates that allowed access to the port itself were closed.

"This isn't good!" Gwyn shouted so that Lucilla could hear her over the cacophony of men and women surrounding them. As they moved about the undulating wall of bodies, Gwyn could only wonder if the rest of her people were safe on board the Kasser. If the Kasser was safe at all.

"Over there!" Lucilla shouted in turn, recognizing one of the guards of the watch who seemed to be trying to calm a young couple with their child. "He was one of the men who let us out this morning!"

Grasping Gwyn's hand so they wouldn't get separated, Lucilla did her best to gently make a path through the crowd to the soldier.

Fortunately the man also recognized Lucilla and Gwyn when they called out to him and beckoned them over.

"What has happened? Have the ships stopped working again?" Gwyn asked the man as he begged the couple for a moment to talk to them.

"No Captain! And that's the problem." The man said as he ran the back of his hand across his brow to clear the perspiration away. "All these people want off of Farro and to be safely on the mainland if the ships do falter!"

That made sense, Gwyn thought, especially for a community with limited resources. If these people were asked to abandon their city, it would take weeks to cross the flats; a trek to the mainland that Gwyn couldn't see many of these people making and surviving.

Gwyn, the soldier and Lucilla continued to talk, with Gwyn asking after the safety of her ship and crew, and if they could be escorted into the port, when one of the two men standing next to them tapped her on the shoulder.

"Excuse me. Did he call you captain? Of one of the barges in port?" The man asked while his partner, who was holding their son, stepped in closer as a crush of people pushed by them.

"Yes."

"We're looking to book passage." The man said with a tone of anxiousness to his voice. "To Canno. If you're heading that way."

Gwyn hesitated. "I'm sorry, but I only haul supplies and. . ."

"We have gold!" The other man blurted out as he hefted his boy into a more comfortable position. "We can pay for our passage!"

Gwyn looked at Lucilla, who gave her captain that look of, we would be stupid not to take their money, and said, "Several of the storage bays will soon be empty and we can double up the crew in their cabins for a couple of days. And Canno is just south of here."

"Can you pay now?"

The men didn't have to think about their answer and said that they could.

"Have you brought your own food?" Gwyn asked as she realized she did not even know how she would feed and influx of people onto the Kasser.

The two men frowned and looked at each other before telling Gwyn they had not, the man who was holding their son once again shifting the boy into a more comfortable position. The boy, too young to comprehend what was passing among the adults, and with a thumb jammed into his mouth, only watched with wide eyed wonder at the spectacle that was playing out around him.

"Five more silver will get you food for the voyage." Gwyn offered.

The couple readily accepted the terms and handed Gwyn the payment of two gold, five silver.

"Now to get us to the ship." Gwyn said as she instructed Lucilla to keep the family between them and described what the Kasser looked like to the men, and where it was berthed, just in case they did get separated.

"That's if they even let us through the gate." One of the men said, hoping they hadn't been careless in giving Gwyn their money.

Gwyn asked the soldier if there would be any problems getting onto the docks and he informed her that the small portcullis on the side of the main gate was still open so they could control the people coming onto the wharf.

"Think there are already men and women from the ships on the other side of the gate selling passage to the mainland for anyone who can pay." The man said as he grasped Gwyn by the forearm to steady her as the crowd suddenly surged towards them.

"Can you get us in a little quicker?" Gwyn asked the soldier, squeezing one of the couple's gold coins into the man's hand.

The soldier stuttered at what he was given, for it was more money than he had ever seen at one time and tried to give it back to Gwyn, who refused its return.

"Just get us inside!" Gwyn repeated and nodded for him to proceed as she grasped the man's hand so she would not lose him.

Pocketing the money with his free hand, the soldier did as he was told and lead the group past another of his comrades as they made their way towards the small side gate. And seeing this as a chance opportunity, Gwyn offered the man more money if he could steer more passengers their way.

"I'm going to leave Lucilla at the dock's entrance. Can you send people her way for us? More like this couple and not like that?" Pointing, Gwyn indicated a woman who had begun screaming at another woman in front of her, accusing the woman and her family of cutting her in line.

"I'll do my best for ya, Captain."

"That's all I can ask for." Gwyn smiled as the man pushed through the ever tightening crowd of people.

***

The distance to the wall from where they had met the soldier should have taken them just a moment to traverse, but the trek took almost half an hour.

Once they were through the portcullis, the soldier hurriedly excused himself so he could get back to his station, nodding as Gwyn reminded him about helping them to fill her ship.

Gwyn was going over some last minute instructions with Lucilla, the small family waiting patiently off to one side for her, relieved to be in a less crowded space, when the commander reminded her of one important piece of information.

"How do you think the prince will react to the news of Birrnians boarding the ship?" Lucilla asked.

Gwyn didn't need to be reminded of Banning, nor of how he had arrived on Iniscarn and why he was now aboard her ship as her guest. Nor did Gwyn know how he might react to finding people from his own kingdom now boarding the Kasser as passengers.

"I don't know!" Gwyn shot back as she left Lucilla to guide the men to her ship. "Just you worry about gathering some passengers! I'll get some crew to help you shortly and I'll think of a way to handle Banning!"

After sending some men to help Lucilla collect and guide anyone willing to pay for a trip to the mainland, Gwyn sought out Banning, finding him in the lower bays already helping her men and women to unload the crates of fruit for their only paying customer.

Any fears Gwyn had were soon quelled when the conversation went a lot better than she would have thought.

"I understand." Banning huffed, more grateful for the break from his labor than having to listen to what Gwyn had to say.

"Do you want me to move in with some of your men?" the prince asked, understanding where this conversation was heading, as he did his best to stick a rag under the leather guards protecting his forearms from getting scraped by the wooden boxes, as he tried to soak up the sweat that was gathering under them.

"If you don't mind." Gwyn watched as Banning then took the rag to wipe his sweat covered face, before retying a long strip of fabric he was using as a cord to keep his long hair in a ponytail. Gwyn's twitched as she refrained from offering to help him with fixing his hair.

"Lyle's still up in the storage lockers. I'll send word to him to see if he or someone else can grab my belongings and move them into the room he's sharing with Mac and Davis."

Gwyn had to head back up to the main deck to oversee the influx of people, so she let Banning know she would talk to Lyle about gathering his things.

"Appreciate it." Banning said as he went back to help the man waiting for him. "I'll talk to you later, Captain." Banning gave Gwyn an affectionate smile before he went back to work with Gwyn's crewman.

So Gwyn went on her way, knowing that her crew would work efficiently in unloading the candied fruits while Lucilla and her team were working diligently on the docks as they signed up over forty passengers by mid-afternoon.

And with the crowds steadily increasing within the port as the day wore on, and with word spreading that this was happening at all of the wharves surrounding Farro, Gwyn decided to forgo taking on any more passengers and left for the mainland that evening.

Of course, as soon as they left port, Gwyn began to regret agreeing to haul these people to Birr. For as soon as they were out on the flats the Farrans began to dog her every footstep, asking the most annoying questions.

"Captain! When will we reach the mainland?"

"Captain! Why are all the larders bolted and why are the cooks keeping us out of your kitchens?"

"We are already stopping in Burne! Why not just fly us to Seruth?"

"I was not expecting myself, nor my children to sleep in a cargo hold! Can you make your crew give up their beds for us?"

"Captain?"

"Captain!"

If Gwyn knew how to make her ship fly faster she would. But as it was, she was making sure her steersman switched positions as quickly as possible, and flying the ship as fast as they could without harming anyone or damaging the Kasser.

The badgering had gone on for two days. With the only breaks from the Farrans being while she was either on the bridge or in her cabin. Which is where she was heading after extricating herself from an elderly man who wanted to know when they would make the mainland

(Gwyn stopped counting how many times this question was asked) when Gwyn found another man approaching her.

"What now!" Gwyn thought irritably, too tired to listen to someone else's complaints or suggestions as to how she should run her ship, only pulling up short when she realized that it was Banning walking her way.

"Your hair!" Gwyn blurted out, for that was one of the drastic changes in Banning that had made her assume a stranger was in the corridor with her.

Gone were the shoulder length blondish brown locks of hair that Gwyn had grown accustomed to seeing on the prince.

"Do you like?" Banning smiled broadly as he ran a hand through his new short, close cropped hair, explaining how he had Davis chop it for him.

"I'm not sure." Gwyn replied as Banning lowered his head so she too could run her fingers through the hair that was left on his scalp.

"And what did he use to cut it? Sheering scissors?" Gwyn tugged on some strands that stood up in odd places on Banning's head. The irregular look made it look like Banning had cut his hair himself. And without a mirror.

"Think he used a small dagger." Banning tugged at another longish tuft just behind his left ear.

"And this is new!" Gwyn's hand moved down to touch the plaid fabric wrapped around Banning's neck.

"One of your men let me borrow it."

Banning lifted the long tubular scarf over his head, turning the worn and hand repaired fabric into a cowl. An article of clothing her men and women used while working on the main deck if the Kasser was moving so that the sand would not scrape their faces or sting their eyes. There were even the traditional stones attached by braided chords to keep the cowl from blowing off one's head.

"You have dirt on your face." Gwyn noticed the grime on one of Banning's cheeks when he pulled the scarf down. But the man pulled away when Gwyn went to clean it.

"It's part of the look." Banning chuckled and explained how the majority of the passengers looked similar to him; lightly tanned skin with blond to light brown hair. "My hair looks darker cut this way and I now look like one of your men rather than someone from my father's province."

"And call me Ban. Banning is a very uncommon name and I don't want to remind these people that they have a prince by that name. But Ban can be short for anything."

"Including just Ban!" Gwyn giggled.

Banning laughed along with Gwyn. "I guess. Just Ban."

"Well, just Ban, you seem to have thought of everything."

Banning's smile broadened, threatening to split his face, and he puffed out his chest in mock pride at his ingenuity, and was about to thank Gwyn for the compliment when the princess jumped at him.

Caught off guard, Banning wrapped his hands around Gwyn's waist, just as she threw her own hands around his neck and found himself returning a kiss as Gwyn's lips touched his.

But the kiss turned out to be short lived as a woman's voice called out from behind Banning.

"Captain?" The woman called out, her tone slightly shrill as she stood behind Banning. "A moment of your time?"

Gwyn sighed disappointingly as she pulled out of the kiss, but not Banning's embrace, to acknowledge the woman. "I'm a little busy."

"I can see that!" The woman drawled as she folded her hands over her bosom and tried to catch Banning's eye, who had turned his head to cough, Banning doing his best to avoid the passenger's gaze.

"I've already told you Mistress Cymru that taking you and your family to Seruth is out of the question."

"I am willing to throw in another gold piece for your troubles."

"Mistress, I am behind schedule and we are expected in Lahunne. So my answer is still no." With that, Gwyn reached up to turn Banning's face her way so she could press her lips against his.

When Mistress Cymru began to protest, Gwyn shooed her away with her right hand.

Insulted by the gesture, the woman stormed away in a huff, cursing under her breath how she had booked passage on a ship run by an idiot.

The two remained as they were until Gwyn was sure the woman had left the vicinity and parted from Banning to catch her breath.

"What was that?" Banning asked huskily, not unhappy that kiss had happened.

"I was afraid that if you spoke your accent would give you away as Birrnian." Gwyn replied as she made another advance towards him.

"Gwyn." Banning's soft plea stopped her just as quickly as if he were going to keep her away with his own hands. "This isn't right."

Gwyn frowned. "Don't you want this? I thought you felt the same as I."

"I do." Banning noticed some of the dirt from his face had made it onto Gwyn's and brought his hand up to remove it from her soft cheek. "But I'm going to have to leave soon. My family. . ."

"Are you leaving in Burne? In Carno?" Gwyn blurted out, not wanting to hear about the arrangements his fathers had made for him nor of his familial duties.

"Only if you want me to."

"I want you to stay." Gwyn said as she stepped closer and kissed him once again. "I'll take you home once we leave Lahunne. If that is what you want."

Banning sighed as he twirled some of Gwyn's long black hair between his fingers. "It's not what I want, but what I have to do."

"I know." Resting her head on his shoulder, Gwyn and Banning embraced each other before she kissed him once more.

And before things became too maudlin, Gwyn gave him another kiss. "But I can do my best, Master Ban, to make sure that you miss me for a long time."

Banning smiled. "Captain, I think you've already accomplished that."

Gwyn's smile matched Banning's. "I was on my way to my cabins. Walk with me."

Banning hesitated before throwing a thumb over his shoulder from the direction he had come. "I was on an errand for Commander Ormin and. . ."

"Pish!" Gwyn said sarcastically and waved a hand in the air, negating whatever else Banning was about to say. "Ban, wouldn't you say my safety around these Farrans is more of a concern than whatever Lhoyt had you doing?"

"Yes, Captain." Banning chuckled.

"Then walk with me."

"Aye, Captain!"

Quietly, the two continued in the direction of Gwyn's rooms. But the silence didn't last long as the captain gave Banning a sideways look and reached up to tug on another of the longish strands of his massacred hair.

"You really should get this fixed."

"That bad?"

"Very!" Gwyn laughed. "I still can't believe you let Davis cut your hair. We've seen how he cuts his meat."

Banning laughed along with Gwyn, agreeing that Davis might not have been the best of choices as barber.

And looking into those deep green, sparkling eyes while the two enjoyed this moment alone, the prince could almost forget about returning home to a life of servitude to his family.

Almost.

Chapter 12
The Lahunne City Sates

When they arrived in Burne to let some of the Farrans debark, Gwyn withheld from again asking Banning if he wanted to leave her company so that he could return home.

Banning chose to remain on the Kasser.

When they arrived in Carno to let the remaining passengers disembark in the Birrnian city, Gwyn was fortunate to find a merchant willing to buy some of the goods rejected by their original buyers in Farro.

"Captain, do you think this is wise?" Ormin Lhoyt asked Gwyn on their second day in Carno as the two watched a crew of men and woman from the Kasser on Carno's docks loading new supplies onto the ship.

Banning made up one of their number, his head covered with the cowl borrowed from a friend.

Gwyn only shrugged as she watched the group work. "Lhoyt, I think you are worrying over nothing."

"But Captain! He could escape at any moment! What would Captain Emmis or your father think?"

"I'm sure they would be quite happy that we had finally unloaded the prince back on his own countrymen!" Gwyn snapped. "Now stop your belly aching over Dar Banning or you will be the one dumped in Carno!"

"Aye, Captain." Lhoyt mumbled, cowed by Gwyn's threat, yet still leery that Banning might yet turn on them all.

And when the Kasser left that evening on its last leg of its journey, Banning remained on board.

Fortunately the rest of the trip proved uneventful while the Kasser hugged the Birrnian coast for the next couple of days before turning west, spending almost another week on the Airgrid Flats before they reached the city states of Lahunne.

Lahunne, a group of islands clustered tightly together in one of the far corners of Gwer, was a matriarchal society where each city and its surrounding villages ran as if each was a sovereign country. The exception to their independence being its military in which a united establishment governed by the elders of the ruling families for the betterment of all and their little kingdoms.

Knowing that Banning had never been this far from home, Gwyn had her ship take its time weaving through the islands as the Kasser made its way to Glain, the largest island in the area, and to Auvereen, the unofficial capitol of Lahunne.

"My uncle is married to Soya Alayna, the ruler of Auvereen, and we'll find him there." Gwyn explained while she and Banning stood at the railing of the main deck, watching another island disappear behind them.

"Okay. But what are they doing?" Some movement had caught Banning's eye and the prince was surprised to see a group of women and men crossing the flats with a fair amount of pack animals.

"All the islands are within a day or two of each other so you can find caravans traversing the flats on a regular basis."

"The Lahunnans can be a frugal people." Gwyn continued to explain as the two of them waved to the travelers as the Kasser passed close enough to cast a shadow over the group below them. "The smaller families would sooner travel this way than to pay to ship cargo with a larger family that might have barges."

"Isn't it dangerous?" Banning asked.

"As dangerous as anything else in the world. But there are enough patrols to keep the area safe. Ahh, finally. We're here!"

Banning looked to the prow of the ship where Gwyn was pointing at a city that the Kasser was now approaching.

"It looks big." Banning couldn't help but notice how Auvereen spread away from its jagged coast. This metropolis of the west surrounded by a vast array of walls of varying height that not only hugged the lower levels of the city, but meandered along the coastline in either direction away from Auvereen.

"The city is big, but looks can be deceiving." Gwyn then explained how the walls running north and south of the city were built by the local clans to protect farmland and their personal property.

"And the structure in that southern part of the wall, the one that looks like a fortification. Well that is a home for one of the clan families."

Banning whistled his appreciation for what the Lahunnans had built here. "And where does clan Soya reside?"

"Wherever it wants!" Gwyn laughed.

"That upper ring of structures you can see on your left? Well those blocks of the city are actually the Soya compound. And Soya Alayna has family and close relations running every aspect of Auvereen."

"Sounds like your uncle married well." Banning replied.

Watching one of her crewman raise the colors of Soya, alongside those of Iniscarn, for being related to Argus Rafe gave Gwyn some liberty of movement around Auvereen, Gwyn explained how the Lahunnans still followed traditions far older than the ones practiced in her own land.

"The people here still worship Cavanna as Mothair Ahn Chead, the First Mother, and follow those first teachings handed down by her."

"So my uncle is only one of about a dozen men married to Soya Alayna."

Banning made a joke about the size of the Soya's bed, eliciting a head shake from Gwyn over his boyish remark, before she continued with his education.

"So, it's the woman who chooses her mates. And a marriage isn't always for love."

"Sometimes the marriage will be for business, like my uncle's had been. Alayna had heard that my uncle had arrived in Auvereen to start a shipping company and that he was brother to Argus Berach. So she proposed marriage to him before he was approached by one of the other clans."

"Now, my uncle maintains Alayna's fleet of barges, and the Soya gets first pick of any product she wants from Iniscarn."

"Sounds like it works for everybody." Banning said while the Kasser slowed as the area around them became congested with an assortment of vessels flying about them. But what he really thought was how sad it was that the wedding arrangements here were so similar to the ones he would have to make.

"Of course, there are ways to annul the marriages." Gwyn continued, oblivious to Banning's change in mood. "But they can be quite scandalous, especially if it is the man who is looking to dissolve the contract."

"Really?" Banning asked, intrigued by what Gwyn would think of as scandalous.

But his companion never explained this aspect of Lahunnan society as the Kasser slowed its flight even more as the ship began to move through a maze of platforms and outlying docks.

"These outer docks are for the smaller houses and Lahunne's military." Gwyn moved closer to Banning so that their bodies touched while she pointed out a landmark with her right hand. "We'll be making for the Soya's walled port."

But that's as far as they were able to go, as they were being turned away by a small skiff whose signaling informed them that all the Soya's berths were full.

"By all that's," Gwyn cursed before excusing herself, her left hand squeezing Banning's right, so that she could join her own man that was returning the skiff's call.

With Gwyn from his side, Banning's excitement over this adventure began to wane. Suddenly feeling alone and realizing how far from his own world that he was, Banning left his solitary vigil at the railing to seek out Mac and Davis in the hopes of finding a distraction for his depression.

Banning was right to seek out the couple, who were with Lyle and several other men towards the stern of the Kasser's main deck. Who could remain in a funk when having to deal with the sophomoric humor of Davis?

Not only did Banning's dark mood dissipate quickly, the Kasser began to move once again, slowly shifting towards the walls surrounding the port so as to be out of the way of any other traffics hat had been trying to skirt about them.

"Have you been here before?" Banning asked Lyle as they watched several vessels leave the port, moving in a tight cluster as they headed north.

"We make the trip once or twice a year." Lyle said as he came to stand closer to the prince. "Auvereen's an old city and worth exploring if the captain gives us leave. Walking the streets of Auvereen is like walking back into time."

Banning only nodded, finding the comment odd, for it was rare to find a city that had not been around for centuries, if not millennia.

"Looks like we've got company." Mac pointed out as a small craft made its way to dock with the Kasser.

A man with two guards, both female, stepped off the craft before it pulled away to hover alongside Gwyn's ship.

Davis whistled appreciatively. "Well I'll be! That's the captain's uncle."

"You sure?" Banning asked, his question answered by Davis and by the man himself, who hugged Gwyn in a hearty embrace.

"You're wanted." Lyle pointed out to Banning for Gwyn was now waving him over to join her.

Banning hesitated for a moment realizing at how much of a frump he must look before resigning himself to the fact that nothing could be done about it now and walked over to join the family in its reunion.

"Uncle," Gwyn said, a smile covering her face, her cheeks rosy with joy, as she reached out to grasp Banning's hand and pull him close, her uncle raised an inquisitive eyebrow at the gesture. "This is Ban, Dar Banning, the younger prince of Birr. Banning, this is my uncle, Soya Rafe."

"At your service." Rafe smiled politely as he bowed.

"And yours Milord." Banning repeated the bow.

His smile not leaving his lips, Soya Rafe asked his niece if they were ready to head into port.

"Just give the word." Gwyn replied.

Nodding to one of his guards, the woman walked over to the railing and waved her sword, its metallic surface reflecting brightly in the sun, a signal for their craft to head back into port.

As it did so, a signal flared from Rafe's ship for the Kasser to follow it into the port as well.

Moving past the towers flanking the entrance into Auvereen's port, Rafe apologized for the inconvenience of momentarily keeping them out.

"We had an incident about a week ago where all of our ships stopped flying for three days."

"That happened about the same time to us in Farro and in the towns we stopped at in Birr." Gwyn interjected. "Isn't that right Banning?"

Banning agreed with Gwyn's assessment of what had happened, but otherwise remained silent, listening to the two banter, comparing notes on the unusual circumstances, while inspecting the man before him.

Although Gwyn had said that the majority of Lahunnans were frugal, Soya Rafe seemed to have taken particular care in his appearance. The man wore a raw silk scarf, of a deep dark blue that was wrapped loosely several times around his neck. And his clothing, in shades of textured tans was of a cut and color to accentuate his tall, muscular form, enhancing the richness of his tanned skin and the blue of the scarf. Other than the scarf, the only other adornment Rafe wore was a brooch made of silver that had a warm antiqued appearance because of age. The object was also shaped like a rounded, many dimpled, five pointed star.

Then there was Rafe's hair; cut to fall just below his ears and of a black as deep as his niece's. A black so rich and shiny that it too reflected some of the blue from the scarf he wore.

Watching the wind catch Rafe's black locks, forcing the man to run a hand through it so as to put it back into place, Banning raised a dirtied hand to his own scalp, now regretting his brashness at chopping his own hair.

Catching Banning's movement, Rafe smiled at the prince, who only blushed in embarrassment at his own cloddish appearance.

"Banning it looks like you have been roughing it for a little too long." Rafe warmly said, purposely dropping the prince's title in the hopes of being on friendlier terms with him. "The Soya lets me keep a small villa not far from the docks. Comes in handy when we are busy, or during these questionable times. You are most welcome to stay with me and refresh yourself."

"Thank you Milord. I'll see if I can fit in some time with the work your niece has me doing on the Kasser."

Rafe joked with Gwyn about being a heavy handed slave driver and asked her how long they would be staying.

Gwyn clicked her tongue and looked at Banning for a response.

But watching Gwyn and her uncle interact only brought on a wave of homesickness and a longing for his own father.

"I should be getting back to my family." Banning said as he looked at Gwyn. "Do you mind? That we leave as soon as your business is done here?" Banning swallowed hard as he watched joy of seeing her uncle, fade from Gwyn's eyes.

"Uhh, sure." Gwyn forced a smile back on her face as she tried to hide her disappointment over Banning's remark. "Uncle, I, uhh, I have some product I need to sell and I can make some deliveries for you. If that won't be too much of a delay for you Banning?"

"No, not at all." He choked.

Poor things, Rafe thought, seeing that there was some complication to their relationship. Hopefully Gwyn would be able to enlighten him about it when they had some time to be alone. But for now though, nothing was going to dampen his mood at seeing his brother's daughter and stepped between the two, throwing an arm over each of their shoulders.

"Now, now!" Rafe laughed. "Docking. Unloading the Kasser. Loading it again. All that work will take four, maybe five days to get done. So I insist that the two of you pull yourselves away from whatever you have going on and spend your evenings with me."

Gwyn nodded, looking up at her uncle, a smile creeping back onto her face with Banning also acquiescing to the proposition.

"Good!" Rafe said jovially, patting both of their backs.

"And here is your berth. I am sorry it's so far out but," Rafe dropped his arm from Banning and guiding Gwyn further along the deck to explain docking procedures, something she was quite familiar with, the two left Banning alone to mull over his thoughts.

***

That night while staying in Rafe's villa, Banning soaked in a hot tub of water, scrubbing off over a week's worth of oil and dirt off when Banning finally found himself beginning to relax.

The clothing laid out on the bed in the room he was using also helped to sooth his mood. All were of soft cotton and ranged in color from pants of a warm tan to a shirt dyed a rich reddish brown.

Banning was trying to fix his hair, a futile effort at best with it being so short, and wondering where his old clothing had gone, hoping that Mac's borrowed shirt had not been discarded out as garbage, when a knock sounded on the bedroom door.

"Enter!"

"If you are refreshed Milord, Master Soya requests your presence in the salon." The manservant, a Lahunnan about Banning's age, said upon entering the room.

"Of course." Banning had taken his signet ring off of the leather chord that had been keeping it secured around his neck for the voyage and placed it on his finger. He had decided that being in such an esteemed household warranted it to once again be worn. "I just need my shoes and I will be ready to go."

The man smiled at Banning's comment. "It is Master Soya's custom to go barefooted while staying here. While your own garments are being laundered he wishes for you to enjoy the luxury as well."

"Then please, lead on."

Leaving the bedroom, the man guided Banning along a hallway paved in a sand colored marble, down to the main floor and across a large portico that surrounded a lawn that surrounded a pond. Both of which were the heart of the villa and opened to the sky, allowing a soft breeze to flow into the home that had been built around it.

Banning couldn't help but be impressed by the spaciousness of Soya Rafe's secondary home.

He also noticed how the majority of the men of this home wore scarves of varying shades of blue while the few women they passed were adorned with jewelry.

Upon reaching the salon, which overlooked the lawn, the two found Rafe and Gwyn seated, bent over a low table, discussing some paperwork.

Banning's guide coughed to get the two's attention. Rafe looked and quickly got to his feet while Gwyn gave Banning the most fleeting of glimpses before returning to the manifests, doing her best to feign interest in them.

"Thank you Gerrit. That will be all for now. Just have our meal brought here when it is ready."

Bowing, Gerrit left the trio and crossed the verdant lawn to make his way to the kitchens.

Rafe offered Banning a seat across from Gwyn before going to pour a glass of wine to match their own.

Banning had not spoken to Gwyn since their arrival, the woman remaining quiet on their ride here and found her continued silence uncomfortable, so asked her what they were working on.

"Trying to unload those unwanted goods from Farro." Gwyn didn't bother to look at Banning while absently moving the papers around as she spoke. "Uncle says we can sell most of it in his own shops and the more bulky items will have to go to a market."

Hearing the dull tone to her voice and not wanting their first meal to be a total misery, Rafe took several quick steps back to hand Banning his wine before grabbing the papers and making a half-hearted attempt at stacking them before dropping them unceremoniously on one side of the couch.

"Ohhh, Gwyn! Enough about that for now." Rafe smiled broadly at the two as he sat down next to his niece. "So tell me Banning, what do you think of our Auvereen?"

"You have a beautiful city Master So," Banning stopped when his host frowned and shook his head. "Rafe."

"And your artwork is unusual." Banning continued, remembering what he had seen tiled and painted on the homes they had passed before pointing to the wall behind Rafe and Gwyn. "And what are those?"

Rafe knew the fresco very well, but turned just the same, just as his niece had. "These were called deiliphs." The man describing how the long bodied, blue grey, bottle nosed, flippered creatures once roamed the seas around Lahunne.

"The Lahunnans were a seafaring people before The Great Rift when Murra drained the seas to end our conflicts. My wife's people have mourned the loss of the waters that once surrounded them and the richness and bounty of life that has now passed from this world."

"There are scrolls that tell of the deiliphs swimming in large groups and of how they used to make their way into the island ports and join the singing sailors with their own voices of clicks and whistles."

Although he was finding this a little far-fetched, Banning was impressed and entertained by Rafe's stories of the deiliphs, and of other sea creatures that lived around the islands, finding that he too now agreed with Lyle's earlier reckoning of the timelessness of Auvereen.

"And what of these scarves you and most of the other men are wearing?" Banning asked, his curiosity for these people was piqued by his host. "Are they the colors of the Soya clan?"

"No, no!" Rafe laughed. Unclamping his brooch, Rafe handed it to Banning. "This is the likeness of something called a starfish. They also lived in the sea and it is the symbol for clan Soya. All of the older clans use sea creatures as their crests so they do not forget what Murra has taken from them."

"And the scarf?" Banning handed the brooch back to its owner.

"Another custom held onto from the past." Rafe ran a hand over the richly dyed fabric that was draped over his shoulders.

Rafe then proceeded to explain to Banning how a deep blue, almost indigo or violet, meant that a man was married. While a light blue scarf meant that a man was betrothed to a woman.

"Black scarves are for mourning and white ones are worn by men whose matriarchs are looking for a merger or something more profitable from another clan."

"And the women wear them as well?"

"No. Occasionally you'll see a women wear a black scarf mourning the loss of a respected husband. Other than that it is not the women's place to show whom she is bound to."

Gwyn, who had remained quiet, mulling over the strong feelings she was having for Banning and of how he would soon be out of her life, added, "The men on my ship who are married will wear scarves while they are about in Auvereen or the other Lahunnan cities."

"Which reminds me," Rafe stood and excused himself, letting the two know he would be back momentarily.

Left alone, the silence between the two became awkward, with Gwyn turning the stem of her wine glass while doing her best to avoid Banning's gaze.

Finally.

"I'm sorry about earlier on the ship." Banning blurted out.

Banning held his tongue until Gwyn looked up at him, ignoring the stony expression on her face.

"It was rude of me to just tell you we should leave after this delivery. But." Here Banning faltered, dropping his own gaze to the gold ring that marked him as a family member of clan Aerin. "But watching you and your uncle made me realize how much I miss my own father."

Banning sighed, frustrated over what he was feeling, his thoughts spilling out of his mouth in a jumbled mess. "Not that I want to go back home. While we were out on the flats I felt free. Like I didn't have to worry about my parents or what they are expecting of me."

"And then there's you, Gwyn. I, I like you very much and I just get frustrated that," Banning quieted, resentment welling up in him over how he could not pick the person he would like to be with.

Gwyn did not need to hear any more from the man sitting across from her. Standing, she went to join Banning on his couch and grasped his hand with her own.

"The thought of this ending hurts." Banning whispered.

"I know."

Not knowing what else to say Banning wrapped an arm around Gwyn's shoulders and pulled her close to him.

Gwyn asked if he was sorry that they had met.

"No, are you?"

"No." Gwyn replied, kissing him before lowering her head to his chest, the soft thump of his heartbeat echoing in her ear.

"I can always drag the flight out." Gwyn offered, running her right hand over the dark colored fabric of his shirt. "Or we can find a longer way back to Kinsale."

"Or we can remain here a little longer." Banning suggested.

Gwyn raised her head to look at Banning asking if he was sure about dragging out their stay in Auvereen.

Banning ran a hand through Gwyn's black hair. "I don't think another day or two matters at this point."

Gwyn smiled and was about to tell Banning how she would give him a tour of her favorite districts of the city when her uncle reappeared, his hands holding onto several different colored scarves that flowed behind him.

"So I see everything is right in the world once again!" Rafe laughed, a sound that came as easily to the man as the sun rising in the morning, as he went and reclaimed his vacated seat.

"For now." Gwyn thought as she and Banning separated and sat upright on the couch. Out loud she asked her uncle what he had in his hand.

"I had these lying around and thought Banning might want to use one for the time being."

Rafe then proceeded to display the scarves on the table between them; one of them being white and another of black, with a deep blue scarf representing marriage and two scarves each of a different shade of light blue. Both of which Rafe explained meant that a man was involved in a relationship.

"Is there a color for not interested?" Banning asked, toying with the silky, iridescent material of the white scarf, noticing the fine detailing of how several starfish, the symbol for clan Soya, had been embroidered onto one corner of the item.

Rafe laughed, his rich deep voice filling the room, shaking his head negatively. "You could wear the black scarf. Men are traditionally given a year to mourn the loss of a wife. But the Lahunnans are a curious people who love to gossip and you would find many wanting to give their condolences and to ask after who had passed."

"Probably not a good pick." Banning frowned, not relishing the idea of having to lie as to why he was wearing it.

Rafe and Gwyn agreed with him.

"What about the white?"

"No!" Gwyn shouted and yanked the scarf that Banning was still toying with out of his grasp.

"Well! That answers that!" Rafe laughed with Banning joining in the merriment while the two watched Gwyn blush in embarrassment.

"You certainly don't need a bunch of women hounding you." Gwyn sniffed.

Banning nudged Gwyn's knee with one of his, forcing Gwyn's already red cheeks to deepen to a dark crimson. "Of course Captain!"

"That just leaves the blues." Rafe spaced the three scarves out for Banning's perusal.

"We can eliminate the deep blue." So, not wanting to be reminded of what was awaiting him back home, Banning took the matrimonial scarf off of the table.

Rafe tugged on each of the differently colored light blue scarves, asking Banning if he wanted to wear one of those or to not have one at all.

Banning leaned forward, cocking his head to look at Gwyn. "What do you think?"

Gwyn asked herself that same question, not backing down from Banning's scrutiny, as she thought of how this man she had grown accustomed to having around would disappear out of her life in a matter of weeks.

And not one to back down from a challenge, Argus Gwyn did what felt like one of the most daring things she had ever done in her life and retrieved the soft cotton scarf that had been dyed a very pale ultramarine blue.

"I think this will look good on you."

Banning asked Gwyn if she was sure as he watched her smooth out the fabric on her lap.

Gwyn inched closer to Banning to wrap the scarf around his neck. Close enough that her warm breath brushed against his ear when she spoke. "It'll bring out the color of your eyes."

Although Banning knew his eyes were a common brown, he blushed at the compliment just the same.

"And you only need to wear it while you are off the Kasser." Gwyn explained as she adjusted the scarf to give it some flair.

"Not on it?" Banning asked with a wink of an eye.

Gwyn only smiled wickedly and shrugged before patting Banning's chest and sitting back to look at her handiwork, leaving that decision up to him.

"Not done yet!" Rafe said to Gwyn as she went to reach for her glass of wine. "Thought you might want this just in case."

Gwyn took the offered piece of jewelry; a gold coin similar to an Argus marker with the clan's crest on its face that had been turned into a brooch.

Gwyn was pushing the brooch's pin through several of the folds in the scarf when Banning asked what it was for.

"Shows everyone who you belong to." Rafe took his own glass of wine and watched the couple over its brim.

Gwyn's hands had frozen at the comment, leaving the golden piece of jewelry unclasped for now it was her turn to ask Banning if he was sure about wearing it.

Banning, who was afraid his voice might crack if he spoke, only nodded for her to continue.

"Ahh! The perfect couple!" Rafe laughed, not too concerned that he was embarrassing his niece and Banning.

As their host went to retrieve the carafe of wine to freshen everyone's glass, Gerrit and several other servants arrived with their meal.

"Just in time!" Rafe placed the carafe onto the table just as Gerrit and the others set their platters down onto it as well. Then shooing Gwyn and Banning off of their couch, Rafe had the prince help him move the piece of furniture back several feet while Gerrit and another man did the same to the couch on the other side of the table.

"I hope you don't mind Banning," Rafe said as he gestured for him and Gwyn to sit on the floor. "But I like to keep my life as casual as possible whenever I can."

What could Banning say as he and Gwyn did as they were told? This would be a first for the prince; almost eating off of the floor when every meal he had at home was very formal and businesslike.

Handing out plates and utensils, Rafe dismissed Gerrit and the others before personally removing the lids off of the platters, allowing a variety of aromas to fill the room.

"What is that?" Banning asked surprised by the triangular face that was staring at him with its opened mouth and one dead eye.

"This is a trosc." Rafe explained as he peeled back the skin of overlapping scales, exposing the animal's cooked, white, flakey flesh.

Then, as Rafe served the meal to his niece and Banning, he told the prince how Murra drained the seas, but left large underground lakes and ponds underneath the Lahunnan islands.

"Not only were we gifted with fresh water, Murra left behind a bounty of food in a variety of fish. And out of respect for what the goddess has given, we only take the fish when the lakes start to become overpopulated. What do you think?"

The flavor of the meat was subtle, with only a hint of the herbs that had been cooked with the creature.

Banning expressed his appreciation for the dinner and held up his plate for another helping.

Rafe obliged the young man, making sure none of the fish's fine, delicate bones made it onto Banning's plate, before proceeding to tell them yet another tale of the seas. A tale about the marriage of two fishes.

"The happy creatures were so busy preparing for their nuptials that they forgot to invite Murra. The goddess was so enraged by this slight that she sent her servant Siorca, a beast that was as large as a house, whose maw was filled with rows upon rows of jagged teeth, to go and devour all of the guests just as the ceremony began."

Gwyn only smiled as she listened to her uncle for she had heard this story on numerous occasions while Banning asked if Rafe had any drawings or paintings of Siorca.

Rafe offered to show the artwork to him after dinner, along with giving him a tour of the villa later then proceeded to tell them another tale of Murra and the forgotten seas that she had banished.

The night remained enjoyable for Banning as the conversation and the short stories continued on into the early hours of the morning. Of course, on that next day, the prince of Birr found that he was quite exhausted and struggled with his labors back on the Kasser.

Another night of dinner and pleasant conversation was had at Rafe's villa, but Banning, as well as Gwyn, were thankful that the man did not turn their meal into another late night of socializing.

In this way a second day of work and yet another evening at the villa of Soya Rafe passed. As did a third.

On the fourth day when Gwyn would have replenished the ship's perishables so they could start their return voyage to Iniscarn, and stopping in Kinsale to return Banning home, the captain of the Kasser gave her crew what felt like a much needed break from their duties.

Gwyn and Banning watched as Tor Lucilla, her mate Varin and her son Micah, along with a group that included Mac and Davis head off to one of Auvereen's many markets before walking off in the opposite direction to finally find some time to be alone.

As Gwyn and Banning spent that day once again walking hand in hand through the streets of Auvereen, the two realized that they did not want to be parted from each other. Knowing this and that it would be tougher to say goodbye as the days slipped by Banning finally informed Gwyn that it was time that he should be getting home.

"I know." Gwyn replied softly, squeezing his hand a little tighter.

Stopping and not caring that they were in the middle of a busy street, Banning raised Gwyn's chin so that he could kiss her softly on his lips.

"If I could I would stay by your side forever." Banning said when they resumed their walk.

"I know." Gwyn repeated, unsure of what else she could say to Banning.

"But my family, my duty."

Gwyn hushed Banning, telling him to say no more as she brought their clasped hands up to kiss the back of his hand.

The couple walked several more blocks when Gwyn recognized several of the buildings and the market square they were approaching.

"This way!" Gwyn tugged Banning down a side street. The homes that lined both of its sides being very tall, casting deep cool shadows across it, giving them the feeling that they were walking through an underground tunnel.

But the sensation was brief as the afternoon sun flooded over them when they entered a large open area.

Banning squinted until his eyes adjusted to the change in light then hissed in surprise at what he saw.

For Gwyn had brought him to a large circular plaza, it's shape dictated by the fact that all the homes surrounding it were all several stories tall and abutted one another, leaving the way they had walked in as the only entrance or exit, and blocking out all sound, save for the fountain in the middle of this hidden retreat.

Banning ignored the melodic splashing of water for the fountain was partially hidden by some trees, red leafed, the branches all gnarled and twisted with age and made for the structure to his right.

The building turned out to be a shrine. A shrine that had no walls, just columns of cream colored marble, three on either side with the front and back open, supporting a roof that was also made of the same marble.

Underneath the roof of the first shrine, carved in a pure white marble was the likeness of Maat. The figure's wings and talons for feet were a giveaway. But just in case no one knew who they were looking at, the air goddesses name was chiseled into the pedestal that she stood on.

Banning went to the next shrine with Gwyn trailing a little behind. Unsure of the figure that was before him, an athletically built man that was also winged, wearing what looked like a harness and a helmet in the shape of a raptor, he read the name on this one's pedestal.

"Shunor?" Banning looked at Gwyn who only nodded that he was correct. "But Shunor was Maat's husband! He was banished with the others during The Great Rift!"

Gwyn smiled, pleased with herself at surprising Banning.

"The god was banished." Gwyn said as she came to stand by Banning. "But images of him can be found in some obscure places in Lahunne. Come."

Taking Banning by the hand Gwyn lead him by shrines all similarly built as the one they had just left, with statues underneath their roofs that were dedicated to Sioda, Ennaya and Barra.

Stopping at the sixth shrine, they beheld a god who had a lyre in one hand with a set of pipes tied to his waist. This was Credne the bard.

Credne had been the god who introduced music to the Gwer. And it was he who taught them how to create their musical instruments and their letters so that the people could record their songs and stories.

Unlike the others who had been banished, Credne chose to leave so that he could continue to sing the tales of glorious battles among the

Gwer who still had the urge to fight each other for the whims of their gods.

Credne, who had also been Barra's partner in this realm, left so that he could also be with one of the other gods going into banishment; Chullain.

They then passed two more shrines. One for Ciaran and the other for Cavanna.

The next was for Mahlan, the husband to Cavanna and brother to Murra and Maat.

It was Mahlan, the father, the creator that used his strength and wisdom to help Aodhagan take the very matter that swirled about them and shaped it into the worlds that the Gwer now lived on.

Mahlan had also been a malicious being and it was he who had instigated the first wars among the people and his brethren. It was his wife that banished him and the others when he ignored her pleas for peace.

Murra's shrine stood next to her brother's. The sea goddess' statue garlanded in freshly cut flowers.

The second shrine on the right from hers was that of Cillach, brother to Cavanna, Aodhagan and Ciaran, with that of his wife Malvina, the goddess of war between them. The goddess held a bow, her weapon of choice, knocked with an arrow, ready to take down whatever came at her.

To Cillach's right was Sobek, their son. Sobek, the Wild, as heavily built as his father whose passions were turbulent and unbridled. Sobek also was the leader of the Great Hunt that drew any creature, friend or foe into his nightly forays into the depths of Gwer's forests.

Malvina and Sobek refused to give up their blood lust for battle and after a great struggle that left thousands dead and sent Cillach to wander the world lamenting, were banished from this world as well.

They walked by the shrine of Dubhas, making the sign to ward off death.

Aodhagan, Cavanna's brother came next. Gemstones, blood red with flecks of gold swirling within them and representing the worlds under his safe keeping, were embedded in his body and sparkled in the sunlight.

The sixteenth shrine was for Chullain, the god of the harvest, of wine making and of feasting. A wine cup was held in his left hand while a sickle was in his right. Chullain, who reveled in the feel of battle and of corn fields being trampled into battle fields so that they could be plowed for corn once again, was with the others in exile.

But in his need for song with his wine and, his desire for Credne, seduced Credne into joining him on their journey into exile.

Coming to the last shrine and full circle about the plaza, the two now stood before the statue of Saffir, goddess of the moon, goddess of the night and of the crystalline snows. A piece of silver shaped into the form of a crescent moon was balanced in the open palms of her hands. And it was she who strived against Aodhagan to quench the sun and to bring an eternal night upon the world.

"Remarkable!" Banning breathed. "To think such a place as this still exists in the world!"

Gwyn beamed, pleased with herself at seeing Banning's pleasure. "But there is one more surprise." Taking Banning by the hand, Gwyn led him underneath the circle of trees and to the fountain in the center of the plaza.

The fountain was tall; almost three times as high as the couple that now stood before it and carved into the likeness of both men and women.

Tritons they were. Men and women so devoted to Murra that they chose to leave the land behind and to be her heralds underneath the seas. Both genders had webbed hands and their feet were elongated and webbed as well. All were garbed in clothing and armor that looked otherworldly.

Banning walked about the fountain to admire the group of figures who seemed to be swimming in an upwards spiral, with the uppermost figures spewing water out of strangely shaped horns, the water cascading over the figures beneath and splashing, with droplets sparkling like diamonds as they caught the light of the sun, into the pool that surrounded them.

"And what of this one?" Banning stopped in front of a Triton, that of a woman, who had been carved to look as if she was swimming through a pond with only her eyes and the bridge of her somewhat flattened nose breaking the surface of the water. But what had caught Banning's interest was how the statue's left hand grasped the lip of the pool with its right arm also raised out of the water while the palm of that hand was turned upward. As if the statue was begging for something.

"You make a wish." Gwyn said as she came to stand by him. "And if the Triton finds you worthy she will return to Murra with it so your wish can be granted."

That being said, Gwyn took a copper out of her purse, clenched it in her hand with her eyes closed before kissing the coin to place it into the Triton's outstretched hand.

"Your turn."

Fortunately for Banning Gwyn had paid him for some of the work he had been doing and he had also won some coin during a couple of hands of cards with Mac and Davis so Banning was able to use a copper of his own.

Looking into the statue's eyes, hoping to see some semblance of life and only finding that he was staring at the glistening of sunlight on the wet, carved orbs of marble, Banning made his wish and kissed the coin just as Gwyn had done before placing the copper into the Triton's hand.

"So what did you wish for?" Banning asked Gwyn as he reached for her hand to pull her towards him.

"Can't say," Gwyn breathed huskily as Banning turned her in his arms so that she was facing him, her butt resting on the lip of the fountain's pool. "It won't come true."

Banning kissed Gwyn, his hands running up her back so he could pull her closer to him while her hand braced herself on the marble facade of the pool.

"Come on," He winked. "I'll tell you mine if you tell me yours."

"No." Gwyn looked down, feigning demureness as the index finger of her right hand trailed a dark vein in the marble's surface.

Banning, who was enjoying this game, kissed Gwyn one more time before asking her to guess his secret.

"Silly!" She shouted before reaching behind her to cup some water in her hand and to toss it at Banning.

Spluttering, Banning let go of Gwyn so he could wipe his face with the blue scarf wrapped about his neck.

Laughing, Gwyn skipped away, moving so that the fountain was now between them.

The shock of getting splashed quickly wore off and Banning's boisterous voice joined in with Gwyn's, the joy in their voices only enhancing the playful sound of the fountain while the prince chased Gwyn, trying to reach Gwyn who kept moving to keep the fountain between them.

But Banning was able to make his move when Gwyn pulled away from the fountain to run under the red canopy of trees that surrounded it and passed the shrines, finally catching her in the plaza's entrance. Of course, Gwyn had slowed her pace so that the arms of the man she found herself falling in love with could be wrapped about her once again.

After a long passionate embrace in that secluded, shaded street of Auvereen, the two separated, their hands still clasped as they continued on with their walk towards the market.

Gwyn and Banning remained quiet, forgetting the past and not worrying about the future. The two were quite happy just to be in the company of the other, smiling smugly as they walked down the street, as if they were sharing a secret they wanted to tell the rest of the world, but were forbidden from speaking, when someone banged into Banning's left side.

Letting go of Gwyn so that he or the person he had struck, or had struck him, would not fall, Banning steadied the person before him, apologizing for the accident.

But the apology faltered on his tongue when Banning looked into the eyes of the woman before him; a woman with the same watery, almost rheumy quality stare that the statue of the Triton had.

"I am sorry Madame." Banning finally muttered as he overcame his shock over the woman's malady which was not unlike his aunts.

The kindly creature, wearing a shawl that resembled a netting rather than knitting, only patted his arm before heading on to her own destination.

Banning watched the woman for one more moment to make sure she had her footing and did not happen to accidentally bump into someone else, a nagging thought of recognizing the woman still gnawing at him, when someone shouting caught his attention.

"Banning, Banning!"

The prince hesitated for a moment even though he assumed that it was a coincidence that someone was shouting his name and was about to return to Gwyn's side when he was stopped by a hand on his forearm.

"Banning!"

Banning froze for a moment, not recognizing the man as one of Gwyn's crew. But the brown hair parted down the middle of the man's head and the longish sideburns and the broad smile on the man's face brought Banning back to reality.

"Kael?" Banning couldn't help but ask, still confused by the man's presence.

"In the flesh!" Kael held Banning at arm's length before pulling the prince into a hug that knocked the wind out of him.

Banning stood numbly in the man's embrace, half-heartedly raising his hands to return his friend's hug, only watching Gwyn who now stood behind Kael, the woman also looking as if she was unsure of what she should do.

Releasing Banning, Kael once again held his friend away from him. "By the gods! We never thought we were going to find you. Especially out here!"

Banning inhaled deeply, hoping to explain how he got to Auvereen and to introduce Gwyn to Kael. But the man was so excited at finding him that Kael was paying no heed to the fact that his best friend's brother wanted to say something and called out to two men dressed in the livery of the Royal Guard that were now approaching them.

"Quickly! Go find Prince Aerin and tell him I found his brother! By the gods!"

"By the gods!" Those words chimed out of Kael's mouth several more times as the soldiers scurried off on their errand. Words that sounded more like a curse to Banning's ears rather than the praise Kael was invoking.

By the gods, Banning thought as it dawned on him that his return to Kinsale was imminent. How I wish I could be away from you.

"But you! You!" Kael's shout of joy interrupted Banning's thoughts. And how could the man not be joyful, overcome by emotion at this chance encounter? A chance encounter, on the far end of the world, for a rescue to find Banning that had started to look bleak and felt hopeless at best.

"I almost didn't recognize you." Kael laughed.

Banning could only wish that he hadn't, not even bothering to smile at the comment.

"You look like a man of the world!" Kael ran his fingers over Banning's fine scarf before cupping the back of his head, shaking it playfully. "And your hair! What did you do to your hair?"

Gwyn saw that Banning was beginning to flounder in their reunion and, finally finding her own courage, approached the two so she could introduce herself to Kael.

Kael's enthusiasm ebbed, just slightly, at finding Banning while Gwyn somewhat explained how they had come to be in the Lahunne City States, Banning remained quiet as his gaze panned across the market square, looking for a chance opportunity to escape before his brother arrived.

That's when Banning saw her; the old women.

Maybe she had become disoriented on her trek. Or maybe she had become part of the crowd which had been intrigued by the clamor Kael was making. A crowd that was now dispersing since it had become bored with their reunion.

In any event there the old woman stood, her cloudy eyes, almost white at this distance. Eyes that were as white as polished marble as the sunlight bounced off of them.

Stunned into silence by the moment, Banning watched the woman, the woman with the eyes like the marble Triton, smile and nod at him before once again hobbling into the ever growing throng of people moving about them.

Chapter 13
The Olean Flats

"Do you know how hard it was to find you?"

"The plan was to not be found."

"Well, He is looking for you too."

"I know."

"He will find you brother."

"Not if you keep following me. It will be you who leads him to me."

"But you need my help!"

"I am fine."

"Brother! You are not fine! I can hide you. . ."

"No!"

"Excuse me Sagart Caittle. Am I interrupting?"

Caittle Anam cursed silently, a curse that would go unheeded if he was lucky, startled by the new voice that came from behind him.

"Liam! What a nice surprise." Anam smiled warmly at the young man who stood hesitantly in the entrance to the storage room. "Come in, come in!"

"I, uh, I thought I heard you and someone else talking." Liam remained in the doorway of the dimly lit storeroom searching for a second person for the only light flooding the room came from the lamp that was hanging in the hallway and from the lantern Liam held in his hand.

The sagart laughed. A laughter that seemed to have a light of its own that chased the shadows into the deepest corners of the room.

"No, no!" Anam laughed again in his deep accented voice. "I wanted to chant one of the old prayers to Barra and I like the acoustics of this room for my voice seems to dance about me. Almost like there are two people singing." The sagart shrugged at the young man who had to yet enter the room. "A selfish and indulgent thing I know. But enough about me. What can I do for you today?"

"Oh, uh." Liam muttered as he took a couple of steps into the room. "Master Yanno asked me to get some salt to replenish the galley's larder. But I can come back later."

"No, no, do not be silly!" Anam walked over to Liam and placed a hand on his shoulder. The sagart's smile and the glow in his dark grey eyes blotting out the rest of the room, lessening Liam's anxiety that he had infringed upon the sagart in some private matter. "By any chance do you know where your father is?"

"He should be on the bridge with the prince and the captain." But then again, where else would Seb Cullen be in the middle of the afternoon?

"Thank you Liam. Maybe I will see you later during prayers?"

Liam mumbled that he would try to be there and watched as Anam left, the man seeming to take some of the warmth and the light with him when he exited the room.

Grabbing the crowbar and the mallet off of their hooks on the wall, and holding his lantern high, Liam began reading the labels on the tightly sealed crates until he found one stamped as containing salt.

As Liam placed the lantern on another stack of crates so he could use both hands to pry the lid off the one before him, his unease returned as the shadows seemed to deepen around him. Liam couldn't help but shudder as a chill ran down his spine, with the hairs on his arms standing on end, for it felt like he was being watched.

Liam couldn't help but stop for a moment and look around to make sure he was alone. Of course he was, Liam told himself as he quickly grabbed several leather pouches of salt before hurrying to hammer the crate's lid back into place.

Once the lid was secured and putting the tools back where they belonged, Liam made to leave the room. But he stopped when he saw some movement out of the corner of his eye.

"Hello?"

There was no response to his call and the shadow of a person he thought he saw appear was not there.

And with a shaking hand, Liam quickly closed the door so that he could head back to the galley, telling himself it was just his imagination when he heard the soft laughter of a woman coming from within the room he had just vacated.

***

"Sounds like you heard the wind scraping against our hull."

"But it really did sound like a person."

"There are no women on the Camalain."

Liam sighed, his back resting against Kael's chest. "I know."

One day had passed since Liam's encounter with Caittle Anam and today Liam found himself with Kael, who had made time to search Liam out so that they could spend some time together. The two, with about another dozen or so other men were in one of the larger storage bays which was now being used as a makeshift bar.

Kael had seated himself upon a crate with his back against the hull of the ship, and with his legs spread wide, had pulled Liam into an embrace, with him sitting in front of him with his arm's wrapped about the sagart's son, while the two of them watched five men who were crouching and throwing dice across the floor.

"See? Sounds like a woman." Kael said as the wind moaned faintly on the other side of the hull.

"But I really thought I heard the sagart talking to someone else."

"Maybe he was talking to a rodent." Kael replied as he ran the fingers of his left hand down Liam's forearm. "You find them on ships once in a while. And maybe that was what was watching you. With its beady little eyes."

Thereupon Kael's hands quickly moved to Liam's sides to playfully tickle him, acting as if mice were nipping at his body. With a yelp that drew the attention of everyone in the room, Liam squirmed out of Kael's grasp.

Laughing, Kael patted the vacated spot for Liam to return, kissing the back of the man's neck when Liam moved back up against him.

"I could have Manus send out men to do a search of the ship." Kael said as he rested his chin on Liam's shoulder, his hands wrapping tightly around Liam's waist.

"That's all I need! Sending the prince on a wild chase over something I said." Liam frowned over the thought of the prince having new fodder to dislike him. Not that Manus needed any new material for his disdain for him came quite naturally. "Thank you, but no thank you."

Their conversation about shadows, rodents and princes ended when one of the dice players cursed loudly at his bad throw. His friends laughing loudly, peppered him with friendly jibes at his misfortune as one of their number scooped up the pile of coins that had been growing on the floor over the past half-hour.

"How's your father?" Kael asked as the men on the floor each slapped a copper onto the floor to start a new game.

"Cranky, tired and for some reason as tight lipped as I've ever known him to be." Liam replied as the losing man of the last game cast the first dice for this one round.

"But I should be asking you." Liam retorted. "Since you have been working on the bridge, I think you see him more than I do."

Kael only made a pathetic moan, the only sympathy Liam was going to get out of him while squeezing him tightly.

Liam closed his eyes, savoring the warmth of the man around him. "He does seem to be overly concerned with Sagart Caittle though. I know if my father's not with him that he is usually asking after him."

"Maybe your father is concerned about who the sagart is talking to as well."

"Maybe." Liam ignored the gentle barb from Kael, keeping his own assumptions as to why Cullen continued to hover around the handsome somewhat exotic Anam to himself. Liam sighed, "This trip just seems to be draining the life out of him. It will be nice for this to be over so we can get him home."

Kael kissed the back of Liam's neck, concerned over what he heard as sadness in Liam's voice. "Hopefully we'll all be home soon."

***

"So he really thought he saw something?"

"No. Maybe. He wasn't sure." Kael said to Manus later that night in the cabin they shared. The two, both partially clothed, were relaxing on their beds with Kael absentmindedly picking at the strings of his guitar.

"But you know how it is on your first voyage." Kael continued. "Every strange sound you hear while we're flying can make you jump. And that storage room is windowless so any swaying of a lantern will make the shadows dance about."

"Personally, I don't think he heard or saw anything. But just the same I asked Lieutenant Cahl to do a search of the lower decks. Said there might be vermin getting into the foodstuffs and that it was your command to take a look. Hope you don't mind?"

Considering that Cahl Goban came into a close second as one of his least favorite people on the Camalain (Caittle Anam was the other man jockeying for that position), Manus was fine sending the lieutenant on a wild goose chase.

Of course holding first place as his least favorite person was Keir Liam, and seeing Liam's timidity as a weakness, Manus mentioned it to his friend, hoping to use it as a wedge between Kael and his new romantic interest.

"What of it?" Kael asked, annoyed by the new attack on Liam by his friend. Kael now wished he had listened to Liam and had kept his mouth shut.

Manus, who had been lying on his bed, sat up and draped his legs over its edge so he could look at his friend while they talked.

"I am sure he is a nice boy," Liam was only a couple of years younger than Manus and Kael. "But wouldn't you want someone that is hardier? More confident in themself? Like someone from the Guard?"

"He's just fine!" Kael snapped. "And you should give him more credit than you do! Everyone else on this damned ship is a member of your father's Royal Guard and he's working just as hard as the rest of them! More so just to impress you!"

Manus ignored the lure to make him feel guilty about his comments, and with his own love for Kael clouding his judgment, continued on. "He's not like us Kael! We're fighters! He's, he'll just run back to his father's temple and go back into hiding when we return home!"

Kael tossed his guitar across the bed, the strings vibrating with a mournful cry. "You don't know that!"

From the frown now forming on Kael's face it looked to Manus that he was making some headway past his friend's defenses and decided to take another swing. "You can't save him Kael!"

"Fuck you Manus!" Kael stood and grabbed his shirt to put it back on. "You're an ass!"

"Where are you going?" Surprised by Kael's reaction, Manus jumped up and blocked Kael's way so that he could not exit the room.

"Out of my way Manus or I swear, prince or no prince, I'll flatten you!"

"You wouldn't dare!" Manus growled.

Kael looked at his friend, the hands he had balled into fists relaxing, his chest heaving in anger and walked away from Manus.

Watching his friend move to the windows to stare out at a world shrouded in darkness, Manus felt as if he might be winning and decided to use the last weapon in his arsenal. "So tell me then, why do you like him?"

Staring at the smug reflection of Manus, the only thing visible against the night sky, made his blood start to boil once more.

"Because he's not like you!" Kael spat. Turning he strode towards his friend who now looked stunned, almost hurt, by the words that had come out of his mouth. Kael didn't care right now.

"He's not like anyone I've met before. Liam is friendly, giving, he's not looking for personal gain. He's nice!"

"I'm nice!" Manus sniffed.

"Only when it suits you! Now if you don't mind M'lord I would like to leave."

Manus stepped aside to let his friend pass by him.

But as his friend slid the door open to the room, the blow of Kael's verbal assault wore off and Manus found a retort for his remarks.

"I am the Prince!" Manus yelled. "It is my duty to be strong and to be tough on my subjects!"

"If you say so Prince Aerin."

"And where are you going?"

Kael, who was about to slide the door shut, thought he heard what sounded like a hint of desperation in Manus' voice. Turning, Kael saw the authoritative stance his friend had taken which was only belied by the pained look in the man's eyes.

But Kael had had enough of this argument and could not take any more of the vitriol that had filled the room and informed Manus that he was going for a walk.

Watching him leave, Manus could only assume that Kael was heading off to Liam's bed. And out of anger at having that vision of the two of them entwined in lovemaking in his head he shouted, "Fine! But mark my words! Either he'll be gone or you'll move on to your next conquest when we get back home! You always do!"

Not knowing what to say and ashamed at having his own promiscuity thrown at him, Kael quickly closed the door.

***

That night sleep eluded Manus.

As hard as he tried Manus could not drown out his argument with Kael.

Their voices echoed violently in his head in a sort of disjointed round robin with what they had said to each other and what Manus would have liked to have said to his friend. Behind it all the prince could hear the sound of Liam's laughter beating on his skull.

Frustrated over their fight and angry over the fact that they had yet to find any sign of his missing brother Manus threw off his covers, got up and began stalking the room.

Mumbling to himself, running his hands through his hair and staring out at the lightening sky did nothing to alleviate his foul mood.

So Manus went back to bed, beating his pillows until they too were hurled across the room. For a while the prince of Birr lay on his back staring up at the ceiling of his room that was still shrouded in deep shadows of indigo before he too finally decided that he needed to get dressed and escape the confines of his cabin.

Many of his men were not used to seeing their prince up so early and their surprise showed on their faces before quickly disappearing as the men saluted him as Manus made his way to the bridge.

Manus also did his best to hide his own surprise (and failing miserably) at finding Kael on the bridge talking amiably with Captain Thear.

The two quieted. The laughter they were sharing over some joke dying on their lips, before Kael asked Manus for permission to leave the bridge.

"Thank you Milord." Kael said politely when Manus curtly nodded at his friend and waved him away.

Sensing that there was some tension between the two friends, Thear Ibor kept quiet while Manus replaced Kael at the captain's side and remained so as the two watched the new day's sun slowly creep over the land.

"How long was Master Karam on the bridge?" Manus finally asked when the silence between himself and Ibor became too uncomfortable for even him to bear.

"All night Milord."

Manus looked at Ibor to see if there was some hint that he might be covering for Kael. And just as he had heard in Ibor's voice, Manus only saw honesty and sincerity on the man's face.

"Talk about anything interesting?"

Ibor only shrugged as his feet tensed within his boots and turned them slightly so that he could keep his balance when he felt the slight turn of the ship that the steersman was making.

Looking back at Croft, whose shift it happened to be, the man staring blankly forward while he flew the ship, Ibor mentioned offhandedly how Kael had asked about learning to steer a ship.

"Told him it would be best if we waited until we got back to Kinsale to learn to fly."

"And Master Karam asked after my family. Seemed most interested when I told him all my boys were sailors. Two captains and a steersman you know."

Manus had not known this and remained quiet as his captain continued on with his story.

"So we just talked about some of their adventures and the foreign lands that my oldest has visited."

"From his questions I got the impression that Master Karam might want to have a ship of his own one day."

Manus found that hard to believe and said so.

"I do not know." Ibor countered slyly as he ran a hand over his neatly trimmed grey goatee. "Not everyone chooses to stay in the Royal Guard for the rest of their life. Sometimes they want more, something different."

Manus didn't respond to the captain's insight of his friend. He just stood there as the words of his parent's consul and now those of Ibor swirled and clouded the waters that were his feelings for Kael.

When Manus thought that enough time had passed so that it did not look like he was trying to escape his captain's company, Manus excused himself so that he could hurry back to his cabin.

Thinking that he would find Kael in the room and disappointed that he did not, Manus walked to the windows in his room and watched the barren landscape of the Olean Flats roll off into the horizon in the morning light, wondering what life would be like without Karam Kael around.

But those thoughts of melancholy loss faltered when the cabin door slid open and Kael walked into the room.

The man was bare chested, his pants hanging low on his waist with a towel draped around his shoulders that he was using a corner of to dry his damp hair.

"Oh, sorry." Kael seemed stunned to find Manus back in the room. "Thought you would be out making your rounds. I'll get dressed and be on my way."

Not knowing what to say for the moment Manus returned to looking out the window, quietly watching the wispy reflection of his friend as Kael stripped and began putting on a clean set of clothing before sitting on the edge of his bed to put on some stockings.

Sighing heavily, his hot breath fogging the inside of the green tinged pockmarked glass, obliterating the vision of Kael, Manus went to sit on the edge of his own bed. The several feet of wooden floor that separated them feeling like a mighty chasm filled with foreboding and despair.

And with the silence becoming unbearable, Manus blurted out that he was sorry about the argument they had that night.

"With looking for my brother I. . ."

"Come on Man!" Kael snapped. Kael had been hoping to hurry out of here before any word was spoken in the hopes of not rekindling last night's fight. It didn't seem like that was about to happen. "Can you not use Banning's disappearance as an excuse for all your outbursts? It's gotten tired and I'm tired of our fighting."

Mollified by Kael's bluntness, Manus ran his hands through his long dark hair before asking how they could get passed this situation.

"I'm not sure there's anything to get passed anymore." Kael kept his eyes averted from Manus as he retrieved his boots to don.

"I know space is tight, but I will see if there is someplace I can bunk for the rest of the voyage."

"No!"

"Manus."

Manus, who did not want to hear of his friend leaving his side, quickly went to sit beside Kael and grabbed one of the man's hands and mumbled an apology.

"Kael," Manus continued. "I'm sorry, I'm so sorry. It's just that I think you can do better."

Kael couldn't help but scowl at the remark and pulled his hand out of Manus' grasp so he could finish putting on his boots.

"I'm not dumping Liam!" Kael stood and stomped his boots loudly on the planks of the floor to adjust his feet within them. "You need to accept that!"

"Fine, fine!" Manus also stood, once again blocking Kael's escape from the room. "If I like him will you stay?"

Kael only shook his head before grabbing his towel to continue drying his hair.

"I'm not asking you to like him." Kael finally said as he combed his fingers through his hair. "I just want you to be happy for me."

I wish you could be happy with me, Manus thought forlornly while Kael belted on his sword.

Not knowing what else to do, Manus acquiesced, albeit halfheartedly, saying that he could handle that before once more begging Kael to stay.

"Where else are you going to find better accommodations on my ship?" Manus forced a smile he did not feel onto his face. "Please stay. I don't want out friendship to end this way."

For once Kael thought he heard some sincerity coming from Manus' mouth and his resolve to escape faltered. "This is true." He said quietly.

"So you'll stay!" Manus didn't wait for a response and unceremoniously and quite out of character, threw his arms around Kael to give him a hug. "I promise I'll be better."

Kael thought the embrace was going on much longer than it needed to so he extricated himself from Manus' arms saying that he wanted to go to the galley for a bite before heading back to the bridge.

And to see Liam, Manus thought sourly. But out loud he asked Kael to grab something for him to eat while he went to get cleaned.

Grabbing his own towel Manus followed Kael out of the room and the two made for the stairwell.

At the landing where Kael asked to take his leave of his friend to head up to the galley, Manus stalled him for one more moment as a thought came to him.

"So the captain thinks you want to leave the Guard." Manus said as nonchalantly as possible, hoping to see what type of reaction Kael gave him.

Manus was rewarded by a look of surprise that was followed by a frown. "He does?"

"Think the captain just assumed that from the conversation the two of you were having." Manus replied. "Was he right?"

"It was just a thought." Kael said as he tried to remember his conversation with Thear Ibor and to recall what he said that might have given him away. "But we can talk about that later."

"Sure." Manus agreed before turning his back on his friend and headed down the stairs to the washroom.

***

So an uneasy truce settled between Manus, Kael and Liam. Manus stopped bothering Kael about his romance with Liam and the prince chose to continue avoiding the sagart's son as much as he possibly could.

Fortunately for Manus and Kael, who had kept Liam oblivious to the argument the two had had about him, the Camalain spent another full day out on the Olean Flats before having the first island that made up the Lahunne City States come into view.

"Are you sure this is where we need to go?" Manus asked Caittle Anam while the two of them, along with Kael, Seb Cullen, Thear Ibor and Lieutenant Cahl stood upon the look-out deck of the Camalain to get a better view of their surroundings.

"Yes Milord." The enigmatic sagart replied. "The priests of Auvereen are of an ancient order and should have some knowledge as to how we can find your brother."

Manus looked to Cullen to see if the man was in accord with Anam and his assumptions. But the elderly priest, the dark circles under his eyes accentuating his haggard appearance, tiredly shrugged in ignorance.

"I hope you are right Sagart Caittle." Manus said as two skiffs that looked to be military in nature flew up to flank them. "I would hate to think that you have purposely wasted my time!"

Anam's only response was to bow and smile beatifically. A smile that Manus had grown to hate as one of the prince's men began to signal the Lahunnan vessels as to who they were and where they wanted to go.

With an escort to lead the way, getting to the island of Glain was not a problem. The issue was that the Camalain was forbidden to enter Auvereen's port and was made to dock at one of the many platforms that peppered the landscape outside of the capital's wharves.

"Did you not tell them that I was on board?" Manus asked his man that was on signaling duty.

"Aye, Prince Manus. But they said only Lahunnans are being allowed to dock inside the walls. Said we'll have to wait for a craft to ferry us to the city."

The wait took much longer than anyone expected, with dusk settling on the horizon, when a ship finally came to see if any of the Camalain's crew wanted to head into Auvereen.

Manus seethed in annoyance, doing his best to hide his anger from the woman who offered her services to them, more so when she gave her price for having to ferry them over to the mainland.

The prince's mood did not improve upon reaching the city. If anything his attitude got worse, slowly curdling like milk left out too long in the sun. For when he went to personally speak to the dock master about moving the Camalain into the port he was informed that only the Soya herself would be granting approval for foreigners to dock within the protective walls surrounding Auvereen's sprawling wharves.

Frustrated at getting this far, and not being able to have an audience with Soya Alayna until the following day, Manus decided to take himself and his small group of men back to the Camalain.

Kael, who had remained silent during Manus' conversation with the dock master, volunteered to take the men and find someone to ferry them back to the ship.

"We don't have time for this!" Manus grumbled as they boarded a small flat bottomed ship that was being steered by a boy in his mid-teens.

Kael agreed with his friend and suggested that they leave the Camalain where it was and not bother to meet with the ruler of Auvereen.

"We should focus on meeting with these friends of Caittle Anam's." Kael continued as the boat left the port, with one of Manus' guards directing the boy towards the Camalain. "If this turns out to be a lost cause we can leave here as soon as possible."

"And where do we go from here!" Manus snapped, for once thinking that they were not going to find Banning.

At a loss for words as they came to dock near the Camalain, Kael remained silent. The man also becoming fearful of what the new day would bring.

✱✱✱

That new day did not start off well.

Manus had the forethought to hire the boy from the previous night, paying him in advance to come fetch them in the morning. But the teenager arrived late, and once his eyes cleared from not being connected to the lodestones, begged forgiveness for his tardiness.

Manus nodded curtly as he silently herded his group that was made up of Kael, the two sagarts, Lieutenant Cahl and several soldiers onto the boy's ship.

The Prince of Birr did not hold his tongue long though for when they cleared the Camalain the small ferry began to fly away from the city.

"Where are you going?" Manus yelled, grabbing the boy's shoulder to get his attention. "Auvereen is in the opposite direction!"

Stunned by the prince's gesture the boy's eyes cleared slightly and the ferry bobbled in the air, sending everyone staggering across the ship's deck, with shouts of surprise coming from Manus' men as they tried to maintain their balance.

"Sorry. Lohd." The boy replied in a clipped garbled tone after regaining control of his ship. "Passengers. More. Others."

Manus stood there impotently, cursing the machinations of the god Sioda and his bad luck with his choice of ferryman as the city got somewhat smaller on the horizon.

"Have patience Milord." Anam said comfortingly as he came to stand by Manus, placing a hand of reassurance on the prince's shoulder, mimicking Manus' earlier gesture towards their ferryman.

The sagart's words were not a comfort to Manus. And coming from a man that the prince did not like only soured his mood even more so that Manus unapologetically shrugged off the man's hand and walked the short distance to one of the railings of the ship in the hopes of some solitude.

Finally, after an hour and a half of making several more stops collecting another dozen passengers, a white gabhar that was bleating nervously by the press of people, it's hooves clacking loudly on the planking, with a hound and two kittens thrown in for good measure, the ferry made its way back to Auvereen.

If not for the serious nature as to why they were here, watching the dark looks that Manus was casting about him, especially at the kittens that seemed to be taking turns hissing at the vitriolic prince and the whining hound that was pulling on its leash to reach them, Kael would have found the entire scenario humorous.

When the ferry finally docked, Manus couldn't get off of it quick enough. Manus even ignored its owner, who with palm held open, asked if he should wait to return the prince and his entourage to the Camalain.

"If you don't mind," Manus said to Anam when his group made it to a more open space where they could gather around him. "Lead the way."

Smiling benignly, Anam guided them into the large prosperous city, directing their eyes towards points of interest as the group headed for their destination.

"If I wanted a tour guide I would have hired one." Manus said in a tone of voice that did not hide his annoyance over what he saw as a frivolous distraction. But the man did not hear the prince's sarcastic remark or chose to ignore it and continued to elaborate on the architectural styles and sculptural icons they passed.

They eventually made it to the city's temple dedicated to Barra which was a tall thing, all columns and carved stone, that was surrounded by a high wall with what looked like barracks on its interior. With its antique, militaristic detailing, the place had the feeling of being a fortress rather than a temple.

The sound of chanting also filled the air, the vocals bouncing off the solidly built structures. So the group followed the haunting cadence into the interior of the temple and found the temple's high sagart presiding over what looked like a prayer vigil.

The elderly priest took the time to talk to them, informing the party that they had also lost all contact with the god of the earth. The man also seemed confused over Anam's inquiries after Manus' brother and apologized for not having any answers for them.

"Where do we go from here?" Manus asked, frustrated that they had already failed in their search for Banning.

Acting as if he was not surprised or bothered by what they had learned at the temple, the sagart from Sliabh Mianach suggested that they should make their way to Ennaya's temple.

"With luck we will find that Barra's sister has the information we are looking for."

Alas, after spending about half an hour traversing Auvereen to reach the temple to Ennaya, luck was not with them and the sagarttas, as well as some male priests, were also baffled by their questions concerning the missing prince from Birr.

Undaunted by the lack of information they were collecting, Anam suggested their next stop should be to head over to the temple to Mothair ahn Chead.

"Who?" Manus asked, unfamiliar with the name.

"Cavanna." Cullen wheezed. The walks across the city were starting to take its toll on the lame sagart and who was grateful for this brief respite. "That was her name at the beginning of our history."

Not one for religion or its history, Manus simply asked as to where her temple was located.

Anam scanned the horizon and pointed to a large citadel-like structure midway into Auvereen that was overlooking the lower districts.

"They couldn't build their temples in one district?" Manus asked, annoyed at the trek they would now have to make.

"You forget Prince Aerin." Anam started, smiling warmly at Manus as if he was too simple to even remember a basic fact of their people's history. "There was a time when the gods warred among themselves with their allegiances to each other changing like the weather. The distances between the temples kept them from being defiled by the disciples of their enemies, with their own legion of worshipers as the first wall of defense against any attack."

"To give one's life for their god as an excuse for war? What an archaic way of thinking."

Anam's explanation seemed to be turning into a lecture that Manus did not want to hear and a waste of time, so waved the sagart into moving.

"And the quickest route if you please Sagart Caittle!" Manus growled, growing tired of the man's company and his ineffectiveness in finding his brother. "We don't have all day to traipse about this city!"

"As you wish Milord."

Manus wasn't the only one who was frustrated by this jaunt through the streets of Auvereen for Seb Cullen seemed just as discouraged by their progress as his prince. Also, the only one who did notice the sagart's distress was the lieutenant. Especially when Cullen let everyone go before him and began to lag a little behind.

"Sagart, is there something wrong?" Goban asked Cullen when he came to walk with the limping priest.

"Just not as spry as I use to be, Lieutenant." Cullen wheezed, his chest heaving heavily as he tried to catch his breath, the knuckles of his hand a blanched white from gripping his staff to keep his balance while they walked.

Concerned for Cullen's health, Goban offered to have one of his men stay with him until he felt rested enough to head back to the Camalain.

"Or we can hire a cart to get you back to the wharves." Goban suggested.

But Cullen only laughed, his chuckle quickly turning into a dry cough. "My thanks Lieutenant. But I will be fine."

The look on Goban's face revealed that he doubted that Cullen would be fine. His own opinion was that it looked as if Cullen was about one step from falling over and dying on the street.

Cullen on the other hand was determined not to let Caittle Anam out of his sight and was emphatic that he would be able to make it to the next temple.

So, not wanting to leave the priest behind, nor to get separated from the rest of the group, Goban got the attention of one of his soldiers and made sure he kept an eye on them as they trailed behind, and to find out the directions to the temple of Mothair ahn Chead just in case they could not keep up with Manus and his party.

The lieutenant and the sagart finally did catch up with the rest of their group inside the temple's courtyard as the prince and his men were being made to wait for the temple's high sagartta.

When the woman did arrive, with a small guard of priestesses of her own, the high sagartta in a tone that the prince found to be quite haughty informed them she had no idea what they were talking about and that no word had come from Mothair ahn Chead about a missing Birrnian prince.

"Please," The woman continued as her eyes fell on the exhausted Seb Cullen, the robes of his order covered with sweat and dust from their travels. Her mind was also clouded with doubt for when she looked upon the other sagart, the one named Caittle Anam, the sagartta was sure she had met him once before. But where and how eluded her. "Gentlemen, please stay as long as you need to refresh yourselves."

Bowing, the high sagartta, along with her gaggle of women dispersed, leaving the men to their own devices.

"Great!" Manus snapped as the reality that they had been on a fools chase and that there was a good possibility that Banning might be dead set in. "That's just great!"

"So where do we go from here Sagart Caittle?" Manus sneered, doing his best to hold back the tears of frustration he felt forming at the corner of his eyes. "Should we make for another temple? We did pass a temple to Ciaran on the way here! Maybe we should go knock on their door and ask if they know anything about Banning's whereabouts!"

Anam frowned. "That would not be advisable Milord."

"Fool!" Manus repeated the word several more times as he stomped about the plaza, finally stopping, his hands on his waist, staring up into the clear afternoon sky, wishing that the answers he sought were in the amorphous clouds that floated overhead.

Sadly, Kael knew that Manus not only was calling Anam a fool, that Manus also branding himself one as well. Wanting to halt his friend's self-abuse, Kael approached Manus to try to comfort him.

But Kael's hand of reassurance was slapped away.

"Back off Kael!"

"Man, I. . ."

"I don't need your pity right now!" A stony look rolled over Manus' face while he attempted to hide the pain he was feeling. "I need to think!"

"Right." Kael said softly, ignoring Manus' verbal assault. "I, I thought it might be wise to see about getting fresh supplies while we are here. With your permission?"

"Go!" Manus waved Kael away before turning his back on his friend.

Before Kael could leave, Goban approached him and whispered that he should take two of the men.

"No reason to go wandering off alone." The lieutenant reasoned. Although what Goban really wanted was to have fewer men around to be verbally attacked by the inconsolable prince. "The sagarts and I will take care of him."

Kael doubted that very much but kept that opinion to himself, and only thanked Goban before pointing to the two guards and indicating that they should follow him.

Upon leaving the temple Kael and his escort did their best to backtrack to a market square they had passed through on their way to the temple. But the trio soon found themselves turned around and utterly lost.

Thankfully the men found a Lahunnan who knew of the market they wanted to get to and gave them directions so they could find it, the Lahunnan repeating himself several times to make sure they knew where they were going.

How I wish Liam was here, Kael thought as they passed a large overly ornate building that he thought he recognized from their previous trek. It would have been nice to have gotten lost and stayed lost, going on an adventure to explore this city.

But then again, even though Manus said he would behave around Liam, Kael was certain the prince, especially in his current state of agitation, would have abused his boyfriend.

Kael sighed, wishing that for good or ill that this adventure would be over and to maybe start off on his own, feeling that he did need a break in his friendship with Manus.

Maybe to even set off on his own ship. Kael was surprised that the captain had deduced that from their conversation the other day. Kael was not happy that Manus had found out that tidbit of information, although he was happy that the subject had not been brought up again.

Would Liam go with him, Kael mused. To pick a point on the map to fly off to and not look back?

No, no, no! The words reverberated in Kael's head to the sound of Manus' voice, while his friend's laughter echoed in derision.

No, Kael thought. Probably not.

"Sir, I think that's the market up ahead." One of the guards said to Kael.

"Right." Kael replied as he and the two men with him picked up their pace and fell in with the traffic heading towards the large plaza several blocks away where a cacophony of sounds and exotic smells was flowing towards them.

Kael was hoping there was a vendor who could supply them with inventory or at least knew of someone that could replenish what the Camalain might need (Kael wasn't quite sure what they were low on) when some disturbance happened further up the street.

He wasn't sure what was happening but it looked as if many of the street goers were making room so that a man who looked to be about his own age with shortly clipped brown hair held an elderly woman, who looked as if she was about to fall.

As they got closer Kael watched how the man made sure the crone was steady on her feet as she began to hobble away.

Cute, was Kael's first thought of the young Lahunnan in his pale blue scarf that was accentuated by his slightly tanned skin.

As the young man scanned the crowd, his eyes passing over Kael before turning to his companion, Kael hissed in surprise for he thought he recognized him.

"Sir?" One of the guards asked, questioning Kael's sharp outburst.

But Kael ignored the man as he took several quick steps forward.

"Ban." Kael coughed. But his soft hesitant call went unheeded.

"Banning. Banning!" Kael shouted with more assurance.

There seemed to be some hesitation in the man and his head turned slightly at Kael's shouting before continuing towards the black haired woman he had been walking with.

Kael swore, confident that it was Manus' brother and ran the distance between them, the guards following in pursuit, puzzled by Kael's actions.

Afraid that he would lose the man in the crowd that was gathering once again, Kael grabbed the man's forearm before once again shouting his name.

Kael could tell that Banning was startled by his outburst and there was a blank look on the prince's face before it dawned on Banning as to who he had been calling his name.

"Kael?"

"In the flesh!" Kael shouted, holding Banning at arm's length before pulling his friend's brother into a tight hug.

"By the gods! We never thought we were going to find you! Especially out here!" Kael shouted excitedly as he pushed Banning back to again take a good look at him.

"Quickly! Go find Prince Aerin." Kael shouted to one of the two men dressed as soldiers of the Royal Guard that were approaching them. "Tell him I found his brother! By the gods!"

If Kael was paying attention to Banning, he would have noticed how Manus' brother seemed to wince every time he shouted that exclamation. But he did not.

"By the gods! But you! You!" Kael choked, his emotions starting to get the best of him. "I almost didn't recognize you."

"You look like a man of the world!" Kael laughed as he ran his fingers over the pale blue scarf, noticing the golden brooch that was attached to it, before playfully roughing the back of Banning's head. "And your hair! What did you do to your hair?"

Banning, unsure of what to say, took a step back as he tried to pull himself out of Kael's grasp.

Gwyn on the other hand had noticed Banning's trepidation and that slight backwards step that he tried to take before she found her own courage and approached the two men, for she too was fearful over what might happen at this encounter.

"Banning, who's your friend?" Gwyn asked as she placed a reassuring hand on Banning's shoulder.

But Banning ignored her as well for he seemed distracted by something in the crowd that had formed around them.

Frowning at Banning's bewilderment Gwyn introduced herself, naming her father as the ruler of Iniscarn and briefly described how one of her father's men had found Banning wandering Murra's Maze.

"Isn't that right Banning?" Gwyn asked of her companion as she squeezed his shoulder tightly to get his attention.

"What?" Banning stuttered as he watched the blind woman smile at him before disappearing into the crowd and returned his attention to the friends before him. "Oh, right, right. The Scarnians found me."

"But why didn't you come home?" Kael asked Banning after he thanked Gwyn for the rescue of his friend's brother.

Once again Banning looked distracted, scanning the crowd as if he was looking for something, that something being a way, albeit a hopeless way, to escape from Karam Kael.

Not sure as to Banning's distress either, Gwyn answered for the man. "My father sent one of his most trusted servants to inform his family that he was with us. We would have already been heading to Kinsale but our lodestones stopped working."

"Ours did as well." Kael agreed. "We were stranded out in the desert for almost four days. Banning, you don't look so well."

Banning turned to Kael, forcing a smile on his face. "Sorry, Kael. It's been a long day. And seeing you after all this time."

"Of course, of course." Kael hugged Banning once more. "It looks like there's a tavern a little up the street. Do you mind Mistress Argus?"

"Of course not." Gwyn smiled, hiding her own concern over Banning's behavior. "We've been out early touring the city and it has been a warm day."

Kael asked the second guard to remain in the street and to send Manus over to them when he arrived.

"It was fortuitous you found us," Gwyn continued as the three took a seat at a table that was underneath a canopy. "Because we were going to leave tomorrow."

"More like divine intervention." Kael laughed before ordering a round of drinks for them. He then proceeded to explain how they had found a sagart in Fomor who had been told by Barra that they would find Banning in Lahunne."

"Really?" Gwyn asked incredulously as she steepled her fingers in front of her face, hiding her smile, Gwyn's eyes glittering coyly as she listened to Kael's story.

Listening to the conversation while keeping an eye on the traffic in the streets, Banning found a new reason to curse the gods, wishing that he had pushed Gwyn into leaving Auvereen days ago.

Or I should have remained on the Kasser, Banning thought as the soldier that had been left behind began gesticulating towards someone further up the street.

And who should appear out of the crowd like some hero breaking through the cloying fog of some mysterious land that tried to consume him? Manus, Banning's brother.

Not saying a word to Kael or Gwyn who were comparing some of their adventures on the flats, Banning watched his brother, his dark shoulder length hair flowing like a war pennant in the wind, a black brooding expression on his face as if a storm was flying across the land, quickly crossed the distance of the street to reach his man.

Banning noticed two other men with his brother as he talked to the soldier that was now pointing in their direction; two men dressed as members of the Royal Guard. One of which who was unmistakably the lieutenant sent as his protector. Cahl Goban.

Like a magnet drawn to its opposite half, its better half, Banning stood as his brother and soldiers now hurried to the tavern, with Gwyn and Kael following suit when they caught sight of the approaching prince.

The look of reproach on Manus' face was as clear as the day but disappeared from view when he pulled Banning into a strong hug.

Several moments went by, with the Birrnian men mumbling prayers of thanks to the gods at finding Banning before Manus, still holding onto Banning's forearms, released him.

"We thought you were dead!" Manus shouted at his younger brother.

"So Kael informed me." Banning replied.

"Father, mother and Fionn have been worried about you! We've all been worried about you!"

Banning averted his gaze from his brother's piercing blue eyes. Second, Banning thought bitterly at hearing his own father's name at the end of Manus' sentence. We'll always be second.

Taking Banning's silence and gestures as an apology, Manus brought his younger brother into another hug. "What were you thinking?"

"The blame would be mine, Prince Aerin." Gwyn started, once again coming to Banning's rescue for she had taken the time they spent at the tavern to gather her wits about her and to not worry as to why Banning had originally come into her company.

"And you are Milady?"

Manus' look of concern for his brother slowly turned into a frown, with deep furrows forming at the corners of his mouth, as Gwyn gave her name and familial lineage.

Scarnians! Manus thought. His own military history had included the formation of Iniscarn by renegade Birrnian merchants and saw this association as a step down in status for Banning. Something his brother nor his family did not need.

But before he could thank Gwyn and whisk his brother away from here so they could make for home, Cahl Goban stepped up and saluted the group, making his presence known.

"It is good to see you Milord." The lieutenant said to Banning, silently thanking the gods that they found him alive, while reaching out to shake the prince's hand.

"Thank you Goban." Banning smiled, finally, at the man who had shadowed him during his entire trip to Ardane. "I hope I didn't put you into too much trouble."

"No, not at all." Goban lied. "I am just happy we found you alive."

"Where are the sagarts?" Kael chimed in when it became clear that only the soldiers had been behind Manus.

"Cullen is resting. He's too exhausted to keep at our pace and Anam is going to get him back to the ship." Manus explained before hitting one of Banning's shoulders. "We almost had a sagart die because of you!"

Banning didn't know what to say and only blushed in embarrassment at the comment as Manus suggested that they head back to port. "We should get you home as soon as possible. Fionn was so distraught when I left. He'll be happy to see you again."

"Okay."

Thanking Gwyn for taking care of his brother, Manus tried to extricate his brother, himself and his men from her so that they could be on their way.

But listening to Gwyn's dismissal by his brother was what Banning needed to perk up and take an interest in what was going on around him.

"There's no reason to send her away." Banning said to Manus, a hint of defiance in his voice.

"I'm sure the Lady has better things to do with her time than to babysit you."

"Well she's my friend," Banning sniffed. "And welcome to join us."

Manus was about to rebuke his brother for contradicting what he thought was best for all of them when Gwyn rested her hands on one of Manus' biceps.

"Please, Milord." Gwyn purred. "There is no reason for this reunion to turn into a row over me. Besides, your brother and I were about to head back to my ship. So if you don't mind me joining you?"

"Yeah." Kael chimed in, enjoying his friend's discomfiture as he tried to control the situation. "If we are all heading in the same direction the Lady would certainly be safer in our company."

Annoyed by Kael's remark, more so when he caught his friend winking at Gwyn as if they were in some conspiracy against him, Manus conceded to the peer pressure and invited Gwyn to join their company.

"You'll pay for that." Manus whispered to his friend as the man paid for their drinks. But Kael only laughed and told Manus to lighten up because they could now head home.

It was fortunate for everyone that Banning and Kael stood up to Manus and had Gwyn remain with the group. For when Manus took a wrong turn that would have sent them in the opposite direction of their destination, Gwyn corrected them and offered to be their guide for the rest of the way.

"See?" Kael smiled, hinting that it was a good idea to have her with them.

Manus only nodded, refusing to admit his friend might have been right while watching his brother, who was several steps in front of them, remaining by Gwyn's side.

The group soon found themselves approaching the wharf, much quicker than Banning would have liked, and would have passed the two sagarts as they made their way into the port were it not for Anam who spotted them in the crowd and the group over to where they had stopped so that Cullen could catch his breath.

Cullen, who had been seated on some stacked sacks of grain, stood as the two princes and their entourage approached them.

"It is good to see you Prince Dar." The elderly priest said as he did his best to bow while holding onto his staff so as not to lose his balance.

"And you Sagart Seb." Banning returned the bow, a pang of guilt filling his stomach at how frail Cullen looked. For unlike his brother, Banning was not a stranger to the temple of Barra and had prayed with Seb Cullen on many occasions.

Banning also bowed politely to the younger priest standing next to Cullen.

"My apologies Milord." Cullen replied when Banning said he wasn't familiar with the second priest. "This is Caittle Anam. From one of the southern provinces."

"He's the sagart who told us we would be able to find you in Auvereen." Kael added. "Seems like Barra knew where you were all along."

"Really?" Banning stared at Anam, disappointed to find out that Barra had such an interest in him. Anam on the other hand simply bowed in return to the prince's query. For what could one say when the eyes of a god were upon you?

"Seems like this chance meeting was meant to be as well, Prince Aerin." Anam said to Manus in a thick accented voice that Banning noticed had the same inflections as that of the Lahunnans. "If you and your men don't mind going ahead of us, Sagart Seb and I will follow and hopefully catch up with you by the time you find a ferry to return us to the Camalain."

"Ferry?" Gwyn asked as all of them moved to one side because men had come to retrieve the sacks that Cullen had used as his seat. "Are you not berthed within the port?"

"No Milady." Manus replied. "Since we are foreigners we were not permitted within the port's protective walls."

"I can remedy that." Gwyn smiled. "My uncle is married to the Soya. I will send word to him so that he can authorize the relocation of your ship to within the port."

Manus thanked Gwyn for her concern but said there was no reason to move the Camalain when they would soon be leaving.

"Come on Manus!" Banning said, seeing an opportunity to prolong his return home. "What's another day? Or two? I'm sure the men could use a break after your search for me."

"The men are just fine!" Manus retorted, avoiding eye contact with Kael or any of the other members of the Royal Guard.

"But Gwyn is also flying to Kinsale." Banning countered. "To make some deliveries on her way home. Two ships flying together will be much safer than trying to make the journey separately. Even you should see that is sound advice."

Manus knew that it was but found that he did not want to agree with his younger brother.

"Besides," Banning continued, "Gwyn let me borrow money for some incidentals and I would like to repay her."

"Incidentals?"

"Clothing mostly. Some other things."

"Well, let me know the amount and I will reimburse the Lady!"

"Boys, please. Please!" Gwyn giggled as she came to stand by Banning, taking one of his hands in hers. "We've become such good friends over these past weeks that I am not concerned with the money."

"But?"

Gwyn, not letting go of Banning's hand, ignored his plea and looked at his brother. "I hope this can be a start of a beneficial friendship for us as well, Prince Aerin. Your country and mine."

Manus wanted nothing to do with Iniscarn, but what could he say to Gwyn's comments? Obviously saying no would not only be an insult to Argus Gwyn and possibly hurt what little relations they already had with Iniscarn. And Manus knew he would not hear the end of it from his father and mother if he blundered this meeting.

"Come on, Man!" Banning blurted out, interrupting his brother's thoughts. "Jump!"

"What? Jump?"

"An old Scarnian saying." Banning smiled. "Just a day or two. I bet even you could use a break."

"He does have a point, Man." Kael agreed.

"I had already decided to concede before the two of you started to badger me." Manus sighed. "How do we go about this Milady?"

"Please, call me Gwyn. Manus, if I may?"

"My uncle keeps several couriers down here to run errands around the city. I'll send word to him about having your ship moved into the port. In the meantime we can wait aboard my ship until yours arrives."

"If it arrives."

Gwyn smiled at Banning's brother. "No worries, Manus. It will"

"Either way I should get back to the Camalain."

"No need Manus." Kael replied. "I can fly back in your stead and work things out with the captain. That way you can stay here with your brother."

Gwyn also offered one of her gliders to get Kael back to the Camalain so that he would not have to waste time hunting for a ferryman.

"Seems like you have thought of everything." Manus said, complimenting Gwyn on her ingenuity.

"Thank you. Now if you gentlemen will follow me I'll take you to my ship. In case we get separated just ask for the vessel called the Kasser."

Banning, who seemed quite relieved at the outcome, mouthed a thank you to his brother before Gwyn motioned everyone to follow her as she took a leisurely pace through the crowd so as not to lose the priests.

"Watch them." Kael whispered as he shuffled next to Manus and nodded towards Gwyn and Banning.

"Uhhuhh." Manus agreed with his friend, grateful that no matter what their differences Kael was looking out for his and his family's best interests.

In this case it was not necessary for Kael to point what was so obvious to Manus. For Banning had not let go of the Scarnian's hand during their entire exchange and it looked as if they would continue with this intimate connection while walking to Gwyn's ship.

Yes Manus would watch his brother carefully and figure out how to end Banning's friendship with Argus Gwyn.

***

True to her word Gwyn was able to talk her uncle in to directing the dock master to have the Camalain moved into port, with the ship being berthed a handful of docks away from the Kasser.

All afternoon the mood had been festive on the Camalain at hearing of Banning's rescue. The crew that had gathered on the main deck (almost everyone who could squeeze themselves around the glider) cheered loudly at Manus' return with his brother by his side.

Among the group whose voices were raised in joy were Thear Ibor and Moro Croft. The captain and steersman were two men who were probably the happiest to see Banning for they had also been on that first trip to Ardane and blamed themselves for the attack. Guilt that finally melted away as Dar Banning and his brother approached them.

"Welcome aboard Milord!" Ibor bowed. "It is good to see you."

"Thank you Captain Thear." Banning smiled. "It is good to see you too. Hello Master Moro. You are well?"

"Yes Prince Dar." Croft repeated Thear's bow. "Now that we have found you."

Banning could only blush in embarrassment at the comment, a pang of guilt coursing through his body at what his absence must have been like for these people.

Patting his brother on the shoulder, Manus steered Banning towards Kael who was chatting with a group of the crew.

"Liam?" Banning couldn't hide the look of surprise at seeing someone else he knew on the Camalain. "You too?"

"You know him?" Manus asked, unable to hide the incredulity from his voice, halting Liam's own greeting in mid-sentence.

"Cullen's son? Of course." Banning replied, surprised at how quickly he had forgotten his brother's penchant for coarseness. "You forget, while you were studying battle tactics with the war masters I was in Sagart Seb's home studying the lore of the gods."

Manus only harrumphed in annoyance at his brother's rebuke before informing Liam of his father's exhausted state and suggested that he should go help him back to his cabin.

"I'll go with you." Kael offered as he and Liam watched the Camalain's crew part so that Cullen, followed by Anam, who had a hand out to catch the older priest in case he stumbled, could board the ship.

"No Kael, I need you to stay." Manus interrupted. "We need to talk."

Banning watched as another man with dark hair that was clipped short, a square jaw that looked like a man could shatter their hand against it, and who was built as if he was ready for a brawl, stepped forward to talk to his brother.

"If you don't mind Prince Aerin I can help the lad with his father."

"Certainly Gorman. Thank you."

"So what's up?" Kael asked distractedly, watching the two men hurry over to Cullen to help Anam escort him to his cabin. The elderly man allowed his son to take his elbow to guide him while Gorman began shooing men back to work so that they could walk unhindered to the cabin section.

"We've been invited to dinner." Manus explained, ignoring what was going on behind him. "Or I should say Banning and I were invited to the home of Argus Gwyn's uncle. I would like you to come as my guest."

Kael readily accepted the invitation for it was quite common for him to be at Manus' side for a social event.

"When do we leave?"

"Within the hour. I'll give you something fine to wear. Banning I have some clothing for you as well."

"Why? Don't you like what I have on now?" Banning joked, fingering the pale blue scarf he had yet to take off.

"Not really." Manus frowned, a distasteful look on his face as he took in his brother's attire. As of yet Manus had not bothered to ask Banning why he was wearing the thing. "You look like a native."

Abashed by Manus' disapproval Banning slid the scarf from around his neck, making sure that Gwyn's brooch disappeared within the folds of the fabric.

Kael asked if anyone else had been invited.

"The sagart's were." Manus replied. "But both declined (an outcome that Manus was quite happy with). Cullen for obvious reasons. Anam because he wanted to pray or something."

"And what of the crew?"

Manus looked upon the dozen or so men that had remained after Gorman's dismissal. Many of them had gone back to work with tasks that they had on the main deck. All were quite jovial, with laughter and light-hearted conversation passing among them for they were relieved that the youngest prince had been found and that they could now go home.

"Kael, looks like we'll be staying here until the day after tomorrow. Have the captain schedule leave for the men." Manus nodded for his brother to follow him towards his quarters. "And have Ibor send them out in shifts. And have them stick close to the port. As far as the taverns outside of its walls."

"Aye."

"And make it quick! We haven't got much time to get ready."

***

So, dressed in their borrowed finery, Kael and Banning along with the properly attired Manus, found Gwyn and several of her own crew on the Camalain's main deck deep in conversation with Thear Ibor.

"Well this is a pleasant surprise." Manus lied as he watched his brother's face light up with joy at the sight of Gwyn, while acknowledging the other people in her group. "I thought we were meeting you at the wharf's entrance."

Gwyn, dressed in a silken gown of grey, almost a dusky purple in tone, strewn with crystals so that it looked like the starry night had come to move about them, curtsied.

"A change of plans." Gwyn began to explain. "Once the Soya Alayna heard that you were here and how my uncle was having you for dinner, she commanded that the meal should be at the main villa so that she could meet you and your brother."

Manus, who missed the smirk that appeared on Banning's lips for he had been considered too insignificant to be entertained, tipped his head to Gwyn.

"We are honored." Manus smiled because a meeting with one of the matriarchs that ruled the city states might prove beneficial for his family, especially if there was a man in the Soya's own family that might be an advantageous marriage for Banning and clan's Aerin and Dar.

"My uncle has already headed up to the villa and the Soya has sent a couple of carriages for our convenience." Gwyn pointed to the two ornately carved wooden vehicles, small enough to maneuver the streets of Auvereen, waiting at the end of the pier. "So whenever you are ready."

"Looks like we'll be later than I expected." Manus said to the captain of the Camalain. "I'll have the guards on duty send word to you once we're back onboard."

"As you wish Prince Aerin." Ibor responded. "Although the usual crew will be on duty if you need anything upon your return. Enjoy yourselves Milords. Mistress."

Manus, his brother and the others made their way to the gangplank so that they could leave. But they weren't the only group of people preparing to disembark the Camalain. Groups of Manus' men had gathered on the main deck and were readying themselves to enjoy a night in the lower quarter of the city.

One such group was that of Gorman and his troop of men, all of whom were waiting politely for their prince and his company to leave.

Kael caught sight of Liam who was talking to his squad leader and the man's partner, and in a not so obvious way raised a hand in goodbye.

"You sure you don't want to join us?" Heath, Gorman's partner asked Liam as Kael turned his back on them and followed Manus and the others onto the deck.

"Yeah." Liam crossed his arms over his chest. "I just want to be close in case my father needs anything."

"Understandable." Gorman agreed as he nodded for his men to head out.

"Stay out of trouble!" Manton chimed in with a mischievous wink of an eye.

"That should be easy with you leaving!" Liam laughed.

It was rare that Liam had a rebuttal for any of Manton's witty, if not vulgar jibes and the others simply chuckled at Manton's attempt to feign hurt feelings over Liam's remark as they dragged Manton away.

So in the fading light of the day, with lanterns being lit on ships surrounding them and a warm orange glow being cast by them, Liam watched his friends, along with several other groups of men from the Camalain, make for the gates that lead into the city.

Liam did check in on his father, who was asleep, murmuring incoherently while Liam made sure that there was water close by in case his father woke thirsty. Liam couldn't help but look upon his father's weathered features and worry about his health before dousing the lantern in the room that had been lit and slowly closed the door to the room so as not to rouse him.

Not knowing what to do and feeling a little lonely Liam made his way to the room of his friend, Moro Croft. But the steersman had also gone off into town with another party to also enjoy a much needed break.

Liam's then headed to the galley in the hopes of having the cook dole out some work that he could do. But with the prince and the majority of men taking their meals out in the city Yanno Crogan had also decided to take the night off and for once was nowhere to be found.

Cutting through the dining hall where about a score of men were sitting about while waiting their turns for shore leave, and not wanting to go back to an empty cabin, Liam made his way back to the main deck only to find Caittle Anam standing at the railing looking out into the silhouetted city.

Great, Liam thought glumly for the sagart had begun to make him feel uncomfortable over the past couple of days. Not wanting to share the railing with the sagart, Liam decided to go back to his room and stay holed up there until his friends returned. But Anam turned before he could leave and beckoned for the young man to join him.

Liam faltered in his retreat as the sagart smiled at him, his face brighter than the hanging lanterns on their posts, while patting the railing beside him.

"Liam, please. Will you join me?"

With nothing else better to do and the grey eyes of the attractive sagart upon him Liam's resolve to escape to his quarters melted and Liam found himself moving to go and stand in the offered space beside Anam.

Liam's sense of unease at being around Anam returned as the two stood listening to what sounded like an accordion being played. The instrument's sharp notes pierced the night, while voices of men and women called out to each other and lanterns held by people moving about their business bobbed over the streets like mythic will-o-the-wisps.

Anam finally broke the silence and the haunting quality of the evening by asking Liam about his father.

"Okay. Sleeping." Liam only gave Anam a sideways glance while other thoughts ran through his head. "Seems like he has the weight of the world on his shoulders."

"The same could be said for you." Anam chuckled.

Liam turned to look at the sagart and found Anam with a smile on his face, a strange knowing look in his eyes.

"If you ever need to talk I am here." Anam added.

And what would you like me to say? Liam thought as a chill ran down his spine and his hands became clammy against the brass railing he was gripping tightly. That I blame you for draining the life out of my father? Or?

Or.

"It's you." Liam blurted out, following that statement with a curse for letting his tongue slip.

"Of course it's me!" Anam laughed in agreement.

"No, it's You." Liam whispered, his eyes not leaving the sagart's, as he did his best to control his body from shaking. "Barra, it's you. It's you."

The friendly smile never left the man's lips but Liam could have sworn that in the lamp lit glow of the night something changed in Anam's eyes.

It also seemed like Anam was waiting for Liam to continue with what he had to say. But with the sagart's piercing gaze upon him Liam found himself at a loss for words.

"Come. Sit."

The words were softly spoken, neither a command nor a plea. Still, Liam found himself following the sagart to go sit down with their backs resting against the wooden wall of the lookout deck.

And while Liam had pulled his legs to his chest, wrapping his arms about them with his chin propped on his knees, Anam had his right leg bent with the wrist of his right arm resting on it while he seemed to be searching for something in the star filled sky.

"Now why would you say such a thing?" The sagart didn't bother to look at Liam when he asked the question as he used the thumbnail on his right hand to pick at the nails on the rest of his fingers.

"Because." Liam started, now unsure of himself. "Because you knew that Dar Banning would be here. Even when my father was only vaguely certain of the direction we should take."

"And then there was the day that we found you. You were all bruised and bloodied and the next day there wasn't a scratch on you."

"Anam, you said my father healed you but I know this cannot be true because he couldn't use any of your, Barra's power, to heal any of the prince's men who had been trapped overnight in a sandstorm."

"Then there was the voice."

"Voice?" The sagart asked as he turned to look at Liam.

With those grey eyes upon him, almost black in this unlit area, Liam almost faltered in his response to the man seated next to him. But he did not.

"About a week ago. When I found you in that storage room? I know I heard you talking to someone else. A woman. Your voices were so distinct. Yet no one was in the room with you when I entered."

"I know I'm not crazy."

"You are not." Anam said in a soft yet reassuring voice.

"And my father always has an eye on you and is by your side whenever he is able. The others joke that he is attracted to you. But he gets uptight whenever I ask him about you and he has taken up a weapon again since your arrival just so he can defend you."

"And it's killing him!" Liam's voice rose slightly as he thought of the now worn and sometimes frightened appearance of his foster-father.

"Between the demands of Prince Aerin and this selfless need to protect you I see the life being sucked out of him. He's always so exhausted now."

"I'm sorry." The sagart breathed heavily, his accented voice barely making the words audible to Liam's ears.

"What?"

"I did not mean to be a burden on your father."

Liam watched as the man that everyone on the Camalain had come to adore and respect lowered his head in what looked like shame.

"Barra?"

"Yes." The man next to Liam sighed heavily.

At first Liam thought Anam was toying with him and waited for the foolery to come to an end. But when the man looked at him Liam only saw sadness and despair etched on his face.

No, this was not a man, this was a god.

Liam hissed Barra's name, surprised at how casually he was sitting next to the god and tried to stand so that he could bow before the deity, but the god grabbed Liam's right hand and stopped the young man from pulling himself upright.

"Please, Liam." Barra said in a voice that was barely a whisper. "Remain seated by my side."

A chill of fear at being so close to Barra ran down Liam's spine as he did what he was told.

And Liam, who was about to say something to Barra, was silenced by the god's hand being placed on his as the man who happened to be on guard duty passed them by. Barra acknowledged the man's greeting while Liam only nodded a hello while they waited to continue their conversation until the crewman was out of earshot of them.

"Barr,"

"No Liam. Use Anam."

"But why? The men would be happy to know that you are among us. And why are you here and not in the Garradh dhe Dia guiding us across the sky and land?"

A sardonic laugh escaped Barra's lips as he slid closer to Liam, much too close Liam thought, so that the sides of their bodies were touching.

"That would make a story in itself. A tale that would take most of your lifetime to tell." Barra chuckled again. "A fine tale indeed."

"So an answer to one of your earlier observations. Yes your father knows. And I have asked him to remain quiet and to keep my identity secret. Just as I now need to ask you to do the same."

"But why?" Liam asked.

Barra's only response was silence. So Liam asked the god another question that he had asked himself, as a child, in the comfort of his bed in the middle of the night.

"Why did you save me?"

Smiling affectionately at Liam, Barra reached over to run a hand over the back of Liam's head. "Because it was the right thing to do."

Liam lowered his head somewhat disappointed by what Barra said. "I thought. . ."

"You thought?" Barra asked as he continued to stroke the back of Liam's head. "You thought that I saved you to be my lover?"

Liam's head bobbed slightly, his face flushing in embarrassment at his own thoughts. For based upon the stories that had been handed down over the generations it was common for Barra, or any of the gods for that matter, to take a mortal lover. Male or female.

"Oh Liam! I saved you so that you could live! If it had not gone against the truce amongst my brethren I would have done everything in my power to have saved your entire village."

"That is the reason I am now among you."

Liam remained quiet, assuming that Barra would continue with his tale. Instead the fallen god asked Liam if that was the reason why he had chosen not to leave the temple.

"That and," Liam shuddered at the truth he had kept buried all his life. Liam started to say what weighed so heavily on him but choked on the words and stopped once more.

Barra placed a comforting hand on Liam's back and whispered some words of reassurance before Liam could find his voice once more.

"I thought that if I could stay within Kinsale, the temple, then I would not have to watch anyone else die."

Barra's hand moved upwards to squeeze Liam's shoulder.

"That is not living." The god explained. "The only one dying is you. And it is a slow death at that."

Liam couldn't help but feel sorry for himself upon hearing those words and swiped at a tear that had formed in the corner of one eye.

"Is that why you also took up masonry?"

Liam's face reddened at the question. "The guild was not far from the temple and I thought it would keep me closer to you. Stupid?"

"No. Misguided maybe. But not stupid. Especially when you are so much better at woodcarving."

"But how did you? I?"

Barra laughed at Liam's bewilderment; a sound so lighthearted that it eased some of the pain that had resurfaced for Liam while the two had talked.

"I always keep an eye on those who I think are special." Barra winked.

"But promise me Liam, leave the temple and get out and live. For no matter what happens," Barra used a finger to poke at Liam's head to emphasize his words. "I will be in there and in your heart."

"If you get back?"

The smile on Barra's lips wavered slightly as his arm wrapped around Liam's shoulders and pulled Liam closer to himself.

"I will not be going back." Barra said in a matter of fact tone to his companion. "Just think of me as you would any of your friends."

Their conversation ended for the moment as a colony of bats, their dark frenetic shapes blotting out the stars with their high pitched squeaks filling the air on their nightly hunt for food. Several hounds began barking in the distance at the routine disturbance to the night.

One last plaintive yip escaped the throat of the dog that had continued its tirade before the muffled sounds of Lahunnans conversing and that of booted feet walking across wooden decks and the docks reasserted its dominance over the evening.

Finally.

"I miss my father." Liam whispered.

"Not Cullen." Liam said a little louder as he tried to correct himself. "But my real father. I wish he were here."

"When it is time you will see him once again." Barra squeezed Liam sympathetically. "He will be waiting for you in Bas Hella, at the feet of Dubhas."

Liam nodded at the remark knowing that this was true.

"And Keir Aldwen will have to be patient for that reunion because I am hoping for a long life for his son. Until then I might be able to help you. I think there is still a spark left from my old body in this new one."

With that Barra instructed Liam to rest his head on his shoulder, to close his eyes and to relax.

While the god's hand came back up to stroke the back of Liam's head, relaxing him even more, his stress flowing away like rivulets of water running down the side of a wall, Barra began to softly chant in a language unknown to Liam. Soon Liam began to feel sleepy resting up against Barra, whose body felt as if it was getting warmer while the chill of the night was chased away.

Liam did stir when a bell in the city began to chime the hour. But Barra shushed the young man and said something to Liam in that alien tongue that sunk him further into slumber.

The bell tolled once more, resonating slowly, its voice muffled as if coming from far off in the distance. It rang again for a third time and then a fourth.

The fifth peal which sounded more like someone grunting softly was followed by several quicker higher pitched strikes.

The pinging's seemed to be coming faster and sounded more numerous. As if several bells were being struck at once, with their annoying clamor bringing Liam back to wakefulness.

Liam opened his eyes and not only found himself blinded but disoriented by what felt like the mid-afternoon sun washing over him.

Liam, his hands shading his eyes for he was still trying to adjust to the new time of day, heard someone calling his name.

At first Liam thought it was Barra trying to get his attention because the man shouting for him had the same type of accent found in southerners.

Liam's name was called again. Turning to get his bearings, Liam found himself standing in someone's yard. Or at least an attempt at one because there was no lawn, only clumps of withered grass dotting the ground with a path that was slightly more gravelly than the land that surrounded it that lead to a home that had its door and windows closed tightly so as to not allow any dirt from entering. On the far side of the home was a barn-like structure and what looked like a lean-to made of hides that sat off to one side of the barn.

The bells, hammering of metal on metal Liam now realized, was coming from the barn where someone shouted his name once more. As

Liam took a step towards the structure a little boy appeared from behind a pile of cumbersome rocks that looked similar in shape and size to the ones being used to make the wall that surrounded the place.

At first Liam thought the boy who looked to be about four or five years old had noticed him. But the boy quickly turned at the shouting coming from the barn.

That's when Liam found himself standing beside the boy. No, not beside him, it was more like he was inside the boy for when the boy moved Liam felt like he was being involuntarily pulled along and seemed to only see whatever the child could see.

"Here Pa!" The boy, or was it him that spoke? Liam wasn't sure because the voice sounded like it had been his own.

"Stay with Keesha where I can see you little man!" A voice shouted from within the barn.

"Okay." Liam and the boy giggled together as they moved towards the lean-to where a black fox was laying under the shaded enclosure and seemed to be gnawing on what looked like it might have been a wooden block.

But the two of them stopped when they walked by the barn opening to watch what was happening inside. There Liam saw a red hot glow coming from a forge made of stone with three men, each working at their own anvils, hammering away on three strips of metal.

Liam took a faltering step that should have sent him towards the lean-to but brought him closer to the barn because Liam thought he recognized two of the men.

One of them was definitely Cosaur Eli who somehow now looked to be about Liam's age and whose face was clear of the scarring he would eventually receive at the hands of the Mendens. The second was his partner, Brogan Giles.

And the third man? The third man who wore a heavy leather apron and was covered in sweat streaked with ash just like Eli and Giles? The third man that stopped in the middle of what he was working on to look over at Liam and smile?

Liam hissed in surprise. Looking at the third man was like looking into a mirror. The man's hair was shorter and he was brawny from his labors, but the resemblance was so similar that this could be none other than Kier Aldwen, his father.

"Pa." Liam whispered before excitedly shouting his father's name one more time.

Aldwen raised his hammer to continue working on the flattened piece of iron before him but stopped when he heard his son's shout, a look of shock appearing on his face as he watched his little boy running towards him.

"Liam! No!"

Aldwen dropped his hammer, its heavy head making a soft thumping sound as it sunk into the sandy floor as the man ran to his son, scooping him up in his arms and intercepting him from running into the barn.

"Now what did I tell you about coming into the barn while the forge is hot and we are working?" Aldwen asked his son as sighs of relief came from his two friends.

"Do not enter." Liam said sadly in his high pitched childlike voice.

"Do not enter!" Aldwen growled.

But the reprimand ended quickly as Aldwen smiled and spun his four and a half year old in the air while making whooshing, flying sounds which set Liam to laughing as his hands stretched out to grasp at the nothingness about them.

"Now be careful!" Aldwen chuckled as he came to a stop and sent pebbles scattering across the ground as the now dizzy man tried to maintain his balance. "I do not want you to get hurt."

Liam nodded and mumbled that he would be good. As he looked into the green eyes of his long dead father, Liam reached out to touch the face of the man that he missed so much.

But with a growl that mimicked Keesha as she worked on her chew toy Aldwen tried to capture his son's fingers with his mouth.

Liam continued to giggle and kick in glee as his father set him down near the fox that momentarily stopped masticating the block and eyed the child warily as he entered her space.

"And you keep an eye on him." Aldwen said as he pointed at Keesha.

The vixen only looked at the man who had nursed her and had taken care of her after finding her injured outside of Fomor. A look of disdain that said she only stuck around because she wanted to and that under no circumstances would she be babysitting his kit.

"That was close." Eli said to his friend as he started to hammer out the shape of a sword from the iron on his anvil.

"Tell me about it." Aldwen replied as he stuck the lump of metal he had been working on back into the forge, hoping that he had not left it cooling for too long. "I just wish they would finish the temple so that there was somewhere he could go while we worked."

"Told you he was going to be a handful." Giles added and ticked off some of the numerous adventures Liam had gotten into since his father retrieved him from Cloras. "Regret having him so soon?"

Aldwen looked over to the lean-to where Liam had gathered the rest of his wooden blocks, very few of which had retained there sharp corners, and had begun to build some type of structure. Aldwen stifled a laugh as Keesha stood, her hind left leg jerking involuntarily, the white gash across her black fur a testament to the fact that her leg would never work properly again, before she knocked over Liam's creation and chose a fresh block to gnaw on.

"No." Aldwen said confidently as he watched the indignation on Liam's face as his son gathered up the scattered blocks while Keesha wrapped herself in a ball, her bushy tail hiding the new toy in her mouth, and wished that he could join them and forgo working for the rest of the day. "No regrets at all."

***

"Well, ishn't tha shweet."

Manus, Banning and Kael had just returned from the Soya's dinner; a dinner that lasted most of the evening. A dinner that went on far longer than Manus personally would have liked and as a result he had imbibed more alcohol than normal in his attempt to make the party more palatable.

On the other hand Banning and Kael had enjoyed the meal and camaraderie of the Soya and her family and were less intoxicated than their leader. Just cognizant enough to flank Manus and lead him to the Camalain so he would not stumble and fall.

But all three sobered somewhat when they walked onto the deck of their ship and found Anam and Liam curled up together. Almost in a romantic way. At least that is what it looked like in their drunken state.

"Ho cute." Manus slurred as he leaned up against Kael and pointed a shaky finger at the two. "Looksh like L'm has found a new boyfriend."

Kael only frowned, unsure of what he was seeing as he tried to push his friend off of himself.

"Uh told you heesh was into olduh men." Manus sniggered.

"Leave him be Man." Banning hissed when he realized what his brother was intimating at and as to why.

"No!" Manus whined, pushing himself away from his brother and hip hopping several steps to maintain his balance. "Lesh go say hi to the couple."

Kael stood numbly, not wanting to know what was happening while Banning tried to stop his brother from making a fool of himself. But that was not necessary for Anam had been watching and listening to the trio for the entire time.

And after slapping his brother's grasping hands away Manus turned and stopped in his tracks when he found Anam looking directly at him.

A look was on the benign priest's face that Manus would not have expected. One of anger, or maybe it might have been loathing because it was hard to tell from the way the lamplight bounced off of the priest's stony expression.

What really kept Manus from moving forward and almost brought the prince in his drunken state to his knees were Anam's eyes. Eyes that now looked like molten lead, swirling about in the man's sockets, that made Manus feel like he would be burned alive if he tried to get any closer to the two.

Manus raised a hand and opened his mouth to try to speak. But held his tongue as Anam, his hand still wrapped around Liam's body, whose head was still resting on the priest's shoulder, shook his own head and silently mouthed the word "No".

Snorting arrogantly to hide his fear, Manus turned to look at his friends and, as if some spell that had been keeping him upright had been broken, fell into the arms of Kael as exhaustion and the alcohol won out over him.

"Mahbe we shhud let them have their alone time." Manus slurred as he rested his head against Kael's chest.

"Let me help you with him." Banning said to Kael as he tried to retrieve his brother who began to slump to the ground.

"Uhh, sure." Kael replied but hesitated as he watched Liam shift in the sagart's embrace and tried to snuggle closer to Anam who was whispering something into Liam's ear.

"Kael! Come on and help me. Before he gets sick or something!"

"Right."

Banning and Kael began to drag Manus away who kept stumbling over his own feet, his eyes closed and his head slack while he babbled incoherently to himself.

Fortunately one of the sentries spotted their predicament and opened the door to the cabin section for them and offered to help with Manus.

"Thank you, but we should be fine from here." Banning answered.

"Very good, Milord." The sentry replied as he closed the door between them.

The dismissal turned out to be premature because Manus gave them a hard time as they climbed the stairs to the prince's room. But when they got to their landing Manus pushed the two away and took a handful of faltering steps to open the door and to throw himself onto his bed.

While rocking his head back and forth and kicking the side of the bed with the heel of his booted foot that he had dangling off the side Manus began to trill on lewdly about the orphan and the priest.

"Shut up Man!" Banning scolded as he rolled his brother over to face the wall before apologizing to Kael for his brother's crudeness.

"Sorry." Manus said as he turned to look at the two. "You can't stay Kael. Banning needs a place to sleep."

"I know Man." Kael replied, not bothering to remind his drunken friend that they had discussed their sleeping arrangements earlier that day.

The frustration to this situation was that Kael had hoped tonight would have been the night he and Liam spent together. But now? Now it looked like that spot next to Liam had been taken by someone else.

Knowing full well that there would be space on their floor and that it was the furthest cabin from the main living section, Kael informed the two princes that he would be staying in the steersmen quarters in the fore of the Camalain.

But before Kael could leave Manus raised his head and called out to his friend.

"See." Manus had a hardened look in his eyes and his voice now sounded quite sober to Kael's ears. "I told you not to bother with Master Misfit. I told you that you could do better."

With that Manus struggled with the blankets beneath him, wrapping them around his clothed body and booted feet and rolled over to face the wall so that he could fall asleep.

***

Kael, Manus and Banning and the numerous men moving about the main deck weren't the only ones to have spotted Anam and Liam.

A presence that roved between time and space in his search for the missing god finally caught the movement that it was looking for.

A being so malevolent in nature that when he laughed at this discovery the most sensitive of Gwerin stirred and moaned at the bloody nightmares overpowering their dreams while those that were awake felt a cold chill run down their spines.

"There." Ciaran hissed coldly, his voice slicing the night like a knife cutting into flesh. "I have found you."

Chapter 14
Auvereen
The Camalain

"So. Do you want to tell me about last night?"

Liam had just gotten washed and was heading off to breakfast before joining Gorman and the others when he bumped into a very bedraggled looking Kael heading his way.

At first Liam thought Kael was just getting in from a night of revelry at the Soya's. But the flat tone of his voice and the hard look on his face chased Liam's own smile away because the unusual surliness in Kael caught him off guard.

"What do you mean?" Liam asked. His own question of how Kael's night had been dying on his lips.

"I mean you and Anam." Kael crossed his arms over his chest as if he was putting on some fleshy armor to deflect the blow Liam was about to lay upon him. "I saw, we all saw you cuddled up together on the main deck."

"You did?" Liam turned pale at this piece of information because the last thing he remembered about last night was the dream of his father then waking up alone in his own bunk that morning.

"Yes!" Kael hissed, maybe a little too harshly, as he remembered Manus' taunts from the night before. "So what was going on?"

"Nothing! We were talking?"

"About what?"

About how Anam was really Barra, a god the majority of men on the Camalain worshiped and would be joyful at having him among them? About how Barra had used his power to allow Liam to spend one more memorable moment with his father?

"Nothing." Liam reiterated.

"Come on Li!" Kael rocked on his feet as he looked at the walls on either side of them, frustrated by Liam's negative response. "It didn't look like nothing. Are you attracted to him?"

"No!"

"Then why were you out there? And what were the two of you talking about?"

Say nothing. Liam bit his lip as he heard Barra's words whispering in his head. No one must know that I walk among them.

"I can't say." Liam replied, finally beginning to understand the burden his father had been carrying for the past couple of weeks.

"Can't or won't!" Kael spat, becoming more frustrated at how Liam was dancing about this subject. "Just tell me what happened."

Looking at Kael and the hurt look that was appearing in his eyes, Liam felt his resolve about to waver, but a group of men came down the hallway, separating the two as they passed by, greeting Kael while Liam turned away from them to look at the blank wall in front of him.

Please, say nothing. Whether real or imagined the god's words for secrecy reminded Liam of what he needed to do.

"So?" Kael called out once the corridor was empty, forcing Liam to look at him once more.

"It's none of your business."

The hardened tone in Liam's voice caught Kael off guard and wasn't quite sure that he had heard what was really said so asked Liam to repeat himself.

"What Anam and I were doing or talking about is none of your business." Liam said more adamantly this time.

Kael was shocked that such a statement came from the gentle Liam. A trait he had found attractive in the man standing before him and muttered something about Manus finding all of this humorous.

Manus certainly was not the person to have mentioned at the moment.

"I know what the prince thinks of me!" Liam said defensively. "I may come off as being naive or simple but I'm not stupid."

"It's not what I meant!" Kael cursed his own stupidity for letting that comment slip and tried to apologize. "You know I don't think those things."

Unfortunately, to the detriment of their relationship, Liam saw a chink in Kael's plea for forgiveness and took it.

"The prince thinks you should be with someone better than me, so maybe you should!" Liam struck back and began to walk past Kael.

"What are you saying?" Kael demanded as he grabbed Liam's forearm, halting him from leaving.

"That we should stop seeing each other!" Liam tugged his arm out of Kael's grasp while trying to do his best to control his own emotions as he watched the surprised and pained look appear on Kael's face.

"The prince was right." Liam said as he twisted dagger in both his and Kael's heart. "This wasn't going to last."

And before Kael could say something in an attempt to salvage their relationship Liam turned and stormed away swiping at the tears that began to roll down his face.

***

Liam and Kael weren't the only ones fighting that day.

"No. That's out of the question. There's no reason for you to go back to the Kasser."

"We're both heading in the same direction. I see no reason why I can't fly with them."

"You'll be safer here."

"The Kasser is a bigger ship and has much more armament then the Camalain."

"Well then, because I say so!"

"Because you say so! Manus, you are not the boss of me!"

"But I am your older brother and because I'm the next in line to rule Birr."

"Next in line! Remember that when I tell you that I am flying on the Kasser!" Banning retorted.

Manus and Banning were on the bridge with Captain Thear going over the best possible and quickest ways to get back home when Banning broached the idea of staying on the Kasser.

Unfortunately Ibor had no choice but to remain by the brothers and listen to their argument as it became heated while watching in frustration as several of his bridge crew slipped out into the hallway to avoid this dispute.

"Still," Manus growled. "You're not going!"

"You know what?" Banning said as he took a step away from the maps the three men had been looking at. "Yes I am!"

"I forbid it!"

"I forbid it!" Banning mimicked. "Now you sound like mother."

"Do not!" Manus sniffed, appalled by the comparison. "I'm just trying to take care of you."

"And that's the problem because I don't want to be taken care of. I want my own life. At least until we get home. Is that too much to ask?"

Manus hesitated in their argument because for once he didn't have a reply for his brother's words.

Looking upon Banning's determined demeanor and knowing the truth of those words, for in the eyes of their mother and his own father, Banning was seen as a prized colt to barter, Manus wavered in his stance to keep his brother by his side.

"Fine! You win." Manus relented.

It took a moment for what Manus said to sink in because Banning thought his older brother would have stood his ground in this argument. But when he did realize what was said a smile covered his face and he thanked Manus profusely.

"The Kasser will need to stay within view and contact with us at all time." Manus said as he tried to quell Banning's enthusiasm.

"Where are we going to go with your eagle eyes upon us?"

"And you'll need bodyguards to protect you." Manus added while ignoring his brother's friendly barb.

"Well there's a group of men that have been acting as escort for me." Banning was about to tick off their names but Manus stalled him.

"No. You'll need protection from our own people."

"How about one?" Banning asked, not really wanting to be chaperoned and looking for a compromise that would avoid having their argument start up again. "Lieutenant Cahl."

"You must be joking?" Manus frowned. "The man couldn't protect you the last time."

"Goban wasn't the only soldier with me and you can't blame one man for what happened to the barge that day. Can you Captain?"

"No, Prince Dar." Ibor said truthfully, wishing he had the forethought to have walked further away from Manus and Banning. "No one person could have stopped what happened to us that day."

Manus wanted to fume over this but having the captain side with his brother didn't help his cause.

"Cahl Goban can go with you."

"Thanks!" Banning beamed. "I'll search him out and have him pack up his gear and head over with me later. Now can we finish planning our trip?"

With that Banning went back to sorting through the maps before them, plotting the best possible routes that both ships could utilize.

Impressed and surprised by Banning's handling of the charts, and after correcting their route to cut across the flats to go to Fomor to be reunited with the Marmairn, Manus asked his brother how he had become so knowledgeable with them.

Banning appreciated the compliment as he memorized what Manus had said about their flight path.

"Brother, you would be surprised at what I've learned since I've been away from home."

* * *

Banning's farewell with his brother turned out to be quick and less emotional than the younger prince expected. The farewell just a goodbye once the details to the first leg of their journey were hammered out and memorized.

Gathering up Goban and his belongings didn't take up a lot of time either. Especially when the lieutenant had been living out of his kit and any necessary essentials that he did need had been stacked neatly to one side of his bunk.

"You don't mind Lieutenant? Following me over to the Kasser?" Banning asked Goban as they made their way across the main deck to the plank that lead to the dock.

"Of course not Milord. Will be like old times." What Goban didn't say to Banning was how grateful he was just to be away from his older brother and the man's intense scrutiny of his every action in the hope that Goban would do something wrong and have an excuse to discharge him from his service with the Royal Guard.

The two were discussing Goban's sleeping arrangements would be and who the other men were that had been safeguarding Banning when they found Karam Kael waiting for them at the gangplank.

"You look awful!" Banning said to his friend who, with blackish blue circles framing his eyes and his disheveled appearance, looked as if he had not slept since before their dinner with the Soya and her family.

"Thanks for pointing that out. You're a true friend." Kael replied before acknowledging Goban. "Just came to see you off."

"Lieutenant, please give us a minute?" Banning requested from his guard.

"Certainly, Prince Dar. I will just wait for you on the dock."

"Keep an eye on him." Kael said as he patted Goban's shoulder as the man headed down the plank.

"I'll keep both on him Master Karam." Goban called back before walking away from the two of them.

"So what's up?" Kael asked Banning once he saw the concerned look on the man's face.

"I just wanted to see how you were doing with you know?" Banning then proceeded to explain how the rumor of his break-up with Liam had already spread through the ship.

"Nice." Kael snorted. But he knew this piece of information, especially when the crew quieted their conversations when he approached them.

"Wouldn't tell me what was going on between him and the priest." Kael continued when Banning remained quiet. "And the only person who seems to be happy about this is your brother."

"Well, he has his reasons."

"I know what they are." Kael replied as he looked at Banning.

"Kael, Liam is a nice guy. Sweet." Banning explained, moving the subject away from his brother. "If I were you I would talk to him again about what happened. Maybe he just got in over his head."

But Kael interrupted Banning saying that a second conversation didn't seem likely.

"Why?" Banning shot back. "Have you told Liam about any of the men you've been with? Would you if he even asked? And by the way, how many men has it been?"

Kael blushed at the barrage of questions, remaining silent as he thought of the men Banning was alluding to.

"Exactly." Banning said as he smiled slightly, relieving some of the tension that had been forming during their discussion.

"But I'm not saying to get back together." Banning finished as he headed down the plank to join Goban who had been waiting diligently for him. "Just be patient and give him a chance to talk."

***

Patience.

This word was on Kael's mind as he made his way down to the storage bays where Liam and the others were stocking the new shipment of supplies for their return journey home so that they could leave first thing tomorrow.

Patience. A quality that up until recently, since he had met Liam as a matter of fact, had almost been non-existent in the gregarious and somewhat impulsive Karam Kael, who now regretted his earlier outburst and hoped to mend things between himself and Liam.

Upon finding the hold the men were working in Kael took a quick step back into the hallway so not to be seen and to gather his thoughts as to what he wanted to say when a conversation that had been going on for some time echoed back to him.

"And what does your father think?" A voice that sounded quite like Gorman's asked someone.

There was a long pause while the sound of wooden boxes scraping against each other filled the air before Liam's voice answered Gorman's question.

"I haven't told him yet."

"As always the father is the last to know." Manton added in a good humored sort of way as he grunted while moving something heavy.

"You should probably do it soon." This was Gorman again.

"I think he'll understand." Kael thought he heard doubt in Liam's voice.

"I don't know Liam." This was Heath. "To just pack up and leave on such a short notice."

"It's not like I'll be living out in the wild. Cosaur Eli said I could stay with him and his family. And since we're heading back to Fomor. . ."

Whatever else Liam said was drowned out as more crates were moved about the room.

"Just make sure you talk to your father." Gorman said in his own fatherly way.

"I will. But he won't change my mind. It just feels like it's time to set out on my own and live my own life."

"If you say so." Now it was Gorman's turn to sound doubtful.

"I do." Liam replied. "A place where there are no princes, no priests and no Karam Kael."

The others bemoaned Liam's sour grapes over his short-lived relationship but Kael had heard enough. Why bother to try and fix what they had when Liam had obviously decided to move on?

Now wondering why he had wasted his time to come down here to talk to Liam, Kael began to back away from the doorway to make a silent escape back to the upper decks. Unfortunately upon turning around to leave Kael found Cyril Yarrow blocking his path.

Kael could feel his skin burn hotly in embarrassment at having been caught by one of Gorman's men while Yarrow apologized for startling him.

"I, uhh, I wasn't here." Kael stammered, ashamed of his own timidity as he moved by Yarrow.

"As you wish Master Karam." Yarrow bowed his head in understanding.

Kael returned the gesture and hurried away as he did his best to ignore the look of pity in Yarrow's dark brown eyes.

Kael spent the rest of the afternoon moving about the bridge and the upper decks, doing his best to avoid bumping into Liam, who was also hiding in the bowels of the Camalain so as to stay clear of Kael, while berating himself at how devastated he felt over their break-up.

Kael stayed on the bridge and worked on into the evening until he was confident that Liam would be holed up in the galley working for Crogan and, in a sullen mood that Kael had trouble hiding all day, strode off to his own quarters to await the coming of his next shift in the morning.

Manus had already made it to their rooms, to the disappointment of Kael who had hoped to be alone for a bit, and was seated at the table in the room revisiting some maps for their upcoming trip, while absentmindedly turning a plate of fruit that was set before him.

"How was your day?" Manus asked, knowing full well the answer to that question.

Kael only grunted an incoherent response while grabbing a handful of grapes to eat before walking over to the bank of windows that made up the back of the room, trying to make out the darkened shapes of men and women in the lighted windows of the ship behind them.

"Something came for you." Manus said. When Kael turned Manus pointed to a wrapped package on his friend's bed. "Guard had it for you when I got here."

Popping the rest of the grapes into his mouth Kael went over to his bed to look upon the familiar shape wrapped in a brownish kid skin. Picking it up and pulling the folds back Kael revealed the present he had given Liam; the leather wristband dyed burgundy with lodestone charms tied to it.

"Nice." Manus remarked. "Who's it from?"

Kael knew that Manus had known what it was and to whom the wristband had been given to and didn't bother to respond as he slumped onto his bed while turning the rejected gift in his hands.

Kael paused in his melancholy musings, for attached to the wristband was the metal star Liam's father had made for his son oh so long ago.

"Must have forgot." Kael said as he ran a finger over the object, wishing that it was Liam he was holding and caressing.

"What?" Manus asked.

"Nothing." Kael replied, his face reddening at realizing he had spoken those words out loud.

Kael turned the wristband one more time in his hands before tossing it towards the foot of his bed where it bounced and flew over the edge, hitting the floor with a loud thump.

If he wants it badly enough he can come ask for it, Kael thought sourly as he lay back on his bed, leaving the wristband where it had fallen.

Manus on the other hand felt a need to twist the knife in Kael's heart a little more, as if to say I told you so, and went and picked up Kael's returned gift, tossing it in his hands a couple times so that the charms clinked sharply before dropping it on the table where Kael had no choice but to look at it.

"Maybe you can resell it once we get back to Fomor." Manus offered encouragingly. "Maybe you can go back to the merchant you bought it from and try to get some of your money back."

Kael only snorted in response to Manus' musings, knowing how foolish and embarrassing that would be; returning the item to its maker.

"Wine?" Manus asked, lifting one of the two wine skins from the floor.

"Sure." Kael reluctantly rose from his bed to take the skin from Manus' hand, tossing the piece of leather cloth over the wristband, obliterating it from his view once more.

"Might want to go find one of these for yourself." Kael said while gesturing for Manus to also hand him the second wine skin.

"You got it!" Manus laughed before going to ask the sentry on duty outside of the room to fetch some more wine and to maybe find something a little stronger to drink.

But Kael didn't want to wait for the guard's return to start drinking with his friend. Nor did he feel like sharing the two skins of wine.

Throwing a map over the covered gift so it was doubly hidden Kael went back to his bed and took a long pull from the first skin, ignoring whatever Manus was now going on about, hoping to not only be thoroughly intoxicated but to pass out before any more alcohol arrived.

***

The men of the Camalain were not the only ones who were having their hearts played with that day. For Sioda, the god of seduction, was making sure that at least one man on the Kasser was having his own feelings toyed with and tortured.

"What's he doing back here?" Ormin Lhoyt grumbled, the old scar that ran down his lower lip and chin turned pale as he clenched his teeth in annoyance. Or was it rage that appeared on his face?

Lhoyt, along with Mac, Davis and Lyle, the Kasser's requisition man who had somehow become a fixture in their little group, were on the main deck taking a break from their duties when Dar Banning and another man dressed as a member of Birr's Royal Guard were seeking permission from Tor Varin to board the ship.

Clune Davis was all too willing to point out to Lhoyt that it seemed as if Banning and his guard would be joining them on their trip to Kinsale.

"But why?" Lhoyt whined. "He's got his own fucking ship he can fly home on."

Lyle looked to Mac for an answer as to why Lhoyt was so irritated at Banning's return. Davis' partner only shrugged, feigning ignorance at Lhoyt's displeasure because few people on the Kasser, with the exception of Tor Lucilla (Gwyn's confidant) knew that their own captain, Emmis Daigh, had kidnapped the prince of Birr.

"I'm sure you have nothing to worry about." Davis jibed, knowing full well the true crux of Lhoyt's discontentment. "It's not like he's going back to Carnuaimh with us. Besides you should just tell him how you feel."

"Why would you say such things?" Lhoyt snapped.

"Because they're true."

"What do you know anyway?" Lhoyt scowled, watching Banning introduce his guard to Varin.

"What we all know." Davis continued. "That you've been mooning over Captain Emmis for years just as he has been mooning over Banning's father."

Lhoyt swore at his subordinate, his friend, while Lyle, the only one confused by this sudden outburst in their conversation, again asked Mac what was going on.

But Lyle was ignored as Davis continued to torture Lhoyt.

"The way I see it you got two options. To tell him how you feel or to finally move on and find someone else."

Neither of those options sat well with Lhoyt.

"Come on Lhoyt," Davis said, noticing the doubt in his commander's eyes. "There are other fish in the sea."

Lhoyt scowled, asking Davis what his absurd remark meant.

"I don't know!" Davis lied. "But the Lahunnans say it a lot. Don't they Lyle?"

Lyle's face reddened at being singled out by Davis because he had confided in Davis and Mac of his own attraction to the sometimes dour Ormin Lhoyt.

Lhoyt, who was oblivious to Lyle's own infatuation with him, ignored the man's mumbled agreement with Davis as Banning and his own man excused themselves from Tor Varin's company. "Great!" He hissed. "They're coming this way!"

"And be nice to him!" Davis whispered with a big smile on his face as he waved to the two Birrnians who were only several yards away from them. "Banning is no threat to you because we both know his eyes set are on someone else."

Chapter 15
The Olean Flats

The Camalain and the Kasser left on schedule the next morning. And Manus, confident to have a second ship accompanying them, and wanting nothing better than to get home, chose to cut across the vastness of the Olean Flats instead of hugging the coastline of his homeland.

The first day was uneventful, with the crews of both ships went through their routine of work and respite.

The second day dawned just as bland and looked as if it would be equally uneventful as the first for everyone; the exception being Liam.

Only a couple of days had gone by since his break-up with Kael and the emotional wounds from the ordeal were still fresh.

Liam also knew that Gorman and the others meant well as they tried to cheer him up. But today, today he needed, no wanted a break from his friend's pitying glances and of how they had been fawning all over him.

Receiving leave from Gorman to miss the day's activities, Liam did the only thing he could think of; to hide away from everyone by staying in the galley.

That's where Cullen found his son. At least, the sagart came across Liam in the dining hall seated on top of a table with his feet on a bench staring out the window watching the dull view of an unchanging horizon behind them.

Liam was so lost in his own depressing thoughts that he didn't hear the taps of his father's staff and didn't look up until a dark shadow appeared in the corner of his eye.

Cullen didn't bother to say a word as he planted the bottom of the metal shod staff onto the bench for stability as he climbed to sit next to his son, slapping away Liam's hand as his son offered to help him.

"The day I cannot climb one step is the day you will need to bury me!" Cullen rebuked as he leaned on his staff to join his son in watching the nothingness trailing behind them. "Do you want to talk about it?"

"Did Gorman send you?" Liam answered with his own question, his tone sullen, for he had also been trying to avoid dealing with his father.

"No. It was Anam who thought you could use the company."

Liam paled at the sound of the man's, no the god's, name.

"Anam told me what the two of you talked about before we left Auvereen." Cullen finally said after realizing his son wasn't about to say anything. "Is that why you and Kael ended things?"

Cullen watched as his son allowed his torso and head to droop between his legs, his back rounded as if the weight of the world had been hefted upon it.

"I didn't know what to do." Liam said as he sat back up and rubbed his face with his hands. "He, Kael kept asking questions and I didn't know what to do say, and I didn't want to lie to him." Liam didn't know what else to say and just shrugged at the hopelessness he now felt. "Why didn't you say anything to me about Anam?"

Cullen turned to his son and saw the downward turn of his lips and exhaustion in his eyes for Liam was starting to look exactly how he felt. Worn.

"That knowledge was not a burden I wanted to share with you."

Liam looked out the window as the Camalain shifted slightly and the sky began to grey as if a storm was heading their way.

"I know it doesn't seem like it right now," The sagart said as he patted his son's shoulder reassuringly. "But you did the right thing."

Liam was about to say something contrary to his father's words when the Camalain rocked violently, the tables and benches leaving the floor and sliding while Yanno Crogan's shout of surprise came from the galley as crockery could be heard shattering as it hit the floor.

"Not again!" Liam exclaimed, thinking that the Camalain would once again lose mobility and be marooned in the middle of nowhere.

"I do not think so." Cullen said while allowing his son to this time help him off the table.

Another groan ran through the Camalain as the ship tilted in the air as if it was trying to stay aloft. Liam kept a firm grip on his father so the man would not stumble and when he looked out the window Liam gasped in surprise at how quickly the sky had darkened to a sickly copperish grey hue. A color that reminded Liam of dried blood.

But through the rusted, sand swirling haze Liam could also make out what like three black shapes heading their way.

Cullen noticed them as well; three ships that looked like arrowheads as they easily cut through the roiling skies.

"Go find Gorman. Never you mind about Crogan," Cullen countered when Liam said that he should go help the cook. "He can take care of himself."

"But why? Do you know who these people are?"

Cullen left his son's questions unanswered as the ship rocked again, the priest's metal shod staff rapping painfully against the wooden planks of the floor.

"Go do as you are told." Cullen said as sounds of shouting and the pounding of booted feet could be heard coming from the hallways of the Camalain as its men began to arm themselves and head to their stations. "Just stay off the main deck and be careful my son."

***

Staying off the main deck was definitely sound advice during this unnatural assault from the elements.

But not all could heed the pit of fear in their stomachs since duty dictated them not to listen to common sense.

So, having to follow orders from Manus, several men ventured out into the open and staggered over to the glider with one of them climbing into the craft while the others began to untie its mooring lines.

Standing at one of the railings, his fingertips lightly pressed against the pitted brass, Anam watched as the glider rose from the main deck and just missed clipping one of the other men as the Camalain tilted awkwardly in the howling wind as the small craft struggled to stay aloft as it went to investigate who the newcomers were.

"Ennaya! He is here!" The fallen god thought as he watched the Kasser's two gliders flit into the sky to follow the Camalain's.

"I know brother." The echo of the goddess' voice sounded strained. "It is he who I am fighting to keep your ships aloft."

Barra, continued to listen to his sister and of her own battle with Ciaran and watched as walls of sand hissed into the air, forcing the Kasser and Camalain to veer back towards their pursuers, the two crewman who were still on the main deck losing their footing and holding onto the mooring lines so as to not slide over the edge of the ship.

"Then land us!" Barra thought as he easily strode over to the crewman, as if he was walking across a sward of grass on a calm sunny day.

"But you must escape!"

"You are not as skilled in the ways of my creations as I am." Barra thought as he raised the two stunned men to their feet. "Land us and save your energy for what may yet come."

"Sagart?" One of the crewmen asked as he unflinchingly laid his hand on the priest's arm for balance and for comfort.

"We must get inside." Barra replied to the man as Ennaya used that little bit of herself given solely to those vessels to help their steersmen steady their ships and to start a slow descent. "Your prince will soon be in need of you."

***

Indeed, Manus who was on the bridge and shouting at Croft to not land the Camalain, was going to need every able bodied man as he realized he might need to defend his ship.

"Are you mad? Get us aloft again!"

Kael, who was helping an injured crewman to his feet, watched as his friend went to the steersman who had slumped in his chair with his hands sliding off of the lodestones and began to shake the man into wakefulness.

"I'm sorry, M'lord." Croft sat up and wiped the sweat from his face. "But I cannot. She said we would be safer on the ground."

"She?"

Manus' question went unanswered as everyone quieted as the underbellies of three metal clad vessels could be seen out the main window while they flew over them and the downed Kasser.

"We are doomed." One of Manus' men moaned as fear overtook him while making the sign to ward off evil.

Doomed is what many felt as Ciaran whispered the word into the weakest of minds on both the Camalain and the Kasser.

Doomed is what the Camalain's glider pilot thought as well. But the word barely registered due to his connection to the lodestones as the three hulking ships made another run over the grounded vessels.

Doom tried to take hold of the pilot while he and the two Scarnian gliders began to weave around their pursuers in an attempt to harry them.

But whether from his strength of character or because Ennaya was whispering encouragements to him while keeping his small ship aloft, chance and hope filled his mind.

And Manus along with the rest of his crew on the bridge watched as their lone glider looped in midair and slammed into a bank of windows on one of the behemoths, its bridge, sending a shower of shattered glass into the enemy crew.

There were no shouts of joy or cheers of triumph, knowing full well their comrade had sacrificed his life to save theirs, as the ship fell from the sky, its lower decks crumbling like the shell of a dropped egg as it slammed onto the desert floor.

Even though it was not the Dotain that had been taken down rage filled the god Ciaran at the loss of the ship and most of his devotees. A rage that, because of the connection he was sharing with his servant Villis Dain, sent the captain to bellowing and swearing on his own bridge at the lost vessel. A rage so malevolent in Ciaran at being thwarted by one mortal that the elements he had usurped from Maat took up his anger by sending a howling wind so strong that the Camalain and Kasser shifted and rocked as the torrent buffeted against their hulls.

But the Birrnian's sacrifice had its desired effect and Aerin Manus watched solemnly as the two remaining Menden vessels landed.

"What are your orders?" Captain Thear asked of Manus as he turned from what awaited them outside while ignoring the oppressiveness and fear that was tugging at his soul.

"Defend." Manus commanded, using a word that his life had been trained upon. A word that now felt foreign on his tongue. "Defend the bridge, Captain. With Croft and the other steersmen. We will need all of you alive if we are to try to make an escape from here. And you as well." Manus added, including his injured crewman.

"The rest of us will go out to defend the ship." With that Manus collected Kael and the remainder of the crew and left to see what awaited them outside.

This assault had been so sudden that no one had time to arm themselves properly, their only defense being what weapons they had at their sides. Fortunately the arms master for Manus' ship had the forethought to call upon some men to help him drag most of the armory down to the lower egress of the Camalain so Manus and many other men found an assortment of weapons and armor to use.

Kael had found some studded armor in the pile that looked as if it might fit and began strapping it on when he spotted Liam across the crowded room already covered in lightweight leather armor with shoulder guards with Gorman's punching daggers covering his hands and its small bucklers strapped into on his forearms.

Kael couldn't help but notice how afraid Liam looked; his skin pale with a thin sheen of sweat already covering his forehead. And when Liam noticed Kael's stares Liam tried to force a smile on his face, a futile attempt, before turning to listen to something Gorman had to say.

"He should not be here." Kael said to Manus who had also finished putting on some armor and was now strapping on some extra daggers to his hips.

Even though Manus agreed with Kael that this was not the place for Kier Liam, the prince told his friend to ignore him and to stay focused on what was to come.

"At least send him to the bridge!" Kael pushed as worry for the man crept into his voice.

"No! We go now!" Manus snapped before ordering the bay doors to be opened and commanding his crew out onto the flats.

As the squads spread out to defend the Camalain from the horde of Mendens heading their way, Kael took up his own position as a bodyguard for his friend, the prince's group of warriors staying close enough to sprint back into the ship if they had to.

"What of your brother?" Kael asked as their handful of archers sent a rain of arrows into the oncoming enemy.

Manus looked towards the Kasser where its own crew, none of them distinguishable at this distance, had emptied from their ship to also engage the enemy.

"Hopefully he's smart enough to keep his head down."

***

"You either do as I tell you or I'll order your man to tie you up and to sit on you! Something tells me he'll obey that command!"

"You wouldn't dare!"

"Banning, don't test me on this!"

"But you need me out there to help you!" Dar Banning shouted back at Argus Gwyn, frustrated at being banned from entering the fray.

The captain of the Kasser had already sent a group of her crew to defend their ship and now geared for the battle was going to join them. Dar Banning was accompanying her, trailing a little behind while trying to don the armor Lyle had given him.

"I need you alive!" Gwyn shot back, stopping in the corridor they were hurrying down to look at Banning, forcing the prince to come up short so he would not bump into her. "I don't need to be worried about where you are on the battlefield. And I certainly don't want to deal with your brother if I have to explain your demise."

Banning was about to tell Gwyn that he could take care of himself but his rebuttal never left his lips as Gwyn caught him off guard by stepping in to kiss him, not concerned that a number of her crew and Banning's man, Cahl Goban, were standing about them.

"No." Gwyn said adamantly, even though a sadness had begun creeping into her voice, as she pulled away from Banning to look at Goban. "Lieutenant Cahl. Take your prince and find Lyle on the upper level. I would appreciate the help from you two in defending our children."

"As you wish Milady." Goban replied, halting his charge from following Gwyn as she and the men and women with her began to leave.

"Be safe, Prince Dar." Gwyn called out one more time, a longing for him in her eyes, before turning a corner and disappearing from view.

***

But who would be safe during this time of crisis?

Neither the Birrnians, nor the Scarnians as Villis Dane's men swarmed onto the desert sands. Certainly not the Mendens whose prey were all too willing to defend themselves to their deaths.

But Ciaran had guided the Mendens to this place in search of Barra and, even though he chose not to be seen by his followers, his presence could be felt by them while allowing some of his power to flow into his new favored pet.

"Just keep the crew of the larger ship at bay." Ciaran's voice whispered in Dane's head. "Focus your energies on the smaller one. Your goal is there."

There was no need for Dane to respond for the god not only shared his body but his very thoughts as well. So the Menden captain, caparisoned for battle with his partner Cremin Vokes numbering as one of his own bodyguards, directed his men into the conflict.

Dane already knew these Sothair Dor were not without teeth and both he and Ciaran fumed once more as the two remaining gliders barreled down upon them to scatter his men and to shatter the bodies of those who were not fortunate to not get out of their way in time.

As Gwyn's men came in for a second run Dane's hand came up and with a sweeping motion, caused the pilot of one glider to lose control over the ship and to slam against the ground. The other glider made for the Kasser in attempt to help his comrades. But Ciaran wanted none of this nuisance and closing Dane's hand, crushed the fleeing glider into a ball of wood and metal. The flesh of the Scarnian inside mangled beyond recognition.

"Leave the injured." Dane commanded, his voice reverberating over the howling winds as one of his men went to help another of the wounded crew. "Our goal is before us and any of the injured who wish to live will find their own means to return to the Dotain."

Doing as he was told Dane's crewman dropped his friend to hurry into the battle. The injured man, whose left leg had been broken when the glider hit him, stifled a cry of pain as he sunk back to the ground and fought to hold consciousness so that he could drag himself back to the ship.

"I can smell him." Dane said as his minions fell upon the clusters of men surrounding the Camalain.

"Who?" Vokes asked, fear in his voice as he watched the dark look of a god's hunger within Dane's black eyes.

"My nephew." Dane hissed as he tried to search out one man among the many battling Birrnians.

Vokes remained quiet, already guessing at which of the two had responded to him and, not wanting to interrupt their dark communion any further, remained silent.

"Come!" Dane laughed. "To victory!"

"Victory!" The Mendens about him shouted, with Vokes adding his voice to the chorus as well, as the group hurried to bring down the men of the Camalain.

**

"Liam! Keep your arms up! To your right! Block! Block!"

The fighting had been going well, as any battle to the death can, with the Birrnians able to hold back the Mendens that had come at them at the onset of the attack.

But a second wave of Mendens fell upon them, joining the remaining warriors from the first, with their numbers swelling enough to break the defenders, sending many of them back to surround Manus while several of the squads splintered away from the Camalain.

One such beleaguered group was that of Gorman and his men.

The squad leader, with his well-trained group of fighters soon found that they were being pushed further onto the flats while also trying to protect the weakest of their number. Keir Liam.

That strategy soon failed as Gorman found himself, Dolan and Liam separated from Heath and the others. The distance of a few feet becoming many yards as the Mendens filled the gap as they tried to take them down.

"Backs together!" Gorman shouted to his two remaining men while his sword found the exposed neck of a Menden that was before him, sending a spray of blood across friend and foe alike. "To your right Liam! Block!"

Gorman not only hoped that Liam would defend himself but saw no choice but to use the young man as a shield to protect his and Dolan's flanks and backs while the two did their best to keep the heaviest fighting away from their charge.

"Keep those arms up! Left, left! Forward! Move forward!" Gorman directed as Dolan cleaved the man in front of him before battering another man with his shield, sending him to death or unconsciousness, who could tell, opening a space towards the rest of his men who were trying to push their own way towards them. Gorman stepped backwards, forcing Liam forward, his shoulder or back continuously touching Liam's, making sure he was still on his feet as the three of them moved towards the Camalain.

The trio did not get far as another group of Mendens engaged them, forcing the Birrnians into another dance of fighting and parrying.

"Liam! Keep your arms up! To your right! Block! Block!"

But this dance of defending their greenest fighter eventually took its toll on them for as Dolan skewered a Menden, taking a moment to catch his breath as the dying man slipped off of his sword, another Menden as tall and as heavily built as Praish Gorman came hurtling through the air. A hammer forged of iron held firmly in both of his hands.

A hammer that connected with the head of a stunned Dolan, shattering it like an over ripe melon, sending the man's limp body into Gorman and Liam who scattered as the Menden used Dolan as a ram against them before allowing the dead man to fall to the ground.

"Liam! Run!"

Gorman's command went unheeded as Liam, numb with shock, watched as the broken face of the jovial Kelman Dolan allowed its contents of blood and pulped brain to seep into the sand beneath him before turning his attention to the fight between his squad leader and Menden.

Gorman blocked the man's swings, taking a blow to his left shoulder that ripped its guard from his body. But it was not the mighty blows that brought Gorman down. But the enemies foot as it connected with his groin.

One kick. Then another to the groin while the man lay on the ground followed by a kick to Gorman's side that finally knocked the wind out of him.

"No!"

Surprised by the shout the Menden turned at the noise, ready to defend himself, only to smile at what he saw; a boy who was barely able to keep himself from shaking in fear.

"Are they sending babies to fight a man's battle?" The Menden laughed, his eye appreciating Liam's boyish handsomeness that was covered by the blood and gore of his friend. "Stand down! I keep you for myself. Yes?"

Between the Menden's thick accent, the blood pounding in his ears and the clamoring of battle raging about them Liam did not understand a word his enemy had said. But Liam certainly understood the leering in his eyes.

"Stay away from me!" Liam shouted as he raised his weaponed hands to defend himself, not realizing he had taken several steps towards his attacker. "And stay away from him!"

If Liam had been better skilled in the art of combat he would have kept his mouth shut. For the Menden clearly understood what he had said and caught the flick of his eyes towards his fallen comrade and turned to see Gorman trying to stand. The Menden quickly sent a kick into Gorman side, breaking a rib or two before kicking the man in the face knocking him out cold.

Turning back to Liam, the Menden only laughed at finding that the young Birrnian had taken several more steps towards him and was only about an arm's length away from him.

"Ahh! Your man!" The Menden said, assuming he understood Liam's predicament when the Menden saw more of his comrades trying to rush to his aid.

"Well then." The tone of the Menden's voice had taken on a businesslike tone as he raised his hammer, ready to end Gorman's life. "Forget this, Sothair Dor. You are Krattis' now."

But Krattis' blow never found its mark for as he was about to take his swing a loud hissing sound filled the air followed by a shout of pain and a gurgling moan as a Menden died.

Several more distinct whines filled the air and another man near Krattis and Liam died as a ballista from the Kasser passed through his torso, pulling most of his intestines out of his body, before the missile sank into the ground behind him.

Another volley of missiles rained down upon the Mendens, killing a few as the ballistae created obstacles for the combatants to move around, before Ciaran took matters into his own hands and crushed the section of hull from which the missiles had emerged.

And as the last of the missiles flew towards Krattis, the man jumped forward as it crashed into the ground behind him, a hiss of surprise escaping his lips as a sharp pain filled his side. Because, whether from seeing a chance opportunity or that the god of war chose to guide his hand, Liam had thrust his left hand forward, his blade slipping through the seams of Krattis' armor which came to rest in the man's right lung.

"You!" Krattis coughed as he grasped Liam's wrist, keeping the blade in place so that he would not bleed out.

Liam struggled in the man's grip, unable to get away. And as Krattis dropped his hammer to get his left hand onto him, Liam began to swing his free hand frenetically to keep the man away.

"Liam!"

Heath, Manton and the others continued to call his name to let him know that they were near, trying to cheer him on, fearful that they were about to watch another of their number fall.

Their shouts, carried on the winds of battle caught the attention of Kael and Manus who turned to watch the struggle.

"Stay!" Manus shouted when he saw Kael about to sprint to Liam's side.

"That's an order!" Manus commanded, countering anything Kael was about to say.

Cullen had also heard the calls of Gorman's men as they tried to reach Liam.

"My son." That sagart whispered in horror as the murderous Menden fell upon Liam, dragging him to the ground, the two obscured by the chaos about them.

"I am sorry my friend." Anam said as he rested a consoling hand on Cullen's arm. But what could a man say, or even a god for that matter, at watching the death of one's child?

But there was something that Anam could do so that the killing might end.

"Truce, Uncle." Anam whispered across the ether as he dropped his hand from Cullen's arm and walked to stand beside Manus. "Let this game between us end now!"

"I know you can hear me Ciaran." Anam thought as the sounds of battle raged on about them.

"And what do you offer me?" Amusement filled Ciaran's voice when he finally replied to Anam's pleas.

"My life." Anam answered.

"Why would I want such a diminished thing?" Ciaran laughed.

"You would not be here if it was not something you still did not want." Anam countered. "Please, have mercy."

"Mercy." Ciaran laughed once more, allowing the winds to subside and the sun to once again be revealed across the land. "Very well!"

"Sagart! What are you doing?" Manus halted Anam as he took a step towards his blockade of soldiers.

Anam did not reply to the prince. Nor did he turn at Cullen's calls as he passed by members of the Royal Guard.

"Uncle?" Anam called out as two Mendens came at him.

"Oh, very well!" Ciaran was in good humor over this victory and had only meant to toy with Anam, as a feline might with a rodent. But he did what was asked of him and not only commanded the Mendens but the Birrnians and Scarnians to halt their assaults on each other.

Anam continued to make his way across the flats, the air filled with the painful groans of the injured and dying, to meet the group of armored men that were approaching him.

"I see you are taking better care of this vessel." Anam said out loud to his uncle as the viciously handsome Villis Dane and his entourage came to stand before him.

"I favor this pet." Dane laughed, his eyes glittering wildly in amusement. "For now."

Anam did not reply as a soft breeze carried the stench of battle to their nostrils.

"So it is agreed? You will let these people go?"

Dane laughed loudly once more for Ciaran was enjoying this game he was now playing with his nephew.

"There must have been a misunderstanding. I said I would let them live. I did not say we would let them go."

"Very well." Anam sighed, resigned to the fact that, although many lives had been spared, the survivors would end their days in the servitude to Mendes. "The two of you may take my life."

"I will not have the blood of my kin on my hands." Ciaran replied as his essence left Dane's body to coalesce into the dark haired and horned being behind the captain.

"But I will gladly take the life of a god." Dane replied while unsheathing his sword.

"Barra!"

Heads turned, mostly those of Manus' crew, at the croak that escaped from Liam's lips as Yarrow lifted the bruised and bloodied man from under Krattis' lifeless body while Heath and Sidri tended to Gorman with Manton on his knees at the mangled corpse of his friend.

"No! Do not do this!"

And as Liam shouted his pleas to the god once more, a veil was lifted from the hearts and eyes of Manus' crew so that all of them came to realize just as Liam had that the god of the earth had been walking among them for this entire time.

Barra smiled warmly at the young man who was struggling in his friend's grasp so that he could run to the god. A smile that tightened painfully as Dane's sword slid into his body.

Except for Dane, Ciaran and several of the Menden's standing about them, horror crept onto the faces of the men at the sight of the captain's sword, blood running down its polished edge, protruding from the god's body.

Dane's first strike had been tentative. The sword only entering into Barra's abdomen, with the god holding his ground when the captain pulled out his weapon before quickly thrusting it back into him.

Groans of agony came from the Birrnians at the shock of how Barra remained silent, while being skewered on Dane's blade, only allowing the smallest trickle of blood to escape from his lips.

Barra couldn't help but stagger, a sharp gasp of pain finally slipping past his clenched teeth, as Dane pulled his blade out of the god, tilting the weapon so it cut into more of the god's mortal organs.

Instinctively Barra brought a hand up to try to staunch the flow of blood and from his innards falling out of his body while forcing himself to stand upright to face Ciaran, ignoring the shouts and prayers behind him, whose own face was a wicked mixture of glee and triumph as he watched the fall of his nephew.

"Uncle, please. Mercy." Barra coughed.

"Of course."

No word was spoken between Ciaran and Dane, the captain knew the intent of his deity and thrust his blade for a third time into Barra's body, pushing the sword underneath the god's left ribcage and letting it cleave into Barra's heart.

All watched, with some of the Menden's gloating of the apparent victory of their captain over this fallen god, while others mourned the loss of their patron deity as one last gasp escaped Barra's lips while all semblance of life finally fled from his grey eyes.

Only when Barra's corpse became burdensome did Dane lower his blade to push the god off of it and allowing him to fall into a heap on the ground.

"If I may Milord?" The Menden captain asked of Ciaran who now came to stand by his side. "A token for clan Villis?"

"Of course my god killer." Ciaran smiled. "A trophy to elevate the name of Villis in the eyes of your people. Status that will eventually help you and your family to surpass clan Lyro."

Dane looked to Vokes to see if his partner understood the implications of what was being said for the man's clan. But Vokes' face was clouded by the shock at what had just befallen and had not paid attention to what was being said between man and god.

No matter Dane thought as he called for two of his men to lift Barra's limp body so that he could behead the god.

Birrnians began to rush forward, comprehension dawning on them, offended and enraged by the desecration that was about to happen when Ciaran raised a hand. A gesture from the god that ceased the movement of the running men.

"Hold!" Ciaran's voice boomed across the land like the sound of thunder that announces the oncoming storm that is just beyond the horizon.

"Though your lives have been spared, thanks to the sacrifice of Barra, they have been given in forfeit. You are now in the servitude to the Menden clan of Villis. But heed my words! Take one more step and I will blot your minuscule lives from this land."

"Enough of this brother!" A feminine voice called out as Ciaran was about to command the two Mendens to again raise Barra's body so that his hand, Dane, could remove the god's head from the rest of his body.

"Be gone!" Ciaran fumed.

But the bodiless woman only laughed. A hearty sound, almost masculine in tone that brought streaks of cerulean, salmon's and pale yellow's into the sky. As if a second dawn was forcing itself upon the afternoon sky while a troupe of men and women materialized around Ciaran and his band of executioners.

"No Gwer shall be put into thralldom this day." The woman who led this group called out as she took in the people of Birr and Iniscarn.

Heads were bowed out of respect, as well as fear, when the most devout realized that it was Cavanna who was speaking to them, with Ennaya and Cillach, Aodhagan and Murra and the rest of the pantheon standing in judgment over the death of one of their own. The exception to this being Dubhas who walked the battlefield calling forth the spirits of the dead to join him in his halls.

"You cannot interfere in this sister!" Ciaran spat. "You are breaking the very rules you created."

"There are no rules to break for it was you who have interfered by taking the mortal life of my son. I am merely here to set things to right." Cavanna countered.

When Ciaran looked to Sioda for support the god of seduction and trickery remained silent, indicating his new allegiance in these matters.

"So be it!" Ciaran acquiesced.

"No! My trophy!" Dane shouted when Cavanna ordered his men to lower Barra's body to the ground.

"Be lucky I do not take your life as surety for taking that of my son's." Cavanna rebuked, her face darkening as if about to let a storm rain down upon Dane and his men. "No more will my son's body be defiled by your hands."

Dane, his men and Ciaran stepped away as the group of gods tightened their ring around Cavanna while the goddess laid out the body of Barra so that she could mourn his loss.

A sight like this, of all the gods standing together on mortal lands, had not been seen in over a thousand years and many Gwer came forward to see this spectacle and to pray one last time before the feet of Barra.

"Do not tarry here too long." Cavanna called out to the men now standing about them. "Once we leave, so too will my benevolence and you will once again be for the taking if my brother and his minions so chose."

"But we would have our dead as well." Aerin Manus said as he boldly approached the group of deities. Standing far closer to the gods than any of his other men were willing. "So that we may also grieve their losses, Mother of Us All, just as you grieve the loss of your own son."

Cavanna gazed upon Manus for a moment, as if she were holding his very soul within her hands and was peeling its layers away, to look at the true nature of the very being that stood before her.

"I hold your mother in high esteem," Cavanna's hard voice boomed out across the land. "The same cannot be said for you Prince Aerin. And even less regard do I have for your brother."

"This boon I will grant you. But let it be known that my favors do not come without a price and I will one day collect payment when I see fit."

"A price I will gladly pay." Manus called out for all to hear. "For the sake of my people."

"And you Menden captain?" Cavanna asked as she turned to look at her son's murderer. "Would you like to also collect your dead?"

"No, Great Cavanna." Dane replied, unable to hide the arrogance at what he had done from Barra's mother. "There is no need to collect their empty shells. We will remember their names and honor them accordingly."

"So be it." Cavanna once again gave little regard to the Mendens or her brother as she laid a hand on her son's forehead one last time.

Standing, Cavanna said some words in a language that only the other gods remembered. As her voice rose to fly across the land and as she raised her hands to the sky, Barra's body hardened into stone before becoming brittle. The little grains quickly slipping away wherever the winds chose to take him.

"Take care of your dead." Cavanna finally said when she looked upon Manus one more time. "You have my grace upon you and your people until the sun dips below the land. After that you are on your own."

"You are most charitable with the time you are giving us." Manus respectfully responded. But Cavanna had already forgotten about the prince and had faded before the eyes of the Gwer, with the rest of the gods, including Ciaran, following after her.

"Remember little prince," Villis Dane said when he was sure that the gods had vanished, his thick accent sounding guttural to Manus' ears. "I killed your god. One day I will come to kill you!"

Manus remained quiet, only watching as Dane collected his men and stormed away, with doubt finally filling his mind over Barra's sacrifice clouding his thoughts before he too turned away to see to the needs of his own people.

***

With the help of his brother Banning, whose only foray into combat was to help the injured out of the ballistae rooms that Ciaran had destroyed on the Kasser, and with the aid of Gwyn and her crew, Manus made quick work of collecting his own dead and injured men.

The one man that Manus could not retrieve was Esten Gilroy, the glider pilot that sacrificed his life for the prince and his comrades. For when they approached the Mendens and asked for his body Manus and his men were answered with harsh laughter and obscenities.

"Runaway Sothair Dor!" The Mendens jeered. "Runaway! You should be away before it is too late for you too!"

"Runaway Sothair! Fly away so that the chase for you will be that much sweeter!"

"Ha, ha! Runaway! For now you are not even worthy to be slaves. And when we find you it will be to send you to join your brethren and to leave your corpses upon the ground for Maat's winds to strip clean."

"Runaway!"

"They are right!" Manus muttered to Kael as they and their group of soldiers retreated back to the Camalain so that they could leave. "Our time is short and we need to be away from these beasts as soon as possible."

"Esten Gilroy was a good soldier and he will be missed and held in high honor for what he did for us today."

Kael did not reply as the jibes continued and small rocks were thrown at them from behind. Manus' friend held his tongue because he did not want to acerbate an already volatile situation. Also, not only he but the entire group of Birrnians silently seethed at being chased away and only wanting to kill the Mendens just as much as they wanted to kill them.

Once both ships were airborne and once again heading for Fomor, Manus and Kael made their way to see that Crogan was tending to the wounded before making their way to the storage bay that was now being used to store their fallen comrades.

This makeshift morgue, which had once been the impromptu bar for the Camalain, had now become Seb Cullen's domain, for it was a sagart's duty to not only tend to the living but to tend dead as well.

"This is not how I wanted to come home." Manus whispered to Kael as he looked upon the dead faces of the men lying out before him while recalling the name of each man in his head.

"What choice did you have?" Kael asked his friend. "It seems that the gods meant for us to be a part of whatever this was. And considering a god died today it's a wonder any of us came out of this unscathed."

"I wouldn't be so sure about that." Manus replied, his eyes resting upon Manton who had yet to leave his boyhood friend's side and was now placing a heavy woolen blanket over the blood drenched linens in the hopes of hiding Dolan's disfigurement.

Kael frowned at Manus' comment, wondering what was on his friend's mind, yet knowing this was not the time or the place to have a personal conversation with him.

"And who'd have thought that a god was on the Camalain?" Kael said as he tried to change the subject. "That Barra sat at our table and broke bread with us!"

"Somebody knew." Manus replied in a flat, matter of fact, tone of voice as he looked at his friend. "Two somebody's if I'm not mistaken."

Kael frowned, understanding Manus' intimation and remained where he was standing as Manus walked away and approached Manton to give the crewman his condolences before approaching the sagart.

Kael watched as Seb Cullen, whose nature had always been respectful and had been a fount of patience and tolerance with the prince, leaned in to hear what Manus had to say before the priest and prince went down to their knees to pray.

Kael could not remember when he had last seen his friend humble himself before another man like this and felt as if he was spying in on something that was very personal and decided to leave and search out Liam.

Returning to the galley, Liam's usual haunt, Kael came upon Crogan, a worried look in the cook's eyes while he stitched a gash shut on a wounded man's arm, informed Kael he had not seen Liam since before the attack.

"When you find that boy you tell him to get his ass over here." Crogan said, drowning out the hiss of pain from the man in front of him as he dug the needle into his flesh. "His mates say he is pretty banged up and might need some tending to."

Kael hurried away, stopping by the sagart's bedroom, only to find it empty. After making some inquiries of men walking the corridors Kael found Liam in the washroom.

The sagart's son was naked to the waist, his face and body mapped in bruises and dirt, hands and arms caked in blood, a blank look in his eyes while he stared at his reflection in the mirror.

"Hey! Here you are!" Kael smiled, acting surprised at finding Liam here.

Liam blinked his eyes as he found Kael's image in the mirror as he stood behind him. Liam raised his hands as if to explain what he was doing here, only to drop them helplessly by his sides as he choked on whatever he was about to say as he fought tears that were trying to form in the corners of his eyes.

"No worries, no worries." Kael quickly grabbed some towels, one of which seemed to have some of Liam's bloody handprints on it, and a glass jar containing a heavy paste mixed with sand and brought them over to Liam.

Removing the jar's lid, Kael scooped out a large dollop of the gritty soap on the fingertips of one hand, working the mass between his hands to make the mass more pliable, before rubbing it onto Liam's hands and forearms.

Surprised at how cold Liam's hands felt to his touch, Kael kept at his ministrations for a bit, quietly, with Liam only staring blankly at the floor between their feet.

Using the already ruined towel, Kael wiped the now pink mess off of Liam's hands and arms before starting the process one more time.

"Your turn." Placing Liam's hands together Kael gently instructed his friend on cleaning the gore off of himself, telling him to get the soap under his fingertips as well, before filling the basin in front of them with water.

Dipping a clean towel in the tepid water, Kael began wiping the dirt and sweat off of Liam's chest and shoulders, exposing more of the purplish discoloration and small welts that covered his skin. The bruises on Liam's body being a testament to the fact that his armor had done what it was supposed to do and protected Liam during Krattis' assault.

"They're all worried about you." Kael began, hoping to pull Liam out of the stupor he seemed to be slowly sinking into.

Rinsing out his towel before wiping down Liam's arms, Kael explained of how even Crogan was asking after him.

"For once it didn't sound like that old proidha was growling." Kael chuckled. "And Sidri. Bumped into him outside of your quarters. He wanted to let you know that Gorman was okay. That Menden beast banged him up pretty bad. Cracked a couple of ribs and dislocated his shoulder but he'll be fine. They got him laid up in, Liam?"

Kael grasped Liam's hands tightly as he watched the man begin to tremble, fighting back a sob, while the tears returned to cloud his eyes.

"My fault." Liam croaked. "If I practiced harder Gorman wouldn't have gotten hurt. And Dolan. Dolan would be. . ."

"Listen." Kael cupped Liam's head with the palms of his hands, forcing the man to look at him, while his thumb wiped away a tear that was trying to cut a path in the grime down Liam's face. "No one could have protected Dolan from that attack. No one!"

"And if anything, you're the one that saved Gorman's life!"

"You did good, Liam! You did good!"

When Liam brought up Dolan's name again, saying that he should have died instead of the soldier, Kael quenched the fire to that thought.

"Enough Liam! Dolan was a member of the Guard and died doing his duty to protect Manus. He may be gone from our world but I would like to think he's now by Barra's side in the halls of Dubhas."

Kael quieted, realizing he might have been a little heavy handed with his comments, especially when he mentioned Barra's name, which brought even more tears to Liam's eyes, and began wiping Liam's face clean, revealing a livid bruise on his left cheek.

"Shit! Sorry!" Kael cursed when Liam winced in pain as his cloth uncovered a cut, about a finger's length, that had been closed by the dirt on his face, with a fresh rivulet of blood running down Liam's cheek that Kael now tried to stop.

Kael had Liam take over and had him press the cloth against his face so that he could soak a fresh cloth in water.

"He got you good!" Kael lifted the dirty cloth, watching as ruby droplets of blood began to form again before giving Liam the fresh cloth to replace the soiled one.

"Think it was my own hand that did this." A tone of disgust crept into Liam's voice when he described the incident. "Think it happened when we fell. I'm lucky I didn't slice my jaw off."

"Well you didn't." Kael replied. "Now press that tight and turn around so I can clean your back."

"About, Anam, Barra." Kael started as he began wiping the dirt off of Liam's shoulder blades. "Did you know he was on board the Camalain?"

Except for the sound of the washcloth moving across Liam's skin, the room quieted as Liam fought fresh tears when he thought about the now dead god.

"At first I didn't." Liam explained. "But I kept having these feelings. Visions. And my father had started to act funny as soon as Barra boarded so I finally asked him who he was."

"When we were in Auvereen?"

"Yes." Liam's voice softened when he answered Kael's question. "In Auvereen. The night you saw us on deck."

"Is that why you broke up with me?" Kael asked as he placed the now filthy cloth onto a growing pile of them beside the basin before holding onto Liam's shoulders with his free hands.

Liam lowered his head and it took a moment for him to answer that it was.

"Barra asked me not to tell anyone." Liam said as he turned to look at Kael. "And I was finding it hard to lie to you."

"So it wasn't us? Nothing I did?"

When Liam said that it wasn't, Kael lowered the cloth Liam still had pressed against his cheek and pulled him in close so that they could kiss, happy that Liam was willing to yield to his advances.

Kael's hands trailed down Liam's back and as he sighed heavily and felt Liam's body respond to their closeness, Kael pulled him even closer so that Liam's naked torso was pressed firmly against the armor that he still wore.

"I don't want to be alone tonight." Liam said huskily when their lips finally parted, with Liam resting his head on Kael's armored shoulder while the man's hands trailed over the small of his back.

"Neither do I." Kael breathed hotly into Liam's ear, hoping that this meant that their relationship would pick up where it had left off. "Neither do I."

Chapter 16
Homeward Bound

Several hours passed as the Camalain and the Kasser put as much distance as possible between themselves and the battlefield where the Mendens had remained. And as the reddish purple sky of dusk turned into the velvety black of night, the two ships battened down hatches and windows, sealing in all light, relying on their steersmen to sense the other vessel, in the hope of avoiding being seen by any searching eyes.

An hour, filled with tension and apprehension as to what was yet to come, passed without Manus' steersman sensing any other vessel other than the Kasser that was only flying about a stone's throw away from them.

When it seemed like they were not being pursued by Ciaran or the Mendens, Manus ordered every able bodied man not on duty to attend the last rights for their comrades being given by Seb Cullen.

Manton was there. For the man had yet to leave his dead friend's side.

As was Sidri who stood by Manton, an arm draped over his squad mate's shoulder as he tried to console him.

"We were best mates." Manton sniffed, his eyes never leaving Dolan's covered body. "Followed me everywhere when we were kids. Followed me into the Royal Guard when I decided to join."

"To see the world and go on adventures, he said."

"Now." A bitter laugh escaped Manton's lips. "Now I'll have to tell his fathers how I wasn't by his side to protect him."

Sidri hushed the man, when Heath, Yarrow and Gorman appeared in the storage bay.

Gorman, whose eyes looked slightly glazed from the herbs he had been given to deaden the pain he was feeling, had his sword arm in a sling and bandages wrapped tightly about his torso, was flanked by his partner and Yarrow who guided the man so that all three went to stand with Sidri and Manton.

Several more groups of men entered the room with the sagart and prince among them. Both men took their time to talk to the crew standing about them as they made their way to the front of the room.

Lastly, Kael, Liam and Croft entered the bay.

Liam's wounds had finally been tended to by Yanno Crogan and Liam now wore a loose fitting cotton shirt that covered up most of the bruises on his sore and chafed torso.

Manus not only noticed Liam's injuries, the prince noticed how he and Kael were holding hands, and of Kael's gift secured firmly around Liam's right wrist as the two parted company with Croft, who went to stand with some of the other bridge crew, while they walked over to Gorman and the rest of the squad.

All greeted the two warmly, with Gorman using his free hand to pat Liam on the shoulder, as if to make sure he was solid and not some apparition haunting this room, before commenting on Liam's bruised face.

"Doesn't look pretty." Liam said as he forced himself not to touch the left side of his face. The shallow cut on his cheek now covered by a poultice to keep it from getting infected.

"Wait until tomorrow." Gorman smiled. "Gonna be as black as the night sky. We're just glad that you're alive."

Liam blushed at the comment and tried to apologize for not fighting better but was stopped by Manton.

"Don't you be fretting." Manton said as he did his best to keep his own voice from cracking while he spoke. "You fought well. And I know Dolan. He would have been beside himself if it was you who had fallen and not he."

"Besides it was you that saved Gorman's life." Heath added. "I don't know how I can thank you for that."

"I told you those daggers brought me luck." Gorman winked.

"See?" Kael whispered into Liam's ear, squeezing his hand tightly in reassurance as everyone quieted in the room as Liam's father began to read scripture from Barra's book, the Bunusacha, the Fundamentals of Rock and Stone.

***

Manus watched as the first group of men, with Kael and Liam leaving with Gorman's squad, exited the room so that another group of men could enter the room to pay their respects to the fallen.

Exhausted and knowing that a third service would be held tomorrow morning for those that could not attend today's ceremonies, Manus made his way to his quarters once the second service was over, and found the room empty.

"Of course." Manus said to the empty room as he walked to stare out the bank of windows before remembering that they too had been shuttered for their protection.

For once Manus' room which always felt like a refuge from the rest of the world, especially when Kael was here, now felt like a prison.

Turning his back to the wooden vista Manus walked over to Kael's bed where his guitar was propped against the wall and plucked several chords from its strings. The sound of the irregular notes bounced about the room before quickly fading away into nothingness.

Manus pulled several more sad notes from the guitar, regretting that he had never truly told Kael how he felt. Manus was also wishing that his brother Banning was here and not on the Kasser when he remembered that there had been a half-finished skin of wine on the table. Turning towards the table to grab the skin of wine so that he could at least numb some of his misery, Manus hissed in surprise at finding a man sitting on his own bed.

"Do you play?" The man asked in an accented voice.

Manus quickly drew his sword and was about to call for the guard stationed in the corridor when the man stood, raising both palms to face the prince.

"Please, Manus. Put your weapon down. I think I have had enough to do with sharp blades for one day."

The man's words were disconcerting as was his presence in Manus' quarters. But Manus soon recognized the golden brown hair, tanned muscular skin and eyes that were as grey as lodestones.

"Ana, Barr, Milord!" Manus stammered as he went to bended knee, his head bowed, his sword making a loud ringing noise as he slapped it to the ground.

"Now, now. None of that!" Barra laughed as he bent and placed his hands underneath Manus' arms and pulled him up to stand.

"But, but, you?" Manus stammered as he lowered his head, unsure of where he should be looking.

"Died?" Manus missed the pained look in Barra's eyes while the god's hand ran over his clothed body, remembering the sword thrusts that had pierced him.

"Yes. Well it seems that my death was punishment for my audacity in interfering in your lives. And my resurrection was punishment for Ciaran at trying to assert his own authority over my mother's. You should have seen Ciaran's when he realized that I would not be staying dead."

"All is in balance once more as my mother would have it." The god said quietly.

"And please! Stop looking at the floor!" Barra reprimanded. "Where is the arrogant prince that did not want to believe in me or my brethren?"

"Sorry Milord." Manus paled, wondering if the god standing before him had ever really heard how he would curse using Barra's name, as well as the names of the other deities whenever he was angry.

"And enough of that!" Barra said as he brushed passed Manus to walk over to Kael's bed. "Do you play?"

"What?" Manus turned, confused by what Barra was telling and asking him.

"Stop calling me Milord. Do you play the guitar?"

"No to the second. And what would you like me to call you?"

"Pity. About the guitar." Barra walked back to Manus' bed and sat back down. "Some music would have been nice right about now."

"And?" Manus asked.

Barra smiled, hearing a slight hint of annoyance creep back into the prince's voice at being teased.

"Anam would be fine." Barra patted the side of the bed so that Manus could sit beside him.

Manus hesitated for a moment, unsure whether the god was serious or not, but took the place near the god when Anam patted the covers again.

"If Kael is not here then I take it that he and Liam have reconciled their differences?"

"Yes!" Manus said sullenly, hunching his shoulders, at being reminded whose arms Kael was in right now.

Anam's left hand reached out to grasp Manus' right. Warmth soon flowed between the two that began to chase away the tension that had been building within the prince.

"Be at peace." Anam whispered, his voice sounding like the slow creak of trees moving in a soft wind. "I can assure you that the two of you were never meant to be together."

Instinctually Manus' hand grasped Anam's a little more tightly at the heartache he felt.

"And not for the reasons given by your father or mother." Anam began to explain. "But that is more than I should be telling you and I do not want Cavanna nor the other gods listening in on us."

"Just be happy that Kael has found someone in this time of sorrow."

"And what about me?" Manus sulked, knowing full well that he should heed Anam's advice and accept that Kael would not be with him.

"I thought we were working on that." Anam replied as he now squeezed Manus' hand.

Unsure of what Anam was intimating Manus looked at the smiling god, noticing a faint hint of sadness in those steely grey eyes.

"You are not the only one who has had failure in romance. Of sorts." Anam said, clearly reading Manus' face, reminding the prince of the stories of how the god Credne had abandoned Anam to go into exile with Chullain.

"A truce Manus." Anam continued, allowing Manus' hand to slip out of his so that the god could run his own hand along the prince's arm. "Until love can be found once more."

Manus remained quiet and closed his eyes, relaxing as Anam's hand trailed up to his face, slightly brushing his lips before the god's fingers moved to twine themselves in his dark brown hair.

Manus did not resist Anam's advances when he felt Anam's lips upon his nor did he fight the god when he pulled the two of them onto his bed with Manus coming to lie on top of the deity.

"What about the guard outside the door?" Manus asked when the two finally parted lips.

Anam smiled, his eyes glittering like two polished orbs of metal as he brought one of Manus' hands to his mouth to kiss its palm.

"He will not hear." Anam kissed Manus' palm one more time. "And no one must know of us."

"Who would believe me?" Manus snorted.

"You would be surprised." Anam stopped what he was doing to look at Manus. "Promise me."

Now it was Manus' turn to take the initiative and he lowered himself onto Anam, kissing the god and tugging at his shirt so that he could run a hand along Anam's taut golden torso, before promising he would remain quiet about their tryst.

"Good." Anam's words slipped into Manus' mind as their kissing resumed, becoming much more passionate as Anam unbuckled the scabbard from about Manus' waist before beginning to undo his trousers. "For even the gods get lonely."

***

The final service was carried out the next day with Cullen once again reading scripture from the Bunusacha while Manus and Kael stood quietly next to him.

At first Kael had been apprehensive about attending the service, expecting some accusatory or inflammatory remarks to spout from his friend's mouth. But none were forthcoming and Kael couldn't help but notice the calmness on his friend's face during the memorial to their dead.

Once the service was over Kael was about to mention his reconciliation with Liam to Manus when a slight rumble ran through the ship, sending all of the crew rushing out of the bay as shouting ran through its halls out of fear of another attack, while Barra's bible slipped out of the hands of Cullen as the man raised one hand to his head, as if in pain, while the other held tightly onto his cane to keep his balance.

Manus was there to help steady Cullen and asked if he was alright while Kael drew his sword, the man readying himself to protect all three of them if he had to.

"By the gods!" Cullen cursed, ignoring Manus' request.

"Sagart!"

"Milord. I can hear him again!"

"Who?"

"Barra!"

"Are you sure? We saw him die?" This time it was Kael that questioned the priest while Manus walked away from the other two so that he would not let anything that would raise suspicious slip from his lips.

"Quite." Cullen said, confidence filling his voice. "Barra lives once again."

"But that's impossible!" Kael stammered.

"Who are we to say what is possible for the gods!" Cullen replied before not only saying a prayer to Barra but to his mother, Cavanna.

"Come. We should go to the bridge to make sure all is well." Manus interrupted, nodding for Kael to follow him. "Sagart? Will you be fine on your own?"

"Who has said that I am alone?" Cullen asked as a look of serenity filled the priest's face. A look that Manus nor Kael had seen since their first meeting with the priest in the temple gardens. "I will be fine."

"I'm still finding it hard to believe!" Kael said after the two passed a group of armed men with Manus telling them to stand down. "Barra! Alive!"

"Seems that way." Manus said, a little too nonchalantly for Kael's ears.

"But you must believe! At least now!"

Manus' light hearted laughter startled Kael and he looked at his friend dubiously. But Manus remained quiet about his beliefs, only continuing to smile as they made their way to the bridge.

"And speaking of good news." Kael added a little hesitantly after they passed several more men. "Liam and I have decided to get back together."

A frown appeared momentarily on Manus' face before quickly disappearing and replaced by a somewhat crooked smile as the prince told his friend that he was happy for them.

Now it was Kael's turn to frown for these were words that were quite out of character for Manus, especially when his friend had been belittling Liam for the past month.

"I, uh, we might spend most of tonight together." Kael replied, testing the waters to see if his friend's true feelings would surface. "Once his shift in the galley ends that is. Though I don't know what time I'll be getting back."

The two were about to enter the bridge when Manus placed a hand on Kael's wrist and stopped him from entering the room.

"I know I've been an ass." Manus started. "And I'm sorry. Truly, I am happy for the two of you and you should spend as much time as you can together."

"What manner of demon are you and what have you done with my friend?" Kael said as he grabbed his friend's face to look him squarely in the eyes.

Chuckling at the immature antics of Kael, Manus simply knocked his friend's hands away before pushing him ahead and following him onto the bridge.

***

Upon entering the bridge Manus and Kael were surprised to find a tension among the crew that had not been felt elsewhere on the Camalain.

"We have a situation Milord!" Thear Ibor told the prince and quickly explained how just after the ship rumbled, Croft, whose shift it was to steer the Camalain, began to call out Barra's name.

"Thought he might be mourning the loss of the god." The captain continued, his eyes darting to where Croft sat connected to the lodestones. "And in his state might harm us all. Was just going to have him land and trade places with Jensen when you arrived."

Manus promptly allayed the captain's fears and informed him and the rest of the crew that Barra had been resurrected and seemed to be controlling the lodestones once again.

"Are you sure Prince Aerin?" Jensen asked, somewhat doubtful of Manus' words as murmurings at this wonder danced among the rest of the bridge crew.

"Yes steersman!" Manus said confidently. "Barra looks over us once again! And Sagart Seb can vouch for my words for he too can hear the voice of Barra within his soul."

Many of the crew began to talk of celebrating over this news but Manus quelled some of their enthusiasm.

"Remember! We have only recently lost friends and loved ones. And we are still two days out from Fomor. Who knows what the gods still have in store for us while we are out here."

"This news is joyous for all of us to hear. But we will not celebrate until our feet touch the soil of our own land."

***

True to his word, even though no threat of attack appeared on the horizon, Manus kept every able bodied man at their post that day, allowing some revelry and celebratory music over Barra's return to be allowed in the dining hall that night.

And when Kael slipped into the galley to drag Liam away so that the two of them could be together, Manus followed suit and headed back to his own quarters where he once again found Anam waiting for him. The world outside Manus' room slowly fading into a momentary oblivion as god and man entwined in an embrace that lasted all night.

Another uneventful day passed. With the crew of both vessels thanking the gods, some even including the vengeful and very vindictive Ciaran in their prayers, for this reprieve as they made for the coast of Birr.

It wasn't until that evening, one day out from Fomor that Manus and Liam found themselves in the presence of the other.

Liam had been given the night off by Crogan and was sharing a meal with Kael, Gorman and the others when Manus, a plate of food in his own hand, came to stand beside their table.

"Mind if I join you?"

"Certainly, M'lord!" Gorman said for his crew as all of them stood politely while Manus picked a spot between Manton and Gorman to sit in, Manus' seat putting him across from Kael and Liam.

An awkward silence blanketed the table as everyone seated themselves and resumed eating their meals with Manus digging into his own dinner. With the exception being Kael, who smiled at his friend around a mouthful of food, everyone else had their heads lowered and intent on their own meals. So Manus decided to restart the conversation.

"How's the shoulder Gorman?"

"Fine M'lord. Almost." Gorman said as he raised his sword arm to show the prince, only wincing when his hand was stretched up over his head. "And Sagart Seb's healing touch mended my ribs as well. That is, with the help of Barra. Couple more days and I should be back to normal."

Manus commended Gorman on his work before tearing off a hunk of bread from the slice he had on his plate, dipping it in the juices from the cooked meat and plopping it into his mouth before asking Liam how he was doing.

"No complaints Milord." Liam answered, unsure of what to say as he raised his eyes to look at the man who would one day rule all of Birr.

"Well your face looks wicked." Manus said as a faint smile appeared on his face.

Liam blanched at the comment, his face turning white and accentuating the vivid blues and greens that were replacing the dark purple on his cheek.

"Seen prettier greens on apples." Kael tossed while winking at Liam to know that this was all in jest.

"More like a rotten plumb!" Sidri laughed as he took a drink of his ale.

"Oy! Plumb!" Yarrow roared.

Liam could only redden in embarrassment as the group, the exception being Manton who had yet to fully recover emotionally from Dolan's death, raised their mugs and toasted Plumb.

"Liam, you fought well that day." Manus finally said as the laughter died down around the table. "Thank you for the service you have given me and my family."

Liam could only bring himself to mumble a thank you of his own to the prince while Kael squeezed Liam's hand underneath the table and whispering encouragements in his ear.

"You'll be able to continue with Liam's training?" Manus asked Gorman.

"If you'd like I can have Heath and Sidri start with Plumb tomorrow."

"Not if you're going to keep calling me Plumb!" Liam quipped, setting off another round of laughter that blanketed the table.

But the good humor had become unbearable for Manton, a man who would have been considered the most jovial of the group, and interrupted the light hearted mood that was forming with his own dark one.

"Begging pardon, Prince Aerin." Manton's hands gripped his mug a little tighter so that the knuckles on both of them turned white from the pressure. "Would you mind if I took leave to return Dolan home?"

The table quieted as Manton, who thought he would be reprimanded by either Manus or Gorman for his bluntness, hurriedly began to explain how their town was only four or five days inland from Fomor.

"See, his folks are still in Rhuad and I'd like to see that he gets a proper burial."

"Only if we can accompany you Manton."

"M'lord?"

That's when Manus explained how another of the men that died had come from Enck, a town northeast of Fomor, and that the prince wanted to return him to his kin as well.

"So if you can hold out for a couple of days, I would like for everyone to honor Master Kelman as he should be."

"His fathers would like that very much, M'lord." Manton took a sip of his ale to hide his feelings over the prince's generosity.

"To Dolan." Manus raised his mug, the others raising theirs as well to the second more somber toast.

"Besides," Manus added while ignoring Manton running the cuff of a sleeve across his eyes. "I see no reason in rushing home right now. Do you Master Karam?"

"No Milord." Kael answered as his hand came to rest on Liam's thigh. "None at all."

***

So their stay in Fomor, once they arrived, ended up being very brief. With Manus appraising the local garrison and Captain Bres, of the

Marmairn, of the Menden attacks and how to better safeguard the town against any incursions.

"You'll be staying on here for a bit longer with the Marmairn, Captain. Until I or someone else can return to replace you." Manus commanded. "But send a skiff with this news to Kinsale to inform my father of these events. And to let him know that my brother and I will be taking a longer road home."

Banning, who had not wanted to return to his family to begin with, was fine with his brother's decision. Especially when it came to making these stops to pay homage to their fallen countrymen.

As was Argus Gwyn.

"Are you sure?" Manus asked her.

"Of course." Gwyn replied. "Your men fought bravely and should be honored. And the detour will give us a chance to trade with your people."

Manus also chose not to fight with his brother when Banning asked to remain on the Kasser. Nor did he say anything about the obvious dalliance that the two seemed to be having. For who was he to judge considering who his own bedmate happened to be?

So just as quickly as they had arrived the Camalain and Kasser left Fomor before dusk could even settle over the land, the two ships making the port of Enck by mid-afternoon of the next day.

The service for his fallen man from this city was held the day after their arrival which gave Manus enough time to not only begin to prepare this town for any attacks but to spend time with the crewman's grieving family before both ships left the flats to fly inland.

"Finally! A welcome change in scenery." Gorman remarked from the main deck as the bland tans and crystalline whites of the desert were replaced by a verdant sea of waving grasses, with a stretch of trees on the horizon slowly creeping their way, while the sparkling blue of a river snaked through the landscape below them.

For it was true that Cavanna had commanded for the seas to be withdrawn to end most of the Gwerin strife; a strife once started by Cavanna and her brethren at the dawn of time as a means of amusement. And by their good graces the remaining gods used their power to keep the land alive so that its people could thrive and flourish.

The crew of the Camalain agreed with Gorman's statement and they finally began to relax in their routine as their road for the time being became less treacherous as they made their way home.

"We're not far now." Manton said on the fifth morning of their flight as the tram line they had been following for the past three days cut through a low mountain range before entering an expansive valley with a large lake at its center and two walled hamlets hugging its shoreline. Rhuad.

"It's beautiful." Liam commented to Manton as the two ships made their way past large fields planted with grains and groves of trees all lined up in neat rows, heavy with fruit just waiting to be harvested.

"It is." Manton replied as he looked upon his homeland wishing that his boyhood friend was by his side. "But not today."

Liam had no words that would comfort Manton, for they had been said over and over again for the past week, and remained quiet when Manton left the railing to head to the bridge and direct the captain towards his and Dolan's home.

Home, it turned out, was a small community of cattle ranchers and goat herders living on the outskirts of Rhuad. Dolan's family tended the latter while Manton raised horned tarbhs; bullish creatures with coats that were as pitch as night.

As is the case in such a community where the men's older brothers are destined to inherit the family estates, especially when there is not enough to split, it was to either eventually tend the land in their sibling's name or to leave and seek their own fortunes.

Seek their fortunes is what the two friends did. Manton and Dolan had set out for Kinsale, oh so many years ago, to join the Royal Guard, promising their parents to come back whenever they could.

But now?

Now.

Now Manton stood before his own family and that of Dolan's as he, Gorman and Heath, Yarrow, Sidri and Liam carried the corpse of their friend off of the Camalain to be returned to the care of his family.

Kelman Ferrer, Dolan's father, his partner and Dolan's older brother were devastated at Dolan's return. But none could discount his bravery and how he died.

"You do us a great honor bearing my son." Kelman Ferrer said to Manus as his son's body, which had been preserved by Cullen's prayers, began to be carried towards their home.

"Your son and a dozen others gave their lives so that I and his friends could live." Manus replied. "He will be sorely missed."

"Will you need help with the preparation for your son's burial? We have a sagart who has been maintaining Dolan's body. If you would like I am sure that he would be willing to help with the services for your son."

But Kelman Ferrer forced a smile onto his tanned and weathered face and thanked the prince for his generosity. Saying that his family wanted to take the rest of today and tomorrow to mourn his son and that a sagart to Ennaya watched over their small community and that he would be the one to help prepare his son for his burial.

Kelman Ferrer was about to take his leave of Manus, wishing the prince a safe journey when Manus asked the man if they could stay for the services.

"You see," Manus began. "I'm sure his friends, Manton especially, as well as myself would like one more chance to say goodbye. That is if our staying will not be an imposition to you."

"Of course not Milord! We would be honored."

With that Ferrer asked for Manus and the others to join him and his family for evening meal on the following day so that they could share stories and rejoice in Dolan's life before his burial.

"Now it is we who are honored." Manus bowed in respect before offering his ships stores and cook if they were needed in preparing the celebratory meal.

Appreciative of the prince's gifts, Kelman Ferrer took his leave from Manus. And gathering men from his household, Ferrer had them replace those who were now bearing his son's body to carry him, with Manton and his own family in tow, the rest of the way home.

The service on that cool clear day was simple. For Dolan, as all Gwer, was considered a gift from the gods and part of the land.

So, bound into a fetal position and wrapped in linen blankets, Dolan was placed into a hole in the family's orchard so that a sapling of a fruit bearing tree could be planted on top of him.

"As Dolan took from the land," Ennaya's sagart preached as friend and family took turns to shovel dirt into the burial hole while someone kept the young tree balanced in its center. "So shall the land take from Dolan. So, that one day when any who have a need, may take from this planting and to continue to benefit from his labors."

Once the service had ended chilled wine was offered with a midday meal to follow. But Manus declined for himself, Banning and his crew, saying that there were still several men to bury as they made their way back to Kinsale.

Again, Kelman Ferrer thanked the prince profusely for what he had done for his son before Manus collected Banning and Gwyn, his own men, including Manton who chose not to stay, so that they could make for their own ships to make their own way home.

Chapter 17
Kinsale
Home

So after the burials of several more of his men, Manus, his crew and that of the Kasser made for the flats to take the short trip back to Kinsale. Back to home.

Knowing full well that news of their flight back would have reached his father's ears almost a week ago, and wanting as little fanfare as possible, Manus made sure they would put into port in the early hours of the morning.

That did not stop Aerin Riocard from having his own family and a contingent of the Royal Guard there to meet Manus and Banning as they debarked from their ships.

Fionn, who was overjoyed at seeing his son alive, could not contain himself and quickly rushed to Banning to embrace him, telling his son how happy he was to have him back home.

"It is good to see you too father." Banning replied because he could not bring himself to say that he was happy to be home.

Riocard greeted both of his sons warmly.

While their mother on the other hand.

"Try not to get lost again." The High Sagartta said to her youngest while commending Manus on his leadership and bravery in battling Ciaran.

Riocard, who was just as proud of his eldest son as his mother, asked for Manus to tell them all about his adventures.

"At dinner? Tonight?" Manus asked as Captain Thear began to escort the remaining dead Kinsalians off of the Camalain.

"And you must be Mistress Argus." Fionn said to Gwyn as she somewhat reluctantly approached the family. "Manus mentioned you in his writings and an old friend told me that my son was in your care."

Gwyn smiled politely, assuming that by old friend Fionn meant Emmis Daigh, and when asked to travel with them back to the castle to hear her stories as well as to be recompensed for Banning's needs, declined straightaway.

"The adventure was payment enough and I would like to return to my own land to repair the damage that Ciaran exacted on my ship, and to bury our own dead. So once I have replenished some supplies to make the trek, I am hoping to leave port."

"As you wish." Riocard replied and told Gwyn to leave a list of what she needed with the dock's quartermaster and she would have those items as soon as possible.

"A gift from my family to yours." Riocard concluded.

Gwyn thanked the ruler of Birr for his generosity before turning to Banning to say goodbye one more time.

"Prince Dar." Gwyn said quite coolly, keeping any emotion she felt for the man out of her voice. "If you ever happen to visit Iniscarn again you will be most welcomed in my father's home."

"Thank you, Mistress Argus." Banning replied. Even though he knew it would create an uproar among his parents Banning could not help wanting to reach out to embrace Gwyn one more time.

And as if reading his thoughts, Gwyn bowed to his family and turned her back on him before he could make the gesture, disappearing among her crew as she made her way back to the Kasser.

**

Banning had once again dressed in the trappings as was befitting the court of Birr, looking upon the tattered clothes he had worn for the past couple of months, longing to put them back on when there was knock on his bedroom door.

"Yes?"

Banning's father entered the room with a plate of food in his hand.

"You missed the midday meal and I, is something the matter?"

"No." Banning said a little too quickly and turned to look out his window at the courtyard below them.

"Are you sure? I can tell that look anywhere." Fionn said as he placed the food on one of the bed's end tables.

"What look?" Banning watched his father's ghostly reflection in the leaded glass of the window as he moved about the room.

"The one where you have this sour looking frown on your face while having your arms crossed over your chest that means you are troubled by something. And you always tend to turn from me when you need to hide the truth from me. So tell me, what is so wrong that it could bother your return home?"

"Father? Are you happy?"

"Of course I am!" Fionn laughed, a little confused by his son's question. "The god's have returned you to me! Why should I not be happy?"

"That's not what I meant." Banning said flatly as he went to sit on his bed pulling Ilwin Mac's donated clothes into his lap. "Are you happy with Riocard?"

Now it was Fionn's turn to frown at the question that was asked.

"Yes." Fionn's one word statement was not a lie. Nor was it the whole truth. But Fionn chose not to expound on his answer as he took a seat by his son's side.

"So you were happy grandfather married you off to Riocard? If you had a choice would you marry him again?"

"It is the life I was given." Fionn said when he realized he did not know how to deflect his son's questions.

"It's not the life I want." Banning said as a matter of fact.

"Then what life do you want?"

"Gwyn." Banning silently cursed himself for screwing up what he wanted to say.

But his father knew what he meant.

"Does she have the same feelings for you?"

"Yes." Banning said as he remembered the times he and Gwyn spent alone. "I believe so. At least I think that she does."

A heavy silence filled the room and Banning was about to apologize for stupidly blathering about his feelings when his father spoke up.

"Then I think you should find out before she leaves."

Banning was surprised at what he heard and asked his father if he was sure.

"No. This is not the life I wanted." Fionn said in response to his son's earlier question. "But if I had chosen differently I would not have had you. Nor would I have been able to tell you to go live the life I could not."

"What about Riocard and mother?" Banning asked, now unsure of what he should do.

"I will take care of them." Fionn said as the two of them stood. "But if I were you I would be away as quickly as possible."

Fionn retrieved the bundle of clothes his son had dropped along with some coin he had on his person and his own royal marker before hugging his son.

"If you do not come back I will know that you got your answer." Fionn said as he squeezed his only child a little tighter. "So take care of yourself if I do not see you for a while."

"I'll come back soon. I promise."

"That would not be wise. At least not for now." Fionn said as he thought of Betrys and what she would have to say on this matter while letting go of his son to look at him one last time.

"Next time Banning, it will be I who comes looking for you."

***

Gwyn had come out on deck to get some fresh air and to see if the next batch of supplies had arrived and was stunned to find Banning, along with his lieutenant, talking to Tor Varin and his son Micah.

Banning couldn't help but smile broadly as Gwyn approached them and allowed Varin to explain how the prince wanted permission to come aboard.

"One last goodbye before we depart?" Gwyn asked.

"No. Looking to see if my room is still empty so that I can book passage with you."

Gwyn thought she must have looked just as stunned as everyone else by Banning's remark. So she simply asked where he wanted to go.

Moving by Varin, Banning grasped Gwyn's hands and answered that he would go wherever she was headed before kissing her.

Micah giggled in delight and Goban hissed in surprise, even though the soldier had thought something was going on between the two, at their public display of affection.

"And what do your parents say?" Gwyn asked when they finally parted.

"My father gave me his blessings. He's the only one that matters right now."

Gwyn was contemplating the consequences to these turn of events when Banning grasped her hand once more and asked her if she wanted him here.

Of course Gwyn only had one answer for the man that stood before her. And reaching out with her free hand, Gwyn caressed his face before kissing him one more time.

"Permission to come aboard?"

For a moment Banning thought that Gwyn was about to send him away. But upon hearing her grant his request Banning brought his own free hand to press Gwyn's tightly against his face, only wanting to feel the warmth of her body flow into his.

The two probably would have remained that way, oblivious to everything else, except that Goban coughed loudly, interrupting the two on purpose.

"Uhh, Milord?"

"You're free to go, Lieutenant."

"But Prince Dar! I have sworn to both your father and Lord Aerin to protect you!" Goban stammered.

"That won't be necessary where I'm going." Banning replied and dismissed the soldier one more time.

Sadly, these were words that Goban did not want to hear. Especially when he dreaded the thought of having to stand in front of Riocard, Manus and Betrys to say that he had once again had lost Banning.

"Please Milord!" Goban begged as a frown formed on the often stoic man's face, his light olive skin yellowing in fear as he thought of his dwindling future prospects. "Let me go with you. I will have nothing left once you are gone."

Even though Goban believed in what he was saying, Banning doubted that whatever his soldier feared would come true.

Still.

"So what do you think Gwyn? Have room for one more body?"

Gwyn paused as she gave Banning's soldier the once over. She had to admit that Goban had proven himself during the battle with Ciaran and he had worked just as hard as any of her crew when it came to helping clear the damaged decks of her ship.

"Welcome aboard." Gwyn smiled.

"Thank you, Captain." Goban said, smiling in relief that he would not have to confront the royal family, or his own for that matter, with what he now saw as list of failures during his command.

"Once we're airborne Master Cahl," Gwyn said, purposely dropping the man's title of lieutenant. "I will have Lucilla figure out what we can do with you."

"Aye, Captain!"

"Now if that's settled," Banning interrupted. "We should go!"

"But I still have two more shipments of supplies to receive!"

Banning forestalled any more of Gwyn's griping by explaining what his father had said to him.

"So you see, the sooner we leave the better. Besides," Banning pulled out the marker that his father had given him. "If we need anything we can stop at the next town to get it. My treat this time."

"Well, you heard the man!" Gwyn shouted so that the crew near her stopped to listen to what she had to say. "Let's batten down the Kasser so we can be on our way!"

"And if I may," Goban said before he was doled out any more orders or Gwyn shooed him below deck. "It might be wise if I go cancel the rest of your shipments. So we have no small craft about us when we leave."

"Fine! You got fifteen minutes to get that done." Gwyn said as she began to tick off things in her head that needed to get done so that they could leave. "Because in thirty minutes, with or without you, we leave!"

***

"We were wondering where you were. Where's Banning?"

Fionn had purposely arrived late for dinner and ignored Betrys' question as he walked into the dining hall and took his seat next to Mihra and across from Manus, for Banning's mother always sat at one end of the table when she dined with them, and draped the napkin that had been set out for him across his lap.

"He will not be joining us." Fionn finally replied before ordering the servants to bring him some wine.

"Is he well?" Riocard asked as a look of genuine concern on his face for his foster-son. "His journey was rough. Maybe I should go sit with him for a while?"

"That will not be necessary." Fionn said before taking a long sip of wine that was just poured for him. "He is not here."

"You allowed him to go out with friends?" Betrys asked as a hint of scorn over Fionn's parenting skills crept into her voice. "Banning should be here. Not out gallivanting about the city on his first night home."

"You misunderstand." Fionn finished his wine, asking the manservant to pour him another glass. "Leave the carafe. Banning has left the city."

Fionn remained quiet as a volley of questions were hurled at him by Betrys and Riocard.

"He and Argus Gwyn wanted to be together so I gave him my permission to pursue the relationship."

"Pursue! Permission!" Betrys sneered. "With a Scarnian no less! We had a line of eligible men just wanting to marry him. Now we have nothing!"

"I have to agree with Betrys." Riocard added, the only hint of disapproval being the frown on his face. The rebuke he had for Fionn would come later when the two of them were alone.

"The princes from Ardane or Tuame would have been a welcome addition into our family. Both strategically and to improve our commerce with them. What were you thinking?"

Without any hesitation, and without any quiver to his voice, Fionn told them he had done what he had thought was best for his son.

Riocard's frown only deepened at hearing these words and asked why he hadn't first thought of what would have been best for their family as he decided to not wait until later to rebuke his partner.

But Fionn remained quiet, ignoring the question from the man he had married, as he thought of what he had sacrificed, and what might have been, because he had done what was right for the sake of his family.

"Forget family!" Betrys shot. "What about Manus? It was Banning's duty to do what was best for him when it became Manus' turn to rule!"

Betrys turned to her eldest son who had remained quiet during their verbal assault of Fionn and asked him what he thought of his brother's abandonment of him.

After the two months of searching for Banning, witnessing a battle between two gods where many men under his care died, and how he had recently, and secretly, become intimate with one of those gods, Manus realized he had only one thing to say to his mother.

"I'm glad he finally found the jar his stones were hidden in so he could start using them again."

Mihra choked as she tried to cover a gasp of surprise while Betrys' mouth dropped open in shock and her skin paled at Manus' vulgarity.

Standing with her hands planted firmly on the table, as if she wanted to push it along with the group of men who sat about it away from her, glared at her son.

"You shame me Manus! I thought of all people you would have known better than to stoop so low."

"Maybe you should talk some sense into these two." Betrys said to Riocard when she realized that her son had nothing else to say to her.

As she made her way to leave, because she was quite disgusted with all of them and was thoroughly finished with the trio, Betrys looked at Fionn one more time.

"Remember this loss." Betrys said as she pointed a finger at the man. "Because there is not enough money in the land for me to ever bed with you again!"

"I know of the ransom that was given for the birth of Banning! And do not to worry." Fionn said, his face flushed from the third glass of wine he had just finished. "Not even the gods could get me to crawl between your legs for a second time."

Betrys was about to say something just as vile to Fionn but one of the servants, who had tried to remain quiet and out of sight during their tirade, snickered at Fionn's comment, reminding the family that they were not alone.

"Stupid man! Mihra! Attend me!" Betrys spat before storming out of the room.

"I will talk to the two of you later." Riocard warned Fionn and his son as he got up to chase after the two women. For at this moment Riocard wanted nothing more than reconciliation with the woman who was not only the high sagartta to Cavanna, but the high priestess for all of Birr.

Several minutes of silence went by and when Fionn realized Manus was not getting up to leave ordered for the cooling meal to be served.

"He'll be fine." Manus said as he watched his foster-father absentmindedly pick at the food on his plate.

"I know."

"In a month or two, when everything here has settled, I can go to Iniscarn to make sure he is doing well."

"Thank you." Fionn said to Manus as he patted the quick note in his pocket that Cahl Goban had jotted and had sent to the castle, informing Fionn that the lieutenant had gone to Iniscarn with his son and would keep an eye on him as best as he could. "But I think it would be best if we let him live his life without us for a while."

***

A month went by.

A month after the Camalain had returned to Kinsale with rumors of Banning's escapade and the turmoil among the Royal Family spreading throughout the city like a plague.

A month in which Liam's and his father's life began to settle back into its normal routine.

A month in which Liam realized he wanted more out of that life than to just flit from building to building in the temple complex that he had been calling home.

"Are you sure about this?" Cullen asked his son while handing him some clothes to pack into one of two satchels Liam had at his feet.

"I think so." Liam replied as he stowed away the clothing. "But I won't know until I go."

"Besides. I'll only be staying in Old Kinsale with Gorman and Heath." Liam said, reminding his father of his friend's generosity to come live with them.

"And Heath has a cousin who is a member of the Woodworker's Guild and has offered to mentor me in carpentry so I can become a member as well."

Cullen knew all this, especially that Liam had never been quite comfortable in the Stonemason's Guild and that the change in work might do him some good.

There was also a third reason for his son wanting to live with his friend's from the Camalain.

That third reason for leaving being Karam Kael, who also lived with his family in Old Kinsale. The very same Karam Kael they found standing in the courtyard outside their home, waiting for Liam.

"Do not ever hesitate to come back home." Cullen said as he watched Kael take the satchels out of Liam's hands.

"So this means dinner is still on for tomorrow night?" Liam smiled as he came to stand before his foster-father.

"Of course!" Cullen replied when he realized that he must be sounding like a silly old lonely man.

But not to Liam who stepped forward to give Cullen a hug goodbye. "Thank you for everything, father. And, I love you."

"I love you too, son."

"And as for you Master Karam." Cullen said to Kael as his son went to grab one of the bags being handed to him by Kael. "You are always welcome here."

"Not to worry sir." The young man smiled. "We'll be here so much it will seem like Liam never left."

The kindly sagart mouthed a silent thank you to Kael and watched as he and Liam sorted themselves out, saying one last goodbye to Cullen, while hand in hand walked past the fountain in the center of the square, before turning a corner and disappearing from the sagart's view.

Cullen stood on his threshold, giving greetings to a couple of sagarts who happened to be walking by, allowing the heat of the afternoon sun to warm his body and soul, while Barra whispered reassurances about Liam's life in his head, before turning to go inside.

Cullen was about to close the front door to his home then changed his mind and walked away, leaving the house wide open to the world. For, if by chance, Liam turned back in need of something, anything, Cullen wanted his son to know that there was no barrier, no reason at all, for him to come back home.

About the Author

A fine arts painter for the last twenty years, "Choices Made" is Scott's first novel and the beginning to what will be the ongoing Gwerin saga.

Scott lives in Rhode Island with his partner Tony and their three cats and one dog.

To find out more about Scott, his artwork and his writings, you can visit him at www.facebook.com/GalleryScott or www.facebook.com/ScottWilliamSimmons.

www.ingramcontent.com/pod-product-compliance
Lightning Source LLC
Chambersburg PA
CBHW051930020726
47501CB00001B/64